Cicisbeo
Diary of an Obstinate, Headstrong Female.
C. C. Burns

C. C. BURNS.

First Edition. Paperback.

ISBN: 978-1-0686805-1-9

Independently published by the author, Claire Burns, 2024, England.

www. ccburns.co.uk

Cover artist: @vikncharlie.

About the Author.

C laire was born and raised in London. She graduated with a BSc (Hons) in Social Sciences from the OU, and a Creative Writing MA from Royal Holloway. She now lives in Surrey with her family where she is fulfilling her lifelong dream of writing, full-time.

ccburns.co.uk

CHAPTER ONE

Prologue: Imminent Departure.

Annalise. February 1822.

Day of the Falmouth Departure.

When Annalise woke to the first shafts of yellowy wintery sunlight casting onto the paint-chipped wall before her, she closed her eyes against the hideous dawn of such a day. She had prayed deep into the twilight hours for it not to break, considered they might both be better off expiring in their sleep and thus evading what horrors lay ahead. But here it was: the sobering light of day stirring the inevasible into rhythm, heedless of her pleas or protests. The clock having no regard for what ill-fate it nudged them towards, or what this meant for her, for them both.

She flung a wayward pillow out of her way and snuggled in close to Eleanor, draping an arm about her waist and trying not to cry. This would be a day of formidable endurance. A test of her forbearance and skill of conviction in the face of abject heartbreak. She had little faith in her ability to manage either. *Yet what choice did she have?* The deal was done. All was settled. It remained only a matter of performance now. Just like the lines in their Shakespeare script at the Barnwell Theatre that day: predetermined, the stage directions set out ahead of her.

She would rise and get dressed, pack up the last of Eleanor's things and smile over breakfast, pretending they were setting out together across the seas. Feigning that all was as well as it could be. Deceiving them both into believing this cruel fate was not looming closer with every weighty swing of the brass pendulum.

It was all to be over and done with by noon, in any case. *What was five hours to answer,* she bargained with herself, considering the clock face that was only half-readable in its shadowy spot beside the satinwood armoire. Less than the journey from Cambridge to London, she reasoned. Far less than the week it would take her to arrive back in Carshalton with all the stops and changes of horses that would entail. Even if she was to travel back by private coach, such inconveniences could not be hastened across so many leagues.

It was all that kept her going, the thought of returning to Poppy and Maggie in Carshalton. Even if she was unlikely to emerge from her room on account of her tears and brokenness, for weeks...months, perhaps. But she would at least have a sense of home to return to, somewhere private to fall apart, unlike Eleanor, who would be inching ever further from her homeland. The thought stabbed at her heart like a white-hot spit. *How would Eleanor bear it with no one to console her? She was already struggling now.* Annalise would need the comfort of her friends now more than she had ever relied upon it. And yet, part of her felt unworthy of comfort or survival at all, like the prospect of recovery was underserved and so should be unobtainable to her after what she was about to do. What she *had* to do…

But as she clung to the warmth beneath Eleanor's limp arm—watching as she purred soft-unknowing-breaths into the pillow—she was sure she could not do it, would fail to see it through, was unlikely to make it past breakfast before falling apart and giving herself away. This was to be the most savage part of the arrangement; to tread this merciless path to their parting beneath a veil of normalcy with such cunning and deceit. She felt sure it would kill her. Perhaps Eleanor, too. And she could not bear to contemplate such monstrous imaginings of the aftermath. She had to tell herself it would not come to that. It would turn out to be for the best…in the end. The lesser evil, even if by narrow margins. And when this failed to persuade her, she reflected on all the betrayal and disgust conjured by the vulgar details Mariella had apprised her of last night. Not that she believed the greater share. Mariella seemed to her not only a venomous liar, but the embodiment of an unlovable creature, if ever there was such a thing. She had never before conceived of such a being. Though it pained her to acknowledge it, even Gint, in all his ill-doings, had occasion to express some modicum of decency now and then. But Mariella seemed entirely incapable of good feeling, immune to it. And as Annalise watched the smug satisfaction on her face as she reeled off one explicit account after another, she knew that it was impossible Eleanor could have ever been in love with her…that *anyone* could ever be in love with such a viper. But still, it remained a poor consolation for the solemn realisation that there remained further withheld truths between them, when they had sworn oaths of honesty to each other only months ago. It smarted worse for how intimate they had grown since then, for how certain she had felt in the knowledge of her love. Only to find there remained secrets lurking in the shadows, cavernous clefts in the accounts she had been furnished with. It was the only thing that took the edge off her own betrayal now, knowing she was both the betrayer and the betrayed.

Her mama had always told her that two wrongs did not make for a right, and that's as may be…but it did help dull the poignancy of one's own offence, of that she felt certain.

So, she held onto this feeble thread of reasoning as she laced Eleanor's stays, poured their tea from the pot, and eventually boarded the carriage with her just before noon. Expecting to falter at every false syllable or reassuring smile, but somehow, just about, managing. Sometimes even by way of fooling herself. Permitting herself to believe her ticket was genuine when Digby presented them to the steward on boarding, or that they were to share the humble little cabin they were led to down decks of rope-railed stairs. Envisaging herself in the narrow bunk Eleanor gave her first choice of, and picking it out as if she was to lay in it this very night, when in fact, she would be face-pressed against the carriage window bound for the county of Surrey as Eleanor sailed off towards the continent.

It was only when the final act commenced, signalled by the arrival of the luggage porter and the staged dilemma of their lost luggage, that she roused herself from the deception of remaining on board and the reality hit her with arctic precision, like a dart of ice through her spleen. She looked between Eleanor and then Giles. His expectant face patient in its silent insistence, and yet still capable of impressing upon her what must be done. Prompting her very feet into motion with the slightest twitch of a brow raise and to following Digby and the porter, not even able to bid an honest farewell. It was then, as she turned about for one last glance at her beautiful, unsuspecting Len, just as she exited the saloon, that she almost dropped to her knees, weak of limb and resolve. But Digby was quick to stoop in behind and steady her, nudge her on and hasten her steps along narrow corridors with low ceilings and flights of dizzying stairs until she emerged onto the top deck and was hurried towards a bridge that was about to be drawn up, making ready for its imminent departure.

'I can't do it. I can't leave her,' she cried at the last, gripping the rails and refusing to move on.

'Ma'am, this is the final call. You need to go now,' said the porter, who was not a luggage porter at all but another of Giles's many stooges. Another disposable pawn in his game where he was always victor, at any cost, by any means.

'I'm not going. Draw up the bridge,' Annalise said resolutely, turning back towards the ship's deck.

'You will go.' Digby stepped up close behind her, prised her hand from the rail and marched her along the bridge, her sore ankle struggling with the speed and force he propelled her on with.

'But I cannot leave her,' she cried.

'You have no choice.' His breath a hot, sour fog at her ear. 'Your word was binding. Besides, you have no ticket and therefore no right to travel with us. One word to the Packet Inspector over there will have you taken off by the Law for attempting illegal passage. Now, come on, don't resist, you'll only get hurt.'

'This will kill her, you know! I cannot do it. I change my mind!'

But it was too late. They had already crossed over to landside, and with a shove that sent her to the floor grazing her palms, he threw her luggage down at her feet. Once she had braced her fall and peered up, he was back over the bridge standing aboard, a rope pulled across the opening as the men began to draw it away. She didn't even try to get up. She only brushed gravelly shards from her scuffed palms and watched on in disbelief as the boat made ready to depart. The crew climbing masts, singing ditties and making busy upon the deck. The chill of the wind whipping against her tear-streaming cheeks, turning them cold as inside she broke into a vapid sweat, an amplified racing of her heart as her breath hung, suspended, as though she refused in protest to permit herself the necessity of breathing. Until she could not. And then she gasped painfully, her chest feeling constricted and narrow as though she attempted to inhale through a thin length of pipe. Swallowing down on the caustic ache in her gullet as she let out a cry that sounded weak, feeble, just as she had become. Yes, a feeble-hearted disgrace. Morally bereft of all the soundness of mind and feeling she had once believed herself incapable of departing from. She was ashamed of herself. Appalled. Then, as she heard the ship fire its departing shot, she felt as though it had gone straight through her heart. *This was it then*—the farewell that was never meant to be, yet, here it was—unwelcome, unheeding, unpreventable.

She watched through the glaze of heavy, tear-filled eyes as the ship drifted away from the harbourside and felt the panic of their separation so despairingly she considered diving in after it, even though she couldn't swim. At least if she drowned she would be spared this impossible suffering that she thought must be akin to being speared by a thousand invisible arrows all at once. She put out a hand to lift herself but she couldn't get to her feet. She felt so ill. Her heart ebbing with every shrinking drift of the ship towing out of the harbour, as if the anchor was hooked beneath her rib cage, every inching yard tugging at her.

CHAPTER TWO

Seasick.

Eleanor. February 1822.

I woke up beneath a veil of stagnant darkness and it took me some moments to orientate myself, collect my thoughts and remember where I was. Bobbing on a rough current somewhere to sea, I remembered with despair as the lapping of the waves against the ship became audible and then loud, with it the rocking sway that made me feel so violently nauseous. I attempted to get up only to find my right arm impossible to move and sighed out in pain as I felt the rest of my body ache sorely as I tried to lift myself using only my left.

'Miss?' Came a voice that made me jump. I could not make out from whence it came in the dimness. I did not recognise it either, young and thick with the Cornish accent I had recently become acquainted with. 'Who is there?' I asked.

'Me, Daisy, miss, your maid.'

She was but a stranger to me, not my maid! I protested silently as the memory of it all flooded back with greater vividness. *Annalise is my maid. Was*, my maid...

A long silence.

'Strike us a light, Daisy, I cannot see a thing.'

'Yes, miss,' she agreed, and I heard her scuttle around the cabin for the tinder box until finally, a warm glow lit the room and I could make out her silhouette beside me. Then, as my eyes adjusted better, a provincial-looking scrap of a girl appeared before me, barely fifteen, lank brown tendrils of sleep-ruffled hair hanging about her ears, creeping from beneath her once-white sleeping cap.

'Are you alright, miss?' she asked, squinting over me.

'Yes, I think so, but I am sore. How long have I slept?'

She frowned thoughtfully. 'I can't rightly say, miss. It could be a week now, or more. Perhaps eight days or so, I fancy.'

'Eight days! But that's impossible!'

She nodded, wide-eyed. 'It ought to be miss, but the surgeon's draft has that effect, told me 'imself.'

'A draught to make me sleep?'

'Yes.' She nodded. 'It was thought for the best, so you might rest and recover.'

Rest perhaps, but there would be no recovery from this. My heart sank further, picturing us now eight days into our journey, floating about in the middle of some dark sea, hundreds of miles from my homeland…hundreds of miles from my Annalise. 'You must help me up, Daisy, this wretched arm ails me too much to depend on it.'

'Surgeon thinks you broken it, miss. I wouldn't try to move it, it's been bound.'

I peered down to see my right hand pressed to my breastbone, a length of muslin cloth tied about my shoulder, holding it in place. No wonder I could not move it. But I could not feel my fingers either as I tried to wriggle them and realised that perhaps the surgeon had been right. 'Daisy, where is my husband?'

'To bed, Miss, but he did say I should call him when you woke – we been expecting you to all day. I'll go and get him for you now, shall I?'

Realising, as I fidgeted about in the bed unable to lift my limbs without pain, that it would be the only practical option, I agreed and laid back down, listening to the sounds of her shuffling about, the open and close of the door and the more muffled sounds outside of it as she knocked on his, and after a short pause, voices.

'You are awake at last,' he said moments later, coming to my bedside and towering over me, casting the light to shadow. 'How do you feel?'

'How do you *think* I feel? You have been drugging me again! I should have expected as much.'

'Hmm, well, this has been on doctor's orders. You were in great need of rest in order you might heal from your injuries. You fell down the stairs. Do you remember it?'

I did not remember, though a blurred image surfaced from a corner of my mind at his words, a view of the boards on the deck below as if looming above them, the sound of calamity about my ears. I remembered the struggle now, yes, that was clear, the vice-like grip of him and Digby so tight about me I could barely breathe.

'Eleanor, there is something I must tell you,' he said with an air of severity, and perhaps, was that an attempt at gentility? I felt his hand press over my own and recoiled at the audacity of him touching me and suffered the pain of turning just enough to move it out of reach.

'You have fallen very ill and injured yourself pretty badly.'

'Well, I see that!' I hissed.

'You have a fractured shoulder, a sprain at the ankle the surgeon believes is now healed, and you have suffered a concussion, though only superficial injuries for the most part.

'Well, I suppose I should be grateful that is all and you and Digby did not murder me!'

'Eleanor, that is not all…the fall caused you to lose the child.'

I was so stunned by this I could not speak. I had thought nothing more could provoke a deeper sense of paralysis to my emotions after Annalise's crying off on me, but when I took in his words, lifted my left arm to run my palm across my navel, I knew it was true. *It was gone.* I felt its absence now. Warm tears rolled down my cheeks and pooled in my ears.

'Eleanor, I am sorry,' he said softly and again tried to touch me in some tender way that made me wince and turn my gaze away to the blankness of the wall beside me. 'No, you are not,' I whimpered.

'There was little choice in sedating you in such a sorry state and with the limitations of the ship surgeon's resources. You lost a great deal of blood and fell weak, so he thought it best to sedate you and relieve your body of the taxation of daily routines in order you might heal faster. He thinks you over the worst now and has reduced the dose of the draught—'

'Please,' I implored him through my sobs, '...just leave me be.'

'Very well. It is late. I will come to check on you in the morning.'

I barely removed from that bed beyond the chamber pot for the next three days. I had spent every tear, tortured every regretful memory and suffered a solitude so tormenting that I hardly knew who I was. I had lost all else, why should I not lose myself into the bargain. What was I anyway without all that was dear to me? *A creature of passive existence.*

Physically, my aches and pains, which had at first been many, had dulled or disappeared entirely once I was helped out of the bed, save my fractured shoulder, which the surgeon, on one of his many visits to me, assured me was mending well. The bleeding and the tiresome cramps had too abated now to a minor inconvenience, and yet, to my mind, these were the pains easiest to bear: the physical ones. It was the maladies of mind I could not tolerate. Knew not how to endure without drowning them in the oblivion of the liquor glass. I considered it often; I hardly had Annalise's reprimands to contend with now. But the beer on board was bad and the brandy and wine so coarse that just one glass delivered me a shocking migraine and exacerbated the sea sickness I was already struggling to manage. So that was the end of that course, for now. Oh, to have a mind and heart mend so easily as blood and bone.

'Doctor, I beseech you, please give me another sleeping draft,' I asked him on his last visit, which had been frequent since I'd woke.

'Mrs Craythorne, forgive me, but laudanum is not to be trifled with. You have taken so many doses these past weeks, I simply cannot permit you to continue as you were. Besides, we expect to dock at Lisbon in the coming week, and it is my duty now to try to recuperate you well enough to change ships and be able to certify you as fit to sail on when we do.'

'Please, Sir, just one small dose. I ask you to take pity on me. Don't you see? I have lost *everything*. I ask only not to have to feel it all at once.'

'Mrs Craythorne, I sympathise with you, truly, but you must understand that the amount of laudanum you have taken these past weeks is not necessary now. You are better. You have made an impressive recovery, the like rarely seen in injured seaman with such haste. I suppose you have the vitality of health and youth to thank for that, but even your constitution shall not resist a dangerous dependence on the drops if I do not act in your best interest. I have weaned you carefully to ease the transition. To give you a larger dose now would set you back days. I would do you far more harm than good in acquiescing to you. If you tell me where you are hurting, I will check you over again and see what can be done. I might manage a liniment or poultice for you to alleviate your symptoms if you tell me where the pain is.'

'My heart, my mind, my dreams, Sir, that is where it hurts so very tartly it is insufferable. If you will not give me something to make me sleep then you might as well have spared yourself the trouble of healing my injuries and ailments. You'd as better throw me overboard and give me some peace, for that would be the greater kindness.'

He sighed, releasing a deeply held breath. 'I see you are very ill at ease. Your nerves are excited, which is to be expected after such a loss. But it is beyond my remit to offer you a remedy for that which even I cannot heal: Time and prayer are the only medicine for such.' He put a kind hand on my own, and I held onto it.

'Sir, please, help me if you can.' It was a desperate plea, but I watched his face soften and yield with a defeated sigh.

'Here is what I will do. Now, I know you have taken no more than a few sips of broth these past weeks; it harmed you not initially, but this far on, it will only hinder your recovery further. You are weak and you need to rebuild your strength. If you agree to take a meal, I will make you up a draught just this once more. Do we have a bargain?'

'Yes, Sir, I thank you.'

Later that afternoon, I was washed and dressed by Daisy and taken out into the saloon for the first time since the day we had boarded. My clothes hung loose and ill-fitting, the whites of my eyes slightly yellowing and my reflection of a ghostly pallor. But I was as respectable as could be made of me now and I cared not for how I looked, nor for who looked upon me; it was all of no consequence. There was only one pair of eyes I wished to rest upon the sight of me and I wondered now if they ever would again. In the absence of that gaze, I cared for no one's envy or approval. And who were these people anyway? Nothing to me. I barely recognised the room beyond the cabin when we emerged from its confines, now so full of unfamiliar faces and lively chatter. I cleared my throat which had turned thick from my lack of speech. The table was fully occupied and a space on the bench was made for me between Giles and his neighbour. I squeezed into it with his assistance as the chatter fell silent and curious eyes fell upon me. What did they know of me to cause such interest? I felt my eyes pinch tight in a reactionary scowl as I surveyed them and my gaze settled upon the face of a pious-looking old maid who pursed her disapproving lips as if to prevent them from speaking the thoughts in her head. I was minded to speak the thoughts in mine when I was then distracted.

'What a hearty saddle of beef this is!' said a gentleman sat opposite me, and I realised afterwards, when the diners went back to their plates and conversation, that he had not said the remark to me but for my benefit in diverting them back to their own business. In better spirits I supposed I might have thanked him or at least acknowledged the gesture. Instead, I lifted my fork, stared at the plate of meat and stewed vegetables upon it, and wanted instantly to permit the churning sea of bile within me to rise and relieve me of its acrid burden. I could not remember the last time I ate and the prospect was repugnant. Ship fare did little to encourage my trying, the presentation and smell adequate to dissuade me in a glance. But I would not waste such a hard-won bargain as the promise of a night of oblivion, so I determined to find the least offensive option. I settled on the unidentifiable soup—watery with an oily scum afloat at the surface— and spooned it slowly to my lips, so slowly, in fact, half the table was gone by the time I surrendered my empty bowl. I was grateful for the lack of host or etiquette at the table in clearing it, but I would have appreciated the kind of light-eating host that stood after only a few bites, as had sometimes been the case in London. But it was only a couple of men who remained scattered about the crumb-laden table now, and the surgeon pushing cold cloches or tureens of this or that in my direction. After insisting that I must at least take some stewed fruit to finish, he eventually left with a promise to return with my draft before bed, and as my stomach bubbled and growled its discontent, I knew it worth the inconvenience.

Thereinafter, one more gracious night of mind-numbing sleep, my pleading requests to him fell on kind but deaf ears, and each day, he placed upon me more demands of taking more meals, walking the saloon for exercise and generally anything he could contrive to keep me from my bed-bound paralysis I wished to linger in. Aside from the perpetual melancholy, the constant swaying of the ship added to my misery and encouraged me to remain in my cabin bunk or a nearby chair for fear of tumbling about. Giles, too, had taken his turn trying to persuade me towards exercise, as did Daisy from time to time, but their pestering only made me more obstinate, and I did as little as I could get away with. Did they really think I had a groat of concern for the risk of muscle wastage or stagnant circulation when my life was no longer of any value to me? It suited me better that body and mind were in sympathy with each other so that the pain in my heart found its physical manifestation place. So that the blood or bruise of limb, could reflect the maladied mind and heart.

Then, one night, at an hour so quiet the saloon was deserted, I came upon an idea that sent the slightest flash of hope through me and stirred me from my reverie. If we were to dock in Lisbon any day now, then opportunity may be about to present itself. Surely, someone here would know how I might go about obtaining a ticket to return back to Falmouth when we disembarked. I might find a way to get back before the second leg of our journey commenced. I knew not what or how it might be possible, but I would need my strength and wits to find a way to exploit this opportunity. I sat at the saloon table restless with excitement and disappointed that after finally feeling *something* above misery again, it must keep until tomorrow once I could make inquiries. Defeated, I waited for a lull in the ship's rocking sway before standing to make back for my cabin when a gentleman emerged from one of the rooms opposite. I recognised him as the same fellow that had done me the kindness of distracting the diners the other day, and rather than continue onto my room, I paused, hovering above my seat.

'Good evening,' he said, surprised to notice me in the vacant saloon.

'Good evening, Sir,' I said quietly, not wanting to wake Giles or Digby.

'You are up late. May I?' he said, inviting himself to sit down.

'Yes. I could not sleep. And you too, I see,' I answered, settling back into my own seat.

'Oh, me, no, I have not attempted it yet. I like to take a night time stroll up on the deck when it is quiet. I find the sea air settles me to bed very well.'

'Indeed. I perhaps should try it myself sometime.'

'You are very welcome to join me, but I own it is a little late to prevail upon my sister. She prefers an earlier night.'

'I do not. Or at least, I do not sleep at all anymore, so it makes no difference what time I retire.' I saw a sympathetic smile twitch about his mouth and thought to try my luck. 'If I do not impose on you, Sir, I would like to go with you, all the same.'

'Not at all. Perhaps you will prevail upon your maid then.'

I did not wake Daisy. Instead, I quietly fetched on my sturdier shoes and pelisse and took Mr Banfield's offered arm into the corridor and up the steps, explaining that the maid was already to sleep and I did not care to wake her.—That I had no intention of trying, was by the by. She was a good-natured enough girl and attentive in her tasks, but she could not be trusted with the most trifling of secrets, I could tell. *He* was her master, not me, and I meant to guard myself very carefully in her company. The less she knew of my new acquaintance or shift in spirits, the better. For she was Giles's eyes now, and I wanted him to remain easy and continue believing in this faux quietude of character he had forced into existence. If he thought me already conquered, there was no need for him to be overly cautious and Digby's studious watch over me be increased after daylight hours. Even devils had to sleep, I supposed.

As we climbed to the top deck and emerged into the open night, the air was startlingly fresh, and I wondered how long it had been since I had breathed it in or felt the chill of it upon my face. Not that it was cold. Certainly nothing reminiscent of the chilly February temperatures of Falmouth, but still crisp enough to find refreshing. The sea was calmer tonight, rocking the boat to a steady bob, though still it dizzied me to walk upon the moving floor, my footing off its usual estimations and a general mistrust of my path. I clung to Mr Banfield's arm a little tighter to navigate the slippery wooden boards as we walked the length of deck open to us. Not having the use of my other arm made me feel vulnerable should I slip upon them. I couldn't afford another setback this close to docking. I needed that clean bill of health if I was to get home. But I began to get the hang of its rhythm after a time and the fresh air seemed to counter the worst of its effects.

It was fairly quiet up here, too, save a couple of the sailors whistling about the decks and a young boy hovering above our heads climbing the rigging. There was nothing to see but blackness all about us, so dense it was difficult to separate the glassy black sea from the night sky, save a glittering canopy of starlight above us, interrupted only by a silvery slither of new moon. It was soothing, the stillness of the view, the freshness of the night, the effervescent possibilities bubbling to the surface of my mind in forming an escape plan...

After we had spent a little while in the vagaries of small talk, I stopped and asked frankly, 'Sir, I wonder if you could tell me if the ship turns straight back to Falmouth once it has deposited us in Lisbon?'

'I own I am not certain, but I would expect it to, after a time.'

'How much time? A matter of hours or days?'

He paused thoughtfully and then said, 'I suppose as long as it takes to unload and reload the post, cargo, and supplies, in the very least, and then wait for the tide to turn in its favour. A day may suffice, but I am no authority on the matter. I am not a seafaring man. This is also my first time at sea.'

'I see. Though you arranged your own travel?'

'Well, yes.'

'Then you might know this: should one wish to obtain a ticket for the return journey, how would they go about the matter?'

He frowned, 'Forgive me, ma'am, but isn't your husband a naval man? Surely, he will be better placed to answer such questions.'

'That man is no husband to me, Sir, but a captor. I daresay he has attempted to forge a different public opinion, but that is the truth. He forced me onto this boat and means to force me onto another if I do not find a means to turn back. But I am unwise in such matters. So I am at your mercy, Sir, to tell me whatever it is you might know beyond my ignorance.'

'My sister and I did fear something untoward with all the frightful screaming rising out from your room, I must admit. Though we had suspected—'

'Me a madwoman, like the other passengers seem to have concluded?'

'Not mad, troubled, perhaps.' He pressed a palm over my hand, which was still wrapped tight about his forearm. 'I shall do what I can to find it out and report back to you tomorrow.'

I determined to make myself a friend of Mr Banfield and his sister when he made the introduction the following day. If I hoped to get my passage back to England when we docked, I would need some help and some strength, I decided, setting myself to the task of taking the surgeon's advice more seriously now and making a fair attempt at my meals and exercise. So slight and waif-like I had grown in such a short time. It was quite shocking now I considered my reflection more carefully. So, I determined to persist with the disagreeable offerings at the table and spent much of my waking hours struggling to force it down me.

My more regular appearances at the table seemed to surprise everyone in the saloon, including Giles, and I was glad that we would soon be to shore and away from these people I neither knew nor liked, but felt unable to escape from in such close confines. I supposed I seemed every part the crank to them, from the screaming lunatic to the melancholy recluse, and now something in between. I was thankful that Mr and Miss Banfield had taken my part and seemed unaffected by common opinion, always kind and diverting as we sat about the saloon table and walked the deck for exercise. They were bound for Lisbon and had a little of the language. It was my hope that since they had taken pity on me, they might be good enough to show me where to put up and survive until the return sailing. To travel alone would be precarious enough, but to put up abroad in a friendless place without the tongue was a daunting prospect.

I had purposely kept my introduction of them to Giles as brief and as distant as I could manage, but from time to time, he would join us on a midday stroll, and where he did not, Digby always kept a distant watch. I was glad Giles, was, for the most part, content to shuffle around papers by day. I presumed some pressing matters of business kept him preoccupied. He was also on terms with the captain and the officers and would dine and drink with them frequently until late hours. I was glad he never invited me to go with him. Although I could see him considering me at times, testing whether I had recovered a reasonable enough level of sanity to be trusted in such circles. So, I was sure not to exclude him from my lower moments of despair now and then to discourage any such notions of inclusion.

But despite my growing improvement and optimism, the night before we pulled into port, I had a painful realisation: the fare of twenty-two pounds, which Mr Banfield had advised me was the cost of the ticket home, was beyond my reach. I had been frivolous with my purse this year and left the last few pounds raised on my wedding ring in Annalise's sewing box for safekeeping, and I did not even have that to rely upon as I had supposed. I would not even be able to raise the steerage fare of thirteen pounds, let alone the cost of putting up at an inn until the ship sailed back, and I was yet to learn how long this would be. I had tried asking Daisy to retrieve my ornaments from Giles, pretending to want to wear them for dinner, but she came back empty-handed, saying master was keeping them locked up safe on board and I was only to wear them in his company for fear I'd lose them, or they'd be pinched. But I knew it was to prevent me from trading them for a way out.

It was in the panic of this realisation that I decided to write to Lady W. for assistance and entrust the Banfields with the duty to post it for me once on land. It was far from expedient, and I could only hope there would be some way I could stall the second leg for long enough to receive a return, but when I later learned that the post might take weeks to come full circle, I began to despair once more. Yet it was all I could do, and since the Banfields were generous enough to provide the means and cover the stamping cost, for apparently, overseas post must always be prepaid, I thought it best not to refuse such an opportunity. A long wait was better than no hope, and so I sat in their cabin one night when all were to bed and made use of their provisions and wrote:

Dearest Friend,

I hope you are keeping well?

How much I miss your society and wise counsel now I am so far away from London.—Further perhaps than either you or I might have imagined just weeks ago when I visited you in Cheapside. There is no easy way to explain all that has since passed, but suffice it to say, he caught up with us in the end and has forced me to travel overseas with him. We are bound for Venice, and though he says it is to be just for a six month, his words are worth so little, I fear I might never see my homelands or those I love, upon it, again.

After over two weeks on the Lisbon Packet, we expect to dock tomorrow if conditions remain favourable and the tide conducive. So much has passed in that time that I hardly know where to begin explaining the whole. But Tulley did not come with us, and I miscarried whilst on board. So I see now his true motive for taking me away is exposed now the child is no more, and yet he persists in the scheme, refuses to turn us about at Lisbon. – He says we are already halfway there, and he has urgent business to attend in Venice. That I might make a holiday of it and meet his extended family. But, I see it for what it is: a transfer from his captivity to that of his family whilst keeping me out of the reach of assistance from my own, and this is the true objective, to isolate me from all support.

It has been the most emotionally taxing time, but I hope to find a way to make the homeward journey alone once I can make the arrangements. – Something I find myself humbled to have to ask for your help in, since I have neither money nor method by which I might make my return. My husband permits me no direct access to money now he mistrusts me, not even a pin, and I find myself penniless and without so much as a piece of jewellery to exchange for a ticket back. If there is any way in which you might be able to help me, I would be forever indebted to such kindness in these desperate circumstances I find myself in, and though reluctant to prevail upon you when you have already done so much for me, I know not where else I can place my trust.

If you can think of a way you might send me a loan for the sum to travel back or might even be able to send me a ticket home, I shall find a way to pay you back and be ever grateful.

Unfortunately, I have no fixed address to supply you with at present, for he withholds even this detail from me for fear of intervention. Thankfully, some kindly persons aboard the ship with me have agreed I may use their address in Porto and will act as an intermediary until I can write to you directly.

Please write and tell me how you do, dear friend, and please do not grow anxious for my sake. I am bearing up as well as I might, and I do not mean to succumb to this false imprisonment and abandon all that is dear to me. I will write to you again as soon as I am able, though it may be some time until then.

Your affectionate and ever-grateful friend.
Ex

That night, as the Banfields and I walked the deck for the last time, I turned to them both and said, 'You have been very kind to me, and I am so grateful to have met you. I shall never forget the service you have rendered me, and I hope, one day, I might repay you it when my circumstances are improved.'

Miss Banfield flashed her kind smile and squeezed my arm. 'Not at all, Mrs Craythorne, we have enjoyed your society equally. We are only sorry there is not more we can do for you. If it was within our power—'

'I know,' I interrupted, sparing them another uncomfortable explanation of their circumstances which prevented them from being able to offer me a place to stay or any greater financial help than the postage fee. 'You have already done more than you know in restoring me to better spirits, and I thank you for sending this on.' I pressed the letter into Miss Banfield's hand. Over the past couple of days, I learned that they were parentless and had lost their case in chancery over the estate that should have been rightfully theirs, which was withdrawn from them on Miss Banfield reaching her majority. England held nothing but bad memories for them now and they were seeking a way to move on from their reduced circumstances. They had only one living relative to rely upon in the world, an uncle in Porto, who had managed to secure Mr Banfield a place at the University of Coimbra and his sister a place as a governess nearby.

They were to start over again in this foreign land, hoping to find a sustainable independence in a society that was more forgiving and less rigid than the English style.

Here, they told me, they may toil for a while, but if they worked hard and saved up, with the humble annuity which had been left to them, they might manage to carve an independence worth having, whereas in England, they could not even keep a horse for the entirety of the sum. They might never again live in the style they were previously accustomed to, but nor would they ever end up in the workhouse in trying their luck here. I certainly hoped it worked out, for their sakes.

'You will stay in touch? I mean, not only the mails, but to tell us how you do?' Miss Banfield asked with concern in her eyes. I knew she had been very ill-affected by my explanation of my circumstances and had struggled over being unable to help. She had even offered me her pewter broach—a family heirloom—as the only thing of value she could think of that might be tradable for a ticket home, but of course, I could not take it, even as desperate as I found myself. 'I will write and like to know how you get along in Portugal, too.'

CHAPTER THREE

Venice.

Eleanor. March 1822.

I couldn't wait to get off that ship, and when it finally docked, I felt like leaping to landside before the moorings were tied. It was too confined a space to be entrapped with Giles's society at such length, especially in such a vulnerable state of mind as I had found myself in after having to abandon any hope of a return ticket back...for the time being.

After bidding farewell to the Banfields in Lisbon, I had no one about to pass even the smallest kindness of speech with. Unlike the packet ship tourists, there seemed to be only men of trade on this merchant ship, and I found myself with either too much time alone to dwell on my many miseries, or no peace at all when Giles was minded to accost my company. With the fresh slate of boarding a new vessel, he seemed keen to present us as a united front. He took up invitations to the Captain's table where he expected me to attend him in some dutiful wifely capacity. It took little to put paid to that idea when I broke into sobs over the white soup on the first invitation, and he was, once again, left to explain my recent 'misfortune' to the party and make my apologies. *Misfortunes*, I had wanted to correct him. It seemed that overnight, I had gained all that was ill and lost all that was dear in quick succession. How could anyone be expected to come back from such a series of tribulation at all? Less still with haste.

Whilst my body regained some of its prior vigour, my mind grew frailer and sicklier by the hour as I considered it all over and over. Searched and re-searched for any trail of hope that might lead me home again, to no avail. I had not managed more than a few hours at a time without bursting into tears over some memory of Annalise and the future that was lost to me. Nor had I been able to brush a palm across my navel without a deep pang of regret. She had wanted so much for us to be a family and keep the child, and I had fought so vehemently against even considering it until now, when all was lost.

Sometimes, the most trifling of things could remind me of a time we had shared such happy contentment and send me into the most profound fits of melancholy. Even in compassionate company I would have faltered, but his inauthentic veneer of sympathy grew more and more transparent with each passing day. I wasn't as surprised by his turn of behaviour as I might have been, given how differently he portrayed himself in company to what I knew of his character. I was but a prop, connection to the ton; beyond that, he had no true tenderness for me. I was just as his dogs and horses were, an excellent pedigree to show off. Except I had less obedience or loyalty to him than such creatures. I was there to do my duty as his wife. It seemed that, and that alone was the extent of his interest in me now he had won the battle.

The only thing that had comforted me through this impossible journey was that the cramped single bunk cabins on board had managed to postpone him coming to my bed. I had at first thought him pensive on account of the Surgeon having forbade such activities until at least two regular courses had passed, then I wondered if he had some minor consideration for my health or my constant tears, but I sensed nothing of true feeling in him that could convince me. Whatever the reason, it was a mercy I was grateful for and one less nightmare to face for now. Although, at times, I felt so numb and so much detached from my reality, I thought I might hardly notice what became of me. I felt as blank as the mirror black waters I would often go up deck to stare upon at night, alone now. On occasion, I would contrive to imagine some new plot to evade him or envision a ticket or banker's draft arriving from Lady W. permitting me a way back home. But I knew I would be lucky if she had even received it in the three weeks spent aboard the *Cappadocia*, let alone hope to receive a return. And even then, if by some fortuity of expedience the Banfields had received it, they could not send it on to me until I had an address to offer them to forward it to. I had memorised their address by heart, sitting over the scrap of paper it was written on in private moments. I had hidden it in the foot of my stockings and it had grown creased and tattered over time. But I had rehearsed it mentally so often, like the arithmetic of my schoolroom days, that I was certain it would be forever etched in my memory long after the paper had deteriorated into an unreadable state. It was the address of Mr Banfield's lodging house near the University of Coimbra, since neither of them would be long at their uncle's and Miss Banfield was reluctant to give out the address of her new employer and be thought to be taking liberties. I thought of them often and wondered how they went along. Certainly, Mr Banfield had the better part of the bargain as far as I could tell of the life of governesses. Still, I hoped that it would be a kinder way of living in Portugal, for Miss Banfield was such a gentle soul it seemed cruel she must be subjected to such a harsh existence. However much impoverished, at least Mr Banfield could look to some meaningful education, a real career and interesting society to keep. At best, his poor sister would be confined to her own or that of a band of brats. And yet, even an existence such as that held more appeal to me now than my own sorry circumstances. She could at least go to bed at night without the fear of being accosted. I knew that at best, I was on borrowed time. So, for now, I meant to take some solace in the reprieve, if nothing else.

Unsettled and bereft, I sometimes waited until he was sleeping and walked up to the deck when it was quiet, save the lapping waves. I would lie on a bench to stare into the night above me and beg the stars to grant me just one wish and no other. *Take me home.* In my hardest moments, I wished for the night to take me, for the ship to sink or to find the nerve to jump into the angry waters. But, like all my wishes, they never came to pass. The following day, I would be disappointed to open my eyes to the creak and crack of the cabin swaying and the sight of him across the room, snoring into his pillow after another night of gaming and drinking with the seamen. For this cabin, he had decided on sharing with me, and though I'd always kept Daisy at arm's length, I missed her quiet proximity once she was sent to her own bed.

I had given up on dressing myself or combing my hair well and refused Daisy's attempts to encourage me to. I was done with pretences. I had lived my life behind a façade of beauty and etiquette, now I wanted the world to see the truth and the ugliness that consumed me. Giles, however, did not. He had complained that I should dress myself 'appropriately for a woman on her wedding journey', but like all his demands, they had fallen on deaf ears. If I hadn't been so disconsolate, I might have taken some twisted pleasure in irritating him, but I had neither the care nor energy. So when he barged in on my scant toilette the morning of our arrival into port and threw down a pile of clothes for me to wear, I let Daisy put them on me with indifference and was grateful he had saved me the trouble of finding some myself. The ornaments, too, came out now, and a set of ruby eardrops were hooked onto my lobes, a matching necklace tied at my neck. He had even bought me a replacement wedding band in Lisbon and slipped it over my knuckle, issued with a warning not to get any ideas.—In retrospect, I realised now he was determined to show me off respectably to his family (or more aptly, my new gaolers) on our arrival. Still, I didn't care for their approval any more than his, and made no effort to dress my hair or face for their acquaintance. I had altogether quit looking in the mirror now, though occasionally I would catch my reflection in some object and jump at the sight of the pale, drawn figure, I glimpsed.

As the mid-March sun rose and the tide drew in we sailed slowly into the port, and the medieval skyline of the city met my jaded view. Though I felt no joy in beholding the marvel of this floating land that I recognised as Venice from paintings, it cut through my dulled senses and commanded my attention all the same. Despite my lack of excitement at being here, there was something poignant about one's first sight of a place so wholly unlike anywhere I had ever before set eyes upon. Lisbon had also made its mark on my memory but seemed nothing to the infamy of this image. *The City of Vice.*— Its familiar appearances in artworks, rather than diminish the spectacle of it, lent a phantasmagorical edge to the antiquated scene as we finally stepped ashore. And whilst I could not fail to be impressed by this bold, eccentric spectacle, I could find only a paralysed hint of wander arising as we were conveyed directly to a smaller boat. We seemed suddenly dwarfed by the city skyline as we were rowed into the arteries and veins of the city, which snaked about floating buildings in the form of a great aqueous labyrinth. Had I come in any other company I might have been awed and enamoured, keen to explore, but a glance across to Giles as he clapped his hands together and reeled on about how good it was to be back, put paid to that possibility and reminded me only of just how far distant I was from home and all that was familiar to me.

He had advised me that we would be staying with his uncle's family in their palazzo, of which there was ample room for us to take apartments and 'enjoy' the entirety of a floor to ourselves. I was yet to decide if that was a good or ill prospect; they couldn't possibly be as vile as him, could they? I knew this scheme was the product of him deciding how best to keep me supervised whilst he concentrated on his business matters here, my new guardians, his substitute eyes, just as Daisy and Mariella had been before that. I supposed taking a house of our own would have left me too free for his liking, and whilst servants could be relied upon to some extent, even they would not be well placed to imprison their mistress continuously. Besides, staff could be turned, even brutes, as he had found out in Falmouth, and he was right of course; the minute I discovered a means of escape, I would take it. If that meant selling the very furniture in the house or food in the larder, I would do it the minute his back was turned and be straight back on a ship to England, however mortifying sea journeying had proved. But I could hardly do so in someone else's house and with so many eyes upon me, could I? He had thought of everything, and it was this knowing that haunted me as we drifted ever closer to my new prison. Whilst I detested the idea of being supervised and spied upon by his relatives, it would at least mean I was not completely alone in his company as I had begun to dread since being back on land. It would not *only* suit his ends. There would be witnesses to his treatment of me. We would be overheard, and I could use *this* to my advantage, too, if I was clever about it.

'Come, my dear, can you not even find a smile for this majestic city?' he said, with unusual cheer in his voice and an unwelcome brush of my hand which was gripping the edge of the boat, the other still bound by a sling. I released it instantly.

'It is very impressive,' I said, in a tone anything but impressed.

'Hmm, I think someone is anxious about meeting their new family. Is that what plays upon your mind?'

I nodded. I cared not to let him into my mind so he could think whatever he might. Typically, of all the many things that took pride of place in consuming my thoughts, he would judge something so trivial as the more pressing over being subject to a kidnap, a broken heart and the loss of a child.

'Do not trouble yourself. They shall like you, I'm certain. Well, if you can show them your better character and not this solemn creature that does not suit you well at all. Rest assured, you will be made very welcome as my wife and have a full provision of servants at your behest as you are more accustomed to.'

'Where is Daisy?' I asked then, realising she was not following behind us in the other boat which carried our trunks.

'Digby has taken her to buy a ticket back to England and settle her to lodgings in the wait—what, you thought she was to stay here, with us? Come, my dear, she is a simple provincial girl, not fit for a household like *Ca' Rosetti*. Besides, she did not wish to stay in a place where she had not the language.'

I shrugged, realising that it was *he* who did not want her to stay in a place where she would not be able to understand the tongue and report back accurately on me. What use was a spy that could not understand the conversations about her? Since I did have the language, however dormant and unpractised, it would be enough to deceive her by, should I wish it. 'What a pretty penny you must have paid her to make such a horrendous trip only to turn right about again.'

'What choice did I have, my dear, when *your* maid abandoned you at the last, than to make do with the only choice available to see you tended to? We were lucky her own mistress was willing to part with her for so reasonable a sum.'

'Oh, who was her mistress?'

'Just an old maid sailing to Lisbon.'

Then I remembered that scowl-faced dame and wondered what story she had been given in excuse for poaching her maid. But I resisted the urge to rise to it, given that I blamed him entirely for driving Annalise to the point of abandoning me, even if I blamed her for not loving me enough to resist it. 'And now, I suspect, you will find me a replacement?'

'My aunt has already made provisions. She is quite adept in such matters. And I'm sure you will find her selection far more agreeable than mine.'

I imagined some old toad of a maid who had been in service to the family long enough to depend upon her loyalty and the pension that hung in the balance.

As the boat pulled into a landing jetty in front of the tall, heavy doors of *Ca' Rosetti*, I did feel something of an anxious stirring within me, though I could hardly reason it after all else. The quaint edifice of the building, rather than impress me as it might otherwise, instead seemed symbolic of the entirety of my circumstances. Of course I should have a pretty gilded cage and not an ugly iron-clad prison. That was, after all, the veneer that all such atrocities as I had suffered could be permitted to pass beneath. Brutalisation and kidnap, which was an offence against the Common Law of England in other circumstances, yet was pardoned on account of the wedding band upon my finger. Now I understood why we ladies were pressed into marriage so young before we grew wise to what a marriage contract really equated to. Bondage. A nullifying contract that amended all sorts of laws, it seemed. Similarly, under such a bond, the child I had lost, that was not his, would otherwise belong to him—the only small consolation I could salvage from the wreckage of my emotions on that account. Why, then, should this not also pass under an illusory guise of a family holiday in a charming Venetian Palazzo...

When we were handed up from the rowboat and stepped through the doors, I was surprised to be met by a view to an indoor courtyard through the other side of them. It reminded me of a scene from a Shakespearean play with its exotic potted flowers, decorative stone statues and trickling water fountains scattered about its sun–streamed flags. But, strangely, there was no waiting reception of the servants or family to be seen, and for a fleeting moment, I feared a repeat of the empty houses he had hired on our journey to Cornwall, with no one about but a scant and nigh invisible staff. Had meeting his family, too, been another of his concoctions to encourage my compliance? *Dear god, let me be mistaken in this.* It had been hard enough before, but at least I had not been alone. The horror at this sudden possibility of being entirely alone with him caused me to trip and almost fall had he not caught me in time by my good arm.

'Ah,' he said, setting me steady again, '... that's the problem with finally getting your sea legs, they become unaccustomed to the land for a time.'

Reluctantly, I let him support me onwards with the bare minimum of proximity. I already had one arm out of use, I could not afford another. And it was true, there was something unsteady about my gait that I could not quite fathom out, though I was certain the heat was not helping. The sun was intensely strong for the season, and as we stepped out of the shade I felt my cheeks instantly ablaze. It was much harsher than the English winter I had left behind me. Though it was only March, it felt more akin to one of those rare but intense episodes of summer heat we occasionally experienced at the height of our better season.

I peered up at the stone stairway which crept up one side of the building and felt a foreboding wave of apprehension overcome me at the prospect of finding the house deserted. I must have paused to contemplate this but quickly felt his arm around my shoulders ushering me on, and was relieved to hear a shuffle of feet audible beyond it, soon followed by an entourage of servants swinging wide open the closed door and funnelling past us to unload the boats. As we drew closer still, I could see the figure of a petite, native-looking lady at the top of the stairs, too elegantly dressed to be a servant, and I felt my eyes grow heavy with tears of relief as I took slow, heavy steps towards her. *We were not to be alone.*

'My dears!' she clapped her hands together. 'I am so happy you are with us at last.' As we drew level and met her at the open door she came straight over to me and threw her arms around me like I was a long-lost relative. Far from the stiff-faced harridan I had expected, her smile was as warm as her greeting and impossible to imagine could be so well contrived for effect. 'It is so lovely to meet you, my child,' she said, still embracing me, and it took me a moment to reciprocate. I was not used to such welcomes, even from my own family, let alone amongst strangers.

'Eleanor, this is my aunt, Isabella,' Giles said a moment too late for an introduction.

'Eleanor, how lovely to welcome you to our family,' she said between kissing both my cheeks.

I managed a smile and thanked her cordially, still reconciling my relief at the families' presence with the intimate welcome I had not anticipated. But I was glad when the remaining servants stepped forth to unburden us of our unnecessary coats and hats.

'Aunt, as glamourous as ever,' Giles said, as it was now his turn to be swept into her embrace and exchange kisses. 'What a bloom of health you are in!' he chimed, and she waved a dismissive hand at him and deemed him a charmer. Though she was indeed a glamourous-looking lady, most definitely a beauty in her earlier years. I could certainly find no resemblance between her and Giles, but I supposed there would be none since she was only a marital relation.

'She is charming, Giles. You have done very well, I think,' she said, turning to me again and then noticing my bound arm. 'Oh dio! You have been in the wars I think?'

'An accident, a nasty slip, though I am quite recovered, and my arm shall soon follow, I am told,' I lied, wanting so much to tell her otherwise and yet finding her far too amiable to disrupt things presently. Instead, as Giles intervened to steer the conversation out of that direction with enquiries of the family's health and the whereabouts of other members of the family who were not present to receive us, I watched with quiet intrigue, wondering at his amiable charade and whether she knew beyond his pretence just how disagreeable he *really* was.

'How was your journey, my child? Not too harsh, I hope?' Isabella said as we walked.

'Long,' I answered, deciding to make no other complaint.

I felt her arm sneak into the crook of my elbow and was grateful to have her as a barrier between me and Giles.

'Yes. You must be hungry and very tired, I know. But your rooms are all ready for you,' she continued, hardly stopping for breath, '...and Benedetta is at your disposal for anything you may need.' She indicated a maid hovering at our side, not dissimilar in years to my own, I considered. Far from the exacting battleaxe I had conjured, though I was not foolish enough to think I could trust her any better for the fact.

'You are very kind, Mrs Harper.'

'Nobody here calls me Mrs Harper, child. You must call me Isabella. It sounds so much more relaxed and younger, don't you think?'

I felt a slight hint of a smile upon my lips at this unconventional intimacy, 'As you prefer.' I perhaps would have returned the invitation if she had not already called me by my Christian name. Yet, instead of feeling the irritation I wanted to feel, there was such an easy warmness to her character that I could not allow myself to be aloof in the face of it. So I contrived enough civility to hide my despair and meet her small talk with a measure of interest and good manner, though in truth, her warmth made me want to collapse into sobs after being so long bereft of company and kindness. I must remember not to let this gull me into a false sense of security. This was *his* family, I reminded myself.

It was a relief when she dispatched me to the care of Benedetta to be shown to my rooms so I could finally be at ease with my melancholy again. Though even that felt impossible in the strangeness of the unfamiliar room, which, although beautifully appointed and catering to every comfort, felt so alien to me in its exotic style. I felt further from home than I ever had, and with it, further from Annalise. I studied the room for a moment to familiarise myself and considered its frescoed panels against a backdrop of pink and green paint, a colour theme that was echoed through the soft furnishings and upholstered furniture. I sunk onto the bed staring through the open shuttered windows into an azure shade of sky rendered blinding bright by the brilliance of the afternoon sun; all the while, winter still raged inside of me.

It wasn't till dinner that afternoon that I met the rest of the family. Mr Harper, Giles's uncle, was a typical English gentleman but perhaps more congenial than I had expected from his strong-featured face. I supposed it was there I could find a slight familial resemblance, but only in looks. Where his uncle seemed authentically charming, Giles' attempts were as transparent as the wine glass I sipped from, to me at least. As to the rest of them, I could not be sure with their warmth being so forthcoming, and yet one of the sons seemed more reserved and less interested in what Giles had to say. I wondered at the length and depth of his acquaintance with them. It could not be so well established given he had only learned of his true parentage more lately and no doubt thrust himself upon their acquaintance since.

'Mr Harper is my Father's younger half- brother, long estranged from that branch of the family, I understand. His mother was English and he was brought up in Chesham,' Giles apprised me as we went into dinner. Marco, one of their two sons, appeared to be of a similar age to Giles, if not a fraction his junior. His brother Dante was perhaps a decade younger than he. Both were exceptionally courteous and extremely easy on the eye. But I was quite disappointed to learn that both the Harper's daughters had left home to begin their married lives. It looked as though my days would be spent in solitude, although that was favourable over the company I would keep for the remainder of my time as Giles's wife.

When we had been shown to our bedchambers earlier, I was relieved to find they were separate as was customary in England. It was difficult to tell how much was transferable or alien from one shore to another as it seemed to follow no certainties, with some things alike and others quite unorthodox, such as dining so heartily at three o'clock during a time they called siesta. And whilst I was accustomed to numerous courses at formal dinners, and Isabella had said this was a celebratory affair on occasion of our welcome, family dinners were rarely such concerns as this; one plate was continuously replaced by another, and yet my appetite had been so reduced I could not keep up.

'You do not want the fish course?' Isabella asked as I pushed an odd-looking tentacle about my plate.

'I am not sure what it is?' I said, somewhat embarrassed to confess it.

'It is Polpo...um, how do you say it in English, my dear?' Isabella turned to her husband and asked.

He finished his own mouthful. 'Octopus,' he told me with a reassuring smile. 'It tastes better than it looks.'

I smiled weakly. I would have preferred to take his word for it, but Giles turned to me and added, 'Give it a go, dear. It is very good.'

I cut the smallest of portions and raised the fork to my mouth.

'You don't have to eat it if you prefer not to,' Mr Harper countered.

I took a complaisant bite and refrained from spitting it back out again.

'Tomorrow,' Isabella said, 'We will go to see the cook together, and you will tell her of some English dishes that suit your liking.'

'Really, there is no need to go to any trouble. The food is delicious,' I offered, which had been true up until this course.

'I insist. I want you to treat this like your own home now, alright? You must not feel that anything is too much trouble. We are family and my home is your home. Giles already knows, but you feel like an outsider for now. I want you to know that you are not, alright?'

I nodded, and the older of her sons said to her in Italian, perhaps in expectation that I might not understand it, 'Mama, do not make a fuss... leave her be. You can discuss it tomorrow.'

'Forgive me, Eleanor,' she corrected herself and changed the subject to one of the forthcoming Easter celebrations and told me that her daughters would come to breakfast on Easter Sunday, and I would meet them then. She explained that I had been given their eldest daughter Maria's old room, and I did my best to commend its appointment and show a little gratitude. But, however comfortable and kind the gesture was, the fact that I did not belong here remained unaltered by it.

Giles spent the evening in the billiards room with the other men smoking cigars, and was already half inebriated when we left the table. I could now appreciate the advantage of this arrangement in having him diverted and in less need of my company. Which was just as well, as I was beginning to feel the suffocation of his proximity so irksomely, I was not sure how much more I could go on in subdued tolerance. Isabella had offered to keep me company in his place, but I felt homesick and sorry for myself and knew she deserved better company than I could be this night. So I politely declined on account of being tired from the journey and went directly to my room. As soon as the door closed behind me, I ran to the bed, threw myself onto it and buried my face into the pillows just in time to catch my tears. They had been welling all day and were desperate for release now I finally had the privacy to allow it. The reality of it all had hit me with its full force now I was actually here. I was without Annalise, far from home, and somehow, I would have to find the strength to bear it alone, without anyone to confide in, to understand the darkness of my isolation.

Presently, my biggest fear was of myself. With no one to reassure me, to remind me of the *whys*—why I was enduring this—how long could I reasonably convince myself to keep going? How long before I fell apart and resorted to something rash, as was my most natural reaction to such situations? The onslaught of tears was both physically and emotionally exhausting, yet I could not sleep that night with so much racing through my mind. Even when I finally calmed, it became like a fog settling over me that I could neither focus on nor evade. But I was distracted, listening carefully to every sound beyond my closed door that might alert me to the possibility of his coming. So far, I had escaped his advances since we'd left Falmouth, but I knew it could not last forever.

It must have been an hour later as I was just beginning to doze when I heard clumsy footsteps staggering along the hall. I listened hard as they grew louder and closer until they paused. *Please no.* I felt my drowsy limbs tense up and threaten to stiffen. The door handle turned and footsteps entered. I had my back to the door so I couldn't see, but I didn't need to, I could feel him there. I kept my eyes closed. I hadn't even realised I had been holding my breath. I exhaled it as softly as anxiety would permit, trying for a convincing attempt at being asleep. The door swung shut and I tried not to flinch as I felt his presence draw closer. My skin prickled, and I noticed every small muscle in my throat tighten and constrict until it ached. He must have leant down close to my face because I had to restrain the urge to cough at the stink of stale cigar smoke and liquor. Then I heard the thud of what must have been his shoes falling to the floor, followed by the rustling sounds of him undressing. The blankets lifted, the mattress sunk beside me, and my stomach coiled. I could feel the heat of his breath against my cheek as his face drew close to mine.

'Wake up, sleeping beauty,' he roused in a ridiculous voice that did not suit his gruff tone.

He's definitely drunk, I inwardly sighed, still persisting in my best attempt to fake my slumber. I felt a clammy palm upon my bound forearm and fought not to shrink from it as the shivers crawled over me inch by inch. *It's alright. You are alright. Think of something, distract yourself.* Then it slid down to my waist and I wanted to scream, cry, and vomit, simultaneously.

'Wakey wakey, Mrs Craythorne,' he continued.

Ignore him, I warned myself, but feeling his hand slither back up and cup my breast, I couldn't do it.

'What are you doing?' I exclaimed, taking care to sound sleepy as I flung his hand off of me.

'Is that any manner to speak to your husband with?' his tone mocking. He reclaimed my breast with greater determination, and when I threw it back off with equal force, I sat up sharp and edged away. 'Am I not to sleep now?' I spat, hugging my breasts protectively in my arms.

'I have been patient with you, Eleanor...' Even in his brandy-laced tone I could not mistake the edge of tenacity in it. '...very patient. All your relentless sobbing into the pillow I have had to endure for weeks. But tonight, I will take what is mine to take, with or without your excuses.'

I edged back as far as I could. 'You know what the Surgeon said! Two courses must pass before we resume such relations. But only one has passed! Do you want me to fall unwell? Do you want to cause me some damage that may injure my chance of childbearing again?' I could think of nothing else.

'Nonsense, excuses, excuses. That was weeks ago. The Surgeon was over-cautious. You are quite well now.' He closed in on me and put his hand firmly on my thigh, spread me open and pushed his finger inside of me. 'Mmm, it all feels perfectly handsome in here, I assure you. Now, let us not make this any harder than it needs to be. Relax, you might even enjoy it.' He grinned, then secured my head with his other hand whilst he forced a kiss against my mouth.

The stench of his sour breath and the clumsy slobbering of his mouth against me was unbearable. I clamped my lips shut. Part of me was saying: *get it over with Eleanor. It is inevitable.* But with every slimy stroke of his tongue, I felt the rage inside me growing fiercely like a rising flame. I had been here before, and the memory haunted me still, but it was anger, not fear, that remained constant to me. I felt his fingers building rhythm inside me and tried to ease myself off of them. When I could not, instead, I pushed him hard off of me, which wasn't difficult in his intoxicated state, even with the strength of only one good arm. 'I am not in the mood. I am tired and still recovering!' I snarled, wiping his saliva from my mouth with the corner of the sheet.

He had fallen to the side of me, landing on his back. He lifted his head and glared at me intensely, and suddenly, the fear set in. It was an icy and determined stare that made my blood run cold as it crept over me. 'I do not care for your mood!' He scrambled back towards me before I could free myself of the sheet and escape the bed. 'You will do your duty, by gad you will!' I made another dash to wriggle away but he grabbed me by the shoulders, causing me to jar at the pain of my healing one, and threw me back down. He was strong but unsteady in his drunkenness.

'Get off me, GET OFF!' I screamed and clawed with my only good hand as he grasped furiously at me and forced his body against mine until I was entirely beneath the weight of him and unable to break free. He put his hand over my mouth, and like a flash, I remembered that vulgar night again. *Bite him; bite like you did before.*

I managed to open my mouth enough to bear my teeth beneath his palm. I looked at him considering it.

He was warning me to 'shut up' in a low grumble through his gritted teeth. Something in his dark gaze made me lose my nerve, so I squirmed and shook my head from side to side to free it, but the headboard was wedged behind me and his hand was firmly wrapped around my jaw holding me against it. 'Mmm mmm,' I mumbled beneath his palm, begging him to release me. But he wouldn't stop; he carried on wildly tugging at my night shift with his other hand. Then I heard the tear of the fabric and felt the cool air against my naked breasts. I opened my mouth wider and barely managed to grasp a chunk of his fleshy palm between my teeth, but I sunk my teeth down with all my bite and he immediately withdrew his hand, gasping.

'You vicious little bitch!' he growled and lifted his arm, shaking out the pain.

I rolled onto my side and pushed up off the mattress to make a run for it, but before I had managed to escape him, I felt the back of his hand wallop painfully across the side of my face. The pain was so immediate at first, I thought he had broken my jaw. I held it in my hand and tried to open my mouth.

He wasted no time as I cowered and hooked his hands underneath my knees, dragging me down until I was lying beneath his weight once more. *I cannot win this.* The realisation sent a surge of panic coursing through me.

He must have read the fear in my eyes because his lips curled up into a triumphant grin. 'Come, wife. Let us not pretend you are a beginner,' he said as he fought past the resistance in my thighs to prise them open and smiled widely when he succeeded in pinning me firmly down, legs astride him. No matter how I fought, I knew this would only go one way now.

'Or do you only whore yourself out, out of wedlock?'

'Yes, a whore, and what's more, a whore that refuses to lie with you!' I managed to scream before the next blow came. But this one was harder and swifter than the last, knocking the last of the fight from me. I could feel the hot sting of tears burning my eyes. I held my wounded cheek and cried silently. I was defeated.

'I am your husband, and you *will* oblige me this night and every other night I wish to have my way. Understand?' he grunted into my ear as he towered above me, wriggling about to find his way in.

This is it. I shut my eyes tight and braced myself as he thrust more aggressively each time. I didn't move. I didn't even *feel* after the first few movements. I wasn't there. It wasn't me. I was somewhere else.

CHAPTER FOUR

Silver Lining.

Annalise. February 1822.

Day of Falmouth departure continued.

Annalise wasn't sure how long she'd sat on the floor crying as the ship nudged away, but by the time she got up, its distant view had withered to half its size, veiled in a hazy mist of sea spray sky. It looked now, much as it felt: *Not real* like a toy ship set to sail upon a pond or lake that had floated too far askew to make out its finer detail. It was hard to imagine it capable of containing them all aboard it now. *Had Eleanor realised yet that she was gone?* She must have begun to question such a lengthy absence by now. The envisaged image of her face as she read the letter Annalise had been forced to compose made her cringe. Would she feel the instant demise of her soul at the realisation of her words, just as Annalise had in composing them? Though they were mostly *his* words. The best she could do was temper the acerbity of tone in a paltry attempt to soften the blow. Not that Eleanor would know that. She would be forgiven for thinking the scheme to be her own, considering how slyly he had staged it all. Consider it a coward's way out of a difficult calamity. She knew Eleanor had already drawn the conclusion before now. That's why she'd been intent on sending Annalise back to Carshalton; she thought it a kindness to provide her with an exit from this impossible situation—made the suggestion in the belief that Annalise either could not, or would not, approach it herself. But she had been wrong. *Oh, so wrong.*

Annalise could not deny that the thought had not crossed her mind in the darkest moments of their capture. She had considered how much easier it might be to return to the life waiting for her in Carshalton and be free, not only of him, but of the torture of watching him punish and reduce her love to a creature of abominable subservience when she knew her to have the heart of a warrior beating inside her chest. That if it were not for her love for Annalise weighing greater than her usual insurgent spirit, then she would not have borne his demands for a minute, to the devil with the consequences. But despite it all, the hardest and most insufferable of moments, she would have lived through a thousand more over enduring the pain of losing her and leaving her alone. But it seemed of late, that Eleanor did not know this, that she had begun to doubt her. What a cruel realisation it would be for her to be left believing herself to have been right all along, that this was what Annalise had chosen. *Surely, she would know better*—if not by way of logic, then by way of instinct.

Annalise was so much overcome she could not remain a moment longer to watch the ship fade away completely as other onlookers did, standing about her, waving off their departed. She looked down at her portmanteau where it had fallen and mustered the strength to pick it up. As she rose from its retrieval, a bird landed on the railing right in front of her, and she wondered what it would be like to have its wings; to be able to fly the distance between the ship and the shore.

She was, of course, supposed to head home now. Reap the scant reward of her betrayal in escaping with her freedom and being at liberty to return home to Poppy and Maggie. Giles had said the coach would await her on the other side of the pier outside the *Maritime Hotel* which they had passed as they drove onto the quayside, and she could see its imposing façade jutting out against the water's edge if she turned her gaze away from the seascape. He said he had arranged for all her boarding expenses to be covered for the many stops along the journey, and all being well, she would be back home by Wednesday next.

But she was not going to find the coach. She was not going home at all. *No.* Who was she fooling? There was no home without Len. It had been an ugly mistake to allow herself to be pressed into such a miserable bargain she knew neither of them could endure, be it six months or more—which was what she suspected, given how everything he said was deserving of mistrust. It would not surprise her if he intended to spirit her off without any intention of returning with her again and keeping her tucked safely out of reach of all who loved her. All who might help her break free of his captivity. It was ridiculous to fix her hopes upon Eleanor returning after six months. But even more ridiculous to her was the notion that she had deceived herself into believing she could return to Carshalton and get on with some semblance of ordinary life in the meantime. That perhaps if she buckled down and got stuck in with all the work to be done at the shop, a six-month would soon fly by. But it was little more than a delusion. She realised that now, in all its profound horror, there was no way she could pretend otherwise under the guise of some feeble hope of him keeping his word, not now she understood its worth.

She. Could not. Live. Without her. Not now. As if it would be any life at all without Eleanor to share in it. As if she could fall into some daily routine knowing that Len was suffering, held prisoner by him, that she would face bearing the child without her. It would be, at best, a painfully hollow existence, at worst, a daily effort to go on breathing. No, it would not even be enough to justify the effort. Not now she knew what verve and vigour life could be full of when the heart was complete, content. Until Eleanor had brought it about to such a state of repair, she had forgotten its true capacity. Had used the heartache and grief of her mother's loss as justification for considering the heart little more than a vulnerability, a source of pain and sufferance. But its full capacity had been restored now, and she had known happiness again when the most she had hoped for after losing her mama was an absence of pain.

She had been content with the prospect of such a bargain then, thinking it such an elevation of spirit to the anguish she had been drowning in since the day she pressed kisses to her mama's closed eyelids and bid her last farewell. But the destination she had been bound for had been much greater than she could foresee, then. Beyond anything she could have dared hope for. And yet, so it was. She had been blessed with so many miracles since, as if her mama was casting them down from the heavens in lieu of her own departure. And now, she had let it slip away again. She was back where she began. No worse, for she knew now what was possible. *Oh, mama, I beg thee to send me another miracle and help me find my way back to her.*

She reminded herself through the aching pangs of guilt that she had done only what had been necessary to protect them both for now, and in that, she had little choice if she wanted to spare them both a life of incarceration, or worse. Eleanor might have been on her way to foreign shores, but at least she was not in the Bodmin Asylum, and Annalise was not rendered useless, sitting out her days in gaol for arson. For that reprieve, she could at least be grateful. But she realised suddenly that this was all it was to be. All it was *meant* to be. A way of buying some time. It was never intended to be a *real* goodbye. Perhaps if she could look at it differently she might consider it a blessing in disguise, a necessary turn of events to permit her a way of intervening. She was not able to affect it from within, despite her vain attempts. But now she was outside of the situation, perhaps she could contrive the means and method to follow on after her and break her free from his captivity now. Her freedom would grant her the ability to plot and plan covertly, and the delay might afford her the element of surprise when he had thought his mission complete, when he may have begun to drop his guard, supposing she was safely out of reach. Yes, that's what this was: an opportunity to achieve what they could not beneath his gaze. And that was the silver lining beneath this heavy cloud.

She would find out the fare, await another sailing, and set out once she could afford it. She would have to write back to Poppy to ask for some money. A great deal of money, she considered, if it was to be enough to get her over to Venice and bring them both back again with all the sustenance such a lengthy trip would require. She hadn't the slightest notion of how to cost such a trip, and then there was the mention of a passport, which Giles had said he didn't include her on, although she wasn't sure if it was true or another of his tricks. She wouldn't have the faintest idea of how to go about obtaining one, but she would have to find out. And so that was what she meant to do. Head over to that packet agent's office she had seen across the road and make enquiries. Focus not on what she had lost but turn her mind to how she might reclaim it again. Assess what must be done, calculate the costs and consider how she would meet them. If they were too obscene to ask Poppy for, she supposed she could try to find some work here and raise part of it that way. Though that would mean delay and she was already back foot.

Then, there was the possibility she could find out how to raise a loan on the dwelling shop if she had to. Would that be any quicker to effect if she could manage it? How much could she hope to raise? At all events, she would try to keep the costs as low as possible. She would not need a grand ticket. Steerage would do if it got her there. Though it would not suffice for Eleanor, especially in her present condition. She must remember to enquire about both classes of fare to account correctly for it. And then there was the matter of timing. Eleanor could not travel too close to her term and end up giving birth on a ship. Given the fact the journey there took weeks, she hadn't long to get there if they were to return home again in time for the birth. What would it mean if her child was not born in England? Would it cease to be a British subject? Would it return an alien? It would certainly render it impossible for Annalise to pretend to be its parent and protect it from Giles. It seemed more sensible that the attempt must be made before its birth, to be on the safe side.

With this multitude of competing thoughts in her head and queries upon her tongue, she arrived opposite the Packet Agent's Office on *Arwenack Street* and attempted to get her questions into some better order and restrict them to those they might actually be able to answer.

CHAPTER FIVE

La Bruna in Gondoletta.

Eleanor. March 1822.

When I opened my eyes to the unfamiliarity of the room, I momentarily forgot where I was. At first, I thought I was at home in Cuddington as the smell of fresh baking drifted beneath my nose. I rubbed my eyes and noticed how my face hurt, and then the memory came back to me in all its vivid horror.

'I brought you a tea tray,' came his voice from nowhere.

I sat up sharp and found him standing at the bedside, fully dressed. The sound of his voice made my skin crawl as I began to remember the filth he had whispered into my ear last night as he desecrated my body with such violence I was sure I had left it entirely at times. I made no reply.

He picked up the tray and placed it on my lap.

I contemplated throwing it at him, but I was all too aware that he was a man without boundaries and decided against it.

'Look, about last night, I apologise,' he said, perching on the mattress beside me. 'Here, let me pour you a cup.'

Still, I gave no answer. How dare he further insult me with an apology, like he was asking forgiveness for something trivial like stepping on my toe! I turned away from him. What he had done was beyond forgiveness. I had never known such vehemence and perversion. It seemed like he had withstood all those nights of abstinence on the ship to intensify his hunger and depravity. I remembered how he made me bleed with the force of him and then mocked my lack of virginity at the sight of it. There was something far beyond a healthy and natural passion to be satisfied in his appetite for me. Something cruel and twisted that frightened me.

'So you are going to ignore me all day?' he said, exasperated.

All day? Try forever!

'Very well, I can see you are still upset. Listen, I do not wish to take a heavy hand with you, wife, nor should I have to. I hope you will take time to reflect and ensure that last night is not repeated. A little effort and accommodation is all I ask. Anyway, I have to go and report our arrival to the Commissary before I head to the docks.'

I felt the mattress shift as he stood up from the bed and exhaled.

'Oh, your ornaments, the ones you had on last night—where are they?'

I welled with disappointment. 'Put away.'

'Hand them over.—I will take care of them.'

'I was going to wear them today.'

He shook his head. 'Eleanor, I don't have time for this this morning. Either you hand them over, or I shall have the room turned upside down by the servants. Which would you prefer?'

I slid the breakfast tray from my lap, got out of the bed, took them out of the trunk and threw them onto the coverlet.

He scooped them up and dropped them into his pocket. 'You may have them back when I am home, in time to dress for dinner. I can't imagine you would need them anytime sooner, shall you?'

I ignored him, crossed the room and peered out of the window.

'You are not to leave the house; the family and staff have my instructions, so if that's what's in your head, I suggest you put it right out of mind. You can't get anywhere beyond Venice without permission from the Police, neither in country, nor out, so any notion of such schemes have already been accounted for. I shan't warn you twice. Any attempt whatsoever will result in my renting somewhere of our own, and Digby will sit over you every hour of the day if that's what it takes. I hope I've made myself clear?'

I held my silence until he finally left. *How was I to endure this?*

It had taken a long time to dress this morning, partly because my new maid, Benedetta, was unfamiliar with me, and my Italian so unpractised it took a long time for us to understand each other to begin with. And partly because it had taken many layers of powder to soften the appearance of my inflamed cheekbone and faintly bruised eyelid once Benedetta had finally mixed the right concoctions from the kitchen to manage the task. But eventually, and reluctantly, I made my way downstairs.

I was hardly in the mood to take breakfast with a family of strangers in an unfamiliar house following such a night. But what choice had I? I couldn't stay in that room all day, not after that. I feared my remaining there above a moment longer would cause me to unleash a sustained attack upon the furniture and allow all the pent-up rage inside me to find its way free. So I forced myself out into the corridor, though I struggled to find my bearings on the journey down. The house was not simply laid out, and I could not remember the way I had come to it last night, so I paused and guessed at each turn of corridor. Remembering the nymph statuette as I passed it, I took the staircase down two levels and managed to navigate my way to the breakfast room. I was surprised to find the table empty and un-laid. *How odd.* Did they also take breakfast at some peculiar hour here? I looked about me, then turned to leave just as a footman sauntered in from behind a gauzy curtain on the far side of the room.

'Buongiorno, Signora,' he greeted me, balanced a tray on one arm and held the curtain aside with the other, gesturing for me to walk through.

'Grazie mille,' I replied, ducking beneath it and heading out onto a large terrace that bridged its way from the breakfast room doorway to another part of the house directly opposite, which I was not familiar with. One side overlooked the courtyard from above, and the other overlooked one of the many winding canals that snaked their way back to the lagoon. I followed the line of the wall, watching as I walked, all the people below me treading the pathways and bridges or gliding beneath in gondolas. They all appeared to have somewhere to be. I wished to be like them, any one of them, whether a merchant or a maid, a seamstress or an oarsman. Anything but myself, any life but my own. Somewhere to be expected; anywhere but here and with him. Someone to know my face and comfort me in my alienation. It was Annalise I referred to in all of my thoughts. I could not even fool myself otherwise. However much I raged at her for abandoning me, however fractured my heart; still, it beat for her. My soul had grown extinct without her in only weeks of separation. What of the time laid out before me? So I supposed it would not matter if I were like the finely dressed merchant I followed with stinging eyes, or the simply dressed maiden who drifted by on a small boat beside him. My freedom would be nothing without her, so what did it matter if I was tied to him and his ways? To suffer her loss was to suffer in all ways, and *nothing* would alter that.

As the scene of the family breakfasting came before me, I pulled myself together and took a steadying breath. The table, which was simply laid for breakfast, had only two occupants and the informality, at least, was somewhat reassuring. For a fleeting moment, I was reminded of my father, the way the gentleman had sunk behind his newspaper so it obscured his face.

'Good morning,' Dante smiled, noticing me once he lowered his paper at the scrape of my chair against the flags as the Butler seated me opposite him.

I was surprised to find it was not Mr Harper and wondered where Isabella was. I could at least find some small conversation with her. As for what I was to say to both their sons, I had no idea. 'Good morning,' I responded as I sank into the seat feeling as though I was encroaching on a private breakfasting at a gentleman's club.

Marco looked up from a letter he was reading and smiled warmly. 'Good morning, Mrs Craythorne,' he said, reaching for a pot of what I supposed to be very strong coffee by the smell of it.

'Please, Eleanor is perfectly acceptable,' I replied, forcing my anxious mouth into a smile.

Marco put his papers down. 'Eleanor it is then. Will you take coffee?' He offered out the pot he had just filled his own cup with.

The smell made me queasy. I had not yet recovered my taste for it since the pregnancy. 'Thank you, no.'

'Chocolate then?'

'Yes, please.'

'I hope you're recovered from your travels?' Dante asked me.

'Yes, somewhat recovered,' I lied and pulled a tendril of hair from behind my ear to cover my powdered brow.

'Not a seafaring enthusiast like Giles, I take it?' he replied, cocking his head.

I stirred some honey into my cup. 'No, not in the least, I confess.'

Dante folded his paper into a neat square. 'Nor I. Building ships is one thing, sailing in them, quite another.'

'You build ships?' I asked, pretending an interest.

'Yes, Giles didn't mention it?'

I shook my head and lifted my cup to my lips.

'Brother, don't bore our guest with talk of ships. I daresay she prefers not to think of them for a while after such a journey,' said Marco.

'Just because you find them a bore, brother, it does not mean everyone does.'

'It's quite alright,' I offered, because I cared not about the topic of conversation in such a head; all words had become meaningless sounds to me.

'My mother should be down soon. She usually takes her coffee in her chamber and then rises about now,' Marco added.

I nodded. I was relieved to hear it. I was grateful for their genial efforts, but I did not know what to say to them any more than they, me. It was most uncomfortable, for all our attempts to pretend it quite an ordinary scene, we were strangers with no common ground with which to tide us by. Then, the pause in our conversation as we struggled for something to fill the silence was broken entirely by the echoing sound of singing rising from the canal below. 'What is that?' I asked, bending my ear towards it.

'It is a passing gondolier,' Dante stood, 'Come, see if you like.'

Feeling obliged now as he walked over to the wall and pointed down, I rose and joined him there to reveal the sight of a gondolier passing beneath. He looked up at us now, lifted his hat to me and continued singing, though our interest appeared to induce him into serenading me quite animatedly, and I was in no mood to receive such marked attention.

'Well, he's taken a liking to you. He changes the very lyrics for you,' Dante said, mildly amused.

I turned away from the gondolier. 'What is he singing?' I asked in the hope of returning to a more reasonable point.

He smirked and his eyes sparkled, 'Well, he *was* singing *La biondina in gondoletta,* but at the sight of you, it seems she has been transformed to the La bruna in gondoletta.'

I felt my cheeks ablush. 'I think I shall sit back down,' I said, and Dante followed, resuming our places at the table as the song continued:

"With you, for you brunette,
on the sea, I will dream,

the purple mouth,
in the shadows, I will kiss it..."

I set my gaze to the table and did my utmost to ignore it.

'You must forgive my curiosity, Eleanor, but I cannot resist the question,' Dante said, taking a pastry from beneath its cover and offering one out to me, '...pray tell me how my old cousin has managed to sweep such a fair maiden off her feet?' He looked half bemused, half serious. 'What?' he said to Marco, who was frowning his disapproval at his brother's question.

'Perhaps brother, you should hold your tongue,' Marco reprimanded him in Italian, likely thinking I could not understand him since we had only spoken in English so far.

But the truth was, I knew the question to be lurking on all of their lips, even if Dante was the only one impertinent enough to speak it. That Giles and I were a mismatch in all ways we could be was no cryptic secret, however well he tried to give an alternate account at our welcome dinner, speaking himself up as the new squire of the country manor at Beddington, as if that justified his angling for a daughter on the *Bon Ton*. Usually, such mismatches were explained away simply by matters of money and rank, but it was made fairly clear I was in need of neither after his regaling of my good stock yesterday. That left the only and rarest of possibilities to account for it: a love match. But any fool could see there was nothing of that nature between us. But what was I to say in answer? *Because I was a fool, who was ripe for trickery and had been spirited here against my will. As it happens, he forced himself upon me under this very roof last night!* The temptation was tangible. 'I think you mean to flatter me, Sir.' I contrived, reaching for a refill.

'Allow me,' Marco offered with a considering expression. 'I think it shall be a very warm day today. Might you prefer to sit where you are better shaded?'

'Oh, it's fine. Nice, in fact, to feel the warmth of the sun after such a long winter.' I was grateful for his attempt at diversion. Even though he and his brother looked very much alike, I could already see the differences between them plainly—Dante: all boyish mischief and overconfident charm. Marco, a pillar of propriety and restrained sensibility.

He put the cup down beside me.

'Thank you,' I said, replacing my hands on the table as they suddenly seemed in the way.

He returned the pot to its coaster and paused to study me a moment. 'You've had an accident?' He frowned and gently swept a ringlet aside to better examine my cheek.

This intrusion shocked me and I blinked, taken aback, then edged away as his smile faded and his expression clouded with concern. 'Oh yes, that,' I dismissed it quickly and replaced my hair. 'I, I'm a terrible sleepwalker, you see. A dangerous thing when in new surroundings. I daresay I shall soon learn where all the obstacles are.' I buttered my bread with trembling hands I could not steady and knew would give me away.

'Indeed,' he replied, unconvinced. 'That's quite a nasty bruise coming up.'

'Well, it certainly awoke me with a start.' I contrived a weak laugh. It must have been the nerves because I was furious now. *The impertinence.* How dare this stranger labour a point upon which he had no right to question me. Dare to touch me.

'Yes. Yes, I'd imagine it did.' The pity in his eyes was unbearable. He was obviously not easily fooled. I turned away to avoid eye contact with him, for I was on the cusp of either breaking out in quite a rage or bursting into tears. I had the strength or desire for neither and before such an audience. I looked across to Dante and was relieved that he didn't seem to understand the direction of the conversation, sat pensively looking between us, chewing on his croissant.

'Well, I better get down to the Shipyard now Giles is back,' he said, brushing the crumbs from his hands and consulting his pocket watch. 'Gone are my leisurely breakfast hours. Your husband's quite the taskmaster,' he sighed.

I dropped my knife into the plate and it made me jump.

Marco cut him an exasperated glance that he clearly couldn't fathom.

'Have a good day!' he said, rising from his seat.

'Are you sure you are well?' Marco asked me when he was gone.

'Actually, I do not feel so well after all,' I told him flatly, hoping he would discern from my manner how unwelcome his interference was. I pulled the chair out gracelessly. 'I think I might lie down a while if you'll excuse me.'

'You haven't taken any breakfast...'

'No, I think I've lost my appetite,' I stood up to leave.

'Shall I have Baldassare bring you something up?' He rose with me.

'No! No, thank you,' I corrected myself. And I quickly turned and left without giving him the chance to detain me any longer.

I sat at my chamber window watching the canal below, replaying the whole morning in my head. It was not going to be easy here. Being in a house full of strangers complicated things in a way I hadn't accounted for. The obstacles seemed to loom from every direction. Under the surveillance of so many eyes, not a coin to my name, nor a pen or sheet of paper to send for help. Even the one thing of potential value on my person—my replacement wedding band—I suspected to be a cheap crude metal, which was why I was permitted to keep it. But if Giles thought I would be thwarted by his confiscations and threats, he was mistaken. I suspected most of them were bluff, "police permission" to travel, indeed. I was not a criminal and would not be fooled by such nonsense. Though the threat of taking me off to some private lodging and having Digby keep watch over me, I could not dismiss so easily.—I knew after all the empty houses he'd arranged on our journey to Falmouth, this threat would be carried out if he felt it warranted, and whilst I suspected he would prefer it otherwise, I knew if I pushed him, that would be the most likely result. So I would have to be careful. I likely would have only one shot at making a run, and until I had money or means, I could afford to take no risks. I must secure the means first, then bide my time until I better understood the opportunities for escape. I must watch and wait patiently to learn the rhythms of the family and staff, keep a keen eye out for any lapses in attention...

When all the men were gone from the house and Isabella was receiving a call in her private parlour, I considered there must be no better time to go on a covert search for paper, pen, and ink. If I could find the means to make contact home and let them know where I was, make a plea to send help, I was sure I could make my stay here a brief one. Then there was Mr Banfield, who likely already sent on my letter to Lady W., but still had no address to forward me any reply, and that must be set right in the first instance. Yes, he must be the priority, for my plea was already progressed, it remained only to see what help might come from that quarter. There must be a way of sending money overseas, though I had no idea how it worked. But my father would, likely Lady W. would, too.

'Benedetta,' I said once she had finished tidying my chamber. 'I don't suppose I might prevail upon you for a tour of the house? I own I got quite lost just getting to breakfast this morning, so it might be an idea to better familiarise myself with the house.—Isabella did offer me yesterday, but I was not feeling up to it then.'

'Of course, Signora, though I shall need to ask the housekeeper for the keys as some places are kept locked for they are little used.'

'No hurry,' I replied, spotting an opportunity in her absence. 'I will wait here for you,' I said, and pretended to busy myself adjusting my hairpiece in the mirror while waiting for her to leave. Once she vanished from the room and I heard the clip of her footsteps dissipating, I rose from the dressing table and headed straight for the interconnecting door between my chamber and Giles's. I trod lightly into the room, taking care to be quiet and checking for any servants, but the coast was clear. Somewhere in here were the jewels he had just confiscated, the others he had bought me, and Leonard's pocket watch, which I knew was worth a good deal of money.—Recovering that alone would likely be enough to sustain a journey home. *Where would he keep them?* I directed a cursory glance about the room, getting the measure of it.

Everything was in pristine order, and I wondered if he had even unpacked yet. I opened the wardrobe doors to find his clothes hung up inside them. I checked the pockets of his coats for any forgotten loose coins, but there was nothing.

Perhaps if I had not hidden the ornaments in the trunk and simply put them away in my drawer, he might have been less suspicious of my intentions, but we both knew what they amounted to, and so I was not expecting an easy find, nor did I have long to conduct the search. Accordingly, I shut the wardrobe door and bypassed all the obvious choices, heading straight for his trunks, which were mostly locked, before trying at drawers and cabinets, running my hands beneath the bed and the underside of tables. But I discovered nothing of note, nothing at all of any value. So I went back to the locked drawer in his desk, took a hairpin from the hairpiece I had just re-pinned, knelt in front of it and began to try to pick open the lock. I was hardly practised in this skill, though I had once seen my brother Henry manage it successfully in my childhood. As for precisely how he did it, I was not sure, but it seemed a persistent wiggling about seemed to achieve it. But I had no time to take such pains, so when it failed to yield after a minute, I moved onto the locked trunks, and presto, the latch clicked, and I lifted the lid.

Now, what was in here that needed locking away? I lifted a heap of ledgers and papers from it, feeling about for any clue of something other than what appeared to be accounting and insurance papers to do with his shipping business. I supposed he must have bought them with him from England, so they must have been important. I sifted through them brusquely but found nothing useful, and once I realised this, I began to restack them back into the trunk in the order I had found them. I picked the lock of the next trunk, too, but that only revealed unpacked shoes and heavy winter coats. There was one more left, but I knew before I opened it with the hairpin that it felt light and I was not surprised to find it empty. There remained only the drawer in his desk, but hearing sounds beyond the corridor now, I had no more time to renew the attempt. I got up quickly, checked the room to ensure it was all in order, and rushed out of it, having ascertained that it was. As I closed the door behind me, Benedetta opened my own.

'Ah, we are ready to go then?' I asked, sliding the hairpin back into place.

She looked at me suspiciously but only said, 'Yes, Signora, I have the keys.'

We went out into the corridor together, and I tried to collect myself. I must do my best to keep my true objective below the radar now. I already knew she was suspicious of me.

'Most of this level is out of use, Signora, apart from you and your husband's apartments, but I can show you if you like?'

'No need,' I said, having already ventured into one by mistake and found the furniture dressed in Holland covers. I supposed the rooms had not been in use since the Harper daughters were at home, and it seemed unlikely there would be anything useful to be found there. And if there was, I would have to sneak a solitary visit to lift the covers and have a proper root around.

She led me down the staircase to the floor below and pointed out the family bed chambers and private apartments, though, of course, I could not expect her to let me into these private rooms, though I thought them the most likely to be furnished with what I needed. We headed next to the *Piano Nobile*. I was somewhat more familiar with this level and had already scanned the drawing room, breakfast room and dining room to no avail. We went in and out of the billiards room where I hoped to find something of use, but there was only a chalkboard and stick of chalk for keeping scores upon it.

It was when she unlocked Mr Harper's study and permitted me to poke my head about the door that I spotted precisely what I needed out upon the desk, quill and inkstand poised. But since it was kept locked, I was not sure how useful it would prove. I was never left entirely alone about the house and could hardly afford to pinch the key and be found sneaking about in there. But I would keep an eye out for any passing opportunity of a door left open whilst the servants were cleaning, now I knew where to find it.

'Is there a library here?' I asked her when I realised we were running out of rooms on this level.

'Yes, Signora, though it is little used, but I can take you.'

'I do have quite a fancy for a good book from time to time, and it seems I shall have a lot of that at my disposal now.'

She nodded and we crossed back through the disused ballroom and into a narrower room beyond it with a mock wall comprised of leaded glass windows and a pair of opening doors. Ornate gold gilt bookcases lined the walls like little cathedrals, with steeples rising from the top shelf. It was small but fully stocked. Though it seemed more of a display room than a well-used one, and though there were a couple of sofas and sideboards, there was no desk or escritoire to be found, and my heart sank. It seemed the only way I was likely to get hold of what I needed was to sneak into some private rooms if an opportunity to do so presented itself. I kept a cursory glance about as she took me down to the service level, but I was unsurprised to see nothing useful there, thinking only the Butler and perhaps the Housekeeper likely to keep them in their private parlours. Whilst I would have preferred to make such an attempt on their rooms rather than the families, it was far too busy and confined down here to manage such an attempt.

It had been a disappointing waste of an hour by the time we'd come full circle, but I supposed I at least knew where the opportunities existed now. I would be vigilant and ready to capitalise on any that presented.

CHAPTER SIX

Yesterday's Shadow.

Annalise. February 1822.

Annalise paused and took a breath at the roadside waiting for the traffic to pass. Just as she was preparing to cross, a carriage she had been waiting to overtake her drew up beside her instead. She stepped back and frowned as the window rolled down. Miss Craythorne popped her head out of it and said, in a tone of poorly veiled irritation, 'There you are. I have been waiting outside the hotel for you for an age!—I am to convey you home, I believe.'

Annalise was so astonished she didn't know what to say for the first few seconds. *Had he really the nerve to expect them both to travel back together like amicable companions?* When he'd said that *someone* would see to all the costs for her, she had been too distracted by the horror of leaving to question such trivialities as to whom. She had suspected a coachman or somesuch. Not for a minute had she considered *her*.

'Well, are you going to get in then?' she said expectant, nudging the door open.'

'No,' Annalise said flatly, closing it again. I do not wish to go with you. I hoped never to set eyes on you again and could think of nothing worse than bearing your company on such a journey!' It was all she could manage not to fly into the kind of rage at her that Eleanor did last night—*the audacity, the brazen-faced impudence.*

'Don't be a fool. I don't much wish to share the journey with you either, but I have given my word to the undertaking, and I am persuaded you will not prefer to walk the three hundred miles back home!'

'Over sharing it with you? I own I should much prefer it!'

She laughed wryly at this. 'You're as blockheaded as her, I see, and I thought you the more sensible of the pair. Suit yourself then,' she said, turned away from the sight of her and rolled up the window.

Annalise took a deep breath and composed herself as the carriage trundled past her. She waited for it to disappear around a bend in the road before she picked her portmanteau back up, crossed the road and headed into the office to find a queue at the desk. She sighed and took her place in the line. But looking about the room whilst she waited, she noticed a board advertising the fares to various places, most of which she had never heard of. Lisbon, she noted: £23.1s Cabin class and £14.13s Steerage. She was reluctant to take out her purse in the line and make a precise count of the amount she had retained from the money Eleanor had raised on the wedding ring, but she estimated that she was presently eight pounds three shillings short of the steerage fare, which was perhaps for the best given the present temptation to act on impulse and buy a ticket and set out fast behind them without a thought for how she might make the rest of the journey, or sustain herself through it.

But she could perhaps manage a request of that sum to Poppy if things were still going as well at the pie shop. It had been a few weeks now, and at two pounds a week profit, it might prove manageable, however much she hated to ask it. Maybe she could raise extra if she found some work to cover the second leg of the journey, assuming the fare would be of a similar price. But she could not be sure of the cost of the inns, especially abroad, or what else she might have to consider along the way. Would there be hacks to hire once she got there? Did such places even have hacks to hire? Then there was this passport, for one, and perhaps there would be other considerations of which she was unaware. And she would need to eat, even though the thought now seemed superfluous, like she might never have an appetite again.

She drew a little further along the queue and reminded herself she was not in line to make a purchase but to inquire when the next departure would be so she could understand the wait ahead and see how long she might need to put up for. Ask where she might obtain a passport or if she even needed one. She had a vague recollection of her mama mentioning something about a passport being required to travel about in France, so as much as she mistrusted his words, it seemed in that, there might be an element of truth. She could have done with a pencil and some paper to note it all. Her head was in such a muddle she wasn't sure she could count on her usual powers of retention.

After a half-hour wait in the queue to see the ticket clerk, it transpired that there was not to be another sailing to Lisbon for a week. By then, they would be half the first leg of the voyage through before she had even set sail, and that was only in the optimistic event that she could raise the funds in time to make the next departure. It seemed more likely it must be the one after.

'Are there other routes I might take to get to Venice?' she asked the clerk, who seemed to soften a little despite his initial perfunctory manner, perhaps noting the despair on her face, in her tone.

'Aye, there is. You could go from here to Messina, though you'd still need another sailing to get to the mainland, and you'd be landing south of the country when you're bound for the north of it.'

'But I would be on the same land? There would be no more boats to travel by?'

'You would. Though you know Venice is a little islet that can only reached by boat, don't you?'

Annalise did not. 'Well, with the exception of the ferrying across to it?'

'Yes, you could go to the closest point. The trouble is, Italy's a more complex land than ours; the peninsula must be easily eight hundred miles long, perhaps more, and it's full of all sorts of different kingdoms within it. The difference between north and south in a place of those dimensions could mean many weeks of travel overland and a great deal of inconvenience in crossing all the various borders.'

'I see. And what of the fare to Messina?'

He ran a finger along a list he had in front of him. 'Sixty-two pounds and eighteen shillings for a Cabin, Thirty-Four Pounds, one shilling and sixpence for steerage.'

Annalise gulped. 'Lisbon then shall have to answer. Tell me, Sir, if you would, what of the prices from Lisbon to Venice?'

'I couldn't rightly say miss. The Post Office has no dealings with matters of foreign transport beyond our own stations. I daresay you'd be looking for a private vessel from that point onwards, most likely a merchant ship, and they have leave to set their fares as they see fit.'

'I see. I don't suppose you might know how I could find it out?'

'Afraid not, unless you happen across the crews familiar with the place, in which case they might have a vague idea. But, from what I understand, the prices on the continent are often favourable when compared to ours. Your coin stretches a great deal farther than what we are accustomed. I daresay that even though the second sailing will be farther, the price mightn't even equal the cost of the first leg.'

This was heartening, at least, even if uncertain. 'Does that count for only sailing fares, Sir, or in general?'

'In many things, as far as I can tell. It is said that for the same amount of coin to sustain an Englishman to penury standards, one might live very well indeed upon the continent with a great many comforts. But as I said, its greater detail is beyond the experience of a land agent: the crew are the ones to ask.'

'Yes, you have been very good, Sir, I thank you. I just had one more matter to inquire about, which I think shall be in your knowing. Will I need a passport to travel on the packet?'

He obliged her despite the audible sighs and harrumphs of the queue behind her and told her that before the war, only those of the fancy classes bothered with such trifles as obtaining a passport before boarding, but those days were no more. Strictly speaking, she could board the ship without one, but she could obtain one beforehand if it so pleased her and might save her the inconvenience on arrival. But if she was minded to set on her way and obtain all the necessaries when she got there, she would likely pay a trifling fee to obtain what might be necessary. However, letters of recommendation attesting to her good character might be worth bringing along to satisfy the issuing authorities. And yes, the ticket would cover her food onboard the packet outbound, though not upon return, and he couldn't vouch for the other ship either way. That would depend, he supposed, on the vessel. And since she hadn't travelled abroad before, it might be a good idea to pop along to the bookseller on *Market Street* and seek out a guidebook which might answer many of the questions he could not. *Coxe's* book—he was sure—was the preferred choice for the Italian regions. And this was precisely what she intended to do later, though presently she could not justify the expense of such a purchase as a new book when she did not yet know how many other expenses she must meet in the interim, though she could certainly take a leisurely browse and glean a few of its pages for the time being. And if it was too much to spare, she supposed she could always write to Mr Harrison and prevail upon him to send one to her on account, ask Poppy to pay it off in instalments.

Despite the sideways glances of contempt when she finally left the clerk's counter, furnished with even these piecemeal fragments of better knowing, heartened her as she trod her way back in the direction of the *Maritime Hotel* to enquire about the price of a room. If the continent really could offer a life of comfort for the British equivalent of one of poverty, she felt hopeful the plan was feasible, and her delay in raising the fare need not be onerous.

Still, she had much to contend with and only a week to bring it all about, but right now, she needed a moment to work it all out and write off to Poppy for some money. Of all matters, this was the most pressing, given the time it would take for the post to be conveyed back and forth. If she went straight there and composed it, she could make the afternoon post, perhaps. And she had often noticed that some of the better inns and hotels would be happy to put ink and paper at the disposal of their guests as a courtesy. But she was not sure that this was *that* kind of establishment. – They had provided it at the *Royal* before Digby swept it out of reach, but she had no purse for such grand lodgings, and she very much doubted she'd be welcome at such an establishment after setting fire to it anyway, she considered, as she pushed open the heavy oak door and stepped inside the *Maritime Hotel*.

She was met instantly with the warmth of lively fires, the slightly bitter tang of stale ale, and an aspect of a smart enough reception parlour that sat on par with the better kind of inns she had stayed in. She rang the bell and set down her bag.

'How can I help you, Miss?' A woman stepped out from a room behind the counterpane.

'Good Afternoon. I am looking for a night's lodging. My sailing has been delayed and I find myself at a loss.'

'You on the *Mary Pelham* too?' said the woman, and Annalise nodded. It had seemed a better decoy should the town still have her on their radar as the fugitive who set fire to the *Royal*. The charges might have been dropped now, but that did not necessarily mean her infamy would be, so soon. So, having heard several gripes from passengers in the line at the packet office on account of their delayed sailing, she thought it might place her above suspicion to assume the same story.

'Hmm,' said the woman, scanning a page in her ledger. 'We are full to the hilt at the moment, though there are a couple of guests we expect to be checking out this afternoon. That would free up a single chamber and a larger set of apartments.'

'The single chamber would be best suited,' Annalise said, considering the costs.

'A'right, well, if you're happy to wait for an answer, I'll find Mr Crompton and see what can be done.'

As she sat in the taproom, waiting for a chamber to be made up for her, she considered the obstacles ahead more seriously. Firstly, there was the fact that she had not the foggiest notion of where they were bound for in Venice and had no means of finding them out between now and then. *How big a place was Venice? Was it like London? Would the odds of happening upon them perchance or succeeding in making local enquiries be likely?* She did not have the native tongue either, which would add to her difficulties, though Eleanor had reassured her upon such a previous discussion that it was said that the French tongue served pretty well across much of the continent and that, at least, she did have. Until such a time as she would, by some means yet unknown to her, manage to locate Eleanor's direction there, she would need to find some lodgings, and for how long and how much her purse would stretch to, she could not know.

These concerns made secondary the dizzying notion of actually navigating her travels alone, which she had not the slightest notion of what might be anticipated along such a route. She had never even left the county alone prior to meeting Eleanor, let alone the country. And whilst she had always dreamt of sailing to France for a visit, she had never *really* believed that someone like her would ever actually get to leave these shores.

She wished she knew a sailor she could ask for the information she desperately needed. She looked about the room for a sign of some such person but found only what appeared to be stranded tourists and ordinary folk, as far as she could tell. Then she thought back to *Merrin Cottage*. She did not know the sailor whose house she had boarded in, but she did know Nancy. Perhaps she could find her again, too. It wouldn't be very hard to enquire after her given that she was the doctor's daughter. How many doctors could there be in a small rural town such as this? Then there was the fact that Nancy was not a stranger to *Merrin Cottage* and might be found feeding the birds if the sailor was bound to sea again. Nancy would surely know about these things; she knew so much that average folk did not from her unusual upbringing in this curious place. And even if she couldn't answer everything, she was confident that she would know of someone who could and might contrive some means of finding out. Then there was the possibility that if the sailor was off to sea again, she might even permit her to board there in the interim, quietly, of course. It would undoubtedly expedite her travels if she could save the four shillings and sixpence a day she was about to part with for a night's lodging here...

She sat thoughtfully over the barely sipped cup of coffee she had accepted the offer of, hoping it might sharpen her mind. But it had grown cold by the time the landlord came to her and advised her that her room was ready and that her attendant would show her up to it just as soon as she had paid up the rate and filled out her details in the visitor's book. She thought back briefly to the inn in Buntingford where the landlord had demanded the same and supposed the custom varied from place to place. So she decided upon a pseudonym as she picked up the pen, settled the bill in full, and was led up to her room on the first floor and furnished with a key.

'Well, if that'll be all, Miss—' said the maid, who was bobbing a curtsey at the door, having made up the bed in her presence and left her a fresh carafe of water and clean glass upon the table.

'Actually, there was one thing. I was looking for the direction of the local doctor—I forget his name now, though it was given to me by his own daughter.'

'Dr Benfleet? I didn't know he had a daughter...'

Annalise shook her head, desperately trying to remember Nancy's family name, a point that had not seemed so relevant at the time of their introduction, but she wished sorely to have better retained now she needed it.

'His understudy, Dr Fredrik?' she offered in answer to Annalise's blank-faced stare.

'No, his daughter is Nancy.'

'Ah, Dr Troon, the naval surgeon.'

'Yes, that's he. Do you know where I can reach him?'

'Aye, miss. We can have a boy sent up to *The Cedars* to convey a message at your convenience if you'd like to make one up.'

'Oh no, I mean, it is a private medical matter; too sensitive to be conveyed by messenger,' she lied. 'Just the direction will be sufficient, and I can go myself if you please.'

'Surely so, miss. You can find him at *The Cedars*, up by the Synagogue on *Smithick Hill*. – Less than a ten-minute walk from here if you have a fancy for walking and don't mind it uphill.'

'Thank you, that's a great help. I don't suppose I might prevail upon you for a leaf of paper and pen, so I might leave a message for Dr Troon should I find him to be out when I call?'

'There should be everything you need in the escritoire, miss,' she nodded in its direction and Annalise realised she had failed to notice it, tucked into the far corner of the room in an unusual spot, but perhaps the only one that leant to it, given the humble size of the room. She understood now why it had been the cheapest one available owing to its irregular shape and a window that faced directly onto a brick wall.

'Thank you and good day,' Annalise said with a sanguinity quite contrary to the fragility of her mood now she was reminded again, by the empty room, of Eleanor's absence. She had only stayed in such places with her and, despite all logic, found herself looking for her within it. It was as though the expectation of seeing her merged with a memory of the same, transported to this very room. That if she turned about quickly enough, she might find her sat at the walnut escritoire, or leaning over the washstand peering into the mirror to fashion one of Leonard's faux brows with the brush of Arabic gum in hand, pressing it lightly into place with the pad of her ring finger.

When the attendant left the room and could be heard disembarking the stairs, her most pressing instinct was to allow a deeply held sob to escape her, now she was at ease to permit its full voracity. She sunk upon the bed and buried her face into the pillow to stifle the alarming sounds of despair rushing forth. *How had it all come to this?*

Then she cast her mind back to last night and reflected on all that had passed. After all the commotion of Eleanor's attack on Mariella, she had been ordered to take her back to her room and keep watch. But even once they'd removed to next door, raging and complaint could be heard through the wall, but with more din than clarity. It was Giles and Mariella's voices that were raised, though, that much could be ascertained, and she'd supposed this was keeping him distracted from dealing with Eleanor, as she presumed he intended. It was this, she thought, which had left them so long unattended. They had wondered at the opportunity of making a last-ditch attempt at escape but had quickly dismissed it on hearing the click of Digby's footsteps along the hall outside. *He was back from his bad business then.* He may still be armed with a pistol, and they could not overthrow him under such a circumstance as they might be willing to attempt if he were not, but Giles was also a man down now, and Digby could not stay up the whole night patrolling the corridor. No, now was not the right time. But later, much later, perhaps, beyond the hour of three or four, when all fell to quiet and the exhaustion of the day sunk them into the depths of weary slumber, *that* would be the time to reassess. They had tried to keep awake, determined not to miss a cue that signalled him to bed, but the toll of the day had weighed on them too, and they fell asleep soon after.

But, at some point in the night, as though her consciousness had taken note even in her sleep, Annalise woke suddenly and remembered. She turned in the bed, stifled a yawn and wiped her eyes. Then, as they adjusted to the inky blankness of the room, she could see Eleanor lying sound asleep beside her beneath a tousle of short curls and a half-twisted bed sheet. She wasn't sure what time it was, but the slightly thinning darkness of the room relieved her and she judged it still adequate enough to pass beneath, deemed it likely the building was still abed. It was quiet too, no sounds in the corridor, no raised voices from next door, just the occasional shrill of the coastal winds coursing through the winding Cornish streets outside. It might be four of five-o-clock-perhaps? They would have to be quick to seize the moment, for another hour or so could be the difference between the servants rising and the last precious hour of their slumber. They could afford no witnesses. They had one last shot at getting this right or they should both pay dear. It was a difficult risk to weigh on either side with the stakes being higher than ever, but however crack-brained she thought the notion of running off in the night with no onward plan and even less money, Eleanor could not be convinced that Giles would not scheme against them. She, too, had seen enough of his character now not to doubt it, though she couldn't fathom how he would manage to so late in events. But, she had agreed that they would get out first and plan thereafter. That one way or another, the ship must sail without them.

She put a hand on Eleanor's shoulder and gently nudged her, 'Eleanor, we must get up.'

'I would not do that if I were you,' came a voice out of the darkness.

So astonished to hear it, she sat up and drew the blankets up to her neck. 'Who is there?'

'Digby. And I bid you keep your voice down, for if you wake your mistress, I dread to think what my master will have to do to contain her if she is still in the head she went to bed with.'

She bristled at his words but saw the sense in not provoking Eleanor or waking her at all now the narrow hope of an escape opportunity had been curtailed. 'Sir!' she said, a low growl. 'What do you mean by sneaking in here in the middle of the night?' she whispered, it dawning on her that her own bed was empty and she had just been discovered in Eleanor's.

'You will get up quietly, very quietly, and come to my master. He will make everything plain to you.'

She felt an immediate dread curdle inside at the proposition and felt tempted to stir Eleanor anyway. Was he about to lead her off into the night at pistol point, too? Now it was quiet and the streets were free of witnesses. Surely not. What threat was she against such stealth? They had only thought about another escape attempt, it was not as though there had been any external clue of a plan to execute one. But maybe it mattered not, and the once had been enough to sentence her. What else could he want her for in the dead of night that Eleanor could not be party to, if it was not to prove some terrible mischief? She knew not. But despite her apprehension, she could not persuade herself to distress Eleanor with another calamity. What good would it do? Eleanor could not stop him, or Giles either if that was their intent. But she would try, of that she was sure. And if she did, it would end badly for her. So she pulled the covers back carefully and gently lifted herself from the mattress as soundlessly as the creaky floorboards would permit.

When Digby delivered her to the room next door, she was not expecting to see Giles sitting up in his chair, fully clothed with a lamp burning so bright it dazzled her bleary eyes as she entered. Had he even been to bed at all? She fancied not by the look of his heavy greying lids.

'Ah, good. Digby, go back and keep watch. I can handle this,' he directed the valet, who bowed obediently and slipped away again.

Well, she knew he was not about to march her off at pistol point after all, but the thought of Digby sitting watch over Eleanor alone, unbeknown to her, sent a chill creeping across the breadth of Annalise's shoulder blades.

'Sit down, Tulley,' said Giles, nodding at the unoccupied seat aside the small table. She sat down with an air of composure greater than she felt.

'Tulley, I think I will be best served speaking plainly to you.'

Annalise sat stiffly in her chair. Something behind his gaze made her uneasy.

'It is no secret to me that you are not *just* my wife's maid. You are her folly, it seems, and whatever the incredulity of such a circumstance, your presence is a hindrance to my cause, you must see?'

'We share an intimate friendship, Sir.'

'And a bed, I am persuaded. Not that I can think of what you propose to do with each other in it, but nonetheless, let us be frank: my wife has some unnatural tendre for you, and it will not do to have you go abroad with us.'

'But, Sir, I cannot leave her, and even if I could, she will not consent to go with you at all if I am to stay behind.'

'Yes, I expected as much, but you see, I cannot let that happen either. You will be sensible enough to know that I could deal harshly with you if you refuse me, but I daresay that will not persuade you?'

'No, Sir, it will not.'

'But, I think if I was to deal harshly with my wife, you may wish to prevent it?'

'Sir, please, do not speak so. She goes with you despite her head and asks only to have the comfort of her maid at her side. I promise you that nothing shall pass between us in my coming. I pray you will just let me attend in my duties, as I should.'

'Tulley, one express to Dr Schmidt, and she will be taken forthwith to the asylum. After her attack on my cousin last night, which was well witnessed, and my cousin's account of *their* unnatural passions, it will not be difficult to convince the doctor to lock her up and throw away the key now she is deemed a danger to others. So you see, if you refuse to cooperate...'

Annalise gasped at this. 'But she is with child—'

'Yes, not mine, at least. If she will not travel with me, then she is no use to me either way. What good is a wife that does not do her duty to her husband? She's as soon as sit her years out in the asylum if she refuses to be at my side and do her duty!'

'Please, Sir, I beg you, she would die in such a place.'

'Yes, there is that possibility, although at least that would permit me the opportunity to find a wife who *knows* her duty.'

'Please, tell me what you want and I will do anything you ask me to. Just don't—.'

He smiled. 'Yes, I thought you would be bought about to reason much better than she might. Now, here is how it shall go. You will go back to her as if nothing is altered, not a hint of anything out of turn.—I warn you now: if you attempt to double-cross me and are minded to wake her and reveal this to her, be advised that Digby will sit up all night outside your door and be aware of the slightest sound in this creaky old place.' He paused momentarily to gauge her acquiescence before continuing. 'In the morning, you will rise as normal, pack up both your things and go with us to the ship, even so far as to board the ship. And when I have you called away on some fictitious errand, you will disembark the boat, and she will not have a notion you have even gone until we have set sail.'

'Oh, Sir! Must it be so cruelly done?'

'Have you a better idea?'

'Pray, let me journey with you, get her safely to your destination and then, once she is settled, you can send me back as soon as you want.'

'Tulley, I am not a fool. How many opportunities will that afford you both to hatch other plans? No, you will not come with us. You have served your purpose. Now, you are but a hindrance. Besides, I have not obtained a ticket or a passport for you, so it is quite impossible. It is settled, as I have explained it. Let me be clear: if she suspects a thing, or you do not get off the ship before we set sail, you know how this will go. I have already sent a note to Dr Schmidt to warn him of my wife's episode this evening, so be sure he will not hesitate to come and collect her at my urgent request. And if you are of a mind to double-cross me and try to stay aboard, put the notion swift out of your head because Digby will be seeing you off the ship himself. He has instructions to act on my behalf should anything turn ill, and I am on excellent terms with the harbour master, who won't hesitate to call the law.'

'Yes, Sir,' she said through her sobs. 'Will you at least let me write her a farewell letter?'

He considered this a moment and then said. 'I will need to see it first, but yes, I think to hear something final will help her get over the idea better should she have any notion of coming back for you. Make sure it is plain that you have severed this thing between you and of your own accord.— You had better get on with it then,' he said, pointing to the writing desk. 'We'll be leaving in less than seven hours,' he added, consulting his fob watch.

'Sir, will you find her a replacement? She will need a maid to tend to her, especially in her condition.'

'Digby is already on the case. You need not concern yourself with my duties. My wife will be taken good care of should everything come about to plan.'

She did not feel much confidence in Digby's choice in the undertaking. From what she could tell, he was no better than his master. What coarse and exacting gorgon would he seek out? But it was out of her hands, all of it. She could hope for nothing more than damage limitation now, and so that is what she turned her mind to as she drew a sheet of paper from the writing desk and wiped her eyes of tears to focus better as she set to filling the page.

When she finished the letter, penned with trembling hands and tear-stained cheeks, she offered it to his waiting hand. After his inspection, he tore it up and threw it into the grate, declaring it a lot of nonsense and verbiage. He directed her to sit back down and insisted he would dictate the words this time. When this was finally done to his satisfaction, he agreed he would give it to Eleanor once the ship was on its way and said he would make the arrangements to have Annalise conveyed back to Surrey after their departure.

It seemed such a trivial consideration against all else, and she did not stay to hear further details. She only considered the last precious hours she had in Eleanor's company and rushed back to the room. She sucked up her tears and swallowed the lump in her throat before going back into their room and climbing into bed aside her, for what she now knew would be the last time.

She pushed this horrid memory from her mind as she felt herself falling into hysterics at recounting it. Once she had expelled this wave of anguish to its full extent, she napped a while with the exhaustion of such an outpouring before getting up and deciding she must write a letter to Poppy to enlighten her of her whereabouts and onward plans. And, of course, she hoped Poppy would understand the reasons for her extravagant request for such sums of money, which she knew would come as a surprise to Poppy to receive such an uncharacteristic request. It pained her to make it. To think of all the toil they'd poured into the venture, only for her to stride along and claim its reward. She had never intended to be *that* kind of landlord. And yet, what choice did she have?

She would as happily have sold the place for half the price she had paid for it if she'd had a willing buyer so that she might not concern herself for money or delays at all in this undertaking. What good was it to her now anyway? But she would not dream of taking back the very roof from over her dear friend's heads, nor their promising trade or newfound independence. No. She would rather ask for a share in the profit now so they could keep their home and trade rather than resort to something as drastic as that. She would make it up to them, vowing never to ask for another penny until the business was in full flourish and Poppy and Maggie's lot was in better balance.

So, with her conscience prickling and her letter ready for the post, she set out a 'to-do list' next to keep her tasks in order, and fashioned an accounting sheet from the underside of the inn's town directory, having used the single sheet of paper in the bureau for Poppy's letter. She adopted the style she had often used for keeping Gint's household ledger, setting out all the anticipated costs against the budget and writing out a balance sheet. It was no easy task considering she could not account for the costs of things properly once she had left British shores, but she fancied if she wrote in estimates based upon the prices here, it would at least provide a starting point, and she may turn out to be pleasantly surprised in overestimating it if it really was so much cheaper out there. She must go and look at the guidebooks. Perhaps they gave an account of such things? Yes, that's what she would do next: head to the post office to get this letter on its way, then to the bookseller. Then, she could try calling on Nancy.

When the attendant knocked and came in before she was quite finished with her list, she had thought it on the undertaking of her placing a dinner order, or somesuch, and was ready to advise her she had no stomach for it and would prefer not to be disturbed. But when she announced that the landlord wanted to see her downstairs, she put down her pen and followed her on, quite bewildered. She had initially feared discovery as the *Royal* arsonist. Still, she thought it unlikely, given the alias and the fact that she was rather well dressed in one of Eleanor's new outfits he had insisted she take for her own.—That would surely not be the description that went about of her that day. Besides, she was on her own now, not a pair. And yes, her hair had been regarded as a giveaway, but she had seen many a fair-haired girl about these parts, so she didn't think it was a particular indication.

But when she followed the attendant into the room, she was shocked to see Miss Craythorne sitting at the table with the landlord and a gentleman she did not recognise. It was no use pretending to be someone else now. She stepped in cautiously and peered at the empty seat.

CHAPTER SEVEN

The Ineradicable Witness.

Eleanor. April 1822.

I avoided breakfast for the rest of the week and took it in my room. I was not fit to keep company, not only the impertinent type I had experienced that morning after our arrival, but even well-intended company. So, I did my best to keep to my room whenever possible. Isabella had put my being 'unwell' down to what she deemed to be a travel weariness and an understandable sense of homesickness she was sure would improve in the passing days. I wished it were so simple, but I went along with it all the same. She ordered my meals be taken at my bedside, which suited me perfectly, until the evening when he came home.

His weak apology had lasted only two nights before I had woken to him in my bed uninvited. I didn't fight this time or the next. I was sure he thrived on my resistance and found it all the more exhilarating. It was true there was little I could withhold from him, but I could at least deny him that small triumph. So I lay beneath him silently and motionless without the slightest hint of resistance, fear, or any emotion whatsoever. But even with my apparent compliance, he was still a brute. My breasts and thighs were bruised and held the shape of his rough fingertips. It seemed he needed more than just my body to get him there; he called me vulgar names and offered crude threats as he ejaculated into me. I was convinced now that he could not manage it without. But I quickly learnt to shut myself off, and in some ways, I was glad he never again tried to touch me with tenderness. The only memory I held of being touched tenderly was from Annalise's fingertips, and I wanted it to stay that way. She might be gone, but I knew the memory of her never would be...

I had at least been grateful for the long days without Giles. His work kept him late throughout the week, and he would often be too preoccupied with the brandy and gaming casinos over the weekend to take much notice of me. But still my days were painfully long and dull and offered me little distraction from my misery, yet I had no desire to be parted from my misery either. It was precisely the most fitting company for my black soul. For though I had revisited his rooms to continue my search at any opportunity, every attempt had proved fruitless. There was nothing useful to be found. Even his ink and paper were locked behind the glass of a cabinet, and my attempt at picking that lock had failed, too. It was clear he meant to take no chances this time, and I was running out of hope. Reduced to a child now, constantly watched by some pair of eyes above an occasional five-minute lapse here or there.

I had limited my—already limited—possibilities of passing the hours by claiming my need for confinement to my room, to the point that even a simple chaperoned walk to get some fresh air was out of the question. I sighed and put down my sewing. I had five months to see out in this place, and I could not imagine surviving it in this pattern, often not even the next five hours, and yet there was nothing to be done but endure.

That afternoon, as I lay sprawled upon my bed, face sticky with drying tears and sweat from the midday heat, I heard a knocking at my door and roused myself from my dark reverie. Isabella appeared in the doorway and not the maidservant, as I had expected from her regular check-ups on me. With Benedetta, I had long given up on pretences of feigned well-being. If I was in the middle of a teary outburst, I would collect myself but take no pains to hide it, nor rise from my bed or dishevelled mess at hearing her cross the room to lay out my clothes or a meal upon the small table. There was little point after that morning of her having to powder my bruised eye or having borne witness to other evidence of my melancholy circumstances.

It was only the family I tried to retain some level of composure with, although I didn't fully understand why. I suppose in the beginning, it was for fear that they could not be trusted and might add to my punishment in Giles's cause if I was thought to be obstinate or disobliging. But I knew now they were not cruel or deranged like him, even if they were blind to his faults or my circumstances. Then I supposed, on realising this, the temptation to expose his many faults to them in the hope they might take my part, became too tempting in the face of such continued kindness and patience with me, that I could not risk succumbing to it. So, it was better to play absentee, for he had already made clear that any attempts in that direction would result in our leaving for a place of our own and *that* I could not bear the thought of. So, since my arrival, I had played the part of a quiet recluse who hid her miseries behind contrived and polite smiles and the barest small talk when it could not be wholly avoided. But they were not fools, and I knew instantly when Isabella came to my bedside as I tried frantically to set myself to rights, that she was about to voice her concerns.

'Eleanor,' she said in that warm, meek tone that often made me want to gush into tears, 'You need not rise on my account.'

I wiped my cheeks. 'I was just dozing. Forgive me.'

She placed a hand upon mine. 'Dear child, may I speak frankly with you?'

I wanted to forbid it, but how could I? I nodded sheepishly as I brushed the creases from my dress and tucked my unkempt hair behind my ears.

'I want you to know that privacy is to be respected in this household by staff and family alike. However, in circumstances such as these, I hope you will understand why Benedetta has felt it necessary to breach this. She has come to me with grave concerns for your health, and reluctantly, I should add, for a lack of not knowing what to do to help.'

My heart sank. I was right to think she could not be trusted. 'I see. What has she told you?'

'That you are suffering deep melancholy. That you spend most of the day at bed, barely take your meals, and are nearly always found in floods of tears or distant contemplation.'

I swallowed hard and pressed my hand to my mouth as if to beg it not to speak and betray my oath of denial.

'Listen, I do not mean to cause you embarrassment. I, too, have known a melancholy episode in my time. It is, I think, a female affliction few of us escape. But it has been weeks now, my child, and I cannot simply watch you suffer so when there seems to be no sign of improvement, the reverse, I fear. – I had hoped that after a time you might settle to life here and find some contentment amongst us. I know you are so very far from home and your family. It must seem a very strange and difficult place to be. But I fear it must be more than that to endure so. I want you to know you have leave to speak to me freely on whatever is troubling you. I cannot promise to have a solution, but I will do my best to make you comfortable if I can.'

The tears were impossible to hold back, and when she gathered me into a mother's embrace, I quickly came undone and let them fall in hysterical bursts. But I promised myself I would not speak of my troubles, for it would only multiply them. So, for all the comforting and gentle coaxing, I resisted the words that raced to the tip of my tongue and only thanked her for her kindness and apologised for my low mood.

'Well,' she said after a time and drew back from me a little once the sobs began to lull, 'Here is what I think: I think your husband has been neglectful these past couple of weeks, working all day, out most evenings, and you are finding married life a disappointment in the face of no companionship. It is a sorry state for our sex when our men are always otherwise occupied and we are left to make do.'

I neither confirmed nor denied, but was willing to go along with this less dangerous assumption.

'You are lonely, and it is to be expected under such circumstances.'

I gushed again at this. *I was lonely.*

'Hmm, and it is no way to pass your days alone in such sadness. So, I realise that perhaps you are not ready to resign your youthful years to paying calls with ladies of my age, and yet we have no other female companionship to offer you beneath this roof, so I have an idea. One I hope might answer. Even if Giles thinks you are unfit for receiving company, I disagree, and think it might prove just the thing.'

I tried to better compose myself to hear this idea, which I knew could not solve my problems, but I owed Isabella a fair hearing nonetheless.

'Now, I know you were not well during their Easter visit, and it is a shame I could not introduce you then, but my daughters are of similar years to you, and I think it would be very good for you to make their acquaintance. Maria is a half-day journey away in Oderzo, but Carlotta is only in Santa Croce – a short boat journey from here. I thought I might ask her to join us for tea tomorrow afternoon if you are amenable?'

I was not in the right frame of mind for social interactions; even Giles had been right in that. Yet I knew I could not rebuff this zealous effort to lift my spirits, so I smiled and thanked her and told her that it was very nice of her. But the dread had already begun casting its shadow over tomorrow in advance. Could I even hold a proper conversation anymore? I was sure I only had words of grief, anger and despair left in me beyond the vacuous façade I contrived to manage the brief necessaries.

'Wonderful! I think you shall get along nicely together, and then perhaps you might feel inclined to be introduced to her circle. The younger ladies have quite an eventful social calendar and it would do you good to get out of the house from time to time, don't you think?'

I nodded. It would, indeed. That he would never permit me to go out without him was quite another matter. Though I supposed he needn't know since he was never in before midnight anymore, and Isabella had proved a willingness to disobey him…

So the following morning, when Benedetta came in to attend to my toilette, I did not send her away with excuses but undertook the ritual with her and made an effort to look more respectable. I could sense her glee in my change of heart and supposed her pleased to have gone to Isabella with her concerns to see the effect of it. I, too, wished it could be so easily remedied, but though it could not, I saw the sense in letting others think so that I might have some greater peace on the matter and they may have some peace of mind. I would have to be more careful now around Benedetta, something I had once been good at: permanent facades around family and staff. Though it was like I had long since forgotten the way of it. All the same, I made my best attempt as I sat in Isabella's private parlour awaiting Carlotta's arrival, which was already a quarter-hour late.

I had already considered that the visit might be over by now, or at least half the way through if the custom differed here. But as I watched the carriage clock upon the mantle tick about another cycle, I wondered how much longer I could retain my composure. It took so little time for my mind to draw me into painful thought loops and reminiscences. Whether good or bad, they always ended the same, in a flood of tears and a sense of feeling perpetually bereft. I had tried hard to distract myself today so that my red-ringed, puffy eyes might settle and not betray my true feelings today. Thankfully, as I grew fretful that I could not keep my emotions in check, Baldasarre announced her arrival.

'Forgive me, mama!' she said in an Italian accent so strong I struggled to understand it. I supposed she had not had the benefit of her brothers' trips abroad to practice the English language as they had enjoyed.

'And you must be Eleanor. Forgive me, cousin, for my late arrival,' she said sweetly and bent to kiss my cheeks.

'Not at all. I am very pleased to meet you, Carlotta,' I said, relieved when Baldassare insisted on helping her out of her coat and bonnet, and she withdrew.

'What kept you, my child?' asked Isabella.

'Oh, the sickness mama. I was all ready to go, and as I stepped into the Gondola, I was caught out and spoiled my last cloak. I had to wait for a fresh one and the boat to be cleaned.'

'Oh, my poor child. Not long now, and it will soon be over with.'

And as I tried to fathom out the thread of the conversation, she threw back her cloak and handed it to the butler, and all became clear.

'Carlotta is expecting her first child next month,' Isabella explained.

I bit my lip as it began to quiver. I had not seen a pregnant form since I had peered at my own in the mirror. I supposed I would have been a similar size now since both babes were due within the same month.

'And it cannot come soon enough!' Carlotta complained as she sat and arranged her skirts around her protruding bump.

'She has been most unfortunate,' Isabella explained, '...and has suffered the sickness all the way through. It is a miracle there is anything left of you!' she said in Carlotta's direction. 'Still, it shall all be soon forgotten,' she added with a gushing smile.

'Perhaps you shall forget, mama, but I shall not. I am never doing this again!'

'Ha, well, that is what we all say. And anyway, it is a price worth paying for bringing us our first grandchild—Eleanor? Oh my dear, what is wrong?'

I could only flee from the table and spare them the outpouring of grief that erupted from someplace I had since thought spent. I ran as fast as I could to my room, despite my weakness of limb from a sustained lack of food, and when I got there, I turned the key and collapsed into a ball of tears at the foot of the door. It was not only the sight of her pregnancy that had produced such a blow, but seeing what such a scenario *should* have been. A time of happiness and excitement, just as it had been with my sisters. Not a dirty secret to be hidden and solved. My lost child was never celebrated by anyone, not even me. And it hurt to think of the unfortunate lot my child had been dealt from start to finish. I suppose Annalise was the only one who thought optimistically about my condition, always trying to help me see it as a blessing and not a curse, prompting me to think beyond the difficulty of my circumstances and trying to find a way to make it work. *Why couldn't I see the sense in her scheme before it was too late?*

Retrospect was a very bitter pill, and I was tired of swallowing them. Tired of my lack of insight and good sense when it was needed and always appearing so startlingly evident on reflection, after the horse had bolted. What I would give to have this head with me back then and make better choices, whatever they may have been. For even Annalise, who had seemed the one redeeming feature of my whole sorry story, had left me broken-hearted and more bereft than I had ever thought possible. Could anything or anyone be trusted in this life, or was I such a poor judge that it was *I* who could never be trusted to make good decisions? *Oh, Annalise, how could you? You have shattered my last shred of faith in life by leaving me.*

When Isabella rapped upon the door, calling out to ask what was wrong, I apologised and told her I was unwell and needed to rest. It was not until later that evening, when Giles, who I suspected had been called back from work on my account, came into the room with his key, that I spoke to anyone.

'What is all this panic you are stirring up amongst my family?' he said, angry but low, as he closed the door behind him.

'I did not mean to. I did not know Carlotta was with child. I did not know how hard I would find it to see someone in the condition I was...should be—'

'Have you confided this to anyone?'

'No. I have not spoken a word. I said I was unwell.'

'Well, that line has grown weary and you have everyone despairing over your health.'

'Everyone but you!'

He pinched the bridge of his nose. 'Eleanor, I have had a difficult day and do not appreciate being torn from important meetings on account of your hysterics. I shall warn you only once that I am in no mood to be trifled with this night!'

'I am not trifling, Giles. I am telling you the truth. I am no more able to bring myself to better health than you or anyone else. My heart is shattered and I have no one I can so much as talk to for keeping your secrets!'

'Just calm down, will you. Here is what we shall say since you have left little choice in confessing something now. We shall admit that you have suffered a miscarriage on our journey, and that shall appease them and relieve you of the secret, alright? But that is all. They shall be told nothing else, no details beyond those bare facts, no explanations or elaborations upon them. That way, my aunt will understand that thrusting your acquaintance upon Carlotta is not the thing, and you may have something to offer her to appease her concerns.'

'Very well,' I agreed.

'Now, shall you tell her, or I?'

'It seems prudent that it should be you since you are the arbiter of truth.'

For a moment, an angry hue coloured his face that I had learned usually preceded his loss of temper, but he only stared fixedly at me and said, 'I shall tell her on my way out,' and he turned and left the room.

I don't know why I expected better of him. How could he understand my sufferance on any account when he seemed absent of a heart at all? And yet, despite my knowing this and having no desire to seek comfort or gentility from him, still it hurt to be so coldly disregarded, as if the pain of losing a child was nothing, just because it was nothing to him. Nothing but a relief or even a blessing in his mind, I considered. But despite my reasoning that the fault was in his lack of empathy and not in the expression of my sufferance, I could not prevent myself from spiralling into the deepest chasm of my despair. It was beyond weeping now but an intense and enduring peak of mental pain that would not abate or surrender. It was like a wave that kept climbing and refused to crash and fall into a calmer rhythm, and I did not know how to contain it. And so I stopped trying to and agreed it may take me wherever it so wished. For I no longer cared for any of it. I was tired of endurance. I was tired of trying to find a way to free myself from him and his captivity. I was tired of trying to understand all the whys and hows that had led me here. And so I gave in. To it all.

The fury manifested in the form of my going to his chamber through the adjoining door and sabotaging his things: clothes and correspondence that had been left about, colognes and other male paraphernalia within my reach. I tore at fabric with my bare hands like a feral beast, poured bottles out into his basin, tore papers into tiny shreds and broke cigars into a crumbly mess upon his pillow. Then, I took my concealing paints from my dresser and wrote upon his mirror with a fingertip, *"I hate you. You are the devil incarnate. May you rot in your miserable hell of such a twisted soul. You shall do it without me!"* I spared the furniture, for my attack was upon him, not his family's house. Then, I found his Brandy decanter and sunk the whole as I admired my efforts.

I must have fallen asleep in his easy chair once I had finished the drink, the entire decanter's worth. But I had not drunk beyond a glass of wine in an age. I had barely eaten beyond a morsel a day for so many weeks that it had the most thunderous effect on me. I woke in the grip of my stomach knotted and my head pounding so violently it was as though the pain in my heart had finally become manifest in my body. And I was ready for an end to it all.

I checked the clock, and through my hazy gaze I saw it was past midnight. I supposed the house was to bed and he might be heading home soon, so I hurried. I peeled the pillowcases from my pillows and took them out of the room with me, checking for sounds along the way. I hastened through the house, downstairs and into the courtyard which led to the landing jetty on the canal. I knew this would still be open for Giles to come in without disturbing the entire house. And on my way through the courtyard, I picked up a couple of the heavy stone bricks that bordered a flowerbed and carried them through the gates to the jetty with me, with more difficulty than I had expected, for I had no strength as I once did. My newly healed arm remained weak and I relied solely on the energy of determination to manage it. I had thought this whole scene through so many times but always succeeded in finding some thread of logic or foreboding—however slight— to talk myself back out of it. Some optimistic idea that I might find a way to write to the Banfields and receive a response from Lady. W. with a ticket, or that Giles might leave some trinket or thing of value about that I could make off with in exchange for passage home. That Annalise might have a change of heart and come and find me...

But these, and so many other desperate fantasies of my salvation, were long since spent and had grown wearied and timeworn. And now I had nothing to talk myself around with and no desire to fight it anymore. I was tired, and the promise of some relief from this continuous agony held more leverage with me than any other prospect I could conjure.

I would deceive myself no more.

I sat upon the edge of the small jetty, one leg dangling over it and the other drawn up to my chest, and, with clumsy hands, loaded the bricks into the pillowcase and tied the pillowcase fast about my ankle. I stared about briefly and took in the stillness of the night, the gentle lapping of the impassive water, the shadow of the looming buildings casting over me like an ineradicable witness. Then, with some difficulty, I managed to lift my anchored leg towards the edge, but it was so heavy and cumbersome that as I struggled with its weight and shifted, it dragged me instantly into the water. Cold and murky, sinking with such speed I was sure I must have been close to the bottom when I ran out of air. It was only then something like panic began to engulf me. A primal instinct for survival found its way to my limbs as they thrashed about to try to resist the pull below. It was futile, and I knew it. I was a practised swimmer, but even I could not hold my breath beyond a minute or so in my greatest attempts, and I had not taken so much as a bracing breath before plunging. And I was weak, powered only momentarily by this primal bodily reaction to suffocation. And then, after my limbs grew heavy and still, I felt something else entirely. Something I had longed for. A sense of peace. Of calm. And I knew then I was close to the end.

Chapter Eight

Falsely Accused.

Annalise. February 1822.

'Miss Tulley, I believe?' asked the gentleman, looking up from his conversation and taking to his feet.

'Yes, Sir,' she confessed.

'I am Mr Carne, the local Mayor. I wonder if you will be good enough to take a seat and suffer an interview with me.'

His words might have framed it as an optional invitation, but something about his countenance and tone was undoubtedly in the attitude of an order. She drew up a chair and sunk into it, thinking she might have at least re-pinned her sleep-ruffled hair and made more respectable if she had realised the formality of the occasion. 'What is this about, Sir?' she asked once she was settled, eyeing Mariella cautiously.

'I will come to that, miss. But first, can you confirm your full name and explain your business here?'

She did as bid and watched the innkeeper frown at the deception.

'Thank you, Miss *Tullier*. I have been prevailed upon by Miss Craythorne over the matter of one particular sapphire pendant of great value and rarity: the property of your former mistress, I believe. Do you happen to know of the item in question?'

Annalise frowned in bewilderment. 'No, Sir.'

'Was it not your charge to care for your lady's ornaments?—You were, I believe, a lady's maid?'

'Yes, at least, it would have been, Sir, ordinarily. But she had none with her.'

He lifted a brow. 'None with her on a trip across the waters?'

Annalise shook her head. 'Her husband would not permit her to wear them of late. He took anything of that nature into his care when we met with him. Not that I remember any such pendant being with her even then. I recall only a gentleman's pocket watch and a ring.'

Now, his brow was furrowed. 'And why would her husband take her ornaments away?'

'I believe, Sir, he was concerned that should my lady have anything of value upon her person, she may be minded to use it to finance her escape from him.'

'Escaping her husband?' he said, his wiry brow knotted with doubt.

'Yes, Sir, he was a tyrant, and she did not want to go abroad with him.'

'So it was not because he was concerned that it could not be trusted to your care for fear you might make off with anything of value?'

She caught the accusatory note in his tone. 'No, Sir!' she replied, affronted. 'I am no thief.'

'Yet, Miss Craythorne, here, seems to believe you to know of the missing pendant's whereabouts, as did Mr Craythorne, according to this witness statement he left with the packet agent before boarding.' He held a piece of paper out before her, but she could not glean the content across the wide expanse of the breakfast parlour table they were sitting about.

'You!' Annalise said accusingly, jabbing a finger in Mariella's direction. 'I might have guessed you had some involvement with this abominable hoax! What are you even doing here? You were supposed to be setting off for home hours ago.'

'I could ask the same of you, *Miss Cranbourne*,' she grinned, emphasising the alias Annalise had used to fill out the lodging book.

'Everything's a joke to you, isn't it? You assisted in the kidnap of a pregnant woman knowing what miseries that disgusting cousin of yours would subject her to. Knowing the violence of which he is capable. The violence you joined him in inflicting upon her! And yet, here you sit, grinning. For shame! You are a bitter and twisted sort indeed. And you wonder why Eleanor throttled you last night. Truly. You deserved it.'

Mariella turned back to the Mayor who had been watching the exchange with interest, sensing there was a great deal more to this claim than met the eye. 'See, I told you she was quite mad, Sir. Mad or just bad, I own, I cannot decide. Perhaps her mistress' malady of mind was contagious?'

'Well, that's for me to concern myself with, Madam. Your assessment is neither needed nor welcome, so if you will mind your tongue and be so good as to let me take the interview,' Mr Carne said to her quite sternly, and Annalise wondered if her words had given him a different opinion of this situation. 'Miss Tullier,' he said, less harshly than before, 'It has been put to me that you stand accused of taking from Miss Craythorne's lodging room last evening, amid some annoyance betwixt her and your former mistress, a sapphire pendant belonging to a Mrs Eleanor Craythorne. What have you to say on the matter?'

'Sir, I tell you in earnest I did not take anything! Steal from my mistress? Never. I would not. I—' she dropped her gaze down to the table and cleared her thickening throat. 'I cared deeply for my mistress. She was not mad. She had a sound mind and knew to stay away from the Craythornes as soon as she got their measure.' She cast her eyes in Mariella's direction and looked at her squarely now, 'They are an abomination to any standard of decency. The real crime here is that my Lady has been abducted against her will and not even her family know of it. And she is with child, Sir, quite alone in the charge of a brute and a rogue, and how cruelly he likes to make her suffer...' tears fell now, and she sniffed them back.

'Miss Tullier, I do not know the circumstances of your Lady's private affairs, and since she is not here to give an account of them, I shan't deign to pry into them. But what I must establish, is whether you stand as accused in this matter. Now, please, restrict your speech to the issue at hand. Did you take a sapphire pendant from Miss Craythorne's room at the lodging house last night?'

'No,' Annalise said flatly.

'Then you will not object, I think, to a search of your things,' Mariella cut in.

'Miss Craythorne,' said the Mayor, his voice raised, tone irritated. 'Is it you or I who is conducting this interview?'

'Well, who is and clearly who should be, are another matter...' she replied curtly.

'Continue in this manner, Miss Craythorne, and I shall consider you deficient of sound mind and deem this matter closed. Do I make myself clear?'

'Perfectly. Though I might remind you that it is your duty—'

He slammed down his pen against the table, and it shook. 'You need remind me of nothing, Madam. Now, Miss Tullier, do you object to a search of your possessions, your room?'

'Not in the slightest. I have little in my possession so it shan't take a moment, please,' she said obligingly, and the Mayor nodded to the innkeeper, signalling they could begin the search and sending the watchman out with him to undertake it, she supposed.

'Miss Tullier, the landlord tells me you paid up your room in full. Can you tell me how you came about the money to pay for it?'

'Yes, Sir, my mistress gave it to me.'

'For your wages?'

'Not exactly. There is more I am owed than the sum she gave me.'

'So a part payment then.'

Annalise shrugged.

'You are, I believe, paid as a lady's maid?'

'Yes.'

'And in so much more besides coin...' Mariella grinned, casting her gimlet-eyed glance up the length of her.

'You know nothing about me,' Annalise retorted before Mr Carne could deliver Mariella the scold his expression seemed to promise.

'And yet all that is necessary to know your type...' she returned.

'If you continue to interrupt me, Miss Craythorne, you shall be bid to leave the room,' he said severely before turning back to Annalise. 'And up until your lady cut ties with you this morning, you were still in her service?'

'She did not cut ties with me at all, Sir. It was her ghastly husband that forced me to abandon her!'

'I see. And why would he do such a thing?'

'He did not want me to go with them. He did not like her...*reliance* on me.'

'Reliance?' Mariella repeated with a snigger.

Mr Carne snapped around in Mariella's direction like a hound about to attack. 'Miss Craythorne, this shall serve as your final warning. One more peep out of you and I shall have you apprehended for contempt!'

Mariella held her hands up in submission, but the mocking expression on her face remained.

'So,' he resumed, '…you deny the charge?'

'Yes. I strenuously deny it. It most definitely was not me. Sir, I declare I should never do such a thing! And to my mistress, of all people. I am the only one that cares for her. *She* does not. Her husband certainly does not. Tell me, if they cannot have a care for her welfare, why would they trouble over a lost ornament? I tell you, it is only to set me up.'

'Well, this statement here by Mr Giles Craythorne says he thought you were a thief, and that's why he threw you off and forbade you from travelling with them. He states that he had noticed things missing from his wife's belongings, clothes, money and other trinkets, but when he challenged you about them, his wife would defend you and say she had made a gift of them to you. Which I suppose would not be so irregular had she not been mentally vulnerable and prone to easy persuasion. He believes you were taking advantage of her state of mind. Accepting what you should not: High-value items, new things, not just cast-offs and candle ends. That's why he was forced to strip her of anything of particular worth. But he maintains that you took the pendant without his or his wife's permission. He also refers to a recent arson attack you made at the *Royal Hotel* this week in an attempt to persuade her to run off with you.—I understand the charges have been dropped against you in that matter now, but—'

'My god,' Annalise gasped in Mariella's direction. 'You are masters of deceit and derangement. Where do you contrive such tales?' she said to Mariella. 'You would better lend your sordid talent to writing novels than harming innocent folk.'

'Miss Tullier, I would be grateful if you kept to my questions.'

'Sir, I say this with all due respect to you as my better, but this woman is a fraud and a trickster. These claims upon me are nothing more than her and her cousin's spiteful attempt to conspire wickedly against me. They did not like my siding with Mrs Craythorne and trying to help her get away from them. I can show you the newspaper cutting where Mr Craythorne reported her missing and put up a reward. I have it upstairs in my portmanteau. I have witnesses to the kidnap he undertook of me and my mistress when someone informed on her. I can prove that I have been in service since I was ten, and my employers have never once made claims of theft or misconduct. They would vouch for me now, Sir! I beg thee to send word to them and they will tell you of my character. Besides, I have no need to steal. I am also the proprietor of a small establishment, which is doing well enough. Pray, let me write down the direction and you may make enquiries confirming that all I have told you is the truth.'

'Well, it might come to it yet, lass, but not now. Let me get back to the interview, and by the time it is done, so shall the search of your things be, and then perhaps we might all go back about our business if there is no further evidence against you.'

She took his gentleness with her and the hint of his speech as a sign that he believed her, however much he was bound by duty to undertake these tasks with sufficient vigour. And since she had not stolen this wretched pendant, she knew there was nothing against her. So she turned to the task at hand now and answered his questions in quick succession, hopeful that it would soon be over and done with. But Mariella was not so minded to permit a swift conclusion to this affair and took it upon herself to contradict almost everything Annalise said, giving some deceptive explanation or levelling some provocative question at her. And whilst it drove the Mayor to several and increasingly severe reprimands, she did not seem concerned to heed them in the least. Proceeding to ask whose fine dress she was wearing now. Yes—Annalise was forced to confess—it was her mistress's, but Mr Craythorne had compelled her to wear it. Who had offered to pay for her return home? Yes, it had been Mr Craythorne, at least, that was before he had discovered the missing pendant and directed Mariella to seek out the Justice. Who had paid the damages to Mr Wynn at the Royal Hotel after she had started up a fire – once again, it had been Mr Craythorne.

When the watchman and the innkeeper returned to the room and Mr Carne rose and gathered in a corner to speak privately with them, Annalise turned and said to Mariella, 'I don't understand what you gain from this bad bidding. How can you tell such lies? To be constantly thrown over by him and yet contrive such menacing schemes on his behalf!'

'He has not thrown me over. I shall be joining him just as soon as he is settled.'

'Are you really *that* deluded that you think so? He is besotted with her, however, twisted his affection. But you, you he discards with the ease she would discard of him. And look at you, still lying and cheating in his cause. What a sorry creature you are! Do you think it will win him when he is so fixed upon his delusion of having her that he goes to these desperate lengths? What stopped him from taking you along with them today? The fact that she was against your going was enough to put paid to that, wasn't it? However, disobliging he is to her feelings, and we both know how evident that is, he is even less concerned with yours.'

'You know nothing!' she snarled.

'I own, it does not take much knowing to see how plainly discarded you have been, and yes, I am a stranger to you and yet I can see the fact. Doubtless, everyone else can see the fact, except for you! Don't you understand? He has taken off with her for good. They are not coming back. He shall not send for you. This is what he wanted, to have her all to himself. He does not care if he never set's eyes on you again, so long as he has her.'

Miss Craythorne, whose hand was trembling around a teacup, picked it up and threw it at Annalise, hitting her square on the side of her forehead, too late for her to dodge it. Mr Carne, noticing the disorder, left the landlord's conversation instantly.

'What the devil!' he declared, removing the cup from Annalise's lap where it had landed and asking her if she was injured.

'A bump perhaps, but it's not as bad as it might have been,' she told him, prodding the spot where it had caught her.

'Not as bad as you deserved,' Mariella scowled.

'Right, the pair of you are headed to the Gaol house. You will spend the night and answer to the Magistrate in the morning!' he declared. 'You,' he fingered at Miss Craythorne, keep to your chair! That was a common assault, and I shall be charging you with it. Mr Crompton, send a maid for a compress for Miss Tullier's injury, will you? And you, Miss,' he said, turning to Annalise now, '...might you explain why my man found this pendant necklace and a bag full of discarded pearls in your receptacle?' He held up the sapphire pendant and unfurled his fingers to reveal a palm full of the marquetry pearls Annalise had stolen from the peacock table at the Truro cottage.

The guilt rose instantly on their account, but she had never before seen the sapphire pendant, ever. 'That, Sir, is impossible! If indeed your man did find it in there and she did not pay the servants a bribe for putting it there for her. I tell you, it is a hoax! I have never before seen that pendant in my life.'

'And the pearls?'

She dropped her gaze to the floor and made no answer to this.

'Miss Tullier, you disappoint me. I own, you are a seemingly gentle and well-spoken creature for your class, and I had hoped to find the search come up empty for your sake. But the fact is, the evidence is compelling and you have left me no choice.'

Annalise began to cry now. 'Sir, I did not do it. I am falsely accused. You must see I could not do it!'

'Nay, lass, I can do nothing more for you now. The evidence speaks for itself.'

'I did not steal it, Sir. I have never even seen the thing before. Please, undertake enquiries of my situation. Permit me to give you the direction of my business and property, and you will see I have no need of the money.'

'That's not what this letter says. Quite the contrary.' he replied, still reading from it, an air of disappointment in his voice. He was holding out the one she had just written to Poppy, explaining her dire need for money and begging her to send it swiftly. How ill the whole thing must look for her now. Though at least her passages filling Poppy in on the kidnap corroborated her story. 'Sir, please, I know you are a decent man. I know this looks very bad for me, but I swear I didn't take the pendant. I *know* you believe me—'

'Well, I don't say I know what to believe, but it does not signify. You can explain yourselves to the Magistrate in the morrow!' he sighed, exasperated, and when Miss Craythorne, realising that she too was to be cuffed in irons by the watchman, broke out in a hysterical protest and attempted to throw him off, chanting insults and threats about her station and that he would pay for daring to manhandle her. Did they know who her father was? They would soon enough.

The Mayor put down the letter, turned to Mariella and warned her that unless she wanted him to add to his statement of events, another violent outburst and obstructing an official undertaking his duties, then she'd do best to sit back down, place her hands out on the table to be cuffed, and keep her tongue between her teeth so the watchman could do his job.

Mariella acquiesced after this and reluctantly laid her gloved hands out upon the polished mahogany table she had revealed from beneath its tablecloth in the scuffle. His tone left little to second guess at his staunch dislike for Mariella, even if he had been forced to apprehend Annalise, perhaps against his better judgment. Little good that did her now. She was to answer for a crime she did not commit and with damning evidence against her that she had no way of disproving. In a last, desperate attempt, Annalise turned to him as she rose from the table with a compress bandaged to her head and the heavy weight of the irons hunching her posture and said, 'Please, Sir, I know you only do your duty, but, I beg you, find out who has planted this ornament in my belongings, for I swear I have been set up, and someone must have put it there.'

He waited for Mariella to be led from the room before making his answer. 'Very well, Miss Tullier, I shall question the staff and see if I can detect any wrongdoing, but I should warn you of the unlikelihood of anyone making such a confession when it would land them in the same position as you find yourself in.'

'I know that, Sir. But will you try? Perhaps someone saw something, and I like to believe that not all souls are so corrupt as to be silenced by coins or trifles and might tell the truth with a little prompting.'

He nodded. 'You, I think, Miss, have a little more faith in the race of men than I. But I am to stay and take witness statements of your assault, so you may rest assured that I shall undertake enquiries.'

'Thank you.'

'Is there anyone you would like me to contact? Let them know what has happened and give them your whereabouts?'

Annalise shook her head. What good would it do to plague Poppy with such unpleasantness when she was too far beyond her reach to see her and explain it all?

'Not even the recipient of this letter?' he asked.

'No. She has enough to be getting on with without worrying about me. Burn it if you will, Sir.'

'I regret that I cannot, Miss, it counts as evidence of motive now.'

'Of course. Well, it seems the evidence is to be my noose, even if it is all wrong. Actually,' she said, remembering at the last, '...there is someone you could tell, discreetly if you would, Sir?'

'As you wish.'

'Nancy Troon at Smithwick Hill.'

'The Cedars? Dr Troon's house.'

'Yes, Sir, I thank you.' And with that, she dropped a curtsey and followed the returning watchman out to the waiting coach.

They were loaded into it together but bound to different iron hooks at opposing ends, so they were a fraction too far apart to attempt to resume the scrapping Mariella had started. It was just as well, she supposed. She was not sure she could trust herself not to be facing the Magistrate for anything less than a charge of murder in the morning had they not been. It stood to reason that if she was to be hung or transported for a crime she didn't do, perhaps she should at least finish the job Eleanor had started last night and rid her of one of these villains and make the hanging count. Then she collected herself, shocked by the wickedness of her temper and resigned herself not to entertain such violent imaginings. She was duly angry but not a murderer.

They sat silently in the coach, rattling about for barely ten minutes until they entered the grounds of the gaol warder's house, which had seemed a charming enough place, until they were deposited in a filthy, damp cell room, hunched against the rear of the building. Once again ironed to opposite sides of the room, a scant crate to make do with for a bed, she supposed.

Annalise was not thrilled with the prospect of spending a night in such a tumbledown place, but it mollified her a little to hear Miss Craythorne's aggravated protests at being subjected to such treatment. Cursing first the watchman, then the gaoler, and generally causing such a desperate raucous that she was attracting the harsher brunt of their rough treatment. Then, once they finally locked up the door, she was clanging her irons against the rails and demanding they come back and let her out. Annalise could see the shadow of her in the low light and could not help but feel some small satisfaction at seeing her in the same state she had reduced her to.

When she finally gave in and ceased clanging, she looked about her, hovering so as not to have to touch anything, and then she threw up onto the earthen floor.

'Got a little more in the bargain than you hoped for?' Annalise said.

She wiped her mouth with her free hand. 'How dare you speak to me, you little peasant. I, at least, will be out of here tomorrow, whilst you are left here to rot whilst you await the gallows!'

'Don't be so certain. By the look of your face, I doubt it will take the Magistrate very long to discern that you are in the habit of getting into such brawls.'

'You think you are clever. Well, how clever does it feel to know you will never see her again?'

'I will again. You need not concern yourself with that. Wretched creature that you are, I'm sure no one would ever miss you, no matter where you were to go.'

'I wonder how much she pines for you this very moment, abandoning her at the last.'

'You know I never did abandon her!'

'But she does not. There is much she does not know. She does not know that by the time she births her bastard, you will likely be swinging from a rope.'

'She knows enough to judge you and your cousin precisely. It was I who could not believe such vile persons existed. She had your measure, though, you may be sure.'

'Does she? I think not. She does not even know the entirety of the truth behind her own marriage, such easy prey she was to catch.'

'What do you mean to imply?'

'We marked her card from the off,' she laughed smugly. 'From that first night, we saw her waltzing about the ballroom, I told him we could bring things around to his plans.'

'Yes, well, I know all about your methods of bringing her around!'

'Oh, that. That was a mere carrot to dangle. I'm not inclined to *your* tastes, although she was a very sweet plaything for a time. Such an innocent! So easy to persuade with a little titillation.'

'Don't you dare speak about her that way.'

'Of course, you fancy yourselves in some deep and meaningful passion, forgive me.'

'You could never understand, could you? Your twisted fancy for your cousin who cares not a groat for you, how could you? Pathetic.'

'What's pathetic is how easy it was for us to convince your little sweetheart that she was ruined and about to bring her family down. A little drop of Laudanum in her arrack glass, a few contrived suggestions, and the fool thought herself sullied with Mr Richards bastard. The best of it was, she ended up bringing about the exact circumstance herself in the end, and now look what she has provoked!' She laughed out loud now, attracting the guard's attention, who was quick to come and hush her up.

'Are you saying you drugged her?' Annalise said quietly once she heard the fading of the guard's steps.

'Oh, yes. That was the first time. The next was the draft I gave her to make her sick and delay her menses. She made it far too easy.'

'You deserve to hang, you vile cretin.'

'And yet it is you that will. What a funny world we live in.'

'You had better hope I do after all you have said!'

'Oh, it's of no consequence to me. The word of a maidservant won't hold much, especially one of a convicted thief.'

'You truly have no conscience, do you? You really would be happy to watch me hang for something you know I did not do!'

'I own, I won't think much on it, but it was Giles's scheme, not mine. I would be happy to let you go and find some new kitchen to scrub away your days in.'

'And that's all you live for? To do his bidding whilst he creams off the rewards and look at you, here in this pit, and where is he?'

'Probably trying to work up your mistress's skirts, for what good that'll do him. He really isn't her type, is he? You are the much sweeter tasting in her mind. Queer taste or no, I can see how her favour is set. All love and sultry glances for you and scorn for her husband.'

'If you know this, what is the point of all this disgusting scheming?'

'Giles wanted connections. Now he has them. I wanted him to have a wife that had no care for him. You can see how well suited to the task she is.'

'And what about what *she* wants?'

She shrugged. 'None of my concern. She would have eventually ended up *someone's* wife, and as you know, he would have never come up to mark in her mind. Not even her precious Elmbridge. What an escape he had! To think by now he would be puzzling over his wife's disinterest whilst she chased her way up the maidservant's petticoats!'

'What happened to you?'

'Me?'

'Yes. I wonder what it must take to create such a heartless and forsaken creature?'

'All that fustian! Look at where it has landed you, such weakness of mind and character. If you want to come out on top, you must use your sense, not your sensibilities!'

'I see. And you have come out on top, have you? With your cousin's head so far turned, he cannot even think of you. Is this how it was supposed to work, him chasing her tail and you chasing his?'

'He will tire of her soon enough. It's nothing more than novelty.'

'I do hope you are right, yet I find it doubtful. You make the mistake of believing her charms so easy to relinquish just because they did not affect you so. Heartless, you might be, but blind, you are not. She captures hearts with the ease in which you attract distaste.'

'Not his. He is finding the challenge of the hunt too much to resist, that is all. Once he has broken her, and he will, he will find her such a bore she will be as good as divorced. What a shame you won't be there to welcome her home when the day comes.'

CHAPTER NINE

Saltwater.

Eleanor. April 1822.

I woke in a splutter, suddenly struck by the return of my bodily senses and the trembling of my body as I coughed up foul-tasting water and opened my stinging eyes to the blackness of the night. The hardness of the stone floor beneath me, its chill radiating through.

'Thank god,' came a voice, and I followed the trail of sound to see, in a bleary shadow, one of the Harper sons sat over me, pumping at my chest so hard I thought my ribcage might give way.

'Eleanor, it's Marco. Can you hear me? Eleanor?'

My answer came in a convulsive wave of water vomiting that near choked me as he climbed off of me, turned me onto my side, and began patting my back as he shouted out for help. It was then I remembered, understood that I was back. That I had been pulled back into this realm of existence when I had just thought I had escaped it. I began to cry then and tremble violently with the cold and heaviness of my lungs.

'Eleanor, you are going to be alright. Just hang on for me. Help is coming,' Marco said, and I felt myself scooped into his arms and held against his warmth. – This I was grateful for. I felt cold to the marrow. Though he, too, was wet, his heart thudding noisily against my ear and drowning out the clarity of the anxious cries rumbling through his chest as they grew distant with my wavering consciousness.

After a while, I felt myself wrapped in blankets and lifted, carried off, and there were other voices, too, asking, 'What has happened?' 'Is she alive?' 'Are you alright?'

'A terrible accident,' I heard him say. 'She has fallen into the canal.'

Then I was laid upon a couch, the flames of a fire rising up against the darkness, and wrapped in the weight of even more blankets. Then Marco's voice again, saying: 'Leo, you must wake Benedetta from her bed to come and tend her until the Doctor comes, but quietly, please. Do not wake the house, my parents are to bed. Dante, if Giles comes back, do whatever you must to delay him, divert him, whatever it takes.'

'Why? He shall wish to know his wife has been in an accident.'

'Please, I will explain later, just trust me, will you?'

'Alright—Giacomo, keep an eye out for him, will you, and let me know?—Marco, what the hell is going on? How did she fall into the canal? What was she even doing out there at this time of night?'

'Not now. Not in front of the servants. Eleanor, how are you feeling?'

'Leave me be,' I said through gritted teeth, but my voice was a mere whimper, my throat in a painful spasm as I tried to speak.

'Are you warming up?'

I must have been, for the sense of my body was returning to me fully, the heaviness, the aching, the pain. And I was so tired again, exhausted.

I must have fallen into a sleep, for this time, when I opened my eyes, I was in my room, in my own bed, dry and propped up on a mountain of pillows. Had I dreamt it all, I wondered, at the sight of the familiar primrose brocade canopy above my head. I was no longer trembling with the cold. I felt warm at last. But then I heard voices in the room, low whisperings to my right and a sense of foreboding came over me.

'Oh, Marco, please, go and get changed now. You will catch your death in those wet clothes.'

It was Isabella's voice, pleading and distressed, but her presence relieved me and shamed me, in turn.

'Mama, I am fine. Please. I want to stay for the Doctor, and then I shall go and change.'

And then the Doctor was there at my bedside, pinching open my eyes and pressing his listening horn against my chest, and it was impossible to remain impervious. But I did not want to open my eyes and see any of them. No, I did not want them to see me or the shame that had begun to rise in me in their knowing what I had done, and having no words to offer them that could explain it.

'Mrs Craythorne, can you hear me?' asked the Doctor.

I nodded.

'I'm Dr Arturo. I understand you fell into the canal tonight. Can you tell me if you hit your head or sustained any injury on the fall?'

'I do not think so,' I croaked, my throat still raw, aching violently as if I'd swallowed the rocks, not tied them to my ankle.

'Will you mind if I examine you for injuries?'

I shook my head and felt the covers lifted from above me. I opened my eyes at last, though they stung, and was relieved to see the curtains about the bed drawn on one side and only the Doctor and Benedetta stood beside me.

'How is your vision?' he asked as he held up the weight of my arm to inspect it.

'My eyes sting.'

'Hmm, the salt water. But you can see clearly? How many fingers can you see?'

'Five. One, Three,' I answered accordingly.

'Good. I do not think you are concussed, and there is no sign of a blow to the head,' he added as he felt about my scalp. 'What of your breathing?'

'Heavy, with sharp pains in my lungs, a terrible ache in my throat.'

'Yes, to be expected. You must allow your body to cough up all it wishes, do not resist. There may still be fluid on the lungs, though I believe you brought the worst of it up quickly on revival, which is reassuring. Your pulse is a little weak, but your colour is good. Any swelling anywhere? In the abdomen?'

'I don't know.'

He proceeded to prod my belly and declared there was nothing notable. And when he had finished all the prodding and lifting, he stood back and considered me more carefully.

'Do you remember what happened, how you came to be in the canal?'

I shook my head.

'Do you remember any sense of being about to collapse or any pain or sensations in the body prior?'

Oh yes, everywhere: body, mind and soul – I wanted to say, but I just shook my head again.

'Well, you have been very lucky young lady. You are not out of danger just yet, but I do believe Marco has saved your life and you may yet recover fully. I shall make up some medicines for her,' he said to Benedetta now. 'I believe you will be nursing her?'

'Si, Signor,' she said.

'Very well, we shall discuss it further. Mrs Craythorne, you must rest now and stay warm. Cough when you have the urge and report to your maid if you feel any deterioration, alright?'

I nodded my agreement and closed my eyes again, but listened hard as he removed from my bedside and walked to the other side of the curtain where I knew not how many stood beyond it, or who was party to my disgrace.

'Dr, will she survive?' came Isabella's cry.

'Mrs Harper, you know I am never one to offer promises, but I do think she has every chance of making a full recovery. Her vital signs are good, considering. I think Marco got there just in time. You have saved her life. But, can you tell me a little more?'

'Of course, what do you want to know?' Marco replied.

'How long was she in the water?'

'I don't know precisely, but the time it took for me to come down from the top floor and bring her out. Umm, perhaps a couple of minutes. It all seemed very fast.'

'That's promising. Did you see how she fell? Was there any loss of consciousness, seizure, or such, before she fell into the water?'

'I don't think so, but as I said, I was not watching for long. As soon as I realised she was in danger, I fled the room.'

'And when you found her, was she floating at the surface or sinking?'

'She had sunk, but not very deeply; she had caught somehow upon a rotten wooden pile beneath the jetty, and once I was able to free her, we were up to the surface in less than twenty seconds, I would estimate.'

'And you say she was out for a minute or less once you rescued her?'

'About that, though, again, I can't be certain.'

'And upon reviving her, she brought up the water swiftly, you said?'

'Yes, she coughed up a gargle right away and once I revived her, vomited out two voluminous mouthfuls.'

'Thank you. That is helpful. I am at a loss as to how she fell; there are no external signs of injury, but I do think the prognosis is a good one. Of course, the next few days will tell if I am correct. There can be complications, damage to the delicate tissues of the lungs, infection from the water and so on—she will need around-the-clock nursing and you are to call if there is any sign of deterioration. Shallow breathing, coughing, and general discomfort about the throat and lungs are to be expected until the fluid is entirely gone and the lungs have recovered. I would hope to see this gradually resolve over the coming days, but anything in excess of this, a change of pallor, inability to breathe, a fever or delirium— send for me at once. Otherwise, I shall put her on my daily rounds to be bled for the time being and will be back in the morning.'

CHAPTER TEN

Bittersweet Birdsong.

Annalise. February 1822.

I t was just approaching sunset when Annalise blinked and bent her ear in the direction of the sound of someone calling her name. At first, she thought it must be Mariella starting up again, but this voice had been soft, almost melodic in its distant hum. She lifted herself from the wooden straw-strewn crate she was resting upon and wiped a flaxen stalk of it from her cheek where it had clung to her. She had begun, at last, to fall into a doze now it was finally quiet enough to do so. Barely half an hour ago, Mariella had been moved to the cell next door on account of the din she was raising, screaming out demands to the gaoler and clanging her irons at regular intervals until he came to deliver her a reprimand. On the occasion of his fifth visit, he seemed to have tired of the routine and told Mariella she was to be put next door on her lonesome. Seeming pleased at this news and making some jest about it being high time she was offered a private apartment separate from the peasantry, the gaoler deigned to inform her that since it was the only other cell in the gaol house, should any other villains be brought into the place tonight, man or woman, smuggler or murderer, she shall have the pleasure of keeping company with them.

It had seemed to quieten her thereafter, and it had finally fallen peaceful once she'd been relocated and the rattle and clack of keys had receded. Afternoon birdsong could be heard now, and it had soothed Annalise to hear something so familiar, so grounding. It was a relief to be free of the sight and proximity of Mariella, even if they were only divided by the boundary of the stone wall, she felt grateful for her seeming absence.

She shuffled down from her crate and walked beside it now, one palm pressed against its callous surface to steady herself as she stretched and tugged her chain across the earthen floor to reach the farthest extent of the ten-foot cell. For it seemed to be the direction from which the sound had travelled from outside. All the sounds from within these walls echoed and bellowed as if choked up from the very pits of hades. But this had made no dilatory rumble along the unlit corridor from which the gaol cells were reached, hunched at the rear of the keeper's house. It drifted gently like the brackish breeze carrying through the window grate. It was, perhaps, less a window than an opening in the brickwork, barred by iron, about the size of a large book.

Squatting low enough amongst the sagging slabs of Cornish stone, she had to stoop just a fraction to place her face against the bars and see out of it.

And there she was. The source of that reassuring sound that Annalise had not dared to hope might be answered. She had not even truly expected the Mayor to deliver the message, yet she was met with the heartening sight of a familiar face.—a thing that seemed foreign to her now.

'Nancy,' Annalise called out quietly so as not to attract the gaoler back again, but loud enough to catch her attention on the second hiss.

She looked up and caught sight of Annalise's only free hand, waving through the narrow gap between the iron bars and turned on her heel to head over in Annalise's direction. She was wearing her red cloak, the one she had loaned to Eleanor on the day of their escape from The Royal. For a fleeting moment, it almost brought her to tears to see the profile of Nancy draped in it and how seamlessly it merged with the memory of Eleanor pulling it tight about her chin, her face nestled beneath the cover of the oversized hood as they scurried along Jago's Slip looking for Merrin Cottage. Oh, to go back to even that moment now and make better choices...

'T'is you!' Nancy said as she drew nearer, eyes bright with recognition and then narrowing with concern. 'I thought there had been some mistake. That prisoner told me there was no one else here.'

'Did she indeed? Well, not a word of truth comes from her lips, Nancy. It's because of her I am in here. But anyway, never mind all that. Thank you for coming. You will forgive me, I hope, for you are the only soul I know in these parts, and I'm sorry to ask it of you.'

'It's alright, I do not mind it. I'm only sorry to find you here when I thought you had gotten away, to be on your way back to London by now. — Are you hurt?' she pointed at Annalise's face where the teacup had hit her. Perhaps a bruise had risen from the place now.

'Not badly,' Annalise told her and shook the creeping memory of the first glance at Eleanor when she stepped off the coach to see that monstrous purple shiner at Leonard's brow.

As though in sync with her thoughts, Nancy asked, 'Where is Eleanor?' She squinted into the grate to see better into the cell.

Annalise swallowed the urge to burst into sobs, though her voice cracked over her words as she made answer. 'She is not with me.'

'But—'

'Her husband captured us at Tresillian, and now I am here, and she is sailing to the continent.'

'Oh no! Poor Eleanor! How dreadful, horrid,' she said, her sweet tone crestfallen, her gloved hand reaching to clutch Annalise's through the bars. 'So you are alone in this place?'

Annalise nodded. 'Well, less alone than I'd prefer,' she slid a side glance towards the direction of Mariella's cell. 'That dreadful woman you spoke to next door has set me up for a theft I did not commit. She is a relative of Eleanor's husband. She came upon us at the inn in Tresillian and sent for the watchman.'

'So it is not because of the fire, then? At The Royal?'

Annalise shook her head. 'No. She has somehow contrived to have a fancy pendant planted in my belongings which she claims was Eleanor's. But I don't think it is hers. I have certainly never seen the thing before. But it is her word against mine and it looks very bad for me.'

'Perhaps you might send a letter to the continent so that when Eleanor's ship comes in, it will not be far behind her. It's said the post runs awful slow abroad, not swift like ours. But if you are quick to pen it, it shan't be too delayed. Then she can write to Mr Carne and vouch for you and have it all put to rights.'

This innocent optimism made Annalise falter. If only it were so simple. It should have been.—a simple misunderstanding that Eleanor's account could have extinguished. But by the time Eleanor did return, if indeed that was ever to be the case, she would be too late. 'The difficulty is, I don't have an address for her or any way of finding it out.'

'Oh.'

'But Nancy, not a soul, apart from me, even knows she has gone. He has kidnapped her quite secretly, and I must get a message to London so that someone might tell her family and see what can be done. I am frightened for her. He is not a kind man. I don't know how things will go for me in the morning with the Magistrate, but if you would not mind—'

Nancy shook her head, 'I will send a message for you. I do not mind in the least.'

'Thank you, Nancy,' her voice trailed off.

'Oh, do not cry! You must not despair. It will all come about. It has to, you're innocent,' Nancy cooed, squeezing her hand a fraction tighter.

Annalise gulped and nodded. 'It is twice you have rescued me now. I don't know how I can ever repay you—'

'You needn't worry on that account. There is nothing to repay. I don't want it or ask for it. I take direction from my own conscience, and that's enough for me. Anyway, you must tell me what I should say and where to send it. It's getting dark and my pa will wonder at my absence if I am not home by the time he returns from draining Captain Merriweather's boil.'

Annalise gave her Lady W.'s direction at Grosvenor Square. It had seemed best to make an indirect approach to Eleanor's family. A scant explanation to Lady Ashlyn in a strange hand might have proved alarming or even be dismissed as a peculiar hoax. But Lady W. would know just how to proceed with it. She may even take it upon herself to intervene, for Annalise was sure she would lament this news almost as much as she did. They had seemed to Annalise the firmest of friends. So she advised Nancy she could speak frankly and concisely to Lady W.

Once she had gone over the details, Nancy nipped back to the waiting tip-dray to fetch her the two warm blankets and parcels of food she had come prepared with,

in expectation of finding both of them here and insisting that Annalise should make
use of both provisions, for she looked tired and cold. Surely, a hearty feed and warm
night's rest would do her much good before she answered to the Magistrate in the
morning. She promised to return then to show Annalise the draft of her message
and to find out what the Magistrate had decided on the matter. —She was sure it
would all come about somehow. And yes, if things were to go well, she could stay
at *Merrin Cottage* again when the sailor went back out with the *Mary Pelham*. Until
then, she could take the barn at her father's house if she would keep to it quietly. And
no, unfortunately, she was unfamiliar with the way of things in Venice. It was not
a packet destination from Falmouth. Had it been Brazil or Portugal, she could have
furnished her with the details she had heard in the stories of many a seafaring fellow.
But no, of Venice, she knew nothing more than that their currency was a coin called
the Lira, and this she only knew because a Venetian migrant had once come off of
the *Swiftsure* with a broken ankle and tried to pay her father in the only coin he had in
his purse. But the travel guide, she might be able to help with for her father had quite
an extensive library and would often be furnished with books and other trinkets for
his services when people couldn't pay in coin. She would have a look this evening and
hope to come back with some news tomorrow on anything she could discover.

Her kindness made Annalise falter, and as she watched Nancy disappear about the
corner of the yard as the evening shadows fell upon the cobbled path, she sobbed hard
until complete darkness fell across the small cleft of a window and the chill of the
coastal breeze grew stronger and whistled its way in through the grate. She wrapped
one of the blankets about her shoulders, deciding the other might make for a pillow
for her sore head, opened up the food parcel, the peppery scent of the pasty drawing
her back into memories she did not want to revisit. But she was hungry now, so
she ate, grateful for something palatable after the gaoler's earlier offering of a cup of
lukewarm broth which Mariella had thrown across the cell back at him. Annalise had
permitted her own to grow cold and congealed in its tankard upon the crate, given
how it reminded her of Mariella's upswept vomit on the floor.

CHAPTER ELEVEN

Survivor.

Eleanor. May 1822 (Three weeks later).

I had survived. So I was told often, and everyone but me was happy about it. I should have been grateful, perhaps, that Marco had bothered, and too, that he had not elaborated on what I had really done, that it was all put down to a terrible accident on account of my drunkenness and falling in. But I knew he knew the truth, for he would not have been able to pull me from the canal without first dislodging the heavy stones, though how he did it, I might never know and would surely never ask.

I had thanked him, of course, on one of his bedside visits, which were at least brief, though more perceptive than I liked. But inside, I raged at his blind interference in what he didn't understand—that he had saved me only to return me to a life I loathed. Something I found difficult to reconcile with the sense of relief everyone else spoke with.

Isabella, too, was a frequent visitor and had apologised profusely for upsetting me with her introduction to Carlotta in her pregnant condition. Had she realised the sorry circumstances of my recent loss, she would have decided against such an introduction, but was only apprised of the matter afterwards. So I assumed she, too, had the measure, or at least her suspicions, and I felt guilty for her guilt. How was she supposed to know? And even Marco, for that matter. I felt remorseful too for bringing my cloud of thunder to bear upon this otherwise happy family and infecting them with my distress, for they were just bystanders, I reminded myself often as they fussed, doted and waited upon me. And because of this, I vowed I must find a way to lift myself out of my despair, enough at least to bring no more to bear upon them. It was not fair that they should have to live with my misery in their own house when they had only shown me kindness and consideration.

Though, as I battled through days of endless coughing and wheezy breaths, illness of the lungs and pain in body and mind, I found it harder to think of Marco in any other way than interfering with my fate, however many counterarguments I had at first tried to balance my judgement with. He was, of course, branded a hero. But to me, he was but another tormentor, bringing me back to my suffering and barring the way of escape. And now, there was no hope of such a possibility because I was constantly supervised by some pair of eyes or other. Giles's instruction was that I was not to be let alone for a moment, not let so far as into the garden unchaperoned, nor permitted to spend the daytime in my chamber unless Benedetta was at my bedside. And so I had returned to a prison far more secure than the one I had—almost— left behind.

But as I began to improve in health and regain the capacity of my lungs and easiness of body, slowly but surely, I tried to embrace the small entertainments to help me pass the time and disguise my close captivity from myself. I would now join the table for all my meals, Isabella for afternoon tea, and calls from her acquaintances. I would join her in the courtyard as she gardened and took up my sewing with her in the evening once we had removed from the dining table. I had drawn the line at her invitations to church, though I had provisionally agreed to pay calls with her next week and see something of this city I had now been resident in for two months and had seen barely a glimpse of beyond the view from the windows.

I took little pleasure in any of it and, deep down, felt just as miserable as before. The difference was that the shame of what I had done had had a sobering effect on me and caused a sense of duty to resurface in me now. A duty to find a veneer of civility that would allow the family to forget all the bad business and move on from it. It seemed, at last, I could finally bring myself to do that if little else. It was made all the easier since Giles had been less severe with me, less demanding of my bed and generally more distant since that night. I supposed I had Isabella to thank for that, for she had confessed she had spoken to him at length to bring him about to understanding the difficulty for a woman in processing such a loss as I had suffered in my miscarriage. 'Men are different from us,' she had said, 'He goes off to his casino and makes himself scarce to deal with it. It is the way of most men who cannot face their heartbreak. But we are different creatures. We feel it all. But you know, there will be other children yet. You are young, in your prime, and you have been married only a short while. Sadly, most of us who have been blessed with a family can count our losses amongst them. But, give it time, and you will be blessed with another infant.'

I did not correct her and tell her that he grieved for no child of his, that any expressed sense of sympathy on his part was not of true feeling but to appear to be in possession of it, or that it would be my worst nightmare to conceive a child to him. Though she was right, I should have perhaps already fallen pregnant again with how frequently he had ravished me in the early weeks of our arrival. But by the grace of a singular miracle, I had not, and hoped it might long continue so. I was only grateful her influence had rendered some peripheral improvement in him and hoped it would remain thus. I supposed it was down to her, too, that he had never mentioned anything of the disturbance to his chamber that night, though I had spent days waiting for his reprimand. Though, it never came, much to my bewilderment.

So, with those pressures somewhat alleviated, I felt more able to fall into this new routine and gradually grew used to being more about the family, particularly Isabella, who, after a time, had felt less of a burden and more of a comfort than previously. Dante, too, had tried to cheer me with his playfulness and our interactions became less formal and easier now. It was only Marco I did my best to avoid when possible.

I purposely rose a little later to avoid being left at the breakfast table with him and would generally divert myself in a different direction if I saw him coming in mine. I could manage his presence in company, but I dreaded any opportunity he might take to speak alone with me, to make mention of what he *really* knew of the events of the night I wished now to forget.

It was on a brief lapse one morning at breakfast when Isabella and I were the only ones at the table, and I was left alone for a few brief minutes while she attended an impromptu call on some matter of church business. She had barely left when Baldassare had brought in the post upon a salver and left it upon the table as he often did, only usually it came earlier than this and I was not left alone with it. I had tried on many occasions to catch a proper glimpse at the address, for I had little more than *"Ca' Rosetti, Venice"* to know it by and was sure that would not be sufficient for postal purposes. I did not know if addresses worked the same way as at home, but I suspected that writing to so bare an address would be akin to writing: "Rose Cottage, London". But now, as I lifted one of the letters and studied it, I could see that the street was named as *rio dei Greci*, and there was another word, perhaps denoting the parish or county, that read "Castello, Venezia". I glanced about for any sign of an ink pot to copy it down. Though rare, I had sometimes noticed one left about the breakfast table if Mr Harper had a hurried reply to scribble over his breakfast. Typically, I was always in company on those occasions, and now I was not; there was nothing to be found.

Had it been in English, I might have stood a chance at simply remembering it all until I could find a way to record it. – Since I was not trusted with ink or quill, I could not even ask to borrow one for the purpose without risking being reported back to Giles. I would have to hope to recite it. But in the Italian, I was not sure I would remember it. Though it seemed simple enough, the translation being "River of Greeks, Castle". But my head was always such a labyrinth these days, I could barely hold a single thought for long without veering into another. I was not sure even remembering it in the English could be relied upon in the days or weeks to come, and so, instead, I searched through the pile until I saw one addressed to Giles, removed it from the tray and tucked it into the sleeve of my dress.

'Is everything alright?'

I looked up, startled, and pushed the salver away immediately. Of course, it would be him. 'Marco,' I said as nonchalantly as I could contrive, 'Forgive me, you startled me. I thought you to have left a quarter of an hour ago.'

'Yes, well, I was waiting for the post. I am expecting something important,' he said, reaching for the salver and scanning through the letters. 'As perhaps are you?' he raised a questioning brow, then found what he was looking for and withdrew it from the pile.

I said nothing but felt my colour up.

'Meddling in his affairs shall only make things worse, you know.'

I feigned ignorance to this.

'If I were you, I would return the letter before he notices it has gone astray.'

'Or what, you shall report me to him?'

He shook his head in disapproval. 'Is that what you think? I speak for your own benefit but suit yourself. I must be off. Good day to you!' he said as he began unfurling his letter and walking away.

I did not return the letter to the salver. I needed a breakthrough if I was not to languish in this place, and this just might be it. If Marco was not going to report me for taking it, how would he ever know it was sent to him? Post got lost all the time. It was nothing new. And so, I decided that at least for a time, until I had either revised the address by heart or managed to get my hands on pen and pot, I would hide it and return it if I saw fit. So, I settled upon a long-known female art of sewing a secret pocket in which to hide it that he was unlikely to find. The brocade pelmet of the bed was where I thought it least likely to be noticed or disturbed. Clothing and mattresses were too obvious a choice and more susceptible to accidental discovery in the course of their use or cleaning, but the pelmet would never be inspected beyond an annual spring beating, and given how clean everything was on my arrival, I was sure that task had not long ago been undertaken, ahead of my arrival.

Now I finally knew exactly where I was, I needed only to contrive a means to get covert access to paper and ink and a means of sending it on to the Banfields. All of which I had no notion of how to accomplish...yet.

But the next morning, since it was a Sunday and the only day of the week Giles could not attend his business affairs, I decided, after we had breakfasted on our small private balcony together, to make another attempt at getting access to the writing materials. See if his recent softening extended this far.

'You seem in better spirits this morning,' he said to me once he had put down his newspaper and emptied the coffee pot.

'Yes, I am,' I lied. Your family has been very kind to me, and now that I have come to know them better, I suppose I feel more at home here.'

'Yes, my aunt did think that would be the case. Well, I am glad of it.'

'But,' I said cautiously, 'I do find that I miss my own family all the more for drawing closer to yours. It has been an age since I have seen them or had news of them now...'

He cast me a suspicious glance and I did my best to look sincere. 'From what I gathered, I thought you and your parents were always at odds.'

No doubt he had that from Mariella's whisperings. 'Well, it is true that we did not always see eye to eye, but my sisters, I was very close to, and my mama, well, I think we had just begun to come to a better understanding. In any case, they are my family, Giles, and I long for news of their health.'

'Then, perhaps it is time you wrote to them. The post is not the fastest from abroad, but—'

'Really?' I asked with genuine surprise.

'Well, of course.—I shall fetch my ink presently.'

I was speechless. Whatever had Isabella said to him to soften him so? He was almost exhibiting signs of human decency. I watched on amazed as he returned to the balcony with paper and pot and laid it out in front of me, moving my plate and empty cup aside.

'Thank you,' I said warily, and when he sat back down beside me, I resisted the urge to delay until his leaving for fear of him suspecting me of my true intentions. But he did not go. He sat back down beside me and rang for another pot of coffee.

I dabbed the quill and paused, 'Oh, I have just realised I do not even know what address to put down.'

'Fear not, I shall take care of that if you leave a space for me to complete it.'

'Of course,' I agreed, keeping an even tone. Of course, I should have known that he would not risk me writing to them without vetting my words beforehand and taking charge of all the details that might be of use to me. But I did not care. I had the address, that was not the object of this task, and even I was not stupid enough to think I could write frankly to anyone right now. This first letter would have to be heavily censored – a whitewash of the truth so that he was not exposed for the villain he was, and so that it did not sound like a direct plea for help. For now, to establish some contact would be enough to begin with. To let them know where I was. To prove trustworthy with paper and ink. Once he grew used to my exchanges, he might permit me my own or grow lax in keeping watch. Then, I could move on to more important matters. So, with perfect equanimity, I began as unselfconsciously as I could muster, given the competing thoughts arising in my mind as I wrestled with the disparity between what I *wanted* to write, and what I *could* write. I struggled over them mentally for a while before I put ink to paper.

'You have had a change of heart?' he asked, watching me.

'No. I am only a little out of practice.' I turned back to my letter and began: "Dear Mother" and paused again. There was so much I wanted to write:

Dear Mother, I have been kidnapped and spirited off to Venice.

Dear Mother, I have wedded a perverse brute.

Dear Mother, how could you allow it?

Dear Mother, I think I'm dying here.

Dear Mother, Giles will be my end if you do not send for me right away.

I felt the heat of his gaze upon my cheek and dipped my nib:

Dear Mother,

I am sorry I have not written to you sooner, but I had not time to do so before leaving. I am in Venice now with Giles, staying with his family while he attends some business matters. It was all very rushed, and the journey long and arduous, so forgive the delay. I had no opportunity to tell you sooner.—I am sorry if I have caused you undue worry on account of my abrupt departure. But I am here now, and I hope you will write to me and tell me how you all do now I have a fixed address to receive word. It may be some time until our return, hopefully within six months.

Venice seems a beautiful city, even more so than the pictures portray it, though the climate is very warm in the extreme, even though it is not quite summer. I am not sure how I shall manage the heat for such a duration, but I am taking care to stay directly out of it as much as possible.

I have found my new family to be welcoming and extremely kind. But I miss home so very much and long to hear news of you and my sisters.

Please forward my address to them. I would love to receive their letters and hope to hear from you soon.

Eleanor. x

All I could hope now was that knowing my whereabouts would be enough. Had I been at liberty to write to someone who understood me and the depth of my true feeling, like Lady W., I could have felt some confidence in her ability to find my words bogus at a glance and read between the lines. But, as much as mama and I had begun to understand each other better, I knew her ideas of a wife's duty may cloud her ability to understand that I would not have had a change of heart towards my husband and that these words could never be my own. Still, I handed it over to him to forward, even if I was only half hopeful that he would even bother sending it. Perhaps it had simply been a test to see what my motives were. If it was, I would surely have passed it with flying colours, externally at least. But on the inside, fury raged so fiercely that when Isabella came to make her weekly invitation to church, I smiled, nodded, and said I would be with her directly. I hated the burden of attending church, and I was not a Catholic in any case. But I would have done anything to escape his proximity and risk undoing all the hard work I had just invested in the scheme by letting my feelings boil over and betray my efforts.

'Eleanor, I am so happy you are ready to attend,' said Isabella when I met her downstairs. 'I own, I thought perhaps you were unreligious, but I have since realised that the last thing one wants at times of difficulty is to be amongst society. I am glad you are finally ready, for I think this is a sign you are feeling much better?'

'I am. I still have moments, I confess, but I am learning to manage them somewhat better.'

'And sometimes we cover the distance just by making small steps, and that is enough.' She looped her arm inside mine and directed me out of the house. It was strange to step out into the world for the first time since I had got here. I was not used to being around others anymore.

The Harper men she had sent on a fraction ahead of us on account that before her daughters had left, it was the fashion in which they journeyed, the church of *Santa Maria della Pieta* being but a five-minute walk away, they would split into their respective sexes and re-congregate once they reached the church. It was not the way we had ever journeyed to church, but then it was not the thing to walk to it either. Not even in London where the streets between *Berkeley Square* and *St. James's* were perfectly walkable. Oh, how far distant such memories seemed now as we strolled along the canal-lined pathway in the already-sweltering morning heat. It was so startlingly unusual a landscape it served only to inflate the alienating sense of being so very removed from all I knew. And whilst I understood it to be beautiful, an architectural marvel of a place, a medieval trove of landmarks, even just from the glimpses I caught from the windows, it was as though I had forgotten how to *feel* it. Like there was a discord between what was known and felt. I *knew* it was a place I would otherwise be astonished by, keen to explore and marvel at. But I could feel nothing beyond a mental recognition of the fact and none of the true appreciation or enthusiasm it *should* have provoked in me. But still, as Isabella pointed out some point of interest along our way, I managed to find the right words of compliment or appreciation to offer in response. Indeed, the church itself was a very grand building with its white marble façade, even if the works to its upper edifice had not been entirely completed yet, and yes, how novel that its neighbouring building, the *Ospedali,* had been the workplace of the famous composer, Vivaldi, and yes, I should very much like to attend one of the highly esteemed concerts to see the *figlie de coro.*

By the time we got inside the church, I had hoped the need for my faux praise and enthusiasm would cease, but I was soon directed to the frescoes painted by none other than, Tiepolo. I was nearly exhausted by the time the opening hymn began. I struggled with the sermon, not least because the Italian was spoken so fast and fluent that I could not keep up with it in its entirety. I had the benefit of a house of mixed heritage at *Ca' Rosetti,* with Mr Harper being an Englishman and Isabella a native. I had not realised how much this blend of Anglo-Venetian tongues had not only allowed the interchangeable use of the languages, but also somewhat softened the accent better for me to grow more accustomed to it. But, just as I had noticed with Carlotta during our brief exchange, the local dialect was far more pronounced than I had been used to hearing, and I must somehow learn to adapt to the lost syllables sacrificed for speed and fluency if I was ever to find a way to get back home.

CHAPTER TWELVE

Marquetry Pearls.

Annalise. February 1822.

A nnalise had not known what to expect of having to present herself to the Magistrate when the gaoler came in early and told her to ready herself to go. But by midday, the bad business was done, and the matter decided.

Despite her unwavering account and increasing concern over Mariella's credibility, she was to be transferred to the Gaol at Bodmin that very afternoon to await trial for theft, or more specifically, Grand Larceny, the Magistrate had explained, though little the difference weighed with her. This was despite Mr Carne having spoken in her favour and apprising the Magistrate of having discovered some witnesses at the hotel who confirmed that they had seen what they supposed were servants of the establishment going into the room Annalise was occupying during the time she was absent and attending his interview. Yes, it was definitely about the hour of three o'clock, for they were on their way to the dining room for high tea. —On this point, all the witnesses aligned. But beyond that detail, the descriptions were vague, and they had no idea what their business was inside the room for they had paid no mind to it, and for all they could tell, it was just as likely to have been to empty a pot or light a fire as to anything more sinister. No, they had not seen a pendant with them, but that is not to say they would have seen it anyway from such a brief and fleeting glance as they paid.

What Mr Carne had found particularly salient and odd, however, was that upon conducting a line-up of the staff and his watchman, the witnesses were unable to identify any such persons amongst them. Surely, this merited some suspicion, he proposed. Particularly when given the obvious display of ill-intent Miss Craythorne had exhibited in violently attacking the accused in his presence. It was, at least, revealing of her feeling towards Miss Tullier, and perhaps suggestive of a motive in bringing a false complaint upon which she had succeeded in planting the pendant, as Miss Tullier claimed. It was, of course, only circumstantial, but worthy, he felt, of the mention, should anything further come to light yet.

The Magistrate agreed to make a note of these points for further consideration, and it appeared for a short while that the matter of having only a written complaint from Mr Craythorne and no opportunity of him being summonsed to answer to the Magistrate's interview was a point of great contention. It seemed an irregular thing to have done in the Magistrate's mind, given that Mr Craythorne claimed to have suspected the maid's wrongdoing for a time and could have come to make the complaint in person before his departure. Time pressures withstanding, it seemed that he had been in the locality for some days, adequate to relay even a written complaint whilst still having the opportunity to answer in person to it. Did they know for certain that this was even Mr Craythorne's hand? It had not yet been verified and no onward address upon the continent had been given by which he could be contacted. Did anyone know how long he was to be gone? – At least a six-month, Annalise told him. Mariella disputed this and assured the Magistrate he was to return within the next eight weeks to prosecute the case and that his attorney would deal in the matter in his stead for the time being, to which he harrumphed and sniffed and threw the written complaint down upon his walnut desk in ostensible despair of it.

For a short while, it seemed that things might turn in her favour over these 'technicalities and irregularities' of case. He had no desire to refer a case that might amount to the prosecutor not present, particularly when the gaols were full and the sessions still more than a month away. It appeared the Magistrate knew not what to do about it and might have been swayed, either way, with just a fraction more certainty of subject.

Mariella was happy to assist to this end and, to Annalise's utter amazement, made an elaborate claim that the marquetry pearls were, in fact, her own, and she wished to add the theft of these to the charges. When the Mayor asked her why she had not reported them missing with the pendant, she claimed not to have even known they were gone, but having been shown them now, yes, she was sure they were the same as adorned her travelling sewing box. And what could Annalise do to dispute this Banbury tale? Admit that she had taken them from a table in a cottage and not from Miss Craythorne? No, that would not do. And so she could raise no dispute to counter it.

Yes, they were genuine pearl, she confirmed when the Magistrate passed one through his fingers to examine it. She had it as a gift from an Indian nobleman, and it had been of great sentimental worth, even if not one of her most valuable possessions. How could she answer to its value when it had been gifted to her and such details were not in her knowing? Yes, her servants and family could swear to the matter, but the box was not with her now; it had been taken, with the rest of her things, back to London, where her servants were to inform her father of what had passed. She could perhaps write to him and ask him to bring it back, for he would surely come at once when he had the news. And despite this quick-thinking ruse and having ready answers for his questions, it seemed she had failed to properly convince anyone.

But it was all as ambiguous as it was untrue, and even Mr Carne's attempts to put to the Magistrate the violence and abhorrence in which Mariella had conducted herself throughout, seemed to indicate that the one and only verified testimony they had to proceed with, was biased and unreliable. Suggested Mariella herself may not be of sound mind given the gaoler's report of her. It all seemed quite the quandary and set to crumble as fast as it had been contrived. That was until he revisited questioning Annalise about the marquetry pearls and the arson attack at *The Royal*, which was not the subject of this complaint, but had at least been verified as a legitimate one before it was retracted. The Magistrate wished to hear directly from Mr Wynn about why the complaint was withdrawn. It was all an odd puzzle, and whilst he was not minded to waste the time and expense of the Crown in recommending to trial an unmeritorious case, nor was he willing to give leave to a thief and troublemaker who thought it acceptable conduct to stage fires in hotels, to drift askew from the reach of justice.

It was true, as the Mayor had pressed, that the accused had conducted herself impeccably throughout and had not changed a single line of her testimony. However, whether this was a testament to her innocence or skill, he could not ascertain. At the very least, further enquiries were due, both on Annalise's account and the Craythornes. There were things that needed to be verified which may sway things in a more certain direction. That was a matter which could be undertaken by the prosecution in the wait for the Lent Assizes, and perhaps by then, a clearer picture may emerge in which it could be decided on by men with a better account than the ambiguous one he was furnished with presently.

But in the end, it was the marquetry pearls that swayed it. Or at least, that's what Annalise believed as she relayed the outcome to Nancy through the barred grate on her return to the cell. She had not been able to account for those and had been torn between the honest urge to confess, and the dire necessity to avoid inadvertently incriminating herself towards a crime she had not committed, by confessing to one that she had. In the end, she said nothing to it, made no answer at all, just fiddled with the corners of the handkerchief in her lap and was grateful to be dismissed after a time.

She despised untruths, but she also knew there were times when the truth could prove a very dangerous thing. She wondered if confessing to the pearls might at least render her credible and of a character less likely to have denied taking the pendant. But no, she had seen enough to know that theft of any kind, however great or small the value of the item or the necessity of the cause, was never looked upon leniently by such men. She was no fool. She understood the Magistrate was not looking for evidence of a crime as so much as evidence of her character, a social problem he had the power to stamp out. She had known persons escape the gallows on matters of violence and disturbance far graver than the case of a stolen petticoat or candlestick, and still seen the latter swing for it. How could she condemn herself to her own death? She knew she was not a *real* thief and saw no justice in answering as one and forsaking her life, when she had every honest intention of reimbursing the owner of the marquetry pearls just as soon as she returned home. And now it seemed she would not get home any time soon, perhaps not at all.

And as she contemplated this miserable circumstance, a part of her rose up and posed the question: did she really want to go on living anyway? Now she had lost her love and feared her heart may never again be whole. She was not sure. She had been devastated to abandon Eleanor but had not lost hope, the hope of going after her, reclaiming her from his wicked clutches. Where her heart had fractured, this fragile thread of faith in their reunion had knitted itself across the cleft of those two hemispheres, with the promise that if she could find a way to fashion this into a story of her rescue, then maybe, just maybe, it might heal again. Was such optimism futile? No, it had narrowed drastically, but it remained by a thread. For the trial would take time to come about, she had been told, if indeed it was passed to trial by the Grand Jury. The sessions were busy and had to deal with all crimes that had occurred since the last Assizes in Summer, which would be no small number by Lent. The passage of time would be a good thing, permitting all necessary enquiries to be undertaken with the proper diligence required to make better sense of the matter so that when the jury heard out the case, they would duly arrive at the right decision.

She did not share the Magistrate's confidence in this but clung to it all the same, for it was all she had now, to trust that between now and then, *something* would transpire, be it a technicality or irregularity made better sense of, that might turn things in her favour. And if it did, in less than two months, she would be freed and ready to resume her plans. If it did not, then perhaps after such a time of enduring the heartbreak that rendered her too pained to consent to its grief, might prove enough to turn her to welcoming the prospect of the rope and an escape from all the suffering.

CHAPTER THIRTEEN

Family Secrets.

Eleanor. May 1822.

T he Church service was a long one and I soon drifted into my head and had given up on trying to keep pace with it when it finally came to an end. It had felt questionable what the lesser evil had been in staying at home with Giles or attending this ritual. It was a much more elaborate affair than the services I had once been used to attending. Giles escaped it on very simple grounds of claiming himself Church of England, and though I too would have been classed as such, I had abandoned such affiliations of late in favour of a more liberal idea that there certainly was a great divine spirit out there, but I very much doubted it was particularly fussy about what branch of Christianity you adopted, or kept count of your attendance at church. Not that I would ever voice such notions. I had grown more towards the understanding that Christianity was less about the establishment and more about embodying the good works it claimed to promote. Annalise had shown me that, the personification of it. I'd felt more aligned with the moral and charitable fabric of myself since focusing more on *doing* good than kneeling at alters or reciting hollow prayers. Though how much charity or faith even remained in my heart now was a mystery even to myself. I felt near dead inside. It seemed that the only real emotion I had experienced in months, ranged from despair to anger and regret. I could just about *remember* what happiness and excitement felt like, though so far departed from it and not enough to re-conjure the sensation, even for reminiscence's sake. *Everything* had become tainted with pessimism in some form or another, like a rampant contagion that had infected every part of me, from the minutest corpuscle of lifeblood to the finest hair on my head.

The purest and most vibrant feelings I had ever experienced had been in my love for Annalise, and so much hate and resentment had overshadowed even that since her abandonment of me. Where at first, I only thought of her with longing and heartache, more and more, I realised how it teetered on deep fury and betrayal. I had always thought I would write to her as soon as I was able, but now I was no longer sure I would have anything nice left to say, even if I did get the opportunity.

'How did you enjoy the service, Eleanor?' Isabella asked me as we rose to leave.

My smile was a genuine one borne of the relief it was at last over. 'Very much, though I admit my understanding of the language insufficient to follow it quite as well as I would have liked.'

'Ah, it will come, my child. Now you are out and about you will pick it up in no time, just you see. I was much the same with my English when I first met Mr Harper, but see, I speak almost as well as he now. Though I had little choice since he spoke not above a few words of the Italian when we met. If I had not revived my English, we would not have been able to pass a simple conversation, less still, progress to marriage.'

Fleetingly, I wondered how their paths had crossed but thought it impertinent to ask such personal questions, even if I was struggling to keep the conversation flowing. So, instead, I gestured towards the strange-looking compartments as we walked out and asked what they were.

'Oh, confession boxes. I forget you are not Catholic.'

'Of course. I am not, but I have heard of those boxes before.'

'Would you like to visit, I mean, privately once the church is empty?'

I wondered what a priest would make of my litany of sins if I ever dared to voice them... 'No, I thank you. I am not sure I would know what to say.'

'Well, if you change your mind. We shall re-congregate at the coffee parlour next door now if you might like to stay a while?'

I nodded and kept walking, mentally preparing myself to endure another social gathering—no wonder the family were always gone so long on Sundays. I had assumed the church journey to be a distant one which accounted for it, but now I noted the elaborate affair a Catholic service was in comparison to those I had attended; it soon became clear it was not only a highly esteemed religious gathering but, equally, a prominent social gathering as we came into the crowded parlour, a large and grand room where people sat over coffee and ices both inside and outside on a terrace of neat tables. It was not a private affair, though, but a hive of familiar greeting and conversation between the parishioners, and I was introduced to so many new acquaintances in that visit, I was sure I must have met the entirety of the parish in one sitting.

'Are you alright?' Marco asked me quietly in a brief moment of repose.

I nodded, but the overwhelm was disconcerting after so long in isolation. I did my best, but had to work hard against the urge to flee from the room within minutes of our arrival.

'I can walk you back to the house if you would prefer to leave?' he offered.

'No, thank you,' I declined, considering the lesser evil. I had managed to evade every one of his attempts to collar me privately since he had pulled me from the canal, and I was not about to alter that now and be drawn into an explanation, a confession, whatever it was he wanted from me.

'I can ask Dante if you would prefer? He would not mind.'

'No, I'm fine,' I insisted, but thankfully, Isabella seemed to recognise my distress and made our excuses after a few sips from our cups.

'It's alright, my child,' she said as she navigated us back out onto the street. 'It is a lot for your first outing, I know. I am only pleased you came and enjoyed a change of scene. Might you like to take a detour and walk about the gardens on our way back? They are very fine at this time of year and shall be peaceful for a while yet?'

I nodded, remembering how the Cuddington woodland would soothe me in times of despair simply by being there. And despite the pretty courtyard garden Isabella kept, abundant with potted plants and vibrant flowers, it was a far cry from the lush English greenery I was used to, and thought such a detour might be just the thing to restore me to a calmer state.

So, with Isabella's maidservant and a footman trailing behind, she led me through unfamiliar narrow streets with tall buildings dissected by snaking canals, connected by small bridges and lines of drying laundry hanging from window to window like irregular bunting. I was grateful for the cover of the buildings that shaded us from the harshness of the sun and enjoyed the respite, even if I was not so fond of the foul and pungent odour rising from the waters. Its familiarity evoked the memory of the unpleasant taste of the water I had swallowed down the night I had tied the brick to my ankle, with a lucidity I could do without reminding of now.

When we arrived in a neatly set garden laid out in the style of formal lawns and landscaped shrubbery, I realised how long it had been since I had laid my eyes upon a simple patch of grass. It was a reassuring sight, but little more than a token reminder of countryside charm given the lack of woodland or vast landscape I had expected based on English standards of parkland. 'Are there any woodlands or forests in Venice?' I asked her once we had completed a lap of the place, with no sign of any such backdrop or clearing becoming apparent.

'I'm afraid not. Occasional wild marshland—quite unwalkable— on the lagoon periphery is as close as you will come to finding anything of a wilderness on this island. We are much a city of stone. But there are other islands close by, far less inhabited, laid mainly to farming that remain largely unspoilt. We can always take a boat trip across to the Lido if you would like to see them sometime?'

'Oh, no, I thank you though. I had in mind a local place to take sheltered walks for exercise from time to time, that is all.'

'Ah, well, if that's your object, then the *Giardini Pubblici* might answer to that purpose and requires no boat journey at all, just a twenty-minute walk from *Ca' Rosetti*. Hardly a wilderness or forest, I confess, much in the style of this garden with many more trees planted and far vaster than any other parkland you will find on the island. We have not the time now, but tomorrow perhaps? I could show you after breakfast and you can see if it will suit?'

'You are very kind, Isabella, but I do not expect to encroach upon your time. You have already been very patient and generous with me.'

'You encroach upon nothing! Indeed, I have nothing fixed tomorrow, and you are a guest to these lands. It is my pleasure to acquaint you with them. Now, shall we breakfast early and decide upon half past nine, then we may enjoy the cooler hours of the day?'

I smiled. 'Yes. I shall look to it.'

She returned my smile. 'I think England is a very green and abundant land, or so my husband tells me. I have never been.'

'Yes, it is, I suppose.'

'Hmm, I would like to see it, but I am not fond of travel. There was a time I thought I might not have a choice but to sample one of these horrific-sounding packet crossings across the channel.'

'On Mr Harper's account, you mean?'

'No. He would not subject me to such, though children can be less considerate in their youth. Both our sons were sent to Oxford for their education – it was my husband's wish that if his sons were to make their homes in Venice, then they would at least know his native lands and ways, grasp the language and manners first-hand. The rites of a Gentleman, he calls it. It was very hard for me to let them go. They were gone for four years in study and a further two making a tour of Europe on the way back. But where Dante grew homesick and was keen to come home, Marco wanted to return to England only months after his return to Venice.— He was offered a position as an apprentice to your famous portraitist, Mr Lawrence, and wished to further his study and be admitted to the *Royal Academy*. I thought I would lose him to the place.'

'He is an artist then?'

'He is. He has his own gallery now, close to Rialto. But in those years of tender youth he was something of an amateur, and it was but an unobtainable dream in his mind. He was preparing for a career in the clergy and had taken theology at Oxford. But Mr Lawrence turned his head, recognised something of a talent in him and made an offer too good to refuse.'

So, he was the clergyman type. That made better sense of his irritating propriety and interference. 'So he moved to England to become Lawrence's apprentice?'

'It was to be the plan. But thankfully, no. Though he visited him from time to time, when wartime peace permitted, always back within a year. But he changed direction, discarded his plans for the church and took up his artistic studies at the *Accademia di Belle Arti*, which, much to my relief, is here in the city. I have never since entertained the idea of stepping foot over the treacherous terrain of the Alps or being thrashed about on a packet boat.'

'No, I do not blame you. I cannot say that sea travel is at all the thing for my constitution, and if it were not for the fact that I must return home by some means, I would be happy to make that my first and last journey.'

'Indeed. I have no difficulty boating about the city or to the mainland, but that is as much of my ancestor's seafaring blood I have in me, I fear. Still, no matter now.'

'Yes, it must have been a relief to you, his remaining, but why did he stay?'

'It was not my pleading I am sorry to confess, but by a stroke of fate. In the weeks of his return home he fell in love, and for a time, it seemed he might be married. Alas, it was not to be, but by the time the circumstances altered, he no longer wished to go and was accepted into the Academia and remained in Venice.'

'Well, a happy outcome all round then.'

'In the end. Though not the circumstances of his disappointment. But it was a long time ago, and he has finally realised his dreams. I think him happy. A mother has only want of three things for her children: their happiness, their security and their proximity. I am thankful. It has not always seemed certain, but I now have only Dante to concern myself with, and he is so much his father's son, his only present wish is to follow in his footsteps and take over the family business in his stead.'

'What is the family business?' I asked, having noticed that on the occasions I was present amongst Giles and the Harper men, such topics dominated the lion's share of their conversation but went quite over my head. With the exception of Marco, I supposed, which stood to reason now I knew him to be an artist and not a merchant.

'Well, for my husband's part, he was with the East India Company for many years, but now he manages the shipyard I inherited on my father's death. My family come from an ancient line of *Arsenalotti* – skilled shipwrights at the Arsenale and, later, merchants in spices and silk and such. Mr Harper approached me with an offer to buy my father's business upon his death, but I had no wish to sell the family legacy nor any idea how to keep it going. I was not intended to inherit or schooled in the way to manage such a venture. Of course, it was my brother who was meant to inherit, but, well, he was banished from Venice some years prior, so there was only me left in line.'

'Banished?'

'Yes. Not uncommon in the days of the Republic. The Council and their spies always looking for signs of betrayal. It was a terrible business. He was accused of being a traitor, but I knew the accusation to be false. There was a great deal of rivalry amongst merchant families back then, and it would not be the first time someone would slip false claims into the lion's mouth to gain an advantage over a rival or ruin them. But I knew him innocent. – I think my father did too, at heart, but had he not gone along with the Council's verdict, the whole family would likely have suffered the same fate, and we would have lost everything. At least from afar, and with trade still running, he was able to support him quietly. Last I knew, he was in Paris before Napoleon struck, but we never had word beyond that time.'

'How dreadful.'

She nodded with a hint of sadness in her eyes before blinking it away. 'Anyway, I would not sell the shipyard, and Mr Harper would not give up on the proposal, and so, after a time, we came to know each other better amidst these futile negotiations and came upon a better scheme. It seemed the perfect solution, to marry and solve it all. He could expand his business interests, and I could facilitate the legacy of the family business and one day pass it on to my sons.'

Marco, being the older of the two, I supposed he was intended for that role, but I suspected he had chosen otherwise.

'It helped that we had grown quite fond of each other by then.' She smiled, 'The business has changed a great deal in that time, particularly since the fall of the Republic. Had it not been for your husband's generosity, we may have lost it entirely after Napoleon arrived. But when we could no longer see a way to salvage the trade we had prospered from in the wake of the war and being tossed between the French and Austrians, Giles proposed a mutual alliance. He had returned from his Naval commission a wealthy man and wanted to expand his small trades of cotton and tea between Asia and Europe, and he needed ships. Built, renovated, repaired, maintained, and so on. So, we were able to survive the type of hardship many Venetians suffered.'

So that was why they were willing to have us here and show such generosity – Giles had been their saviour. I found it hard to believe any such act was a charitable one on his part.

'So, we thrive once more by the custom of your husband and, of course, the grace of God.'

'So Mr Harper's business and my husbands are one and the same, a partnership?'

'No, they are quite distinct, though their interests are in common. We own the shipyard, and Giles contracts us with the production and maintenance of his merchant vessels. His fleet grows ever larger, and it keeps our small yard quite busy. We take on contracts for other merchants, too, and retain a little of our former shipping activity in trades of salt, Burano lace and Murano glass, though it is much reduced from its former magnitude. And so, Mr Harper has diversified our investments, so whatever happens with the shipyard in such times of uncertainty, we have other means to rely on beyond it. I suppose it is for the sake of passing on the family legacy that we continue with it now. It would be worthwhile for Dante's sake alone, for he carries the ancestral blood and talent quite potently and desires to bring our name back to the former glory it enjoyed in our heyday. Marco never had an appetite for it, though he was schooled for it.'

'It is important to you,' I said, still surprised at the frankness and intimacy in which Isabella confided such detail to me, a stranger. I knew not if it was on account of me being 'part of the famiglia' now and therefore seen as worthy to being privy to such family secrets, or whether it was simply a cultural discrepancy in custom which accounted for it, or maybe, I considered more thoughtfully, she understood my unhappiness with Giles and hoped to promote his character in a more favourable light out of some misguided sense of gratitude or hope of improving my estimations of him.

'Very important. Anyhow, I have told you much of my history. What about you, Eleanor? Tell me about your family.'

Though it held no great interest, I would have rather stayed on the topic of shipping yards and merchants than have to poke at the painful wound of my own family story. 'There is not much to say. My life has been a simple one in the country for the most part. I know not if it is the same here as it is at home, but females of my class live simple and sheltered lives and are then married off as soon as we come of age.'

'Come, you are modest. I believe your parents to be of great rank and account. You must have enjoyed an education.'

'Yes, that is true. I suppose, in many ways, I was fortunate. I had the benefit of an education and a life of privilege, but, well, I am not sure I was ready for marriage at all.'

She gave a reassuring tug at my elbow. 'I am not sure we ever really are. I was three and twenty when I married Mr Harper, an old maid by all accounts when all the girls I knew were wives by their sixteenth birthday, mothers by their next. And despite my being so delayed in that course, I still found it a difficult adjustment to begin with. Give it time, my child. You are still so young. You will adapt and find new things to bring you comfort. There has been no greater pleasure or comfort in my life than becoming a mother. And I know it is a very sore subject for you now, but once it comes to fruition, I am certain you will know such joy.'

By the time we returned to *Ca' Rosetti*, we had been gone far longer than I think either of us had anticipated, having completed several laps of the small garden as we moved from one topic to the other, but still, we were surprised to find Giles in such a fidget, pacing about the marble tile of the entrance hall.

'Where the devil have you been?' he asked me before we had quite stepped in.

'For a walk,' I said, flustered. 'Whatever is the matter?'

'Giles, what is it?' Isabella asked, rushing towards him.

'Nothing. I was anxious and worried. I thought you would be back from church with the others, and when you were not, I grew concerned. That is all,' he said in a far more reasonable tone than the one he had used on me.

'All is quite well,' Isabella reassured him. 'And I am to blame. Forgive me. I should have kept better watch of the time. We ladies do sometimes get lost in conversation, I confess. But a little exercise and a good chat is excellent medicine for our sex. Now, let's get something to drink, it is very hot.'

I knew, as we walked upstairs and relieved ourselves of our bonnets and pelisses and sipped on lemon water, that what Isabella took as an overly concerned husband was not the half of it. He had suspected me of some new mischief, some escape attempt or the like. He, of course, would never admit it, but I knew his mind. It was disappointing to see how little trust I had won in the weeks of my bare existence and complacent confinement. If I was ever going to break free, I would need at least a little of his trust to begin with. So, I endured his questioning with perfect equanimity. Where had I been, who had we met, what had we spoken of? I answered frankly on most points and was careful to gain his consent to go to the *Giardini Pubblici* with Isabella tomorrow morning. I had considered withholding the detail since he would be gone to the shipyard in the morning anyway and would be none the wiser, but if I was to build his trust, I must at least appear to be frank with him.

CHAPTER FOURTEEN

The Penalty of Truth.

Annalise. March 1822 (Six weeks later).

'T ullier! Visitor for you,' came the matron's voice through the rattle and clang of her key chain in the iron lock.

Annalise opened her eyes against the gloom of her cell. It was familiar now, after six weeks of confinement within its narrow walls. Apparently, Bodmin Gaol was an oddity for housing its prisoners in single cells, which she would not have minded so much if it were not for the meagre size of it, which was scarcely bigger than her bed and lacking the better daylight and that fresh, briny breeze she had grown used to at the Falmouth Lock-up. The window here was larger but tainted by a thick residue of grime upon the glass panes and overshadowed by the shade cast upon it from the neighbouring cell block, which towered over her second-floor aspect.

It was, arguably, slightly better furnished, with a bed and coverlet, a wooden stool in the corner, and above it, two slate shelves set in the brickwork holding her comb, tankard, wooden spoon, and a small bible that there was rarely enough good light, or time, in which to read from. The better light was allocated to her two hours of Oakum picking, after which her eyes and fingers were so sore from the strain that she had no desire for reading. On the floor of the far wall sat two buckets, one filled with fresh water and the other for slops.

But despite these extra provisions, she missed her old cell in Falmouth. It was perhaps no greater in length but at least double in width, feeling somewhat less oppressive than the tomb-like enclosure of these walls. She missed, too, above all else, Nancy's visits at the grate and her parcels of pasties and ale. She had at least had something to look towards to punctuate the long days and nights and something kind and familiar to anchor her when all else felt like obscurity. But it had been short-lived. She had been moved to this new gaol three days after being presented to the Magistrate, so even the small kindness left to console her new fate had faded to dusk. She had been lucky to enjoy even this. Her three-day spell at Falmouth had proved longer than anticipated due to Bodmin being already full on account of some long sought-after smuggling gang having been recently apprehended after a wrecking at the nearby *Maenporth Beach*. So, the plans for her transfer were delayed, and she had enjoyed longer in Nancy's company before being transported all the way up here.

She'd wished desperate not to have to leave Falmouth, to remain there until the trial, for she had no complaints beyond her loss of liberty, and she knew it bearable. The gaoler had been kind to her, both on account of her amicable behaviour, which likely provided a stark contrast to her neighbour, Mariella, but also, she suspected, due to her acquaintance with the Troons, who were not strangers to him. He would often turn a blind eye to Nancy's lengthy visits and the passing back and forth of small items of clothing, food, and letters when they came.

There had been two arrived on the morning just before her departure, both from Lady W. One apprising her that she would indeed pass on the dreadful news to the Ashlyn's, and another, promising to seek the guidance of her legal man to see if he might recommend someone she could send to give Annalise counsel. She was grateful for both the courtesy of her replies and the offer of assistance, given how little she knew her. But she dared not set much store by it since all of late, had turned against her favour.

For weeks, she lamented leaving her little ten-foot square cell that overlooked the gaoler's planted grounds, where seagulls cawed beyond her window grate and the wintery sunlight fell upon a single flagstone at about two o'clock each day for just a quarter-hour where she could sit beneath its warming rays. She did not miss Mariella's sporadic bouts of raucous and clanging, however, and was sure that this sentiment would be much shared by the gaoler too, when he finally had leave to load the pair of them into the Sheriff's chaise, bound for Bodmin.

He had indeed delivered on his promise to put up the other villains in Mariella's cell: a drunk, a vagrant, and a tinker woman had all been and gone in the passage of those three days. But as to whether it had caused the gaoler, or Mariella, the greater grief was uncertain. Having only overheard the scene next door, from what Annalise could make out, she had been scrapping with her cellmates who had taken offence to all her clanging and complaint, and she suspected they had gotten the better of her in the brawl if Mariella's grievances were anything to go by, and the extra bruises she noted as they were once again, faced with the sight of each other in the coach.

She had not again seen Mariella since their arrival at Bodmin and had only heard her raising a din on the first night. Since then, it had all been quiet, and she had wondered whether Mariella had met her match in the harsher regime of the Bodmin matrons, who stood for no-nonsense and were quick to see their orders enforced one way or another. Or whether she had managed to contrive some unscrupulous means of release as she had continuously bellowed on about, "once her father got word of it".

It seemed unlikely now she had increased the charges levelled against her to include attempting escape from the travelling coach when pleading the need for the necessaries as a ploy to attempt to flee, and instead trying to hit the Sheriff with her irons. She had aimed poorly and missed but had further charges laid against her, nonetheless. She had also heard the matrons threaten punishment if she did not observe the rules of silence which prevailed around the clock here, no excuses. It made little difference to Annalise with no one to speak with anyway now. Only that it seemed to increase the audibility of the clink and clunk of the operations of the gaol as iron doors were unlocked and slammed shut, and the matron's steps could be heard clipping up and down the corridors with an unnerving tread against the flags. She was surprised she had not noticed it as the matron entered the room.

'Well, what are you waiting for? Get up! You 'ave a visitor, I said!'

Annalise stood up sharp, 'Forgive me, ma'am, I must have been dozing. A visitor, you say?'

'Plenty of time for that, your legal man is come. Now put your cap on tidy and I'll let him in.'

Annalise did as bid.

'Right then, that's better. I shall send him in directly,' she said, picking up the slop bucket on her way out, presumably to spare the finely dressed gentleman the unpleasantness of its stench, which had started to grow worse with the warming temperatures of spring creeping upon them.

'Miss Tullier?' said the fellow ducking beneath the door arch, who was surprisingly tall and unsurprisingly well-spoken. The scent of wet wool and woody cologne followed him in, and she supposed it was from the rain that had dampened his coat.

'Yes, Sir,' she dipped a curtsey, reached for the wooden stool, and pulled it out for him. 'Please,' she gestured for him to sit and took a seat for herself on the edge of her bed. She had quite given up hope of Lady W.'s promise of assistance after all these weeks without a word. She had wondered if she would even know where she was now that she had been transferred and Nancy could no longer pass on letters to her.

'I am Mr Langley, a barrister acting on the instruction of Mr Jeffers.'

'Mr Jeffers?' Annalise frowned.

'Lady De Whittaker-Hollingford's attorney in London.'

So that was why she was known by her friends simply as Lady W. It was quite the mouthful. 'Yes, Sir. She did say she was to send someone. I hope you have not come far?' His accent told her otherwise.

'From London, directly, as it happens.'

'Oh,' she said, surprised at the trouble taken on her account and more than a little ashamed that it had been at Lady W.'s expense. She'd supposed she would send a local man.

'I am down for the duration of the assizes. I have a few cases to attend to, and Mr Jeffers felt I would be best placed to serve your cause. Grand Larceny, I am told, though very little else, which is why I am here. Anyway, I haven't long. I have much to investigate and prepare, so you will forgive me if we set right to the task.'

'Yes, of course,' Annalise said, remembering the purpose of his visit and reprimanding herself for indulging in pleasantries. It had felt like an age since she had spoken above a perfunctory word to anyone, less still, someone connected to something familiar to her, even if it was both a kindly patron she knew not very well and a city she had only frequented briefly.

'Right, well in the first instance, I shall need you to make your mark on this Power of Attorney permitting me to present for you at trial.' He opened a leather satchel upon his lap and fingered for the correct paperwork before handing it to her and offering her a quill and a dab of ink from his pot. It appeared, from his raised eyebrows as she scrawled upon it, he was not expecting her elaborate signature in the space he had indicated, less still for her to pause to read it before adding it to the page. 'Thank you,' he said, taking it back from her and shaking out the paper to hasten the drying of the ink before sliding it back into his satchel. 'Now, I shall start by informing you of my duties to assist you in your trial. My powers are limited insofar as I cannot make the defence for you; you will have to present this for yourself. However, I can advise and intervene on points of law, call and examine your witnesses, and question the prosecutions to better frame pertinent matters. I can also help you construct the best defence you might give. But in order to do so, I must first be apprised of the whole case against you, the entire truth of the matter, all the offences alleged, and a verbatim relay of the discussion at the Magistrates hearing, for your account is all I have to go by. That means you must give me even the most singular and perfunctory of detail, the damning stuff, as well as the advantageous. You have the benefit of my confidence, so you may speak freely, do you understand?'

'Yes, I shall tell you all I can, Sir.' And so she began to enlighten him about the events that led up to and culminated in the bogus accusations made against her. The matters debated between the Magistrate and Mayor, and Mariella's sudden manipulation of the stolen pearls to transfer the claim to one of her own interest when realising the weakness in her cousin's absentee attempt. She also confessed to him about the theft of the marquetry pearls and the fire at The Royal. And as she spoke, he scribbled notes upon his book and looked up occasionally at a particularly interesting or peculiar detail from time to time, as though trying to read her authenticity, she thought.

Then, once he had the whole, taken down the names and direction of the Mayor at Falmouth and those she might prevail upon for a character, he closed his notebook and said as if remembering, 'I should have asked it before, but I assume you intend to stand by your not guilty plea?'

'Why yes, of course, on the matter of the pendant. But if pressed, I feel it my duty to confess to taking the marquetry pearls. I must hope that if I explain why I took them—to help my mistress, and with every intention of reimbursing the costs—then hopefully they may understand that it was not so ill-conceived an act as it appears, and too, that Miss Craythorne is lying in having any interest in this matter.'

He frowned at this and shook his head in disagreement. 'Miss Tullier, I much admire your wish to speak honestly with the court, and I don't say *I* disbelieve you. But you must own what a famous tale all this will sound to them. Notwithstanding the sole benefit of discrediting your accuser's account, it will only be of use if they believe it, and I do not think they shall take your word once you have sullied it with confession. It is not worth the risk; if you take it, you leave the judge no choice but to sentence you if you make any admissions and cannot prove the pearls did not belong to her in the first place.'

'You do not believe me either. What hope have I if my own lawyer thinks me guilty?'

'Miss Tullier, I do not think it in the least, and it matters not what I think in any case. I am a defence barrister. Do you think I only assist the innocent? I would have a trifle of the work if I did. Listen, it is my undertaking to do my best to obtain the most lenient outcome for you, and that I will, but I cannot do it alone. We must work together to this end.'

'Sir, do you ask me to lie?'

'No, I ask you to withhold the whole, for your own good sake. You must understand that the evidence is so poorly set against you with the ornaments found in your possession, Mr Craythorne's statement, and his cousin's testimony. You shall be deemed as good as guilty before you even take the stand. Our joint endeavour is to discredit this account.'

'But I have been set up, Sir. Surely, we can both discredit them and tell the truth. And then there is the dwelling shop I mentioned, surely that shows I was not in need of the proceeds of stolen jewels. And I shall be able to get characters from all but my mistress, unfortunately, but they shall be good.'

'Yes, and all these things will help us to build a case upon your good character, and that is perhaps our best card to play unless something further comes to light to weaken the prosecution. You mentioned a few things that might be useful: a point of law on the verification and admissibility of Mr Craythorne's statement and the likelihood of his appearance at trial. If he does not come, you may be acquitted on account of prosecutor not present. Though even that is complicated by Miss Craythorne's claim over the pearls. That is where I must focus my investigation, on weakening her account. Then there is still, to your advantage, her attack upon you in front of credible and impartial witnesses, which will no doubt assist me in deconstructing her good character and reliability. But if you confess to taking the pearls, it matters not to whom they are considered to belong. It shall cast enough doubt in the jury's mind to consider you a thief and overlook our strongest defences. And even if we prevail, what's to stop the true owner or the parish themselves from coming forward and bringing an action against you for the same? No, it will not do. You must hold your tongue.'

'So it is all a game, the truth matters not?'

He pressed his fingertips together to form a steeple before him. 'Miss Tullier, I know it must appear to common folk that the law is a straightforward matter of right or wrong, but I regret to inform you that it is not that simple and rarely even just. It is generally more concerned with who can offer the most convincing presentation to those who sit in judgment. Who they take pity on or find reprehensible. Who they think will repeat villainous behaviours and who they think repent of them. They will not accept your fantastic story of Miss Craythorne and her cousin's schemes, true or not, less still if you cannot provide convincing evidence of them, and I do not see how you can if your Lady is gone away. They will probably not accept your plea of innocence against their word, either. But, what they will do, I hope, if we can cast enough doubt on their argument, is go easy on you if they like your character and think you worth the sparing.'

'And how will I accomplish that?'

'Your natural disposition is amiable, and your letters of credit will do much good. If we could get a witness or two to speak of your good character, it would be better still. Just forego the details of the rest of the story, and I think you will come off suitably.'

'Who can come to speak for me now with such a journey to make?'

'I could see what might be done locally.'

'But I do not know anyone locally, that's the difficulty. Apart from a young girl at Falmouth I have known less than a couple of months.'

'That is not what I meant. Anyhow, have you been told of the value of the items it is alleged you stole? This shall have the greatest bearing on the indictment we might expect at trial.'

Annalise shook her head. 'I can't remember, Sir. I was so preoccupied that day I had to answer the Magistrate that I have quite forgotten the sum. Only that it was a very great one for the necklace, not far short of a hundred pounds, I think.'

'Hmm. That is not going to bode well for hopes of leniency. I shall see if I can find anything more out about it. But in the meantime, Miss Tullier, let me tell you this – you simply cannot afford to confess to stealing *anything* if you hope to survive this trial. You are facing the sentence of a capital offence once over the worth of forty shillings, which clearly this is such.'

'Death...I know.'

'Well, I doubt it would come to that. You are young and amiable. I would expect a recommendation to mercy—'

'Mercy? You mean I will not hang?'

'No. At worst, you might be transported, possibly for a great many years if the value is as high as you recollect.'

'How many years?'

'No less than seven, to be sure in even the best case, but more reasonably, I would expect somewhere between fourteen and twenty–seven years for such a high-value item.'

'Twenty-seven!' The thought seemed somehow worse than the rope and filled her with tangible horror. Twenty-seven years thrust to some derelict land and foreign clime, forced to live and endure at such length...

'Look, it is my job to do my utmost to spare you such a fate, and if you take heed of my instruction, Miss Tullier, I am confident there is a chance that the jury may be easy on you. But, you must pay heed. Is that clear?'

She nodded, though noncommittally. 'You said, Sir, that if my accuser did not attend—'

'Then you shall most likely be acquitted on the charge of the necklace, but it still leaves the issue of the pearls. If Miss Craythorne had not claimed them as her property, you would otherwise be free to go in such an event.'

'I do not think he shall attend, Sir. He told me he meant to be away for six months, and it has been but a little under two. Even if he wanted to, the duration of the return journey would deem it unlikely now.'

'Well then, we may hope yet. I shall make some enquiries at the cottage you took them from to see if I can find out the owner and suss them out. If you are right about Mr Craythorne, it may be our best line of enquiry to follow. I don't suppose you know who acts for the prosecutrix?'

Annalise shook her head.

'Well, I shall see what I can fathom out.'

'Thank you, Sir.'

When he gathered up his things, bid her farewell, knocked on the iron door to be let out, and ducked to exit, Annalise felt, for the first time in weeks, less alone and less troubled. For she did not think Giles would be able or willing to return to these shores in time, particularly given that Eleanor's abduction had now been relayed, and the Ashlyns would likely be raising a dust. Or at least, she hoped.

Perhaps, she might finally dare to begin to look to the end of this miserable affair and the return of her freedom in as little as another sennight. Perhaps she might venture to rekindle her plans for following on to Venice, after all. The prospect filled her with a sense of optimism so dangerously tempting she dared not entertain it just yet, not entirely, alas. But she felt more at ease that night than she had in weeks after Mr Langley's visit. She sank into a blissful, restful sleep against the hard bed and scratching blanket, without the usual calamity of mind and discomfort of body.

CHAPTER FIFTEEN

Colourblind.

Eleanor. May 1822.

Rising earlier for breakfast the following day meant the table was almost fully occupied when I arrived at it. Isabella was still absent, but the men were sitting over plates of pastries and cured meats in the full swing of conversation. Without her presence, I felt inclined to turn back again, but it was too late; I had already been spotted, Mr Harper indicating the men at the table to rise at my appearance, something of a stickler for such conventions.

'Good morning,' I said to them all as they put down their cutlery and rose, taking my seat quickly to enable them to return to theirs.

We exchanged the usual small talk, which soon faded into more important affairs, such as a meeting in Mestre that Giles and Mr Harper were to attend, and then the usual complaints on the falling price of silk owing to the competitive French market and the cost of duties imposed by the Austrians. I sat peering at Isabella's seat, hoping to conjure her into it and relieve me of the irksome topic, even if I was not participating in it. But it was not only me who kept my silence throughout such exchanges, Marco often did too, unless pressed for his opinion on some matter of hot debate, and now it made sense to me why. He had knowledge, yet no interest in these matters either. Although where he had his newspaper to amuse him, I had nothing at all without Isabella's company. Not even so much as a letter to look forward to, though I hoped at least that would soon alter, that my letter to my mama might reach Cuddington soon.

When the rest of the men pushed their plates aside and bid us farewell, only Marco and I remained at the table. I helped myself to more tea and was pleased he did not offer to pour it for me. Then, with precision timing, the singing Gondolier passed below, and his rendition of *La Bruna in Gondoleta* echoed up to the terrace. I sighed and cut my bread into triangles.

'Listen, Eleanor,' Marco swallowed his mouthful and put his knife and fork down on his unfinished plate.

I felt the dread of his speech instantly.

'I'm not exactly sure how I have managed it, but I think we have got off on the wrong foot. I am sorry if I have upset or offended you in some way. It was certainly not my intention.'

I looked away and busied myself with the pastry tongs. I wished he had spared us both the embarrassment of this unwelcome candidness. Why couldn't he have kept to a mindless speech on the weather or some such talk that is perfectly comfortable between strangers? 'Not in the least. I have been a little out of sorts, is all. Forgive me,' I managed with reasonable conviction, and was relieved when he nodded and returned to his breakfast.

I considered changing the subject and at least making use of the uncomfortable silence left in the wake of that awkward speech and asked him how long the post took between here and England. Having understood him to have spent time in both, I was sure he must know.

'Better than it used to be, but still some weeks each way,' he answered.

'Some weeks? How many precisely?'

'Well, that depends on the method and the route. How did you send it?'

I had no answer, for I had not sent it and had no idea how Giles had. 'I haven't posted it yet. I was considering the fastest option,' I lied.

'Well, the fastest option is often the most expensive, by private merchant ship usually. But I regularly use the Austrian postal service and find most things arrive within a fortnight or thereabouts, notwithstanding any calamity such as a new outbreak of war, a blockade, or some travelling delay such as bad weather and so on.'

'Thank you, that is most helpful,' I said, hoping Isabella would be down any moment. It was now nine o'clock, after all, and we were to leave in half an hour.

At nine-twenty, Isabella joined the table after a painful episode of scant and awkward conversation between the two of us trying to avoid anything above the perfunctory. I was relieved to see her at last and surprised that by nine-thirty, she had managed to drain her coffee cup, eat a pastry, and summon Baldassare to ready the maid and footman to accompany us for our walk. It was at this moment when we were waiting for their arrival as we fastened on our bonnets, that Baldassare returned in a fluster and beckoned Isabella to permit a private word with him.

When she returned, her expression was altered, and I feared some dreadful news had been delivered.

'Marco, are you going to the gallery soon?' She spoke hurriedly in their native tongue.

'Not until this evening, why, what is wrong?' he replied in the same.

'It is Carlotta, she has been taken to child bed and asks for me.'

'Then is it not happy news?'

'Yes, but I promised to show Eleanor the *Giardini Pubblici* today, and now I cannot. Will you take her?'

'I am sorry, mama, but I cannot. I am painting in Torcello today and have already hired the batela.'

'Marco, it has taken weeks to convince her to go out at all, please.'

'Isabella, do not trifle on my account,' I interrupted them. 'You must go to Carlotta at once. I will be fine. I will take a walk with the maid.'

She looked startled that I had got the measure so well. I supposed I had never revealed to anyone the true extent of my understanding of their language. It was not as fluent as my French, but it could hardly be considered an ignorant comprehension either.

'We can't have you walking about Venice alone, my child. It is not like England, all meadows and bridleways. To unfamiliar eyes, it is like a maze here; you will get easily lost, and then there are all the beggars and pickpockets to consider.'

'Well, we have those in London, too. I have nothing valuable to steal, so I can't imagine myself a worthy target, and I could take a map perhaps, if you have a pocketbook of the city I might refer to?'

'No, it will not do. Marco, you must take Eleanor to Torcello with you.'

We glared at each other. Apparently, even he had not bargained for this.

'Really, there is no need. I am perfectly happy to—'

'Forgive me,' he said, noting the severe glare his mother cast over him, 'It would be my pleasure.'

'Excellent, that is settled then,' Isabella congratulated us, clapping her palms together.

I wanted to vanish.

'You will like it very much, I'm sure Eleanor. Torcello is very picturesque and peaceful. There is even some woodland. I'm sure you will find it the perfect spot to read your book there or take a walk without getting lost. It is one of the rare places you will find such beautiful greenery without going to the mainland.'

I smiled compliantly and wished Carlotta and her family good health.

I was brooding all morning whilst I waited for Marco to have the boat loaded with all his artistic accoutrements. Why couldn't he have put his foot down and declined on account of being too busy or some other reasonable excuse that would have prevented our having to spend the day in the uncomfortable sufferance of each other's company? We could barely manage to get through breakfast. I paced my bedroom floor trying to find excuses, but I knew none of them would suffice. The truth was not that I might get lost, for the maid would surely know the way even if I did not. It was that Giles's instructions dictated I must be chaperoned at all times, like a child. If some member of the family or other could not account for me, and I managed to make an escape attempt or threw myself into the canal again, it would be on their head. And so I knew that if I declined to go, Marco would cancel his outing, stay home, and watch over me until Isabella returned. At least if he was occupied with his painting, we might stay a little more out of each other's way, and I could not be blamed for entirely sullying his day.

I took my seat in the boat with mixed feelings. One moment, feeling guilty for encroaching upon his plans, and another, feeling incensed for being made to tag along like an unruly child in need of supervision. I hoped the journey was not long, for this proximity was inescapable. I had packed a book, put my walking boots on, and vowed to put enough distance between us on arrival to avoid any further discomfiture. But as I settled into my seat and surveyed the surrounding waters, I felt uncertain of my state of mind. It immediately brought back to me the memory of the time I had been in a much smaller boat at Cuddington: the day spent by the lake with Annalise. I replayed it with bitter-sweet fondness, remembering how we had laughed when we fell in and got soaked through, and almost laughed aloud as if it were now. Then I remembered, more sombrely, that first kiss, considered how distant that day seemed, and wanted to burst into tears. However much I tried to banish it, her memory seemed woven into my every thought and action, still, and there seemed no escaping it. Sometimes, I wanted nothing more than to wallow in every detail and keep her close to me in the only way I was able. But sometimes, times like this, it was too painful to bear, and my pain would soon bubble into anger. But pent-up anger was like a dose of potent venom to my already plagued soul, and I knew not how to move beyond it without an outlet.

I heard Marco instructing the oarsmen in Italian and realised I must compose myself before my thoughts betrayed me. I inhaled deeply as the boat shifted and began to glide out towards the middle of the narrow canal that wrapped itself around the western boundary of *Ca' Rosetti*. As we moved out from the shadows into a stream of sunlight, the lagoon changed colour from cloudy grey to aquamarine. The morning heat was already rising, and as much as I adored the sunshine, I doubted even I could enjoy it for too long in the open. I pushed my parasol open and propped it over my left shoulder to shade my face. I could feel his eyes on me; a contemplative gaze that I refused to meet. I tilted the hood of my parasol ever so slightly forward to limit his view of me and concentrated on the sights around us. Seaweed and moss clung to the water-stained walls of the canal as we meandered our way beside high buildings speckled with paint-faded shutters and sprays of colour from the window boxes below them.

'It is hard to imagine the laying of each brick, is it not?' he said eventually.

Spare me the history lesson. 'Yes, quite a marvel,' I said flatly.

'You look lost.'

I knew he was not referring to my lack of geographical navigation here, somehow, disturbingly, he could read me. 'I was just thinking of a friend.'

'It cannot be easy to be so far away from home.'

I wish you would mind your own business and leave me in peace! 'I am a little homesick,' I said eventually to appease him.

'I was the same, to begin with, when I came to study in England, but I soon grew accustomed,' he replied, and I pretended I knew nothing of what Isabella had confided to me of his history. 'But, indeed, there is no place quite like home, as the saying goes,' he smiled as he looked about him, his Carmelite brown eyes shining in the sunlight. I could see the contentment in them, and I envied it.

'Did you like it in England?' I asked, feigning a look of interest.

'A great deal. I confess the weather and the food took some getting used to, but it is a great country, and I still visit from time to time. Though it has been a while.'

'You still have acquaintances there?'

'A great many from my days at Oxford, mostly. I am expecting one such friend to pay me a visit soon, in fact. I received a letter only yesterday.'

I could feel the emergence of an opportunity in this news, though I knew not quite how it might be useful yet. But even word from home, however general, and sight of my own kinsman, seemed somehow like a beacon to me. 'What is the fellow's name? I wonder if I know him?'

'George Holland-Bury,' he said, waiting for a sign of recognition.

I did not know the name at all, and I was disappointed at the fact. But it did not rule out the possibility of some mutual acquaintance, I considered, more desperately. I shook my head.

'He is an artist too, though perhaps not very well known outside artistic circles.'

'Your mama tells me you have a Gallery. You must know a great many artists.'

He looked thoughtfully. 'Yes, I suppose I do. Though we are a small affair, our exhibitions grow each year, and we show the work of artists from far and wide. I like to think we are curating the modern collections of artists that will one day be as well known as Tintoretto and Da Vinci, but time will tell.'

I noted the passion in his voice, his face softening into a shape I had not seen before. Something lighter and more effervescent than usual. 'It means a great deal to you?'

He nodded. 'It is all I have ever wanted to do,' he said, staring out towards the open lagoon as we left the small canal behind us and drifted into the wider expanse. Then, he turned fully to me. 'You know it won't always feel like this.'

I frowned. I had finally spoken more easily in the hope of discovering more about his contacts and English friends, but this return to an invasion of my privacy set my guard back up about me.

'—a strange and unfamiliar place. We adapt to change far quicker than we expect of ourselves.'

'I'm sure you are right,' I replied, trying not to sound too clipped. The day was young, and I wanted to at least get through the journey in relative amity. And, of course, I knew even I could adapt to a foreign land in time, even the weather and the food! If only those were the root of my unhappiness. But I could hardly explain that the foreignness of the country was the least of my troubles, and yet, I suspected he, above the rest of the family, understood that with the greatest acuity, which was perhaps why I found it so difficult to be about him.

We sat silently again for a while, and I knew he was trying to find some safer ground on which to direct the conversation. I was clearly not so good at hiding my contempt as I thought, for he always seemed to catch it, however brief or fleeting.

'Have you plans to tour the sights while you are here?' he asked when the silence had become stifling.

'No, not yet, at least,' I told him vaguely.

'Perhaps Giles will show you about when he is not so tied up with business.

I felt myself stiffen in my seat at the mention of him. 'Yes, perhaps.'

'There is much to see: The Academia, the Doge's Palace, the Basilica...' And then, when he observed my lack of interest, he fell silent again and looked away.

The conversation carried on in this style for the entirety of the journey, and it was not a short one as I had hoped. I had no way of keeping the time but was sure it had taken well above an hour.

It was a relief when we finally arrived on the island of Torcello. The close confines of the boat had made the need to fill the silence a tangible pressure that could now at last disperse. It was a bumpy welcome, the oarsmen navigating through a sludge of boggy mudland and sand banks that the boat struggled to move through with ease before they finally managed to moor it and hand us out. It certainly was a wilderness of sorts, seeming neglected and primitive at first glance. But once we were afoot, the view of all the greenery improved my interest, and I felt some relief to set my eyes upon a more familiar landscape. I studied it at length, hoping to induce some response in me. The grass and trees were a lush and brilliant shade of green in the luminosity of the sunlight, stretching over hills cresting against the backdrop of scant ancient buildings that met the skyline. It was a beautiful wilderness, I supposed, with only a scattering of structures at the centre, disturbing nature's glory. Yes, I could make the observation, see what was before me, but I remained all ice inside.

'It is beautiful here,' I told him anyway, once we had walked long enough in silence along unkempt natural pathways thick with weeds. I could sense the expectancy in him. He was obviously in love with this place and struggling to understand my indifference. He was not the only one. I remembered back some years, waving off my brothers as they left for their Grand Tours of the continent, asking mama when I would set out on mine. She had chuckled at the question. The innocence of it made me sad because I wished to return to it so desperately now it was lost to a reality far harsher than the one I had dreamt up as a girl.

"Dear girl, why would you need to acquaint yourself with the world? That is a gentleman's pursuit and one we need never trouble ourselves with," she told me. I could still feel the swell of disappointment in me now at the thought of never laying my eyes on all the places I had read about in books, seen in pictures, heard great tales of, and learnt the tongues of.

'I hope it pleases you to see something more like the countryside. My mama says you grew up in the country and have a particular fondness for it?' Marco cut into my reverie, and I collected myself.

'Yes, I am a provincial girl at heart, I suppose, and I like it very much here. It seems peaceful.'

'It is a special place. So peaceful. It is the least inhabited of our islands, and as much as I love the city, sometimes, I, too, crave the comfort of nature. Perhaps it is the Englishman in me,' he smiled.

'I suppose it is easier to paint here than in the city, without the bustle.'

'Yes, it is true, but a Venetian artist knows that attempting to paint the city in anything but either the early morning or twilight hours is a fool's errand, though sometimes a necessary one. I painted a scene of the last Regatta, so it is possible but hardly a peaceful endeavour. But in those small windows of time when Venice is sleepy, it is quite transformed into something majestically still and silent and perfectly paintable in such conditions.'

'Then what is it you travel such distance to capture here?'

'The mood of the place. The combination of nature thriving against the remnants of a lost city in decay.'

'City?'

He nodded, 'You are standing on the very first Venice, the centre of it all, in the beginning. The capital of trade and commerce and the grandest of Palazzo and Basilica...'

I frowned, wondering how the landscape before me, comprising of a few stone precipices rising from the centre and a scattering of more ordinary-looking homes, could have ever been such.

'It is true. Torcello was once Queen of the Lagoon. At least it was, until about the tenth century, it is said.'

'What happened?'

'Mother nature reclaimed it, I suppose.' He pointed to the lagoon we walked beside with the wooden stool he carried in his hand. 'First, the canals swelled with silt and grew increasingly impassable as sandbanks emerged and the ships could no longer navigate the waters here. Then the swampy canals provided a breeding ground for Mosquito's and the Malaria drove even more people from the island.'

I cringed at this and looked about me.

'We are quite safe at this season, providing we stay away from anywhere overly sodden.'

'So what happened to all the people?'

'They dismantled their Palazzos and rebuilt them in the Venice we know today. At the time, Venice was more alike to this place now, even more of a wilderness perhaps, for some traces of the lost city remain even all these years later,' he pointed again to a square a little ahead of us with old buildings set about it.

'So they switched roles.'

He nodded. 'Some fear that one day Venice will be nothing more than this – the scant remains of a wilderness, deserted, or worse, flooded in the acqua alta, all but remaining of its ghost: scattered clues of sunken stone.'

It seemed an impossibility to my mind.

'But it shan't be in our lifetime, and I hope may never come to pass.'

I nodded my agreement. We were now at the foot of a Cathedral.

'This is the *Basilica di Santa Maria Assunta*. It is one of the few buildings that remain in use to serve the small population. It is mainly agricultural families which inhabit the island now.'

'Is this what you mean to paint today?'

He shook his head and directed us on. 'No, I have already captured the remaining buildings here in their own right. I come now for the natural landscapes and to attempt to capture the mood of the place.'

I wondered how you captured the sense of a lost city, a ghost town, and translated that into a work of art. We walked on for a further quarter-hour or so, uphill in the heat through wild meadows and lofty trees, beads of sweat escaping our brows. Then, he finally stopped and set down his receptacle and easel. 'This is the perfect spot; you see how the bell tower peeps above the trees and the sunlight catches just that side of these overgrown ruins before us.'

'Yes, quite the view indeed,' I agreed and tried to coax some passion into my tone. After his impromptu attentive tour, I owed him that much, at least.

'Can you paint?' he asked then, looking away from his landscape and meeting my eyes.

'No, not really,' I said and hugged my arms around the book I was carrying, borrowed from Isabella's private library. 'Please, carry on as you would. I have infringed on quite enough of your time. I will find a spot to read this, and once I have recovered my strength, I might go with Benedetta for a stroll about the copse, if I may.'

He nodded and stretched out his easel, and I wandered over to a shady patch beneath a tree.

Benedetta laid out a canvas mat for us to sit on, which she had been carrying rolled up beneath her arm and we settled upon it. However tempting it was to chance a bit of sun exposure now I was at ease to rest in it rather than walk beneath its beating rays, I knew I would likely burn if I dared to sit freely in a heat of this intensity. Then back flooded memories of me and Annalise scrubbing our tans off with *Milk of Roses* after falling asleep in it. I laughed out loud then, remembering the shocking pink sight of her, and then sighed a long, shallow breath to rid myself of the melancholy as the thought began to curdle.

'Are you alright, Signora?' Benedetta looked up and asked me.

I must have seemed an oddity to her. I nodded, sat down and opened my book out in front of me. But I wasn't in the mood for reading. I had neither the focus nor interest right now, even though I craved distraction. I looked over to Marco, still setting out his things. He pushed his dark hair back with his hand, took off his jacket, hung it on the back of his easel, pulled his collar loose, and rolled his sleeves up. Then he stood there a while, contemplatively, turning at different angles, frowning at the vine-covered ruins. When he started painting, I turned away and forced my eyes over the printed words. *Focus Eleanor. This will be a long morning without a distraction.*

So, I had no choice but to persevere with the pages before me. I was reading *Frankenstein*. Not my usual choice of reading matter, but I was limited in my selection since most of the library was in Italian and this was one of the few volumes that were not. Besides, I needed something that would take me far away from myself and help me to forget for a while.

It was a quarter past two when I grew tired of persevering and went over to Marco, minded to enquire after when we would be leaving. But he was engrossed in his work, and I was remiss to disturb him. So I stood at his side, looking between the canvas and the landscape, and when he noticed me at last, I said, 'You have a remarkable talent.'

His surprise at receiving a compliment from me was evident, but he put his paintbrush down and thanked me evenly. His skin had browned deeper in the sun, and his forehead was aglow with a film of sweat. He wiped his shirt sleeve across it.

'I am not convinced I have captured enough yet, but I shall try not to be too much longer,' he said and stood back from it, smudged a finger across it in a few places and bit his lip.

I watched how the light caught his eyes and illuminated the honeyed flecks of contrast in them. Though distinct from hers, his reminded me of a hue I sometimes caught in Annalise's eyes and I turned back to the painting. 'Do not rush on my account. I have nothing better to do at home,'

'Would you like to try?' he offered, gesturing at his paintbrush.

I shook my head. 'I have not used a paintbrush for years. I was a perpetual frustration to my watercolour master—'

'No matter, I see people far beyond your years take it up for the first time and surprise themselves.'

I raised a sceptical eyebrow.

'I hold classes every week at the gallery. It is always surprising how little people think they are able to achieve in the beginning. Won't you have a try, if for nothing else, to pass the time?' He spoke with passion, his smile was bright, his whole face animated at the prospect, and it suddenly felt impossible to refuse him.

'Very well. I might start with a little sketching. I am somewhat better at that, but I warn you in advance to expect no masterpiece.'

He laughed at this, even though I meant it in earnest. 'I expect nothing at all. You don't even have to show me if you prefer,' he smiled at me again and then bent down to arrange things for me to use. He pulled out pencils and many different-sized brushes, a few stained cloths, a roll of canvas and a small hammer as he emptied the contents of his box onto the dusty ground afoot.

'So, do you have good attendance at your classes?'

Sweat ran into his eyes as he stretched some canvas over a wooden frame and knocked a nail into it.

'In the evening class, I have about twelve men, and in the afternoon ladies' class, I have five or six at most.' He straightened his back as he adjusted the height of the easel.

I blinked at him. 'Ladies' class?'

'We're small but growing. Perhaps I might persuade you to come along and improve the number?' he offered as brightly as his smile, which I was not able to forget, even when I turned and stared at the blankness of the canvas in front of me.

I started out well enough with the sketched outline, but when I moved on from sketching, dabbed my brush with an earthy shade of grey paint, and agonised over where to place it, I began to lose focus. I felt silly looking over his picture; the colours all merging into each other and still perfectly catching the shape, the detail, the shades of light and shadow.

He must have noticed my pause, for he looked up and asked, 'May I?'

I shrugged.

He came up close behind me and peered from over my shoulder.

I don't know why I felt so aware of his proximity, but I grew increasingly uncomfortable.

'Finding a starting point is always the hardest part. Start small and build the colour.'

I took a small step forward to put some distance between us and swept my first stroke across the canvas. But the moment had passed and I was back in my head. I put my brush down. 'Forgive me. I don't think I'm able after all.'

'Do not be so easily defeated,' he said, picking it up and handing it back to me. The aim is not to capture it in perfection or accuracy. Art is about expression, about how you see what is before you and conveying your unique interpretation to the page,' he told me gently.

I turned my head and looked at him unconvinced. If it was about expression, I was sure I should paint something awful and ugly as I felt inside, not the beautiful sweeping hills and cloudless sky.

'I think you are putting too much thought into it. You must step out of your head and into your heart,' he said, pressing a palm to his chest. 'Close your eyes.'

I hesitated before complying.—I was not sure I had a heart anymore.

'Now relax, breathe.'

This is stupid. I peeped then, and he saw me.

'Just trust me,'

I trusted no one anymore.

'Now I want you to feel what is all about you, the essence of the place. Listen to the sounds, the trees rustling, the birdsong.'

I concentrated on the sound of the crickets in the grass, the occasional rustling of the leaves, the rasping of his voice, and more and more, they grew louder to me, everything else fading, slipping from my grasp.

'There. Now take a breath.'

As I exhaled, I felt the tension in my body begin to ease. I took another breath and drew it deep into my lungs. Then I felt a calmness I recognised from my life before hell, so overwhelming that it almost brought me close to sobs as I remembered it. I *felt* something, something above misery.

'Now, when you are ready, open your eyes.'

I had almost forgotten his presence. I blinked against the sunlight as my eyes adjusted to its glare.

'Now look at your landscape, and as soon as you see it, beneath your unique lens, put your brush to the canvas and let your hand guide itself. Do not think about it.'

I did as he instructed and was surprised when I drew my hand up and put the first proper strokes to it.

He moved back to his own work, and I caught a glimpse of satisfaction on his face.

We didn't speak for a long time after that, but we shared an awkward glance now and then when we went to dip our brushes into the rinsing water at the same time, or caught each other looking in the direction of the other's canvas. But there seemed to be some peace between us now, and I was willing to put my grudges aside. I was, perhaps, a little hasty in my judgement of him. Yes, he was irritatingly perceptive, and he had interfered where it was not welcome. But. He had been patient with me today, generous with his time and effort, despite not wanting to bring me here as much as I wanted not to come. Though where he was pleasant and diverting, I knew my company to be dull and disappointing, even if he was too well-mannered to show it. So, as the day progressed, I made more effort and shifted towards feeling grateful to have come, relieved at this newly forged truce between us, hoping it spelt an end to awkward breakfasting and poorly stifled resentment. It was time to cast the bad feeling aside and extend the cordiality I felt around the rest of the family, to him.

I was surprised at how effortlessly my mood had managed to lighten through the course of the afternoon. How doing something physical again demanded my attention in a way that distracted me from the circular thoughts that had plagued my every waking minute since leaving England. I was grateful to learn it was still possible; that I hadn't lost my ability for distraction altogether. I could not call it pleasure or enjoyment per se, but to feel occupied in and of itself, was a reprieve from all the gloom.

I was contemplating the shades of the sky when he turned from his easel and looked over at me.

'How are you finding it?' he asked.

'I'm finding it very refreshing, actually. But I can't say my pleasure for it has improved my hand,' I told him, frowning over my canvas to evaluate it. True to my word, it was certainly no masterpiece, but it was not quite so bad as I had predicted. It was fairly recognisable.

'Well, that is the most important part: the pleasure of it. – May I?' he asked, gesturing with a paint-streaked hand.

'If you must.' I stepped aside to make room for him.

He stood for a moment in quiet contemplation, looking it over, and his silence made me nervous.

'You think it's terrible, don't you? And I'm sure it is.'

He looked softly at me. 'No. Actually, I was thinking you have captured the ruins well and something of the sense of haunting grief I still feel about the island.' He stared back at it. 'I think your use of colour is a little confused, but that is easily improved with guidance and practice.'

'I think you are generous with your praise, Sir, and kind not to tell me what you really think.'

'I have told you what I really think,' he corrected me and took up my hand with the paintbrush still in it. The surprise of it silenced me. The Italians were much more tactile than I was used to, and I still had not adjusted to it.

He dipped the brush into a blob of white paint and dusted it lightly over the darker shades of blue. 'Just a light stippling. It softens the colour, helps it blend, see,' he said wisely, and when our eyes met, he let go of my hand and left me to continue on my own.

When we got back, the rest of the family were still out, and I supposed Carlotta was still in childbed since there had been no word to the staff. Given how tired I felt from being outdoors in the sunshine for so many hours, I decided to take a nap. It was the most I had done for months and I was excessively fatigued. Besides, the luxury of having no one about to coax me from my room for a change was not to be wasted. I was sure Marco would be content to leave me be, and he had already headed off to his attic studio, taking our paintings with him. He told me he would hang my picture to dry with his, varnish it, and return it to me the next day. Out of curiosity, I had wanted to go up with him to see this studio, but no invite was forthcoming, and I decided against inviting myself after all the time I had already taken from his day.

So, I took a short nap, which revived me a little, but I had dreamt of Annalise, which stirred up my thoughts again and transported me back to my desolate mood. It did not help that when I went down for dinner in the evening, Isabella had still not come home. So I was left to endure another evening in the company of solely male society and enjoyed no diversion beyond more talk of shipping contracts and business meetings. I ate quickly and left them to it as soon as I could. If there was any consolation, it was that I was left in peace and to suit myself for a change. Benedetta, of course, still hovered over me like a shadow, but she was one of the few who could not issue orders or strenuous coaxing. So we sat in relative quietude as I tried again with my borrowed copy of *Frankenstein*, to no avail. But the time to think freely had not been in vain. As I reflected on my day, I considered all I had learned. Marco had contacts in England. One was soon to visit and presumably would be returning home at some point thereafter. If I could perhaps continue this effort towards being on better terms with Marco, I might get an introduction. I might try to befriend this acquaintance and manage to travel home with him when the time come.

Failing that, I may learn better of the travel details: my options, the costs and how to arrange it all. Though still, I would need money, and I could see no solution to that presently, given all my precious ornaments and valuables remained locked away in Giles's drawer, for which I had no key. But there was time yet to consider it all, and I had made more progress towards that end in the past couple of weeks than I had since boarding the packet. I had an address now. A letter I hoped was making its way to Cuddington. It would be the first time my family would come to know where I was. Who knew what interventions may come to fruition on that head. And then there was still the possibility that Lady W.'s return had likely reached Porto. For all I knew, it may be sitting on Mr Banfield's desk waiting for a forwarding address to post it on to.—That must be my most immediate plan, to furnish him with it as soon as I could. Now I was going out more, I was sure an opportunity to post it might present itself. Surely Isabella would think nothing of my making a detour on a walk to send a letter to my 'family'. Where could the harm be in that, as far as she knew? But first, I needed paper and ink. Then I considered my free access to the very same all morning. I remembered my painting drying in Marco's studio, and the way became clear.

CHAPTER SIXTEEN

Bonjour.

Annalise. March 1822.

The matron swung open Annalise's cell door with a clank that made her jump and lift her head from the pillow to fathom out the disturbance. It seemed it was not for the usual purpose of conveying her new buckets and two pounds of Oakum for the day's picking, but instead, ushering in male wardens carrying a bed frame into her cell.

Annalise sat up sharp. 'Matron, why have I another bed? Is there something wrong with this one?'

'You shall be joined by a cellmate this afternoon, that's what for.'

'But, I—'

'Never mind your protests. The gaol is full to the brim and someone shall have to share—several of you, in fact.'

'Forgive me, matron. I make no protest. I was only puzzled.'

'Oh 'ark at her,' she said to the men who were struggling to squeeze the frame into the narrow spot beside her bed. 'She makes no protest! La!'

Both the men grinned in response.

'Well,' she said, jabbing a distant finger in Annalise's direction, '...you don't have a say, felon. Remember that, and remember too that the rules remain the same, so don't be turning your mind to making mischief with your cellmate or thinking you have leave to break the silence or dally on your work, is that clear?'

'Yes, matron.'

'Good! Now get up and make your bed up neat before breakfast.'

Annalise did as bid, wondering how she might be expected to make her bed up with the gap between the two frames barely wide enough to stand in, but she thought better than to raise this point, or any other for that matter, with *this* matron. She seemed of a rough and wicked temperament and not someone she would like to find herself on the wrong side of.

She had noticed this was the common way of the many she had encountered since her arrival: exacting, pugnacious and unrelenting. Though there were exceptions. She could account for at least two in possession of a milder nature and seemed to have something of decent feeling about them.—The matron from yesterday, for one, who had been kind enough to find her a pot of lard in which to dip her sore fingers in her early days of learning how to pick apart the Oakum. The other she had not seen for some days but had, on one occasion, found Annalise sobbing and placed a kindly pat upon her shoulder, took her bible from the shelf, handed it to her and told her gently, 'Find your peace, child, and have some faith. It gets easier after a time, and you are not condemned yet. You may still dare look to the prospect of your liberty. The Assizes shall soon arrive, and you will learn your fate. Until then, take heart.'

It was not until another afternoon of toil at the picking, and after a supper of bread and onion, that her new roommate was deposited into the cell without ceremony. Only a brief instruction that she did not speak a word of English, and therefore, she may have to look to Annalise to learn the way of things, for matron had given up on trying to explain it to her.

'It shall not be an excuse for idleness,' the matron warned the new prisoner as she let go of her arm. 'You might not speak the tongue, but you have eyes in your head and can see the way things are done here. Pay mind! Now, I'll be back with some soap and a comb, and you shall wash before you sully the bedclothes with your filth, do you 'ear?'

The young woman remained unmoved in expression and shrugged noncommittally before the matron let out a despairing hiss and stomped her way out of the cell.

When the door was locked again, Annalise looked her over more closely. She was perhaps in her later twenties, thirty at most, dark-featured with heavy lashes that fell thick across her eyes as though they had been generously sooted. Her features were quite hard, but her eyes, though untrusting, had something softer about them as she peered up at her cautiously.

'I am Annalise,' she whispered once the sounds in the corridor had tapered off. 'Would you like to sit on the stool until matron returns with the soap?' she asked, pointing at it.

She followed the direction of her gesture and pulled out the stool. 'Je m'appelle Ninette,' she said sitting down upon it.

'Vous-êtes Française?' Annalise asked, a little too excitedly, before reminding herself to have a care to be quiet. She had rarely come across French-speaking folk, rarer still real French persons.

'Oui. Parlez-vous Français?' Her eyes brightened and her face softened with something like relief.

'Oui,' Annalise confirmed. 'But we must speak very quietly, and if the matron comes, we shall be as silent as the grave. Those are the rules here. If we are found breaking them, we shall be punished.'

She nodded. 'You have been here a long time?'

'Not very long, about six weeks now. Matron will return shortly. She is to bring you some soap and expects you to wash before you go to bed. That is what she said to you before she left.'

She nodded, disinterested as this speech and began to unlace her boots. 'Why are you here?' she asked once she had taken them off and set them against the wall.

'I have been set up for a theft I did not commit, and well, one I did commit. –It's complicated. Anyway, what about you?'

'I struck my master in the eye with a weaver's bodkin,' she said flatly. 'It is not complicated. –He was a pig.'

Annalise cleared her throat. 'I see. Did he survive it?'

'Unfortunately, yes.'

Annalise did not know whether to judge her dispassionate speech as mortifying or droll. 'Well, at least you shall not face a murder charge, I suppose.'

'If I am spared the rope, I shall be sure to finish the task properly next time and add his wife to the tally.'

Annalise was grateful for the return of the matron's clipped steps, for she had no answer to this and felt a little disturbed by the ease with which she spoke on such a macabre subject. It was perhaps for the best that others could not understand her if this was the flagrancy with which she spoke of her crime.

Later, when they were to bed and at liberty to speak again, she did not know if she wanted to revisit their previous conversation. It seemed a topic most disconcerting to go to sleep on, locked in with an aspiring murderer to bed but a yard away from her. She had, at length, as was common in the spirit of such silence, contemplated the *why* of it all. What would drive her to do such a wicked thing, and then not only to fail to repent of it, but to revel in the hope of a second chance to finish what she had failed to execute on the first. What a way to wish away your liberty if there was even a slim hope of her reclaiming it. It seemed a doubtful thing to Annalise, though she was no expert. But violence from subordinates never went down well from her understanding. Between themselves was one thing, but against the prevailing order, quite another. She wanted to ask her how she intended to plead and what she meant to say of her defence if she was to make one. It did not seem like the kind of act which would attract leniency or sympathy, even if her employer was a miser or brute. But in the end, it was not she who dictated the direction of the conversation, but Ninette.

She could see her outline in the dimness as she lifted onto an elbow and swept her long plait over her shoulder before asking, 'How did you come to know my language? Nobody here seems to know it but the lofty ones, and they don't speak it well, or at all, to people like me.'

People like her? An aspiring murderess... 'My mother taught me when I was very young.'

'You speak well, not native, but passably enough.'

She wondered what she sounded like to her ear. Her mama had always pressed upon her the native pronunciation and always understood her with ease. But she supposed she had used this tongue much less frequently since her passing and had perhaps become lax. 'And you, do you really speak no English?'

'A little, just a few simple words, but not enough to fathom much of use. Here, they have a strange accent that makes it harder for me to discern what is said. When I was in London when I first came, I began a little better, but since I settled to these parts I have found it very difficult.'

'Yes, it is much altered here,' she agreed, thinking that to a foreign ear, it must seem tricky. It had taken her a while to adjust to the difference. 'So what brought you all the way here, from London?'

'My sweetheart.'

'Is he also a Frenchman?'

She shook her head and Annalise tensed a fraction at the sudden movement. 'No, he is an English gentleman. That is the problem.'

'But how do you converse together if—?'

'Why, in the language of love, of course. And he speaks a little French, not well like you, but enough that we managed by it. Have you a sweetheart?'

Annalise felt a hot sting of tears threaten to well. 'I did, but we have been parted of late, and it has been tough.'

'Oui, oui. The same for me and my love. It is a terrible suffering, is it not? It is the worst of things.'

'It is a dreadful affliction. Especially whilst languishing in such a hellish place as this, and to be deprived of even the comfort of good friends. I have suffered a great deal in this silent confinement, and yet, somehow, as time passes, you become accustomed.'

'I will not. My pain is carried everywhere with me, and so I shall be as miserable here as I was before I came here, silence or not.'

'I am sorry to hear it, truly. But for my part, I must not lose sight of hope, for I think it is all that is keeping me alive now, however fragile it seems.'

'I have nothing left to hope for. It is too late for all that. If I have any hope at all left within me, it is the hope to see the light go out in my master's eyes before my soul departs this earth.'

Annalise swallowed and contemplated whether to press her further or change the subject. After a brief pause, she decided on the latter. 'So, where in Cornwall did you live before they brought you here?'

'A place called Wadebridge, it is not very far away.'

'Was it nice there?'

'It was pretty enough, and I thought it was a good place to begin with...'

'It does seem a beautiful region, even if very rugged in parts. I confess the beaches and countryside are far superior to that which I have previously known.'

'In France, we have places that are more beautiful and also more terrible. It depends where you go.'

'Do you miss France?'

'Of course. I miss my homeland, my language, the beautiful white-capped mountains that could be seen in the backdrop from my hamlet, and the warm climate. But I do not miss Paris, or the poverty and rioting I left amidst. The aftermath of the revolution and wars has been hard on the French people. It is not as it was in my childhood.'

Annalise wondered if she was a little older than she had first thought, given her nostalgic references to pre-war days. '

'My mama said as much. She was from a place called *Annecy*, do you know it?'

'Oui. I have heard of it. It is by a lake, close to the Swiss border, but I have not been there. It is many leagues from my birthplace in *Ille-sur-Tet*, in the South.'

'What kind of place is *Ille-sur-Tet*?'

'Rocky, full of limestone and quarries, vast meadows, and a view to the Pyrenees. And it is warm and lovely, and the boulangerie bakes the most delicious bread you will ever taste anywhere.

'It sounds like a charming place to live. What made you leave for England?'

She shrugged. 'The riots, Napoleon, the prices, the lack of progression for our sex after the revolution...so many things. I thought in the beginning I had made the better choice when I met my sweetheart in London, but even that did not last. I might have been better off never coming to this place if I had known how it would go.'

'But you might be able to return to France, to your birthplace perhaps, one day.'

'For what? To consider all that I have lost?'

'No, to try to regain it, or some sense of what is missing.'

'I cannot. What has been taken from me cannot be restored. All I want now is justice for my sufferance, and if or when I get out of here, one way or another, I shall have my satisfaction.'

This was precisely the territory Annalise had hoped to steer away from, and knowing not what else to say without exciting her passions, she feigned exhaustion and the early hum of sleep, though her thoughts seemed more alive than ever as she tried to settle them.

It was perhaps an hour after their conversation ceased, most of which Ninette had been lightly snoring when suddenly, she let out a terrible shriek and fast descended into what Annalise could only consider some kind of nervous fit. Her first instinct was to flee, but she was soon reminded of the impossibility of this as she felt the cold iron of the cell door against her back. She could only watch silently as Ninette thrashed and screamed in her bed, crying out half-sentences that were difficult to make sense of.

Before she had decided on how to proceed, a flood of footsteps descended, and the matrons were soon in the room, lighting the cavernous dimness with their lamps and demanding silence.

'What is the meaning of this raucous!' demanded one of them as she cast her light about to see better over the bed.

Annalise was cowering in a corner now. 'I do not know, matron. – I think she is suffering a nightmare or some such terror.'

'Prisoner, prisoner!' she said to Ninette as one of the matrons squeezed along the narrow path between the beds and tried to still her with a rough shake of her arm. It seemed only to make things worse, and Ninette, appearing not at all come to her senses, and yet disturbed further from her sleep, began to thrash about more violently until the matrons wrestled her back down to the bed and issued several hard slaps and reprimands to her.

'Matron, please, I do not think she is awake! Please...' Annalise pleaded in the hope of interrupting this violent apprehension. But one of them threatened her with a dose of the same if she didn't pipe down, and she remained silent thereafter, pressed into a corner at the furthest extent, sobbing at the scene before her. It all then seemed in third person as more matrons were called to bring up a straightjacket, and Ninette—now awake and cursing foul in the French tongue only Annalise could understand—was weighted down on the bed whilst her upper body was bound and her ankles tied with rope.

When they finally achieved this cruel binding of her, and the silence was restored, they uttered a warning to Annalise to get back to bed and disregard what had happened, and locked the cell back up again.

Annalise crept carefully back to her bed, the mummy-like figure of Ninette still and foreboding as she returned to it. 'Are you alright? Are you hurt?' Annalise whispered as she passed her.

'Would you be alright if those fat bitches had treated you so!'

'Shhh! You will bring them back,' Annalise warned her.

'I think my nose is bleeding and it is running down my throat. Will you help me to turn?'

Reluctantly, but unwilling to leave her in such a circumstance, Annalise edged her way over and assisted her to roll onto her side, propping her with the coverlet so she did not roll straight onto her back again. Then, the blood began to flow onto the blanket, and she felt, rather than saw, the evidence of it. 'I think I shall have to call for some rags.'

'Do not call them brutes back. Pinch my nose for me, it will stop.'

Tentatively, Annalise did as bid, which was no easy feat in the dark and beneath the fear of the matrons returning to check on them. But she followed Ninette's guidance and held the pressure until a few minutes later, it staunched the flow, and she was relieved of her duty and free to return to her bed.

CHAPTER SEVENTEEN

Attic Encounter.

Eleanor. May 1822.

'What was that?' I asked, starting with fright and turning around at an outbreak of a raucous rising from the lower floors of the house.

'I don't know, Signora, shall I go and see?' Benedetta offered, and I bid her go. She was just readying me for bed. I picked up the hairbrush and carried on myself, catching a glimpse of my scant frame in the mirror as I leaned in to see my hair. It had now grown past my ears but was still short and perfectly manageable for me to tend myself. In the daytime, I was forced to wear a hairpiece fitted to hide the "abominable haircut", as Giles called it, until my hair returned to a "respectable length".

Like most things of late, I cared not either way and did as bid for a peaceful existence. But in many respects, I was pretty unrecognisable from my former looks. It was not only my short hair but my stature, which had diminished so drastically that I no longer seemed to hold my former shape. My chest depreciated, my hips less pronounced, and a general boniness about my limbs I had not seen since girlhood. Alongside my plain wardrobe and simple hairdress, I resembled something of a fusty governess, slight, pale and unpretentious. It was only half accidental. It had been my ardent hope that the less attractive I became, the less appeal I would have to Giles's senses, and whilst it had taken some time to effect to such a degree, it seemed, at last, to have paid off.

So, when he ordered me fitted for new gowns as my others grew increasingly ill-fitting, I picked the drabbest and plainest patterns and fabrics to be made up for me, in keeping with the rest of my looks. I was sure the family must have thought me a rusticated dowdy, dressed beyond my years, particularly given how fashionably and elaborately they dressed here, even in their dotage. Despite my lack of keeping much society, I noticed that in Venice, looks mattered a great deal. With the exception of the poor, people of most ranks made an effort with their image and were rarely seen looking anything less than impeccable.

'What news Benedetta?' I asked when she returned.

She looked unsure of what to tell me.

'Is something wrong?'

She shook her head.

'Is Isabella returned?'

She shook her head again.

'Is there any news of Carlotta?'

'Yes, Signora, she is in good health,' she admitted cautiously.

'And has she birthed the child yet?'

'Yes, Signora.'

All this tiptoeing about the matter was becoming irksome now. 'Well? Is the child in good health? Has she a son or a daughter? Come, give me the news!'

'I was told to wait until Signora Harper returns.'

'Well, it is too late for that now. Are you to tell me, or shall I go and find it out for myself?'

'She gave birth to a son not yet an hour ago. All is well. Signora Harper shall remain until tomorrow. The gentlemen downstairs are celebrating.'

'Thank you. I am glad,' I told her, and I was. My own miserable circumstances had not degraded me to the point of wishing the family ill. I would not wish my circumstances upon any woman, not even an enemy. I was pleased for Carlotta and the Harpers, even if it seemed my well wishes were neither expected nor welcomed presently. So I did not take pains to re-dress and go downstairs to offer my congratulations, since I was not yet supposed to have learnt the news. Instead, I finished my toilette, got into bed and dismissed Benedetta for the night.

It was only then I let out a few tears at the thought that I, too, would be cradling a baby now. May, the physician had advised me to expect the child's arrival. It could be me now, lying-in with a babe at my breast, counting little fingers and toes. How had I not realised that I *wanted* that? Perhaps I had not wanted it until now.

I lay in bed for a while, staring into the darkness, making shapes out of the shadows. I could not sleep with all the hullaballoo from downstairs, yet I had nothing else worth rising for. So I fidgeted, tossed, and ran in circles about my head until, finally, the house fell quiet, and I began to drift. Then, through the mist of my inertia, I heard the familiar sounds of footsteps against the marble floor outside the room, then the turn of the door handle and the sound of *him*.

I knew instantly he was drunk by the clumsiness of his steps and the haphazardness with which he undressed when he came into the room, but I pretended to be asleep throughout the disturbance until he shook at my arm and called out to me, 'Wake up wife. I bring news!'

'What?' I said when his persistence could no longer be ignored.

'Carlotta has had a son!'

'That is excellent news. I shall offer my congratulations in the morning. It is late now.'

'A son on the first try. Now there is a triumph.'

'Indeed.'

'A wife that knows her duty.'

'Giles, a wife has no more say in whether she births a son or a daughter or conceives at all!'

'Perhaps. But what is certain is that she shall never perform the duty at all if she does not make an effort in the trying.' And with that, he flopped down beside me, crawled against my back and parted my legs with a clumsy hand.

I had not anticipated this tonight. I had grown used to the recent reprieve and assumed he was getting what he needed in some other quarter. But I see now that even that would not serve the purpose on his mind. News of Carlotta's son had amplified the lack of his own, and now he meant to try to correct the matter. I turned over patiently and made no complaint at all. Of all the various avoidance tactics I had tried with him in recent months, nothing seemed as effectual as this one. Complete complacency of body and speech had made the quickest and easiest work of the task, and resulted in the longest lulls between visits.

So, against all feeling, I rolled over in the bed to permit him access to me.

I was met instantly with the breathy tang of inebriation and stale smoke.

I lifted my shift to above my breasts and braced myself as he clambered about to find me in the dark.

'When are your courses due?' he asked me then.

'I don't know, perhaps in a week or so.'

'Hmm,' he grunted, clammy hands navigating over my flesh to make it out. 'You know, there are some in this region who believe that in order to conceive, the chances are better if a female is incited to passion. Pray tell me what I should do to provoke you?'

Jump into the lagoon, I thought, shocked at this deviation. 'What nonsense,' I replied.

'Perhaps, and yet it is the only thing left to try, is it not?—Come, don't be coy, what tricks did Richards turn to fill your belly?'

'Giles, please. I don't want to speak of him.'

'Or perhaps your little handmaid had a way to bring you about? Hmm, are you going to tell me what they did to you, or shall I have to try until I discover the method.'

The prospect of either was repugnant to me, but I would never tell him what passed between Annalise and me; it was sacred to me, still. Moreover, it was impossible he could ever re-enact the tenderness between us. Genuine passion and emotion could not be conjured through some base act or means, it had to precede such acts, and it had to be *felt*. And besides the impossibility of ever feeling any such thing with him, I could feel almost nothing anymore, anyway. Those bodily regions that had once been brought to the heights of sensations so powerful to overwhelm body and mind, had been dead to me for months. Their sole use of perfunctory bodily function, not of pleasure. Not even on occasion. It was like an entirely different body than the one that would tremble and quake at Annalise's faintest touch. I had felt neither desire nor base urges since leaving her bedside, and thought it unlikely I ever would again, unless I could find my way back to it.

'Giles,' I said, irritated now, '...please stop, that is unnecessary. The usual way is perfectly fine.' He was stroking me intimately and making a terrible hash of it. I was grateful he never usually bothered, but tonight, the drink and Carlotta's news had made him fanciful, and I could tell he was determined to test this new theory.

'Is this what she would do to you, frig you to completion? How do you like it?'

'I don't like it, Giles. I wish you would stop.'

'Very well,' he said and then crawled down between my legs, and I felt the heat of his breath against me, but my body did not respond; there was no need to compel it to refrain, for all his slobbering did was remove me further from my sense of having a body at all. Even when he grew tired of the attempt and found his way into me, I only mentally noted the change.

But once he was done and rolled over and fell into a stupor, I could not return to sleep. The whole thing had disconcerted me deeply. If he was intent on impregnating me, then no harlot would keep him from my bed, and I feared that tonight would become a new precedent for those that followed. Then I might end up with child again in the weeks or months to come, and I did not want to bear *his* child. On that account, I was certain. *I had to find a way out, and soon.*

When I was confident he'd sunk quite into oblivion and was snoring into the pillow, I decided there was no more time to waste. I had wasted so much already, sunk in the depths of inertia and stagnation. I had perhaps given up for a while. But now, something not quite as substantial as faith, perhaps dogged desperation, had resurfaced in me and my survival instincts were revived. I got up, put on my robe and soft slippers and struck up a light once I was in the hall.

I went quietly about the house, stepping light upon the stairs, easing the doors open and closed carefully, and navigating my way up to the attic where I had hoped to find Marco's studio. I had not been shown the attic floors on my tour of the house, and I had never ventured further up beyond this floor. I didn't know precisely where it was or how to find it, but I did know that this floor was entirely given over to us and our apartments, so I had no concern about stumbling into someone's bedchamber and startling them awake.

In a logical fashion, I went about the corridor and gently opened and closed doors, looking for some staircase that might lead up to it. —Upon finding them no use, moving on to the next until I came to a small stairway that curled its way up into a dark room above it. *This had to be the stairs to his studio.* But on following them carefully to the top, I found that they led to a dormitory, and I realised I had inadvertently intruded upon the staff sleeping quarters. I went out again as quickly as I came, fearing I had disturbed someone. Thwarted, I took a moment at the bottom of the stairway and listened hard beyond my beating pulse for any signs of disturbance, but nothing came.

I had two choices now: take the risk of continuing to look, or to accept the disappointment of returning to my chamber having accomplished nothing for my trouble. I had resigned myself to the latter and was walking back toward our apartments when, in the incandescent glare of my lamp, I caught sight of an opening in a recess I had not seen before. It was slightly obscured by a pillar of white marble rising before it, but on closer investigation, I noticed a door set slightly deeper into the recess, and the door itself was slightly ajar. Was this too to lead to another servant's quarters, I wondered, as I pushed it tentatively. I supposed I could always pretend to be looking for Benedetta if someone noticed me. I would say it seemed too late to ring the bell and disturb the house. Yes, that would suffice. So, I didn't return to my chamber. I came to the foot of another staircase beyond the open door and began treading it soundlessly. Then, as it turned about a corner landing which opened to the next level, I knew I was in the right place; I could smell the residual tang of linseed oil and mastic.

Holding my lamp out ahead of me, it illuminated a row of collapsed easels against the walls, an overburdened coatstand with paint-stained shirts and aprons hanging from it, and a few bare wooden frames, constructed but not covered.

There must be some paper and a pencil somewhere in here amongst it all, for sketching purposes, if nothing else, and Marco would surely not miss one or two. The thought had crossed my mind earlier, to slip my sketching pencil into my pocket, but then I had grown distracted. More fool me, for it would have proved an easier task than this one, as although I was here now, where to find them was another matter. I walked on further, extending the lamp's glow farther ahead and realised that the small, plainly plastered room was not as I first thought it. I followed a narrow opening into another concealed part of the room and turned a corner where I suddenly noticed the shadow of low light flickering. As I drew in closer still, I realised it was not a trick of my lamp casting onto something reflective, nor the glow of a dying fire in the grate, and jumped back.

A long screen was stretched across half the room's width, and through its fabric, I saw the shape of Marco standing at his easel with his back to me. *Whatever was he doing up at this hour?* He should have long retired to his bedchamber. I turned around sharp to make a quick exit, but in the panic of trying to get away unseen, I knocked something to the floor, which I couldn't see but was loud enough to disturb him. *No!* I stooped to find it but heard his footsteps close and realised it was too late. I crouched there with my lamp at my feet, searching frantically for the thing that had fallen.

'It's you?' he said, frowning, standing directly before me in an open-necked shirt, half covered in paint.

I stood up slowly. 'I'm sorry, I shouldn't be here,' I said, embarrassed, finding the thing I had knocked over: a wooden ornamental figurine. I set it on the nearest surface I could see. 'Forgive me, I didn't expect, I mean, I couldn't sleep, and I wanted to see if my painting might be dry.' I knew I sounded ridiculous and felt the colour rising in my cheeks as I stumbled over my words.

He stepped in closer and lifted his light to better see me. 'I could not sleep either, ' he said, and half-turned towards the rear of the room and held out a gesturing arm, 'If you give me a moment, I will find it for you. It is dry now.'

I hesitated and pulled my robe tighter around my waist. 'It is late and you are busy.'

'Well, you are here now. It will not take a moment.'

Uncertain if I had simply shocked him or irritated him, I followed him on, wanting to leave on better terms than I had entered. When I stepped beyond the screen, I blinked against the glare. It was bright with lamplight, and I noticed for the first time that the walls were painted like a giant mural. I recognised scenes of Venice and London and what I guessed may have been Rome, a waterfall, a garden and a seascape. 'Did you do this?' I asked, thinking aloud as I turned about in a circle to examine it.

He turned around and followed the direction of my gaze. 'Yes, over the years when I was practising at murals,' he explained, putting his light back down and taking a cloth to wipe his hands on.

'Impressive,' I replied, running a finger across the surface of the wall.

He tossed his cloth to the washstand and came to stand with me. 'I'm not sure I would agree. I was more of an amateur artist in those days. My mama permitted me the space to practice as a compromise for my remaining enrolled in University,' he said, looking about the walls as though he had not looked at them in detail for some time. 'This,' he pointed, '...is the Basilica in St. Mark's Square, The Rialto, The Academia. And this, the most recent addition, is my gallery. He pointed to a narrow Corinthian columned building set opposite a small walkway alongside the canal. 'Some other sights you know well, he gestured to the scenes of London: St. Pauls, The Royal Opera House and Westminster Palace.

It reminded me of the time I had spent in London with Annalise last summer, and I quickly turned away. 'Where is this?' I asked, spotting a bright, colourful seascape flanked by lemon groves on the opposite wall.

He followed me over to it. 'Amalfi, on the South of the Italian Peninsular.'

'It looks so exotic, picturesque. Like a scene from a fairy tale.'

'It is a true likeness.'

When we reached the end of the murals, I wandered to some of the uncovered canvas paintings: Mostly landscapes and a few charming townscapes of people sitting in squares having coffee, an old Italian man smoking his pipe outside his shuttered window.

'And here is your painting. I have varnished it,' he directed me, taking it down from what I presumed was a drying rack.

'Ah, thank you.' I tried to look delighted at the recognition of it. It was, after all, what he thought the object of my visit. Though it looked no better for the drying time. Worse, perhaps, in the dimmer light.

'A promising attempt,' he said, handing it to me. 'Perhaps you might come to my class on Monday afternoon? We can work on your colour and blending if you are minded to improve?'

I thought back to why I had come and the plans I had hoped to set in motion. The letter remained unaccomplished, but that was no reason to abandon my other schemes. Besides, regular access to paper and even a pencil would serve me well beyond my initial task. 'Thank you. I'll think about it and let you know.'

'Of course, you will need to ask your husband first.'

I bristled at this assumption, though he was right.

He tilted his head, brows lifted with uncertainty. 'You think he will be against it?' he asked

'I don't know. Perhaps.'

'Would you prefer I ask on your behalf?'

I shook my head. 'No. Not for now, at least.'

'Very well. The offer will remain an open one.'

'Thank you, that is good of you.'

'Well, I'm in the business of helping budding artists flourish, so...'

'I'm not sure I fall into that definition, but I did enjoy it today. So, I would very much like to continue if I can.'

He nodded thoughtfully. 'Well, see what he says. If he is not amenable to the idea, you know where my studio is now should you want to come and practice in the daytime when we are all about our business,' he offered. 'I have teaching books too, though it is not the easiest way to learn.'

'Really?' I exclaimed, eyes wide, lips parted with surprise. "Thank you!" I said with such excitement that it seemed to shock him to see me in such a head. I suppose it did seem a disproportionate response. How could I tell him it was not. That this alone would make all the risk-taking tonight worthwhile. When everyone was out to work tomorrow, I could send Benedetta on some errand and write my letter up here in complete privacy. 'Forgive me,' I said more evenly. Only I have very little to do all day and it grows irksome. To have something to occupy me...'

'Naturally,' he smiled. 'Well, then consider it at your disposal. I shall leave the key on top of the door frame. If the door is unlocked, I am in here, but I am generally only here in the evenings so you will be quite free during the day. If I might ask you to take care about the sculptures and covered works.'

'Why, of course. In fact,' I considered, looking about me, 'Maybe it would be best if I set up a little spot just beyond the screen. That way, I shan't need to disturb your studio much at all. It seems that area is little used.'

'True, but the light is poor, which is why I use it for little more than storage of light-sensitive works or materials. But see here,' he pointed, and I looked up, 'That entire wall is comprised of windows. Smaller than the windows on the other floors, but at an unobstructed height to receive a generous illumination in daylight hours. You might prefer it here to better see. It is no easy task in the dimness,' he gestured at the several flickering lights on the surrounding ledges and floor.

I did not comment that a lamplight was perfectly adequate for letter writing, which is all I intended to do up here. 'Very well, then I shall be careful.'

'I will have a bit of a tidy-up for you. It shall make it easier to find things.—I should perhaps give you a tour: Pigments, oils, brushes, cloths and the like can all be found on the shelves above the washstand. Paper, vellum, canvas, and so on are in that cupboard there. Easels, well, you can take your pick. And I never light it at this season, but the fireplace can kick up a bit of dust if it gets windy, so I never remove the screen until it's back in use in winter. It is no fun cleaning soot from paintings. And one more thing, the servants are entirely forbidden from coming here and attempting any cleaning, so I would be grateful if you could tidy up after yourself and forbid them entry, should they come.'

'Of course, but why are they forbidden?' I asked, a curious tilt of the head.

'The last time, one of the housemaids knocked a very rare sculpture to the floor, and before that, I almost lost half my collection of canvasses to a fire that had been lit and left unattended. The loss would have been irreplaceable if I had not returned to fetch my satchel just in time. I keep few such valuable items here now I have the gallery, but all the same. I prefer to manage things myself in here, which is perhaps why it is not the most orderly, but I know where everything is.'

'Then I thank you for your trust in permitting me here. I shall be very careful. But please, do not feel you must tidy it all for my sake.'

'It is due anyway, and Holland-Bury will be here before I know it and shall likely come up here too, so I will do it early and be better prepared.'

'When is your friend expected?'

'He sets out to sail to Calais this week, so, early next month, all being well.'

'So soon? It took us much longer, I am sure.'

'Yes, if I remember rightly, you took quite an irregular route. Via Lisbon, was it not?'

I nodded not wanting to recount the memory.

'He comes via Calais, and for the most part, by carriage, which proves faster than by ship from England, with the exception of crossing the Alps, at least, which can slow things down a deal.'

This was welcome news. This is how I must return home to spare myself the agony of so long at sea. All the men I had known travelled to the continent via Calais. But it was also spoken of as a matter of great expense, logistical organisation, and danger.

'Are you alright?'

'Sorry,' I said, noting his furrowed brow, realising I had abandoned the conversation in favour of my racing thoughts. 'I was just thinking, you have no portraits here and I understood you to have been a portraitist.'

'Oh?'

'Your mother mentioned that you were connected with Mr Lawrence. – I think she was proud of the fact.'

'I see. Well, it is true. I was once more of a portraitist, but I have settled on a preference for landscapes and scene painting. I don't paint portraits anymore at all.'

I sensed something clipped about his tone but thought better than to press it.

'But I hold classes on it sometimes, it's amazing how many artists hope to improve on it. It's big business, I suppose. One of my first students has an exceptionally rare talent for it. He was asked to go to Rome with Lawrence and help paint Pope Leo a few years ago. He is doing very well indeed now.'

'Did you not want to go in his place? I would have thought such a commission—'

'No,' he said flatly. 'I don't do portraiture anymore, as I said, which is why I made Lawrence the recommendation of my student.'

I thought this strange: why would a Catholic pass up an opportunity to meet and paint the head of his church, a Catholic who was once inclined to become part of the clergy?

He leant forward to pick up one of the candles on the floor and blow it out, and I noticed the shape of his chest as his shirt gaped with the motion, which was hanging loose and undone about his shoulders.

I looked away. 'You must be very proud of your student.'

He crossed the room and set the candle holder on a nearby sideboard. 'Indeed, I take little credit; the talent is his, but I was happy to help him realise it. I'm very pleased for his turn in fortune. It is much deserved,' he said thoughtfully. 'Would you believe he was an unskilled migrant worker at the docks when I met him? Now he lives out his true purpose every day and is paid more for one sitting than he could hope for in years at the docks.'

I felt the warmth of admiration in my eyes as I smiled. 'Then it is an even better story.'

'It is.' A thoughtful expression crossed his face before he fixed me in his gaze. 'I suppose it reminds us all that when life gets difficult, no matter how bad things seem, there is always the possibility of a turn in fortune, a better ending.'

I did not like the pointedness in which he emphasised his words. I no longer felt we were talking about the portraitist at all. 'Well, I have kept you long enough, and it is late. I should get back to bed now, but thank you for your time. Today has been a better day, and I am grateful for it,' I said, picking up my painting and arranging it under my arm. 'Goodnight.'

'Goodnight,' he replied.

I returned downstairs to bed, relieved to see that Giles had not moved a whisker in my absence. The risk had paid off and the foundations of a plan were beginning to form. I tucked my canvas behind the dresser to hide it and climbed back into bed, keeping as far away from him as the expanse of the mattress would permit me.

CHAPTER EIGHTEEN

The Seamstress's Favour.

Eleanor. May 1822.

I woke up later than usual and was glad Giles was already gone from my bed, and the breakfast table when I joined it.

'I believe congratulations are due, I said to Marco and Dante when I sat down. 'You are uncles now, I am told.'

'Yes, so we are,' said Dante thoughtfully. 'Though I am sure I am too young to be called so,' he added.

'Fear not, baby brother, he shan't speak for a couple of years, and then you will be six and twenty, perhaps even married yourself by then if mama has her way,' Marco teased him.

Dante cut him a look of disgust, then tossed a toast crust towards him. 'And that shall make you seven and thirty and likely still unshackled, so by your example, I shall have a decade before mama can complain of it!'

'True. Though she shall complain if we don't get a move on, so less throwing your breakfast and more eating it.'

I watched them with mild amusement. 'Is your mama trying to match you, Dante?' I asked.

He sighed wearily. 'Sadly, yes. It seems now she has given up on him, I am to be subject to the effort.'

'And you are not so minded?' I added, and he shook his head. 'Is your mama returned now?'

'No. She is waiting for us to collect her,' Marco replied.

'You are going to see your new nephew then?'

'We are,' Marco said hesitantly. 'Father has already left but must go directly to the shipyard afterwards, so we will pay a short visit and convey our mother home.'

'Would you like to come, Eleanor? There is room enough in the boat,' Dante asked, and Marco cast him a look of rebuke, which signalled to me that he knew about my miscarriage and, from what I could judge, perhaps Dante did not.

'That's very kind of you to offer. But I think your sister will prefer a little recuperation before entertaining strangers. I hope to see her and the baby when she is better rested.'

I saw the sympathy in Marco's gaze, though he said nothing and looked away.

'But please, send her my regards and congratulations, won't you?'

'I shall,' Dante agreed before draining a whole cup of coffee in one sip. 'Right, I've just got to tie my cravat, then I will be ready,' he told Marco.

He rolled his eyes with irritation. 'We don't have time to wait for your dandying about.'

'Five minutes, I swear it,' he pleaded, leaping from his seat and taking the stairs in the hall at double stride.

Marco's tone softened with empathy. 'I'm sorry. He is not insensitive. He does not know,' Marco told me once the footsteps grew distant.

'And yet you do,' I said, mindful only after, of my acerbic tone and the pains I had taken to move to better terms with him.

'Because I asked, after...well, after the canal accident. I was concerned, and my mother only meant to explain your circumstances better to me, not to flaunt your privacy.'

It took all my complaisance to remain calm in the face of this intrusion. 'Concerned about what?'

He shifted uncomfortably under my gaze. 'That you may make another attempt.'

So it was certain, he did know what I had done, even though he had told the doctor I had fallen in. I suppose it was foolish of me to hope otherwise. I hadn't seriously believed he did not, but it still made for hard hearing. I cleared my throat, 'I was drunk that night,' I explained.

'I know.'

'You do?' *Was there anything he didn't know?*

'I saw Giles's chamber, found the empty glass and decanter,'

I bit my lower lip and felt myself growing hot.

'And what you wrote upon the mirror—I do not mean to pry or to embarrass you, but cousin or not, I know Giles is not an easy man.'

'Well, like I said, I was drunk and cross with him. Spirits always make me hot-headed so I usually do not take them. It shan't happen again.'

He nodded. 'There are a number of places in the city, charitable houses for women in difficult circumstances and such—'

'What?' I said, my tone laced with incredulity.

'I just mean that there are other options in moments of desperation that do not require the penalty of your life.'

'I did not come here for a sermon,' I stood up. 'If you will excuse me, good day.'

'Eleanor—' he called after me, but I did not turn back, and as I approached the stairs, Dante came bounding down them.

'See, under five minutes!' he said to Marco, and I hurried up to my room.

After our falling out, I felt reluctant to go to his studio at first, but I realised there would be no better opportunity than when the house was this quiet. I did not know how long it would take them to make a return journey to Carlotta, but I knew I was on borrowed time, which, in the end, was enough to sway me.

I sent Benedetta on an errand to brush and hang my winter wardrobe in the courtyard for an airing on the excuse that I wanted them packed away in storage trunks since they no longer fitted me and it was hardly the season for such heavy layers. She was initially reluctant to leave me unchaperoned, but when I opened the contents of my cupboards and chests all over the room to sort through them, she reluctantly took an armful downstairs to set upon the work.

I waited until I caught sight of her appearance in the courtyard from the corridor window before seizing the moment to go up there. My rooms were on the fourth floor of the building, the studio only one flight above. Even if she was fast at her work, I was sure I had over ten minutes before she could finish and climb the four floors between us. So I went immediately, finding the key above the frame as he said it would be and rushed up the stairs, slowing only when I came past the coat stand, in order to cause nothing to fall, or worse, break, this time. So I trod carefully about the natural pathways that lent to walking about the room, most rendered narrow with clutter until I passed the screen. It was more open here and somewhat less chaotic for his tidying, but hardly organised in a fashion that would make it easy to find things, especially small things like pencils or slate. But it was transformed by day, the brilliant light streaming in through the windows as he had said, and that at least might aid my search. I walked over to them and, as I looked out, considered the view before it, directly overlooking the canal and their private landing jetty where I had tied the brick. *So that's how he discovered me that night.* I was right before the view of his windows. I shook the thought, remembering my time constraints.

The paper was easy to come upon, I recognised the cupboard he had mentioned and found it straight away. It was more than I needed, cut in sheets almost as large as the great canvases, but I could take one and trim it down into several pieces that would no doubt supply me with many a letter-sized sheet in the weeks to come. It would be more work to trim them down to size now, though, and I hadn't the time, so I cut just one square from it, put the scissors back, and simply rolled the remainder up beneath my arm and continued my search for a pencil. – This, however, proved a much trickier task, and I had been through every shelf, cupboard, and draw in reach, to no avail, when I heard the distant clip of footsteps on the stairs below. I took my paper, locked the room and raced back to my chamber, tucking the paper roll into one of the open trunks and throwing a dress over it.

Benedetta came into the room only moments after, and I did my best to conceal my ragged breath and to look busied with folding and consideration of the dress nearest to me. 'Ah, you are back. This pile may go out next,' I said, pointing to one I had sorted out before she left.

She nodded and stooped to pick up the pile, then paused as she rose and said, 'Are you alright, Signora? You are sweating.'

'Yes, well, I thought I would try a few dresses I was not sure fitted, but without your help, I thought it might be easier just to put it over the top of my clothes, and it is definitely not the weather for it!—I shall wait until you return before I try any others,' I smiled, though she looked mildly puzzled by my answer and in fairness, it would seem a very stupid thing to do.

It took another two rounds of searching the attic and returning periodically to the chamber before I finally gave up on finding a pencil. Instead, I settled on attempting to mix an ink substitute out of Marco's painting ingredients. I was poorly practised in this art, trying to remember something from my painting lessons. I stumbled my way over ingredients, picking up glass vials of pigments and holding them to the light, unstopping bottles of oil and playing with the ratios until I found the consistency of a murky dilute paste I hoped would suffice. I took the smallest, finest paintbrush I could find, stoppered the paste mix in an empty vial, and was just about to tidy up after the mess when I heard footsteps much closer than before. I had lingered too long this time. *Benedetta*!

I rushed towards the attic staircase but knew I was already too late by the loud clip against the tile. Then, before I had conjured an excuse for my absence, I heard the footsteps heading closer in my direction, edged back beyond the door, and closed it as quietly as I could. I would have to wait for her to give up and go and then contrive some excuse for my absence. I could say that I was looking for another trunk in Giles's chamber, I considered. But when the door handle turned, I pressed myself flat against the wall and held my breath. *So much for servants being forbidden to enter the studio.*

But it was not Benedetta who stepped into the room and closed the door. It was Marco, and by the time we had both discovered the sight of each other, we each jumped and gasped in turn, me surprised to see that it was him, him surprised to find me behind the door.

'Forgive me!' he said, turning about on the stairs, 'I did not mean to startle you, but what are you doing hiding behind the door?'

'I thought you were Benedetta! I did not want her to discover me up here—' I began, but I heard her call out for me beyond the door before I could continue. I pressed a finger to my lips to plead his silence, and he seemed to consider me a moment before stepping out into the corridor and saying, 'Did I hear you call?'

'Yes, Signor, I am looking for Eleanor. She was in her chamber, and now I cannot find her. Have you seen her?'

'I have not. I daresay she has ventured down to greet my mama, perhaps she saw us arrive from her window. Why don't you try my mother's parlour?'

'Thank you,' I whispered when she went away again, presumably to continue the search.

'Will you tell me what is going on?' He frowned his confusion.

I did not quite know what to say without sounding mad-brained. 'I have not spoken to Giles yet about taking up art. He was gone before I rose, and I did not want Benedetta to tell him ahead of my asking about the classes.'

'You think that she would?'

I shrugged. 'I don't know. But I know she acts on his instructions, barely giving me a moments peace unsupervised, like I am a small child she is charged to watch over and report on.'

'I am sure Benedetta is just doing her duty to you. Perhaps she does not realise you feel stifled by her diligence.'

'Or perhaps she is paid extra for her diligence, for the work of a spy and captor as he made of all his other staff before!'

'What do you mean?'

'I mean, he has paid his servants to spy on me before, and worse—'

'Well, she might be in his employ now, but Benedetta has been in the family a long time, she was my sister's maid before your own. I do not think her of the type of character you suspect.'

'Well, of course, you would assume me imagining it! The madwoman can surely not be trusted above the conduct of a servant!'

'Calm down, do not put words upon my lips. I did not call you a madwoman—'

'You needn't, I can see you all think it. The fragile lunatic who cannot be trusted with paper or ink, scissors or precious ornaments! Dare I be given news of your newborn nephew, and god forbid I step a moment beyond anyone's sight! And you wonder why I would rather tie a stone about my ankle than exist in this prison? I live the life of a caged bird.' I broke into tears instantly at the relief of my speech. It had been so close to the surface of late I could no longer contain it. But even as I felt the warm gush of tears rolling down my cheeks, I realised the sabotage I had committed to my plans just when they showed some small sign of promise.

'Forgive me,' he said softly, unsure how to proceed. Then he put his arm around my back, directed me up the stairs to the studio, pulled a stool out for me to sit on, and found a clean length of cloth for me. 'I did not mean to upset you, Eleanor. I am sorry if I have spoken out of turn. I knew you were miserable, but I did not realise you had been denied such simple things. What can I do?'

I regained my composure as he pulled up a stool opposite me. 'Nothing. There is nothing to be done. I am entirely at my husband's mercy, and he possesses very little of that virtue.'

He sighed uncomfortably, 'I will talk to Benedetta, ask her to relax her watch a little. She will heed me.'

'No, it will only make things worse. If she is spying for him, she shall tell him of your interference, and if she is not, he may notice her lack of diligence and swap her out for someone else.'

'What is it you want leave to do? To attend the class?'

'My ambitions were aimed far lower than even that. I wanted only a piece of paper and some ink to write a letter to my friends.'

'But your husband would not deny you such provisions, surely?' His expression altered as he read the gravity in mine. 'Very well,' he said, astonished, '...you shall have use of mine. I will bring it to the studio directly and you shall write your letters.'

'You would?'

'I confess, I would prefer not to keep secrets between man and wife, but these are less than ordinary circumstances. I see that.'

I sniffed back tears of gratitude. 'Then I thank you for your generosity, truly. You know not what this means to me.'

He nodded. 'Go and find Benedetta and show her you are around. When you return, I will have the things you need here. You will forgive me for having to rush off. – I came only to pick up my workbox and am expected directly at the Gallery.'

'Dear Mr. Banfield,

I hope you are well and settling into your new life in Porto. Please send my regards to your dear sister.

You find above, my forwarding address. Apologies for not sending it sooner, but I have only just had the chance.

I thank you again for your generous assistance in forwarding my letter to London and humbly make this last request to forward me anything you have received by way of reply so I may, at last, relieve you of any further burden in this undertaking.

I hope to write to you and your sister properly when I have time. Unfortunately, I have very little at my private disposal at the moment, and I imagine that you, too, are busy in your respective endeavours.

Wishing you good health and fortune.

Your ever-grateful friend,
Eleanor Craythorne.

I swapped my letter out with Giles's, which I had hidden in the pelmet pocket, and I would wait for an opportunity to slip his back onto the salver one morning. I had yet to figure out how to send mine, but it was a relief knowing I was finally closer to my objective. I was grateful to Marco for making it possible, though I had the distinct sense that he had been avoiding me since that meeting.

Where he might usually be found at breakfast, he was already gone. In the daytime, he was absent longer than usual, and in the evening, he was shut away in his studio. Even Isabella had noticed it and asked him what he was about, hardly ever in above to eat and sleep lately. He told her he was working on the plans for a new exhibition in time for his friend's arrival, but I suspected there was more to it than that. I had distressed him with my outburst in the studio. I knew it even then, saw how I had divided him from his sense of moral duty in being brought into my bidding and knowing not how to placate me. I suppose he felt guilty for it and hoped to avoid further such outbursts or requests being made to him by ensuring himself absent and never alone in my company for a passing second. I could hardly blame him. I had been surprised he had aided me thus far given how much propriety he exuded, and after all, his loyalty should have been first to Giles, and he had kept my secrets in spite of the fact. But I had hoped to find a moment in private with him to ask him the favour of sending the letter on for me ,or at least apprising me of how to do it here. I did not have the first idea or opportunity, and there was no postage prepayment to offer either.

But on that head, at least, I had finally come to a solution. One that had been staring me in the face all along. I had nothing in the way of petty cash or jewels to bargain with. I did not even know what the currency was here. But having pondered long and hard over the problem as I had my trunks of winter clothing aired, folded and packed away, I realised that there was much value in those muslin and silk skirts and quilted petticoats, particularly since most had so little wear and were almost as good as new. They comprised of the wardrobe Giles had furnished me with on my capture. I had been in Leonard's clothes when he had apprehended me, and everything else was at Stapleford. His provisions had been far from paltry and consisted of fashionable patterns and fine fabrics from India, though only a couple of them ever fitted me well since they were fashioned from the dimensions of an old dress I had left at Beddington, prior to my advancing pregnancy, and now they were far too big. Had I not been determined to remain in dowdy style and shun their flamboyance, I would have simply had them altered. But I had no need or desire for them now. Where would I wear them anyway – about the courtyard or to mass?

But they would be useful to *someone*, and I had a plan now to realise their value. I told Giles I was in need of some new clothes now that I had shut away my winter ones and made more space in my wardrobes. As always, such matters were never trifled over, so long as I had no direct handling of the money, he approved any rudimentary applications for his credit.

The seamstress was arranged to come to the house the next day. I endured the usual ritual of thumbing through fabric swatches and patterns in my dressing room whilst Benedetta assisted the dressmaker with measuring me. Once this was undertaken, I sent Benedetta away to fetch us some refreshments and swiftly took my opportunity to be alone with the lady.

'Signora Sartore,' I said to her, drawing closer, 'What is your most expensive fabric and design?' I asked her, watching her eyes light up and reach for one of the earlier ones she had tried to persuade me towards. 'Very nice,' I assented as she handed me a velvet swatch in a shade of deep Corbeau.

'Tell me, Signora, do you perhaps buy, as well as make dresses?'

She frowned and looked offended. 'Signora, I am not a rag woman. I serve only the best houses in Venice, and all my fabrics are brand new.'

'Of course they are, but I expect you might know where to pass on such things and get a fair price for them?'

'I don't understand.'

'Very well, I shall make it plainer since I have little time. I have some very fine dresses I wish to sell, secretly,' I whispered. 'They are of high quality, but gifts to me, not to my taste and yet how can I return them without causing offence?'

She nodded now, seeing the sense in that at least.

'So, I thought that perhaps you may discretely sell them for me, take them away with you today, and when you come to fit me for my new clothes, you may bring me the money?'

'I do not trade in this way, Signora. You might try the Inns at Rialto or the Bastioneri?'

'Impossible, I am practically housebound. I would see it less as a trading agreement and more as a great favour to me, and of course, in return, I would like to order several more dresses and perhaps a Spencer in that beautiful velvet since I will have all the more space for them once these are gone.' This was the clincher. I saw it in her eyes as they flashed hot with calculation. 'What do you say?'

She nodded, 'Si, I will do it. As a *favour* to you, Signora.'

'Excellent, and I am most obliged to you.'

I lifted the lid of the foremost trunk and allowed her an inspection of my offerings, asking her to take away the ones she thought might fetch the most. She agreed to take no more than two today, but would take more if she could pass them on without difficulty. She suspected this would be relatively easy given the quality, but maintaining that this was not her usual line, she would prefer to make enquiries. I knew it to be fustian; she would likely unpick the hems herself, but I did not care what she did with them, so long as she kept her promise of discretion and bought me a fair price. So I placed my order with her charged upon Giles' credit, and closed the disturbed trunk before Benedetta returned with our tray.

It was the better part of a week before I had word that she was to return for a fitting, and I looked to it so impatiently I think Benedetta began to suspect me of something. Again, once her assistance was no longer required, I sent her away on an errand while Signora Sartore passed the money to me and selected another two dresses to take away with her. It was the first time money had passed through my fingertips since Cornwall, and though it was not a coin I knew, and understood nothing of its relative worth, it felt a triumph to be in possession of it again. For now, I might be able to buy my way out of this situation, one dress at a time, perhaps, but eventually.

Content that I now had the means to send my letter, I still needed a means to execute it. I considered all the options but realised that it would be risky to ask anyone in the house, family or servant, or to do so myself in any of their presence. But I had an idea that would require neither if I could pull it off.

The very next day, I passed a note down to the singing gondolier as he passed beneath the balcony by dangling it on a length of wool. He was not quite a stranger to me and seemed to have taken a bit of a shine to me on him seeing me each day upon the terrace as he went by on his boat. It was a simple note stating that if he could assure me of discretion, I had an errand for him to undertake and to name his price for posting a letter with the Austrian postal service. He sang his response to the tune of three lire, and I nodded my agreement. I lowered Mr Banfield's letter and the silver coins inscribed one Lira in an envelope I made from Arabic gum and stiff paper, setting out the terms. If he undertook the task in earnest, once I had a reply from my correspondent, proving its safe carriage, he would have another lira and be trusted to future errands.

And so, at last, my hard-won mission was accomplished in passing on my address to the Banfields, and I felt more optimistic than I had in an age. I hoped it would not be too long before I might expect the forwarding of Lady W.'s reply, which I was sure must be with him after all these weeks. We had parted in Lisbon in February. It was now nearing the end of May, ample time by any standards.

After this first expenditure for posting Mr Banfield's letter, I was careful with my small stash of foreign coin as it began to grow from week to week with the coming and going of the seamstress. I planned to continue keeping her busy until my trunks were entirely empty. I had all summer before anyone would open them again and discover them gone. By then, I was certain *I* would be gone by some means or other, now I had begun to set things in motion. I had composed more letters, too, in the privacy of Marco's studio, including one to the pie shop in Carshalton, though with hurt and angry words that I was in two minds about whether or not to send. But I hid them all for now, tempted to send them on, but considering it best to be sure of a reply before trusting any more of my hard-won coin to the Gondolier until he had proved himself. So, for now, I only added to my bounty, never subtracted, and looked forward to when I could work out how far it could stretch. I knew little of Venetian currency or costs since I never encountered any. All I could tell was that my portion was significantly less than the increasing bill I was racking up on Giles's credit with the seamstress.

Nonetheless, it was all the money I had, and I guarded it like a treasure trove, hiding it beneath a loose floorboard in Marco's studio when he was not there. There seemed no safer place than somewhere all else were forbidden from going, even the servants, and as yet, my visits there remained a secret. I was always careful to choose only the moments when I was entirely alone on my floor to visit it. Benedetta was so used to being sent off on trifling errands about the house for me now that even she was less suspicious of such minor absences or excuses, and I could usually manage a clear ten minutes or more to add to my coffers or make use of ink and paper when I needed to.

As for Marco, we had still not spoken above a passing good day, but I knew I still had leave to use the studio for the key was always left on top of the door frame for me, and he occasionally left scribbled notes with messages such as: "take care – paintings drying" and the like, which I was careful to observe.

I went out more often now, too, so the time seemed to pass easier than before. Always under family chaperone and rarely anywhere of note, but I grew used to weekly mass and the coffee house soiree. I had grown familiar with the hackberry-lined gravel pathways of the *Giardini Pubblici*, which sufficed for walks when it was cool enough to take them. I paid calls with Isabella at times and even visited Carlotta and baby Pietro, managing to keep my tears at bay until I was in privacy.

All in all, I was less miserable than before, even if I was still deeply unhappy and homesick. But whereas previously I could not be roused from my low spirits, now I could move between moments of despair and equanimity with greater fluidity. I could maintain a better façade around others and, sometimes, even dared to dream of a life beyond this one.

It was only Giles's obsession with impregnating me that brought me low now. It had not been solely a result of his drunkenness or the novelty of a new birth in the family, as I had hoped. It was something he had fixed resolutely upon now, and I saw no sign of him relenting until the deed was done. It was not every night anymore as it had been in the initial days after, but followed a pattern of sustained effort that waned after a few days, followed by a determined renewal once I declared myself to be finished bleeding for a course.

He sulked through the duration of my courses as if I had the power to grant or deny conception and had wilfully intervened in letting nature proceed thus. It was true that I would have done so if I could, despite my mixed feelings when I would hold little Pietro on my lap and feel maternal stirrings so poignantly I would have to hand him back. I wanted to be a mother now, but not enough to bring *his* child into the world. And so, when his enquiries came as to my courses, with timely precision, I grew anxious at the possibility and was relieved to eventually bleed and disappoint him. But once another had passed, he made mention of seeking out a doctor's opinion if I continued to fail in my duty, and I agreed to it, knowing that no amount of medical observation or wives' tales would fill my womb. Only nature's will, and if I had any say at all in the nature of my own body, I hoped it might heed me and continue to fail.

CHAPTER NINETEEN

R.S.V.P.

Eleanor. June 1822.

B y the first week of June, I had finally rid myself of all of my dresses, but one, that Signora Sartore insisted she would be unable to sell, and my money stash was as full as it would ever be, unless I could contrive another scheme. I could think of nothing presently and could only hope that I had enough to yield to my plans or I might receive help from home. Each day, I took pains to be to breakfast when the mails were usually distributed and kept a studious eye on them, waiting for anything for me. I expected a reply from my letter home and for Mr Banfield to have sent Lady W.'s reply by now. Yet every day proved another disappointment.

I sometimes caught Marco watching me, no doubt understanding my thoughts as my expression fell from studious to disappointed. But he said nothing and only looked away if I caught him. But today, for the first time in an age, when the other men vacated the table, he did not join them, but remained behind like he had used to before.

'You are waiting for a letter?' he asked me, to my abject surprise.

I nodded.

'How long have you been waiting?'

'Weeks,' I sighed, '...above four for one of them, perhaps only two for the other.'

'Two is likely premature, but four? That is usually adequate. Any day then, hopefully.'

I smiled, thinking surely the one from Porto would be swifter, having not so far to journey as London. 'Yes, to be sure. You are setting out later than your usual habit. Are you to take a day off?'

'Yes, as a matter of fact. Mr Holland-Bury should arrive at midday.'

'Oh. Will he be staying here at *Ca' Rosetti?*' I asked, trying not to sound too enthusiastic at the prospect.

He laughed, 'No, that would not be a good idea. I have arranged some lodgings for him in *San Polo*, which is for the best.'

'Why? Do your family dislike him?'

'No. But they would grow to if I ever permitted him board with us here. He is a good fellow at heart, but Venice is a city of temptation and vice and, for fellows like

Holland-Bury, something of a novelty. My mama would never approve of the hours or the company he keeps.'

'I see,' I said, feeling somewhat concerned that I had pinned my hopes on making a travel companion of this man and wondered if that would now be impossible. 'Though you do not trouble over it?'

He shrugged, 'Why should I? Holland-Bury is his own man, an old friend and a talented artist. What he loses at the gaming tables or how often he is in his cups, and so on, is his own affair.'

So, drinking and gaming. It certainly did not sound promising. 'How long will he stay for?'

'A few months, four at most. He will want to be back over the Alps before everything freezes over. But fear not, he shall be on his best behaviour when he visits here, you may rest assured. Anyway, if you will excuse me, I have some things to attend to before he arrives.'

I barely saw him for the rest of the week after that. He was always out and had not yet brought Holland-Bury to the house even once. And so I began to grow disappointed at the possibility of not getting to make an introduction at all, less still judge whether he would make a passable travel companion or prove a willing accomplice. I grew disheartened too at waiting on the post and could feel myself slipping into more regular fits of the blue devils. But just as I became aware of this deterioration, good news came in another direction in the form of Giles announcing he would have to go away for a week on business, an important negotiation in Treviso that could not be passed up. I attempted a show of indifference to this news but wanted to jump in the air and shout hurrah! A whole week in his absence was not to be sniffed at, but I saw it as not only a reprieve, but an opportunity...

So, in the run-up to his leaving, I made my best efforts to seem more stable and obedient than I had managed since arriving. It was all going so well, and I was hopeful it was a sign of better things to come. That in return for months of sufferance, the heavens were finally clearing a path to my liberation, one small turn at a time. Then, on Saturday morning at breakfast with the family, the salver came as usual, but this time, there was a letter on it: for me.

I was not the only one to notice it. Marco saw it first and cast me a warning glance that I could not act upon with everyone at the table. It was either a delayed response from my mama or Lady W.'s reply from Porto, and whilst I hoped that either one might be delivered in his absence, I *needed* it to be the former now.

I continued with my breakfast with growing trepidation, aware as the tray was passed about that it would not come to me until after he, and I would have no chance to swipe it. I could only hope for some help from Marco's quarter now, though I was uncertain whether he would volunteer it.

Mr Harper took up his pile first, and it went counter clockwise next, to Dante, who shuffled through and took something from it, then announced, 'Oh, Eleanor, there is one for you today.'

Oh, Dante! My heart sank.

Giles's head sprung up from his plate.

'Ouch, what did you do that for?' Dante said to Marco with a grimace, then slapped his arm as if in reprisal.

'Sorry brother, I was pulling my chair in,' Marco replied.

'It felt like a kick!' he said, then passed the salver along to Marco.

'News from home perhaps, Eleanor?' Isabella smiled. 'You boys, at your age, I thought you might be beyond squabbling at the table!' she chided them.

'Yes,' I said, ignoring them, 'I wrote to my mama many weeks ago. I had suspected it lost in the post or some such, but it seems I was mistaken. Will you excuse me?' I asked brightly.

'Yes! Yes, go and read your letter, child. I can see you are excited to have news,' Isabella encouraged, but Giles put down his cutlery and I felt instantly on edge.

'I will join you,' he said, not even looking at his letters, rising from the table with me and following me on.'

Marco and Isabella exchanged a glance of concern but said nothing more.

'Where are you going?' he asked me as I continued towards the drawing room and not back up to our chamber. I hoped my caution was unnecessary, but the last thing I wanted was to be at the top of the house alone with him should this letter *not* be the one from my mama. But it was not to do; he insisted we return upstairs, and I knew precisely why. – He wanted no audience to his unreasonableness. And he was, of course, unreasonable, as good as snatching it up from me as he closed my chamber door.

'Giles, it is my letter!' I protested.

'And you shall read it after I have.'

'Can we not read it together, at least? I have not had word from them in an age. I am too excited to wait.'

He held a palm up to stay me, 'Patience is a virtue my dear, it shan't take long, and he broke the seal and walked away from me as he read.

I grew sick with worry but did my utmost not to show it. Then, when he lowered the letter and came marching over to me, his expression told me all.

'Who have you been writing to!' he shouted.

'What do you mean?'

'Who is Mr Banfield?'

'Oh, him,' I inwardly shrunk. 'He was the fellow on the boat to Lisbon. You remember, he and his sister sometimes took walks with us.'

'You wrote to him?'

'I—'

He slapped me swiftly around the face, 'Do not lie to me! I shall have the whole.'
'Please, Giles, do not harm me.'

A knock came suddenly at the door, and the sound of clattering in the hall.

'You—' he tucked the letter into his pocket, pointed and mouthed the words, '...do not move a whisker.'

I nodded and watched him go to the door, fighting hard against my hysterics and temptation to shout out for help.

'Ah, you are still about, cousin. I hate to ask, but I am up against the clock and I know you are heading in my direction shortly. I wondered if I might take a lift in the boat with you? I've got all this stuff to get to the Gallery before the exhibition later, 'Marco said.

I saw the irritation in Giles's face immediately. 'What is wrong with your boat?'

'Holland-Bury has use of it to run errands for the gallery, but he should have been here an hour ago, and my parents are leaving for the Lido in theirs, so, well, I have only you to prevail upon cousin, if you would be so good as to help a fellow out.'

Giles sighed, 'Very well. Give me ten minutes and I shall meet you down there.'

'Thank you! I shall be much obliged. Me and Dante shall start loading it now then.'

Giles nodded, closed the door, then turned back to me and said quietly. 'You have five minutes to tell me what this is all about.'

'How can I when I do not even know what the letter says?'

He threw it to me, and I picked it up off the floor. It was brief.

Eleanor,
I hope this letter finds you well and that you, too, are in good health and settled in Venice now.

Thank you for your well wishes. My sister and I have settled well on the whole, though the climate takes some getting used to. But thank you for asking.

I will indeed pass my regards to Alice and tell her she may look forward to hearing from you in the future. You find her address below. A friendly correspondent would no doubt do her much good now we are so far parted and she has little in the way of company.

On the other matter, I regret to tell you that though I posted your letter as directed, I have never received an answer to forward on. I am sorry for it, but rest assured, if anything comes, I will certainly pass it on without delay now I have your address.

Ever pleased to be at your service, your humble Svt.,
Mr Banfield.

I was so disappointed by this news that I almost forgot my company. I thought quickly. 'Alright, I shall tell you the truth,' I told Giles cautiously.

'You'd better, for I will have it, even if I have to send a man to Portugal myself to demand it of this, Mr Banfield.'

'Giles, there is nothing between Mr Banfield and I, I assure you. How could you imagine it otherwise when you were with us on the ship, as was his sister.'

'I did not until I saw he dares to correspond with you, which means you wrote to him first! Why?' he narrowed his eyes. 'And how indeed?'

His rising temper was interrupted by the sound of something smashing in the hall outside and Dante shouting, 'Sorry, Marco, it was only a paint jar! Giacomo, will you please ask Leo to see to this.'

I was reassured by all their clanging and clomping about in the hall. Knowing they were just beyond the door helped me find the nerve to go on. 'You are right. I did write to him first, just as you say, and the reason is because I wanted to enter into a correspondence with his sister and, because I asked them to post a letter for me when they got off the boat and forward on a return. Which is why I had to write to him when I got here for I had no forwarding address at the time.'

'Who did you write to?'

'You have to understand, Giles, I was in distress at the time. I—'

'Who?'

'Annalise.'

He seemed not to know what to make of this, then burst into laughter.

'What is so funny?'

'A love letter to your little maidservant—'

'I was upset at the time of her abandoning me. I meant to tell her as much. I am quite over it now, but at the time—'

'If you were over it, why did you even bother to forward your address? Did you think she might have had a change of heart? Come and join you here, perhaps?'

'No. I mean, maybe I did back then. It was a long time ago, before things had improved between you and I—'

'Unlikely, don't you think that she should abandon you then cross the continent to find you, and on a servant's purse?'

'It is ridiculous, yes. But I was not in my right head then, Giles, you know I was not. But I feared that she might have made reply in all those months, and so I knew I must retrieve it from Mr Banfield for fear that if I did not, he would be in possession of a letter quite scandalous. I wanted only to destroy it now, and I confess, I had hoped a correspondence with his sister might give me something to do.'

'Well, he would have it that she has not even bothered to reply. That, or he never even bothered to send it on. And as for a correspondent, you shall soon be with child and have no time for such frivolities.'

'Yes, it is true.'

'Is that the whole?'

I nodded profusely.

'Then that leaves just one matter…how did you manage to send him the letter in the first place?'

I gulped.

'Well?' He cocked his head, waiting.

'I—I sewed the words into the fabric of one of my old shifts,' I explained, remembering the escape notes Annalise had embroidered into fabric in Cornwall, '…then I starched it stiff.'

'Am I to forbid you even needle and thread now? Is that what we have come to with all your wily schemes?'

I shook my head, 'No, Giles. I have only done it once. It was arduous work and took me an age, which is why I only have word from him now. I have not done it since, and nor shall I again. I only wanted to retrieve my reply. Why should I need to resort to such anyway now? The only other person I want word from is my mama, and you have already sent my letter to her… haven't you?'

He nodded dismissively, and I knew he had not. It made sense now why he was so intent on coming back with me to read this. I thought the letter was one of two possibilities. He *knew* it could not be from my mama because he had never even bothered sending it. No wonder he was suspicious.

'So, pray tell me, how did you manage to send it with no money? Foreign posts must be prepaid, so *someone* has given you coin.'

'No. I found some coins in the *Giardini Pubblici* one day while walking. Isabella didn't notice, I pretended a stone in my shoe.'

'Really? Very unlikely to come across money just lying about on the floor in a place full of beggars! Do you think me a fool, girl?'

'No, I—'

The door knocked again. It was Marco. 'Sorry, old chap, but it's passed ten minutes now, and I'm rather on the backfoot. Will you be ready to go soon?'

'I am coming directly,' he said, irritated. 'Eleanor, bring me my jacket.'

'Ah, is Eleanor about too?' I heard Marco say, and I grew anxious as I picked up the coat and headed for the door.

'Why?' Giles asked with a frown.

'Well, I wanted to invite you both to the exhibition this evening should you fancy it? I know you are not much interested in art, cousin, but it shall be full of society and a chance to make acquaintances if nothing else. – I would quite appreciate the support too, to be honest, I am not sure how much attendance I can be certain of. You know how these things go; everyone says yes when you mention it, and as it grows closer, they begin dropping out on all sorts of accounts and excuses. Anyway, Signor Serrano has just confirmed,' he said, shaking a letter in his hand, '…so that's a relief. He usually can be relied on to make a purchase or two.'

'Signor Serrano?' Giles echoed, mildly surprised, impressed perhaps. 'Come, we shall discuss it on the way,' he told him and left the room with a warning glance back at me that told me this matter was not yet closed.

I sighed my relief into my palms and sunk onto the chaise, my hands still trembling. I was not sure if I had come off well or if it was only Marco's disturbance that had moderated him. But he seemed mildly amused by my answers, and I could not fathom why. I could only hope that now I had the expanse of a whole day to ponder it, I could come up with something more convincing on account of coming by the money, for it was true, Venice seemed equally full of wealthy as poor and the more I had gone about the place, the more accustomed I grew to seeing beggars and vagrants about it, and it did seem a most unlikely line for coins to found on a patch of path. He seemed to take no convincing that I had written to Annalise and not suspected Lady W., whom I'd actually written to. He appeared not overly surprised at the story of me having sewn the letter either. But the money was the sticking point, and I would have to do better on that account.

The answer came to me quite inadvertently in the end. Isabella and I were walking about the gardens, as was often our habit on a Saturday afternoon once the peak day heat began to wane, when a commotion broke out and the Austrian white coats arrived in force. A man was apprehended, and we were warned to take care of our person, for there was a band of pocket thieves operating in the area, and they were yet to capture them all. It had given Isabella a bit of a fright, and she vowed that we would bring Mr Harper in the future and come by way of Gondola rather than on foot.

So that afternoon, when Giles returned from the shipyard and reconvened our conversation, or more aptly, interrogation, I thought, as I sat before him trying to steady my trembling hands, I gave him a more elaborate account.

'The truth is, Giles, I was scared that if I told you the whole, you might put an end to my walks and think me very bad. The matter is that we were walking along the gardens, and Isabella stopped to speak to one of her acquaintances from church. While she was busy talking, I noticed a pickpocket slip something from a gentleman's coat. – I did not see what it was, but I was not the only one to notice, and someone behind me shouted, "Stop! Thief!" and came running up behind him. He was only a boy of perhaps ten or so, and he grew frightened and began to run. The chase was chaotic, but I saw him toss the thing into the shrubbery before being detained. Anyway, once the boy was apprehended and things were calm, I went over to the place with the honest intention of retrieving the thing I saw him throw. It was a small leather pocket purse containing coins. I know I should have returned it immediately, Giles. I am ashamed. I took the purse and put it in my pocket. Everyone was so consumed with talk of the thief that it was not noticed and—'

He laughed hard now. 'Well, what would your haughty mama make of that? Her daughter, a thief!'

I lowered my gaze. 'I did not steal it, Giles. I did find it on the floor, and I did return it after a time. I handed it in to a guard and told him I had found it precisely where

I said. Only, well, I took enough to cover the posting and to pay for the trouble of a street scamp who conveyed it for me, first.'

'A conscionable thief then,' he laughed again, then his face fell grave. 'Well, you never cease to amaze me with your schemes, Eleanor, but I am growing weary of them, I confess. I own I had thought you had at last come to some greater sense—'

'I have now. Though it has taken a while, I admit it, but Giles, I don't want to fight anymore. Our goals are in common at last and—'

'They are?'

'I too want a child, Giles, so very much it near breaks my heart...' A few tears fell because my conviction was in earnest; I just failed to mention that I didn't with him. 'I see Carlotta and her son and their beautiful home, and I want that too now, Giles. It has taken me some time to know it, but I am ready now to settle for a better way—'

'And how do I know you will not concoct other schemes and find ways to send other missives.'

'I will not concoct any other schemes, Giles. But I would like to write to my family occasionally, and it would be all the easier if you wouldn't forbid it. If I could just be permitted ink and paper. It is no fun embroidering a letter, I assure you. Forgive me, husband, I have been a terrible wife, I know. But I mean to do better now. Don't you see that?'

'Well, you shall prove it so or prove it otherwise. And if you do prove it otherwise, if there is one more matter you keep from my knowing—'

'There shan't be.'

'If there is, you shall leave me no choice but to forbid your leaving the house.' I nodded my assent.

'Well, you may make a start in demonstrating your contrition tonight. We are to go to this exhibition thing, and I want you beside me for all to see.'

I was astounded. He cared nothing for art, and I doubted he cared much more for Marco's sake. 'Well, of course. I shall look forward to seeing the pictures.'

'That is not the object, though you may, so long as you play your part. There is a very important guest there tonight, Signor Serrano, a diamond broker with whom I have been trying to negotiate a contract for an age. You shall behave prettily in his presence and help me to persuade him.'

'Me? But Giles, I do not know the first thing about your business. I have tried to take an interest, but you never like it when I do—'

'And nor do you need to. I will do the talking on that head. These Venetians are all about family and image. They trade much on good faith and standing as good business sense. You are a Baron's daughter, and my wife, play the part of each with the charm we both know you are capable of, and you can leave the rest to me.'

I nodded. 'I can do that.'

'Good. Now, we are to leave in an hour and a half. I suggest you smarten up and wear something...impressive.'

'Of course,' I acquiesced, smiling as I rang for Benedetta, wondering what I would wear now I had given all my fancy dresses to the seamstress. All but one, I then remembered and rushed to the dressing room to fetch it out of the otherwise empty chest before she arrived to notice the fact.

It was certainly not the most impressive of those I had passed on to Signora Sartore, but relative to my current style, it might just about meet the definition, providing I could make it fit so it did not hang poorly from me.

'We have some work to do tonight, Benedetta,' I told her when she arrived. 'Fetch the sewing box, I need you to take this in at the waist and bust. We have little above an hour, but I will help.'

We darned in large, hurried stitches with thick thread once she had finished pinning the slack. They would not do to be seen so shoddily executed but were concealed beneath my arms and would not be noticed if I had a care about lifting them. It was not as though it was a ball we were to attend, and I would have dancing to consider. I was confident they would hold for a night at a gathering such as this. Which is what I reminded myself of as I permitted my toilette to transform me into something more akin to my former self.

It was one night to appease him. To please him and do his bidding. In return, I would earn both his forgiveness and restore enough trust that he would go to Treviso on Monday morning as planned, and leave me free for an entire week with no further restrictions on my outings. A week I was even more determined to put to good use now, even if I had yet to work out the detail.

CHAPTER TWENTY

Night Terrors.

Annalise. March 1822.

I n the days that followed Ninette's arrival, Annalise became familiar with this disconcerting pattern of "night terrors", as she called them. After the brutality of the first night and those that followed, where Ninette was taken down to the solitary confinement cells and, on one occasion, made to visit the whipping room, Annalise did her utmost to prevent a reoccurrence of the same.

On the first night of Ninette's return to the cell, Annalise stuffed her coverlet into the small hatch opening in the cell wall beside the door. She swiftly returned to Ninette and put a hand about her mouth to muffle the sound.

It had been no easy feat with her thrashing about so, but it had eventually brought the episode to an end, and before the matron's notice was attracted. And so she fell quickly into the routine of repeating this each night to avoid Ninette succumbing to any further brutality. Then, after a time, she learnt, through the accidental habit of falling back to sleep with her hand over Ninette's mouth, that the attacks could be even more swiftly interceded by simply holding Ninette close and whispering soothing reassurances into her ear. And so, this became routine thereafter. She would hold her until they fell asleep, and if an attack ensued, she was close at hand and could intervene quickly.

It had been a difficult errand to bring herself about to, prompted only by the fear that if she did not bring herself to bear on the situation, Ninette would likely end up dead at the hands of the matrons if she was submitted to any more whippings, rough slaps and nosebleeds she was left abed to choke on. It had been hard to place herself in such vulnerability with someone who was but a stranger, self-confessed to be violent, mentally unsound and difficult to reach. It was hard, too, to wake in the night with the warmth of her body against her own and, for the briefest moment, forget she was not abed aside Eleanor and face the dreadful disappointment she felt in realising it, as the time between the memory and the habit grew ever more distant. But she persevered all the same, being so much distracted with the care of Ninette that she had little time to lament her own troubles in the days leading to her trial.

She had, however, eventually gotten to the bottom of the trouble that had led Ninette here, and begun to understand somewhat better. Finding now, more tragedy than repugnance at her part in the story. She had told her one night how she had been employed in the willow holt weaving business owned by her sweetheart's father. They had contrived her employ in the family business to allow them to be close at hand and continue their clandestine affair. They had met in London when she was in service, and he, a guest to the house on his term breaks from Oxford.—The round trip home to the West Country proving a lengthier affair than the holidays themselves, save the summer one. So, he would stay at Russell Square with his aunt during each term break.

'It was love at first sight,' Ninette explained, when they had perchanced upon each other about the house quite accidentally. They had to have a care about the place, but they soon both lived for the holidays when they could be together.

When he completed at Oxford last year, he returned home to Wadebridge to learn the management of the business in readiness to take it over on his father's retirement.—They supplied withy pots to the fisherman and employed a legion of weavers for the purpose, the family having distanced themselves from the labour of the trade for some time and managing only the makers and supply.

But when the time came for them to part ways, the lovers were not ready to surrender, and he was not yet in a position to support a wife. So, between them, they concocted a plan.

Ninette was given a faux letter of recommendation to bring to Wadebridge, and directed to follow on a little after his return to the West Country. She was soon employed by the family as a basket weaver by day. But by night, her sweetheart would creep into her bed and continue their love affair.

They made plans for their wedding, which was to take place in the summer when he reached the age of his majority and could rely on an income to support them.—They were to elope and return when the contract was too late to retract, given that the family would object to the match... But they never got beyond the planning, for Ninette became pregnant, and his mama discovered their affair. This had been their undoing. Her sweetheart was promptly enlisted in the Navy by his father and sent away to prevent any attempt at an elopement. Ninette had then been subjected to a forced abortion, so late in her pregnancy, she described it as a bloodbath of a murder where she had endured a labour only to birth a dead and injured child, almost dying herself by a fever soon after. She had lost her love, her child, and her future happiness in a matter of days, all at the hands of his parents.

When she finally recovered from her sick bed and was put out by the family, she returned one night to burn the place down, but had not got so far as lighting the tinder when the barking hounds discovered her. It was then she stabbed his father with the bodkin as he tried to wrestle her off of the estate.

Her night terrors seemed to be the way the horror of the labour and the memory of her bloodied child, was revisited in her mind. She would often cry out, 'Stop, pray, stop! You are killing my baby!' Once Annalise had learnt of the connection between the words and the circumstance that gave rise to them, she would console her as best she could. Reassure her that she was safe and she would eventually grow quiet and calm again.

But this was as far as Annalise's intervention could suffice. No matter how much trust and confidence grew between them, Ninette would not be persuaded to defend her actions at trial or give up her plans to avenge her suffering. 'An eye for an eye,' she often quoted to her, and they would quickly reach an impasse on the subject and be forced to retreat to silence, or continue in a change of subject thereafter.

As for her own troubles, there had been both good news and bad. Mr Langley had returned to visit her a few more times since, and had imparted to her that he had received confirmation of her ownership of the dwelling shop and a dazzling character from Mr Harrison, who was saddened that he was not able to make the journey in person for the decline of his health. This news had hit her hard. She should be there to nurse him and help run the bookshop if he was in decline, not be kept away so far. What if she was transported and never again to see him? He had been like a father to her. She would never recover from such a blow, she was certain.

Mr Langley had also received a character from Mrs Crawford, for Annalise had expressly warned him not to seek it from the Cook, and he had even managed to obtain one from Gint, which left her feeling odd and unsure of whether to permit Mr Langley to use it or not. Then there was Miss Lockheart, who had agreed she would not disclose the situation to Poppy or any of their other acquaintances until the outcome was decided. And finally, much to her surprise, even Lady W. had furnished her with one, describing her as a loyal and proficient lady's maid of the utmost professionalism and a credit to her trade.

It had been what she had needed in this point of lowness, to be reminded of the kind thoughts and words of those who knew her, and even less familiar acquaintances who had taken the trouble.

Mr Jeffers, the attorney who had been undertaking these tasks from London, had also managed by informal means, to undertake to make enquiries after the Craythornes. Through his contacts, he had discovered that news of Mariella's apprehension had indeed reached home. A Mr Truscott, a very prominent West Country barrister, had been pursued to act in her defence, instructed by an attorney in London. This had made it difficult for Mr Jeffers to elicit the kind of information he might have managed to glean from a London barrister, but he had discovered by way of the attorney, that Mariella was to be charged with only misdemeanours and that her father, whilst not concerning himself with attendance in Cornwall, was using his influence from afar to attempt to secure her bail and have the charges diminished further. As far as he knew, she was still at Bodmin.

With regards to his enquiries at Falmouth, Mr Langley had managed to convince the innkeeper to hint at the direction of the witnesses at the inn, but having found most of them to be tourists since departed, he had only managed to secure the testimony of one: a local washerwoman who serviced the wardrobes of travelling guests. One detail that had been of interest, however, is that the watchman who had searched Annalise's room and recovered the evidence, had reckoned that the pearls he'd confiscated had not been genuine, but cheap replicas, likely made of paste. This led Mr Langley to make enquiries with a jeweller who had explained to him how to tell the difference between a genuine pearl and a paste replica.

'But what does it matter whether they are genuine or not?' Annalise had asked as he explained this to her.

'Don't you see?' he asked, evidently puzzled by her failure to follow. 'The Craythornes are wealthy people. They would not parade about in cheap replicas when they are proud of their wealth. If we can get Mariella to confirm a belief that they are genuine when, in fact, they are cheap replicas, I suspect it will cast doubt on her ownership of them and therefore, her claim against you. And, it might even devalue their worth to below the capital threshold.'

'I see,' Annalise had said, failing to glean how such minutiae of detail held such power and was something to rejoice in, less still, to carry much weight in the scheme of such charges against her. What she needed was some slip-up on Mariella's part, a hole in her account, for which she knew there would be many. There always was with liars, especially those contrived fast and on the spot, as this one had been. But Mr Langley had explained that he could not formally access any case reports or evidence of the prosecution's claims, nor fully understand the indictment until its introduction to the trial itself. He had elicited what he could informally and could do no more in that regard.

How then, she protested, was he supposed to find the weakness in Mariella's story?

'By quick assessment and thinking on the spot,' he told her, which was something he was well versed in. But that concern, he reminded her, was best left to him. The errand of his visit had been to assist her in constructing the kind of defence he wished her to make. Purposeful, simple and short. She was not to elaborate on the backstory of her former mistress and her husband's situation. It would be sufficient to answer that it had been an unhappy marriage and Mrs Craythorne wanted a separation from her husband, which he had prevented by taking her off to the continent. – Lady W. had already corroborated this circumstance through a witness statement sworn under oath by Mr Jeffers's observation. As with much of the evidence he'd collated, it would depend on the Judge permitting him to rely on reading out such testimony for the lack of any of them being able to attend from afar. It was only the Falmouth laundress he had managed to secure the attendance of by covering the expenses of the trip and time from her duties. Nancy Troon had expressed a willingness to testify, but her father was reluctant to permit her to become entangled in the business.

Annalise was not to mention a word about the arson attack, and if questioned about the pearls, she was simply to deny all knowledge of them until the moment they were presented to her – just like in the case of the pendant. As for the letter she had described writing to Poppy, she was only to mention this if prompted and explain that it was an immediate circumstance she found herself in, having been offloaded from the ship only a couple of hours beforehand and finding herself in temporary difficulty. – One she could not have foreseen or planned for. Until then, she had no need of the money in the employ of her Lady and could not have predicted this circumstance would change, quite literally, overnight. At all times, she must emphasise that she was of clean record and had both a comfortable home and income to return to after her dismissal from service, and nothing to be gained in the abhorrent act of stealing. Indeed, why write to Poppy at all to ask for the sending of money if she genuinely was in possession of stolen jewels she could have sold? That would be a faster solution than awaiting the conveyance of the mail.

So this is what she kept to mind when she found herself standing in the dock with all eyes upon her. The very sight of the crammed Court as she entered, and the questioning pairs of eyes surveying her, was enough to make her sweat beneath her shimmy. But she did her best to remain calm and contrite of appearance, and as the Court rose and the indictment was read out, she became distracted by fathoming out all that was taking place before her.

CHAPTER TWENTY-ONE

The Art of Impressionism.

Eleanor. June 1822.

'By Jove, you do scrub up well!' said Dante, when Giles and I came down to the courtyard to take the boat to the Gallery.

'Dante!' Isabella scolded him. 'Where are your manners? Apologise to Eleanor at once!'

'Mama, it was not an insult, a compliment in fact. It is an English saying. It means she looks nice,' he told her, and her face softened. 'Though it probably was a pretty shabby way to say it, forgive me, Eleanor, you look bello!'

'Thank you, Dante,' I said evenly, trying to hide my smile. He was such a cheeky fellow, he often made me want to laugh, but I feared that Giles would not be happy to consider behaviour he might deem as flirting. Though a glance across in his direction suggested he was not at all put out by Dante's reaction, pleased perhaps, at having confirmation of the fact I looked improved and he was not escorting a dowdy tonight.

'You do look very beautiful,' Isabella said. 'I am pleased to see you looking so well, child.'

'As do you, Isabella, striking. I love this colour on you,' I told her as we ambled out towards the jetty and were handed carefully into the boat, lifting our skirt hems to spare them.

Marco was already there when we arrived and the Gallery was filling up with guests, sauntering about the paintings and sculptures, sipping from narrow wine glasses as he moved between them, stopping to talk about an exhibit or simply to greet them. A small string quartet played Vivaldi's *Allegro Pastorale*, and a neat troupe of footmen handed out glasses about the room. It was not a large gallery, but it was very well appointed, with a sleekness and modernity quite in its own style. We were there above ten minutes before he noticed us congregated in the foyer and made his excuses.

'Marco, it looks beautiful in here!' Isabella said, kissing him. What fine work you have done! Look at the mural above the staircase, Edward. Isn't it spectacular?' she said to her husband, and he looked up and nodded his assent.

'Thank you, mama, the paint had barely dried by three, but we pulled it off, largely thanks to Holland-Bury's efforts,' he told her, and I saw him catch sight of me and glance away again.

'Yes, not too shabby at all, big brother,' Dante added. 'They'll be summoning you to the Vatican to paint their ceilings before you know it, though I'm not sure how well Holland-Bury will fit in there,' he added with a twinkle of mischief in his eyes.

Marco laughed, shook his father's hand, and nodded his greeting to Giles and me, thanking us all for coming and directing us to the different exhibits and handing us a programme.

'Is Signor Serrano yet arrived?' Giles asked him.

'Not yet, though he is rarely on time.—Oh, you will have to excuse me, the Contessa Albrizzi is arrived. George,' he turned and said to the man I assumed must be Mr Holland-Bury, 'There you are. You will take my family about, won't you, whilst I greet the Contessa.'

He was presentable enough, I considered. Blond hair combed up in a neat quiff, fashionably dressed but not in the dandy style. He came over to us directly. I could see his fair English skin had already been scorched by the sun and wondered if I must have adapted to it since I had yet to suffer the same. It seemed strange to hear another Englishman speak entirely absent of the Venetian accent as he went about the party with handshakes and cheek-to-cheek kisses, saying how good it was to see them again and how well they looked, in the style of perfect English gentlemanliness that gave no clue away of the gaming and drinking reputation that preceded him. *There was hope yet*, I considered as he made my introduction and ventured to kiss both my cheeks. It was extraordinary to me that this style of intimacy was all the thing here. We shared a brief look of recognition at how unusual it was to greet a perfect stranger in this style. Had we been in England, it would be outrageous. Alas, we were not, I reminded myself, but consoled myself with the idea that soon, we might be...

He took us about the paintings exhibited and gave commentaries on the scenes and artists with great aplomb, and we followed him about accordingly until Giles noticed the English consul, Mr Hoppner, and broke us away from the rest of the party, wanting to make my introduction to him. I did my best to play my part and mustered the remnants of the polite and elegant teachings of my etiquette training to impress him on the introduction. I retreated from the conversation meekly once it descended into trade and taxation talk. Smiling serenely as I took a back step, though I was standing quite bored now and struggling to maintain it when Dante came upon us and asked, 'Can I borrow her, Giles? My mama would like to introduce her to my latest *intended*,' he said with an exasperated sigh.

Giles looked up briefly and nodded his assent. I took Dante's arm and let him direct me through the thickening crowd.

'Your mother invited her here?' I asked him as we walked.

'Yes, though I am doing my best to subvert the attempt.'

'Will you not give her a chance?'

'Never mind all that. Are you alright?' he asked, once we were out of earshot.

I frowned. 'Yes, of course, why wouldn't I be?'

He shrugged. 'I don't know. Marco told me to check on you. Seemed to think you were caught up in some bad business with Giles this morning and sent me to find out if you were alright?'

'So it was not your mama, he sent you?' I said, puzzled.

'Well, he's a bit tied up tonight—'

'Well, you may tell him I'm perfectly well. Though your brother would do well to mind his own business.'

'True. But he means well. Anyway, I better get you out of the way before Holland-Bury collars us. I think you have quite turned his head.' He laughed, and I cast a glance over to him and saw him looking in my direction. I was quite astonished. It had been a while since I had had that effect on anyone, and had it not been pointed out to me by Dante, I would have likely mistook it altogether or thought him gazing at someone beyond my shoulder. But it was a good sign. I would need some way of drawing him closer into my acquaintance to see if my plans were feasible. But my chance to dither and permit Holland-Bury a conversation was quickly lost when Signor Serrano finally arrived.

Giles plucked me from Dante's arm to meet this guest of honour I had been dragged here to play pretty to – that I recognised the very same look of desire in his eyes, without anyone needing to drop me a hint, was quite disconcerting.

Perhaps I *had* scrubbed up better than I realised, I considered as his eyes danced with fire in them as he bent low and kissed my hand on Giles's introduction. 'A pleasure indeed,' he said, holding my gaze for a while before releasing my hand and turning back to Giles, who wasted no time descending into merchant talk.

However, he, too, was to be disappointed in his objectives when the announcement was made that a series of auctions for the exhibited paintings were to follow. The Contessa called the room to attention and began in quite a eulogistic speech recounting Marco's achievements and talents and commending his continued contribution to Venice's art legacy in bringing it into the modern age with all the grace of the forefathers and the fresh vision of the future, inducing much applause before she handed over to him. We all turned to listen in silence as Marco thanked the Contessa and us all for attending, and explained that half of the proceeds of tonight's sales would go to charitable causes. That the benevolent Scoule and Charitas of the city were in such scarcity and decline that it was the duty of all Venetians in more fortunate circumstances, to resurrect the spirit of the former auspices of the lost age and support those in need, and that the need remained great. Then he went on to introduce a lady who addressed us on her founding of a charity house. Her speech was impressive, and though I had not been much moved by anything of late, this reached me in a familiar place, and I, too, felt moved to help. That I could not even help myself anymore was by the by. Giles was here tonight, and I meant to make him cast up his pockets in this endeavour and make a bid.

So when the applause settled and the auctions began, I turned to Giles and said, 'Husband, it was a very moving speech, was it not? All those poor girls who would otherwise have nowhere else to go, not a soul to rely upon?'

'I suppose,' he said dismissively, keen to resurrect his arrested conversation with Signor Serrano now a light whispering of chatter broke out in the room on the display of the first auction painting.

'Will you make a bid then?' I continued, 'It is for a good cause and—'

'Ah, a woman with a charitable heart,' said Signor Serrano with a look of endearment.

Giles glanced between us then and seemed to have a change of attitude. 'Well, yes, of course, my dear, you shall pick whichever you should like to bid on.'

'And you shall pick for me too if your husband does not mind it?' Serrano said, and Giles agreed that he did not mind. So I considered them carefully as they were exhibited, and when a lively scene of the Regatta was moved to the stand, I said to Giles, 'I think this one would be nice to take home to Beddington. What do you think?'

'If it pleases you, my dear, by all means. You know you have a finer appreciation for such things than I do, so I shall leave it to your judgment.'

'Very fine judgement, too,' added Serrano. 'I confess I had my eye on the very same piece. I hope I will not offend you, Signor Craythorne, by also placing a bid.'

'Not at all, Signor. I am sure my wife shall have other fancies if we do not match your bid.'

I said nothing, only smiled, for though I liked the Regatta scene, I was motivated by the cause more than the means, and did not care much for procuring any paintings to sit on Beddington picture rails since I had no intention whatsoever of becoming mistress to that house if I could contrive otherwise. And as the bidding war ensued, it seemed the Regatta would not be destined for Beddington anyway, for we could not match him, or at least Giles had reached the limits of what he was willing to sacrifice in his pursuit of impressing the old man when it was called in excess of five thousand lire, receiving raucous applause from the room. One not again matched throughout the entire auction, even when I chose another exhibit, the one I had watched Marco paint in Torcello, and Giles procured it for a not-so-shabby three thousand.

When all the excitement was over, and the rest of the family came to congratulate us on our winning bid, Giles wasted no time beckoning his uncle into a corner with Serrano to resume a more practical conversation. And though I was excluded from this particular endeavour, I was forced to remain smiling and endearing, for Giles and Serrano's eyes stayed fixed on me for much of it.

'Eleanor?' I turned away briefly to find Marco at my side with the lady speaker at his. '...might I introduce you to Ofelia Barozzi, who would like to thank you personally for the generous donation you and your husband made to the charity this evening in making your bid.'

'Of course, my pleasure,' I smiled at her with authentic ease, 'Signora Barozzi, I am very humbled to meet you. I was much moved by your speech this evening and the inspiring work you are undertaking.'

'And I, humbled by your generosity, Signora Craythorne, for I see you were the driving force behind our donations reaching such a record tonight. The proceeds raised have exceeded our imaginings. I am delighted. We shall be able to get much underway that has been long envisioned but held back for lack of funding. A new communal kitchen for a start, where meals can be offered. An extension to our women and children's dormitory, too, I hope.'

'That is wonderful, Signora, truly, and yet I'm sure it is only a drop in the ocean of what remains to be done, but if there is anything I might do to help, I would be very happy to.'

'Well, we are always grateful for help, Signora, and your patronage would be held in such great esteem. It is not every day we might boast the patronage of the English aristocracy.'

I cast Marco a questioning glance, and he cast his eyes at Dante to blame.

'Well, I am only a Baron's daughter, Signora Barozzi, and no longer of much standing, I confess, so I'm not sure I would be a very good ambassador for the charity, but I am willing to offer whatever practical support I can.— I could perhaps help a little with administrative tasks or the educational interests of your beneficiaries?'

'Wonderful, that would be very welcome. Perhaps you will accept an invitation to visit us and we might have further discussions?'

'A visit to where my dear?' Giles was back at my side.

'Ah, husband, may I introduce you to Signora Barozzi,' I offered.

'Signor Craythorne, a pleasure. I was just telling your wife how grateful we are for your generous contribution to our cause tonight.'

'Ah, the pleasure is ours, to be sure.'

'Giles, Signora Barozzi thinks it would be of even greater benefit if Eleanor might offer more ongoing support in the charity's works,' Marco cut in.

'Yes, I was just going to ask you, husband, what your thoughts are on my paying attendance to discuss what might be done?'

'An angel in appearance and heart, Signora Craythorne, your charm knows no end,' Serrano threw his hands up, impressed, and Giles cleared his throat.

'I suppose it would be alright, so long as it would not place too many demands upon your time.'

'Wonderful, wonderful,' Signora Barozzi said, clapping her palms together. 'There will be no fixed obligations on your time, Signora, only what you can spare us.'

'Then I should be very happy to accept your invitation, Signora, and if you might send word to me as to when it would be convenient, we can discuss things further.'

'Which inspires me to make an invitation of my own,' Serrano cut in, 'You and your wife must dine with us at *Ca' Serrano* when you are free, Signor Craythorne.'

Giles's eyes flashed at the prospect. 'Well, Signor, that is very kind of you. We should be delighted, shouldn't we, Eleanor?'

'Yes, honoured. I shall look to it,' I beamed, though I was growing weary now of such playacting and was relieved when Signora Barozzi moved her attentive thanks to Serrano now, just to take a breather.

'You do me proud tonight, wife,' Giles said to me when they turned aside from us.

'I am glad. I hope you see I have tried, and I can be trusted to better now my spirits improve.'

'Yes, I do see you are still capable of remembering the woman you were when I first met you. I hope to see more of the same now you are.'

I nodded, a fitting answer failing me as I caught sight of Marco's eye-rolling expression and assumed he had overheard us, even though he was in conversation with the Contessa now. I felt suddenly embarrassed, though I wasn't sure why. But I had no time to linger on it, for Serrano soon returned to us and said, 'Forgive me, I did not mean to turn my back on you. I was wondering, perhaps, since you are here with family, you will not think it an impertinence if I steal your husband away for a round at the Casino tonight, Signora Craythorne? – Just the one. What do you say, Giles? I always like to sit down to a game of Faro with a man before deciding whether to do business with him. You can tell a lot from it,' he said to me now, winking.

'Would you mind terribly, my dear?' Giles asked me, and I returned a genuine smile.

'You shall be missed, husband, but what wife would deny a man his trifles.' I tiptoed to kiss his cheek and said, 'I will be fine to return with your aunt and uncle. I shall sit up for you, but don't rush back on my account.' A hint of playful seduction in my tone. 'Look after him for me though, won't you, Signor,' I said more innocently, but cast him something of a less innocent smile as he looked on impressed before granting me a bow.

However, my antics seemed to have less of an impressive effect on Marco. When I turned about to find the family, he was gone, and they were nowhere to be seen.

I knew as I walked through the crowd to find the Harpers that I had restored much good faith this evening, however exasperatingly. I was sure that tonight, Giles would have granted me almost anything in exchange for my performance with Signor Serrano, and he would surely go off to Treviso as planned without any undue concern about leaving me. If it had not been for the elation of this triumph, I knew I would have felt quite qualmish at having to play up in such a style to him and the Signor. Did he think me one of his harlots to dangle like a carrot beneath the gaze of a fellow nearly thrice my age? A shudder passed over me as I watched the pair of them walk out together, the Signor's arm over Giles's shoulder and Giles not even pausing to look back. *That was what had made it worthwhile.* I finally had some leverage over him to bargain with, and I had every intention of pondering how to put it to good use.

'Ah, Mrs Craythorne, are you looking for Marco?'

'Mr Holland-Bury,' I smiled. 'Um, no, my aunt and uncle, actually. Have you seen them?'

'Yes, they left about five minutes ago. Your uncle had a terrible headache, I believe.'

'Oh,' I said, astounded. 'Is Dante still here?'

'Yes, he is. I will help you find him if you'd like.'

'Thank you,' I said, taking his offered arm, thinking the timing quite impeccable.

'Marco tells me you are from the County of Surrey.'

'I am, do you know it?'

'I know Putney, whereabouts are you?'

'Not so very far, near the Epsom races – well, within a few miles.'

'Ah, then yes, I do know it, though only by the Derby, I confess. I am better acquainted with London than its counties.'

'Is that where you live?

He nodded.

'Where? I, too, am fairly well acquainted with the metropolis. My parents have a house in Berkeley Square.'

'Nowhere quite so grand, I have to say. Bloomsbury, do you know it?'

'I'm not sure, though the name rings true.'

'Well, I am not surprised. It's hardly quite the circles you might move in. But it is close to the British Museum.'

'Ah, yes, then I do indeed know the district. If I recall, there seems to be much development in the area. The Dukes of Bedford have some significant plans to bring it about.'

'Yes, they have not long completed our very own shopping arcade at Woburn Walk, so I believe we are rising up a fraction in civility.'

'Indeed. Soon, it shall all be developed, they say, even the slums south of the river. And what is truly in a league? You seem a perfect gentleman to me, Mr Holland-Bury, so I am sure we are not so very different. Pray tell me, how long are you in Venice?'

'Loosely, for a few months.'

'Loosely?'

'Well, I shall either have to go before travelling conditions turn difficult with the seasons or wait until after they pass. I am not wholly decided just yet. I suppose it depends—'

This was not the definitive answer I had hoped for, but if it was malleable, it remained a possibility. 'You will travel to Calais?' I asked and pressed him with a series of questions on this when he told me he would. Was he to travel privately? Well, that depended on how his fortunes fared by the end of the trip. He preferred it, but would take the Diligence for part of the way if need be. Were the inns so very bad along the way? Some were dreadful, though he had been making the journey long enough to know which to avoid now and rarely suffered any great inconvenience. Was he to travel alone? He and his valet, which he'd brought with him from England. What was the likely expense of such a journey? It, too, depended, but he usually managed it within the range of fifty to sixty pounds. What did that amount to in the local currency? He was not entirely sure now the local currency had switched to the new Austrian Lira this year, but he estimated in the order of one thousand two hundred and fifty to one thousand five hundred lire.

'Mrs Craythorne, you do have an awful lot of questions,' he said after a time.

'Forgive me if I am overzealous, only I am very keen to convince my husband that we, too, should travel home to England by road and not sea this time, for I found sea travel not at all the thing, and yet I know little about the arrangements for going over land.'

'Well, I would be inclined to agree with you, but your husband is a naval man, is he not, so it is perhaps unlikely he would share the same view.'

'Precisely my predicament,' I sighed. 'Though still I must make a try, for the very idea of stepping back onto a ship...Perhaps if he insists upon it, I might instead pair with you, and we can both have our way,' I proposed, with a note of jest in my voice just to test him, and though I saw the corner of his mouth shift playfully at this idea, I never got a reply, for Dante discovered us then, sparing him the need to answer.

'I turn my head for a minute!' Dante cast an accusatory scold at Holland-Bury, which I was relieved to find was also in the spirit of jest when Holland-Bury slapped his shoulder and said, 'We were just coming to find you as it happens.'

'Oh yes, but in no great hurry, I see.' He raised his eyebrows.

'Dante,' I said gently. 'Mr Holland-Bury was doing me the service of escorting me to find you when it seems I have been quite abandoned.'

'Abandoned?' He frowned, casting a glance about the room. 'Where's Giles?'

'Gone off to the Casino with Signor Serrano. An offer too good to be refused, it would seem.'

'What, and he's just left you here alone, with predators on the prowl?' he said with a theatrical air. 'Typical Giles, though, business ahead of all other considerations. I daresay he has his eyes on the diamond contracts. Still, it would be an excellent catch.'

'It would seem so, though he thought your parents were still here and I could return home with them, but I am told they are already gone?'

'Yep, papa done his usual.' He rolled his eyes. 'But I don't think Marco minded. They did stay a couple of hours.'

'What do you mean?'

'Ah, family politics, I shan't bore you. Anyway, you are safe under my chaperone, fair lady.'

'Yes, probably the only one she is,' Holland-Bury retorted, and Dante cast him a scornful glance, took me by my arm and said, 'I'll take over from here.'

'Thank you, Mr Holland-Bury and goodnight,' I interjected, thinking it quite rude how Dante spirited me away from him so abruptly. 'Don't you like Mr Holland-Bury?' I asked him when we walked on.

'He's alright, so long as you don't drink with him, game with him, or leave pretty young ladies with him.'

'He seemed perfectly honourable to me,' I protested.

'Know you not how to spot a libertine when you see one fair maiden?'

'Dante, you are never serious, are you?'

'Everyone else is serious enough, so...'

'Anyway, I am sure Mr Holland-Bury is not a libertine. – Your brother is far too square-toed to keep such company.'

'Alright, Libertine may be a slight exaggeration, but he is certainly slow to cast off his youthful follies. And that's coming from me. But then, nor is my brother square-toed, so I return the charge of exaggeration.'

I laughed a little and felt easy in his company. 'Very, well,' I accepted. 'You are the greater authority on both counts, but I assure you that Mr Holland-Bury was perfectly civil in his dealings with me.'

'Hmm, for now perhaps, but you have been given fair warning.'

'I have, but Dante, what shall I do? I doubt Giles will come back for me now.'

'Well, you can come home with us, of course. But the trouble is, I'm in with Marco in his boat so we are going to have to wait about for him and he does not seem to be kicking them out even though we are beyond the finish time.'

'He is trying to build his business, Dante. How can he prove a poor host?'

He shrugged, 'Well, I don't know about you, but I am fairly bored now. We can either cause some mischief to hurry them along, or hide up in the studio until they all get gone. What do you say?'

'I say, Mr, that some might argue you sound more of a libertine with such proposals to lure me upstairs alone with you.'

He burst into laughter at this, 'You may rest assured, you are perfectly safe with me, cousin.'

'Oh, and I am to take your word for it? What, have you a change of heart in conceding to your mama's match-making efforts then?'

'Absolutely not.'

'Then a sweetheart, I suspect?'

'Something like that.' He winked. 'Well, if you do not trust my honour, then mischief it must be...'

'I do trust you,' I said, with a gentle shove of rebuke. 'Let us go to the studio. My feet are tired and I hope there will be a chair up there.'

There were chairs and chaises adorning the entrance to the portrait studio, which was quite the neat and orderly polar opposite of Marco's home studio. Here, it was elegant, organised, clean and exceptionally comfortable. I wondered that he ever bothered with the paltry confines and clutter of his home attic when he had this as an alternative.

'Pretty plush, isn't it?' Dante said, pulling a footstool over to me and presenting it with an exaggerated roll of his arm. 'For the lady's piedi delicati...'

'Thank you, gallant, Sir,' I said, flicking my shoes off in a similar tone of frivolity and making him smile now. It was then I realised how long it had been since I had laughed, smiled in earnest, and had fun, and it struck me as a shock to witness it in myself. It was the perfect antidote to the taxing evening I had endured before now. I accepted the glass he poured from the pilfered wine bottle and took a long, contemplative sip.

'Cin cin,' he said, clinking his glass against mine and settling in the opposite chaise. 'Ah, that is better, capital choice. I am too tired for mischief.'

'I don't think you ever tire from mischief.'

'Well, I am told that one day I shall grow up, and that shall be the cure of it.'

'Then don't grow up. Stay just as you are.'

'Ah, my mama would be fast to break friends with you if she heard such counsel.'

'Your mama adores you!'

'True, and who could blame her with a face like this,' he beamed saucily. 'But, in you, I have a fresh audience. Where they are quite tired of my antics, you find them novel. Still, it is the first time I have seen you laugh so I shall take credit for that.'

'No small triumph,' I said more sincerely.

'Well, you are not the first to pay me such compliments, but—'

'Dante!' I said aghast before breaking out into another fit of laughter. 'You cannot say such things to ladies!'

'So I am told, often, and yet it is never them that seem to take offence to it unless, of course, we include my mother...'

'Stop. I shall split my dress hems if you keep making me laugh so.'

'Well, that's a new one, I confess.'

'Seriously now, no, I mean it. How are you and your brother so very different? I can barely believe you were brought up in the same house.'

'Well, I always think instead of us having an equal share of charm and good sense, I was given his share of charm, and he the sense. I speak in jest, but truly, you have him quite wrong. My brother is a very good man. But he has had a difficult lot and, well, I suppose he is a decade older than me, so he has earned his right to be a, what did you call it earlier, oh yes, a square toe.'

'Difficult lot? Really, how?'

'Well, it's not really my place to say, but he had a run of bad luck and was never quite the same after. But I wouldn't change him, the only fellow I know that would climb mountains for a stranger in need and want no one to hear of it. Not even the stranger himself, if he can help it.'

'Yes, your mother said he was once meant for the clergy. I suppose I see that good Samaritan in him. Why did he—'

'Gosh, you do like to ask all the awkward questions don't you, but if mama told you. —He was initially meant for the shipyard. Father spent years trying to mould him to it, but he had no interest; wanted to be an artist. When I came along and fell into the picture, mama gave father the idea that perhaps now he had two sons, it was not so important to school Marco so heavily, and I have to say, she had a good instinct even though I was not yet out of dresses, for I did take to it quite naturally. Anyway, as Father loosened his stance with Marco, the problem became one of what he was to do for his living. Father did not think art a legitimate pursuit, so mama pushed him in another direction, towards the church. At first, he seemed open to the idea. Though likely any idea would have captured him that got him out of the shipyard. But I don't know, I was too young to pay mind to it all back then. Anyway, he goes off to Oxford and falls into this artistic set, a society set up for extracurricular purposes. Anyway, he writes to my parents and tells them he is to stay and take up an apprenticeship in it.'

'With Mr Lawrence?'

He nodded. 'All hell broke out at home, though he was not here to see it. My mama begged him return and my father demanded it, lest he fetch him back himself. In the end, he came home. But he was very unhappy. Then,' he paused and searched my expression.

'Your mama said he fell in love and decided upon staying.'

'You *are* well informed. Well, I hope she has not been so forthcoming with *my* secrets,'

'No, only that she thinks you were born to the life of the shipyard master. I think she is very proud that you shall carry her ancestry forward in the trade.'

'She is a stickler for tradition, my mama. Anyway, he begins to rebuild his life here, meets Eliza, proposes to her, and all looks well for him, though he must give up the church, of course, for she is Protestant and he, Catholic. That caused its own problems with father, but mama brought him about to see that Marco settling down to marriage and a family was more important, so in the end, he conceded. Anyway, it never got that far in the end. Her family were not so relenting and would not have her marry into a Catholic family despite Marco converting.'

'My gosh, how tragic'.

'It was, and he lost his way for a while, and his art eventually brought him back to himself. And here he is, at last, come about,' he raised his glass. 'He deserves this, you see.'

I nodded. Feeling guilty about how I had been with him before. 'To your brother, a very talented and deserving artist.' I raised my glass, too, now.

'That's why my father has gone home early. He has no headache. He still finds it difficult to come to terms with Marco's path, though I think he is trying now, and mama is truly proud. Family politics, every family has them. Anyway, I have disproven the claim that I cannot be serious, and you've had our secrets now. So will you tell me what's up with you? And don't say you are homesick like mama always does, for I have lived away for years and never suffered it in your style.'

'Fair is fair,' I agreed. 'Can I trust you will not repeat it to anyone? Especially not your family.'

He nodded. 'You have my word.'

I wondered where to begin. 'I did not marry your cousin for the right reasons. I fell into some scandal and my reputation was at stake. But he proposed to me in spite of it and I blindly accepted. It was a terrible mistake. We were not well-suited and I have been pretty miserable ever since.'

'Well, that explains a lot.'

'It does?'

'Well, I'm not au fait with much in the way of marital concerns, even if my mama is keen to alter the fact, but it definitely makes a lot more sense than being homesick,' he smiled.

'Yes, I suppose it does, and if I had been happy in my marriage, well, then I perhaps would not have come to feel so very alone. But when you are not happy, it is very hard to be away from those you love.'

'Well, I do not know how poor a substitute we are, but I hope, as you come to know us better, we may suffice until you get back to your own family.'

'Thank you. I hardly know what I would do without your family's kindness. I dread to think how much the worse it could have been.'

'Well, you may rely on me to try and coax smiles from you when I can. Now, enough of this melancholy talk, I feel quite worn out by it. Shall we have a little fun and leave a surprise for Marco's students on Monday?'

'What?'

'In there, the teaching studio,' he pointed, 'come,' he said, pulling me up from my chair.

This studio was less plush and more practical, but large, orderly, and well-equipped for its purpose: Great looming windows to its rear, rows of easels set at the centre with a neat perimeter of tables, dressers and washstands to the periphery.

Dante rattled about in a drawer. 'Now, here is a pencil: you take the front row, and I shall take the back.'

'To do what with?'

'Whatever takes your fancy. I know what I mean to do,' he said, heading for an easel and beginning to sketch the shape of what soon became clear to be a figure of the male anatomy.

'Dante, you cannot!'

'Too late, already have. Go on, choose your mischief.'

'I shan't sabotage your brother's workshop!'

'It's in pencil, it will all come off with a light scrub. A little funning never hurt anyone.'

'I'm not sure your brother would see it quite the same.'

'Even *he* has a sense of humour, you know.'

'I have not seen it.'

'And I had not thought you possessed one until tonight, and I own you were starting to persuade me otherwise until you started to behave like...a square toe!'

I could not deny him his point or another laugh.

'Come, take up your pencil, I shall take the entirety of the blame if he takes offence.'

CHAPTER TWENTY-TWO

Ponte delle Tette.

Eleanor. June 1822.

We spent another hour larking about before we finally got into the boat after midnight. Holland-Bury and Marco at one end, me and Dante at the other as the gondolier broke through the shiny dark waters beneath a brilliant moonlight. The city still swelled with the residual heat from the days beating sun, though it was a fraction cooler now, I had no need of my shawl which lay resting in my lap. We were first to take a detour in dropping Holland-Bury back to his lodgings before heading home, and I was anxious at yet another delay to my return, fearing Giles would be back ahead of me by now, growing wild with my prolonged absence and suspecting me of scheming. But I could not say anything to hurry them without seeming impolite and ungrateful. And after my heart-to-heart with Dante tonight, I had no wish to be either. It had been a good night in the end, the merriest time I had had in so long. I had forgotten what it was to feel so vibrant, to laugh so heartily. It was not just gratitude for an interlude in spirits. I knew now that Dante and I would grow to be fast friends. He was a breath of fresh air to my constricted lungs, and I needed a friend like him who could remind me of the better parts of myself. So I felt hopeful once more as I sat with him, talking in the nonsense styles we had grown comfortable with. He gave me a comical tour of the city and its residents as we passed through the towering stone perimeters of its architecture.

We were just passing beneath a small bridge when Holland-Bury began to say his farewell in preparation for docking when a woman appeared upon it, garishly dressed and thick with face paints, leaning over it and watching us before lifting her breasts out of her dress and exposing them to our sight.

'What the devil?' I gasped.

'Come on, gentlemen, what do you say?' called out the woman. 'I can give you a handsome price for all three of you', she laughed and fluttered her fan across the tips of her nipples. 'I'll even let you watch...' she said to me now.

'Eleanor, turn away,' Marco said as Holland-Bury looked fit to burst into laughter, and Marco shot him a warning glare. 'Dante, put your coat about her, will you?'

'What, over her head so she can't see? You know she shares the same anatomy, don't you? And is perhaps more used to seeing a pair of those than even you, George,' Dante replied, and now I broke into laughter, too.

I don't know if it was the shock of seeing my laugh at all, but when Marco bit his lip and abandoned his reproach, I put it down to the surprise rather than his approval of the coarse subject matter. In any case, it diffused the situation, and we continued down the canal towards the landing where Mr Holland-Bury was to disembark.

'Well, I take it you understood her trade well enough to require no explanation?' Dante said to me with a smirk.

I nodded, remembering the streetwalkers who had tried to lure Leonard into alleyways and carriages that night in Piccadilly.

'Ah, so you know she's a reformed nun,' Dante added.

My belly began to ache with the strain of such hysterics. When I calmed enough to catch my breath, I said, 'I understand her trade, but what I don't understand is why she did that?'

'What, exposed herself?'

I nodded.

'It's nothing new about these parts. As any good market vendor knows, displaying their wares is the best way to make a sale. There's a whole bridge full of them about the corner on the Ponte delle Tette.'

'Bridge of...no,' I said, looking up at him and smacking him lightly on the knee. 'You are such a tease, Dante.

'Honest.'

'Bridge of *tits*? What do you take me for?'

'Marco, do I tell her a lie?'

'No, brother, but I wish you would not speak of such things at all. Eleanor —'

'Eleanor does not mind, do you, Eleanor?'

'I do not. It makes a change to be spoken to as an equal and not a fragile counterpart.'

'There. So, shall we take you to the bridge of tits and show you it is true?'

'Dante!' Marco glowered, signalling this was a step too far in his estimations.

'Yes!' I said, 'Take me.'

'Giacomo,' Dante called out to the oarsman, '...to the Ponte delle Tette!'

Marco shook a despairing head. 'And what will Giles think of us taking her to such a place, Dante?'

'Well, I'm certainly not going to tell him. Are you Eleanor? And anyway, it's not like we are taking her to see male flesh! Pity, though.'

'Dante, you have had too much to drink. Giacomo, ignore that, turn around, and take us directly home.'

Dante shrugged. 'Sorry, Eleanor, you shall just have to take our word for it.'

But I was not minded to take their word, for I wanted to see this sight for myself. Not out of any indecent intent, for I could not even think about loving another woman again. It all still hurt too much. Nor did I have any stirrings of that nature despite the other awakenings of former parts of myself tonight. But I was astonished and intrigued by this possibility. By this shocking overt display of female sexuality so brazenly exhibited in public. A one-off occurrence as we had encountered, I might have put down to a peculiarity of character, but a bridge filled with such sights, a namesake in honour of it, accounted for something much more interesting. Did Venetian society accept and tolerate this conduct? It was, after all, famous for its vice. Did they have some greater recognition that these women existed symptomatically to serve the men who sought them out? That without them at the root, ready to consume such services, she would cease to be? Out in the open was at least honest. It was at least acknowledgement of something more than societies that hid them away and pretended their sons did not seek them. I had not thought the Catholics so liberal, and yet I had no way to understand this information. But, I would seek to. I would find a way to pay a visit myself next week when Giles was absent. – That, of course, was providing my late return had not angered him to the point of retracting or placing a blanket ban on my leaving the house.

I needn't have worried. When we returned to *Ca Rosetti*, Giles had not yet come home. *One game indeed*, I thought, as Benedetta pulled my night shift over my head. I hoped that meant I could rely on a peaceful night tonight. I was certainly tired from my adventures, perhaps even a little squiffy myself, and perfectly ready to sink into happy oblivion now I knew no harm had been done to my hard-won efforts.

I was up and ready for church before Giles rose from his chamber and supposed him to have returned home exceedingly late and too far in his cups to bother me when he did. I sat on our private balcony on my own, enjoying the morning sun and freedom, not only from his absence at breakfast, but his promised absence to come. I could certainly grow used to this, I thought, sipping on my coffee and watching the world go by in the streets and canals below. People walking their dogs, others carrying bread and vegetables by the basket, gondoliers sailing by with smartly dressed persons making an early journey to mass. I felt altered today, renewed with possibility and hungry to explore it, though a tad ahead of my time. This time tomorrow, I smiled to myself...

For now, though, the church bells rang, and I went downstairs to meet the rest of the family in the hall to set out. This time, it was not Isabella who hung behind for me on our walk, but Marco.

'Eleanor, about last night, I hope you were not offended—'

'Not in the least, truly.'

'My brother was much in his cups, and he can forget himself sometimes. He is not much used to being about female company and—'

'Marco, your brother's company was precisely the medicine I needed last night. I have not laughed so hard in…longer than I care to remember, though I, too, was a little in my cups. But I owe him a great debt for reminding me that I still know how to laugh at all. It is my hope we shall become firm friends.'

'Well, I am pleased you are in brighter spirits. It suits you.'

I smiled. 'Thank you. I might say the same about you. It was lovely to see your gallery and works yesterday. You have done an impressive job, and the charity sponsorship is so very generous of you. Did it go as well as you hoped?'

'Thank you. It has been quite the labour of love, but yes, I think we did better than we expected last night. All in all it was a great success and we already have commissions coming from all sorts of directions, so I am hopeful it shall continue thus. Though I think I was not the only one to make an impression last night.'

'Well, I had very little choice in the matter, but I played my part.'

'Yes, I see that.'

'What, I am so transparent to your wily eyes that you understood the playacting, or that I am simply a terrible actress and made a poor show of it?'

'It was a very good show, perhaps, to less wily eyes, as you put it.'

'Well, we all have to do what we must, and it wasn't all bad for it got Giles and that old merchant to cast up their pockets, didn't it? And for a very worthy cause.'

'The cause was good, though the means, I think, expensive. But I am glad you agreed to meet with Ofelia. I am sure that you might both be of benefit to each other.'

'Yes, well, I hope to go to her this week once Giles is out of the way.'

'Is that what you look to?'

'Is it so very obvious?'

'If your improved spirits are the measure, then—'

'Well, whatever the cause of them, I mean to make the most of it.—I wondered, about the art class we spoke of before, is the offer still open?'

'Yes, of course. Have you spoken to Giles now?'

'I have not. But, well, as he is away next week—look, I know what you shall say, but will you hear me out?'

'Go on.'

'I shall level with you. I am not an art enthusiast; at least, I am all for admiring art but little for attempting to produce it. I cannot confess that my motives for wanting to come will be for its own sake, or because I have some latent, undiscovered talent, or even because I expect to improve to a great degree. But I enjoyed it that time in Torcello because it got me out of my head, the very act of doing, and I have spent an awful lot of time in my head of late. But I think I am ready now to try to move beyond it and to have some occupation, the opportunity of some society, and I think joining the art class might help me to that end.'

'Then your reasoning is sound. I, too, have found art to be a therapeutic practice at times.'

'The trouble is, I do not think Giles will see it that way, and yet I know it is unfair of me to expect you to keep secrets from your cousin. So I have given the matter some thought, and I was thinking that if I was to attend this week whilst he is away and see how it goes, if I think I am suited to it and inclined to continue, then I will ask him on his return. No excuses.'

'Eleanor, what do you believe your husband's reasons might be for forbidding it? I mean, he was amenable to you helping Ofelia with the charity house, so is it not simply about you going out?'

I swallowed a little, considering how much I should say. 'He does not trust me, Marco. He would say with good reason.'

'Because of the canal incident?'

'No, there have been other incidents, never of that nature, but ones he finds no less displeasing.'

'I see. Well, perhaps your coming to the art class and helping at the charitas might help to regain his trust too.'

'Maybe.'

'What do you think it will take to regain it?'

Be bound, gagged and caged, I thought silently. 'I don't know, but I am trying to, though it is not always easy.'

'I see that, and so I will keep my silence. But I urge you to speak with him on his return and try to get him onside. I will even talk to him myself if you would like me to.'

'Thank you. I shall see how things transpire.'

'Well, if you are to attend tomorrow, I can convey you there and back.'

'That is very kind of you. I am much obliged.

On the way back from church, I switched walking partners and kept Dante aside while we gained some distance on the others. He was the one I felt I could trust the most, so I decided there would be no better person to risk seeking assistance from. I told him I wanted to see the *Ponte delle Tette* tomorrow and take up Marco's offer to try the art class, but Giles would disapprove and Benedetta might report on me.

'Well,' he said thoughtfully, 'You can either pay Benedetta for her silence—'

'I don't have money to pay her.'

'Don't you?'

'No, and even if I did, I wouldn't have a clue what to offer. I don't understand your currency.'

'I don't think anyone does anymore since these Austrian lire were minted, but a few centesimo should do the trick. Here, take this,' he said and felt in his pocket and put some coins into my palm.

'No, Dante, I was not asking you for money.'

'It's not much, change from the coffee house.'

'What are the coins?' I asked, longing to know what the colour, shape, and weight of the ones I had in the attic were worth and how far short of the sum George had estimated his travelling costs at last night.

'Those? Centesimo. The smallest denominations, similar to the pennies you have in England. One hundred make up a Lira.'

So, the gondolier had been very fair in his price for conveying my letter after all, and I knew for certain now he had undertaken the task given Banfield's reply. It was safe to trust him to more, and yet I was reluctant to part with any more coin until I better understood the value of the ones I had. So, I went on to ask Dante to show me examples of the other types of coins. He apprised me of their various names and English equivalents as we passed them from hand to hand, and though I was pleased to have some better framework for understanding them, I was disappointed at just how little money I suspected I had in the attic now. Of course, until I could make a proper count tomorrow when everyone was out of the house, I could only guess, but I suspected it was nowhere near the sum Holland-Bury had quoted, and it filled me with dismay. I passed all the coins back to Dante now he had finished showing me the ones he had with him.

'Don't you want to keep some for Benedetta's bribe?'

'No, I don't want to bribe her, but thank you.'

'Why not? It is customary, and it wouldn't be the first time I've asked her to keep her tongue on some account over the years.'

'I fear it would be a costly undertaking for whatever Giles will pay for her reporting on me.'

'Hmm, I suppose he shall prove victor in a tug of war.'

'Precisely.'

'Then what you need is some excuse to shake her off, but even I would not encourage you to go about the city on your own, so who could replace her as a fitting chaperone? —Not my mama, certainly she will not be willing to visit the bridge of tits unless it is to deliver sermons to the unfortunates and get them to repent of their wicked ways...'

I nudged him playfully, 'There is no one else.'

'Ah, well, perhaps not to visit the bridge because even I have no desire to join you in that pursuit now I am not in my cups, but what about if we say that I am going to give you a ride in the boat to see Carlotta on my way to work in the morning and that Marco will be returning to collect you on his way back? – That way, Benedetta will not be needed. However, that still does not solve the problem of your going about the place alone.'

'But it is an excellent start! Do you think your sister will mind being adopted as an alibi? And I can't be sure Marco will be willing to conspire in the scheme, though he did offer to convey to and from the class, but not for spurious purposes, and I don't think he'd be too pleased at finding I have ill-used him for such.'

'I daresay he would not be, but if he is simply asked to bring you home in the boat after the class, he shall be none the wiser. Sometimes, with Marco, it is better not to put him in such predicaments as require him to make any moral sacrifice, but Carlotta shan't mind a bit.'

'Truly?'

'Not in the least, she is of your sex and quite used to pulling off such schemes in her youth to get a bit of leeway. Here it is—I have it! How about I send word to Carlotta, asking her to provide an alibi, not for you to see the tits, but for you to attend Marco's class. She shall see no harm in that at all, and I could prevail on her to offer to send one of her maids over for you in the morning, and then you shall not be alone nor reported to Giles for a higher bargain. And, if you happen to lose your way on the journey to the gallery because you are unfamiliar with the city, you might just stumble across the *Ponte delle Tette* quite by accident, and no more shall be thought of it!'

'You are a genius!'

'I am, aren't I?'

On Monday morning, I waved Giles off with such a sense of relief I could barely contain myself. It had even lightened the misery I felt as I lifted the floorboard in Marco's studio and stacked my coins into piles to count them out. Three hundred and fifty lire and thirty-four centesimo had been the sum total, well, to the best of my memory of Dante's explanation and the collection of silver and bronze coins I returned to the calico purse I had sewn to contain them. Not a single gold one was in my possession, and whilst it mattered not in what denominations the sum was made up, the fact was, I was drastically short, and at most, might manage the cost of board and lodgings, my packet ticket from Calais to Dover and the stage to London, as things stood. But I was not to be defeated now. I had had a taste of my former self this weekend and I meant to cling to that glimmer of hope and find a way to navigate myself out of this life with Giles, whatever it took. And whilst my coin had been a disappointing discovery, I was grateful for everything else that had fallen into place, thanks to Dante. It was all settled and I set out with him and Federica—Carlotta's borrowed maid—for a 'visit to Carlotta'. Benedetta, though mildly puzzled by this arrangement, was none the wiser to my actual whereabouts and seemed not in the least displeased at being granted a half-day off. So, I hoped this might prove enough for her to raise no concerns by the time Giles returned from Treviso.

Dante dropped us close to *Campo San Polo* and had already apprised me of the directions I needed to follow to reach my intended destination. All I had left to do now was convince Federica to occupy herself for an hour and meet me at the gallery, for I did not come to the Ponte to see the tits at all, but on more serious private business, and I could not have anyone party to it, not even a borrowed servant. And so, I pulled out some coins I had retrieved from my stash and asked her to explain something of the relative value to me. How much a loaf of bread, a bustle of wheat or a pound of flour might cost, to get a better bearing on it. And then, when she answered, I said, 'And how much would it cost to take yourself off to get something nice to eat and meet me outside the gallery in an hour?'

She looked confused at first but then realised what I required of her and said that four centesimo would be sufficient, so I counted out the coins, pressed them into her palm and watched her disappear into the square. Then I turned about, slipped my hood over my head and redirected myself into a *calle* in the direction Dante had given me.

I felt a nervous flutter in my belly as I scurried along the narrow street. I was unsure if it was simply being at liberty to walk about alone for the first time since *Leonard* roamed freely about Piccadilly, the intimidating look of some of the vagrants I passed from time to time, or the contemplation of what I was about to do. But I had little time to ponder it as the walk was short, and I did not need to get even as far as the *Ponte delle Tette* before I was met with the sight of hawking harlots all about me dangling in doorways and leaning over the canal edge to beckon the men in passing boats. However, these had their breasts (barely) covered by their dresses. But as I made out the bridge ahead where women congregated heavily about it, I saw more breasts in one glance than I had seen in a lifetime. They were equally abundant in the windows of surrounding houses and in small clusters about the surrounding streets. I was no less astonished for my knowing precisely the kind of district I was entering. Nor did my memory of the woman on the bridge soften my surprise at beholding the scene before me.

I, however, was invisible to them, all their attentions turned towards passing men, whether passing by on foot or on the canal. I watched on as they called out to them, sang out tunes, waved fans and cast seductive glances. One even threw her handkerchief at the feet of one of the passing gentlemen and kissed him on the nose for retrieving it. But after a while of growing accustomed to the scenes before me, I mustered enough courage to approach one of them. A girl of less garish dress and seeming somewhat more reserved than the others. She was leaning against the wall of a house on the corner of the *Carampane*.

'Signorina,' I said, approaching her and lowering my hood a fraction, 'Might you spare me a moment of your time?'

She looked me over dubiously. 'But it is my time as well as my body for sale, Signora.'

'I have money, but I don't require that. Will you talk with me?'

She sighed, 'Look if you have come here seeking your husband, lover or brother, I am afraid I cannot help you.'

'That is not why I am here.' Though I supposed it probably the most common occurrence for seeing an ordinary woman about such parts.

She studied me more carefully. 'Are you from one of those charities, for I require no assistance or rescuing—'

I shook my head, 'No, I am not. I come here on an entirely different matter, and I bear no ill intent towards your profession or spurious ulterior motive, I promise.'

She looked about her. 'Well, it is not busy. You can sit down with me for fifteen minutes for six lire.'

I nodded my agreement.

'Come in then,' she said, leaning into the doorway she had been lurking in.

I followed her in.

'We shall have to sit in here,' she said as we entered a small bedroom hung in heavy pink brocade.

'Very well,' I agreed, taking the offered seat, the only one in the room, whilst she leant against a tabletop waiting.

'Well?'

I took off my hood and handed her the coins.

'What do you want to talk of?' she asked, counting them.

'I want some practical information about your trade. Not for any dubious purposes. I wish to understand it better.'

'Why?'

'Because I need to find a way to earn some money, and fast.'

'You do not seem in need of money,' she said, casting a glance up and down my attire.

'Well, I am in desperate need or I would not be here.'

'Alright, what would you like to know?'

'What might I expect to earn in the first instance?'

'You are pretty, English, I think?'

I nodded.

'Have you an education?'

'Yes.'

'Are you a good conversationalist?'

'I believe I can be.'

'Then you would do better amongst the higher ranking Courtesans.'

'I cannot afford to be known to the higher ranks.'

'Because you belong to them?'

I nodded again.

'Well, it is better work if you can get it. You can become very rich for less fucks, in those circles. Here, you can get by, but the work is unpredictable and not always easy, and you will certainly never be wealthy.'

'In what sense is it unpredictable?'

'Men often come to us for two reasons: a last-minute urge when they are in their cups or because we are all they can afford. When they are in their cups, you don't know what to expect: they may be demanding, violent, or fall asleep mid-romp. When they are poor, they sometimes want a lot for their coin and try to press you into unhappy bargains.'

'And what do they pay?'

'That is up to the matron. She will decide your worth, and she takes half. But the usual rate is about thirty to fifty lire, less for bringing about by hand or mouth. If they have singular tastes or are particularly unpleasant or difficult, you can sometimes negotiate a higher price.'

I was disappointed by these figures but remembered that I did as much by Giles without having a single coin of my own for the trouble.

'And what does the matron do for her part in the bargain?'

'She provides this room and takes care of the linens. She arranges protection and helps you find custom.'

It was clear who had the easier lot.

'Some houses include your board, meals, and clothes, and some—like this—provide the room only when you are working. We are somewhat more independent here. We can come and go as we please, so long as we cover the agreement cost.'

'And, if I wanted to start out. How would I go about it?'

'If you are serious about it, I can introduce you to the matron. She will decide whether or not to accept you and, if she does, upon what terms.'

'Would you be willing to arrange an introduction?'

She nodded. 'Come back tomorrow afternoon. I will speak to her later.'

'Alright. Thank you.'

'Is that all of your questions? You still have five minutes left? Unless you would like some other value for your payment?'

I hesitated. 'How do you find it, I mean, the actual work?'

'I do not find it terrible if that's what you mean. I find it nothing either way...for the most part. But in the beginning, it is different, harder to manage. After a while, one prick or another makes no difference. It is only the manners you trouble over.'

I nodded, recognising the similarity to how it had developed with Giles. I would never be alright with it, but I had at last grown more ambivalent. 'And would I be required to bare my breasts outside of the house or from the windows?'

'Not required by law anymore, but if you don't want to be mistaken for a *berdache*, it can help.'

'I'm sorry, *berdache*?'

'You know, for a man who takes men by the arse. If you have the tits to prove it, you will get men of ordinary tastes. If you do not, you might attract the *battone* who think you are only dressed as a woman.'

'But surely that is a rare occurrence.'

'Not here. That is why we were first permitted to bear our breasts at all. To keep the men from straying to their own sex, or so the church said.'

'The church?'

She shrugged. 'It was their idea.'

'And,' I asked more nervously, '...are there likewise females serving females in your trade?'

'Not many that I know of, though sometimes the men will ask us to pair up. You do not have to do it if you prefer not to, though they will sometimes pay you extra if you are willing.—Are you willing?'

'Well, I think that's time,' I said, glancing at the clock and standing up. 'Thank you for your help. I shall come back tomorrow. Who shall I ask for?'

'Me, Giulia,' she said and opened the door.

My head was so full of calculations as I left the bordello that I had nearly forgotten my promised attendance at the art class as well as my directions towards it. I had left the bordello just after noon but had walked for more than a quarter-hour before I realised I was lost and remembered Frederica, who would be waiting there and wandering where I had gotten to. It did not help that the streets were so busy from the nearby markets, so I had inadvertently opted for the smaller calle which were quieter, so I could think better as I reflected on all I had learned.

I had taken my time strolling along them, taking in the quaintness of the buildings, stacked closely together with their shutters and colourful window boxes, winding canals and small bridges linking them like floating pieces of a great puzzle. But when the clock tower chimed the hour of one, I suddenly remembered where I was due and realised I was entirely lost.

'Excuse me,' I asked passersby, '...how do I find *Riva del vin*?'

I had to make several requests at each turn until I found myself on the right street. It was easy to know it, for it was directly aside the Grand Canal, and the Rialto was a landmark you could neither miss nor mistake. Marco's gallery was, but a single turn somewhere off this street, and I was relieved when I finally found it.

I stood at the steps of the gallery peering up at its great columns and debated whether I should go inside. I was anxious, not so much over the class, but where I had been, what I had done, and Marco's disconcerting ability to seem to see past what most could be relied on to overlook. I peered up at the plaque with the words *Galleria d'Arte Moderna* carved out in bronze lettering, and underneath it, in smaller print, I spotted Marco's name. There had been no time to make such observations at the exhibition with the keenness with which Giles marched us in.

I walked up the few steps and went over to a large notice board beside the door, where various pieces of paper were pinned behind a sheet of glass. I saw details of

current and forthcoming exhibitions across Venice, art lectures being held in the
Academia by someone called Giovanni, a few small adverts for portrait artists offering
their services and advertisements for his classes. *"Ladies' afternoon class, Mondays,
1-3pm."* I read from it, and beside it, I saw a notice requesting models for life drawing,
"apply within", it said. I looked at the door and hesitated. It was a quarter past one.
Would he think me ill-mannered to walk in now when they must already have started?
I turned around to leave but remembered I needed Marco to convey me home later if
all was to go to plan.

'There you are, Signora!' Frederica appeared beside me and I jumped. 'I have been
looking everywhere for you!'

'I am sorry, I got lost.'

'Well, are we going in?'

I nodded, pushed the heavy door open and went over to the attendant who had
been looking at me strangely since I had arrived upon the steps. I lowered my hood
and told him I was here for the art class and he gave me the direction, which was
just as well, for I didn't remember it from mine and Dante's visit. I did, however,
remember the indecent images he scrawled and hoped that Marco had at least received
my offering first, which I had written on a scrap of paper and left upon the desk on
our way out. *"Warning, mischief awaits. Check the easels before you use them!"* I had
written.

But after a brief, private chuckle at the memory, I grew nervous as I trod each step,
in two minds as to whether I should turn around and wait out the time perusing the
paintings instead. I had hardly gotten the chance on Saturday having to pose much
as an exhibit myself, but Federica looked at me expectant and I urged myself on. As
I grew nearer, I could hear Marco's voice echoing from beyond the door that was
now in sight. It was strange to hear him speaking in Venetian when I had grown used
to hearing him in English. His Venetian was fast and native sounding now, and I
supposed he must have troubled over slowing it down for my benefit on the occasion
he spoke it in my presence.

I considered knocking when I reached the open doorway, but I didn't want to
interrupt him mid-flow. He was sat perched on the edge of a table with his back to
me, and in front of him were six of the easels Dante had defaced on Saturday night,
laid out in a crescent shape around a scene set out of a picnic rug and various baskets
and refreshments set upon it. I noticed a clock on the far wall, and seeing it was half
past the hour now, I felt even more embarrassed for my late coming. I lost my nerve
and was about to edge my way back out when a lady stepped out from behind her
easel and gestured in my direction.

Marco looked over his shoulder with a frown that quickly merged into a smile when
he recognised me.

'Excuse me,' he said to the class. 'You may begin,' he nodded and then headed
towards me. 'You came. I thought you had a change of heart.—Federica?' he frowned,
recognising his sister's maid, 'Would you like to join in too?'

She shook her head. 'No grazie, Signor.'

'Well, do make yourself comfortable out there then,' he said, indicating the plush seating area Dante and I had lounged about in prior to venturing into here. I wondered what he'd made of Dante's sketching when he discovered it, but I had no intention of bringing it up.

'Why is my sister's maid here?' he asked as she settled upon a sofa.

'I borrowed her. I didn't want Benedetta to report my attendance to Giles before I was certain.'

'I'm sure she would not have, but I'm pleased you have come. I shall introduce you in a moment, but for now, we better get you set up.'

I was relieved at his warm welcome. 'Yes. Although I am very late, I do apologise. I got a little lost.'

He looked back at the clock. 'No matter. We were late starting today. We planned to go onto the square to paint the pigeons, but the ladies thought the sun too strong. So you must forgive me for such a drab display, but it was a last-minute effort.'

'Do you often take the class outside to paint?'

'Not often, though I try to when the subject matter suits. Right, it's time you were introduced. You are creating quite the intrigue.'

I stepped forward nervously and took his lead, noticing faces sneaking around the edge of their canvas to look at me as I walked.

'Ladies,' he clapped his hands together, which startled me. 'We have a new addition to our class today. Will you join me in welcoming Eleanor.'

They stepped out fully from behind their easels now and I could feel their gazes casting over me. I was rarely shy or embarrassed, but I felt it painfully now. I was greeted with smiles, curious frowns, and "piacere's."

'Eleanor is over from England, so if you would consider speaking a little slower, I'm sure that would help her understand you better,' he told them next, and I was met with renewed expressions of intrigue.

'I am Margarita, pleased to meet you,' she said, holding out her hand, and then a procession of personal introductions ensued where my Italian was tested beyond its usual practice, and I was left with so many names I knew I would not remember.

'I remember you from the auction on Saturday. You were with those donors who bought the Regatta scene. I am Guistina, pleased to meet you.'

'Yes, I was,' I told her, and then I must have mispronounced something because we reached an impasse and one of the other ladies who could speak a little English played at translating for us.

When the introductions were finished, the women slowly returned to their work, with just the odd glance in my direction every now and then.

'You are our second new addition today, Camilla is also new. There must be something in the air,' he said as he rallied around, gathering up different things for me to use.

'That's very good news.'

'It is. We still have space for a few more, but we are slowly catching up with the men's class. Today, we are focussing on sketching and proportions, so it is quite a technical activity rather than a creative one. But, we shall progress to adding paint next week where there is much more scope for it.—Before you arrived, I had everyone draw a faint cross in the centre of the paper to divide it and study the scene, apportioning the right items to the corresponding quadrant. Too often, the mistake at this stage is to focus on the item the eye is most drawn to, usually those at the centre, and put your efforts into that at the expense of the others. The difficulty, then, is that you rarely fit everything else in and have to start over. So, we first divide the scene into four with our eyes and apportion it lightly on our page. Once we are satisfied we have everything in the right place, we can then focus on adding more detail.'

I nodded, catching the scent of his woody cologne as he pointed and gestured his arms about, as I had noticed the Venetians frequently do.

'Any questions?' he asked, handing me a pencil.

'Not yet.'

'Well, have a go. I will give you a little extra time to catch up with the others, and then we will move on to the next step.'

I did as bid, though not so ineptly as I had in Torcello since I had more aptitude for sketching than paints.

But as time progressed, I noticed that some of the ladies were incredibly talented, and I felt slightly ashamed of my best efforts once we turned our easels about to exchange critiques. They were kind and generous with me, though, and I was grateful not only to be spared embarrassment, but to understand them to be a considerate group who did not seem at all frosty to an outsider like me, as I at first expected. Indeed, by the end of the class, I had grown much more comfortable with them, even if I was struggling to understand the occasional word or colloquialism amongst the din of voices. I had never before had to speak so consistently in the tongue over such a duration and amongst so many at once, and there was variation between the Italian and Venetian words that threw me further off. I had begun to understand this better recently, with Benedetta's help, but there seemed always to be more undiscovered. I suspected I would improve more in my fluency of tongue than artistry, in this class, though that was no bad thing given how reliant I would soon be on it in my new pursuits. Not that I thought talking would be the greater part of the language I would be relying on in those quarters anyway, body language was at least something more universal.

It was on pondering such thoughts and my plans to return to the bordello tomorrow that I considered a fitting excuse to get me out of the house to attend to it. I decided to leave my cloak here so I had an excuse to retrieve it tomorrow. I had others, of course, but it was all I could think of, so I had Federica slip it into a gap between the wall and the chair before we left.

CHAPTER TWENTY-THREE

The Indictment.

Annalise. March 1822.

T he charges laid were read as, 'Grand Lacerny, theft over forty shillings; for feloniously stealing one Sapphire pendant on a chain of Indian gold, value: eighty-five pounds, property of Giles Craythorne, and, a quantity of marquetry style pearls, value of two pounds ten shillings, property of Mariella Craythorne.'

Annalise, struggling to find her voice at all, eventually entered her not guilty plea. This followed a very tiresome and dishonest setting out of the alleged theft by Mariella's barrister, Mr Truscott, who begged leave of the Judge to call first to the stand, the second prosecutrix, Mariella Craythorne, on account that the primary one, had not yet arrived.

This was allowed, and Mariella entered the witness box looking all the part regally dressed and as lofty in countenance as ever. Unfortunately, the bruised and rough look of her that Annalise recounted from her last sight of her, bore no resemblance now to that sad and sorry creature. She was dressed in fine pea-green silk and had fashioned her hair neat beneath her bonnet. The scuffs and scrapes on her face had healed, the bruises had disappeared, and the only sign of any imperfection was a raised pink line of a scar running from the corner of her mouth to just above her chin on the right side. This was not something Annalise had seen before, and she assumed it to be a result of her stay at Bodmin.

'Miss Craythorne, will you tell us about the pearls that were wickedly taken from you?' Mr Truscott asked.

Mariella cleared her throat. 'Yes, Sir,' she said in an accent far more genial than Annalise had heard her speak in before. 'The truth is, I had not even noticed them gone until the Magistrate presented them with the stolen necklace they recovered from the prisoner's things. I knew instantly I recognised them as the pearl decorations that adorned my travelling sewing box.'

'You refer to the prisoner in the dock?'

'I do, Sir. That is she.'

'Where did you get the box?' asked Mr Truscott.

'It was a gift from a Maharajah in Madras, a friend of my father's from our time abroad in his diplomatic service. It was a beautiful kindness given on our parting some five years ago now.'

'So, a gift of some sentimental value, I would imagine?'

'Indeed. I shall certainly not be able to venture back to India and ask the Maharajah for a replacement!'

The Court chuckled at this and Mariella smiled demurely.

'No, indeed, a rarity of craftsmanship. No doubt worth far more than the two pounds ten shillings you have estimated its value at.'

'How do you put a price on a gift from a Maharajah?' she said with a shrug.

'Certainly.' He smirked. 'Now, if you will describe when you last saw the box intact.'

She nodded. 'It was at a boarding house in Falmouth the night before my cousin and his wife sailed for Lisbon. My cousin's wife suffers from a nervous instability of the mind. She had one of her nervous fits that evening and I caught the brunt of it, unfortunately. She ripped the sleeve off of my dress in attacking me, and afterwards, I instructed my maid to repair the damage. It was a favourite.'

'Do you say Mrs Craythorne was violent to you?'

'She was, Sir. She attacked me most viciously in front of several persons.'

'That must have been quite the ordeal?' he said with a sympathetic air. 'But you have recovered well, it seems.'

'It was, to be sure, and I was in a very sorry state. But I am, by the grace of the almighty, healed and well again.'

'Mr Truscott, if you would move along, this is not the only case the Court must hear today!' said the Judge, looking irked.

'Forgive me, my Lord. Miss Craythorne, when you last saw the box, was it intact, with the pearls in place?'

'It was.'

'And where was it?'

'It was left on the side-table by a sofa once my maidservant had finished using it. I sent her to bed. It was so late by the time she had attended my injuries and mended my dress.'

'And when did you notice it gone?'

'Well, the next morning when we left the boarding house. I assumed my maidservant had packed it away with the rest of my things and thought no more of it.'

'Which was why you had not noticed the theft until the Magistrate presented the pearls?'

'Yes, Sir. I was quite shocked at recognising them. I had to check for certain with my maidservant afterwards. She confirmed that the box was missing. I had thought the prisoner had just stripped it of the pearls in the form the Magistrate had shown me them, but no, the whole box was missing.'

'And the prisoner, she had access to the place from which it was kept?'

'She did. She was present in the room at the time of the attack and a little while later.'

'Thank you, Mrs Craythorne. No further questions.'

'Mr Langley, do you have any questions?' asked the Judge.

He stood up from the table. 'I do, my Lord. Miss Craythorne, you claim that the pearls are your belongings. I assume you know them well having enjoyed the gift of them, some five years, you say?'

'I do, Sir.'

'Hmm, and you are certain that these pearls,' he gestured to them, sat on the table in front of her barrister, '...are definitely *your* pearls?'

'Yes, as I said.'

'If I may, my Lord, show the pearls to the witness for her to examine them.'

'Yes, yes, but hurry, Sir!'

He did as bid and presented them to the witness stand. 'Miss Craythorne, these are the pearls you know well?'

'Yes,' she answered in a tone of boredom, casting the briefest glance over them.

'Very pretty, are they not, though a little aged and worn now, would you agree?'

'Well, I have had them about five years now, Sir, and the box gets much used.'

'Indeed, but good, genuine pearls can take a little wear, wouldn't you say?'

'Yes, I suppose.'

'Mr Langley, where is this going? I bid you make your point,' the Judge pressed him.

'I shall. Miss Craythorne, are these genuine pearls?'

'Of course they are, Sir,' she said, irritated, unable to hide the affront she felt at his question.

'It would be an insult to be given replica jewels from a Maharajah, would you agree?'

'I would, Sir. I would say it an insult to the Maharajah that you would insinuate them to be anything but the best of pearls.'

He pressed a palm to his chest. 'Forgive me, no insult intended. I only wished to clarify that these are indeed your own, genuine, pearls.'

'As I have told you many a time!'

'You have, though it is fair to say you have not seen the box from which you claim they were taken since the night you saw it on the side table. You have only your servant's word for it that they are gone at all? That the box itself may very well be intact, misplaced perhaps, or even incorrectly packed up in the chaos of the events that night and leaving in the morning?

'Well, had they not been discovered in the prisoners belongings, I might agree that it was not impossible, but they were. And if you mean to insinuate my servant is a liar, Sir?'

'I do not. I only wish to make it known to the Court that you yourself have not had sight of the box, that you rely on second-hand knowledge, and that others, including your own maidservant, had access to this box and could have just as easily removed it from its place on the table.'

'Well, you may construe it so, but I know it to be true, just as I knew she had taken the necklace when my cousin discovered it missing.'

'Is there a reason your maid has not been called to give her statement?'

'Yes. She cannot speak English, Sir, only Urdu.'

'Convenient.'

'Objection!' said Mr Truscott. 'My Lord, it is not my client's fault the witness cannot give testimony.'

'Yes, move on, Mr Langley, you are exhausting my patience with this line.'

'As you say, my Lord. Miss Craythorne, can you tell the Court why you have been unable to examine the box for yourself?'

'Because I do not have it with me.'

'You mean you do not have it with you in *Gaol*, which is where you have been for the past seven weeks.'

A hiss of surprise rippled across the room.

'Miss Craythorne, have you, or have you not, been imprisoned these past seven weeks awaiting your trial?'

'I object.'

'Mr Langley, state the relevance of your questioning or withdraw,' the Judge intervened.

'I shall state it indeed. It is relevant because of the many charges for which Miss Craythorne has lately been imprisoned; one of them was for attacking Miss Tullier by throwing a china cup at her head in the witness of the Mayor of Falmouth and the local watchman. Is that not true, Miss Craythorne?'

Whisperings erupted amongst the gallery and the jury.

'Answer the question, Miss Craythorne,' warned the Judge.

'It is true I have been imprisoned,' she said reluctantly.

'It is true that you hit Miss Tullier on the head with a china cup in a wholly unprovoked attack as she sat across the table from you on being questioned by the Mayor?'

'Objection, my Lord, my client must not be forced to confess to a crime she has not been yet tried for.'

'Move on Mr Langley.'

He nodded. 'I put it to you, Miss Craythorne, that the very same frustration with which you attacked my client, was the very same that inspired you to fabricate these thefts, with intent to harm her, for no other reason than that she tried to assist her mistress in preventing her being taken abroad against her will and without her family's knowledge. That is what this is really about, isn't it? A servant helping her mistress, remaining loyal to her service and care when you and your cousin had only ill intent towards her. A woman made vulnerable by her pregnant state and taken away from her family against her will and thrust upon a ship to who knows where? Were you and your cousin frightened that Miss Tullier would be free to go and report on all she had seen? Is that why you concocted this sham?'

The Judge coloured up, a cherry mottling about his heavy cheeks. 'Mr Langley! You forget yourself. Jury, disregard what you have just heard. Miss Craythorne, you shall answer no more questions.'

'Forgive me, my Lord.' Mr Langley withdrew.

'Mr Truscott, do you have any further witnesses to call at this time?'

'Not yet, my Lord.'

'Then Mr Langley, have you anyone to call?'

'I do, my Lord. I call Mr Plumpton, Jeweller.'

He answered swiftly to the call, entered the stand and was sworn in.

'Mr Plumpton, please tell us of your trade and experience, if you will,' Mr Langley said, pacing before him.

'I am Mr Plumpton, jeweller this past thirty years for *Plumpton's* in Truro.'

'Thank you, Mr Plumpton. I think it's fair to say you are well qualified to know a genuine pearl from a replica?'

'Certainly so.'

'My Lord, may I present the pearls to the witness?'

'You may.'

He fingered them for a moment, held one up to the light, and ran one across his teeth before putting it down again.

'Mr Plumpton, what is your evaluation of them?'

'They are paste. These are not genuine pearl.'

A gasp of surprise from the gallery.

'How can you tell?'

'Well, firstly, they're too smooth. Real pearls have a grit to them. You can feel it against your teeth. These are smooth as glass. Then there's the colour—not milky enough by half, altogether too uniform, no natural marbling. Then there's the encasing—paste needs encasing, but real pearls don't and would not be likely on the type used to adorn furniture, in any case.'

'You are certain?'

'I am.'

'And what would you value these replicas at, Sir, market value?'

'New, they might have fetched twelve shillings or thereabouts, now, perhaps nine, at best.'

'Nine shillings. So, not the two pounds ten shillings they have been estimated at then?'

'T'would be a sham to ask above ten shillings.'

'Thank you, Mr Plumpton. I believe you have brought some of your own pearls today, genuine pearls, to show the difference. If my Lord will permit me, I will show them to the jury for comparison.'

'First to me,' said the Judge, gesturing for them.

'Mr Plumpton, one final question before you go. If I put to you that these replica pearls were commissioned as a gift, a gift by royalty, would this surprise you?'

'Aye, it would, Sir. I would expect to sell such trinkets to a working man of modest means, not at all to the polite classes and would not conceive of showing such wares to a Royal.'

'So we agree. This is highly unlikely to have been the gift of a wealthy Maharajah, as the prosecutrix has falsely claimed. No further questions.'

'Mr Truscott?'

'Yes, my Lord,' he said, rising. 'Perhaps Mr Plumpton should like to give an appraisal of the value of this sapphire pendant?' he took it from his desk and presented it to him.

The Judge nodded.

'Tell me what you can of this, Sir.'

He draped it from his forefinger, held it up to the light and examined it for a moment, then looked up and said, 'It's good gold, Indian, twenty-two carats, clean purity, about an ounce and a half I'd guess, without my scale to confirm.'

'Ah, so not a fake! And what of the gemstone?'

'Good clarity, eye-clean. True Sapphire, to be sure. Padparadscha, I would dare to guess, but so rare, I have never handled one such.'

'And what would you value such a piece at?'

'A piece like this, very rare indeed, Sir,' he sighed and looked thoughtfully. 'I would set the price for one hundred pounds with the expectation of bargaining no less than eighty-five.'

'Close enough. Now tell me, what would be the chances of procuring a replacement of such a piece, should one be unfortunate enough to have such a precious thing stolen?'

'Very scarce indeed. You might find something of half the weight and quality if you were fortunate, but this, no, you'd like never come across such an example again.'

'Thank you, Mr Plumpton, no further questions.'

'Who do you call next, Mr Truscott?' asked the Judge.

'I have no one to call presently, my Lord.'

'Mr Truscott, pray, where is the prosecutor?' The Judge asked.

'I believe, my Lord, he is on his way.'

'From where?' he asked impatiently.

'From the continent...'

The Court broke out in laughter at this before Mr Truscott could complete his sentence and the Judge slammed his gavel to silence them. 'The continent, Sir?'

'Yes, my Lord, I believe him to have been due into Falmouth on *the Walsingham* this morning and making his way directly to the Court. —Apologies, my Lord, I assume him delayed.'

The Judge checked the clock and sighed. 'Right, it's almost twelve, we shall adjourn for refreshment. Mr Truscott, make sure you gather an update on the status of *the Walsingham* before we return to session!'

'Yes, my Lord, I thank you.' He bowed.

Mr Langley came directly to the bar and lent in to speak low. 'Miss Tullier, how certain are you that Mr Craythorne shall not appear?'

'I cannot be at all certain. It seemed unlikely, but if what Mr Truscott says is true...'

'Very little Mr Truscott says is true. He is a slippery fellow indeed. Had I known such a character as he had the brief, I might have warned Mr Plumpton not to fall prey to his ill use. Damn it! We had better hope he does not show.'

'Do things go badly, Sir?'

'They were going well enough before he twisted them to serve his purpose, but he is not an honourable man and you must prepare yourself for his tricks when he comes to summarise his case. Now I must hurry up to the mess and be sure he does not have the Judges ear.'

Mr Langley's disconcerted speech was all she needed. If it wasn't tormenting enough to endure this process, knowing not if she was to walk out today a free woman or meet a crueller fate, now she was to have the matter drawn out. Worse still, she would be taken back to that abysmal holding cell in the basement that was pitch black and stifling for want of airflow, with only room enough within to walk backwards and sit directly down before the door was pressed shut, almost against your knees. She expected no refreshment either, even though she had grown hot, weak, and nauseous, standing in the box waiting to learn her fate.

CHAPTER TWENTY-FOUR

The New Recruit.

Eleanor. June 1822.

I returned to the house in Carampane the next day and called upon Giulia as agreed. Though it proved far more difficult to plan it with the precision I had managed yesterday with the benefit of Dante's help. I now had no reasonable means I could construe to borrow Federica again or put off Benedetta, and even though I had planted the excuse in advance in leaving my cloak at the gallery, I would be forced to improvise for the rest. So, after convincing Isabella that I would be fine going to the gallery on foot, that no I did not want a message sent to Marco for him to bring the cloak back this evening, nor did I want a boat put at my disposal because I wanted the exercise, she finally agreed to accompany Benedetta and me as far as San Marco where she was headed to the flower merchants at the *Frezzeria* and let us continue alone from there. It had, I realised, been out of genuine concern for my welfare rather than to prove another obstacle. But, it had been a hard-won battle to get so far today, and I still had the problem of losing Benedetta, which was precisely what I did in a moment of desperate spontaneity.

Once we had collected the cloak from the gallery and set out for our return journey, I had to think fast to rescue my failing plan or concede to letting it all come to nothing. *That* was not an option.

In the scramble of the Rialto, which was reliably chaotic and disorientating at this hour, I managed to contrive to lose a shoe buckle as we climbed the steps and set us both to search for it. I had kicked it off on purpose, of course, but I made a convincing effort to look for it before gaining enough distance and distraction from her to duck into a seller's booth for long enough for her to walk by in the other direction. As soon as she did, I rushed across to the opposite arcade at the rear of the bridge, darted back down the other side and pulled my scarf over my head to better conceal myself. It was a cruel trick and I wished I could have found a better means, but I was all out of ideas and time and *had* to get there somehow. All I could do was try to be quick so her panic and search did not grow too wearisome, for I knew she would be at odds to return without me and throw the house into alarm. It was the last thing I wanted either, and so I had to hurry if I hoped it might not come to that.

I ran most of the way there, arriving near breathless and my cheeks burning hot.

'What is wrong with you?' Giulia asked when I found her lurking about the doorway of the bordello.

'I have been rushing and I am in desperate need of the chamber pot, but I don't have long.'

She gestured me inside and opened the bedroom door. 'It is under the bed,' she said and turned away from me.

'Thank you,' I hesitated, feeling more than a little self-conscious lifting my skirts and using it in her presence, even if she was not looking. Though I supposed I must soon grow used to far worse audiences to far more intimate acts.

'You can leave it under the bed when you are done. The servant girl will take it.'

'Thank you. I should never have lasted another minute,' I sighed, letting my skirts back down and feeling better for the relief of it.

She turned around again now.

'Is your matron about?' I asked.

She shook her head. 'I am sorry, but you have had a wasted journey.'

'Why? Will she be out long?'

'No, she will be back soon, but it is no use. She says we are full and she is not looking for the burden of a new girl to train. It's hard enough to find work for the rest of us with people struggling, so,' she shrugged. Perhaps you can try the other houses? Matron Beppo's house is a bit classier and she might take a fancy to you.'

I was devastated at this news after taking such pains to get here. 'Where is that?'

'In Carampane, just about the corner, come, I will point the direction out for you, but do not say I sent you; my matron and she are rivals and I don't want any trouble.'

'I shan't then, rest assured,' I told her and followed her back out onto the street half-heartedly. I neither wanted to waste my journey nor have to start over again, especially when the time was so much against me now. But what would I contrive to be let out again tomorrow if I did not manage the business today? I would have to seize the opportunity and make a try for it, I considered, and followed her up to the junction of the street.

'It is just up there and on your left. Follow it all the way down to the little square and it is the building that will be facing you, *Ca' Beppo*. The door is to the left.'

I was about to take my leave and thank her, but as I went to do so, I noticed her expression alter into something like mortification. 'What is wrong?' I asked instead.

But it was too late for her to make reply.

'Giulia! What are you doing away from the house? You are supposed to be supervising,' came a voice of reprimand a few yards ahead of us.

'Matron,' she addressed her, and I understood then. 'We are not busy. I was just showing this lady the way back out.'

She looked me over thoughtfully and stopped. 'Well, are you going to introduce me?' she asked Giulia.

'This is the lady I spoke of last night, who said she would call here today. The English lady—'

Her eyes widened with surprise. 'Ah, yes! I remember now. Signora Crivelli, piacere,' she said beaming at me.

'I'm pleased to meet you, too, Signora. I am Eleanor,' I told her, not wanting to give away more of my identity than I needed to now I was thwarted.

'Eleanor, I am happy you came, but you are leaving so soon? Will you not come back to the house and we can chat over a cup of coffee?'

Giulia scrunched her face up in confusion but said nothing.

'I thought you were full, Signora?' I said with mild surprise.

'Yes, it is true, in *this* house, but for a beauty like you, I should find some other rooms to rent...hmm. Come, let us go inside and we can discuss things further.'

So I followed the pair of them back into the house, still anxious of the time but relieved not to have been turned away after all.

This time, we went past the room Giulia had taken me into before, followed the corridor about and took the staircase to the first level, where we entered a parlour overlooking the view below by way of a small balcony and tall glass doors that had been left open so the ladies could lean out of them and display their flesh to the passing boats. They turned about at the sound of our entry and Signora Crivelli clapped her hands and sent them away—Giulia included—before she ordered a servant girl to close up the parlour doors and fetch us some coffee.

'Please,' she said, once we were alone, '...take a seat, Eleanor, and if you will, remove your scarf so I can see your face better.'

I did as bid and felt her appraising gaze crawling over every inch of me, sizing up my worth like a fat hen ready to have its neck rung for a feast.

'Tell me, Eleanor, have you been educated?'

'Yes, in Literacy, Arithmetic, Music, French, Italian and a little History.'

A propitious sparkle lit her eyes. 'I see. And of your situation?'

'I am the daughter of an English Baron, though I am estranged from my family now. I can tell you no more than that.'

'You are a true English Rose,' she said, satisfied, and taking her seat opposite me, she continued, 'A rare thing in these parts, and yet I think you will do very well here as something of a novelty and in the service of your countrymen who abound in the city on their tours once again. Yes, I see you in some pretty apartments by the Piazza San Marco. Tell me, do you intend to live in and have your board?'

It was tempting to consider the possibility of escaping Giles immediately, but I was not foolish enough to thrust my security onto a self-serving stranger who would have me in her debt for rudimentary needs. Or, to cause the Harpers distress and be forced into hiding for fear I might be recognised and recaptured by Giles. No, I would have to play the long game, the safer route. 'No, Signora, I have a place to live. I shall only require a place to work, and I shan't be able to work all that often either, for you see, I am a married woman and my husband cannot know about this.' It seemed prudent to level with her from the outset and spare myself the complication later.

'I see. Well, that is a shame, but how often do you think you could be available?'

'I wish I could offer you a plain answer but it will be complicated for me. I cannot pretend it won't take some refining to work it out, but in general, the daytime is most convenient, but not on the weekend. Evenings rarer, but not always impossible,' I added, thinking how much Giles was out at the hells or probably frequenting districts like this when he had a fancy. 'Will that be a problem, Signora?'

'Usually, I would say so. You see for yourself that the girls are loitering about with nothing to do at these hours. They may have a regular or two who comes during his siesta to pass a few hours, but on the whole, the daytime is not good for business because most of our patrons are engaged at work until the evening. But I have something different in mind for you: the type of patrons who are richer and have more time at their disposal to do as they wish. It has been in my mind for a little while now to open another house, a discreet and exclusive house in a better part of the city, for girls like *you*—a cut above the rest. The path of the *cortigiana onesta*, I think, shall suit you better and to be exclusive, not always available at the beck and call of gentlemen, shall only make you more in demand and mandate a higher price...Yes, the usual rules do not apply here, and so I think it possible we can make it work, so long as you can promise yourself to me at least four times a week?'

'I could,' I answered, not yet having the faintest idea how I would manage even one more visit, let alone four a week, '...but the thing is, Signora, I am not certain that scheme will be a good one, for I am amongst those classes you speak of—'

'Yes, which is why they shall desire you! You shall have things in common and know how to amuse them.'

'But I cannot risk being recognised, Signora. If I was found out—'

'You won't be. Your service shall be a discreet, elite service. We shall be very careful.—Look,' she said, pointing to a painting of a masked lady on the wall. 'This is how we shall present you. Mysterious, alluring, captivating! It will only add to your demand, the only way to reveal you being to call upon you privately.'

I supposed it would not be the first time I had assumed something of a disguise to good effect. 'What would I be paid by such men of wealth?'

'*That* we must negotiate, do not run ahead. There is much to consider. The cost of your rooms and linens, and we shall need to hire servants too, for men of that rank shall not expect to pour their own drinks or hang their own coats. Then we shall have to put you in the best catalogues to raise an interest.'

'An approximation then?'

'A hundred lire per patron, in the least.'

That equated to an awful lot of encounters to meet the number Mr Holland-Bury had quoted, but I knew she was pitching low to consider her share, and it was still a vast improvement on what Giulia had reported, and the more I could earn, the quicker I would be on my way to England. 'Very well, if you can be certain of my anonymity, then I will consider it.'

'Consider it? Come now. I shall have to go through great pains to find you suitable rooms and servants, not to mention ensuring news of you reaches the right calibre of callers. I shall need more than your consideration; I shall need the bond of your word to take such pains.'

'Well, when you have made your enquiries and sought *actual* prices, we can finalise a rate, and then you shall have it.'

She smiled narrowly, I thought, unused to having to bargain in this fashion and more used to laying down the law. But I was no featherheaded youth, not now. I knew what it was to be breached by a man you did not care for, and his being rich or poor did not alter the experience. I was not about to take a penny less than I could get for the trouble, nor bind myself to terms that were not finalised.

'Well, you are spirited, I see, but a little of that shall titillate your patrons all the more. Will you need dresses, or shall you use your own?' she asked.

'I expect I will need to have new ones made up, more *suitable* ones, though I can take care of that.'

'And what of your toilette? You can manage it yourself?'

'For the most part, a hand with my lacing should suffice. An ordinary servant will be adequate to assist me.'

'Alright, I will need some time to make enquiries after suitable rooms and then we shall meet again to fix our terms. Where can you be reached?'

'I cannot be. My identity must remain private if I am to manage to proceed with this at all.'

'Very well, we will manage for now. Going forward, I shall need some means to communicate with you, even if it is indirectly. I suggest you come back in a week, and by then, you will need to find a way we may pass messages, even if it is by way of a third party. You understand?'

'Yes, I shall find a way.'

'Good. Now, you are married, so you shall not be in for any particular surprises with regard to your duties, at least. However, you are new to this profession, so it might be advantageous to consider a little mentoring. I can put you with my best girl, Perla, for some pointers and practice. You could even come this week to suit you.'

'I don't know,' I said reluctantly.

'It is in your interest, Eleanor. The better you are at bringing them to completion effectively, the quicker you shall earn your coin. Do not mistake our work as the same as that of wives. No, ours is the art of practice and skill. If it was as simple as just rolling over in the marital bed, why would husbands ever fill ours? They come to us because they know they shall get precisely what they ask for here and not leave disappointed. But not all girls are equal and the skilful girls do better, to be sure. A pretty face and handsome form will certainly lure them to your bed, but how shall you keep them coming back to it time after time to fill your purse? You need to know what you are doing and practice the art until you become the best.'

'Very well, I shall accept the mentoring, but I would like to ask Giulia if she would be willing to teach me.'

'Giulia,' she laughed the name, 'Perla is far superior and makes twice as much as Giulia on a bad week.'

'Well, I feel comfortable with her. She has been kind to me, and if I am to undergo this initiation, I should like it to be with her.'

'Very well, to begin with. Though I shall want Perla's assessment of you before we get to work so I can be certain of what I promise to your callers.'

If I had not been so full of haste as I left the bordello, I might have revelled in my triumph today, and began to run more calculations through my mind based on these new figures. But I was in even more of a fluster and hurry as I ran down towards *Campo di San Silvestro* and back up towards the Rialto than I had been on my way here. I had checked the clock on Signora Crivelli's mantle as I stood to leave and realised I had already been about three-quarters of an hour. Poor Benedetta, what would I say? How would I find her now or know if she had returned to *Ca' Rosetti* and started up a panic? I kept my eyes peeled for sight of her as I hurried back over the Rialto, retracing our earlier steps in case she was still there. But of all the many bodies I had to meander through, she was not amongst them. And now I faced a further difficulty I had not foreseen in advance: how on earth would I ever get back to the house without her to direct me, for I did not know the way. I knew we had come via St. Mark's Square, but I did not know how to reach it or where to go thereafter.

Once again, I resorted to asking passers-by for directions and eventually found myself in the pigeon-pecked square of St. Marks. From here, I remembered to head towards the *Palazzo Ducale* and the lagoon front. I was sure that if I stuck to this stretch and avoided the backstreets and calle, I would eventually end up at the church we attended for mass and should remember the way once I saw it.

I had been correct. Once I met the white façade of *Santa Maria delle Pietra*, I was able to navigate myself, and bar a few wrong turns I quickly corrected, I found my way not a moment too soon. I was almost there now, crossing the *Ponte Dei Greci, Ca' Rosetti* obliquely opposite and a mix of relief and trepidation at the sight of it as I considered whether Benedetta might have returned now. But as I reached the top of the bridge, I saw Marco pass beneath it in his boat, an anxious Benedetta beside him.

'Marco! Marco!' I waved, and Benedetta turned about and saw me, pressing a palm to her chest and pointing out to Marco where I stood. He directed the boat over to the walkway where I could alight and I ran back over the bridge to meet them, wondering what she had told him.

'Signora! I have looked everywhere for you!' Benedetta exclaimed, close to tears.

'What happened to you?' Marco said, 'We have been all over and could not find you.'

'I got lost. Terribly lost in the calle. It has taken me an age to find my way back!' I replied.

'You should not be about the city on your own!' Marco griped, an agitated hue in his cheeks. 'Do you know the worry you have caused us? We feared something dreadful had happened to you!'

'I feared the very same with some of the places I ventured to,' I added for effect and was pleased to see it elicited a softening in their expressions. 'I don't know how we lost each other. I tried to find you, Benedetta, but I ended up astray and did not know my way. If it were not for the directions of strangers, I would have never found my way back. I am sorry for worrying you. Both of you,' I pleaded, for I was sorry for that. It had been an act of desperation, not malice.

When we went into the house I was pleased to learn that they had not been back beforehand since Bendetta had gone directly to the gallery after losing me, and therefore, no one else in the house was aware of what had come to pass. Had I arrived but a couple of minutes later, I would have been too late to prevent it, for they were defeated, having searched at length, and after a final try to see if I could be found at home, they intended to raise the alarm and seek help in the endeavour.

On learning this, I took my chance to plead with both of them to hold my secret for fear I would not ever be permitted to leave the house again if Giles got word of my faux pas. Benedetta was easy to convince, no doubt on account that she did not want to be blamed for it any more than I wanted it known, but Marco was restless and reluctant.

'Maybe that shall not be such a bad thing if you cannot be trusted to stay close to your maid!'

I broke into tears. 'It was an accident, Marco. I got set apart from my maid in the crowds and could not find her. What else could I do? I do not know this maze of streets and I got lost. And for that, I am to be shut up like a prisoner!'

He paced anxiously, pressed his palm to his forehead, then swept it up towards the ceiling. 'Don't you see the danger you could have encountered? Anything could have happened to you—'

'And yet it did not. I am fine. Please, Marco, if he finds out, I shall not be permitted to church on Sundays, for my walks with your mama, or to your art classes I hope to convince him to agree to. My entire existence shall be confined within these walls, and I cannot bear such a meagre existence.'

There was a long silence before he looked up at me and said, 'Then you will promise not to venture out again on foot unless you are properly attended. If you are not with one of us, you shall have a manservant *and* a maid.'

'But I have no manservant, no means of travel other than my own two feet.'

'Then I shall make sure that you do. If you warn me in advance of your need, you shall have Giacomo and my gondola at your disposal.'

'Thank you, Marco. I am so very sorry for distressing you and Benedetta.—Do you think she will report me to Giles?'

He shook his head. 'You have her quite wrong, you know. It is not with your husband that her loyalty lies. She has been in tears for fear you had been harmed.'

'Yes, probably for fear of her position,' I said, thinking aloud. A mistake, I realised instantly as his expression grew despairing.

'You don't trust anyone, do you? You think everyone is as bad as him. Well, she is not, and neither am I. Is it really so impossible for you to think someone might actually care for you, even if you seem to have little care for yourself?'

'Forgive me, it was undeserved.'

I considered this long and hard as I brooded over how I would ever find a reliable means to attend my business for Signora Crivelli if I did not place my trust in her. I needed allies amongst the staff and none so much as her. So, I decided to test her this week while Giles was still abroad. I would begin with some small secrets and matters of little consequence to see if she could be relied upon. I would also need to consider some regular excuses for getting out. I still waited on Signora Barozzi's invitation and hoped there might be scope there, but until it came, there were only so many walks I could claim to need for exercise.

By evening, I had come up with a shortlist. I would start up a new interest in sightseeing and taking tours of city landmarks. That, after all, is what tourists like me came for, to see the sights and learn something of the history and culture. There could be thought nothing odd in that. Though until now, I had not bothered to do more than pay a passing glance, but that was about to change. It would be assumed to be on account of the return of my better spirits, which all seemed keen to encourage. Then, there would be an expansion of my religious activities. I would ask to go to confession on weekdays; not even Giles could dare to deny me that in a house of devout Catholics. Then Isabella was always undertaking some charitable efforts for the church, arranging the flower dressings and charitable donations of clothes and such. Perhaps it was time I joined her and widened my network. Then there was a female pastime I had long parted ways with, shopping for fashions and trifles. Where better to reconvene the habit than in a city of merchants. And finally, there was the art class and the new society that had acquainted me with amongst the ladies. I would consent to Marco speaking to Giles on my behalf. If it was anything like female society at home, once we become more familiar, there would be invitations to take up and calls to pay. And whilst not all of these activities would provide cover—for no doubt Isabella would attend some—it was my hope that if Giles and the family became more accustomed to my absences and coming and going as a matter of routine, then they were less likely to be suspicious of the times I was not where I professed to be. Less likely to question it with greater frequency. And so long as I took care to conduct the greater part of my outings when Giles was to work, then he would have no need to find complaint, particularly if he came to enjoy a more affable and complaisant welcome from his wife as his reward.

So the next day, I decided I would stay at home and send for Signora Sartore to visit me with the latest fashion catalogues to commission some new dresses and lighter silk cloaks for my new enterprise. Although this was not my only motive. I needed an anonymous way to pass messages between myself and Signora Crivelli, and I knew after our previous business dealings that so long as it was worth her while, she could be trusted to discretion. So I told her that if she agreed to the undertaking, she could rely on my ordering two of her finest dresses each and every month. It was an easy deal to broker, for her prices were as exorbitant as this new arrangement. By far, the gondolier would have been a low-cost means to make a go-between of, but it was too risky, and the coin would have to come from my own purse. This might be expensive, but only to Giles, and it was by far the superior arrangement, for not an eye would be batted at my receiving messages from my dressmaker.

I wasted no time and set her the first task of passing a message immediately to seek a time when I could visit Giulia for instruction before the week was out. I needed to make as much progress as I could before Giles came home at the weekend if I was to get ahead on my scheme. I also made up some harmless faux messages addressed to myself to test Benedetta.

And so Benedetta undertook her first commission in taking in the messages for me to see if she could be trusted, and it seemed that perhaps Marco had been right and I had got her wrong. Not in terms of her spying on me and reporting to Giles, but in her intentions. For she was a great deal more open with me than I had expected. She admitted that Giles had approached her when we first arrived, to remind her who would be paying her wages now and to bid she keep a close watch on me. She would be well rewarded for her vigilance, and he had proved generous in his veils. She had not minded the arrangement to begin with as it seemed borne out of grave concern for my health, my melancholy state, and echoed the family's concerns. But, as time went on and she saw more of us, together and apart, she had come to suspect that he was as much a contributor to my melancholy mood as anything else he attributed it to. She had noticed the change in me in his presence or in the aftermath of his coming to my chamber. She had even seen bruises and felt so distressed she had voiced this to Giles.—A mistake, of course, for he had told her plainly that if she dared mention this to anyone, he would see her out of a house and a job by the next day. Precisely what I would have expected of him, so I knew she spoke in earnest. After that, she'd retreated to her own judgement and would only report on my general state of health and answer direct questions about my activities in his absence. All of which had been non-eventful until recently. But she had learned to hold her tongue now. She did not tell him when she noticed the empty trunks my winter wardrobe had been kept in, but had been concerned about what she should say if he discovered it. She did not mention that she had noticed my comings and goings to Marco's studio, and I knew if she had reported anything of that nature to him, the consequences would have been swift and disastrous for us both. 'Thank you, Benedetta,' I told her. 'I should have trusted you, but you see, I have misplaced my trust so often that I am cautious now. It is because of misplaced trust that I am in this situation.'

She nodded, understanding. 'It is alright, Signora. You do not have to explain. I know you are fearful of him.'

'With good reason, I assure you. Listen, I do not want to compromise you. I understand you have been in the family a long time and I hope that bond will offer you protection beyond his power. But the truth is, he is a wicked and scheming man, Benedetta, though I know he shows such an example to very few, and takes pains to contrive a contrary impression on others. But it is the truth and I cannot pretend I can protect you from his wrath, though I would certainly speak up for your sake to the family if it should ever come to that. But, I suggest, for your sake and mine, that you continue to report on me in general and trifling matters so that he does not suspect you of conspiring with me.'

'As already I have been, Signora. I give him reports of insignificance. I think he has come to accept that to be normal at last.'

'Then that is a good thing because—and I shall repay your courtesy of openness now—I am about to embark on things of far greater significance and much higher risk. Things that, if he discovered, both you and I would know the full extent of his wrath. So, fair warning, Benedetta, it may be best for you to see if you can be assigned another role within the house or even look for a place elsewhere, for though I mean to be as careful as I can, I cannot promise you won't be compromised if I am discovered.'

'Then we must make sure you are not.'

I was pleased for confirmation that my missive had been conveyed when I was admitted to the bordello at Carampane with the expectation of my arrival. Signora Crivelli confirmed that the Bottega at *Procuratie Nuove* had sent a boy to bring the note, and she wanted to confirm that she was to address her messages to me via Signora Sartore at the same. I had no idea what arrangements Signora Sartore had put in place, nor what these "Bottegas" who seemed to be commissioned with the undertaking were. Still, I smiled serenely and nodded my confirmation, for whatever the arrangements were, they had succeeded.

When I found myself in the familiar little bedroom with Giulia, I had expected our lessons to be of a theoretical nature and had not come at all prepared for anything so practical. So when she announced that a patron was due to arrive in half an hour for the purposes of demonstration, I was more than a little thrown out of countenance.

'Giulia, I don't want to watch you have intercourse with this man. Surely you can just explain what must be done?'

'You will not be watching. You will be participating.'

'I don't have time.'

'Well, I suggest you make time, for matron never pushes the boat out like this for any of us, so you would do well to know when you are better off. Besides, she wants me to report to her how you do, and I cannot if I do not know.'

I was being tested then, the old lady was not foolish enough to take me at a pledge. 'Who is this patron?' I asked.

'His name is Andrea. He is perhaps approaching thirty and a fisherman by trade. He is a regular and by far one of the better of our patrons, so it will be an easy beginning.'

'What will I have to do?'

'I shall demonstrate, you shall then take over.'

I nodded, feeling that familiar creeping of dread I felt when I suspected Giles would come to my bed at night. I would *have* to move past this if I wanted a way out of my lot. 'Alright, but I am not at all prepared.'

'Well, let us begin there,' she said, gesturing to the washstand. 'You shall always wash between patrons, especially their spending's from you. Do you intend to use a sponge?'

I shrugged.

'Do you use anything with your husband? Signora says you are married.'

'What do you mean by use anything?'

'Anything to prevent a pregnancy?'

'Oh, no,' I said with interest, 'I did not know I could.'

'Well, there are things that can be tried, though there are no guarantees, and it is a risk we all suffer the burden of. But there are long-known ways to lower your chances, and they work more often than not. Heaven knows I should have had a brood by now if they were useless, and yet I have only one.'

'You have a child?'

She nodded. 'A daughter. She is three and the reason I persist in this unhappy life. I have no husband, and the father is unknown, though it would likely make no difference if he were. So, I am all she has to rely upon, that and the love and care of her nonna who looks after her when I am at work.'

'And you support them both?'

She nodded, and my heart wrenched for her.

'Anyway, we shall run out of time. Now, you can go with prevention or cure, or both if you have the wherewithal.'

'Both, I think.'

'Well, the easiest way, above all, is to try to have them withdraw at the penultimate moment; you can take them by hand or mouth for the last few seconds. But not all men will accept this, and you have two other preventative means if they won't. The first, and it may well succeed with the greener, younger men, is to trick them into using your thighs and not your cunt.'

'Really?' This sounded much more preferable.

'Yes, to the less experienced or less pushy, it can manage the task if you mimic it well enough. Now, let's clean up, and I shall show you.'

I watched as she proceeded by way of demonstration, mimicking her actions as she washed in soap flakes before she straddled and hovered above a separate bowl of steaming water, pouring a mixture of potash and mugwort into it. It smelt so caustic I was already uncertain about lowering myself above it as she did, but when she looked up at me and said, 'It stings a bit,' I was frightened to follow suit.

'Well, what are you waiting for? He will be here soon, and there is much to be done.'

I flinched at the sting as the acrid steam met my delicate folds.

'You shall grow used to it if you do not wish for a child to deal with. Anyway, we needn't linger now, for you are unsullied, and I have already taken a steam after the baker this morning. But it is after the act you shall need to stay here a good while longer. The soap and water to remove the free-falling spendings and the steam to reach the places you cannot.' She stood up from the bowl, blotted herself with a clean rag and stood in front of me, and I was faced with the level sight of her thickly curled pudenda.

I turned away.

'Give me your hand,' she demanded, reaching out with her own.

I baulked at this. It was one thing to remain indifferent to the opposite sex, but I was not sure how well I would fare in contact with my own. Annalise and our lovemaking was still so fresh at mind that I could not bear the idea of stirring up such sensations and memories, especially in so base a circumstance as this.

'Do you want to learn or not?'

I reached out, and she placed my wrist between her thighs, a whisper of hair ticking my forearm as she began to tense and squeeze her thighs vicelike around it.

'Do you feel it?' she asked, and I nodded. 'This is where you shall let him thrust his cock in exchange for your cunt, if you can either trick or persuade him.

'Right, your turn.' She released my arm and waited, expectant, as I dried myself and stood. 'Open up then,' she nudged between my thighs and I was relieved to find no stirring reminder of delight as I proceeded to grip her arm in the fashion she had mine. 'Good,' she declared, and I released her.

'Now, of course, the natural lubrication should be flowing by then, which helps too. You can even cross your ankles to make a better effort, though it depends on your position.—Talking of such, the next easiest way, at least once you have grown accustomed to it, is to let them take you by the arse instead. You can't get pregnant by it.'

'No!' I said instantly, the memory of Giles's assault on me at Beaulieu coming starkly to my mind from its buried archives. 'I shan't do that.'

'Well, some customers will likely ask for it, but suit yourself. Shall I show you how to douche in case you change your mind?'

'No,' I said flatly. 'I shall not.'

'Fine, let us move on to other tricks for when they insist upon your cunt. Sponges,' she picked one up from the washstand and held it out, 'soaked in vinegar and inserted as high up into the cunt as you can get it. There is a bit of an art to it at first. You know you have done it right when your patron is not even aware it's there. Mind, it is unlikely to work if you do not get it close to the cervix. Here, have a go. You can put it on before Andrea gets here.'

She went on to demonstrate this too, but it was impossible to see what dexterity it took to accomplish the task as soon as it disappeared inside her, and on my own failed attempts, I eventually had to succumb to her managing to place it for me in the end. Once it was done, I got back up off the bed and looked at the clock with a sense of foreboding, noting that we had little above five minutes left before this fisherman arrived. Had she not kept me distracted with so much talk, I might have fallen into a dreadful fit of panic and ran from the house that very moment.

'There is also one last thing that I don't profess to be familiar with first-hand, but under such circumstances as your being married, it might be wise for you to consider the use and cost of a guantone. Sponges, potash and mugwort might spare you a babe, but not the clap. Since I suspect you can afford the expense of greater safety and you likely don't want to be infected or to infect your husband, I would seriously consider my advice. And if you want one, I shall be able to tell you where to buy it.'

'What is it?'

'A sleeve that goes on the cock beforehand to protect you from making direct contact with his seed. Not that all patrons will be willing to wear one, though, and you should be careful to use it only with men you think are not overly religiously minded or high amongst those ranks. We are already thought unholy enough, but at the peril of such efforts to prevent a child, they draw the line. So you have the other ways now, all the same. Mind, to be on the safe side, you are not to conduct such things as I have shown you in front of your patrons, or leave evidence of them about, for the church takes vehemently against such affronts, and so you must always deny and denounce such practices. If there is no proof, your chances of evasion are much better.' At that, she rang for the servant girl and had her clear away the things we had used.

I wondered what on earth I was getting myself into with such words of foreboding before the gentleman had even arrived to defile us. But I said nothing, holding dearly to the thread of why I was here, what was at stake if I gave into my growing trepidation and failed to follow through—a *time-limited number of forced intimacies, or a lifetime of them.*

So when, some moments later, I was introduced to Andrea— a coarsely spoken but cordially mannered man of average looks, and I was particularly pleased to note, groomed to a reasonable standard—I tried to keep my focus level. It seemed extraordinary to me that I was about to lift my skirts to this perfect stranger and permit him such a liberty, and yet I reminded myself of the transactional nature of our union and that it was *that* which should simplify my willingness. It was not a love affair or romantic tryst I was trying to emulate here, nor was it under the duress of a husband I detested, but just as it had become with Giles, reduced to an act of bodily mechanics. I thought of Maillardet's automaton then and saw my own arms and hands forged from wound-copper coiling and polished wood, and told myself I was, as he; removed, automated.

I persuaded myself of this often as Giulia began to undress Andrea and play with his flaccid cock.

'Gently, to begin. Keep your touch light and tantalising,' she directed me as he stiffened and began to breathe a little heavier. Then she told me with her gaze that it was my turn to try. So I did, forcing my hand to replace hers and holding my expression and motion as steady as I could, which became trickier as he began to wriggle and grope at me as Giulia took off her clothes and then began to take off mine.

As I walked back towards Rialto to meet Benedetta at the vegetable market where we had agreed to reconvene, my thoughts ran in every direction. Surprise at my eventual indifference, disgust at what I had reduced myself to, relief at being able to push through with it, and something a bit like triumph at having earned my own money for the first time in my life. Not that I accepted my paltry share of it on this occasion. I did not want to take money that was needed to support a family of three anyway. Whilst I often felt my desperate need of money had grown into a matter of life and death at times, I still needn't worry for my roof or my bread, and nor did I have loved ones reliant upon me for it. Giulia's circumstances played on my mind often, and I realised, as she conducted the business with a routine attitude, that this *was* her lot. She was likely to be doing this for the entirety of her days, or at least until she could do it no more. Then what would become of her and her small family, I did not know. I was fortunate. I would eventually disappear from this place and this career when I had my fare, never to look back upon this low chapter in my life again. But to Giulia, it was a matter of course, day in and day out, and it saddened me to see the equanimity with which she bore it—the bleak acceptance of this in her casual speech.

But what else was she to do? She had no one to support her and not even the freedom from burdens to choose one of the few alternatives, such as the convent or a life of service, to break free of it. Neither would take her baby and her nonna, even if she were so minded and at least in this line, she could exercise some modicum of autonomy over her life and remain with her loved ones.

I wondered sometimes how womanhood could be such a dichotomy of marvel and curse. And yet I knew the answer, as always I had. Women were marvellous creatures, but it was men's fear of the fact that kept us bound beneath their boots. Lest that should ever alter, we might never know just how capable we might become, of just how capable we really were if ever given an even footing on which to take a stab at life. But it was by the by. Perhaps one day I might assume Leonard's character again to test the possibilities further; I would certainly need cover on the run again. But for now, I was to bear this path as best I could in the hope of getting off of it, and quickly.

So when I returned to the Bordello on Saturday to go with Signora Crivelli to look at a shortlist of rooms she had enquired after, I made my mind up that it would not only be she who shares a cut of my earnings, but Giulia too. A finder's fee of sorts, I considered. For it was her, above all the girls of the many houses I could have approached, that caught my eye in the doorway with her demure and sensible demeanour. It was she who showed me patience and kindness, and she who petitioned my cause to her matron. And so why should she not benefit too from her part in it? Ten per cent seemed fair to me, before Signora and I split the rest. Of course, that was not the way Signora Crivelli saw it to begin with, but a reminder that there was many a house I could apply to in place of hers was adequate to obtain her agreement, however resentfully. I was, of course, playing a dangerous game with Signora Crivelli. She was no pushover, and I was treading a fine line between leveraging her desire to use me as a springboard to a more lucrative retirement, and threatening the pride and authority she had long cultivated and was used to exercising over her charges.

But it was a risk I was willing to take, for I knew she would not have gone to the excess of effort that she had if she did not hold an honest belief in my proving worth all the investment. And when I viewed the rooms, I realised just what an investment she was making. These were not the shabby, paint-peeling, tired rooms of the bordello. No, these were entire floors of apartments, not wholly dissimilar to the one me and Giles occupied on the fourth floor of *Ca' Rosetti*. Yes, far more scantly furnished and with other residents occupying the other floors, but still, I could not imagine for a moment the rents would be insignificant, even in a city in decay.

We agreed upon one a stone's throw from the Grand Canal on account that it had the advantage of being closer to the *Hotel Gran Bretagne* and likely to be more appealing to the type of clientele she intended to attract. She was to order new linens for the bed and procure a manservant and a maid to tend me, then have a pamphlet printed to introduce the new and exclusive services of her "Rosa Inglese."

I, on the other hand, had only to figure out how to smuggle my new dresses from *Ca' Rosetti* to my new apartments, for they were to be cut too indecently low and made up so decadently, that it would be impossible to leave the house in them and not be suspect. I also visited the wig maker to have a complete wig made up in a colour not dissimilar to the red wine at the dinner table. If I was to build a reputation whilst retaining my anonymity, I must differentiate my two personas adequately enough for Giles not to put the two together. From what I could gather, there were not many English women in Venice, and I was certain less still in the same trade. The wars had not left my countrymen untarnished, but it was nothing to the ransack the Venetians had suffered. We were still deemed a wealthy and rank-retaining expatriate in a place where only the faded glory of a golden age still prevailed, like a gilded ghost. If word was to get out of the *Rosa Inglese,* or one of these pamphlets were to fall into the wrong hands, I risked recognition in the similarity of description. So reluctant as I was to encumber myself with such an expense as a new wig, particularly before I had even earned a single coin, I decided it was a sensible measure to take to preserve my anonymity. So I accepted Signora Crivelli's loan for the sum, and I would pay back as I earned, pushing my fare a little further back, but a delay I was willing to bear if it kept my cover.

Chapter Twenty-Five

All Rise.

Annalise. March 1822.

As Annalise contemplated the stuffy darkness of the holding cell, she dreamt of a heartening sip of freshly brewed black tea with just a little honey and a dash of milk. How long had it been since she had enjoyed the sweetness on her tongue, the warming heat of the liquid in her belly. She could not remember. Nor when she had last enjoyed anything warm at all, be it food, drink or fire. The broth and gruel were the only hot offering and they never arrived warm; by the time they were left on the hatch shelf, they were, at best, somewhere between lukewarm, and stone cold and congealed. But, she reminded herself as she stared into the gloom, despite the setback of Mr Truscott's examination, Giles may still not show. He had not thus far. And that it was every part possible that tonight, she might well be at liberty again and enjoy a fire and a pot of tea. Reinstate her plans and reclaim the life that had been stolen from her these past seven weeks. That was the *real* crime, on nothing more than a false claim she had been robbed of her freedom and all the possibilities that bestowed upon her.

Even if she walked free from the Court today, those precious weeks would never be restored to her, a period of time that might have allowed her to have already reached Venice by now. The trauma of such a dreadful ordeal would never be erased from her memory. Her only consolation was knowing that Mariella, too, had been subject to the same and had borne some of the cost of her own contrivance for a change. She might have enjoyed the luxury of clean clothes and smartness today, but she knew her time incarcerated had brought her every kind of misery owing to her foul attitude and smart mouth, which there was no place for in an establishment like this. She looked forward to the day she could retell the circumstance to her Len, when they were reunited again as she knew they must be.

She held on to that hope as she was released from her cell and led back to the Court and her place in the dock, praying that this would be the time things were set to rights and she could move on from this dreaded episode.

Mr Langley came directly to her as the courtroom was still filling up and said quietly for her hearing, 'We have some very good news, Miss Tullier. Two character witnesses have arrived for you just in the nick of time.'

'But who, Sir?' Annalise asked, bewildered, looking about the place to find them out, seeing no one to answer.

'A Miss Lockheart and Miss Gubbings.'

'What? she said, astonished. Poppy was not even supposed to know of her situation, not yet. Had Miss Lockheart gone against her instructions? There was no time to ask anything more for the Court was made to rise, and the session resumed as the Judge entered.

'Mr Truscott, is the primary prosecutor arrived yet?' was his first question.

'No, my Lord, but I have confirmation that the *Walsingham* arrived at Falmouth seven hours ago and must expect him any moment.'

The Judge raised his brows. 'Seven hours to drive from Falmouth to Bodmin, Sir, hmm, I would expect him by now.'

'Any moment indeed, my Lord, I am certain of it. If I may suggest that I read out to the Court Mr Craythorne's witness statement so that the trial may proceed without any further delay—'

Mr Langley stood up, 'I object, my Lord. The prosecutor is not present. Everyone else has managed to get themselves to Court on time today. Must we make exceptions for those who do not when there are numerous cases to be heard today?'

The Court fell into laughter again and Annalise began to wonder if her barrister was more showman than legal man. In any case, it seemed to win him favour with all but the Judge.

'Overruled. We shall permit Mr Craythorne the benefit of the hour given the breadth of his journey. Mr Truscott, it is now one forty-five. I shall give him until two o'clock, no more.'

'Thank you, my Lord...I read to you now the statement made by Giles Craythorne on the third day of February 1822, the morning of his departure from Falmouth.'

'Objection!'

'What is it now, Mr Langley?'

'Mr Truscott has not stated if this is a sworn statement taken by the Magistrate when the complaint was made.'

'It is not a sworn statement, my Lord', answered Mr Truscott, irritated.

'Not a sworn statement, made upon oath and honour, Sir?' repeated Mr Langley. 'Then of what use is it to this Court, pray? It is no more than a letter any of us here could write and enter into evidence if the mood shall take us?'

'Mr Langley, I ought to remind you that this is my Court. Jury, you may hear it, and the prosecutor shall be asked to swear by it when he arrives.'

Mr Langley sat back down and Annalise listened carefully as the statement was read out by Mr Truscott in a style of great theatrics that seemed to affect the jury and gallery alike with various hisses and sighs at one point or another elicited from them in response. It had been every part the fiction she had expected it to be, sometimes employing the subtlest of twisting of events and, at others, shocking absurdities of truth, always, of course, painting himself in a respectable light she knew never shone on him, and casting her character into the shade of a wanton cretin.—Perhaps it was just as well Miss Lockheart had subverted her decision and come anyway to speak for her, for if it was left to this damning obloquy then she would certainly be looked ill upon by those who knew no better of her. She knew that any scrap of good character she might have hoped to salvage from this litany would be quickly diminished as soon as he read out the passage about her setting fire to the Royal Hotel. – That she was not on trial over that matter would be of no consequence now the idea had been seeded in the minds of the men who were about to pass judgment over her. Who were such men of middling and merchant sorts to bestow the benefit of the doubt to, a man of like standing, a hotelier who was painted as having a rampant villain set loose upon his respectable establishment, or a maidservant like her?

For the first time, she began to seriously contemplate the fate that awaited her. It had been easy to keep the dread at arm's length like a lurking shadow that never quite caught up with her but never left her side. When she was first apprehended, she was still in shock at Eleanor's departure, which had not even ceased before the shock of her imprisonment was laid before her. It had taken weeks for even those matters to feel tangible and not some surreal imagining, some fantastic nightmare. Then, when she had finally sobered from this stunned existence, Ninette had come, and she was so distracted by all the madness and misery of her afflictions that she had little private time to seriously ponder her own.

But now, standing here with the heat of so many assessing gazes levelled at her, trying to stop her irons clanging as her hands trembled, she suddenly saw it in all its horror. The juror with the long beard and greying hair would stand up and pronounce her guilty and her life would not be her own anymore, may not even be long in existence.

'Thank you, Mr Truscott,' said the Judge when he was finished. 'I remind the jury that until our prosecutor arrives to swear to the events you have just heard, you shall hold such matters lightly. He has but ten minutes left, Mr Truscott. Have you anyone else to call in the interim?'

'I do not, my Lord.'

'Mr Langley?'

'I call Miss Lockheart, my Lord.'

And suddenly, there she was, coming through the door and led to the box by an officer of the Court. The familiar sight of her caught Annalise's breath. It was the sight of home and a life she had left behind, a life she no longer felt anchored to. And yet, there she was, her best Sunday clothes pressed neat, her kind smile of recognition at the sight of her. She felt a tear drop at the sight of this warm smile as she returned it.

She was now sworn in and Mr Langley rose and stepped forth towards her.

'Miss Lockheart, thank you for coming today. I know it has been an arduous journey for you to make, all the way from Surrey, some two hundred and eighty miles from here, and yet you are on time.'

Laughter rose and fell in the Courtroom.

'Thank you, Sir. I would have made thrice the journey to speak to the character of Miss Tullier, for she is a worthy soul to take the trouble for.'

This was met with surprise and interest from the onlookers.

'High praise indeed and not the trouble one would expect a respectable woman like yourself to take for a thief or troublemaker, I would suggest?'

'No, Sir, I know Miss Tullier to be incapable of such villainy, and if I thought it otherwise, I should not have come. I have come today in the hope that a terrible injustice does not befall this kind and Christian woman.'

'Miss Lockheart, you are, as you say, here to speak of the defendant's character. Can you begin by telling me something of yourself and how you know the defendant?'

'Yes. I am Lillian Lockheart. I live in Ewell in Surrey where Miss Tullier once lived. I am daughter of the Rector in that village and reading teacher to the parish poor. I first came to know Miss Tullier by her weekly attendance at church when she was but a child. I knew her late mother well; she was Housekeeper at a local gentleman's household and assisted in teaching children from time to time.'

'The accused mother was a learned woman?'

'A consequence of her former class, she was very well educated, Sir, as is her daughter, taught by her mama in both moral sense and women's educational pursuits. We enjoyed a congenial acquaintance up until her sad and premature death over a year ago.'

'Thank you. Can you speak to Miss Tullier's character?'

'I can indeed. I have known her since her childhood but have come to know her more intimately since the passing of her mama. She is all you will find proper and good in a soul and far above her years in wisdom and sense. She nursed her mama in her illness until her last days with such selfless devotion whilst undertaking all the duties of her station. Despite how this kept her busy, she always found a half hour to go along to the poor district and offer alms. She is renowned in our small village as a person of very charitable heart and most kindly regarded. And of late, she extended this generosity when she inherited a sum and brought a dwelling shop with which she has permitted her friends to move into, rent-free, and set them up with the beginnings of a fine baking establishment. She now employs two of the children of the poorest houses in our village as apprentices to provide them with a trade and the opportunity for honest work. I own, I do not know of the circumstances which have led to such unconscionable accusations against her, for she has been away in the service to her Lady these past months, but I do know that it is impossible they could be true. Anyone who knows her would say the same. She is of honest character and good moral sense, and whatever has come to pass, there has been a dreadful mistake of some sort. She has already been much missed these past months, but to lengthen her absence under such a misapprehension will injure a great many with whom may call her friend and benefactor, as well as permit a gross injustice.'

'Thank you, Miss Lockheart. Unless Mr Truscott has any questions for the witness, I call Miss Gubbings.'

Mr Truscott waved his hand, indicating that he did not. How could he, she supposed, when they were wholly unconnected with the sham?

If Miss Lockhart's speech had not already moved her to tears, the sight of her dear Poppy was the final frontier. She smiled through them as they fell thickly, and wiped them away with a handkerchief Mr Langley had given her on one of his visits. She dabbed gently beneath her eyes as Poppy was sworn in.

'Miss Gubbings, you too are here to give testimony to Miss Tulliers' character. Can you tell the Court something about yourself and your relationship to the accused?'

'Aye, I can, Sir. I am Poppy Gubbings, Annalise's friend of nigh on twelve years or thereabouts. I run the pie shop and live within Annalise's dwelling shop in Carshalton at her expense. Before that, we were servants together in the great house at Cuddington for the Ashlyn's, and before that, at the gentleman's house in Ewell.'

'So an extensive history and one, I am sure, positions you to know the accused most intimately and reliably?'

'I do. She is the best friend a person could 'ave and should not be in that box,' she said, breaking into tears and clutching for her handkerchief now.

'Take a moment if you will, Miss Gubbings. I realise it must be most distressing to see your good friend so wrongfully circumstanced—'

'Objection.' Mr Truscott stood. 'My learned friend is addressing the jury, my Lord, and not questioning the witness.'

'Mr Langley, keep to your questions. Miss Gubbings, will you continue?'

'I will milord. Sorry milord.'

'Miss Gubbings, have you ever known the accused to be in the habit of stealing or other such behaviour?'

'No, never!'

'And yet, your years in service together would no doubt have given her access to a great many valuable things.'

'Yes! 'specially in the grand house at Cuddington for Lord Henry. A very fine estate, and she 'ad access to the lot, for she was promoted to Lady's maid within months of her employ as her conduct was so much esteemed by her Lady.'

'So, she could have stolen things of great value had she been in such a head and yet, I suspect, no such accusations were ever made since she continued in her Lady's service until her apprehension in February.'

'Never, she'd not steal a crust of bread if she were starving, I tell yer. It's not in her heart. She always gives more than she ever asks of anyone, even her Lady. She went over and above what most of us would think reasonable of a servant, answering to her every whim, abandoning her home at her request to attend her on her travels, even though it broke her heart to have to leave us for a time. Poppy, she said to me, I must go, my Lady needs me, and it is my duty. I will come back...' she trailed into another sob.

'About her Lady. You refer to Mrs Craythorne, lately wed?'

Poppy nodded.

'Did you, yourself, know Mrs Craythorne?'

'I did. Not well. But I knew her as one of the family in the great house before she married and a little better when she returned.'

'Would you describe her as suffering any nervous or mad episodes?'

'No, Sir. Not as far as I ever knew, and you come to know a lot within a house, and I 'ave never heard it said so.'

'And you say she returned to the family home after she was wed?'

'Aye. She moved back into the house shortly after she wed.'

'Why was that?'

'I don't know the whole, Sir, and I'm not one for gossip. But it was said to be a very bad match. The Craythornes were thought of as being very low and not altogether respectable. The man she married was thought a coarse and unpleasant sort, I believe.'

'The kind of brute who might kidnap and spirit off his wife on a ship—'

'Objection. Whose character is the witness to answer for, the prisoners or Mr Craythornes?' put in Mr Truscott.

'I shall rephrase the question. Miss Gubbings, you say that Miss Tullier was a devoted servant. If her mistress was to have fallen into difficulty or suffered cruel treatment, would Miss Tullier remain loyal in the face of it, in your opinion?'

'Yes. No doubt that's what's landed her in this mess! I told her not to be ill-used and drawn into the marital troubles, but she said she was needed and could not abandon her.'

'And what do you make of the likelihood of the accused stealing or taking advantage of a mistress she had only ever been loyal to.'

'Impossible. It's not in her heart to be so wicked.'

'And finally, Miss Gubbings, if Miss Tullier had written back to you with a request for money, having found herself suddenly and unexpectedly stranded and in financial difficulty, would she have been in likely expectation that you could meet the request and send forward the money she needed?'

'She could indeed! She knows it. For it was only a few months ago she paid us a visit and I forced two pounds into her luncheon parcel, a share of the profits from the shop. She would not take it when offered, said she did not need it. But it wasn't right. She should 'ave her share since it is all thanks to her that we 'ave enjoyed such good fortune.'

'And the business continues to bring good fortune?'

'It does very well, better than before. I 'ave twelve pounds put by in a jar for her share-taking when she comes home. I would 'ave sent it right away if I had known she needed it.'

'You could not know Miss Gubbings, for she was apprehended the very day of writing to you to make such a request. A request she would need not have made at all if she had at her disposal jewels worth circa eighty-five pounds to dispose of.'

'Objection. My learned friend makes a case to the jury and does not examine the witness.'

'I withdraw, my Lord. No further questions for the witness.'

'Mr Truscott, it is now ten past the hour. Has Mr Craythorne yet arrived?'

He exchanged whispers with a gentleman beside him then turned and said, 'I fear he has not yet arrived.'

'Call for him, usher,' indicated the Judge, to which he did immediately, but no one answered.

'Mr Truscott, I shall grant no further requests for patience. Your witness has been called for the third and final time and has failed to appear. As the witness, in this instance, is also the prosecutor in the case of the Sapphire pendant, I am left with no choice but to acquit the defendant on the first count of charges brought against her on the grounds of the prosecutor not being present.'

'My Lord, I –'

'That is my decision, Mr Truscott. Do not interrupt me. You have stretched the bounds of my patience and the demands of this Court quite enough already.'

'Forgive me, my Lord.'

'Miss Tullier, for the purpose of clarity, the charges against you for the theft of one sapphire pendant, valued at eighty-five pounds, no longer stand. Jury, you need no longer deliberate on that matter. On the second count of the theft of the pearls, we shall continue to hear. Do you understand?'

'Yes, my Lord,' Annalise replied, feeling dizzy with the relief of this alteration. Deep down, she knew he would never come. He would be too busy guarding Eleanor like a hound dog. But she supposed, for the briefest time today, with all the trickery and bluff of Mariella and Mr Truscott in construing the expectation of his arrival, she had begun to fear that perhaps she had been wrong and he really was due in upon a ship this morning with a view to heading directly to the Court. But now, it mattered not whether it was as she had suspected, or whether he turned up this instant. It was too late. And whilst this alone did not confer her freedom, and in fact, she still faced a penalty equally as severe in the case of the pearls, now, she could at least feel at ease with the greater justice of the matter. She had not stolen the pendant, and now she would not be punished for a crime she had not committed. There felt a sense of fairness in that. In the case of the pearls, she hoped her better luck might continue, but knew deep down that if she were punished for it, it would at least be a truth and not merely the contrived result of the Craythornes scheming.

'Counsel, have you any further witnesses to call?'

Mr Truscott shook his head.

'I have one more, my Lord,' said Mr Langley. 'I call Miss Trent.'

She was called three times without answer before the Judge said, 'Right, then all the witnesses have been heard save the defendant?'

'My Lord, I humbly request the same courtesy is afforded of waiting a little time for the witness to arrive. I have a number of sworn characters and statements I can read out in the interim.'

'I daresay, but this case has cost us enough time already today, Mr Langley.'

'My Lord, the witness is important. She is a laundress at the hotel where the jewels were said to be discovered and saw persons' unknown going into the accused's room at the very time before the discovery of them.'

'And why is that relevant?'

'Because, my Lord, it proves, as is my client's defence, that the items discovered there were not taken by her but were planted there to set her up. Persons going into the room but moments before the search is undertaken, who had the opportunity to plant them, and who cannot be recognised as the hotel's staff.'

'Ten minutes, Mr Langley, no more. You may read what you can in that time and we shall hear from the accused if she means to speak, before the jury deliberate.'

'Thank you humbly, my Lord.' Mr Langley shuffled through some papers in his leather satchel and settled upon those of interest. 'I read to you now a sworn statement made upon oath and signed in the witness of Mr Treleven, Magistrate of Falmouth, made by Mr Carne, Mayor of Falmouth, who apprehended the accused and Miss Craythorne on Third February 1822. I, Mr Peter John Carne, Mayor and acting Sheriff of Falmouth, offer a statement of the prisoner's good conduct. My watchman called me to attend the Hotel in Falmouth on Third February 1822, at the request of a Miss Mariella Craythorne, who awaited my arrival and furnished me with allegations of theft, the details of which are recorded in my report to the Magistrate of the interviews conducted and evidence seized. Details of which can be found therein. On request of Mr Langley, counsel for the accused, I make an honest appraisal of my knowledge of the prisoner's conduct during her time of interview, arrest, and incarceration at the Falmouth Gaol House. Miss Tullier was called down from her chamber at my request at approximately three o'clock. She presented herself in fine manner and willingly participated in the interview, seeming not to understand the cause of the occasion. She was met with great hostility and provocation from her accuser, Miss Craythorne, who attacked her verbally and physically, in my presence, unprovoked. Despite this, Miss Tullier conducted herself throughout with great civility and patience. My report from the gaoler was the same, with her conduct being peaceful and obliging throughout the three days she was held there. This is the limit of my knowledge of the prisoner's character. Signed, Mr Carne, Mayor, witnessed by Mr Treleven, Magistrate.'

'Pass it over, Mr Langley,' the Judge requested. 'Have you any response, Mr Truscott?'

'Yes, my Lord, I point out that Miss Craythorne had just been the victim of crime at the hands of the prisoner and recently subjected to a violent attack from the prisoner's mistress. Is it not the likely case that any one of us would be in high anxiety to have such valuable things stolen and be faced with the guilty party? Indeed, anyone may fall foul of high emotions on such an occasion.'

'That may be so, but most of us would not consider violence, and in the face of the authorities, I would suggest to my learned friend,' offered Mr Langley, and the Court offered a titter of agreement.

He proceeded then to read out the other characters to the Court, next Lady W.'s, then Mr Harrison's. After which, the Judge declared he felt the Court adequately had the measure of Miss Tullier's character and that we had exceeded the ten minutes already.

Mr Langley gave Annalise a reassuring smile which she took as meaning it had all gone well.

'Usher, call Miss Trent for the final time,' the Judge directed. No answer came. 'Right, that shall be all. Now, Miss Tullier, do you mean to speak to your charge or address the jury?'

'I do, my Lord.'

'You consent to be examined?'

Mr Langley shook his head to indicate she should not, but she had already fixed her mind on having her say. She would not add to the notion of her guilt by remaining silent. 'I do, my Lord,' she answered, refusing to meet Mr Langley's eyes.

'Very well. Mr Truscott, your witness.'

'Miss Tullier, the Court has heard today, much to sing your praises and much indeed to your credit, that cannot be denied. However, these persons have not been closely connected with you for some months and perhaps had not understood the desperate circumstances you found yourself in of late, being let go of your employ and stranded in a place so far from home.'

'That is true, Sir.'

'Is it not also true, Miss Tullier, that when in such desperate circumstances, one might be inclined towards irregular behaviours, ones that may not, in ordinary circumstances, befall a character such as yours, but, in the panic and desperation of such a calamity as being cast out of your employ, may induce one into thoughts and actions not normally conceived of?'

'Objection. That is not a relevant question, my Lord.'

'I rephrase the question. Miss Tullier, have you, of late, found yourself in circumstances dire enough to alter your usual behaviour? Has it not been a very eventful and difficult time for you?'

'It has, Sir, and I do not deny that I have been out of sorts, but enough to commit these acts I have been falsely accused of? No,' she said, unconvinced of her own speech as her eyes travelled to the pile of marquetry pearls on the table.

'You are described as having great loyalty to your former mistress. I ask you, does that loyalty extend to encouraging and assisting her in attempting to disobey her husband? Escape from him?'

'She needed no encouragement, Sir, he was most cruel and tormenting to her, that's why she left him.'

He scanned a piece of paper as he spoke, 'Did you not tell the Magistrate and Mr Carne, in your interview with him, that you staged a fire in your hotel room to create a diversion in which you might both escape?'

'I did, Sir. But please understand that the fire was not serious in the least. It did not and was not intended to harm, only to distract momentarily. It was contained within a bucket with a jug of water beside it to put it out. It was only smoking within, and it was told to me after that no real harm had been done. —I do not say it was the right thing to do, but we had by then been held captive for a week, and he would not let us go. What choice did we have?'

The gallery broke out in gasps of surprise and Mr Truscott permitted adequate pause to let the effect be felt before he continued.

'Was it not Mr Craythorne who relieved you of the charges and settled the sum for damages suffered by Mr Wynn's Hotel?'

'Yes, under ultimatum that if my mistress did not return with him of her accord, she would be incarcerated in the madhouse at Bodmin, and I be given over to the constable for Arson. She agreed to travel with him in exchange.'

'An odd embellishment to the tale of a man who went out of his way, and his purse, to see you a free woman and not a prisoner at his majesty's pleasure? Yet you would lead this Court to believe that he and his cousin have contrived to have you falsely accused now? What possible reason would he have to arrange such a circumstance when you so willingly offered such an easy opportunity if what you claim is true?'

'I do not pretend to understand the workings of such a mind bereft of decency. Perhaps it was a worthy price to gain his wife's consent or a vindictive afterthought. But it is, as I told you before. It was not done out of any sense of goodwill but as a bargaining chip to induce my mistress to go with him.'

'To induce his own wife, whom he had as much right as every man sat in this room to enjoy the comfort and society of her person, to go with him?'

'Yes. She required such inducement after all she had suffered at his hands, as you heard for yourself in Lady W.'s statement.'

'Miss Tullier, is it fair to say that you dislike your master, Mr Craythorne?'

'He was not my master, Sir. I was employed directly by my mistress.'

'A mistress that did not pay you these past? How many months?'

'I don't rightly recall, Sir, but she did much for me and would have paid me in due course had we not been kidnapped by Mr Craythorne.'

'Kidnapped? You suggest Mr Craythorne kidnapped his own wife?'

'And me, and another woman he let go eventually, once one of his violent brutes had menaced her and left her with a split cheek.'

'It almost sounds like a story from a novel, Miss Tullier. It grows more gruesome and outlandish by the moment! But then the Court has heard you had the benefit of an education and are, perhaps then, familiar with such fantastic novels.'

Laughter in the Court.

'A horror story was precisely how it felt to us both, Sir! Locked up and rattled about in the coach for days, not knowing where we were or where we were to be taken, and for what purpose—'

'And if that is what you believe to have been occurring, I am certain this would cause you to feel anger towards Mr Craythorne?'

'Of course. Any person of decent sense would feel revolted by such treatment of any person, more so his own wife, his pregnant wife.'

'Angry enough to steal his property, Miss Tullier, in the panic of the ship's imminent departure, in the hope of contriving another escape for you and your mistress, perhaps?'

'Objection. The property of Mr Craythorne is no longer a concern of this Court,' Mr Langley said, but she would not meet his eyes, though she felt their flame upon her.

'Sustained. Mr Truscott, withdraw the question. Jury, disregard that line.'

'Withdrawn, my Lord. Miss Tullier, I put it to you, that you were driven to steal property to raise funds to hatch another escape like the one you had attempted previously. That you did not have time to write to your friends for assistance with the imminent departure of the sailing, and so, in your desperation, perhaps quite without thinking and being in your usual sense and reason, you saw the property in the room at the lodging house that night when your mistress attacked Miss Craythorne, and saw an opportunity. In that moment of distraction when all eyes, except for yours, were focused on breaking up the attack and tending to Miss Craythorne's injuries, you sought your opportunity to take the valuable items, knowing no one should notice in the chaos of it all. Hoping that in the night, you and your mistress might have the means to make off yet again! Is that the way of it?'

'No, Sir! That is not true. I swear I took nothing from the room. I did not even see the items in the room, even if I had been of such a mind, which I was not.'

'Would you have not done *anything* to protect your mistress, your loyalty being what has been so much spoken of in credit to you?'

'Yes! I did my utmost to help her, but alas, it was not enough. But I did not steal from the Craythornes!'

'I put it to you that you did do so. That there were no limits to what you would do for your mistress, mad as she might be, for your affection for her was not at all in the ordinary way, was it, Miss Tullier?'

The Court inhaled in astonishment.

'Objection!'

'Sustained, clarify your point, Mr Truscott.'

'I put it to Miss Tullier that her affections for her mistress were not of a natural order. That in her mistress's insanity and her own foolishness, they were of a mad-brained notion to be in love with one another.'

More gasps and disgusted shakes of the head from the gallery and even the jurors now.

'Is that, or is that not, the case Miss Tullier? Did you harbour fancy and feelings for your mistress that directed you to these out-of-character, foolish and villainous ways? Causing you to depart from your usual sense and reason?'

'You will answer the question, Miss Tullier,' directed the Judge when she said nothing in reply.

'I did love her! I do love her! But I did not steal from the Craythornes.'

There was now such a raucous in the courtroom that the sound of her own sobbing did not drown it out. Even when the Judge slammed his gavel fiercely and finally called the Court to order, she did not notice it until Mr Langley came upon her and placed a glass of water into her trembling hands. 'Collect yourself,' he whispered, '...you must continue with me if I am to have any hope of salvaging this.'

'I have no further questions for the witness, my Lord.' Mr Truscott took his seat at the table, his expression triumphant as he took in the effect of his mastery.

'Mr Langley?'

'Yes, my Lord. Miss Tullier, I know you are distressed by Mr Truscott's provocative line of questioning. I remind you that your private affairs are not on trial, nor would any such matter be a concern of the Court or the law, even if it were true. The matter before us today, the *only* matter, is the alleged theft of Miss Craythones' property. Will you tell the Court if you are guilty of it?'

Annalise dabbed at her cheeks and cleared her throat. 'I am not, Sir.'

'Thank you. Perhaps you might offer an explanation as to your own account of events surrounding the discovery of the jewels in your belongings.'

She nodded. 'I believe the things were planted there.'

'Out of fear that you would return home to tell the whole of what had passed in your direct witness and the Craythornes would be scandalised?'

'Yes, Sir.'

'And when do you believe the planting of these items to have taken place?'

'There are two possibilities; one is when my luggage was taken on board the ship and unattended by me when we were first admitted onto it. Mr Craythorne directed me to keep up the appearance that I was to travel on with them or risk another episode of alarm that would likely induce him to commit my mistress to the madhouse should such an event occur. I did not want to, but nor did I want her to be incarcerated. She was not mad. She only did not wish to go with him. I agreed to go on board with them and settle her, and when I was diverted off of the ship just prior to its leaving, Mr Craythorne's valet gathered my luggage and threw it at my feet.'

'So there was time and opportunity enough for someone to interfere with your luggage without your knowing?'

'There was, Sir.'

'And the other occasion, I believe, was at the hotel where you were apprehended?'

'It was. I was called down to speak to the Mayor and my things were in my room. I had not yet unpacked them so I cannot say whether they were already put there at that moment. But when I was asked if I had any objection to the search of them, I had none, and readily agreed.'

'Because you had no reasonable expectation that anything would be discovered?'

'Yes, I knew it was false, so I had no objection to proving my innocence.'

'You were surprised then when the watchman returned with the jewels?'

'I was astonished. So much so that I asked the Mayor to make enquiries of the staff should someone have been bribed to place them there in my absence. He did as bid and told me and the Magistrate the next morning that there were witnesses who had seen the comings and goings of persons in the room at the very time I had been downstairs in my interview with him. That they were not members of the hotel staff.'

'Indeed, as corroborated by our absent witnesses account, a laundress who had seen such persons.'

'Objection.'

'Sustained, Mr Langley, you do not speak for an absent witness. Move on, and swiftly if you please.'

'Of course, my Lord. So, there were at least two separate occasions you can attest to, presenting ample opportunity to plant these alleged stolen items into your property?'

'Yes.'

'And tell me, did the watchman present the items to you on their discovery?'

'He did.'

'The pearls were shown?'

'Yes.'

'And Miss Craythorne saw them?'

'She did.'

'And did she claim them to be her stolen property?'

'She did not.'

'When did she make this claim?'

'The following morning when the Magistrate interviewed us.'

'Straight away?'

'No. It was after the Mayor and Magistrate expressed some difficulty with the prosecutor, Mr Craythorne, not being present to answer his accusations. It was discussed that there could be a difficulty in securing a conviction if Mr Craythorne was abroad.'

'Indeed, a case of prosecutor not present, just as it has been shown to be the case today. So what happened next?'

'There was a lengthy debate betwixt the Magistrate and the Mayor and whether or not he must recommend the case to trial or to dismiss it on grounds of no prosecutor. It was then Miss Craythorne claimed the pearls to be her property.'

Another round of gasps broke out.

'Indeed. Fearing her scheme was about to fail, Miss Craythorne falsely claimed the pearls on realising they had overlooked this important detail in their hurried scheming, and hoping to rectify it, and succeeding in doing so and making a mockery of you, and of the Court, and of justice itself. Likely the faux pearls were mistakenly left in the room by the previous guest which is why neither you or Miss Craythorne recognised them. But not wanting to let an opportunity go astray. she turned this to her cause at the last. And there we reach the crux of this entire case, a claim that is nothing more than a vindictive and malicious prosecution—'

'Objection!'

'Mr Langley!' the Judge thundered.

'No further questions, my Lord.'

'Right, this matter has taken up enough of the morning. Miss Tullier, have you anything to say in your defence?'

'Nothing I have not already said, my Lord. I am not guilty. That is the honest truth.'

'Jury, you shall confer and return a verdict forthwith.'

They huddled in together and whispers were heated and hurried.

Annalise felt her pulse throb beneath her ear as she watched them leaning in and exchanging words too quiet to fathom. It was perhaps only minutes but felt like hours before the Judge interrupted them and asked, 'Have the Jury arrived at a verdict?'

'We have not, my Lord. The jury cannot agree.'

'By gad! Then the jury shall retire to make a decision and shall not return until they do!' the Judge almost shouted and then rose. 'Bring in a new jury for the next case, Mr Thomas. We shall hear that whilst we await the return of this one.

Before Annalise was led back to her cell, Mr Langley came to her in the corridor. 'What on earth was that?' he demanded. 'I told you not to consent to the examination. Only to a brief address to the jury!'

'I know. I should have heeded you.'

'Indeed you should. We were heading for a victory. Now we must both pray for a miracle!' he sighed, and then she was taken back to the cell.

CHAPTER TWENTY-SIX

The Launch of the Rosa Inglese.

Eleanor. July 1822 (One Month Later).

Presenting the Rosa Inglese.

An educated lady of distinction. Red hair and creamy pale skin adorn this rare beauty of eloquence and fine manner. Fair of face and form, you shall find no other like her in Venice. Versed in English, French, and Italian with an informed appreciation of music and the arts, she now makes her Venetian debut and invites a select few to come into her acquaintance. She occupies comfortable apartments close to the Hotel Gran Bretagne.

Exclusively by approved appointment only. 150 Lire shall admit you to her chamber if your manner pleases her.
Go between – Signora Crivelli.

My career had not launched as quickly or profitably as either Signora Crivelli or I, had hoped. In the first fortnight of the pamphlet's circulation nothing at all came about from it and it seemed destined for failure. Had Signora Crivelli not been bound by the rental agreement on the apartment, I think even she would have given in to my suggestion that I work in the bordello for now and try to earn *something*. The mystery of an exotic unknown Courtesan had served not to pique interest and create a climate of allure as predicted, but had proved too mysterious for anyone to seek me out at all. It was likely not helped by Signora Crivelli's association with low houses. I knew the rigidity of class structure well enough to discern that a climber like Signora Crivelli could be spotted a mile off from such ranks. They would not take her word on it just because she claimed to have charge of a rare beauty of distinction or circulated a pretty pamphlet. She would have to show them at least a preview of her goods if she hoped to gain their interest or custom.

It was in this head I decided to take action of my own accord. She might have been the authority in this profession, but I was the greater authority on class conventions, and whilst I was not a Venetian, and although redundant now, I knew its Patrician class structure to be a rigid one. If we wanted to bait the plump-pocketed gentlemen of this city, we would have to invest a little more and be seen in the right places.

So, with a little more persuasion and perhaps desperation on even her part now, I concocted a scheme to get us under the right noses.

I had heard it discussed over dinner one evening that there was to be a private ball given at the La Fenice Opera House and that the Harpers had not been invited and were somewhat put out by being so shunned. They were known to the hosts and had, before the fall of the Republic, enjoyed good terms with them. But there had been great political divides since then, ones that I knew not enough of the backstory to discern the extent of, but gleaned sufficient to understand that their political preferences for Austrian rule had put them out of favour with these Bonapartist supporters who had taken offence to the lifting of the Mincio Barrier, where the Harpers had supported it. The bottom line being, that they would not be found on this particular guest list. It was precisely the opportunity I needed, somewhere highbrow enough to be seen by the right people, but safe enough not to be discovered by any of the family. The only obstacle now, was how to get myself onto the guest list.

It was not as difficult as I expected once I had set Signora Crivelli to the task of finding out who were the gentleman most likely to be in attendance. She had to make some enquiries of her own in this regard, but once she had fixed her mind to the matter, she came up with a preliminary list based first on sound logic. There would, of course, be the ambassadors to be relied upon, and the former high-level administrators remaining from the Bonapartist former regime. Then, from there, she thought about the associations she knew them to keep, some by way of repute and some by more intimate *on dits* that fell through the grapevine of her network of industry matrons.

So we compiled a shortlist of those known to be of a likely political persuasion and who, of them, had reputations for keeping courtesans, which was the greater majority, leaving Signor Crivelli the somewhat easier task of using her contacts to seek my introduction to one their courtesans. It was an expensive endeavour, though, not only in terms of the fee extracted from Signora for the privilege, but also the number of favours she had to call in to execute such a haughty introduction.

'The good thing,' she told me when we were puzzling over how to overcome the rank divide between us and the higher courtesans, '...was that everyone had to begin *somewhere* in this trade', and not all the higher courtesans had started out so lofty as they had since been exalted. There was one such named Rachele Tanto, who had started as a low Meretrice at the Rialto, but had been accepted into Matron Beppo's house and enjoyed the good fortune of being accidentally discovered by Lord Byron one evening on his way back home from *Café Florian* a few years ago. A temporary spell in his society had been adequate to raise her to the interests of higher ranking gentleman, and she was currently paying attendance on the former Governor of Venetia. But since she had once been in Matron Beppo's house, there remained a fragile thread upon which could be tugged to make contact, if only Signor Crivelli could humble herself to petition her arch-enemy for the purpose. A prospect she found more difficult to sacrifice than the sum demanded to render her the introduction once it was finally granted, and it was, for all favours had a price in this world, not only of the intimate kind.

And so, before I had earned so much as a penny, I was now indebted with not only the expense of the wig, but now my half of the portion of Matron Beppo's bribe. It was hardly how I meant to begin, saddled with debt.

I was given leave to go directly to Tanto's apartment in San Marco on the night of the ball. I was to be her plus one and receive her introduction into society by way of attendance upon her. We were to travel to and from together, and there her obligation ceased, and my fate was decided, one way or the other. And so I made my best efforts to present myself with the right balance of allure and distinction, a task once effortlessly routine but now a greater test of discernment. But as I lifted my masque to check myself in the glass one more time before I left the apartment for Tanto's, I was satisfied I had not lost my touch. A recognition I noticed in her reception of me when I arrived in the sumptuous palazzo she occupied, hung with every example of fine tapestry and extravagant brocade, as though in this small quarter of Venice, there had been no plunder at all.

She was perhaps a few years my senior, a slight and slender lady, striking, with raven black hair dressed high, glossy ringlets falling to her face, a fine-set mouth, and narrow but alluring brown eyes. 'Signorina Tanto, I thank you for permitting me to accompany you tonight.'

She received me with relative equanimity, slightly cool in tone and expression to begin with, but warming to me fast, I could tell from her surprised satisfaction.

'It is no trouble, really. You are only fortunate Carlo did not need me tonight.'

'Indeed, it is certainly my good fortune. I understand you to be very well regarded in your profession, and you see that I am only starting out.'

'Well, you look the part. If you can convince the rest of the company you *are* the pure quill, this may just fire you off,' she said, lifting a ringlet of my wine-red wig to better see my face.

I held her gaze, 'It is certainly my intention.'

She smirked her approval and then conceded to a more leisurely conversational style with me from there, and we covered greater introductory ground as she finished readying herself for our departure, offering me the shared use of her parfum and rouges as we talked more familiarly. Then I asked her, when I felt able to broach the subject, whether she had successfully managed to convince her patrons in the use of a *guantone*, for I had not yet purchased one for fear of discovery, but had grown increasingly anxious over the threat of disease and pregnancy since my encounter with Andrea.

'Not often,' she replied, though I find the more devoted husbands can be more willing. I rarely service more than one patron at a time nowadays so I don't concern myself overly.

'And you have not suffered any consequence for the times you have not?'

'No, none as yet. The pregnancy risk is easy enough to evade if you employ the proper methods, but the disease risk is one we bear by only the grace of good fortune.'

'I have employed the potash and mugwort wash and vinegar sponge most diligently, but I cannot grow used to it. I find the exercise quite a trial.'

She looked at me, appalled. 'You don't need to resort to such coarse means. There are far better ways. Go to the apothecary and ask for some Queens Anne Lace; tell them you suffer a digestive complaint but take the ground seeds as a tea or in your morning chocolate. You will thank me.'

'Are the sponges, potash, and mugwort washes thought to fail then?'

'No, not fail precisely, but the side effect can be to burn layers of delicate skin from you when you use them as regularly as our profession requires.'

'I see, and the seeds work efficiently?'

'Well, I have no complaints or abrasions, so I would vouch for them. I once used the methods you speak of, too, though not for some years, and I remain no worse off for avoiding them.'

I made a mental note to visit the apothecary on my next outing. I would at least combine the methods until I was certain of my courses.

'Well, I believe it is time for us to leave. I wish you well,' she said, kissing me gently on the cheek, a disconcerting surprise but one that sufficiently whet my appetite for faux flirtation as I took her arm into the *Sala Grande* at *La Fenice,* my breath steaming from the constriction of my masque in the early evening heat so contained by the crush of bodies in the room. Though I was grateful for its cover, and enjoyed the odd spectacle of seeing all the other attendees in such a theatrical style. I had never been to a masked ball before.

She had explained that before the Republic fell, it was commonplace to see the city itself so adorned for half the year. Being only a young child then, she had found it daunting to behold and was not sorry that such masquerading was now confined only to private soirees.

As we made our way through the crowded ballroom and up to the mezzanine to lean over the rail and observe the spectacle from above, she pointed out the various persons she recognised and how she could distinguish them despite their masks. The names meant nothing to me, and the ranks very little, but I gleaned enough to understand I was in the right place now. I needed only to muster the courage to let my mask slip briefly in the company to offer the preview that this was all contrived to achieve. An opportunity I took when the dances began, and Tanto took up invites whilst I remained at the sidelines, to begin with at least. For by the time I had retied my mask and the second set was called, I too enjoyed an equal share of such invitation, and whilst I did not recognise the dancers or, for the most part, the dances either, I was sure to do the pretty and make my best attempts at restrained flirtation and mimicry. The result being that I did not return to Tanto's apartments alone, but with my first won conquest, my first full paying patron.

The following day, Benedetta came to me once Giles had left for the shipyard to bring me a note from the dressmaker conveying the message that I was wanted for a 'fitting' on Tuesday evening. This was to prove our shorthand cypher thereafter. On the off chance of any discovery of the messages, there would be nothing but discussions of dress fittings and fabrics to be revealed by them.

By the time Tuesday came and I arrived at my apartments to undertake this next seduction, I was met by Signora Crivelli, who thought it easier to come with her diary to negotiate all the appointments she needed to arrange with me.

'You are launched, dear Rosa! I knew it should be so. The messenger boy has come to me six times with enquiries in one day! I could not convey it all by note. I need to confirm with the patrons right away. What can you manage?'

We discussed the possibilities as I underwent my preparatory toilette and pinned my wig. Since I could not get out under cover for as many six occasions in the week, it was decided we do our best to fit them all into a span of two separate daytimes I could rely on good excuse. One of them under the alibi of Signora Barozzi's charity house, which I had finally begun attending, and one by using my art class time, which meant missing it and having to explain my absence to Marco. Both tenuous, and yet both accomplished with a bit of thought and care. For Giles was no longer my greatest obstacle to freedom, so busy in business in the day and profligately engaged most nights as though still a bachelor, it became easy to convince him in my improved complacency that I was undergoing something of a spiritual transformation in my commitment to long confession, church attendance and charity works. Something he was not in sympathy with, but appreciated the meek and contrite effect it seemed to have on his wife. Marco, however, was much harder to gull, so I knew I would have to make a more earnest appeal for his assistance.

'If you are not coming to the class, why does my mama think you are still going?' he asked me when I told him at breakfast not to return to collect me this afternoon.

'I need an alibi Marco, that is the truth of the matter.'

He frowned, 'An alibi for what?'

'If I confide in you, Marco, it can go no further. I need your word.'

I watched his contemplative eyes struggle over the sight of my more pleading gaze. 'Are you in some difficulty?'

'Well, that is the thing, *I* am not, but there is someone else who needs my help on a very private matter—'

'Who, and what kind of help?'

'I cannot say, for it is not mine to divulge.'

'Then, if you will not tell me who, tell me what business you are to undertake in it?'

'First your word.'

'Very well, you have it.'

'I am to attend on a young woman. She recently had a most unfortunate decline in health since she prevailed upon a midwife to help her out of a very delicate situation.'

'An illegal abortion!' he said, appalled. 'She is lucky to be alive.'

'I know, but she is, by the good grace of god, and she already has a child to tend to and cannot in her current state.'

'By God, Eleanor, I recommended you to Ofelia to help you find some greater occupation, buy you some freedom, not involve you in such low dealings as this.'

His assumption that I spoke of someone from the charity house was false but better not corrected, for I told no lie on account of the circumstance. All was true of Giulia from the bordello, and I *had* paid attendance on her and her small family to offer the little aid I could. Only she was now in recovery and had no further need of my calls with alms as she was when unable to work. She had returned to the bordello only yesterday, though I begged her to remain away longer.

'Marco, you promise you will not mention this to anyone, not even Ofelia. I hold you to the bond of your word.'

'Fine, but Eleanor, I shall extract your word that you will not take such an example of how matters of this kind are to be dealt with.'

This alarmed me. Why would he presume such a thing? I had certainly never made plain to him my feelings about not wanting to bear Giles a child, whatever other minor indiscretions I had let slip. 'Well, of course, I wouldn't. I am a married woman.'

'Just promise me.'

'I promise,' I told him, feeling uneasy beneath his gaze, somehow exposed, discovered. A feeling I was to grow used to hereafter when I answered questions about other late arrivals home and missed classes.

CHAPTER TWENTY-SEVEN

The Verdict.

Annalise. March 1822.

S he passed what she supposed was little above an hour in the darkness of the holding cell, sobbing for most of it, reprimanding herself for the remainder. Why had she not listened to Mr Langley's counsel? Had he not told her himself that the Court would have no interest in her honest accounts? Had he not known better how her honest words could be turned so cruelly against her? Weaponised in such ruthless fashioning. It might not have made so much of a difference had she not confessed her love for Eleanor; it was that which had seemed to set the Court asunder as it broke out in gasps of disgust and horrified whispers. Was she even awaiting a verdict for Larceny anymore, or the sentence for her moral conduct, or lack of, as seemed to be the persuasion of the courtroom after her confession.

She was prepared for the worst when she was called back to the Court.

'Jury, do we have a verdict?' asked the Judge, weary of patience.

The bearded foreman stood. 'The Jury has arrived at a partial verdict, my Lord.'

'Very well.'

'In the case of the theft of the marquetry pearls, we find the prisoner guilty but accept Mr Plumpton's valuation of nine shillings.'

Annalise's heart fell as quickly as it had rejoiced at the first acquittal earlier that day. What did this mean?

'Very well. Miss Tullier, you have been found guilty of theft under 40 shillings.' He consulted something laid out before him, and he then said: 'It is therefore ordered and adjudged by this Court, that you be transported upon the seas, beyond the seas, to such a place as His Majesty, by the advice of His Privy Council, shall think fit to direct and appoint, for the term of seven years.'

'No!' cried out someone from the gallery. Annalise looked up to see it was Poppy. 'Mercy, milord. I beg thee, mercy! She is innocent!' she continued until Miss Lockheart led her out of the Court.

Annalise followed her escort from the courtroom in a mist of disbelief. She had her life but seven years to face in some desolate land before she could lay any claim to it. And how would she even get back if she could endure such a lengthy sentence and survive it? Where would Len be by then, seven years lost to her? She supposed she should be grateful that the efforts of Mr Langley had spared her the noose, but her heart was so much broken at the prospect of such a separation from Eleanor, her dear friends, and her homeland, that right now she felt the noose the lesser of the miseries to bear.

She was in an inconsolable fit of hysteria when she was removed from the holding cell some half an hour later. She assumed to be deposited back in gaol whilst arrangements were made for her transportation. But she was advised by the warder that before she was transferred back to the gaol, her barrister had begged a debrief with her. She followed him up the stairs accordingly and along blank walls of rugged stone corridor until she was deposited into a room to await him.

She stood instantly as he came into the room. 'Mr Langley, forgive me for not heeding your advice. I have been foolish. It has cost me dearly, as you see.'

'I do see, Miss Tullier, and I am sorry for it. It seems you were punished not on account of the theft, but on account of Mr Truscott's character assassination. With the jury's partial return, your good character, and first offence, you should have looked to a six-month imprisonment—a year at most. I can only assume the Judge was responding to the moral outcry in the Court in sentencing you so harshly.'

'Moral outcry?'

'Yes, the odd confession you made claiming to love your mistress. I think this is what has done the injury.'

It was as she had feared then. 'You did not think it on account of the fire and my helping my mistress to escape?'

'I daresay that did not help your case, but I fear, from the Court's reactions, that the curious nature of your relationship with your mistress did you the most harm. The Judge, no doubt, felt he must respond accordingly. That, or Mr Truscott has managed to get him in his back pocket!'

'What do you mean, Sir?'

'A bribe. If it was a London court, I would be sure of it. But nay, on the Western Circuit, these country sorts are usually not so easy to turn. It is my supposition that the Judge felt duty bound to give the public what they wanted and took a harsh line with you. The good news is, if that is so, privately, he may be willing to make a recommendation to pardon, a matter your friends have busied themselves in beseeching him. Presently.'

'They have? They are still here?'

'They are. And they wish to see you, though they are in such a sorry state I daresay it will prove no good to your spirits to see them so.'

'I want to see them, Sir, if I can.'

'Very well, I shall see what can be done.' He tapped on the door for the warder and said something to him she could not hear. He took a few coins from his pocket and passed them on before returning to the room. 'They will come soon, but you shall not have more than ten minutes with them. If they want to see you beyond that, they shall have to apply to the gaoler once you are returned.'

'Thank you! How long shall I be returned to the gaol before—'

'We must hope it will not come to that. I shall write directly back to Mr Jeffers and apprise him of the outcome. I will give your friends his direction, and when they return, they can draw up their affidavits with him and make the applications to the Home Secretary to stay you here, in the least. But, if the worse happens—and I do not deceive you, it often does, even when the best petitions are laid—you might expect to be gone in the next month or two, depending on what arrangements can be made.'

'I see. Where do you think I shall be sent, Sir?'

'Most commonly to Van Diemans Land or New South Wales.'

She had never heard of them. 'What is it like in those parts?'

'I do not know, and let us hope you shall not know it either. Now, I must prepare for my other cases, for who knows when they shall be called up, too. But Miss Tullier, I shall write to you in due course with any updates on your petitions. If I have the time before I return to London, I shall call into you if you would like me to, should you have any further questions once you have had time to take it in, but I cannot promise I shall have the time.'

'I would like it, I thank you.'

He held out his hand and she shook it. 'I am sorry things did not go better, but all is not done yet. I bid you farewell, Miss Tullier. Your friends should be here directly.'

They did not come for a great while and in this time of solitude, she retraced all that had passed in this last couple of hours and tried to absorb the sobering austerity of it. Was it truly so that she had been sentenced on account of her love for Eleanor? Was love truly a crime? She had said it was not a crime betwixt women, and yet, it seemed it was to some minds. She should not have been so easily provoked into that confession, yet something inside would not permit her to repress the truth of her feeling. It was only then she considered the fact that Poppy and Miss Lockheart, too, were party to hearing this confession. What would they make of it? Would they even want to see her now? Perhaps that was why they had not yet come.

But they did arrive some minutes later, sobbing and grasping her into tight hugs and damning the Judge and jury and that awful Mr Truscott who said such dreadful things and made such sport of her.

'He did say awful things,' Annalise agreed. 'But not all of them were untrue,' she added.

Miss Lockheart looked between her and Poppy and stepped back to offer them all the privacy she could in a room so small it was nigh on impossible.

'But what about Mr Leamington?' Poppy asked her, puzzled. 'I thought you were to be engaged.'

'Oh, Poppy,' Annalise sighed into her palms. 'Nothing makes me more sorry in all of this than all of the untruths I have misled you in to keep you from discovering my affections for Eleanor.'

'So you really do have that kind of affection for her?'

Annalise nodded. 'I love her, Poppy. And she loves me too. We did not plan it so, but it fell into the way, and I—I have never known such happiness.'

Poppy bit her lip.

'I'm sorry, Poppy, I disappoint you.'

'I do not think Poppy is disappointed in you, Annalise, but very surprised, in shock. She has never before heard of such a circumstance...' Miss Lockheart cut in with a gentle, compassionate expression.

'That's it. I can't get my 'ead around it, luv. But I do love you too, in an ordinary way,' she clarified, '...in the way of a sister to me which I have always thought of you as, and I don't say I understand it, but I will say, you are, as you 'ave always been, my dearest friend in the world and nothing shall alter that! I only don't know how I shall live without you. Seven years!' she began to sob.

'Come, come. You know there is still a chance for mercy, and we shall set right about the task when we get home,' said Miss Lockheart, with a reassuring tap at Poppy's shoulder.

Poppy nodded, sucked in a deep breath and wiped her eyes again. 'Yes, yes, we will set right about it to be sure. But what will become of you in the meantime? You shall waste away in a rotten gaol house or be taken with some terrible fever in the filthy place and—'

'Poppy,' Miss Lockheart intervened, '...have a care for your words.'

'I'm sorry, luv. Ignore what I said. I'm just overcome and speaking nonsense.'

'It's alright. I know it. And, I have been in the gaol house for the past seven weeks, and as you see, I am still here, still well.'

Poppy nodded and sniffed back her tears. 'You are thin, my luv, too thin.'

'Well, I own I have not had much of an appetite with all the worry, but—'

'I shan't even be able to bring you pies and visit you. You are so far away...'

'I will write to you, Poppy. We may stay in touch that way until I can return to you. To you all.' She, too, began to falter now. 'Pray, tell me, how is Mr Harrison? I had word that he has fallen ill?'

Miss Lockheart returned her desperate imploration with a look of pity and reluctance. 'He has been somewhat down on his luck, first his gout and then an infection of the waters. But he is stable and being taken very good care of by a local nurse, you may be sure.'

'Do not spare me the truth, Miss Lockheart. I must know if I am at risk of never seeing him again!'

'Dear girl, not any one of us can give such assurances, and I own, there was, for a brief while, some fear of his decline, but he is stable now, and there is every reason to hope for a full recovery.'

'I shall pray for it,' Annalise said. 'Has he had to close up the bookshop?'

'He did, for the briefest time when he was at his worst. But I ran the mornings for him thereafter, and he has employed one of the village boys as an assistant, too. So all is being managed, do not fear.'

She nodded unconvinced and turned back to Poppy, 'Poppy, do you still have that twelve pounds in the jar for me?'

'I do.'

'Then will you give it to Mr Harrison for me, please? He has done so much for me, and it should be me there nursing him, running the shop in his stead, but I—'

'Annalise, he shan't want for your coin,' said Miss Lockheart gently.

'But it is all I have to offer him, presently.'

'I will luv, I promise it,' Poppy agreed.

'Thank you. It may go some way towards his nursing bill and the assistant's wage.'

'I do not think he will accept it, however kindly meant,' Miss Lockheart added.

'You are probably right. But it would ease my mind to know it could be put to use for him.'

'Then we can but try,' she agreed.

'What of your burdens, Poppy? How do you manage now in the shop? Easier, I hope?'

'Much easier. We 'ave a little army of helpers now and they are finding their way by and by. Jane rolls the pastry, washes the pots and pans, and cleans the tables. Thomas goes out delivering pies on his push wagon and sweeps and scrubs the floors at close. Ruth sees to the customers, and Maggie divides her time between helping me cook and going out for supplies. It is all coming together splendid, you need not worry about that.'

'That is very happy news! I am so proud of you, Poppy. You have brought me great pride in the measure I have brought you trouble and disappointment, I fear.'

'Don't be daft! You've brought me a brand new life—a happy one of worthwhile industry and comfort. And even if you hadn't, it would take more than this to turn me away from you! We are family. Now stop such talk and let me hug you!'

She remembered the warm, comforting feeling of her friend's arms around her when she was back at the gaol waiting for a cell allocation. She lay on the hard bench, cold and exhausted but unable to settle. She had been there for four hours so far. The gaol was still oversubscribed, being only the first day of the sessions. It was hoped that they would thin out somewhat by the end of it and that more wards might be put to the convicts' use. Until then, she was stranded.

She had requested to return to her cell with Ninette. The thought of being alone again with so much darkness swirling about in her thoughts, was too much. Even though Ninette's troubles were no easy thing to manage, it was a welcome diversion and someone to talk to. Besides, she was not sure how Ninette would fare without her. But she had been told she could not return to the remand wards now. She might have left this morning as someone as likely innocent as guilty, but she had returned a convicted prisoner, and so she would board with convicted prisoners. She was reminded, too, that this gaol would seem akin to a luxury lodging house once she was put on the hulks to sail.

It was hard to conjure any sense of hope or consolation in all the gloom. Hard to see into any sort of future at a distance so far off as seven years, whether she was to hedge her faith in a petition to stay in gaol or be sent away. In either circumstance, it felt endless and foreboding, like her very life had been stolen from her in an instant, and yet she was forced to bear witness to its absence. All plans, hopes, and dreams, were suspended, and in their place where such things were seeded, an empty void of nothingness to wallow in.

All she had now was her memories, and those were only permitted to remain because they could not be taken from her. So she reflected on them at length. Remembered the kind comfort of her friends and news from home with something like a smile to remind her that the world outside was still permitting others to foster their dreams and hopes, even whilst strangling hers. She imagined the transformation of the extension at Carshalton, which Poppy had described to her. It was now furnished with tables and chairs as an extra dining parlour at busy spells and somewhere for Poppy to lay out the cooling pies when the kitchen became too overcrowded with pots and pans and rolling pins. Every second Wednesday, it also served as a teaching room, where Miss Lockheart had expanded her learning of letters to the children of Carshalton. It warmed her to see so much good come from it. Hearing how well the Bartlett's went along with fewer mouths to feed and more money sent back home. To think of the children learning their trades and finding a place in the world that would secure them better futures than otherwise promised them.

But as gladly as these things heartened her, others haunted her mind in equal measure. The despair and grief in Poppy when Annalise was asked to relay all the details of how she had fallen into such a circumstance as this. The thought of Mr Harrison battling his ill health without her. And the dread of what had become of Eleanor these past weeks under his wicked regime. The pain and unknowing of all these things weighed her down like lead and made her wish for just five minutes' freedom to throw herself from a bridge or beneath a passing carriage. She simply did not know how to endure this kind of torment, how she could carry it for seven long years. Would it get better after a time? Would she become accustomed to the way of it? Or, as she feared, would it get worse as the time stretched out without news or word to at least know she was alright.

Yet despite all this, something as subtle as a whisper and as gentle as a breeze told her not to lose hope. That one day, she would see her again. And by the time she was released, Eleanor would be returned home, and she might find her far easier than in a foreign place. She imagined then, their reunion, and such a long-awaited reunion it would be, and this same imagining, in slight variations, would come to be her sole comfort for many a night that would pass so lonely.

CHAPTER TWENTY-EIGHT

The Pseudonymous Meeting.

Eleanor. July 1822.

I shall never forget that first day when I was passed from one man to the next in such quick succession and had to undergo the potash and mugwort washes three times in one day. For since Giulia's misfortune, I meant to take no chances and employed all methods now in my preservation. When I had visited the apothecary for the Queens Anne Lace for myself, I also procured some for Giulia and bid her take them and spread the word about the house.

I now better understood the perfunctory tone of Giulia's descriptions of our work when the gravity of such acts came with such frequency: you became fast desensitised from the acts themselves. You had to, or it was all too terrible to contemplate. So, my body became something of a fine-tuned automaton as well as a commodity, even if far more complex and sophisticated in its function. But I was grateful for the swift conclusion to my anxieties it brought me. This was an act, nothing more. It was that day that truly broke me into this way of life. A deep-end dive of what it meant to be thus employed. One cock after another, as Giulia had once put it. After that, it came so effortlessly I barely thought of it by the time I removed my wig, got back into my demure dress, and made my way back to *Ca' Rosetti*.

What I did think about, though, at length, was the money. Every day, I passed my earned coins into Benedetta's hands once we reconvened at our meeting point, and she would subtract her trifling compensation and hide the rest until I was free to convey it up to Marco's studio and lift the floorboards.—This I always did alone and when I was certain the floor below was vacant. Sometimes, posting Benedetta at the main staircase to alert me should someone come up. The sound of her dropping the bell was to be the signal, but we had yet to need to use it.

Once I had cleared the debts I held with Signor Crivelli for the wig and bargaining price of Tanto's introduction, things finally began to look up, and my totting up of coin told me I was near halfway towards meeting my fare, and I had only just fired off at the beginning of the month. Each time I would travel to the apartments with the natural apprehension that would overcome me on that journey of wondering who I was to meet and what they should demand of me, I reminded myself I was already almost halfway to my goal. This would all soon be over...or so I thought.

On my next appointment, which was an evening one this time, I completed everything as usual and sat ready in a seductive poise upon the chaise, wig, and mask in situ. I waited for the servant to let the gentleman in. I was expecting a new patron: Mr Rudolpho. Who I recognised coming through the door, was Signor Serrano. I tried to retain my composure. I was, after all, masked and disguised, a protocol I followed with all new introductions for precisely this purpose. As a preliminary precaution, I had always demanded of Signora Crivelli a run-down of prospective patrons by way of name and brief biography, to ensure they were not one of the family, especially not Giles, before I agreed to see them. Mr Rudolpho's description came as: *"Mr Rudolpho, approx. fifty years, a foreigner. Merchant and Venetian speaking. Married."* This had not rang any bells, for I knew no one of that description or name. But how easy was it to give an alias? How likely for a married man who also wanted discretion and anonymity?

'Mr Rudolpho?' I said, the question in my tone perhaps a little too critical to pass for a welcome greeting.

'Si, Si and you, the Rosa Inglese. Well, well, Signorina, the pleasure is certainly mine.' He bent to kiss my hand the way he had the night of Marco's exhibition and I felt instantly paralysed by fear of what to do.

'Signor, you are very good, but pray, forgive me, I fear I have come over quite unwell. I must ask you to be so good as to take pity on me and reorganise our meeting for another time.'

'Come, come, what is wrong? You do not like my manner or my looks? I mean to pay you double the paltry fee you ask, I see you are worthy of more.'

'No, Sir, I do not fault you on either account, only I feel quite ill all of a sudden, a migraine, perhaps...'

'Oh dear. Well, what a pity for both me and you. But I should never wish to put you out, so I shall withdraw and meet with you when you are better if you will permit me.'

I nodded. 'Thank you, Sir. I am so very sorry. I shall have your fee returned to you at once—'

'Nonsense, you shall keep it with my compliments, sweet flower, as a pledge of my much-anticipated return.'

'That is very generous, Sir, but I cannot take your money for nothing. I insist—'

'Very well, I shall make one request of you for the sake of it before I go: pray, take off your mask and show me this beautiful face I have heard much spoken of and admired. A token I can keep to mind until we meet again.'

I swallowed hard. 'Next time I shall, Sir, to be sure.'

He looked suspicious of me then. I noticed the transient flash in his black eyes. 'Do I know you, Signorina?'

I shook my head a bit too vigorously to convince anyone of a migraine, 'No, I don't believe so. I am new here.'

'Well, there is only one other English Rose I can think of that is new to Venice, and now I think of it, she bears a striking resemblance in form and voice to you, sweet girl.'

I stiffened but tried to keep my speech easy. 'Well, I suppose us English must sound much alike. Now, I really must insist you leave now. I really am growing very ill.'

When he rose, I thought to leave, but then he cocked his head to one side, shook a contemplative finger and said, 'That English merchant's wife, yes, that was she. The one always dangling after a contract.'

I panicked. 'Please, Sir, I beg you do not mention the similarity, my reputation is all!'

'Well, if you give me an honest answer, I shall not mention it to a soul. You have my word.'

'Very well, you are correct, I am she.'

'That was not my question.'

'What is it then?'

'Did you feign illness because you knew yourself recognised, or for genuine reasons?'

I bit my lip. 'I feared you would recognise me if we continued,' I admitted.

'Well then, that is a relief. I have never induced such an effect on a woman before. I began to worry I had lost my touch.'

'Forgive me, I panicked.'

'There is nothing to forgive,' he waved a dismissive hand. 'Your anonymity is important to you, and you protected it. Who can blame you for that? I did the same, as you now know.'

'My husband does not know—'

'I gathered, but you are quite mistaken if you think *I* would be the one to tell him. What do I gain in that, other than casting you further from my reach?'

'Are you not in business together now?'

'We are negotiating, but what does that matter?'

'It just complicates matters, I think.'

'It needn't alter anything. You know, I was taken with you that night we were introduced at the auction. I never knew my luck would turn so favourably in finding you here. Signora, since you are not unwell, may we continue our appointment now?'

'Very well, if I have your word as your bond—'

'You have my word and my heart, sweet flower.'

It took a while to fall into less stiff conversation after this, but we began to grow easy after a while. So long our conversation, I thought we might only talk the entirety of the allocated time. There was but a quarter of an hour left, and he had not moved beyond tactility and flirtation, and I had begun to think this a very happy bargain for my coin, especially if he did mean to double the fee. But eventually he leaned in for a kiss, bid me remove my wig and then my clothes.

I stood before him with my short curls bouncing about my bare shoulders, my exposed breasts poised at the level of his gaze, and then he pulled me into his lap, and it began...

At first, I expected it to follow the usual formula I had come to glean from other patrons. Once they were aroused enough, it was a matter of understanding what they wanted me to do, performing accordingly, and then offering some invented signals of pleasure as Tanto had shown me: breathy noises and sighs, the occasional expression of delight, and usually, before my features had softened, the business was done. But I had sensed something different in Signor Serrano's manner this evening, something confirmed when I asked him what he would like me to do.

'Lay down on the bed,' he said at first, and I did so, expecting him to remove his breeches and fuck me. But he did not. Instead, he only removed his jacket and boots and lay next to me on the bed and began sucking at my breast and stroking between my legs so tenderly I felt aghast and stiffened. A signal he seemed to take for a reaction to pleasure and encouraged him on. What disconcerted me now was that I felt something that hinted of pleasure, and I did not want to feel anything above the ordinary, anything that might prevent me from paralysing the link between body and mind, the strategy I had relied on so faithfully until now.

It had never been difficult, never required any effort or resistance on my part. I had felt not a stirring of intrigue with any of my patrons, ones that had proved both superior in looks and charm than he. But it had all failed to penetrate the ice of my soul even when I had to perform to the contrary. Why, then, was this old merchant managing to wake something I wanted to remain dead to me? I could not understand it at all. I opened my eyes to look at him in the hope it would shake me out of this odd reverie, and whilst a part of my mind expected to see Annalise peering up at me, the inevitable disappointment of seeing him instead did not rouse me from it in the way that I had hoped. He began to work harder at my glance at him, and I began to feel my legs trembling and threatening to give way. *Whatever was happening? Why now? Why him?* But it was no use. I was too far lost in the sensation that I did the only thing I could before it was too late: perform an enactment of my completion to very vocal effect so that he would stop and withdraw before I could no longer contain its authentic successor.

It was not easy to manage as I struggled against the betrayal of my own body to give in to his frantic fingertips now, but by sheer dogged will, I resisted until he finally removed his hands, and I was left with a yearning throb so exceeding, I feared he might manage to continue this assault of my senses if we proceeded on to fuck right away.

So I delayed him, recovered my composure and undressed him slowly, took him in my hand and even in my mouth—my least well-tolerated duty that finally delivered me to the stark repulsion I had looked for before, but could not find. In this pursuit, I was rendered perfectly indifferent to any sensation above boredom and impassiveness by the time he pulled me on top of his cock. The relief was reassuring, and I performed for barely a minute before the final act was done. Then, unlike my other patrons who would, after a few moments of repose, come about to their usual senses and get dressed before bidding me farewell, he lingered in the bedclothes kissing and stroking me like a lover, not a whore. Whispering compliments into my ear and pressing his body close against mine. Oh, how I wanted to crawl from the bed in disgust. No other had made me feel so vilified and repulsed at myself, and it disconcerted me gravely. I could explain none of it in any logical form. It was a mystery and had unsettled all my assumptions of bodily indifference and control that I had relied upon until now. Knowing this was a possibility, for my body to react this way and after such a time...it now made the prospect of continuing seem impossible.

As I crossed the canals in the gondola hired to take me close to home, I was persuaded that I must give this up at once and look for another way to raise the rest of the money. I had at least made an expedient and lucrative start, but no amount of money was worth sabotaging the peace of mind I had finally wrestled back from the depths of hades.

I cast a glance out of the window. The evening sun smouldering honey and gold in a burnished amber sky, casting the domed and steepled skyline into silhouettes against it.

'Are you alright?' Benedetta asked me, sitting opposite me in the boat beneath the privacy of the felze that concealed us from open view.

I nodded, 'I think so. Benedetta, what other ways might I make some money here? Can you think of anything, an investment perhaps, now I have a little to invest?'

'I do not know about such things, Signora. Did something happen tonight? Was you harmed?'

'No,' I said, wanting to answer, yes, I was violated, but not knowing how to explain the sentiment, even to myself.

I avoided Signora Crivelli's messages for the next few days. Finally, when they became overwhelming and risky in such abundance, I sent her a return pleading illness and asking her to cancel my appointments for the rest of the week. I wanted to tell her for eternity but knew it unwise to try to convey this via a messenger. I would need to tell her in person and warn Signora Sartore to cancel the conveyance of messages before I risked her overwhelming me with protests and demands. I had been foolish and negligent in not agreeing a specified end to our arrangement at the outset. It had crossed my mind to tell her I expected to be gone by Autumn, but since she could take the lease for no less than six months, I feared she would not take it at all if I apprised her of that detail, and so I worried not about it further, because I would be gone from the city by then in any case. But now I regretted it sorely. There were still over three months remaining on the apartment lease, and I wanted to be free of it *now*. I wondered, as I enjoyed a reprieve of duties in those days, how she would react to the news. I knew the answer would be badly, but I wasn't sure what to expect in consequence of that. Would she try to pursue me and find me out? Would she succeed? Would she bring Giles's awareness to the matter and foil the entirety of my plans? These questions began to trouble me, and I considered how she might be placated. I could lie and tell her I was being taken away from Venice by my husband and had no say in it. I could compensate her for the remaining three months' rent. If I got desperate, I could threaten to report her to the Austrian authorities. My trade was not outlawed, but hers was.

In the end, I decided to do nothing immediately but put her off for as long as I could. I sent a message to Signora Sartore telling her that no matter how many messages were received for me, to hold them until I saw her next week for my next dress fitting.

So, for a while, I enjoyed being at liberty and burying my head in the sand, not needing to conspire cover and sneak about. I think Benedetta enjoyed the reprieve as much as I. It had grown harder and harder to keep up with the demands of concealment now I had grown so much busier than before, often having to find ways to accommodate an average of six patrons a week, many of them compressed into multiple sessions to reduce the number of excuses to find. It was not always easy to execute, and excuses for delayed returns home or deviations from plans, such as attending art class, were starting to wear very thin. It simply wasn't sustainable, even if I was willing to continue in it, and after this last encounter, I remained adamant that I was not.

For now, I made the most of the reprieve and looked forward to my art class today, having been patchy in attendance over the past few weeks, just when I was gaining some rapport with the ladies and even with Marco. We were not intimate friends in the way Dante and I had grown to become since the night of the gallery exhibition. Not that I saw him as often as I would have liked anymore, for just as things had grown busier for Giles of late, they had also grown busier for him and his father, and so it was common for all of them to return so late home most nights, that they had to have their own separate sitting for dinner.

But Marco and I grew more familiar in this absence, though we remained largely very formal in our dealings. Though he would now break jokes with me from time to time, but never in the way Dante did, daring and often ghastly, but always hilarious. No, his brothers were suitable for his mother's ears and never in bad taste. We would talk at length now, too, around the dinner table in the evening with his mama, or if he was giving me a lift in the boat to some place as often he would. But our conversations were always based on some subject of objective neutrality, like the history of one of the buildings we passed or a commentary on a painting. They were interesting conversations, not only because I learned a great deal from his vast knowledge, but because he did not speak to me with the dismissiveness men often spoke to me, and my entire sex, with – like we might struggle to follow the subject matter with our inferior logic. No, he spoke to me with zeal and complexity from an assumption of my comprehension unless I stated otherwise, and even then, he would answer my questions with patience and diligence until I understood. It was the same in his classes, too, and I knew that to be the reason the ladies held him in such high esteem. What he taught us was above and beyond how to sketch or paint, great lectures in art history, great encouragement in our endeavours, and the way he delivered it always made you feel equal to your counterpart. And so I grew to enjoy these conversations immensely, looking to them with anticipation when he would offer to convey me to the dressmakers or the charity house in his boat, considering what we might discuss today. But it was always contained to this style, and what we both avoided, was anything too personal. I knew why on my part; it was because I was always careful of arousing his disapproval or slipping up on some spurious detail or another. For where Dante was easy, he was vigilant. And I did not want to lie to him anymore as I had about attending Giulia, something I think we were both keen to avoid a reoccurrence of.

Where I looked to Marco for interest and good sense, I looked to Dante for quite the contrary: silliness and funning, even small earnest confidences from time to time. All in all, though differently composed, we went along very amicably now, and I had realised that the family had become very dear to me. That the bond of duty that had pushed us so arbitrarily together, proving awkward to begin with, had altered into something voluntary and valuable for its own sake. And though it would not be equal to inducing me to remain as Giles's wife, I occasionally lamented the idea of having to sever my ties with them so brutally and abruptly when the day came. They, like so many others I had lost touch or favour with, would join my list of lost loves to the sacrifice of this man I married. One sin that had cost me everything dear to me, and still, the sacrificial count grew.

But Giles, at least, was easier to manage now he was so preoccupied with the restoration of his new ship and all the business of this new line of trade he was preparing for. He had not spoken in any detail to me about it, but then he never did. I knew he regarded me much like an ignorant child and not worth discussing such high-minded matters with. But on rare occasions, I caught details of his discussions with the Harpers at the table, and what I did know, was that much of this new effort had to do with a new contract between him and Serrano. If the thought of what had passed between me and the Signor had not been so harrowing, I might have taken some smug pleasure in harbouring the secret of letting him have his way with me behind Giles's back. Especially when he came home late and disturbed me in the night to mount me like a broodmare in his continued quest to impregnate me.

It was quick at least now. He would enter the chamber, lift my chemise without a word and make a fast and vigorous effort, lasting little more than a couple of minutes. Some nights, he would not even bother to wake me and I would gasp in fright to find myself pinned beneath his weight in the bed. But even this was a great deal more manageable for me than his previous ideas of attempting to pleasure me or sleep all night in my chamber, even if he now insisted on me lifting my legs in the air and holding them upright against the bedpost afterwards.—No doubt another peculiarity he had discovered to increase the chances of success. He usually waited five minutes to observe that I had done as bid, then left for his chamber. In many ways, this was an improvement, but it was the sporadic nature of the duty that troubled me.

When I had first learned about the sponges and washes from Giulia, I was not only pleased to have stumbled upon a solution to protect myself in my new career but to protect myself from Giles's objectives, too. I had brought a small supply back from the apartment and charged Benedetta to keep it hidden away for me and bring it to my evening toilette when requested if I suspected his attentions that night. It had worked out well to begin with, but his increasingly late nights and impromptu demands had made it difficult to prepare for in advance. So even though I took the tea from the apothecary as a regular course now, I also took the precaution thereon of placing a sponge every night so as not to be caught out, but even that failed to answer once his schedule grew more demanding. Sometimes, when he would not come home before midnight, he might accost me in the morning, demanding I put down my coffee cup or hairbrush and hurry in lifting my skirts, for he had only five minutes to spare. He would sometimes burst into my toilette, send Benedetta away and bend me over the washstand without saying a word other than to direct me to lie on the bed with my legs up once it was done. There simply was no way to prepare for all the arbitrary times or places he might chance upon me, and I feared his eventual success if I could not manage to thwart it. So I took careful note of the dates of my courses now so I could detect their absence or lateness, which so far had proved no cause for concern above a day of apprehensive miscalculation. I placed the sponge each night and dared not remove it again until he was gone in the morning and rose immediately from the bed to squat over the wash basin as soon as I could. It was a tiresome effort with no slight discomfort, the caustic vinegar and potash aggravating my delicate depths and causing growing irritation now, just as Tanto had warned me of. And yet, still, it remained the lesser evil.

Tonight, however, I suspected myself safe since Mondays were usually particularly detaining for Giles at the shipyard. If there was any day I might hope for some relief, it would be this one. So I left out the sponge this morning, taking only my tea, and got into the boat with Marco and Benedetta to head to the art class with a particular sense of buoyancy. Today, I was to enjoy myself and be at *no one's* beck and call.

I was met with smiles of surprise when I came in and set up my easel as if I'd never been away. I gathered that Marco had told the class I had been unwell since they all asked after my health and said how glad they were that I was recovered enough to return. When we were all set up, Marco sat on the edge of the table to give his usual brief.

'We have moved on from the still life in your absence, Eleanor. Last week, we looked at portraiture, not in a detailed sense, but in terms of properly mapping the outline and proportions, much as we did with the still life before we advanced it. This week, we shall have a model again to sit for us and attempt to impose her face upon last week's outline sketch. We have a different model coming today...'

This news was met with unwelcome sighs. 'Why change the model when we have already begun?' Guistina complained.

'It could not be helped, I'm afraid, she was rendered unavailable at the last,' Marco explained. 'But it is not to be despaired of. In fact, it is a good opportunity for you to adopt an important skill in portraiture, for artists often have to use differing models when commissioned to undertake someone's portrait. Few subjects are willing to sit for the many hours and days often required to do justice to a portrait, and so using a substitute and learning to improvise is something not to be spurned, but to learn how to master.'

'But how shall we reconcile this new face with what we already have?' Lia asked.

'She shall assume the same pose, and so everything you sketched last week remains transferable, for the finer details will be added from hereon. Now, retrieve last week's sketches from the drying store and prepare for her arrival, which should be imminent.—Eleanor,' he added, once the class had dispersed to find their sketches. 'You shall be behind a step, but that is no matter. If you will permit me to get the others started, I will come to you and talk you through what you missed last time. In the meantime, have a look at their sketches to get an idea.'

I nodded. 'Thank you, I shall.'

'Right, I must find out where Holland-Bury is if you'll excuse me.'

'Mr Holland-Bury is joining us?' I asked, my interest piqued. I had not seen him since the exhibition and had been keen to advance our acquaintance now my purse was growing fuller.

'I hope so. He is procuring our model, though he is late!'

As the ladies returned to the room and pegged their sketches to their easels, I went about them to get the measure and joined in with the small talk that inevitably broke out in Marco's absence.

When he returned, he had the not-so-easy task of bringing us to a lull and directing us back to our stations.

'Right, our model is here. She will join us directly,' he said, and then I noticed Holland-Bury come into the room with a woman following behind him. 'Ciao, bella donna,' he greeted us all with a low bow and the smile of a rake. I saw the intrigue rise in their expressions as they returned his smile and greeting, though more formally.

Marco cut him a glance of muted reprimand and I bit my lip to keep from laughing.

'Ladies, this is Mr Holland-Bury, a portraitist from London. He will be assisting me today, so feel free to make use of his extensive knowledge in this practice. Marco pulled a chair into the centre of the room. 'And, this is Lena,' he added, leading her to the chair and directing her in how to sit.

Unlike Holland-Burys welcome, Lena's was met with stiff nods from the ladies that at first I did not understand until she emerged fully to my view and with an audible gasp, I recognised her as the bare-breasted lady from the bridge that night we all returned home late. Yes, she was certainly altered now in her plain, drab gown and absent of the garish face paints that had adorned her into something of a caricature in the poor light that night, but if I had any doubt I had been mistaken, it was quashed by the other ladies' reaction to her. I was clearly not the only one to recognise her. And once we had finished the sketching later that afternoon, her farewell was met with no greater decorum. But Lucia and I offered our thanks and farewell more freely than the others.

When she left, Guistina came marching over to me and said, 'You were right to show your disgust at her arrival, Eleanor. It is an insult to have her in our presence.'

'I was not disgusted, Guistina, only surprised to have recognised her, that is all,' I corrected her, feeling terrible that my gasp had been misconstrued for disapproval. How could I disapprove of her now? I was no better than she.

'That is the dirty whore always hanging about the Rialto, isn't it?' Rosina came over and whispered and Guistina nodded.

'Marco, how can you bring the meretrice here with respectable ladies?' Guistina protested.

Marco shot Holland-Bury a hot glance of admonishment, and he threw up his hands in admission, 'Come, ladies, be reasonable; she shan't taint you!' Holland-Bury said. 'Every great artist has painted such ladies! Do you think respectable ladies will bare themselves to the greats? Yes, Tintoretto and Caravaggio used such subjects in their famous works, the *Penitent Magdalene* and *Joseph and Potiphar's Wife*, because they are easy to procure and not shy of standing before a gentleman painter. The *Madonna of Loreto* was painted with the model of a courtesan of the day: Maddalena di Paolo Antognetti, hmm, you did not know.'

'Well, we were not painting bodies or nudes!' Guistina protested. 'Only a face. Do you tell me no respectable lady would bear her face?'

'Holland-Bury, you are not helping,' Marco said, irritated. 'Ladies, please accept my apologies. I did not realise, and there was no intention to offend your sensibilities. But, try to think more charitably of ladies like Lena, hmm? She earned her fee in honest pursuits in our studio today—'

'Yes,' said Lucia in surprising defence of Lena, '...and if she could find more honest work like this, I'm sure she would prefer it over the other kind.'

'Well, then, why does she not go the *Zitelle*?'

'You are always so judgemental, Guistina, just because we do not starve. You see the poverty they live in. How many more would have died in the famines had they not found a way to feed themselves? The *Zitelle* can't take all the women—'

'No, and is it any wonder when the number of them far exceeds the number of rats in the city?'

'So you would choose your virtue over your belly, would you?' Lucia retorted.

'Of course, you would not?' Guistina barked.

'I should rather starve,' Rosina put in now in allegiance.

But Lucia was not to be cowered. 'Easy to say when you do not understand the meaning. I wonder how you would have fared during the famine on a diet of straw and manure!'

'Ladies, Ladies, please!' Marco cut in, 'This is an art class, not a debating forum. Argue no more. The fault is mine and I mean to remedy it. Next week's model I shall be sure to procure by better means.'

'Oh, so now her honest work is to be cut short because Guistina protests, and now we shall all have to alter our work yet again?' Lucia directed her objection at Marco now.

'No, I shall pay her the same and she shall not lose out, alright? Now, can we settle this matter and put our things away?'

Reluctantly, they began to unpeg their sketches and tidy their stations, but there was a stiffness in the atmosphere now and an exaggerated clatter and clang in their movements as they did.

It was not uncommon for them to squabble. Venetian women seemed to me much more openly spirited than I had been used to, and though it had come as a bit of a surprise, it had been the very thing that had warmed me to them so quickly. The fussy pretences I had been surrounded with in my circles growing up had been precisely what I had come to loathe about them. Here, they spoke directly and were not afraid to press their point and make up after it. I liked it immensely, and yet I was reminded now that despite it, they, too, were not free of their class conditioning. If they knew what I had become, they would have shunned me with equal disgust, more perhaps, because they thought me one of them, because once upon a time, I had been even loftier.

Even Lucia, for all her charitable speech, would be forced to spurn me, even if she would do so with a great deal more pity than the others. But as much as it evoked shame in me, it helped to further solidify my resolution to put an end to this career. I would visit Signora Crivelli this week to give her the news. It could not be put off any longer.

It had also given rise to a new idea, one that still required the selling of my body, but only to be looked upon now, not vilified. I thought back to Holland-Bury's lecture about the greats, to the notice I had read outside the gallery door, "Life models wanted, apply within". Yes, there was another way I could earn the rest of my fare, though I was not willing to be paid the scant coin Lena most likely had been. But then I was willing to bear all my flesh for a larger fee, and whilst I was sure it would prove no comparison to my share of the hundred and fifty lire I had grown used to receiving, I could at least retain more dignity, which would be worth the sacrifice. Of course, I could not approach Marco with this proposal, but Holland-Bury was a different matter. So, as I put away my sketch and waited about for them to return from the office, where the pair of them seemed to be having an argument of their own, I meant to decline Marco's offer to take me home today and try to convince Holland-Bury to help me in this new pursuit, instead.

I sat on a stool in the empty studio now, listening to their raised voices as I waited.

'We are not at Oxford now,' Marco said, '...amongst a group of men. These are *Ladies*, most of them from highly-ranking families. George, you should know better!'

'How was I to know they would recognise her? I told her specifically to dress down, and she looked very humble, I thought.'

'Yes, she did, and had you at least gone to the trouble of procuring such a woman from one of the houses, then perhaps it would have gone unnoticed, but a meretrice about the Rialto, flaunting her flesh whenever she thinks it safe to try? Come Holland-Bury, even Venetian Ladies visit the markets and main streets of the city.'

'Alright, I'm sorry, I thought she was altered sufficiently that no one would know her.—You didn't at first. Look, I was running late and didn't want to let you down. I shall take better care next time, upon my word.'

Marco sighed, 'If you were not so useful in this skill, I am sure I should ban you from attending any of my classes again! "Hello, beautiful ladies." Remember your company, George, you are not in a house of ill repute.'

'And yet you hate portraiture, and I am every bit as good as you claim. So you shall have to give me a chance to make it up to you and prove I can do better. I'm not used to teaching ladies, who is?'

'Then imagine them your own sisters, that may prove a start.'

'Is that your trick to keep your gaze level?'

'No, George, I respect them, there is no trick. You should try it sometime. Even you may learn something and come to draw a distinction between female flesh and female company!'

'Come, you needn't be coy with me, even you have eyes. That Guistina is a pretty little thing, and as for that vixen of a cousin—'

Vixen, I thought, wanting to object then remembering I was not supposed to be listening.

'Do not, George, you push your luck too far now.'

'Alright, alright! I shall say no more. I will be the perfect gentleman next week, in manner if not mind. But what shall we do about Lena? I'm not sure I will manage a lookalike from a more limited selection, and they have done too much work today to start over.'

'Well, I cannot have her back. You saw the disturbance you caused, and I need not referee them again. You will have to do your best to replace her, or we shall have to work from memory. I daresay they shan't like it, but it will be preferable even to them. Go to Lena, pay her for next week and make her an apology. And do not pick the next model from her situation. Now I have to take Eleanor home, but I will see you this evening for the men's class, where there at least, I hope I may not find you wanting.'

At the mention of this, I went directly out to Benedetta in the lobby to brief her that we would be walking home today, and so it did not prove apparent that I had been listening in on their discussion.

'I'm Sorry, Eleanor. I am ready to go now,' Marco told me as they emerged from the studio together.

'It's no trouble. But you needn't escort me home today after all. Benedetta has just reminded me that I am to stop in for the dressmaker. I waited only to tell you that I will walk today.'

'Oh, well, I can walk you there instead if you prefer and pick you up after?'

'Marco, we will be quite safe. She is only at St. Marks, and it is the middle of the day. Please, do not trouble yourself. You have work to do and I must hurry, for your mama is expecting me to go to confession with her at five.'

'I can escort you as far as St. Marks,' Holland-Bury offered, 'I'm off to Florian for a bite, so I'm heading that way anyway.'

'Perfect,' I said to Marco's warning glare to his friend.

I waited until we were some way beyond the gallery before approaching Holland-Bury with my enquiry. We had spoken only lightly on the subject of the class, and now, as we pushed through the crowds on the Rialto and ventured into quieter streets, I wondered how best to broach the subject. 'Pray, tell me, sir, was it true what you spoke of in class, that the greats used fallen women as their models?'

'It was true, I assure you.'

'Is that where all artists seek their models?'

'No, not necessarily. But it is by far the easiest and most common way.'

'I see. So there is no space in such a market for a more respectable woman to serve as such?'

'Anyone may apply, it is hardly a prerequisite, but as I said before, artists usually require models for nude substitutes, not ordinary portraiture, for they have their subjects for that purpose. It is only because this is a ladies' class you are spared the kind of painting that most artists seek out models for. So you needn't be concerned at finding another fallen woman at class next week if that is what is troubling you, and I hope you will accept my sincere apologies if bringing her into your company has offended you.'

'It did not offend me. So where shall you seek a face model instead?'

'I don't know. I do not usually trifle over such matters, but I shall try a humble tradeswoman, maybe one of those market vendors or a servant perhaps,' he looked at Benedetta then and looked away again as if thinking better of it.

'What shall she be paid for her service?'

'As little as I can negotiate her down to. Why, have you someone in mind?'

'No, not for that at least, but tell me, if someone was looking for the other kind of work—?'

'Nude modelling?'

'Yes, where might they find such work, and what might they expect to earn?'

'What? No.—This isn't about Lena, is it? You ask on your own account?'

'I do—but I must beg your confidence. Marco cannot know of what we speak.'

'By gad! No, he cannot know, to be sure, or he will have both our guts for garters. And it is for exactly that reason we shall close the subject there.'

'Fine, if you answer my questions, I shall ask no more of you.'

He smirked at this. 'He said you were headstrong. Tell me, Mrs Craythorne, why should a wealthy woman like you be interested in such matters?'

'I am not a wealthy woman. Few of my sex are unless they are widows. I have nothing of my own.'

'But your husband is very well situated, I understand... and by the look of your fine wardrobe, I cannot suspect he denies you his money.'

'He does not deny me exactly—'

'Ah, you do not want him to know how you shall spend it. I see. Have you fallen into difficulty over the faro table?'

'Yes,' I lied, grateful for him inventing the excuse and sparing me the need, 'So you see, I cannot ask my husband or he shall be cross with me and—'

'Well, I see your predicament, though I cannot imagine you will land yourself into less of one by taking your clothes off for a trifling debt.'

'It is not so very trifling.'

He looked at me incredulously, then asked, 'How much do you owe?'

'Eight hundred lire,' I told him, estimating the shortfall in my fare by the time I had settled the three months' remaining rent with Signora Crivelli, which I suspected I should have to resort to in the least when delivering my resignation.

'What, eight hundred lire? Who have you been gaming with?'

'I cannot say, only that it is with some ladies—'

'Crikey, Mrs Craythorne, even I don't pledge those kind of sums at the table, what possessed you?'

'A moment of foolishness, I now see. You know how easy it is...'

His expression told me that he did. 'Well, if it had been a more reasonable sum, I might have been able to help you out, but dash it, for an amount like that you shall have to try Marco.'

'Oh, and you think that will be any better? No, exactly. I shall suffer great lectures in his direction, too. Besides, I don't expect or ask you or Marco to bail me out of my dilemma; why, indeed, should either of you? No, I am quite happy to pay my way if only I can discover the means by which I can.'

'Yes, I daresay he will box your ears over it—lord knows he boxes mine over the very same—but he will settle it for you, I've no doubt about that. Then, you can give up this scheme, which will land you in far worse trouble than your debt. Swallow your pride is my advice—god, am I giving advice...I surprise even myself.'

'I could not prevail on Marco for such, it is out of the question—'

'Of course, you could. He would do anything for you.'

I frowned at him then and he bit his lip.

'What I mean is, you are in far better credit with him than I. He has bailed me out too many times to count, but I don't believe you are in the same boat?'

I shook my head. 'I shan't ask him, so will you help me or not?'

'Look, I wish I could help you, Mrs Craythorne, in earnest. By gad, I'd pay to paint you myself...but I can't, my hands are tied. I'm already in enough trouble with him after today's faux pas. I don't intend to be blamed for helping you lose even more than your coin in such a mad-brained scheme as this. Haven't you some pretty trinket you can sell?'

It was a mad-brained scheme. At least, I saw it seemed to be from his perspective. But that I had done far worse, that this would be an improvement upon it, I could not disclose. 'No, I don't. But you would paint me, you say? How much would you pay for me to model?'

'No,' he said sternly, 'that is not what I meant. Disregard it, a stupid passing comment.'

'Oh, you would not wish to see this little *vixen* with her clothes off,' I said then, falling into desperation now.

'Ah, so you heard us, I see. Well then again, I must apologise—'

'Fuck, Holland-Bury, give up all this pretence. I understand your type very well,' I was not sure if his expression was simply shock or amusement at this turn, both perhaps.

'Oh, you do? Well, it seems I was mistaken in thinking I had the measure of you. Don't let the family hear you speak like that, will you,' he laughed.

'This is not a joke. I am in difficult straits and I need to find a solution quickly!'

'Alright, calm down. I shall level with you. Even if I *were* to tell you how to go about things—and I'm not—the sad fact is, you won't earn nearly enough to justify the sacrifice of bearing yourself nude. I'd dread to guess how many sittings you would have to undergo to earn even a quarter of the amount you mean to raise. There are not enough artists in Venice, less still with purses that plump.'

I was disappointed at this but still suspicious of his claim, 'If you are trying to gull me in the hope of putting me off—'

'I'm not, well I mean, I am, but that is to say, I speak the truth. I have never paid more than a guinea for a model, and that was in London. The money here is worth a meagre fraction of our coin at home. The place has fallen into harsh decline. Everything's cheap here, whores included, and they are plentiful. To be sure, I am never so well off as when I visit these shores.'

I knew him to be in earnest now. Signora Crivelli had expressed the same view and tried to angle my marketing towards the "foreigners", my own countrymen included, precisely because she thought them more likely to manage the higher fee. They had more to spend on such luxuries than most of the Patricians in such times, with them fleeing to the mainland whilst their Palazzo's crumbled. No one had escaped some degree of ruin in Venice, she had said, though they at least bore it far better than most of the population. It made me wonder just how cheaply I was giving myself away for in comparative terms. What was my lire to the English equivalent, I wondered. But right now, that was neither here nor there. If I ever wanted to get back to my country and escape Giles, I needed to find a way to fill this void in my fare. And then it come to me. If I could not pay the rest in coin... 'Well off, you say?' I said to him then and held back from Benedetta a little farther, and lowered my voice. 'Well, Mr Holland-Bury, I wonder, if you are so plump in the pocket now you are here, and you are certainly a rake, so do not waste your time in trying to deny the charge, simply tell me: how much would you pay to fuck this little vixen?'

He almost tripped over at this and was barged along the alley by passing traffic. But even as he recovered his misstep, I saw the flash of temptation in his eyes. 'Dash it. I should never have offered to escort you to the seamstress if I had known how you would make me suffer—'

'Suffer? Mr Holland-Bury, George, I *could* make you suffer, you know, if that's what you would like, or perhaps you would prefer to take pleasure from me?'

He gulped and edged away from me now. 'Have you lost your mind?'

'No, but I do believe you are on the brink of it. Come, how hard must I work to convince you to accept what we both already know you desire.'

'There is more at stake here than what I desire.'

'Really, you fear my husband's wrath or Marco's lectures in greater measure than wondering what it feels like to know my cunt?'

'Jesus, I have to go. Call back your maid. I shall have to leave you here.'

But I did not. Instead, I shoved him into an adjoining calle and pressed myself against him until he could not move, and then he stopped trying to altogether. I spoke to him now with my lips almost touching his. 'My cunt is at your disposal, rake, what will you pay me?' I said again, but this time I ran my hand across his breaches and found the swell of his stiff cock bulging from them. He pulled my hand away with such a pitiful show of restraint I did not move aside when he bid it.

'Look, you are not a whore, and I am not so ill a friend as to—'

'Who will know? I shall speak of it to no one, you may be certain of that. Come, name your price, take me back to your lodgings now and have your way with me. I know you long to.'

He seized me with a kiss, something I often tried to avoid with patrons, but under circumstances such as this, I was willing to indulge him. For if I succeeded in winning him around, then I could fuck my way to England with him instead of taking the risk of so many others in raising the money. The solution seemed so obvious now I realised the foolishness of my scheming when the answer had been here all along.

I supposed I had not entirely failed to see the possibility from the outset. I knew Holland-Bury to be a rake, and I knew him to look at me in that flesh-defiling way I had become ever more astute at recognising now. I suppose the difference was that back then, I feared the possibility of travelling with such a companion, being so vulnerable in his charge and trying to fend him off on a journey so long as that. I had hoped to disprove him as a rake or to discover enough about him to know if he would at least be safe to travel with. But that was *before*. Before I had lifted my skirts and defiled myself with so many men now that it seemed ridiculous to me that I would not have reconsidered simply exchanging the bargain for the regular attention of just one man, instead. Yes, one man in place of several, instead of splitting fees with Signora and contriving to escape the house at the beck and call of some patron or other, or risking more acquaintances arriving like Serrano had. This would solve *everything*.

I was at half the fare now, a fare he would have to pay regardless of whether I journeyed back to England with him or not, for the hire of coaches and horses would be no less for my joining it. It would only be singular costs, like the packet ticket, board and sustenance, that would inflate the price, and my half should surely cover that much. For the rest, payment in kind should have to suffice. And so I replaced my hand at his breaches as he kissed me hungrily on the mouth, found the buttons and began to open them when he withdrew suddenly and threw me off. 'Stop!' he said, 'Please, stop. I cannot.'

'You already have. What's wrong with you?'

He threw his hands over his head and sighed. 'If you were but any other woman...but you are not. You are—'

'A married woman and so what? Even married women have affairs.'

'Your marriage is not the difficulty, you are Marco's—'

'Oh, I see, the bonds of friendship. Well, I am not Marco's sister, nor even his cousin by blood, and so what offence can he take? What bonds are to be broken? I could understand if I was Carlotta or Maria, but—'

'You don't understand, do you?'

'No. I have never understood why men behave so. What I understand, though, is that we are both adults, and we could both give a little something the other wants. And that is no one's business but our own.'

'We have no business, Mrs Craythorne, and nor can we. Look, I am sorry for my lapse, I really am. I shouldn't have let things run so far, but please, believe me when I say that I *cannot.*—If you are serious about modelling, the *Academia di Belle Arti* are often seeking nudes, and you might also try the guild noticeboard, that is the best I can do. Forgive me. Good day.' And he stole away at such a pace, he was vanished from the street by the time I stepped out from the alleyway.

CHAPTER TWENTY-NINE

Hemmed in.

Eleanor. August 1822.

I was furious for the rest of the day. I would not be put off so easily because Holland-Bury viewed me as some blood relation of Marco's. It was a ridiculous reason. If he could disregard Giles's rights over me, he could certainly forego Marco's—who had none whatsoever. Such misguided bonds of honour between men never ceased to amaze me.

On the one hand, they might call a fellow out for flirting with his sister but then happily fuck someone else's wife. It made no sense to me, this misplaced double standard. But Holland-Bury and this scheme made such perfect sense to me now that I could not let it fail without putting up a fight. It was the answer to all, if only I could bring him about. More persuasion might be needed than I had hoped.

My reasoning was only further enforced when the next day Signora Sartore came to measure me up for my monthly subscription of new dresses and brought with her a pile of messages so excessive, I could barely suffer the reading of them. They were mostly of the usual sort: an appointment request for this gent or another on this day or time, a few pleading notes to ask if I was yet recovered and when I would return, and then a few less patiently toned ones that demanded a reply. But out of all of these, there was one in particular that had disturbed me above all. It read:

I have excellent news! Snr. Rudolpho has made an offer of exclusivity to you and will pay a handsome sum to cover all your losses on his account, as well as double his fee! This is the breakthrough we have been waiting for. Hurry your reply. We cannot keep him waiting!

So much for our cypher. As I watched the notes sink into the murky canal water below, I wished I could drown more than just the paper they were written on—my agreement with Signora Crivelli, for a start. I would have preferred the satisfaction of burning them in the grate, but since no fires were lit in the house at this season, it was the only safe way to dispose of them in a hurry. The occasional message, I might burn over the flame of a candle if I was sure I was quite alone. But this thick wad would have the servants running about shouting 'fire' if I dared the attempt, and so I tore them into pieces and dropped them into the water, watching them disperse with the current of passing boats.

How could I have got into such a fix trying to get out of another? I did not want to go on as the *Rosa Inglese* anymore. Nor did I want to become Serrano's exclusive mistress.

I was willing to try applying to the art academies Holland-Bury had suggested, but I held little hope in them if what he said was true. *He* was the only hope I could see now—the answer to it all. Perhaps I had judged him too harshly and pitched my seduction far too base and low, even for his taste. It had seemed the right approach to take with a rake, but if there was some thread of honour in him, as appeared to be the case, I perhaps would need to raise my seductive game a little higher. I still had time to draw him out.

So when next Monday's class came about, I made a far greater effort with my looks than I ordinarily bothered to. No, I did not resort to *Rosa Inglese's* wardrobe, but I picked one of my finer dresses and had Benedetta pin up my curls à la mode, which were now long enough to do something with at last. I even puffed myself with scent and sooted my lashes, something I had not done in a great while in my ordinary life. So when I arrived in the studio and set out my place, I waited anxiously for him to arrive. When he failed to show up after Marco's briefing, I knew it had all been for nothing. He was not coming. *He was avoiding me.*

I was utterly miserable throughout my sketching. It was this I blamed on my subconscious sketching of something reminiscent of Annalise's face when Marco announced that today we would try to sketch something from memory. I was surprised as I recognised her beautiful hazel eyes and pert smile peering back at me from the page. I had intended to just make something up. Something that required no real effort or thought with my mind racing everywhere but to the task at hand. And yet, inadvertently, I had produced her likeness. It was a shock to remember her so poignantly after so long, and it was all I could do to stop myself from bursting into sobs in the middle of the class.

I felt so cornered by it all: enduring Giles, as always, the ceaseless struggle for money, Signora Crivelli's increasingly frustrated messages, and my failed attempt at Holland-Bury, which may have just cost me my journey home. It was all *too* much. For all I had tried to escape this asylum of my existence, it seemed futile once more. Autumn fell in only three months' time, yet I knew not how to even travel the distance to the final lap. And now Holland-Bury was avoiding me, I could not even be sure he would permit my going with him at all, after all else. In any case, how was I ever to persuade him towards either idea if he meant to continue avoiding me? I could hardly seek him out. I didn't even know where he lodged beyond the vague canal-side spot we had dropped him off that night, and I was not even sure I remembered where that was now.

It was in this low mood and state of desperation that I forced myself to Signora Crivelli's bordello after class and accepted to resume my duties, against all my better judgement. I needed to make sure that one way or another, by Autumn, I had my fare to travel home, even if it was to be a lone journey or a sea voyage. And perhaps that would prove a cheaper means, by sea, even if a less appealing one. Or there was the other way he spoke of, the Diligence, I remembered now. Some enquiries were in order on both accounts, I considered as I walked the stairs to Crivelli's drawing room.

'Where the hell have you been? I have sent you message after message! Two weeks, I do not hear from you! What is the meaning of this disrespect you show me?'

This was the welcome I was met with on my arrival, she shouting down the house and throwing around her hands in exaggerated, angry gestures.

'I told you, I have been ill,' I said levelly.

'Ill, well, your illness has cost us over a thousand lire! Unless your head is hanging off, I don't care how ill you are, you come to work!'

'Fuck you,' I said then and got up to leave. 'Who do you think you are? I am not one of these defenceless girls you push around with your will and might. I could have you closed down by the end of the night if I was minded to!'

She bristled at this and grew angrier still. 'Oh, and you think I could not go to your husband and tell him what you have been doing? Ah, you think I do not know you, but I, too, have my ways.—yes, I know he is that rich English Merchant.'

I was fuming. 'You have dared to spy on me?'

'What choice did I have when you vanish like that?'

'You had no right. I am leaving. I shall go over to Signora Beppo's and see if she wishes to take charge of me. I am sure she shall not sniff at the hundreds of lira I line your pockets with! You do what you will!' And I crossed the room to make for the door.

'Listen,' she said more calmly now. 'I sent no spies. He came to me, seeking the *Rosa Inglese*, and I put him off when I realised who he was. So you see, *I* have protected you. It is in neither of our interests to quarrel so when our cause is in common.'

So he had come. I was close to discovery. I turned back. 'I did not come here to quarrel with you, but you are so fixed on feathering your own nest, you pay no heed to my difficulties, and you cannot seem to know when to temper your manner.'

'Fine, I will apologise. I am sorry.'

I was shaking with such fury I wanted to tell her what she could do with her apology, her apartment, and her job, and yet she knew now who Giles was. I took a steadying breath and sat back down.

'Now, you were ill, and now I think you are better, yes?'

I nodded.

'Well then, let us go from here. I suppose you have at least read my messages?'

I nodded again.

'Well then, you will know we have had an excellent offer from Signor Rudolpho.'

I held up a hand in protest. 'The answer is no,' I said flatly. 'I do not want to be his mistress.'

'You shall be so much more than that! If you take up his offer, you shall reach the height of your profession in one swift move. You shall be as Rachele Tanto. It will be the making of you. You will have jewels, gondolas, servants, and maybe even your own apartment brought and kept for you if he is as rich as he says he is. Everyone knows the *Cortigiane Oneste* comes at a very high bargain. What you earn now is a trifle. You shall have whatever you desire.'

All I desired was a one-way ticket home, to the devil with the rest of it. 'I don't want to be exclusive to him, whatever he is offering.'

'Well, if that is your objection, we shall negotiate a non-exclusivity clause in your contract and see if he agrees. You can perhaps propose certain times and days that are exclusive to him, that would solve it.'

'Fine put it to him, but I shan't budge if he refuses.'

This appeased her, along with my agreeing to see some of the other gentlemen who had been longest in the wait now. So I left on better terms than I had arrived on and with no earnest intention of agreeing to Serrano's contract, even though I was confident he would refuse this counteroffer anyway. Men like him wanted exclusivity so they could lay claim to something that would be denied others – there was the intrinsic worth in making such a bargain. Otherwise, why not just continue to seek appointments for the usual fee whenever the fancy took him? No, it was a power grab, a one-up on Giles, which I would not have objected to for that sake, but after how he made me feel, so defiled and appalled at myself. No, it was impossible. And with the memory of that resurfacing as I walked away from the bordello, I directed Benedetta to take me to the Academia di Belle Arti to see what work might be found there.

'Where have you been?'

I jumped as I closed my parasol and handed it to Benedetta in the hall. Giles was never home this early, and it was barely above five. 'To my art class, as you know... and then I went to the Art Academy to look at the gallery there – a study task Marco suggested to the class, and I thought I might attend to whilst I was already out. I would have come directly home had I realised you would be home early, husband.'

'Where is that do-gooder cousin of mine? Still filling your head with nonsensical ideas, and you still fancying yourself to become the next *Vigée Le Brun*.'

'No, Giles, nor ever did I. I told you it helps me with my melancholy to have something to attend to, and I don't know where Marco is. Still at the gallery, I would presume.'

'I thought he undertook to bring you home from your classes?'

'He does usually, only I had errands to run, as I said.'

'Well, you shall have plenty to attend to soon enough. I am early home because I have just received word from Dr Heimlich in Padua,' he said with a sprightly air. 'It seems my pleas to move us forward in his appointment list have finally paid off. He will see us next week. I am to write him a return now and make sure we secure it—Come, let us go into the drawing room, you can pour me a Brandy, and I will tell you about it.'

Benedetta, correctly reading this as her dismissal, dropped a curtsey and left.

I followed him up the stairs, poured him a drink, and we sat in the drawing room. The late afternoon sun was still burning bright and streaming in through the tall windows casting shapes upon the Turkey carpet.

'Well, husband, will you tell me what this is about?' I asked as I settled into my seat.

He took a long sip from his glass. 'I have procured the most renowned expert in—what does he call it again—of yes, matters of conception and fertility. We will go to him next week and he shall see what is wrong with you and help set things right.'

'Oh, how fortunate he will see us so soon,' I answered. I did not tell him that there was nothing wrong with *me*. After all, I had proven my ability to conceive at least, though not by him. Nor did I want him to suspect me of the efforts I had taken of late to curtail the risk of him succeeding, so I went along with it affably.

'Yes, well, it was not an easy feat. It cost me a large donation to his research project, but it has done the trick, which is why we must not delay. He is a busy man, and his waiting list would have put us another two months behind, so we must make plans to travel to Padua next week.'

'Padua, next week? Will he not come to us?'

'No, Dr Heimlich is engaged at the University medical school there and holds his clinic thereabouts. We can reach it within a day if we go directly via the river. I need to speak to my uncle later and see what their plans are, for it's possible we might all make something of a little holiday of it. They have a Villa along the Brenta they should have long since removed to, but on our account, they have remained. But I am mindful of taking up the entirety of their summer, and I know they have not been able to go so often as they used to in recent years. I think they would be very happy to join us there and remove from the city. Certainly, my uncle would benefit from the rest after all the work of late. And it shall do you good, too, my dear. Dr Heimlich recommends an extended stay so that you can take the healing waters at *Abano Bagni* while we are in the region. He tells me your overall health is paramount to our cause, so a change of air and scene shall do you good. He recommends a stimulating diet too and has asked you to complete a diary of what you eat ahead of our visit to bring with you so he might consider where improvements are to be made. You have grown rather skinny. I would not be surprised if you've fallen malnourished and that is to blame for all this trouble. Still, it will all be set to rights now.'

'Well, I have actually put a little weight on, according to Signora Sartore when she last measured me, so I am sure I am already heading in the right direction. Anyway, it all sounds very hopeful,' I offered, wondering what on earth I was going to tell Signora Crivelli now, having just made plans to resume my services. 'How long do you think we shall be away for?'

'Ahh, I don't know yet. I am still very busy finalising matters for this new contract, so I can't away too long. I daresay I can spare the better part of a week if all remains at hand, but no longer.—That's not to say that you cannot stay beyond a week, dear, if my uncle and aunt take to the idea of a holiday, you might stay in the country with them a while if Dr Heimlich thinks it good for your constitution. I shall let you know once I have spoken to my uncle.'

'Thank you. I should let Signora Barozzi know in advance if I cannot help at the charity house and Marco, too, that I will not be at class.'

He waved a disinterested hand at this. 'Well, it's hardly a matter of importance. Your pastimes I accept to keep your spirits up, my dear, but they are hardly a consideration. Besides, you shall soon have a family to take care of and no time for such trivialities, so as I warned you before, do not grow too attached to these amusements, for you shall soon have to give them up. As soon as you succeed to be with child, I want you rested and taking no chances.'

What, like the chance of you and Digby wrestling me down a flight of stairs again! I thought. 'Of course, husband,' I said with a weak smile, images arising of being confined to my room and reduced to an invalid if he ever did get his way. I was adamant he must not, more so now I was to be *remedied* by this Dr Heimlich, whatever that entailed. 'Giles, do you know what practices the doctor shall wish to undertake upon us?'

'*Us*, why would I need to undergo treatments, my dear?'

'I don't know, I suppose it takes both of us to create a child—'

He laughed out loud at this. 'It does, and as you have seen for yourself well enough of late, I have no issue fulfilling my end of the duty.'

'No, I know that I just meant—I mean, I know that men probably do not like to discuss such things with their wives, but I am not naïve about such matters. Giles, have you ever fathered any bastards?'

'What?'

I thought of Mariella and wondered why she had never fallen with his child or whether she knew how to take means to prevent it. Indeed, I would have expected her to know how. 'I do not mean to make a fuss of such things. They are irrelevant to our marriage, I know. I only supposed that you might have by now.'

He tossed his empty glass across the carpet and towards the chair I was sitting in. It did not smash but bounced along the carpet and hit the leg of my chair too softly to crumble. 'How dare you!' he roared. 'Who have you been speaking to?'

'No one, honestly.' I leant to pick up the glass. 'I did not mean to anger you, Giles. I am as keen as you to get to the bottom of this matter and only thought it thorough to consider whether we were both in ample health, that is all. You have been under a lot of pressure at the shipyard.' I put the glass upon the nearside table.

'You fail in your duty time and again and think *I* should be the subject of Dr Heimlich's efforts? You really are dicked in the nob, aren't you!'

The door knocked then, and Dante came in. 'Ah, I thought I heard voices,' he said cheerfully.

'Dante, good evening. You are back earlier than usual today, too,' I said.

'Yep, even us menials get time off once in a while,' he winked at me, then turned to Giles. 'You alright there, old chap? I am not interrupting, am I?'

'No,' Giles grunted. 'Is your father home yet?'

'He is. I believe he has gone directly to his study.'

'Ah, good,' he said and got up, crossed the room and left.

'And good evening to you too!' Dante said in his vacated direction and I offered him a smile.

'Are you alright?' he asked me more seriously.

I nodded. 'Yes, I am, thank you.'

'I heard him in one of his tempers and thought you might appreciate a rescue effort. I know I'm not as good at it as Marco, but it seems it did the trick, and I am far better company anyway.'

'Is that what accounts for these timely interruptions? Do you and Marco have a secret pact to thwart him whenever you are in earshot?'

'Something like that. Anyway, enough about your husband. How are you, Zuccherino? I fear I have neglected you of late, I have been so very tied up.'

'Not at all. I know you are kept very busy, but I do not deny that I have missed you.'

'Good, I was starting to think you preferred my brother's company over mine.'

'Dante, I prefer your company over and above *everyone* else's. You know it well.'

'Honey-tongued minx you are. But who can blame you? Now, tell me what I have missed in my absence?'

'Not very much, no surprise, I am sure. Though my husband seems to have it in his head that we are to go and see a specialist about the ongoing saga of my unfilled womb.'

'Ah, that's what all that was about, was it? Gosh, must you make it sound quite so grotesque? Wombs and such talk are definitely not for my hearing. As lovely as you are, my sweet, I think better save that kind of talk for my mama.'

I laughed, 'I shall not subject your ear to such female matters again. But, I shall ask you something else.—Giles said you have a house in the country somewhere close to Padua, and he means to suggest a holiday to your parents as part of our visit to see Dr Heimlich.'

'Ah, one of those Austrian fellows, vell das ist most zerious zen!'

'Dante!' I chuckled. 'What I wanted to know is whether you think they shall take up the idea of going to the Villa? I believe that is what he is gone to speak to your father about.'

'What, you fear being stuck out there alone with him if they decline?'

I nodded.

'Well, it's hard to say. I know they will both want to jump at the idea. They miss it greatly, and as you have seen, the city is not so pleasant in summer. But the trouble is, my mama shan't want to go without my father, not after all the bad business, and my papa is simply far too busy overseeing this new ship Giles expects to be ready by the end of the month.'

'What bad business?'

'All the wars and the famines.'

'But is that not all history now? Surely your mama does not fear another outbreak of either.'

'Perhaps not war, so long as the Greeks keep to their own quarters, but the famines are still much to mind. People grow desperate in such times, and it became a lawless place. Banditti all over the provinces holding people up, peasants stealing from the farms out of desperate hunger, horses killed for their meat, the Villa even got broken into and pillaged at the height of it all. It's put mama on edge ever since, and even though matters are improved now, and she truly loves her gardens there, I do not think she will consent to going unless one of us strong fellows is about to protect you sweet flowers.'

I gave him a little shove, for he always liked to toy with me so. 'So you think your father will say no, and therefore your mama will too?'

'Sorry to say so, but I think it is likely. And I can't go if that's what you're thinking because I am even further down the pecking order and can't be missed at the shipyard at all as I am charged with managing the workers. You shall have to look in Marco's direction for a plea for help there, though even he has the gallery to keep him tied. But it might be worth a try. He could always ask Holland-Bury to keep an eye on things for him. He might as well be of some use.'

'Why do you say that, you do not like Mr Holland-Bury?'

'It is not a matter of liking him or not. I daresay we would get along well enough in small doses if Marco were not my brother. But the trouble with Holland-Bury is he always looks to my brother to help him out of a scrape, but where is he when my brother needs him? Ah, well, it is his choice, and I don't deny even Holland-Bury has a good effect on him too sometimes, encourages him to lighten up and not take life so seriously, but he leaves a lot wanting in a fellow's friend, that's all. Not that you are to repeat a word of that missy.'

'My lips are sealed. But thank you, I might approach him. I shall have to see what the outcome is. I don't want to inconvenience anyone for my sake—'

'But nor do you want to suffer a week alone with your *darling* husband? It's alright, my lips are also sealed. See what they say, and if Marco can't help, I might even be able to talk one of my sisters into going and bringing their husbands. I'm sure there will be a way around it.

It turned out there was no need to be concerned after all. In a much-improved mood, Giles came to me while I readied for dinner to announce that we would set off for Villa Rosso on Monday morning. His uncle and aunt would go with us and open up the house; they were minded to check on the early harvests anyway, and whilst Mr Harper would have to return on Wednesday (the day of our appointment with Dr Heimlich), Isabella was happy to stay on with me and Giles until we were ready to return. She also wouldn't mind taking the waters in *Abano* for her rheumatism, so it was all settled. The only problem I had now, was letting Signora Crivelli know I would be absenting myself again for another unspecified period, now I had just given her leave to fill my diary. It would be a problem for tomorrow, I decided, as I was too fatigued to keep going over matters. It was far from ideal, but I knew my compliance with this trip was fundamental to keeping Giles sweet and non-suspecting, so I had no choice but to find a way.

CHAPTER THIRTY

No Complaints.

Annalise. July 1822.

'Matron, you carn't mean us to finish these today?' Tabby protested as another wagon of soiled linens was tipped into the laundry crate.

'Oh, can't I?' said the matron. 'It is not even three o'clock yet, so I think you can manage to see half of it hung for drying before dinner!'

'We'd be better treated in the plantation fields than what is expected of us here!' Tabby replied.

'Enough cheek, prisoner, and be grateful you are not still picking Oakum,' matron reminded her, half tolerant, half steel.

'But it is boiling hot today. Look at our poor hands!' Tabby demanded, holding her palms stretched out beneath the matron's great shelf of a bosom. 'Swollen as sausages and wrinkled as prunes, and you'd have us scrub until the flesh falls off the bone! La!'

'Mind your mouth, prisoner, and get back to work. You shall have some lard to tend them once the laundering is done,' matron told her, but not harshly as she might others who dared take such a line, with the customary threats of the basement cells and whipping room. No, such threats were not dished out to Tabby. Tabby was able to push her luck much farther with the turnkeys than most would have got away with, owing, in part, to belonging to a well-known local family of villains in Bodmin who the likes of the turnkeys were frightened of, and too, to Tabby's cheeky and scampish nature that was taken with a very large pinch of salt.

It was said that Tabby's siblings had once terrorised the family of a former turnkey who had delivered her a lashing on her first stay at his majesty's pleasure at the age of only twelve. That the matron and her family had left the county for the torment they received in return for it.

'Don't be fooled by their bravado', she told Annalise one morning when in a scrap with one of them over her food provisions, '...they might strut about in here like they are all the thing, but trust me, out there, they are as frightened as lambs when you's know where they lives and what their habits are, who their family is. And they quake at the sight or mention of the Spargo clan, to be sure. So don't you put up with none of their lark. You are my friend now, and if they make trouble for you, they make trouble for me!'

Annalise had not quite known how to feel about this. She was grateful for the sentiment in which it was intended, but for the thought of some woman's family being terrorised for undertaking the duties of her employ, she did not wish to entertain. So she did her utmost to stay out of trouble with the matrons, even the difficult and meaner-natured ones who could test even her patience at times.

'Fusty old bitch,' Tabby said low when the matron stepped away again, and Tabby returned to the sink beside her. Annalise pretended not to hear her as she scrubbed at the washboard. She had learnt in these past months that feigning ignorance was sometimes the best course of action with Tabby, for if you warned or chided her against such speeches, she would often take it on as a challenge to do worse, and if you agreed with her, she would often press you to join in similar observations or mischiefs. Neither of which Annalise had a mind to take the risk of indulging in, given that she had seemed to fly below the radar these past months and not be hoisted onto a ship.

But after a tricky start to their acquaintance, Tabby being unimpressed at having to share her cell with Annalise, they had learned to go along quite well together these past months, quite to their mutual surprise. It had been the kindly matron who had decided upon their sharing when unable to rouse Annalise from her bed or bring her about from days of endless sobbing on her return to the gaol after the sessions. She took no water or bread, picked no Oakum, and responded to none of the punishments the harsher matrons attempted to bring her about with for a fortnight. She was warned she would be force-fed or die a death of emaciation if she continued so, but even that could not rouse her into caring. In truth, she had rather hoped for any outcome that might bring her suffering to a swifter close. But in the end, the kindly matron had decided on drastic action in moving her in with one of the gaol's most accustomed and renowned pickpockets who was, it seemed, as frequent a boarder at this place as she was her own home—twelve times she had been imprisoned and released in her young life, and whilst it seemed to her nothing to answer, to Annalise it seemed as though life itself had ceased to be worth the trouble.

In this disparity of attitudes, the matron thought one might bring the other to better balance. That Tabby's spritely and resilient countenance might lift Annalise from her melancholy and show her how to manage her time here with better equanimity, and that Annalise's un-quarrelsome and meeker character might have a calming effect on Tabby.

At first, it had seemed like putting tinder to flame, and neither liked the arrangement well. But after a time, it appeared the scheme had played out according to plan and they had learned to coexist in companionable society with one another. Annalise being forced from wallowing in her deep state of paralysis by Tabby's animated spirits and regular rifts with the matrons, and Tabby kept entertained by drawing stories from Annalise, both of her knowledge of London and her life as a servant to the stories of old she knew from books she had read. All of this had been a great wonder to Tabby and was one of the few things that could fix her attention for any length of time. It had served Annalise too in convincing Tabby to help her to get a job in the laundry room, where the work, although almost as tedious and laboursome as the Oakum picking, at least permitted a change of scene from the tomb of a cell and allowed opportunities for talk and movement. And there were windows in that room that, though barred and set up high, were often left open to allow air to flow into the humidity of the washroom and light in which to work by, and even that seemed a luxury from what they were usually accustomed.

Tabby had worked in the Laundry since her most recent arrival three months ago, and on account of the sway she held with the matrons, when one of the other girls finished her sentence, Tabby petitioned Annalise's cause to take up her abandoned post in the Laundry. It had been an unexpected saving grace to be permitted air, light, and industry in which to wear herself out to ensure sleep each night. The days turned quicker, and her mind had less time to torment her with unanswerable questions while she was busy. And for that, above all else, she was grateful. Not that it had soothed her heartache and longing for what was lost to her, it still smarted just as cruelly when she pondered it. It was that she pondered it so much less now she found a way through.

They had barely finished mangling the last of the day's wash when Annalise was called away from her duties and told she had a visitor and was to discard her apron and make ready to receive him.

'Mr Langley!' she said when she was delivered to the anteroom where he had been waiting for her. 'What are you doing here?' she asked, surprised at the sight of him, especially since he had never visited her again since their day in Court.

'Miss Tullier, how do you do?' he asked, and she took her seat opposite him.

'I do better than before,' she managed. 'But why are you come? I thought you long since returned to London.'

'Indeed, it is so. And already the Western circuit descends for the Summer assizes.'

'Oh yes,' Annalise remembered, having heard the complaints of some of her fellow laundresses that they might soon have to share their cells too, having only recently enjoyed reclaiming them after a wave of releases.

'It is a courtesy call I make, part in apology for never making it before I left, and on Lady de Whitaker-Hollingford's request that I make a report to her on how you do, how the conditions are here and perhaps, see if I can procure a report of good character from the governor, on your behalf. Since nothing else has yet moved the Home Secretary to look into your petition, it is hoped that a good report from the governor might help things along in staying your sentence. Will it be possible to apply to him? What I mean is, you have not come into any bother that would cause him to give a bad report of you?'

'I see. Well, that is very good of her, and no, I daresay I am quite unknown to him, for good or for ill. But, I must confess, I do not know if I wish for that to change by being brought to his notice now. I had come to consider in all these months that perhaps I had been quite forgotten by the prison authorities and might be left alone to serve my time here. It has been almost four months now without any mention of my being transported.'

'As sometimes the case may be, if there are more prisoners than spaces on hulks awaiting to sail, it is not uncommon for the ones with longer sentences to be prioritised. But at any moment, that can change and directions can be issued. There seems at present some demand in the colonies for young women such as yourself to become maids and wives, so you see, it is important we still petition your cause, Miss Tullier, if you do wish to remain here.'

Wives. 'So you are certain I have not been forgotten?'

He shook his head. 'No, just in a very long queue at present, and whilst not impossible with the rate at which the judges are transporting, it is still possible you are shuffling your way up the queue, unbeknownst to us.'

'Very well then.'

'Am I to assume, from your wish to remain here, that you are kept in proper conditions?'

'As proper as they can be in such a godforsaken place, I suppose. But I have no complaints.'

'Well, it is not often you hear that from a prisoner, I must confess. But I am glad to hear it.'

'Tell me, Sir, do you bring news of home for me?'

'Ah, yes, I do have letters for you and am asked to send a reply before the sessions are spent.' He ruffled around in his satchel. 'With regards to your petition, I can confirm that several excellent affidavits were drafted and issued to the Home Secretary back in May, so your friends have done all they can to be expedient and thorough in their efforts. Sad to say that our Home Secretary is not nearly as efficient and it is anyone's guess as to when he might be pressed to consider them. But Mr Jeffers tells me Lady de Whitaker-Hollingford has taken a particular interest in the effort, so you should remain patiently hopeful.'

'Why?'

'Because, quite frankly, Miss Tullier, there is no better hope of consideration than having friends in high places.'

'I see.'

'I do not say that your case does not have merit, I simply say that it is the nature of the beast.'

'I understand, Sir. I wonder, did you happen to find out the outcome of Miss Craythorne's trial? I had expected to be called to the Court to bear testimony to her attack, but I never was.'

'I did. I'm sorry to say it did not go through to trial in the end. It seems she pleaded guilty to avoid the public spectacle and was rewarded with a respited sentence on account of pleading her belly.'

'What? Is there nothing in this land that is not tainted by corruption?'

'Very little in this line of business, I am sorry to say. I daresay she pleaded guilty on a pre-arranged assurance by the judges, but it would likely have made little difference anyhow, her being with child.'

'So you believe she really was in that condition and that it was not just another well-plotted scheme to get her off?'

'I believe it was the very reason her family insisted she put in a guilty plea, to spare the news of her condition breaking into the public sphere. But I can tell you no more. That is the limit of my knowledge on the matter, and that is only through the medium of a mutual acquaintance between her attorney and mine.'

A secret, then. How ironic: Giles was now a father to Mr Richards' child whilst Mariella veiled the existence of his own. Or at least she assumed it was the case. 'Thank you, Mr Langley, and for bringing me my letters. I fear I shall be unable to reply without pen or parchment at my disposal here, but if you might convey my thanks and well wishes and assure them of my health, I would be most grateful.'

'I will indeed, Miss Tullier. And I shall do my utmost to procure a favourable report from the governor.'

She knew not whether this had been possible, for she did not see Mr Langley before the assizes were over and supposed him to have left the county again. But she was grateful for the letters she received from Poppy and Mr Harrison and clung to their words of kindness and comfort. The news that he was now out of danger and well enough to train his new assistant in managing the greater share of the work in the bookshop and spent more time at leisure after the scare. It heartened her. She had prayed day and night for his recovery, for Eleanor's safe delivery of the child and for some kind of benevolent resolution to this circumstance.

CHAPTER THIRTY-ONE

Gift Horse.

Eleanor. August 1822.

At breakfast the following day, I was surprised to find the whole family at the table for a change. I had also forgotten my excuse to Giles yesterday about my impromptu visit to the Art Academy, so when he turned to Marco in answer to some part of the conversation I hadn't heard and said, 'Well, you shall be pleased to know that you have at least one pupil who is dedicated in her learning, cousin, what gallery did you go to yesterday to comply with your study task, dear?'

I gulped down a mouthful of too-hot coffee. 'The Academia di Belle Arti,' I said nervously, looking at Marco.

He considered me briefly. 'Oh, you went. I hope you found it to your liking?' he said, looking up from his pastries and brushing crumbs from his hands. Dante must have mentioned it to him, for I had not. It seemed to me that perhaps the pair really did collude, as I had begun to suspect, though I was grateful for it. Even my own brothers could rarely be relied upon to take such pains for my sake.

'It was beautiful, as were the works.' This much was true. I had noted the marvel of the great frescoed walls as I made my enquiry to the attendant about the modelling advertisement.

'Did you see the *Vitruvian Man?* It has only just been returned to us in Venice.'

'I did. It was every bit as interesting as you said it was.' This part was entire fabrication, for I had not been permitted so much as a peep into the rest of the gallery as I was led along the corridors to the principal's office, who, after having inspected my naked form and granting his approval of my application, had me escorted back outside again after with a promise to contact me when they had suitable work. I had given him Signora Sartore's details for the purpose of this correspondence, too. She was certainly paid well enough for her troubles, what difference would another messenger make?

'Well, that's excellent. The proportions are useful for us to consider in portraiture. We shall discuss it further in Monday's class. Perhaps you might encourage the others to go along, now you have.'

I smiled, 'I would be happy to, though I shall not be about on Monday—'

'Of course, we were just speaking of your trip to *Fiesso di'Artico.* I think you shall all enjoy it very much.'

Giles looked satisfied by this—by what he presumed was my prioritising this trip above such trivialities of insignificance, as he liked to call them. I made the most of pandering to this idea to keep him off the scent of other less favourable activities I would be up to later today in his absence. 'Yes, I look forward to seeing the Villa and the countryside and taking the air,' I smiled in Giles's direction.

'You will love it there, Eleanor,' Isabella said. 'It is a beautiful spot by the river, and I know how you love your English countryside, so I think you will appreciate the natural landscape and the gardens there. Though I cannot pretend to know what condition they have been kept in in my absence.'

'Giuseppe will have kept them neat and orderly if nothing else,' her husband put in.

'Yes, I daresay, but whether anything more has been pillaged or planted, I do not know.'

'My wife is very proud and fussy about her garden, Eleanor. Do not worry, it shall be perfectly presentable for your arrival, even if it has missed your green-thumbed diligence, my dear,' he said now to Isabella, who beamed at him.

I was pleased to see that this trip, far from seeming an inconvenience imposed upon them, had cheered the family greatly and seemed to fill the room with excited chatter on one topic or another. Though it made it all the more apparent to me what an inconvenience I had already proved in denying them to go there long before now as they had used to be accustomed. Their summer ruined by having to nanny me and work double time at the shipyard to meet Giles's lofty ambitions. Still, I would be gone from under their feet by Autumn and then they could return to their regular routines unhindered. Until then, I meant to enjoy my final weeks amongst them, for they had grown into a very fine substitute for my own lack of family now. A family who had not even bothered to send word to me in months, and this time, I had taken pains to send my covert letters and knew they must have reached them. I daresay it was something of a relief to know where I was and that I would not be able to cause any more mischief to sully them with in their society, at least, now I was under my husband's diligent watch. It was just as well I was so far away, too, for I would never want them to learn what I had been reduced to. Even if they had cut ties with me, they would never suspect I would sink so low as I had.

'Do you ride Eleanor?' Mr Harper asked, and I realised I'd drifted from the conversation.

I put down my cup and swallowed. 'Yes, I love riding. Do you keep horses at *Villa Rosso*?'

'Sadly not, anymore. Only a donkey for the farmer now. Before the war, we kept four horses, but, well, we have had no need of them since and so the expense could not be justified any longer, and we could hardly move them here with us.'

'No indeed, I should think even a single horse would not be feasible in the city, though I once saw one of the white coats on horseback approaching the Palazzo Ducale.'

'You will see them at the Arsenale, too. They are used to pull the boats along the canal during construction.' Dante added.

'Yes, well that's perhaps the only place you will seem then in the city.' Mr Harper added. 'Aside from the occasional ceremonial appearance, they are rarely used here unless there is military trouble, and thank the lord, there has been none of that for a very long time now. Though most fond riders keep stables on the Lido for their riding sports. Perhaps Giles, you might think of hiring some if Eleanor is so fond of it. I know of an excellent stable close to *Malamocco* I can give you the direction of,' he offered.

Giles wiped his face with his napkin. 'I'm sure Eleanor can manage until we return to England, and then she can fill the stable with as many as she likes.' I knew he meant there was no way he would trust me with the provision of a horse on these shores should I take flight on my own and cross the continent to get back there and flee from him. And it was true. I was so desperate now to be gone before I fell with child on one account or another, that I would have preferred to brave even the Banditti and treacherous terrain to prevent that fate, even if I would prefer better means.

When Giles, Dante, and Mr Harper bid us farewell, I felt a little easier, and the conversation fell into the usual natural flow it did when it was just Marco, Isabella, and me. Then she excused herself on account of having much to do in preparation for our trip, and then it was just Marco and I, remaining.

'Thank you for covering for me,' I said when I was sure we were alone. 'I'm sorry, I should have warned you. I was caught out on the spot—'

'Dante told me, it's alright. But did you go?'

'I suspected he might have. I went there but had no appointment and was turned away,' I lied.

'Shame. Perhaps we might go together after class when you are back. I can make the appointment when you are decided when to return.'

'Yes, that would be nice. Though I'm not yet sure how long I will be gone for. I wonder if Dante also told you the purpose of our trip to Villa Rosso?'

'Yes, some doctor Giles insists you consult.'

I nodded. 'And some medicinal spa I'm to attend.'

'Do you wish to go?'

I shrugged. 'Not with him, though I think it will be nice to go with your parents...You will not join us?'

He shook his head. 'I cannot. I have the gallery to think of and I am already having difficulty pinning George down to help me out with classes.'

I dropped my gaze to my empty plate. 'Yes, I noticed he has not been about much lately. Was he supposed to be?'

'He was supposed to be running a full series on portraiture for me, but he has begun to let me down with the Ladies class, though he just about manages to get himself there in time for men's. I should have known better than to rely on him and make promises to the class to keep up the programme.'

I felt terrible. This was clearly my doing. 'Well, why do you not hold him to his bargain? It's pretty shabby to let you down after starting out.'

'That's George all over.'

'Can't you cover the subject?'

'I can, though I am out of touch. George lives and breathes for this, it is his craft, and I wanted to offer something beyond my repertoire to the students.'

'I am certain what you offer is more than enough, Marco. The ladies adore your classes, as do I. You are no inferior substitute for your friend, though I am sorry he has let you down.' I pressed a gentle hand over his, feeling guilty. I hoped that now I was to take a holiday and be absent, he might be willing to resume them and honour his part for Marco's sake.

He reached for his cup. 'So, why did you go to the Art Academy yesterday?'

'Well, I mean to take in all the sights whilst I am here and the Academia I had not gotten about too, and Benedetta knew the way—.'

'I'm glad you wish to see it. Perhaps I *should* set it as a study task for the rest of the class. It's a good idea. Tell me, though, why did you throw your sketch away after yesterday's lesson? I found it in the bin when I was tidying away. It is the best work I have seen you do, Eleanor. It shows great promise.'

'I did not think it very good at all.' It was true that it was my best work. I had even surprised myself with its precision, yet it was the last thing I wanted to be reminded of now that I had relegated Annalise to my list of regrets and disappointments.

'It was very good, truly. Who is she?'

'Someone I once knew, no one of consequence.'

'She is very beautiful. I see why you chose her portrait.'

I wanted to let out a painful groan of disagreement, but instead, I just said, 'She is, though I daresay I have not remembered her in complete accuracy.'

'That is not what matters in that exercise. It is that you can sketch so well without a subject to sit for you. It is truly impressive. I would like you to continue and finish it if you will. I took the liberty of salvaging it from the bin and have hung it in the attic studio. Perhaps you will take it to the Villa with you and find some inspiration to keep trying there since you cannot come to class.'

'I shall,' I said, thinking I would have to add retrieving it from the studio and burning it later to my list of things to do today. If Giles came across it, he would certainly recognise her features. Even if they were not entirely accurate, they were certainly telling enough. But it was to be postponed until later. I had much to do today in keeping with *Rosa Inglese's* appointment schedule, so I excused myself and went to get ready to attend the apartment.

By late afternoon, I had serviced three patrons and endured three potash and mugwort washes and changes of the vinegar-soaked sponge. I also had another two hundred lire to add to my purse, a fact I reminded myself of as I winced over another steaming bowl. I was concerned now I was to be examined by a specialist of such renown, whether the irritation I felt from all this abrasive washing and steaming would give away a clue to what I had been doing. I remembered back to Giulia's warning about never disclosing such things for fear of the authorities. Would Dr Hiemlich suspect my efforts to prevent a child? Would he have seen such irritation before and understand the origin? It began to concern me. I only hoped it was needless or I could put it down to some other cause between now and then.

At four o'clock, I was ready to meet my final patron for the day and look to the relief of my duties being over. I was expecting Mr Scott, an Englishman on his Grand Tour who was staying at the hotel next door. He was young and fairly green, a quick and easy conquest who had fallen for the thigh trick, and so I looked to his arrival with equanimity as I took my seat upon the chaise. But when I looked up towards the opening door, it was not he who came into the room, but Serrano. I jumped out of my seat instantly.

'Sir, there is some mistake. I have no appointment with you.'

'Forgive me, I know you were not expecting me but Signora Crivelli changed your appointment as a generous favour to me.'

'And how generous did you have to be to her, I wonder?' I said flippantly.

He held up his palms. 'I have offended you. Forgive me. I have no wish to. I only want to talk.'

'Sir, I know why you are here, and I have already given my answer.'

'I will agree to any term you ask, but that one.'

'I cannot alter that, Signor. It is far too dangerous for me to promise so much to a man so well-known to my husband. Surely you understand that? I take a great risk in seeing you at all, but exclusivity, your mistress—'

'We will be careful. Discreet.'

'It is too risky, I'm sorry.' I stepped towards the door to indicate him leave.

'Then tell me how to ameliorate such risk? What will you have? Your own apartments somewhere quieter like Murano where you will not be discovered? Your own gondola and gondolier to convey you there under the cover of its felze?'

'Sir, your generosity is not in question here, truly.'

'There must be *something* that you want. Why don't you name it?'

'Well, if you could get rid of my husband and Signora Crivelli whilst you're at it—'

'You tease me, yet if it would answer...'

'And now you tease me, Signor. Please, I shall be honest with you: there are only two terms that hold any weight with me, one as I already put to you, and the other is that there is no attempt to pleasure me,' I said more uncomfortably.

'You break my heart, Signora, truly. I offer you anything and you settle for such fripperies as denying your own pleasure and being well-kept by your most fervent admirer. I cannot fathom you.'

'I daresay I seem quite the puzzle, but I have my reasons, Sir, I assure you, and however peculiar they seem, they are sensible in my mind.'

'Here's what I propose to put your mind at ease. I will send your husband away on some distant task this very week. I will find some errand or another. You will consider it a token of what I can offer, and you may see for yourself how easy it will be for us to go on unhindered by his presence. In that time, I want you to reconsider my offer.—Say not a word about it now, pray, hold your tongue and I will return to you this time next week to have your answer.'

I could not deny it was not tempting, despite my obvious misgivings. But I was reluctant to throw myself into one man's trap to free myself of another.

But when Giles announced, only two days later, that he would have to cancel his coming to Padua for the sake of an urgent business trip, I was impressed and already trying to talk myself around to the idea. Was it possible he could render me free of Giles for my remaining weeks in Venice and supply me with the remainder of my fare, as well? It seemed an offer too good to refuse, yet I would always come full circle at the memory of my undoing that day. I had no reason to suspect that it would happen again. Indeed, I had felt not an inkling since, yet the possibility was still enough to deter me. But just because I meant to refuse him again did not mean I was not at liberty to enjoy the gift of Giles' absence to the fullest, even if it seemed I would not be spared my trip to Dr Heimlich, as I had hoped on this announcement. No, I was still to go, and since it was me who needed treatment, his absence, whilst unfortunate, should make little difference to the main objective of the trip.

'It is all settled,' he said that night as I held my legs against the bedpost for the mandatory five minutes.

'Marco will join the party, so when my uncle leaves on Wednesday, my aunt agrees to remain and accompany you to the clinic and the *Abano Bagni*. He cannot manage above a fortnight, but perhaps I can join you by then if the doctor thinks you should stay on longer.'

I knew he had spent the entirety of dinner trying to persuade the family to salvage the trip. I had expected his attempts to fail, so I went along with them, hoping Marco would decline on account of the gallery as he had told me, and yet it seemed even he was not beyond Giles's persuasion.

It was still an improvement by all accounts, except for the foreboding matter of Dr Heimlich, which it seemed there would be no way of escaping for all my prayers. I wondered at the state he would find my lower regions in, having grown used to thrice or more daily alum and mugwort washes in the preceding days of our trip as I tried to pacify Signora Crivelli over my renewed spell of absence in fulfilling as many appointments as I could before departing for the country.

I would at least have a few days' reprieve before I saw him. Giles left on Saturday morning and I made that day my last in service to the patrons. By Wednesday, I would have had four days off of the abrasive cures and hoped it would be enough to render some improvement. If not, I would have to blame some harsh reaction to cheap soap or some other such unlikely excuse. Either way, I was relieved of the anxiety of any such discussion unfolding in Giles's company now.

CHAPTER THIRTY-TWO

Villa Rosso.

Eleanor. August 1822.

T he river Brenta and its surrounds were precisely the breath of fresh air I needed, I realised, as we drifted and meandered about its expanse in the Burchiello on Monday morning. Isabella and Mr Harper kept to the shade of the elaborate cabin below, Marco and I sat on the balcony over a game of *vingt et un* as he pointed out various aspects of our view. I felt then that I was happy for the first time in an age, though the sensation seemed so foreign to me now it took me some time to fathom it. I had put it down to the simple relief of respite from Giles, first and foremost, but also from the demands of Signora Crivelli and the patrons, even the confines of the city itself in the full swell of summer heat. But it was something more than only that, I realised now. This reminder of what it was to be happy I took as something of a token of a future I no longer thought possible. I knew in my heart I would never get over the loss of Annalise, but I had thought I might never know comfort or hope again at all. Sitting in agreeable company, removed from the weight of all else, I finally saw that it was possible to recover some sense of a future better than my most recent past.

Soon, I would be free. I would be home. My purse was certainly stacked well in favour of managing a fare within a matter of weeks if only I could get back to Venice within a fortnight and Dr Heimlich did not mean to detain me here for longer. 'Marco,' I said then, with this in mind. 'How was it Giles persuaded you to come when I thought you unable?'

'I did not do it for Giles's sake,' he said vaguely, then laid his deck down to expose his winning cards.

'Argh! I have certainly lost my touch,' I complained, surrendering my losing hand. 'Best of three?'

I nodded, and he reshuffled. 'Thank you for coming. I hope it has not made things troublesome for you?'

'The pleasure is mine, and so long as Holland-Bury can be trusted to keep things afloat at the gallery, I'm sure a couple of weeks off will do me some good, too. I cannot remember when I last took a holiday.'

I smiled. 'I am glad of it then. I think your parents are happy too.'

'Very. They love it there. They mean to retire to it once my father is ready to hand the reigns over to Dante.—Though when that will be, I do not know.'

'Is Dante not ready?'

'Dante has been ready for the past few years, but as for when my father will be ready to let go, I cannot say. Soon, I hope. The war years and famines have taken more toll on them than us younger generations. I would like to see them enjoy some peace now that things are more stable.'

'Yes, well, I suppose it is harder for those of the old order to adapt to a new one after such a time.'

He nodded. 'For my mama mostly. Her family rose from humble beginnings to their better station before the Republic fell. Not patricians, of course, but as close as you can climb. She places the loss of their once great fortune as something of a failure on her part in managing her family's legacy, but it is not the case. Some of the most powerful houses in Venice have fallen in recent times. No one can withstand such downturns as the economy here has suffered. Even the Pisani's had to sell their house in Stra, to Napoleon, no less.'

'Napoleon. Well, I think we are all glad to see him take his final bow. There was merriment all over the country last year when he was announced dead.'

'It was much celebrated here too, in most quarters, though perhaps more privately. We do not enjoy the sovereignty of country the English do anymore. Even if we are marginally better off under the Habsburgs, we are a long way short of our former glory.'

'Was it very terrible under the French?'

'Abominable. There are no words for the state in which our country and people were left. The poor, of course, suffered the worst of it. So much starvation and death, the charity houses overrun and yet no proper support for the funding anymore. All our riches plundered, public and private, when it came to taxation. I would wish it on no one, which is why, though I still see much need for economic improvement, I am not against the Austrian's hold. Emperor Francis is a preferable ruler to that Franco war criminal. Of course, Francis has his critics, too, but it is often overlooked that he has been left to sweep away the ashes of Napoleon's destruction, though at least he makes some effort towards it rather than sacking us of everything. And heaven knows the Republic was not perfect. Corruption and spies, profligacy and inertia all played their part. Some like to blame the Portuguese, but the decline of the Republic was on so many accounts, not simply chance or the opening up of alternative shipping routes and competitive markets. But there's no doubt that Napoleon put the final nail in the coffin with savage style.'

'I am sorry for it. I never fully appreciated all the talk of war and how fortunate we were not to fall under Napoleon's reign. I was but a child then, and apart from the chatter of adults, I felt nothing of the threat.'

'A fortunate circumstance indeed. I, too, enjoyed my share of shelter in England for a time. Father paid us out of conscription, but they took no chances and sent us away as much for safety as for the sake of our education, I believe.'

'Who can blame them? You have the most loving of parents, and in that, you have certainly been the more fortunate. As for the city and its inhabitants, I hope it returns to its former glory one day, for it is an astonishing place, even in decay. Spending time at the charity house has made me realise the extent of the damage in the aftermath.'

'I see it has grown on you at last, then.'

'It has. I own, when I first arrived, I was indifferent to everything, but now—now I am sorry at the thought of leaving, especially your lovely family, when the time comes.'

'Well, let us hope it is not for some time yet. By the sound of Giles's ambitions, it shan't be anytime soon.'

'Did he tell you so?'

'Not exactly. But he is hopeful that taking on Serrano's diamond runs and equipping his ships with enhanced manning and security will attract more of the same work.'

'I see.'

'He did not mention that to you?'

I shook my head. 'He told me when we arrived, we were to stay for six months before returning home. But then my husband thinks females are not worth mentioning matters of business to, even if such issues do dictate my living arrangements.'

He offered me a sympathetic smile. 'Well, he is greatly mistaken, certainly in you. But I hope you are no longer unhappy here.'

I smiled back. 'Here...no, not anymore. But, I am not sure I will ever know anything above unhappiness in my marriage.—Forgive me, I should not have said that.'

'To me, you mean?'

'I suppose so. I sometimes forget you are his cousin. Forgive me, I meant no offence.'

'Eleanor, the only thing that offends me is how he treats you. Be assured of that.'

And yet you know not the half of it, I thought. 'You are very kind, Marco, all of you, and it is to you all that I owe any peace of mind I have recovered since I got here.'

He held my gaze then, and for a moment, it seemed neither of us knew what to say until he declared the cards dealt.

'Right, let's see if I can redeem myself,' I said, considering my hand. 'Oh, we have stopped?'

'Only to have our passports checked and to be tied to the horse. We are pulled by horse the remainder of the journey now.'

'I see,' I said, watching as a fellow began attaching a rope to a horse's harness on the riverbank pathway. Uniformed officials spoke with Mr Harper as he showed them the documents. I thought instantly of Samson at the sight of the horse's shiny chestnut coat gleaming in the sun.

'The sight of the horse pleases you better than our game, I think.'

'No. I was only distracted. I miss my stallion sometimes, that's all. It is my hope that when I get home I can bring him with me, for he remains with my parents. I have had him since I was a child and he is as much a friend to me as a means of riding.'

'It is quite alright. We can save our game for later if you prefer. There is much to see now of the countryside and palaces on this stretch of the journey should you like to take in the view.'

'Alright, if you do not mind, we shall play on later. I would like to pay attention to the scenery, for I am never happier than when I am amongst the majesty of nature.'

'I see it in your eyes. It is a worthy delay. Look ahead, as we reach the rivers curve, we shall soon approach Villa Malcontenta, one of Palladio's marvels.'

'Oh, I see it. It is very grand. But pray, why is it called Malcontenta? It seems quite a peculiar choice for such a picturesque place.'

'Oh, forgive me. It is something of a local nickname. Its correct name is *Villa Foscari*, after the Foscari family who commissioned Palladio to build it some two hundred and seventy years ago, I believe. The Foscari's were an important Venetian family and boasted our longest reigning Doge to the Republic. But it is uninhabited now and, like much else, is falling into ruin, sadly.'

'It does not appear to be in ruin, though I see the land is not so well tended. But you did not explain the local namesake?'

'Oh, yes, it is owing to an old myth or legend, who can tell.'

'Well, will you tell me this old myth that has endured for a quarter of a century?'

'If you like. The story goes that it served as a gilded cage for one of the Foscari wives. It is said she was locked up here alone for thirty years until her death.'

'Why?'

He shrugged, 'It depends upon which version you favour. Some say it was on account of her infidelity, others on account of her refusal to adhere to conjugal duties,' he explained, somewhat uncomfortably.

I was guilty of both. Perhaps she had been, too. Though I would have settled for such a cage away from Giles as preferable, I considered.

'It is harsh, I know.'

'I don't know. Perhaps she preferred it to her husband's company. Who is to say that it was not, in fact, a relief to her rather than a sufferance? Perhaps the malcontent was attributed to him and not her.'

He puckered his lips thoughtfully. 'Perhaps. I have never thought of it like that but I suppose you would be better placed to judge.'

I realised then that I had spoken too freely and that he had wisely drawn something of a parallel between the mythical Foscari wife and my marriage. Whether he thought me guilty of infidelity or refusal, I did not venture to guess, but I was on dangerous ground and thought it wise to change the subject. 'The willows are beautiful, the way they soften the river's curve.'

'Yes, I fancy I shall do some painting while I am here. You are welcome to join me in place of the classes you shall miss.'

I thought back to Annalise's sketch, which I had not burned after all but packed in my trunk to come with me. 'Thank you, that is good of you. I shall be the envy of the class having your private tutelage at my disposal.'

'I don't know about that. I only hope Holland-Bury keeps to the programme in my absence.'

'The ladies adore you, Marco. You are far too modest. Will Holland-Bury be taking their class then?'

'Yes, which is not a problem, so long as he turns up and sticks to *teaching* portraiture. It is his area, and he excels in it. They are, in fact, lucky to have his eye for detail.'

'Then why do you seem concerned?'

'Oh, I am not concerned over his teaching skill, so long as he remembers that the ladies are there to be taught and not to be flirted with.'

'I see.' I thought back uncomfortably to my failed attempt to persuade him.

'I have my assistant in attendance to ensure things are kept in order.'

'I'm sure it will be fine then. Perhaps he learned from his mistake at bringing Lena to the studio that day.'

'So he tells me. Anyway, I am going to get a drink. Would you like something?'

When we arrived at *Villa Rosso* late in the evening, I was pleased to have come despite my appointment with the doctor. I met the view of our new home by the fading amber light of a retreating sunset as the Burchiello was harboured before its view.

The Villa stood quaint and pretty at the river's edge and reminded me of something reminiscent of Stapleford in terms of its more modest stature and air of faded decadence. Of course, it was very much in the native style, painted in a shade of Russian Flame adorned with window shutters of sun-bleached Spanish fly, but it held an atmosphere of retreat about it that reminded me of those happy days spent in the dower house in Cambridgeshire. A retreat much needed, though for somewhat different reasons now. But above all else, what delighted me in beholding it, was the surrounds. The acres of sprawling farmland and grass meadows laid out beyond the pretty formal gardens. The lazy river views with its trailing willows and sense of peace radiating from every leaf and shrub. I had missed country life more than I had realised, and whilst I knew it was not home, it served as a charming reminder.

As I surveyed the view from my chamber window and paused to take a break from the unpacking, I noticed another similarity in the familiar smell of straw and dung drifting up from the farmlands. It was so reassuring and soothing to be close to the land, something so comforting to me after all this time. I was even looking forward to helping Isabella in the garden as she spoke of her plans for it at dinner. I was no able gardener, but I was of a willing mind to try and perhaps learn something of the skill.

For I was truly at leisure here, free of any demands, and it felt exhilarating to be so at liberty having been so captive and burdened for months. And in a fortnight, when I hoped to return to Venice, it would be a matter of only a few more weeks' endurance until I was ready to make my move towards home and *true* liberty.

I would give Holland-Bury one more try and see if he could be brought about to permitting me to travel with him, but I would not be put off should he decline. No, not after this reminder of the sweet taste of contentment. However dreadful the journey by land or sea, I meant to make it one way or another, for this was to be the prize: a return to a self I had thought deserted me. A free-spirited self that, this time, would return to my country under *no one's* regulation. Not my husbands or my fathers, or societies, for that matter. For I had no intention of returning to Cuddington and seeking my parent's refuge, not now they had made clear their position. This time, I was to start over new, assume a new identity altogether in some place I should never be found by anyone I did not wish to be. I knew not the means or finer details yet, but I would fathom it all out once I got there. And in the meantime, I knew I could rely on Lady W.'s support whilst I found my feet. She might not have written to me yet, but I suspected not her loyalty but some issue in the carriage of either my letter or her return. Soon, she would receive my second attempt, and I was confident I would hear back from her this time. Especially since I had told her to address the letter to Benedetta and not me, just in case there was some foul play involved in the lack of responses. But for now, I settled into bed in the easiest of spirits I had known since my capture. It was all going to be alright. For the first time, I *knew* this.

This knowing grew stronger each day as I exhaled into this new lightness of being. Family mealtimes on the terrace and walks along the riverside, planting with Isabella and picking the early harvests with the servants on the farm: fresh berries and ripe tomatoes, apples and apricots in sweet abundance. I was even permitted to help in the kitchen as I once had enjoyed in Stapleford. I remained a novice but was keen to learn. After all, I would need to know how to feed myself in my new life, for it would be a humbler existence than I had been used to.

When I was not kept busy in some pursuit or another, Marco and I would play cards, or he would tell me something more of the history of the house and sometimes of his own life too, which was new and welcome after such a time of him remaining relatively closed to such questions. My only wish was that Dante could have joined us all and completed our happy party. I missed his teasing and frank company, though I understood why he could not submit to my pleas to come even for a brief visit. It was a chance for him to be left holding the fort and proving to his father he was more than capable of the task. I hoped it succeeded for all of their sakes, for I saw how happy the Harpers were in the refuge of this little paradise and shared in Marco's wish they retire to such a way of life. There was a restorative medicine in the surroundings of nature I had always been subtly aware of. But now, I felt its presence in such profound measure, saw its effects not only on myself but also on everyone here, and it heartened me. I was only sorry for Mr Harper that he'd had to depart again so soon, just as he began to fall into the leisurely rhythm of the place.

Even Doctor Heimlich's visit this afternoon filled me with less foreboding because my courses had come early in the night, and I knew then I was to be spared my greatest fear of submitting to an intimate examination. Not that I was certain he would undertake one, but now, as I sat in the anteroom of his clinic, I felt sure he would not on explanation. In any case, the evidence of any irritation would be well disguised now.

I flicked through the pages of the diet diary I had completed over breakfast as Isabella gave me a gentle squeeze on the arm.

'Would you like me to go in with you or to wait here, my dear?' she asked me when my name was called up.

I had already considered this beforehand and asked her if she would accompany me. Not only would I feel less anxious in her presence, but having a witness to my compliance with the doctor could only be an advantage now.

The doctor was a stern-faced man with thin wisps of dark hair combed across a balding head and tiny spectacles that magnified his eyes disproportionately as he looked me over with a darting gaze. There was some difficulty at first in understanding his strong accent in the Germanic style and my Italian comprehension, which I was not used to hearing spoken in this inflection. But, with occasional help from Isabella, as well as some things spoken in broken English, we found a way through the interview.

The first twenty minutes of the consultation proved something of an interrogation into the entirety of my health history and menstrual patterns, which was easy enough to explain and seemed to arouse no particular interest. But when more personal questions ensued, I wondered at my thinking in inviting Isabella in.

How often was the marital bed attended? Did there appear to be any difficulty on the part of my husband in performing the act of generation? Had either of us ever displayed any symptoms of venereal disease? Were either of us in a habit of self-abuse? Had I reason to believe my cervix had suffered any damage or injury?

I had not foreseen such intrusive questions and stumbled over clipped answers and tried not to look in Isabella's direction. Then we moved on to matters he had been apprised of in my husband's letters, namely his reports of mental disturbance and nervous episodes.—This seeming in his mind to be the primary concern in the first instance. Since I had conceived before, it seemed reasonable to expect that everything had been functioning as it should, that the cause of my miscarriage seemed circumstantial in my "falling" down the stairs, and in and of itself, did not seem to suggest any anatomical obstruction to nurturing a pregnancy. Yes, it was unfortunate that my courses would delay an examination of my cervix to rule out any damage suffered by the fall, but this could be undertaken on our next review visit in six weeks' time. Between now and then, I was to consult the dietary sheet he gave to me in place of the one I had submitted, eat a diet rich in good meat and vegetables, and take no more than one glass of wine a day. I should seek to gain weight, though not too much. And whilst I was here, every day I should take a glass of the terme waters, and when possible, to visit the baths too. It might help to restore not only a tranquillity of mind, but also prevent spasms of the womb, all of which would be conducive to bringing my health into greater balance.

On my husband's return, we should resume conjugal activity, but not to excess. This point at least was worthy of the interrogation, even if I felt ashamed as I left the clinic with Isabella, and Marco handed us into the hired chaise he had been waiting in to convey us back. It was his presence I attributed to the lack of conversation on the doctor's visit on the journey home. Beyond a brief mention that she would speak to the cook about my dietary needs and we would go to Abano tomorrow to take the waters, no more was said.

I was grateful to have it over and done with, though. I was now free to enjoy the remaining time here to suit myself, and I meant to do precisely that. However, I had not anticipated anything beyond my usual ambling and pottering about the place until Marco called me outside after tea.

'I have something to show you. A surprise,' he said.

I frowned and placed a hand across my brow to see him better against the glare of sunlight. 'A surprise, for me?'

He smiled, 'Yes, of course for you. My mama would not find it thus, perhaps a punishment, but you, well, I realise you are very fond of horses, and so, since we must make so many journeys to and from Abano, I thought I would hire the horses for the duration rather than for each trip. Would you like to go for a ride?'

My mouth fell wide open with astonishment. 'Really?'

He laughed a little at this. 'Yes, really.'

'Oh, Marco, thank you! I should love nothing more!' Without considering the impropriety on my part, I leapt in towards him and hugged him with a lack of restraint that surprised him. 'How thoughtful of you,'

He released my hold on him and stepped back. 'A worthy endeavour to see you in such spirits. Come, let me introduce you to Volatore and Angelo.'

I followed him down to the farm buildings at speed, struggling to contain my excitement. He led me into a stable where two fine white stallions drank from a water trough in their shared pen.

'What are they? They are beautiful!' I said, taking up a bucket of apple halves ready to make an offering.

'They are, the breed is Lippizano, very sturdy creatures,' he said, slapping the haunches of the one who came over to us and stuck his head over the stable gate.

'Hello boy, aren't you a handsome chap indeed,' I said, offering him an apple slice from my palm. 'And which are you? Volatore or Angelo?'

'Hmm, now I know that Angelo has a patch of pigmented skin upon his rear thigh, though I cannot see from here who is who.'

'It is Volatore, then. Look, do you see?' I said, pointing to the other horse, looking up from the trough and taking a slow trot over to us to see what he was missing.

'Yes, you are right, you do have a good eye.'

'Oh, hello, Angelo, would you like a piece of apple too? Yes, I thought so.'

'I think he likes you.'

'I think he does, and oh, how I adore you both. Oh, you like that, a little scratch where you can't reach,' I said, ruffling behind his ears and pressing the tip of my nose against his, 'Beautiful boy you are.—What?' I said then to Marco, who was smiling in a way I had not seen him smile before.

'Nothing, I am only not used to seeing you so—'

'Silly? Well, I am afraid that horses have that effect on me so you should grow used to it.'

'No, not silly...animated.'

'Very tactful,' I teased. But I saw then he was not funning in the least. His expression was quite transfixed. 'Are you alright?'

'Yes, yes, I am fine. Now, it should be a little cooler in about an hour. Will that give you enough time to prepare for our ride?'

'Yes, though I have no habit. I have had no need of one for such a time.'

'And neither I, so we shall go in rustic style. It is too warm for all that fuss anyway, wouldn't you agree?'

'Yes, alright, I shall see what I can find to answer.'

I would not have cared if I was in the finest ball gown or barest scrap of shift as we rode along the river side by side in the early evening sun as it waned and settled into pink and amber hues beyond the trailing willows. I had not felt so invigorated since I had ridden Annalise and I back from the Buntingford Inn that snowy night. I eschewed the memory and focused ahead on the winding path which obscured the onward course of the river. I was not to be sunk into low spirits today, not on any account. I was as free as the breeze blowing against my face, and I meant to make the most of the sensation, to commit it to memory so fervently that I would not lose sight of my objective in the final phase of my escape plan, however difficult it might become.

'Slow down,' Marco called across to me then, and I brought Angelo to a more moderate pace, realising we had galloped ahead.

'What is it?' I asked when Marco levelled with me.

'We are approaching the Pisani Villa. Would you like to stop and see it?'

'Yes, alright, I will follow your lead.'

I needn't have. Its façade was so commanding of the entirety of the view as we approached it that it would have been impossible to miss. Its extensive blanc façade flanked by gatehouses stretched across the vast expanse of riverbank it dominated.

'Well, what do you think?' he asked.

'I think it is magnificent.'

'I thought it might remind you somewhat of the English country estates you are used to.'

'It does.'

'Would you like to take a break now and sit a while?'

'Yes, I think the horses might like a drink.'

He jumped down, tied Volatore to one of the boating moorings and turned to help me. It felt strange to be handled by him, almost intimate in some unfathomable way as I slipped down into his arms and found my footing on the floor below. Then, releasing me a fraction too late, he turned away and tied Angelo to a neighbouring mooring before taking a blanket from the saddle bag for us to sit on. I accepted his offered hand to lower myself to the ground and waited for him to settle beside me.

'So, how was your ride?' he asked, knees drawn up in front of him as his arms rested lazily atop.

'Amazing. Truly. I had forgotten how much I missed it.'

'I am glad.'

'What about you? Did you enjoy it?'

'I am perhaps not as keen a rider as you and certainly far less practised, but it has been pleasant.'

'I confess that even I am feeling a little rattled. I daresay we shall both be suffering the ache of impractice by tomorrow, but it is a worthy cause, in my mind.'

'I know, and therefore, likewise in mine.'

'Thank you for this, Marco. You have brought me such joy in your consideration. I know I had you quite wrong in the beginning, and I realise more and more that I was not always very kind.'

'I do not blame you, and there is nothing to apologise for. I am only glad we have arrived at better terms, even if it did take some time.'

'I, too, am glad. But I wonder at your patience with me sometimes.'

'I have wondered at it myself,' he said, teasing now. I liked the animation in his features and let out a small laugh, which he joined me in.

'Well, I am grateful for it. I want you to know that.—Gosh, I am not very good at these speeches, am I.'

'No worse than I.'

'Oh, and what would you like to say to me?'

He bit his lip and pondered this before answering. 'Only that I want you to know, you are not alone in all your troubles. We are family, and, well, you can trust me.'

'I do trust you, Marco.' This, too, had taken some time to come about, but it was true.

CHAPTER THIRTY-THREE

Full Spectrum.

Eleanor. August 1822.

'Oh my, I am not sure I can drink this,' I said to Isabella, bringing the glass to my lips and smelling the sulphuric aroma of the water rising to my nose.

After a pleasant amble around the local flower market and a brief stop at the coffee house this morning, we were now standing in the pump room at the Abano Bagni, having queued to obtain our share of these alleged miracle waters. Peering into the glass as I swilled it around, I wondered if the miracle was the forbearance it would take to swallow them.

'Come, my child, we shall do it together,' Isabella encouraged, holding up her glass and taking a long sip.

I followed her example and resisted the urge to spit it out as the warm metallic pungency filled my mouth. I swallowed hard and grimaced at the aftertang. 'Urgh!' I shivered and dabbed the corners of my mouth with my handkerchief. 'If it is so good for us, why must it taste so ghastly?'

'I do not know the answer to that, but I do know it is worth the inconvenience. I used to take it whenever we were in Padua, and I am certain my rheumatism has grown worse for not visiting for a time.'

I forced the remainder of the glass down.

'There,' she said. 'See, it wasn't so bad.'

'I cannot agree,' I replied, meeting Marco's amused expression with a glare as I pushed the empty glass aside.

'It will be worth it, child. You want a family, don't you?'

'Yes,' I lied, feeling Marco's scrutinising gaze cast over me as if he detected it a false answer. I looked instantly away.

'Then we must bring you back to health as the doctor instructed.'

I *was* returning to health now that I was away from Giles; it required no curative waters, only his absence.

'Mama, Eleanor knows that. You need not bend her ear,' Marco interjected.

'I am not bending her ear. I am only reminding her that it is for a good cause.'

'You are quite right, Isabella. Forgive me.' I ignored Marco's cynical pout and said, 'Will you try it?'

'I have no need,' he replied curtly.

'Surely we all have a need of good health?' I countered with a wry smile.

'She is right, Marco. Why don't you take a glass since we are here? It will do you good,' his mama coaxed him, reaching for another glass.

My lips curled with amusement and he cast me a look of contempt. 'There is nothing wrong with my health.— Alright, fine, if it will give me peace,' he conceded, taking the offered glass from his mother's hand and downing it in one swift gulp. 'There, are you happy now?'

I resisted the urge to laugh aloud and turned away to hide my face.

'How many bottles shall I request to be loaded into the coach?' he asked his mother.

'Half a dozen will do for now. We will be back again next week to attend the bathing pools, so we can pick up more then.'

'Well, I won't be joining you in *that* endeavour before you conjure up some needless benefit for me,' he said pointedly.

'That, I will spare you,' Isabella smiled. 'You can drop us off and go to that vineyard in Montegrotto and get some of that Paduan wine your father likes.'

'Certainly. Now, are you ready to go?'

The week was passing all too fast for my liking. I had accomplished what I needed to in coming here and satisfying Giles and Dr Heimlich of my compliance, yet as I fell into this quiet and leisurely pace, as if following the very echoes of the earth's own heartbeat, I could not imagine returning at all. Every moment had become its own prize, opening itself so fully present to me. Whether helping on the farm or in the kitchen, riding Angelo, or enjoying the company of the family, I honoured every passing second of this borrowed time. Every easy night's sleep and dawning new day and the realm of possibilities I awoke to contained within it. Every cerulean skyscape and marbled crimson sunset. And the world was filled with the vibrancy of all its vivid hues once more.

Even Marco noticed the improvement in my colour palette as I joined him in painting a river scene beneath the shade of a lofty willow in the afternoons. My use of colour was indeed improved because I no longer saw the world in monotone. My vision was at last restored to its full spectrum, and it translated into everything I did. However simple, however complex, I felt its expanse in every breath now, every glance, and the idea of returning to a world so void of all its richness seemed impossible to me.

It was not only the greater presence I celebrated, but the absences, too. Of course, the obvious ones that required no explanation. But even the simple things I was at liberty to abandon now, be it my daily cup of Queens Anne Lace, the fiddly application of the sponge, the burning of messages, the conjuring of excuses, the telling of lies. Every burden lightened, and I became almost childlike in my easiness once more—living for the sake of being, not existing for the sake of being alive.

I noticed this spark of *joie de vivre* reflected in the family, too. Isabella as she tended her garden with Guiseppe, and Marco as he painted in such styles of genius as I had not before seen in his work; however in awe I always was of his talent. It certainly wasn't only the sulphuric waters we had brought back from Abano that could be credited with it. Even if I did insist that Marco suffer a cup with me and his mama at the breakfast table every morning, just to tease him and distract myself from this one inconvenience, as we raced to see who could finish first. It was always him, but I grew better at it too, and often slammed my empty glass back down upon the table just a second or two behind him as Isabella declared us children with an endeared chuckle.

It had proved everything a glimpse of paradise should be, yet always framed by the knowing it was to be only a glimpse, not a forever. I had not let that taint the moment, though. In fact, I had banished all such thoughts from my mind the instant they encroached upon it, until one day, as we breakfasted on the sunny patio terrace admiring the improvements to the garden, the post came.

'You have a letter, Eleanor,' Marco said, passing it along the table to me, and I thanked him and set it aside. I was in no rush to open it. Quite the contrary. It could only be from Giles, and I dreaded the news that he had now returned to Venice and was ready to join us directly. It had been such a beautiful week, I could not bear to contemplate polluting this happy place with his presence now I had grown so comfortable in its refuge.

So I put it off all morning as I rode out with Marco, helped the farm hand pick apricots for this evening's dessert course, and tried at making Gnocchi with the cook, which proved a great deal trickier than it looked.

It was only when the day drew on, and Marco reminded me of it sitting unopened on the dresser top that I took it up reluctantly.

'You don't want to read it?' he asked me.

'Not really, if I am honest.'

'Would you like me to leave the room and give you privacy?'

I shook my head. 'No, please stay,' I said, tearing the seal.

'It is good news?' he asked to me after a minute.

I nodded. 'He cannot come,' I gushed, unable to keep the relief out of my tone. 'He is returned home but sent directly to Trieste to meet the diamond agent there. He thinks it best if I return home with you and your mama next week, for he does not know how long he shall be detained there. Where is Trieste?'

'On the most eastern border, close to Istria.'

'Is it a long journey?'

'A full day by carriage, though I daresay Giles will be joining one of Serrano's ships from Venice, and I don't pretend to know if that proves any quicker.'

'What do you know of Serrano and his business? It appears Giles will do anything to please him.'

'He is a very successful businessman.'

'I gathered that, but so is Giles. There must be something more?'

'True, Giles is successful,' he acknowledged. 'But we are talking leagues apart. Serrano is from a noble family, originally of Armenian descent, renowned for amassing vast fortunes from gem trading worldwide. His ancestors settled in Venice long before my time and married into Patrician families. A strategic alliance to further their trades from the city in the age of the Republic. Like all trades, they have declined here since the fall, but Serrano's network is vast and dynamic. He is one of the few who has suffered little from the decline of our city and simply diversified his fleets in other ports to go on trading. If Giles secures ongoing contracts through him, he will become an even richer man, vastly richer, I suspect. And therein is your answer.'

'I see. And do you think he will succeed in his ambitions?'

He shrugged. 'I see he is determined to, and knowing Giles, I suspect it means he will pursue it until he does.'

I nodded. It certainly seemed like an accurate assessment in my mind. 'Yes, it seems you know him well.'

'Not very, but I have heard enough about the dinner table to understand him ruthless in his business endeavours.'

'Ah, and not only in them,' I said without thinking.

He frowned. 'What do you mean?'

I shook my head as if to shake some sense into it. 'Nothing,' I replied, and noticed the disappointment in his eyes, then urged myself on. 'Let's just say his pursuit of me was not so very different.'

'I do not doubt it. Even I know enough of English society to tell the doors to your hand would have been firmly barred against him, no matter how much money or determination he threw into your pursuit. —so will you tell me, how was it possible?'

I considered his question and resisted the default compulsion to throw him off with a clipped answer or an implausible excuse. I was to vanish in a few weeks' time, and there would be so many questions I could not answer then. So much left unsaid to those who were due my apology and explanation. I could not tell them all, and certainly not that I would soon be gone. But I could trust to him some greater detail now, that he, in turn, could pass on to the rest of the family in explaining the gravity of my unhappiness with Giles and understanding my affront was not directed at them.

'Well,' I began, his eyes searching mine, '...we both know it was not a modern romance story where love conquers all.'

'And not all marriages are, even modern ones. But I cannot imagine any other explanation.'

'You said before, when we were up at Stra, that I could trust you...completely in confidence, no matter what I tell you?'

He nodded with sincerity. 'You have my word.'

'Very well. But not here. Take me somewhere we will not be overheard by a soul, and I will answer your questions.'

He took me on the river in a rickety old rowboat, and though I had my misgivings about the state of repair of the vessel, I at least felt sure we were pretty safe from any risk of being overheard.

He laid out a blanket and a cushion before handing me into the boat.

'Are you quite certain this is seaworthy?' I asked as I settled tentatively into my seat.

'Seaworthy, definitely not, but river worthy, certainly.'

'Very well, I suppose I can at least swim if it all goes ill.'

'Impressive, though it won't be necessary, you are in safe hands. Us Venetians might not be the best of whips, but when it comes to boating...'

'Then I shall put your claim to the test, Signor, and hope you live up to your Venetian heritage.'

He laughed at this and climbed in with the mooring rope about his forearm. 'Which direction would you like to venture in?'

'I suppose we must go beyond Stra, for I have not yet seen beyond it.'

He raised a brow. 'You realise it is nearly two miles just to get to Stra, and I am rowing, not being pulled by a horse.'

'Fine, I will help you,' I said, picking up the other oar.'

'You row?'

'I do. Or at least I used to. There is a beautiful lake on my parent's country estate that my siblings and I enjoyed boating and swimming in when we were young.—What you think girls like me are always kept indoors?' I teased.

'No. I am only impressed...Do you have many siblings?'

'I have two brothers and two sisters. But I have not turned out much alike to them at all.'

'What do you mean?'

'I have disgraced my family, Marco. That is the truth of the matter. You wanted to know why Giles's way was not barred, well that is the answer.'

'You mean in marrying below your rank, or before then?'

'Before then, the very circumstances offered him a way in, and I thought me, a way out.'

'I see.'

'You think ill of me?'

'No, I do not,' he replied with a gentle sigh, his eyes wandering to the horizon. 'Foolish perhaps, but were we not all once fools in our tender years?'

I shrugged. 'Well, I was particularly so, though, of course, I never realised it then, not until it was too late.'

'So what happened?'

'Do you know the branch of the family in Cuddington? I own, I do not know if you and Giles share that lineage or if it is a marital relation.'

'A marital relation, I believe. I do not know them, but he has spoken much of his uncle there.'

'Well, his uncle and his family moved into the estate bordering my parents. Their daughter, Mariella, befriended me, I thought on genuine terms. But her aim turned out to be to contrive the most elaborate and deceptive matchmaking scheme it is difficult to conceive of. She tricked me into Giles's acquaintance and, when my reputation was in question, offered him up as the solution. I had no idea then that he had put her up to it from the outset.'

He paused rowing and leant forward. 'What?'

'He bid her to contrive it all from the beginning in ways and means I cannot bear to repeat. Only to say that they went to great lengths to convince me I was in need of saving and that he was the answer to my problems. It was not all their doing. I had been reckless and green, and so very careless with my reputation that I was ripe for their deception, that much I own. But when I realised what had gone on, when the pieces of this elaborate puzzle began to fit together, it was too late. We were already wed.'

He cocked his head to the side with interest. 'How did you find it out?'

'On my wedding night. I found them together in his chamber.'

'What, you mean *together*?'

'Yes, that is the first I came to understand something was amiss. They had been having a clandestine love affair long before I knew them when the family was in Paris. He used her to make an alliance with me, and she did it in the hope of maintaining a position as his mistress once I had served my purpose of elevating his position in society, and naturally plummeting my own to a depth that tainted my whole family.'

'Eleanor, I am so sorry. I had no idea.'

'I know that now. When I arrived, I did not know what to think after all else. I hardly had high expectations from the example of that branch of his family. So, I hope you understand that my poor manner was not a personal affront. I simply did not trust anyone of his acquaintance after that.'

'Naturally, why would you. But, I hope you know better now?'

I smiled warmly. 'I do. I am very fond of you all, don't you see that?'

His face softened. 'I'm beginning to.'

'Anyway, when they were discovered and would not stop their affair, I separated from Giles and returned to my parent's protection for a time, of course creating even more scandal. I had hoped there could be an annulment, a divorce even, but it was impossible. I would have been happy with a legal separation, but he would not hear of it and would not stop pursuing me. In the end, he pursued me all the way to the distant countryside, where I went into hiding, and he captured me there and brought me here against my will.'

His expression was lost somewhere between rage and disgust. 'He forced you here?'

I nodded. 'There is more, though, for this part, the fault is mine. I fell pregnant at the time of our separation; needless to say, he was not the father. My miscarriage was not of his son, as he says. It was the child of a music master, who was kind to me at a time I felt very lost.'

He had stopped rowing entirely now and we simply drifted in the boat, a heavy silence hanging between us.

'So, you see, I am not entirely innocent either.'

Fury danced in his eyes. 'My father will have him out from under our roof this night if he knew—'

'And what good would that do? For I would be dragged along with him, and believe me when I say I could think of nothing worse than being alone with him.'

'Then you can go to the convent and seek refuge from him there. I will take you myself.'

'And do what? I am no nun, Marco. I could not remain in such a place.'

'You would not have to, only for a time.'

'And then what?'

He looked away and peered into the distance for a moment. 'You do not want to get away from him?'

'Of course I do. But he pursued me for months across half the country and found me. How difficult would it be for him to do the same again? He has money, Marco. He throws it in any direction he must to execute his will, and in the end, it pays off. And now you tell me he is on the cusp of growing richer still. If I am to find a way, it must prove infallible, because I cannot go through this ever again.'

'Forgive me,' he said, a hand outstretched to me. 'I hate to make you cry. I—'

But they were not tears of sorrow but relief, to at last have spoken the unspeakable truth.

'I'm going to moor the boat alright.'

I nodded because my words were caught in my throat and washed back down in a gush of tears so long resisted that I could not prevent them. When I felt the weight of the boat shift and looked up, he stood before me, raised me to my feet, pulled me into his arms, lifted me onto the riverbank, and held me. 'It is alright, you are safe with me. I promise.'

When I woke the following day, I wondered at my wisdom in divulging so much to him. He had been so gentle and patient with me at the riverbank, offering me the comfort of his embrace and reassurance of his words. Yes, I could trust him. He would keep my secret, no matter how difficult. And no, he did not think me a disgrace, and neither would his family. They would, however, deem Giles to be one if they knew what he knew. He did not know how, but he would help me if he could. I need only ask and if it was within his power...

And yet, despite his kindness, I sensed a brooding and restlessness in him and feared that if it did not run its course before we returned to *Ca' Rosetti*, my telling would be betrayed, not by his confession, but by his difficulty in containing his disgust.

I peered out of my window when I rose from my bed and watched him thundering across the meadows on Volatore's back. We usually rode together, but I supposed he might have needed some space from me to digest all that I had revealed to him. He was a moral man, and though he said he did not blame me, I knew my past indiscretions would not sit well with him, however much he denied it. I had altered his ideas about me, as well as Giles, and it was perhaps best I gave him time to adjust to them. And so I did not ask after him as Isabella and I, sipped down our daily dose of the Abano waters. Nor did I enquire as to why he was not returned for luncheon. It was only when he had been absent all day that I grew concerned. I had noticed Volatore returned to the stable when I came to groom them, as I often did in the late afternoon when it grew cooler, but there was still no sign of him.

Finally, as I walked through the orchards to pick a few apples for the horses, I saw him across the field, axe in hand, splitting trees into firewood at the wood keeper's shed. His back bare and glistening with sweat, the side of his face that I could see, flushed hot, and a pile of firewood quarters so high, I knew he had been here for some time.

I considered whether to interrupt him or not when he was so fixed upon his task, and yet I was troubled to see the fury in his movements, the force in which he smashed the axe into the wood, the sounds, something between a sigh and grunt he elicited as he worked. It was disconcerting to see someone always so well contained so very untamed. It was all my fault. I had meant to offer him an explanation so that when I vanished, he understood on who's account. But I wondered now if I had done more harm than good in speaking so freely.

'Marco,' I called as I approached him across the yard, but he did not hear me and continued. I kept my distance from the flying wood debris and waited patiently until he paused to wipe a trail of sweat from his eyes. 'Marco,' I called again now, and this time, he looked up and lowered the axe to the ground.

'What are you doing all the way up here?' he asked, catching his breath.

'I came to get some apples.' I held up my basket. 'Are you alright? I have not seen you all day—'

'I'm fine. I just thought I'd help Giuseppe get ahead for winter,' he replied, gesturing towards the wood stack and taking a swig from his hip flask before offering it to me.'

'No, thank you. Would you like an apple? You missed luncheon.'

He shook his head. 'I'm not hungry. Just hot. Do you mind if I sit down for a moment? I have only a tree stump to offer you, I'm afraid.'

'Please, sit. I have no desire to.'

He sank onto the stump, picked up his discarded shirt and pressed it to his face to blot the sweat from it, then sucked at his hand.

'What are you doing that for?'

'I have a splinter. I have already picked out three today, but this one will not budge.'

'Here, let me take a look,' I said, walking over to him and picking up his hand to inspect it. In the crease between his thumb and forefinger, there was a buried splinter raised angry from his attempts to dislodge it. 'We shall need a pin for this one, it is quite submerged. One moment,' I said, untying my bonnet and pulling a hat pin from it. 'Here, put your hand upon your knee,' I directed him, coming down to my knees now and resting my palm beneath his own to stretch it out whilst I gently picked his skin with the pin. 'I'm not hurting you am I?'

'No.'

I carried on picking, 'You know, I did not mean to distress you yesterday. I thought I owed you an explanation, and yet I fear I have done you harm—keep your hand still, I nearly have it.'

'You have done me no wrong, Eleanor. I knew you were desperately unhappy even before I pulled you from the canal. I suppose I had always thought it a loveless, incompatible match, but not the result of such calculated malevolence—Ouch.'

'Sorry, I have it now. Just hold still while I pull it. There, it's all done.'

'Thank you,' he said, and I looked up at him now. His dark hair flopped to one side, a few sweaty strands stuck to his face, his cheeks still flushed hot, and his eyes unreadable. He withdrew his hand to inspect it, and I got up off the floor and brushed down my skirts.

'Will you come back to the house with me?' I asked. 'I think dinner shall be ready soon.'

'You go on. I will be back once I have finished this.'

When I returned downstairs after dressing, I half expected not to see him at dinner. But I heard voices as I headed towards the small patio terrace where we often took our meals and enjoyed the view out to the river.

'Marco, you are not yourself. Are you worried about the gallery?' I heard Isabella say and halted.

'I am perhaps a little anxious now it's been a week, but I'm sure it will all be fine. No news is good news, and so on.'

'Is that all that concerns you?'

'Yes, mama, why do you press me so?'

'Because I know my son, and I know when something is troubling you. Won't you tell me what it is? You know I shall worry until then.'

'Please do not worry, mama, I am well. Forgive me if I have given you cause to think otherwise. I shall put the gallery out of my mind from here on.'

'So it *is* that. I'm sure it shall remain standing for a fortnight's absence, il mio regazzo. If you are worried, you can always send a messenger home and have Dante check in on the place.'

'Dante is busy enough, mama. It will be fine, you are right.'

'Well, you will soon be back in Venice. Try to enjoy the remaining week here, won't you? It was doing you so much good.'

He stood and kissed his mama on the cheek. 'I will. Now let me wash before dinner is on the table.'

We exchanged an uncomfortable glance as we passed in the hallway. But by the time he returned, he seemed much more like himself, though whether out of authenticity or an effort to throw his mama off the scent, I was uncertain. Still, we chatted and discussed our plans for the rest of the week as we usually did, opened a bottle of wine from the cellar and enjoyed a game of *vingt et un* once the plates were cleared. Then Isabella went to bed with her usual punctuality and left us at the table.

'I think I might retire to bed too. It has been a long day and I am tired,' he said, rising from his chair.

I raised my gaze to him. 'Marco, please don't go. I want to make amends, but I don't know how to make things better.'

'You are not at fault, Eleanor.'

'Then why does it feel like I am? I know you are angry. Are you angry at me?'

'No!' He threw his hands up to his head and ran them over his hair. 'It is me at fault, Eleanor, not you. Just know that and give me some time to ride this out.'

'But I don't understand.'

'I realise that, I do. Let me sleep on it, and I will try harder tomorrow. I promise. Now, will you come inside so I can close up the doors?'

I nodded and got up from the table, too unused to his impatience to question him further, and so I bid him goodnight and went upstairs feeling so deeply regretful of thinking it wise to confess to him the things I had.

The next day, we went back to the Abano Bagni. He had kept his word and had been more cheerful and like himself about the breakfast table, and when we rode in the coach, he offered me the usual commentary on places we passed on our journey, and on the surface, it all seemed as it should be. Yet somehow, I knew that it was not. It was not only me who was unconvinced, but Isabella who brought it up as we settled into our private bathing pool, steam rising about our heads from the heat of the water.

'Eleanor, has Marco said anything to you?' she asked me.

'About what?'

'About something that he is anxious over or that has happened?'

'No. Though I get the sense that perhaps he is restless and keen to return to Venice now.'

'Yes, I do too. I just wish I understood what troubles him. I know my son, and when he stays up all night painting, it is rarely a good sign.'

'He was up all night painting?'

'Yes, he often will when he has something on his mind. I just wish he would tell me what. He has not received any letters or messengers, has he?'

'I do not think so. He has not mentioned anything. Perhaps now that Giles is not joining us, we should return to Venice a little earlier to ease his mind. We can take some more of the waters back to drink and we need not come here again.'

'No, my child. You are here to restore your health, and I see how transformed you are in a week. I shall be pleased to see your progress by the end of another.'

'You can?'

'Yes, you are thriving child, radiating such happiness as I never before saw in you. It is doing you good, and we shall continue our holiday. It seemed to be doing Marco a great deal of good, too. He needed some time off. I am sure he has not taken a day off beyond the Sabbath since he opened the gallery. No—even if he does not realise it, he is better off here. We all are. I think tonight, I will have the cook make his favourite dinner, and I shall play a little music on the pianoforte. He always used to enjoy my playing. That should cheer him.'

When we returned, I helped Isabella plant some lilies by the terrace in a bed Guiseppe had turned over for her yesterday. It seemed best I afforded Marco some more space in the hope of appeasing him. He was painting by the river now, just outside the house. But he looked tired and preoccupied and disappeared to his chamber at some point and slept all the way through dinner. A dinner I had spent the latter half of the afternoon preparing with the cook. His steaming plate of Osobuco left to cool in his empty place about the table. 'He is better left to sleep,' Isabella said, 'If I wake him now, he will be up all night again.'

But her plan did not succeed. In the middle of the night, I woke to use the chamber pot and pour a glass of water, only to smell the scent of linseed oil in the heavy air. I headed back to my bed and then hesitated. *Don't*, I warned myself, and yet, despite my better judgement, I found myself moving along the hall in light-footed steps until I reached the far extent of the corridor where I knew his room was, though I had never dared venture into the vicinity of it. A single line of light illuminated the foot of the doorframe and gently, I tapped.

'Come in,' he said, and with another tug of hesitation, I reached for the door, easing it gently open.

'Eleanor?' he frowned, 'I thought you, my mama.'

He was stood in only a pair of long johns tied about his waist, a makeshift studio set up in the middle of the room where he was painting. I averted my eyes and said, 'Marco, what are you doing up so late?'

'I could not sleep. Why are you still up?'

'I woke, it was hot, and I was thirsty.'

'Then why are you not back in your bed? You should not be here,' his tone was irritated, dismissive. I knew he was right, but I stepped further into the room despite it.

'Look, Marco, your mama is worried about you. She spoke to me today and is trying to understand what has altered...as am I.'

'I will talk to her in the morning. Find something trivial to offer her so she can be at ease. I shan't mention anything if that's what concerns you.'

'I am concerned about *you*, Marco. I have not known you like this before, and I don't know how to fix this void between us because I cannot unsay what I have said. If you think me low and shocking for the things I told you, I am sorry, but I cannot change them, even if you disapprove.'

He let out a hint of a sardonic laugh at this. 'You have it quite wrong. I do not think ill of you. I told you who I think ill of. The problem is with me, alright.'

'Balderdash, you cannot even look at me. I would sooner you be honest in your feelings than mislead me with such nonsense.'

'Eleanor, please, just go to bed. I have no wish to fight with you.'

A tear rolled down my cheek and I wiped it away. 'Then don't. Can we not just return to the terms we were on before I spoke? Be as we were?'

'No, and that is the trouble. Don't you see, you took away the only barrier between my containing my feelings in confessing what you did to me.'

'What do you mean, Marco?'

'You do not know?'

But I did know. Or at least I had begun to suspect somewhere in the periphery of my mind.

'What are you painting?' I asked, coming up behind him and looking at the canvas he was hovering in front of, paintbrush still in hand.

'A portrait of someone I once knew.'

'She is beautiful. It is brilliant, Marco. I thought you did not paint portraits anymore, you should.'

'There is much I thought I did not do anymore—' His eyes glistened with tears, and it shocked me. And then, I felt the urge to hold him like he had held me so patiently that day on the riverbank. I moved closer to him, took the paintbrush from his hand and put it down. He did not move, but his eyes, so dark and incandescent, followed my movements until I stood before him, wrapped my arms around him, pressed my nose to his and closed my eyes. We both sighed, and then I felt his reluctant arms shift and embrace me back, enveloping me in his heat, his woody, sweaty scent, and the clamminess of his skin against the parts of mine left exposed by my shift. And I needed the strength of his arms to hold me up because I thought for a moment I might lose my footing as the overwhelm of realisation took me. I *felt* things.

Things I had not felt since... no, I could not acknowledge it. Yet I could not deny it either. *It could not be.* How many men had ill-used my body since I got here, and it mattered not, for I had managed to leave my body entirely whilst they consumed it without stirring anything beyond repulsion in me. Even the exception to this rule in Serrano's encounter, I had begun to finally understand since I got here and reflected on it. It was never a matter of his skill or some inexplicable attraction, but a sadistic part of my own appetite for avenging Giles in such a style.—Bedding a man more powerful than he, humiliating him as he had me, which had caused anything to stir within me that day. Not out of any genuine arousal but in the triumph to at last deliver a blow rather than take one. It was not pleasure of a good or organic nature. But this, this I felt standing here now...was. And yet. *I must not.* And he did not either, so I pulled back from him and said, 'You need to sleep, Marco, you are tired. Come, get into bed and rest your tired mind,' and he let me lead him there and sit him down upon it, and I kneeled on the floor beside the bed and stroked his face as he sunk against the pillow. We did not speak, and I did not leave, until finally, his glazed eyes gave into exhaustion.

When I returned to my bed I could not sleep a wink. I felt undone, disordered, mystified by my self-deception. I thought *that* part of me was dead. I thought *that* part of me belonged only to *her*. I rose then, remembering my sketch of Annalise that I still had not destroyed, though so many times I had intended it. I opened my trunk and tossed out my clothes until I found it at the bottom, wrapped in a blanket as I'd left it. I pulled it out and held it to the lamplight, and there she was, her endearing eyes peering back at me, the hues of innocence and enchantment captured perfectly. I felt a hot tear roll down my cheek. *Oh, Annalise, how did it become thus?*

Once I'd finished crying, I gathered my resolve, the lamp and my sketch, went over to the open window and looked out upon the airless night, seeing nothing but different shades of darkness. I perched my lamp upon the window ledge and lifted its glass cover, burning my fingers and almost dropping it. Then I stared at the naked flame and brought the picture above it. 'It is time to let you go as you let me go long before now,' I said to the paper-sketched Annalise. Then the corner of the page caught alight and began to burn, and I began to panic, withdrawing it and flapping it about like a fan to put it out, sparks flying into the air, glittering before settling to ash, until it was extinguished, until it was saved, all but a missing blank corner of the page frayed grey now. *I cannot.*

Hours later, I was sat on the floor beneath the window, first light breaking and pouring in through it, her portrait resting against a book in my lap as I sketched her back into life, adding detail that was missing drawn from my memory of her sitting in Mr Darracott's studio in Cambridge as she posed for her lover's eye. I wondered if it was still at Stapleford in my dressing table drawer. I longed to look at it more than ever I had.

One day, I would return for it, and it would be the sole remnant of her I could keep, treasure as I once had treasured her so dearly.

And then my thoughts darkened as they descended into other memories of the nights we spent at Stapleford, and I pictured her image one particular night as she sat straddled above me. I put my pencil back to the page and began to sketch in her shoulders, then the curve of each breast, the peak of each rosy nipple, until I ached inside and found my hands between my legs, fingertips slick with want. I climbed into bed then, removing my shift entirely, bringing her to rest on the pillow beside me as I answered the demands of my body. Demands it had not made upon me for so long that the completion was astounding when it came, and I must have soon fallen to sleep.

CHAPTER THIRTY-FOUR

The Ebb of Time.

Eleanor. August 1822.

'Eleanor? Mama mia! Forgive me. I did not know you were unclothed,' came Benedetta's voice as I opened my heavy eyes to the hazy sight of the sketch beside me on the pillow. I snatched it away and sat up in the bed.

'Sorry! I was hot last night,' I told her. The room coming into better focus now. 'What time is it, Benedetta?'

'It is ten o'clock,' she said, crossing the room to put a jug of water on the washstand. I would have come sooner, but you usually ring for me when you are ready. Isabella was wondering where you were. I think you were supposed to help her in the garden today.'

'Yes, that's right. Where is she?'

'In the garden making a start.'

'Tell her I will be down shortly. I had a troubled night. There was not a wisp of a breeze to soften the heat.'

'No, it was particularly close. Shall I bring you up some coffee before your toilette?' she asked, casting a sideways glance at the chaos I'd spilt out of the trunk.

'Please.'

When she disappeared back downstairs, I got up, and returned the sketch and all the tumbled-out clothes to the trunk before slipping my shift over my head and venturing over to the window. The brilliance of the August sunshine dazzled me for a moment as I lifted my face to the clemency of the morning air. Then I noticed Isabella crouched over her crocuses pinching at dead leaves, and Marco sat beside her, holding a basket out to catch them.

The sight of him sharpened my laggardly gaze, and it lingered over him now. They were talking and smiling, and it warmed me to see them much as they often were. He said he would make amends with her and I felt better to see that he was able to.

I watched on for a while as so many different thoughts darted through my mind that I could barely catch one, and then a particular line of thought seemed to crystallise. I went back to the chest, lifted its heavy lid again and pulled the sketch of Annalise from it. This time, I set it in the grate above a candle and watched it smoulder into ash. 'You are dead to me now,' I said to it.

I was not sure what kind of reception I would receive from Marco when I joined them in the garden, but I was pleased to find it not a hostile one, even if somewhat subdued. I offered him a half-smile of uncertainty as he pushed his dark hair from his face as I approached them.

'Ah,' said Isabella, following his gaze and turning about to see me. 'Buongiorno, how are you now? Benedetta said you could not sleep.'

Marco and I shared an uncomfortable glance. 'No, it was too hot. But I managed eventually. What is on the agenda today?' I asked more brightly, gesturing at the flower bed.

'Much. I have oleanders, peonies, and a laurel bush to plant this morning. The boat just came in with my delivery from the flower market, and I must try to get it all out before the sun dries the roots.'

'Well, I am at your disposal, where shall I begin?'

She showed me to a barren patch of earth that she directed Marco to turn over for me, where the peonies could be planted in rows of six, spaced a hand apart. Neither of us protested, yet I sensed our mutual reluctance to be forced so much into company when we neither knew how to manage it anymore.

Isabella made a visual check that we had all we needed and said, 'Giuseppe and I will be at the front of the house planting the laurel if you need any further direction. Oh, what's this?' she asked as Benedetta approached with a letter in hand.

'For you, Signora', she said, passing it to her.

'Were you expecting something?' Marco asked.

She shook her head as she pulled off her gardening gloves and broke the seal. When a smile formed across her face, I saw the relief in Marco's.

I watched her scan the letter.

'It's from your father. He will be joining us in the morning! He will stay to bring us home on Monday. Dante has everything running smoothly and has insisted he can do without him. He will take me to dine in Padua tomorrow evening at the *Croce d'Oro* for our Anniversary. He did remember.' She beamed now and we both beamed back at her and then found each other's gaze.

'How many years will you be celebrating?' I asked her.

'Thirty-five.'

'That is wonderful, Isabella, congratulations.'

'Thank you.'

'Funny that, I shall be celebrating the very same birthday in October,' Marco teased and she smacked him playfully with her gardening gloves before putting them back on. 'You are too cheeky. What will Eleanor think of us!'

'That perhaps love knows no time, and you found it from the outset,' I said, avoiding Marco's eyes.

She smiled gratefully at me, picked up her spade from the bed, and announced that we should get to work. The sun was already burning hot for the hour. And so we did as bid, Marco forking and turning, me retrieving the flower plugs from their crate and soaking them in the tepid bowl of water as she had directed, readying them for the soil.

'Thank you for last night,' Marco said to me when Isabella set off with Giuseppe for the front of the house, wheelbarrow in hand. '...for your kindness.'

I hardly knew how to respond. I had not expected such frankness. 'Well, if I have learned anything since I have come here, it is that the only thing that can reach us from a state of torment is the kindness of others.'

He nodded. 'I'm sorry for how I have been. I lost my way for a moment, but—'

'You have nothing to apologise for, Marco. Heaven knows you have seen me so far departed from sense that I might not be here at all today, if it were not for you...'

He seemed to consider this, perhaps because I had never before really acknowledged what he did for me that night, not even to myself. How could I when I wanted only to escape, and he seemed but another obstacle to my trying? And now, I wondered if he presented an altogether different kind of obstacle to the same.

I wondered it more and more as we worked beneath the beating afternoon sun, filling the landscape with points of brilliant colour as we tried, somewhat haphazardly, to avoid the brush of the others arm when working close to set the peonies in the ground or, when inadvertently reaching over to the watering can at the same moment. Equally, there was a reluctance to let our eyes meet above a necessary second, and yet I'm sure he caught my searching gaze as often as I did his.

And so this continued through the day and into the next until at last Mr Harper arrived at the Villa, and his addition to the company seemed to moderate the strain, attenuate it just enough to ease its silent importunity.

'Ah, you do look well indeed,' Mr Harper said when he found me in the garden arranging a posy of wildflowers for them as an anniversary gift. I had spent the morning walking the local riverbank searching for the perfect offering.

'Thank you, Sir. I do feel some improvement. It is good to have you back. Happy Anniversary,' I said, remembering.

'I thank you. It seems I am not the only one who has a special anniversary this week.'

'Sorry?' I frowned.

'Giles tells me it is yours on Friday and he is sorry he cannot spend it with you, though he asked me to bring you this.'

'Thank you,' I said after a pause too long to pretend I had remembered the fact. I took the parcel he handed to me and tried to smile.

'Don't worry, I shan't tell him you forgot,' he winked. Then he bowed and left me holding the parcel in my hands, staring at it with contempt.

Had it really been a year since I signed away my liberty to that monster? How could I forget such a monumental failing as that to have come about only a year ago. Sometimes, it felt like forever. It was hard to contend with the fact that this time last year, I was still free. I still held within my power the opportunity to shun the wedding and call it off. If I had known how it would go, if I had followed my gut feeling, if I had understood then what it was to feel true love...Oh, damn the foolish naivety of youth. By this time Friday, my younger self had committed me to more suffering in a year than I had felt in twenty combined. It seemed more worthy of a funeral ceremony than a celebration, in my mind. The mourning of a self long lost to a contract that was irrevocable, however poorly the terms and conditions had been disclosed. However, null and void my feelings.

And yet, as I watched the house swell with romance between the Harpers as Isabella readied for her night out with her husband, I knew I would have to appear merry on Friday and accept their well wishes as gladly as they had accepted mine today.

'What's that?' Marco asked me when he found me in the stables brushing down Angelo and Volatore.

I looked at the unopened parcel I had set upon a hay bale and entirely forgotten about. 'It's a wedding anniversary gift from Giles,' I explained, and his face fell as darkly as my own heart had at the sight of it.

'It's your anniversary, too?'

'Friday, apparently. Though I did not know it until your father brought this to me.'

'Come, do not cry. You do not have to open it if you don't wish to, not for now at least.'

'I can't believe it, Marco, but a year ago, I signed my own death warrant, and I did not know it. Do you have any idea what I would give to go back to that moment and change the whole course of the miserable life I have endured since that fateful day?'

'I do. But. We cannot change the past, Eleanor. That is as about as much as is certain in this life. Our only choice after is what we do with what remains, be it good or ill.'

'I know, and that is the hardest part to accept.'

He came over to me now and rested a palm upon my shoulder, its weighty warmth causing me to stop brushing as I pressed my forehead against Angelo's flank.

'It is not a death warrant. You have your life still, and whilst you have that, there is always hope.'

'It has felt like one. Worse. I feel like I have died a thousand deaths since I met him, and yet I still live to endure another. At least they say we rest in peace in death or go to the heavens. *Why* couldn't I have made a love match, a match of mutual convenience, failing that. Instead, I chose a monster when I could have chosen—'

'Anyone, I am certain.'

'Yes, at one time, perhaps, before I was so tainted. Though I struggle to remember such innocence of virtue as I once possessed.'

'And yet when innocence departs us, wisdom takes its root.'

'Wise but miserable. I'm not sure I reckon much of the exchange.'

'Wise and beautiful, still,' he said, and I turned around to face him. His expression disarmed, caught out as if he regretted the saying, betrayed by his own tongue.

I stared hard at him, his pronounced square brow framing eyes so dark and alluring that I often struggled to hold his gaze without feeling unravelled, for they seemed somehow to lure me in, even when I did not want them to. I had noticed it from the outset, and even then I knew him handsome. But his brooding manner and my indifference to everything in the beginning made it easy for me to dismiss the detail...then. 'Is that what you think of me?'

'That...and so much more I wish I did not...'

'What do you mean?'

'I shouldn't even speak of what I mean. And yet...I see you doubt yourself. It is like you do not understand what you possess. But I have come to realise there is a great deal more to you than meets the eye. You are not only beautiful, but intelligent, kind of heart. Those gifts are worthy of so much more than what life has dealt you so far, but that does not mean it shall continue so. I have often felt as you have, like life is not always worth living, especially when I have been dealt its harshest blows. But I have lived to come about the other side of them, and I *know* things can turn.'

I nodded. 'Thank you, though I fear you do not know the darkness in me if that is what you see.' I staunched another flow of tears with my thumb.

'We all wrestle that battle, Eleanor, even if no one else sees the struggle.' And then his eyes smouldered contemplative, and I wondered what battle he was struggling against in the realms unknown to me. I was starting to believe I understood it, beginning to dare to hope that in this struggle, we were in common. 'You are right, there still remains hope,' I said, and then I let my gaze be drawn to him, permitted those eyes to take me wherever they so wished. And it took a course entirely of its own, and I kissed him, and then he kissed me back, and for the first time, I remembered what it was to feel so hungry for such tenderness as I felt in his caress. *Oh god, how long had it been since I knew this sensation?* To *want* to feel something, to be stirred to passion and have no desire to repress it. This was not the unwanted kisses of patrons at my lips or Giles's forced attempts; this was something so tender and responsive that it caught me entirely off guard. Not because I had not spent the entirety of the last twenty-four hours wishing to know his kiss and trying to talk myself out of it, not because I had not known such sweet kisses before, but because I had not been sure I was even capable of such feeling anymore.

And now I knew. And I was transported by it. By the taste of him, the feeling of him—strong but sweet-tempered—and I began to feel the ache of longing so deeply I knew myself beyond a simple spell of lust. I knew him beyond it, too, when he held my face between his soft palms and kissed me more urgently. I dared to let the brush slip from my hands and gave them permission to feel the taught muscles I had ventured to glance at and admire, but never thought I might touch. Stroke the tawny sun-kissed skin I had often seen glazed with beads of sweat beneath the light of the sun or a candle's glow. And now I pulled back, pressed my lips to the tender skin of his neck, ran my fingers through the silky black hair that hung about his ears and felt his hot breathy sigh warm my ear. 'Eleanor,' he said as I traced my tongue over the hollow at his clavicle and drew myself closer to him. 'Eleanor,' he said again, and I began to open the buttons of his shirt and trail my kisses close behind my busied fingers. 'God. You have to stop. We cannot do this.'

His words came like lead.

'I want you, Marco, I want this.'

'No, you don't.' He pulled back and held my hands in his, preventing them from reaching the remaining few buttons. 'Not wanting him does not mean you want this,' he said.

'I know that. But being his wife does not render me immune to the feelings you have stirred in me, either.'

This stunned him and, in truth, even me as I spoke them aloud.

He groaned. 'Nor does it eradicate mine. But it does not change the fact that you are *his* wife, Eleanor, not mine.'

'Please, Marco, don't. I cannot fight this anymore. I have tried.'

'We have to try harder. It isn't right. I have to go. Forgive me.'

I cried a while when he left and accepted Angelo's gentle nudging and Volatore's attentive sniffs at my ear as they were meant, to console me. I hugged them, petted them, and finished brushing them, hoping my tears would dry before I had to return to the house and face the rest of the family.

'Ah, here she is now. You can ask her for yourself,' said Mr Harper as I came in through the open terrace doors. He was standing with Marco, who looked equally put out at being accosted.

I forced a smile.

'Eleanor,' said Mr Harper, 'I thought you stabling with the horses tonight! Isabella said you were fond of them, but—'

'Forgive me, I did not know I was wanted.'

'Well, I wanted to put something to you. I thought it might be nice to invite you both along to the hotel with us this evening if you had a fancy for it. The food is excellent and—'

'Oh, Mr Harper, you are very generous, but I could not impose on your anniversary outing, absolutely not. Besides, I am having a bath drawn and planning an early night. Though I thank you for the offer.'

'Ah, well. As you please, then.'

'You have a lovely time with your wife. Thirty-five years of happiness is no trifling celebration.' I kissed him on the cheek and excused myself to my chamber.

I came out again only to wave them off and then returned to my room to help Benedetta draw a bath for me. It was easier here, given there was not so much water to boil up as the very air swelled with heat, and the method here, too, was better. In the day, buckets drawn from the well were left to sit in the heat of the day's sun, so they already made a tepid tub before the water from the kettles was added. It was just as well, for aside from the farm hands, there were no armies of servants here to carry the buckets, only an aged cook-come-housekeeper and Giuseppe who seemed to answer to almost every other office. So I was pleased we could manage it between the two of us with far less trouble than it usually took, and looked forward to soaking the grime of two days of gardening from me. If I was honest, I was equally grateful to have something to keep me distracted from all else.

I had taken my dinner downstairs with the cook so that Marco and I were not left peering awkwardly at each other over our plates. And though it was not easy to physically remove myself from his proximity when I knew us in the house alone, I found it somewhat easier than separating my thoughts from him, which would not stray far from the memory of his kisses. But they had brought me as much sorrow as joy, for I had not meant to get into this kind of scrape again, *ever,* and certainly not now, and not for a minute with him. With any "him". After Annalise, I had thought myself certain of my preferences. The previous encounters owing only to the naivety of not knowing any better. And yet now I wondered if I was no different than the ladies Theo spoke of who entertained both sexes. I digressed then in bringing Theo to mind and wondered if she had returned home safely as Giles had insisted. I wondered if I sent a letter to the Theatre at Bury addressed to her, whether she would receive it, and then I let out a little laugh at wondering if I would ever be referred to as "Queenie" again. I hoped so. I hoped that when I finally removed myself from this impossible situation and arrived home, I would find her at the Theatre in Bury and have a chance to thank her for what she did for me and apologise for how she suffered for me, too. I needed friendship now, of the true kind, as she and Lady W. had shown me. I supposed it had been friendship I had sought in Marco and Dante. I suspected that was why I had not at first noticed when those lines had started to blur into something more. *I should have had my guard up better.*

I had been particularly cautious with the ladies at the art class and even those I had been introduced to at the charity house and bordello, even with Tanto, who had not been so easy to resist. For I had spotted the danger in those kind of persons ahead of myself, and took great care to remain at surface level with my female acquaintances where I considered they could pose a risk. I never saw the need with men, not now, and yet here I was, reduced to such longing on account of one I thought least likely of all.

Perhaps I had not grown equally in wisdom as I had descended from innocence, after all. Why was there always more to learn, more of retrospect's stinging lessons ready to catch you out when you were still smarting from the consequences of those that came before?

I sunk back in the tub and excused Benedetta after she had finished washing my hair. I could manage the rest from here, and I wanted to be alone with my thoughts, for they were so scattered and pervasive that I required no audience to detect my troubled mind. I might fall into laughter or rage as swift as tears with the pace at which they raced. I lifted my knees over the edge of the tub and submerged the rest of me beneath the water. Perhaps I would return to the Bagni again tomorrow. It had been nice to bathe in the thermal waters, and not for the purposes of preventing my womb from spasming or whatever such nonsense Dr Heimlich claimed, but for bringing me a sense of relaxation to my mind, I could credit him. I would need to find some way to absent myself from Marco as far as possible for the last days of our holiday, and between the journeying to and from Abano, that would certainly account for half a day I could rely upon.

When I had finished scrubbing mud from my fingernails and sponging myself down with soft soap, I rose from the tub and felt the steam rising from my pink skin. I had perhaps had it a little too hot, and I trod carefully out, feeling a little heady. I opened the windows back up, lay the bath sheet on my bed, and reclined against it as my pulse throbbed at my throat. And then, just as I felt myself drifting into something close to sleep, I heard a flap above my head and thought I had imagined it. But when I opened my eyes, I saw a large bird flying about the room. I jumped up, startled, screamed and ducked as I ran for the door and slammed it behind me, barely clutching my bath sheet to wrap around me. But I was a fraction too late in wrapping myself back in it as Marco came thundering down the hall from his end of the corridor.

'Are you alright?' he asked me, charging in my direction as I fought with the tangled sheet to cover myself. 'What is it?'

'There is a bird, a huge bird, flying about in my room!' I told him and saw the relief in his face.

'A bird? I thought you liked birds?'

'I do, but not in my chamber, not that big.'

'Alright, go somewhere else and I will shoo it out.'

By now, Benedetta was up the stairs and ushered me along the hall to an empty room. The furniture was still draped in covers, but the windows were at least shut, and I explained to her in excited bursts what had happened.

'Would you like some wine or sweet tea for your nerves, Signora?' she asked me, and I nodded. 'I will see if I can find you something to put on.'

But Marco was back before she was, calling out to me from the hall, 'It is gone now. You can return. I have closed up the windows.'

I tucked the bath sheet tight about me, opened the door and poked my head around it. 'You are certain?'

He threw me an incredulous look. 'I assure you.'

'Thank you,' I said more sheepishly now, stepping fully into the corridor again.

He averted his eyes.

'You didn't hurt it, did you?'

'No, I didn't,' he said, defensive.

'Sorry. Thank you, again.'

'Hadn't you better get dressed? And next time, don't open the window in the nude. Perhaps don't open it at all if this is the result.'

I felt my cheeks flush hot with embarrassment. 'I didn't think anyone would be out there at this time of night.'

'Well, Giuseppe and I were bringing the harvest crates in.'

I pressed my palms to my cheeks.

Benedetta returned then, carrying a tray in her hands and a shift draped over her shoulder. 'It is gone?' she asked, and Marco nodded. 'All gone, perhaps you might see if there are some light curtains that can be hung in your mistress's chamber. Goodnight to you,' he said to us both.

'Goodnight.'

I felt like such an imbecile as I calmed down and sipped on the tea Benedetta had brought me. Once I was recovered and in a clean shift and slippers, I joined her in the task of emptying the bathwater out of the window, bucket by bucket, and taking care to close them back up straight after. Though how I was to sleep tonight without the modicum of air that made it tolerable, I did not know.

When the tub was empty, she said she would ask Marco to help her carry it back to the scullery because Giuseppe had already gone back to his farmhouse.

'No,' I said, standing up from the chair I had just sat back down in. 'I will carry it with you. You needn't disturb him again.'

She looked at me oddly as she sometimes did, usually when I either misinterpreted or mispronounced something in the Italian.

'We are strong and capable, are we not?'

'Yes, Signora, as you wish.'

So we wedged the bedroom door open and took an end each. It was more cumbersome in size than in weight, and we struggled about corners and bashed it down a few of the steps, but we managed all the same and deposited it in the scullery with some relief. 'Thank you, Benedetta. I shall require nothing else, so by all means, enjoy an early night if you wish.

'Thank you, Signora. Goodnight,' she said, and we parted on the basement stairs.

When I came back up, I had not expected to see Marco at the top of them.

'What was all that clanging about?'

'Sorry, did we disturb you? We were taking down the tub.'

'What? Why did you not ask me to do it?'

'Because I didn't want to disturb you again, and we are quite capable, you know, us females.'

He smirked as I drew level with him at the top of the staircase. 'Very well, I shall go back to my painting then, but do feel free to call on me if there are any more birds or bathtubs to tend to.'

'Goodnight, Marco,' I said and walked past him.

But when I got into bed, I was once again restless. All the good my bath had done in settling me had been entirely undone by all the excitement afterwards. It was only half past nine, and I was so wide awake now that I knew it might be hours until I exhausted myself to sleep. Then came a tap at my door, and I wondered what Benedetta had forgotten. 'Come in.'

She appeared in the doorway. 'I found some window netting in the laundry room, as Marco asked. I didn't know whether to wait until the morning or if you would be too hot to sleep without the windows open.'

'Thank you, Benedetta, but you should have gone to bed. But I will help you, and we can make quick work of it. We need only do one of the windows tonight, the rest can wait. How do we hang them?'

'There should be some hooks in the wall,' she said, casting her lamp about them to find the place, but there were none. 'I think we will need to hammer in some new ones.'

'Well, then, it shall have to wait till morning. Perhaps you can ask Giuseppe to see to it then.'

But when she went, and only a few moments later, the door tapped again, I did not bid her come in; instead, I said, 'Go to bed, Benedetta. It can wait.'

'I am not, Benedetta.'

I sat up sharp. 'Marco?'

'Can I come in?'

I got up from the bed, smoothed down my hair and opened the door. 'Yes?'

He held up a hammer and a fistful of nails. 'Benedetta said you needed a curtain hung, or you might boil in your bed tonight.'

Benedetta! 'Come in,' I said, stepping aside to make way for him. 'I told her it could wait until the morning.'

'Well, she is right. You won't get through the night with the room shut up like this. Where is it going?'

I pointed to the window closest to my bed, and he opened it up before tapping a nail into the bottom two corners of the wooden frame. I stood hovering at his side, holding the netting, not knowing what to say to break the silence. Then he turned and said he would need to get a stool from his room to reach the top of the window frame and, accordingly, went off to fetch it.

I remained cautiously at the window, enjoying the relief of somewhat cooler air and supposing Benedetta had been right after all. At least I might sleep tonight, at some distant point.

'Here, mind yourself,' he said, returning now and putting the stool down beside me. He handed me some nails and the hammer and asked me to pass them up to him as he climbed upon it. I watched him tap in one nail, and when he came down to reposition the stool and do the other corner, our eyes met uneasily as I swapped sides with him. *Oh, how were we to manage the next four days when the next four minutes seemed impossible?*

'Eleanor?'

'Yes?'

'The hammer?'

'Oh,' I said, passing it up. 'I hope your parents are having a nice time. I suppose they will be back fairly soon.'

'They will be having such a merry time I doubt they will be back this side of midnight.'

'Oh.'

'Right, pass me the net, and I will see if this works.'

I passed him one corner and then the next, and though it would need some cutting down to size, it would suffice for tonight.

'There,' he said, stepping down, '...entirely bird-proof.'

'Thank you, I appreciate it. I might actually manage to sleep tonight now.'

'No problem. My talents are not restricted to bird shooing, it seems.'

I smiled, and he held my gaze.

'Marco, I—I'm sorry if I made you feel uncomfortable earlier. I don't want it to be like this between us. If for nothing else but the sake of your parents suspecting us enemies, might we manage to at least pretend to be as we were?'

'You are right. We will have to learn to make a better show of things, but you have nothing to be sorry for. It is my fault we find ourselves in this fix, and I mean to put it right.'

'I kissed you,' I reminded him.

'Well, that may be so, but if you had not, I am certain it would have ended no differently. I think perhaps it will be best if I return to Venice tomorrow. Now that my father is here, there is no sense in my remaining and making this harder than it already is.'

My heart sank. 'You need not go, Marco. I mean to go daily to the Bagni anyway, so I do not think our paths will cross so very much.'

'It is for the best. I will tell my parents in the morning that I am anxious to return to the gallery, and they will think nothing of it.'

I nodded.

'Well, get some sleep now. I will see you at breakfast before I go. Goodnight.'

'Goodnight,' I replied, but I did not want him to leave, and as I watched him close the door behind him, I felt oddly bereft. Then I saw the stool beneath the window, snatched it up and went out after him.

He had barely reached his chamber when he turned about to see me.

'You forgot your stool,' I said, glancing down at it.

'Oh. Thank you.'

I handed it to him. And then, when I turned about to leave, I turned swiftly back again and followed him into his room, closing the door behind me. And then there was nothing to be said, for the look we shared said all. And I could not tell if it was I or he who seized the other first, for we seemed instantly to collide towards each other and quickly found ourselves kissing with even greater urgency than we had earlier in the horse pen. And this time, I was persuaded neither of us would find the restraint to prevent such a high passion from taking its course, for we kissed our way towards the bed and tumbled upon it without breaking our embrace.

'Eleanor,' he said, pulling back.

'No,' I told him, 'I will not leave unless you tell me you do not want me.'

'I was going to ask you if I could take your chemise off.'

I smiled and sat up enough to lift it over my head and watched the delight dance in his eyes as he took in the view of me. I was used to seeing men crumble at this trick, and yet this was not the same, for he looked at me with such earnestness in his eyes that I felt nothing but enriched by it, whereas, beneath other men's gazes, I always felt diminished.

I lowered myself back down, and as he found my lips again, I tugged the shirt from over his head and drew the warmth of his skin to mine and delighted in the shock of it as he kissed my neck and stroked my breasts so gently I shivered and jerked beneath his weight. Then he trailed his kisses to my breasts, and I felt the astonishment and relief as he took my nipple into his mouth and I cried out with such alarm that I surprised myself at my fragility.

I ran my hands through his hair, across the planes of his broad shoulders, not knowing what I wanted most. To let him continue in his tender caressing, to explore the sight and taste of his body, or to bid him remove his breeches, which were all that remained between us now. But before I could decide, I felt his hand stroke the length of my inner thigh, and it was too late. I was rendered in paralysis as I anticipated the stroke of his fingertips, which seemed torturously slow in teasing their way to the stiffening heat of me, but when they did, they caused me to cry out and writhe like I had never been touched there before.

I knew I would not last long in this and felt the familiar tremble in my lower limbs, the arching and lifting of my back and then the wet surprise of his tongue as he crawled between my legs. I lifted my head and opened my eyes to see him there, but I had already arrived, building waves of tension meeting his mouth and breaking now, without restraint, as I held his face to me and sighed with such abandon I could hardly catch my breath, for it was an enduring release that seemed to know no end, that kept on building and climbing until my body fell weak with its accomplishment.

When I opened my eyes, he was just staring at me from above, brushing hair from my face, and his sparkling dark eyes and handsome face loomed above me. I reached up to him and smiled before kissing him again and finding the buttons of his breaches. When he lifted to wriggle out of them, I cast my eyes over his body, thinking it a marvel of the kind used to inspire the carving out of bronzes and marble statues, for it seemed he had been so cast in those lines of perfection. Then I felt him stiff against the soft flesh of my thigh as he lowered himself back down and, with the gentlest of probing, found his way into the slickness of me. We both gasped then and opened our eyes, and I wanted to peer into the depths of them as he traversed the depths of me, so snuggly, so gently, I had to bear down hard against him just to appease the aching throb. I could not take this slow torture. I was too ripe, too sensitive to every sensation in my body, as if the reunion with my mind was restored to a vigour I had either never known, or failed to remember after such a time.

I wrapped my legs around his back and he began to move faster now, to build momentum, which opened me fully to him, and we shared the same look of astonishment as we climbed and writhed together with growing determination to feel the full extent of each other. Without words, I bid him deeper, and he delved. I bid him faster, and he thrust more frantically as I lifted my weight, clung to him with every limb and all the internal force I could contrive as I followed the urges directed from that single point inside me that yearned to keep close contact with the stiffness of him. And we were both breathless with the effort now, our sighs falling into rumbling exhalations as we worked to the inevitable end that revealed its promise with each new thrust, each surprised glance, and then I could do no more but scream out 'faster', and from my innermost depths, I trembled and quaked beneath him only moments ahead of his own undoing as he stared into my eyes and cried out in relief. Then he collapsed against my bosom, panting, sweat pouring onto my chest, and I stroked his face as we both recovered.

I felt tears rolling down my cheeks now, but they were borne not of regret or despair but of gratitude. No man had ever made love to me so openly, so tenderly, and I did not know it possible to feel so moved. That an act that had become so commonplace and tainted could be restored to something so sublime. 'Marco,' I whispered after a time.

He lifted his head from between my breasts and peered up at me, 'Yes.'

'You are like a dream to me.'

He rolled onto his back, scooped me into an arm, and kissed my forehead. 'And you I shall never be able to stop dreaming of.'

I brushed a palm across his chest and pressed a kiss to his shoulder. 'Then let us not hurry to wake from it.'

We did not hurry. Instead, we kissed and stroked and lay in contented silence until we heard the thrash of hooves beyond the window and knew his parents were back. I tilted my head and looked at him. 'I am sorry to have to leave you,' I said.

He kissed me tenderly. 'I wish it could be otherwise.'

'Promise me you will not go in the morning. We have four days left. Let us enjoy them while we can. After that, we will not be the free spirits we are now. Might we enjoy the dream for just a little longer?'

And we did precisely that with what remained to us. Like a well about to run dry, a fire burning down to its last embers, or a sunset that might never rise again, we relished every moment we could steal to be alone with one another in all ways.

It was easier with Mr Harper about to find greater opportunities now our pairings were equal, and we left the house early in the mornings to ride out to Stra. Whilst we rested the horses, we found a patch of meadow to lie in and share kisses and caresses. On my trips to the Bagni, he would escort me alone most days, for Isabella was content now to remain at the house with her husband and put him to use in the garden and in directing the harvests.

We held hands as we travelled in the coach and stole kisses when the roads were derelict. We procured a private bath at the Bagni and sunk into the steamy water together. He took me to walk the vast square at *Prato della Valle* and to see *St. Antony's Basilica* in Padua and gave me a tour of the city, and at times, I felt it precisely what a wedding journey should have amounted to. And oh how I wished it was such and that this might be only a beginning and not a slow farewell.

If we discovered a chance outing of his parents to the flower market or the Botanical Gardens, we would climb into his bed and make love, every time as though it was the first and last combined, and when we could not, I would throw him down upon the haystack in the horse's pen and climb on top of him and cover him in kisses. But however we spent our precious hours, it was always in a state of natural bliss. For now there was no turning back from it, it seemed the only thing to do was embrace this shrinking opportunity we both knew was moving ever closer to its end.—I refused to think about it, and he never mentioned it, yet as the days passed, I knew we both felt its inevitability chasing at our heels.

We were merry in company too, though, and our evenings became full of gaiety, from lively conversation about the table to games of cards, evening walks along the river, and even Isabella playing at the pianoforte on one evening. I often thought how happy I would have been to have married him instead. I adored him and his family; it would have been a happy life to settle to amongst them all. I'd pondered this most of the morning of my wedding anniversary as they congratulated me with words of hope and generosity and made a concerted effort to cheer me since I could not be with my husband.

The irony was difficult to bear. If I had married your son and not your nephew, I thought, I would indeed be sorry to spend my Anniversary alone. I would receive gratefully your well wishes that I would soon be counting my tenth and twentieth years as they had, and that in that time, we would grow a family of our own, and our happiness would be multiplied. But it was not so, and I could offer them only empty words and platitudes.

It was Marco I had felt the most sorrow for in all the talk, for I knew that however much we ran headfirst into this affair, he remained in conflict over the situation of my marriage. In his mind, a married woman was off-bounds, and he was not *that* sort of fellow. I saw it in his eyes as they pressed me to open my parcel and discover my anniversary gift. I did as bid and tried to contrive some joy and surprise for their sake as I revealed a set of diamond eardrops and a matching necklace. And even in that, the irony thickened. I had not been permitted access to any ornaments beyond my replacement wedding band unless Giles was attending me, and yet here he handed me something I could have sold this very day and been on a ship home by tomorrow. And yet I was not sure now that I wanted that, at least, not yet.

Though the note that accompanied it did give me pause to reconsider. *"Happy first Anniversary, dear wife. I hope you like my gift. As for yours, I wish only for the fruit of your womb and your safe return to me."* This, I did not share with the family and burned it when I returned to my chamber.

But beyond that difficult day, I hardly remembered the existence of a husband at all as I enjoyed the charms of the one I wished to call the same. He was handsome and kind, and his more advanced years of wisdom and intellect kept my interest as much in mind as in body. And I felt safe with him, so safe, like I could trust him to anything at all, and oh, how I wanted to. I considered it now as we sat on the bank of the river, sipping wine, the little rowing boat moored before us, bobbing at the water's edge. 'I can't believe we are to return tomorrow. I don't know how to face going back.'

He drained his glass and then considered me. 'Eleanor, we need to discuss that, you know. We have run out of time for putting it off.'

I cast my gaze to the ground. 'I know.'

'You know how I feel about you, Eleanor. At least, you should by now.'

I nodded and picked a tuft of grass to fiddle with. 'But?'

'But, we both knew when we threw out the rule book that with the rise would come the fall.'

I felt my lip tremble. 'I knew it, but I did not know just how impossible that might grow to become.'

'Nor I. But you do realise we have to stop now, don't you?'

'Do we? We can be careful, discreet. God, we could leave and be together.'

He held up a hand. 'Eleanor, you say nothing I have not considered a thousand times each night when I am alone without you next to me. I have not stopped thinking of a way that we might be able to salvage something after tonight. But I cannot find one that does not lead us to creating so much damage, so much hurt to others.'

'I thought you were angry with Giles—'

'I am. I don't speak of him. And I don't know how I will manage to share a roof, a table, or a word with him without wanting to...lose my restraint. I don't know how I will lie in bed at night, knowing that you lay in his arms above me when mine are hungry to hold you. But for your sake and my family, I will find one. But that is one thing. To destroy my family, break their hearts, leave them...I cannot.'

I nodded. I didn't want him to be right, yet I knew he was. 'I know well enough how that goes, Marco. I cannot ask of you what I know would be the cost to bear. I would hate to see you or your family suffer, even more than I have loathed myself for causing the same to mine. For mine is not like yours. Your family are close, kind, and supportive; everything a family should be. I want no harm to come to them, either. And yet, I do not know how I will give up this happiness. I know not how to give up on something so full of promise and hope and...'

'I feel the same as you do. I meant never to open myself up to the possibility of love again. I meant never to lie with another man's wife. But all has come to pass. I cannot change that now. But my eyes are wide open. There can be no future for us, and we must find a way to bear it.'

'I am tired of finding ways to bear it, Marco, all of it. Is it so wrong to want to be happy? Must the ransom always be so high?'

'Eleanor, our life together could not be a happy one under the circumstances upon which we have met. I would want to love you as a husband should love a wife. I would want to share you with no other man, however insignificant the regard between you. And I would want you amongst the people I love, not hidden away as some forbidden, scandalous secret. Though we might know happy moments, it is blind to think we could enjoy a happy life.'

'I know what you say is true...I do.' I gathered my knees before my face and wept into them. He shuffled beside me and hugged me beneath his arm. After a time, he pulled me up from the ground, walked with me, hand in hand, and said, 'We will have time enough to be miserable and apart, but for now, let's just enjoy it until the very last.'

I squeezed his hand and nodded. 'Just tell me one thing, if it were different...'

'I would not wish to separate myself from you for the barest moment, for all my days.'

I smiled at this.

'The gallery has been my life's endeavour. Holland-Bury likes to jest that *that* is my wife and master, and I suppose, in many ways, it is true. I live and breathe for my work, for a dream that took so long to bring about. It has taken everything I could give to it, and I thought that was enough for me. You have made me question everything I thought I knew about myself. And though I dread the days that will follow, I confess that I do not regret the time we have had. I will always be grateful to carry this memory with me for always.'

'I, too, regret so many things, but I don't count this among them either. But, what I know I will regret is to endure my marriage and let the days of my life pass so miserably, now you have reminded me that life can be so much more. I want you to know I will not be accepting my lot. I plan to leave him. It has been a plan a long time in the making, and I mean to do it soon. And when I do, I want you to understand there was no other way for me.'

He stopped and looked at me with such concern. 'I do know. And I don't want you to remain in misery just because I can't be the one to bring you joy. You must do what you have to do, Eleanor, for I never want you to end up in the dire state of desperation I found you in when you first came here. So, save yourself, and know that I wish I could have saved you first.'

I kissed him then and felt both our tears streaming down our cheeks.

'Just promise me you will take care,' he said when he pulled back from me.

'I will. I *want* to live now.'

Then, the last hues of daylight faded from the sky, and it grew dark. We climbed back into the boat. I thought to row home, but when he unmoored it, we lay down in its narrow confines and let it drift as our passions ran their final course. And then, when we had exhausted ourselves with one release after another, we stared into the sky, holding each other, bidding the dawn not to break.

CHAPTER THIRTY-FIVE

Fading Dream.

Eleanor. September 1822.

'Giles, please, I feel the coming of my cramping. I cannot manage it tonight. I am in pain, and the doctor said not to excess, remember. And certainly never attempted upon the commencement of my bleed.'

He sighed. 'Very well, but it is not the greatest welcome home a fellow could look to, and it certainly won't fill your belly.'

'I know, the timing is off, forgive me. But if my courses don't run as they should, a child will not be possible at all now, will it?'

'Yes, yes. But I have missed you all this time. Won't you find some other trick to make up for it?' He drew my hand down to his bulging breeches and I felt qualmish at the mere thought. Likewise, I felt repugnant at the thought of letting any man near me after Marco.

We had been back from the Villa not quite a fortnight and I was already bereft at our separation. Though even that had not been on Giles's account, for he had only returned from Trieste today: "an extended gift", Serrano's letter had read, "to demonstrate my devotion". But it was not his devotion or Giles's I hungered for, and it had been torturous to be beneath the same roof as Marco, sometimes even alone, knowing we could not share even the simplest of kindnesses together, for the dream was over now.

We no longer chatted at the breakfast table when everyone else had left, for he went earlier than all. He no longer escorted me from art classes but sent his oarsman to convey me back whilst he remained. In the classes, I was treated with the same courtesy we all were, but not a modicum more. Even to church, I would never enjoy his escort, but Dante's, or at best, the pair of them, which proved more impossible still, for it was difficult to hide the discomfort between us in company even more than it was to bear it in solitude. And that, of course, was why we had to continue thus, for it was a dangerous rope to tread, and we were already stumbling. I dreaded to contemplate how much more dangerous it would grow now Giles had returned. He had been back less than a few hours, and already Marco had left the dinner table and the house, on some poorly hashed excuse that was so out of character everybody noticed it.

And yet it was the cost we were to bear now, the terms we had agreed to, to know such tenderness. I lived ever more in the memory of those days than the present moment now, for these had proved so desolate a downfall I could not remain steadfast to the present anymore. At least when it was optional, I considered, as Giles directed my head towards his exposed cock.

It was the only one I would be forced to tend to, though, for I was not able to return to the apartment now, however many threats Signora Crivelli made to expose me. I couldn't be the *Rosa Inglese* anymore. I had no stomach for it. If she was to expose me, I supposed it might even be a blessing and expedite my plans to leave the city, for my enquiries at the biglietteria had proved I already had enough money to buy my sea passage home. I needed only to set the date and make the purchase.

And yet, every day, I resolved to do it; every time I approached the office with a purse full of coins, I turned about at the last, knowing I would never see him again if I did. I already knew what that felt like when Annalise had deserted me. Could I go through it all again, and so soon? I did not think I could. Besides, though I had the fare, I discovered a complication I had not foreseen: needing the authorities to sign my passport to permit me to travel. It had not been a falsehood as I had suspected when Giles had said so. Here, you needed permission to go anywhere. It had only recently been signed for our trip to Padua, but Mr Harper had surrendered it to Giles on our return, and he locked it away in his desk drawer. I had no key, but this could be overcome at the right moment. Yet I knew I would have to act swiftly in executing both its retrieval and the signing, as well as the ticket purchase and travel date, before one risked the chance of revealing the other. And I was not sure how long it would take to effect, given that Giles had always taken care of such matters.

In the meantime, I took up work I had been offered from the art academy, modelling for artists, usually with my clothes off, although sometimes otherwise. I had sat for a private sitting too, arising out of that line and earned a far better rate for the trouble.—For Holland-Bury had not been gulling me, the fees were atrocious, and it was irksome work, posing statue-like for so long and trying not to let my thoughts show on my face. But it was better than enduring another man's cheap assaults upon me.

Before, I had been low enough in spirits to be willing to dwell amongst lowly habits, but now I was altered and wanted to preserve the little I could to his memory. I could not foresee how I would manage it now with Giles at home. But I came upon an idea that would buy me the rest of the week and hoped beyond that, the threat would urge me to effect the travel plans I kept shirking.

So that evening, once I spat the taste of Giles from my mouth and had Benedetta ready me for bed, I asked a favour of her. 'Is there any chance that there will be blood in the kitchens from some slaughtered creature?'

She frowned at me and said, 'Your Italian is wrong. You asked me for *blood*.'

'I meant to ask you for blood. – Look, I know it is a strange request, but I must convince Giles I am on my courses, or I shall know no rest.'

'Ah, I understand.'

'Will you be able to look in the kitchen and bring me my rags? He will suspect me if there is no evidence of it.'

She nodded, 'I will look.'

She came the next morning with a half cup full, and I soaked the rags and left a stain upon my sheet and the back of one of my shifts, as was often the unsightly clues it resulted in. My actual courses would return in about a week, so I would either have to ensure I was gone by then or pretend something was amiss and it had proved an extended affair. I knew this was at least possible, for the doctor had asked me of it. And I would certainly have to be gone before his review appointment—for that was only three weeks distant now—or I would really have some explaining to do. Giles had already mentioned our forthcoming visit to Padua at the regaling of our merry trip to the Villa the Harpers had apprised him of at dinner, and it had given him notions that we should enjoy such a holiday together this time and make a late celebration of our anniversary.

'Yes,' Mr Harper had said, 'You and Eleanor should stay at the Villa on your own and take a week to yourselves, we insist, don't we, Isabella?'

It was at that point Marco made his excuses, and I understood why. That place was sacred to us both now, and the very idea that it could be tainted with such a contemptible denouement was inconceivable. All that was left to us now was the memory of those magical days spent so blissfully together. I would have to leave before they could be distorted with less savoury ones, if for that reason alone.

So it was certain I must recover my passport and *carte di sicurezza,* which at least I knew now to be locked in his drawer with my valuable ornaments and other such things he meant to keep from me. I needed only to choose my moment carefully when I could retrieve them, for the only way would be to bust it open, for picking the lock had always failed me in past attempts to break out my gems in the hope of pawning them with the bastioneri. But once it was broken, there would be no return for me. So I decided the most sensible thing would be to find somewhere I could stay in the interim, between breaking the drawer open and boarding a ship. If I had not the complication of getting my passport signed, there need be no delay at all if I timed it right, but I could not account for the time it would take to manage it. However brief, I decided it would not be wise to consider staying in the city for that time. Though vast and busy, it was also too obvious, too convenient. I would have to think of somewhere else. Perhaps one of the less inhabited islands, Murano, might serve, but then I was more likely to stick out amongst a smaller society. Then there was the mainland, which, beyond the trip to the Villa, I knew nothing more of, beyond stories of Banditti and poverty. And so, not knowing where else to turn, I realised I would have to resort to asking for Marco's help, even if all that amounted to was his counsel. He would know best where I should go and likely how long it would take to have my passport signed. So I waited until Monday's art class when I knew it would be safest to approach him.

These had become so difficult now I'd almost persuaded myself to stop going. But, it was the only time I could be sure to see him at length now, even in this diminished capacity, and so I could not deny myself the opportunity, for soon there would be none at all. So I set up my easel in my usual spot, hoping he would show at any moment, for he had skipped the class entirely the week of Giles's return. We had suffered a rather uninspiring lesson with one of his gallery curators, who had us sketching a rather scantly filled flower arrangement in a vase snatched up from the entrance hall. But in truth, it wouldn't have mattered if we had sketched the Basilica of St. Marks or if Canaletto himself was taking the class; it wasn't *him*. But he had returned since, and I hoped he would show today, as I sensed in the others, too, as we grew restless in the wait.

'Where is our teacher today?' Guistina asked me as we settled behind our easels. She, too, had been absent for some time and had spent the last ten minutes appraising the class of her summer travels to Rome.

'I'm not sure, perhaps running a little late?' I offered, still holding onto hope.

'But you live under the same roof? He said nothing to you?' Rosina added, stepping away from her easel now and joining the conversation.

'I am not his keeper, Rosina. I have no idea,' I answered, perhaps a little more irritated than I should have been.

'I know that, but he might have mentioned something. I cannot bear another lesson with that curator. I would rather slip away now if he is not to come,' she complained.

'Perhaps he is too busy with his mystery lady to teach us now, I'd imagine,' Lia teased before I had the chance to reply, and I took this as my cue to leave the conversation and busy myself with mixing my palette.

'Ooh, la la! What have I missed? Tell me more.' Guistina put her paint board down and went over to Lia's station. 'Who is the lucky lady?'

'Well, it seems it is quite the mystery. Nobody knows, but he is certainly in love. We all see the change in him since he returned from his holidays. Rosina thinks he has been secretly holed up with her and has not been away to the Villa at all.'

'Hmm, well, he is a very private man, but I never had him down for the secret tryst type. If he is in love, then surely he will want to bring it to the notice of society to put all the mothers off if nothing else, and then there is his mama who would have surely let something slip into one of our mama's ears? She used to try so hard to match him. She even tried with you, Guistina, before you were married, remember,' Margarita said.

I feigned disinterest but could not help casting a sideways glance over Guistina now, considering her in a different light. She was pretty and talented, yet I had never noticed him pay her any particular interest.

'Yes, I remember it well,' she declared '....and how sorry I am that she failed and I am left with Paulo,' she sighed.

I grew tense and dropped my pot of brushes over the floor.

'Well?' The pair of them had joined me on the floor to reclaim them. 'You must know the identity of your cousin's mystery lady?' Guistina pressed me, her eyes bright, expectant.

I stood up and looked at the crowd gathering around me. 'I'm sorry, ladies, I know nothing of Marco's private affairs.'

They sighed their disappointment. 'Spoilsport,' Lia complained, and I ignored her.

'I'm sure he has his reasons for his secrecy, and if he means for us to know of it, we will, soon enough.' Lucia conceded.

Rosina sighed. 'Come now, Marco will not marry, he has never propositioned anyone.'

'It is true. Do you think he is otherwise inclined?' Lia suggested.

'Lia, lift your mind from the gutter, he is not one of *those*. Some people are just not suited to marriage, I suppose. Let's face it, how many of us would be married if we had the choices a man has?' Guistina said.

Lucia was the only one to raise her hand.

'Well, you are not yet a year married and your husband has been away for most of that time!' Guistina said to her.

'It is not impossible to love your husband, you know, Guistina, just because *your* marriage is in trouble,' she replied.

'Trouble? My marriage has never been better.'

'That, Guistina, is because you spend more time at your summer house with your cicisbeo than you do at home with your husband!' Rosina cut in.

'Exactly, it has never been better.' They all laughed a little at this, and even I could not resist a little flourish, for though I had never before heard of the word, I gleaned the measure of it.

'What is your husband like, Eleanor?' Guistina asked me then, and it wiped the laughter clean from my lips. 'If Marco and Dante are anything to go by, I am sure you have not done badly with the Harpers,' she added.

'Like Lucia, we have been wed only a year, it is early days,' I said and sought a diversion. 'But yes, you are right. I have found the Harpers to be a very fine family, and I have been most fortunate in my attachment to them.'

'But you truly don't know who this woman of mystery is? He has brought no one to the house?' Guistina made her last plea, and I wondered if she could sense the contrived denial in my tone. I shook my head. 'I'm afraid I do not,' I said flatly. I hoped my discomfort was better concealed than it felt, for I was sure I read something in Guistina's expression that warned me she was suspicious.

'It was probably no one of significance at all, a courtesan perhaps, hence the secrecy,' Lia offered.

'Hmm, perhaps,' Guistina muttered, unconvinced.

'Well, if his own family does not know of her, there can be nothing of importance to it; certainly, there will be no wedding bells in tow.'

Then we all fell silent as footsteps were heard in the hall and Marco came running in, breathless and flushed. I exhaled my relief at his appearance.

'Apologies, Ladies. You will forgive me, I hope. I was detained and could not get here sooner. I did not mean to keep you waiting. I do apologise.'

I saw the shared glances of suspicion pass between them as they offered him waved hands of forgiveness and told him it was no matter.

'We are only glad to have you back, Signor,' Rosina offered, '...we feared we were to be left in the hands of that curator again, and I must be frank with you, Signor, I would sooner not come to class if that is to be repeated.'

'Lucca was just helping me out as a favour. He is not an artist, so you will perhaps be kinder with your criticism of his efforts, Rosina. But no, rest assured, it was but a one-off. You shall rely on either myself or Mr Holland-Bury, I promise you. Now, it seems you are already set to go, so I shall introduce you to your model. Please be kind in welcoming Chiara, who shall sit for us over the coming weeks as we undertake a series of full-length portraits now we have grown used to capturing faces.

This was met with wide approval, though Lia stepped forward and asked, 'Will we only capture female portraits, Signor? Will we not also learn how to capture men?'

'You could always model for us, Marco, we have not yet sketched a man,' said Guistina with a grin. The class broke out in giggles, and I felt sorry as I watched him blush.

'Maybe,' he said to quieten them, '...though it shan't be me.'

'And nude. We have not yet sketched a nude,' Lia said with a smirk, setting everyone off with laughter again.

Marco took it with good grace and smiled at their cheek.

Margarita's eyes flashed. 'That's a fantastic idea!' she shrieked, loud enough to make everyone turn to her. All the best artists paint nudes, Mr Holland-Bury told us so himself. But I did not mean you, of course, Signor,' she said to Marco, looking embarrassed at how her enthusiasm had poured out. But another fellow, surely?'

'I do not think your husbands would approve of you attending a class on the sketching of nude men, Margarita, do you? Now, we are late to start, so let's get some proportions on the page shall we.'

I think we were both relieved when the class settled down and fell into concentration at last. I saw the strain behind Marco's patience and composure and felt it in my own forbearance. The atmosphere of easiness and funning had always been a feature of the class and one of the things I had enjoyed immensely in the company of it, but today it all seemed too much. Too close to the truth. Too contrary to how I felt inside.

I was glad to finally have the peace to watch him from a distance as I settled to make a start. Though my concentration was poor, and when I asked him for assistance, he was brief and perfunctory in his attendance on me. I had hoped to test the water, see if it would be possible to approach him for help, but I gleaned nothing from his demeanour, and as we cleared our things away, I knew I would have to take a chance and hope he would hear me.

So I took my time clearing up, working slowly, letting everyone go before me into the store room and painstakingly rinsing my brushes in the turpentine as the class began to filter out in a swathe of thanks and farewells.

'Marco,' I said when the class had finally departed. 'Can I have a word?'

He looked at me with mistrust. 'It will have to be quick. I have much to get on with this afternoon,' he replied.

I nodded, and he led me into his office, offering me a chair while he stood anxiously at his desk.

I cleared my throat. 'I need your help. I did not want to ask you, but I have no one else I can trust who would know how to advise me.'

'Alright, what do you need?'

'I need two things: to obtain a signature on my passport so I can travel and to consider the best place to go into hiding in the meantime.'

He cast his heavy gaze to the floor and bit his lip, pausing there for a protracted moment. 'It is time then?' he said when he looked up again.

'Yes, I fear it has to be.'

He raised his hand to his mouth and sighed. 'You mean now Giles is home?'

'That, and other matters.'

He nodded. 'Alright.'

'I know I must have it signed at the Police Headquarters in *San Severo,* but I do not know how long it will take to obtain an appointment, and I have to get my timings right to keep my cover until the last.'

'I am not sure if it runs the same for foreign travellers, but usually husbands sign for their wives' passports. But it may not be required since you already have one in issue, and I presume Giles would have had it made up for a year, though they will want to see your *Carte di Sicurezza.* I do not know how fast it will be. The bureaucracy under the Austrians is never speedy, but I will make enquiries for you with the *Commissario Superiore* this afternoon, if I can.'

'You do not mind? I don't want you at odds about it, but I would be grateful.'

'No, it is better I take care of it. If you are seen there, he may discover your intentions. I will not be suspected.'

'Thank you, Marco.'

'Now, how long will you need somewhere to stay for?'

'It depends on how long it will take to have the passport signed, for I should warn you, Marco, I am going to have to break into his drawer to retrieve it, and once I do, he will know, and I must be gone.'

'Is there no other way?'

'If there is I do not know it.'

'Let me think on this, alright. See if there is something else to be done before resorting to such risk-taking. Once I know more, I can consider where you might be safe to wait it out. The convent is perhaps your safest bet, for he will not be admitted to it no matter what he tries.'

It would not have been my first choice. 'Will I be able to leave it when I am ready to?'

'It depends on the story we admit you with. You are a married woman, so you are in your husband's charge. We might have to come up with something so I might have leave to sign you in and out of it. But let's not jump ahead. I will start with the passport. We will go from there.'

'Yes, I am grateful and sorry to ask it of you.' I stood up.

'Have you considered your travel plans?'

'I have. There is a boat from Genoa that travels first to Marseille, and from there, I can transfer to another that sails directly home. I need only consider the timing because it leaves on the twenty-sixth day of the month. If I don't put arrangements in place by then, I shall have to await another, and I cannot afford to.'

'Do you need money?'

'No, I have money. I meant I cannot afford the delay. He means to impregnate me, Marco, you know that, and I hold him off by a whisker. The best I will manage is perhaps another five days, so you see, I have to be gone by then. I cannot afford the complication of a child to think of now, and I do not want to bear him one in any case.'

'No, you cannot be put in such a position if you are to travel alone.'

'I cannot be put in that position at all. I will not be able to return to my family when I get back to my country, Marco. He will look for me everywhere he knows I have a connection. I must disappear now, leaving no trace if I ever want to be safe. I cannot care for a child when I do not even know how I will look after myself just yet.'

'No. No, of course not. But…is there someone you can turn to there he would not suspect?'

I shook my head. 'Not now. He turned over all of those cards in his last pursuit of me, and there is no one left. But I have a very powerful friend I can rely on. If I can find a way to communicate with her discreetly, I know she will do all she can to help me, even if at arm's length.'

This seemed to relieve him. 'Then that is something. Shall I write to her for you? I can have her reply directed to the gallery and he will have no way of intercepting it.'

'It is perhaps a little late for that. Though, once I am certain of my travel dates, it might be worth writing to her again so she at least knows to expect me back in the country.'

'You already have?'

'Yes, twice. Once, through a third party in Lisbon who I met on the journey here, but something went wrong somewhere along the line because when I managed to forward him an address, he replied saying he had sent the letter to London but had received no reply. And even if he had by now, I would not have got it. Giles intervened in reading his letter and threatened to send men to Lisbon if I ever wrote to him again.

Needless to say, I did not, and have heard nothing more since. Whether that is because there was nothing to convey, or whether he got to any such reply before me, I do not know. Only that I hope not.'

'Is that the letter you had at breakfast that morning when he came after you?'

I cast my mind back. 'Yes. I told him I had written to someone else though, another person I knew. At least Mr Banfield did not disclose any details.'

'That's why he was so enraged.'

'Yes...you noticed it?'

'Of course I did. Why do you think Dante and I caused such a fuss in bringing down the exhibition things from my studio? It was why I had Holland-Bury put off from collecting me and asked Giles to convey me. I could not think how else to intervene then. You did not seem to want my help.'

I did not realise it was anything more than coincidence and the fortuity of good timing. 'You did all that for me?'

He nodded.

I frowned. 'But, that was before...'

He nodded again.

'How long, Marco, did you harbour these feelings for me?'

He brushed a palm over his head. 'I don't know.'

'Yes, you do.'

He sighed and sat down in the chair opposite me. 'What does it matter now? You are to be gone in a fortnight and it shall all be as if we never were.'

'I thought that was what you *wanted*.'

'You think I wanted any of this?'

'Well, it is what we agreed upon then. Though—'

'Don't, Eleanor, can't you see it is hard enough for me to hold on to this thread of resolution as it is? That the thought of you taking such risks, travelling so far alone, disappearing into some inconspicuous anonymity with no plan to support yourself is not already tearing me apart? That the idea of you disappearing at all...' he looked away.

I crossed the room and, though frightened to even touch him, bent over him and wrapped myself about his back as he bent forward with his head in his hands. I pressed a kiss to the side of his wet cheek and held him. 'I'm sorry, I knew I shouldn't have come. I know you are struggling. Forgive me.'

He lifted a hand to my cheek and pressed his palm against it, and I was relieved not to have taken another misstep. To finally feel his touch and smell his musk after dreaming of it all my waking hours.

'I didn't know I would miss you this much, and you are not even gone yet,' he said, a muffled complaint into his hand.

'I miss you too. I can barely function anymore.'

He pulled me into his lap and I held his head against my chest. 'I am not very good at keeping my own promises anymore, am I?' he said.

'I have never been very good at that,' I offered.

'I have never been so reckless.' And then he kissed my neck, and I shivered, sighed, and pulled back from him. 'I don't want to increase your suffering, Marco.'

'I already suffer, every moment since we left *Villa Rosso*. It seems inevitable.'

'I can leave now, or I can stay...only if you want me to.'

He answered me with a kiss and I returned it. Then he told me to get up and took me by the hand.

'Where are we going?'

'Somewhere I can be with you properly.'

I let go of his hand when we reached the lobby where Benedetta waited for me. 'She can be trusted,' he said, taking it back up. 'You think she does not know about us?'

I looked at her with bewilderment.

'Who do you think kept a look out for us when we were alone at the Villa?'

'I—'

'Benedetta, will you have Giacomo ready the boat, please? We will be down directly.'

'Si, Signor,' she said, smiling at the sight of us.

'But,' I stopped myself short of the rest of my thoughts, which were that she knew of my other life, the life of the *Rosa Inglese*.

'She dislikes your husband almost as much as we do. You need not fear. She is a good woman, I told you.'

I nodded, not trusting myself to say anymore.

We soon arrived at a hotel, not so great a distance from the gallery, though precisely where I was not sure, for I had lost my sense of direction after getting out of the gondola and continuing on foot. I had spotted the great dome of the *Santa Maria della Salute* up ahead as we landed, but I could not think of anything other than how desperately I wanted to be alone with him. And when we finally sunk our naked bodies beneath the sheets and felt the familiarity of each other, I knew it was worth the risk to be with him again.

He did not mean to rush or give in to the urgency of my impatience; he wanted to make love to my body with reverence and tenderness and would not be hastened. And I suffered every torture of his tenderness and returned him the same, venturing to touch him in ways I had not yet had the courage to, to taste him in ways I had not before had the chance to, and when he entered me at last and began to build some rhythm, I directed him onto his back and straddled him. 'What, you do not like me being in charge?' I said to him when he looked at me with confusion, then astonishment.

'I think I shall leave you in charge,' he smiled and curled up to meet me as he writhed in pleasure, and I joined him there with an abandon I cared not to restrain this time. For I did not know if there might be another, but I had now, and I meant to throw caution to every doubt and show him exactly what I felt for him in no uncertain terms.

When we were spent in all the ways one can be, he did not bid us to dress and leave as I thought he might. Instead, he pulled me against him and held me close, saying, 'Maybe I could at least travel part of the way with you, see you safely onto your next boat at Marseille.'

I lifted my head from his chest to look at him. 'The timing would be suspicious. I am told you never take holidays.'

'My family might know it, but he will not. Besides, I used to often take holidays to England and beyond before the gallery.'

'How long have you had the gallery?'

'Five years now, so not very long. Perhaps it is time that I did.'

'I'm not sure that will ease our separation. I am not sure I could be trusted to board my boat from Marseilles if you were there with me.'

'Then maybe I should have to escort you all the way, make sure you arrive.'

I gushed at the thought. 'It is too much.'

'It is not enough...'

I lifted up and rested my head on my elbow to see him better. 'Marco, I know in heart, you want what I do, and yet I know that when you speak from your rational head, you are right.'

'Maybe I don't want to be right anymore. Maybe I just want to be with you.'

'But I have nothing to lose but misery. You have everything to lose, everything that matters to you. Believe me, I know what that is like and I would never wish that for you. I would never want to be that consolation prize.'

'You could never be that to me. Though I daresay I am getting carried away. But that does not mean there is not a way that it might be possible to stage things so that he leaves Venice in search of you and we remain close by. If he suspects nothing between us, Venice is the last place he will ever expect you to return to.'

'No, but he may come back in time, to tend to his business if for nothing else. I have never been a match for that priority at the best of times, so I am sure he will not risk Serrano's contract for my sake. If I know anything of Giles, he will send spies everywhere for him while he oversees his business ventures.'

'Then maybe Venice is not a good choice, but there is the Villa. My parents will frequent it more now that my mama is at ease again. We could find somewhere close enough to visit them there.'

'You think your parents will ever want to know me again after turning you into an Innamorato?'

'They are fond of you, Eleanor, and I do not say they would be easy, and it would not take some time. You know my mama's recitals of the commandments, but she is a woman of great heart, and even she would not blame you if she knew what he had done. As for my father, he will take her lead in matters of the heart.'

'And what about the gallery?'

'I could still oversee it, paint from home and come in occasionally. I would need to appoint someone to manage it for me in the day-to-day course of business, but it's what most owners do anyway. So long as *you* stayed away from the city—'

'But you love your work, Marco, you said yourself, you live for it.'

'Maybe because it is all I have had to live for...until now. Besides, I cannot work. I have produced nothing of note since I returned. I cannot concentrate; my thoughts are always with you. Perhaps you will become my muse?' He laughed, but I did not find it funny. For I realised how much he did not know about me and yet all he was willing to sacrifice for me. Maybe I had grown in wisdom, for if I had not learned the cost of dishonesty in losing Annalise, then it truly had all been for nothing. I could not let Marco risk all that was dear to him for someone he did not really know. Someone I *knew* he would disapprove of. I had only two choices: to decline his offer and return home without his escort and, in doing so, maintain his untainted image of me, or to confess everything I had not and run the risk I would disgust him so terribly, it might save him from such sacrifice. In any case, I could not let him choose blindly.

'What's wrong?'

'I don't know what the time is. I must be back before Giles gets home.'

He leant over to the floor where his clothes lay heaped and pulled his pocket watch out. 'It is a quarter to six. Will he be due now?'

'Soon, I think. I had better get dressed.'

'Alright, but when can we be together again?'

I got out of the bed and began to gather my clothes. 'I think we should have a talk first, a proper one, before we—'

'About what?' He came to meet me, gathered me up from behind and rested his face on my shoulder.

'I just think you should have some time to think more seriously about the things we have discussed today. It is no light matter. We should talk about it in a better head.'

'Then we will, and then I will hold you again, and you can make love to me again. When can you manage it?'

'Tomorrow is Tuesday. Your mama is usually at the church organising the flowers between two and four. Can you come home then?'

'Now that *is* a risky business. Anyone could come home unexpected.'

'Well, maybe we should just talk then. The last thing we need now is to blow our cover this close to my leaving.'

'You are right. You are not *always* reckless, then...' He nuzzled at my neck and stole a parting kiss from me that made me doubt this fragile shred of reasoning in wanting to confess.

CHAPTER THIRTY-SIX

Confession.

Eleanor. September 1822.

I waited tentatively that morning, taking notice of all that was spoken at the breakfast table about the family's plans for the day, relieved that everything appeared as ordinary as any other Tuesday. I paced about in the house when Isabella left for her errands in the afternoon, waiting for him to arrive, wondering how I might bring matters up or even if I could manage to go through with it at all.

When I saw the boat pull into the jetty and watched him leap from it, excited, handsome, unsuspecting, I was sure I'd lost my nerve.

I had Benedetta arrange for coffee to be served in the drawing room for us when he arrived. It would look ordinary, we would sit about the table like we had used to, and no one would think anything of it if we were disturbed.

When he came into the room, I was not expecting him to accost me with kisses before we had barely exchanged a greeting and I lost my nerve entirely.

'What? It's alright. Benedetta is keeping watch. She will alert us if anyone comes home and keep the other servants away.'

'I know, I just feel strange here, ill at ease.'

'Then let me take you somewhere else where we can be ourselves.'

'No, because if we are to be ourselves, then you must know me first.'

His expression was puzzled. 'Do I *not* know you?'

'You know me as I am now, but you know little of my past, who I was before, who I had to become to survive.'

'Why do I think this is not going to be the conversation I was expecting.'

'Because it is not, Marco. Because I have never had such a conversation before, and because of that, I once lost someone I loved.'

He let me go now and sat down. 'The music master who fathered your child?' he asked, looking up from the table.

'No, not him.'

He frowned. 'There were others?'

I nodded.

'I'm not sure I want to hear this,' he said, running a palm across his forehead before shrugging off his apprehension. 'You were young, naïve, and we all have a past we would rather forget. I don't care what you were before, I don't even care that you are his wife anymore. All I want is for us to find a way to—'

'Well, you have to hear this, Marco, for I cannot let you lay down sacrifices and take risks for my sake without you knowing all. If you still want me after, I will join you in any plan you choose, but I will not let you choose me blindly.'

'Jesus, Eleanor, what have you done, murdered someone and escaped the noose?'

'Don't be ridiculous. Though that you might prefer I had, I suppose you will not know unless you hear me.'

'Alright, alright. Calm down. If it matters to you this much, I will hear whatever you want to tell me, but I want you to take heart; I will not abandon you like others have just because you have made mistakes. You mean more to me than that.'

This heartened me a little, but I knew better than to set much store by it given what I was about to disclose. It would be impossible for him to contemplate the things he now must hear. 'I don't know where to begin,' I said, joining him at the table and sitting down beside him. I stared at the steam rising from the coffee pot, the empty cups laid out.

He put his hand on my knee. 'Take your time then.'

I cleared my throat. 'When I befriended Giles's cousin, Mariella, I was, as I told you, an innocent. But in the course of our friendship, she schooled me in *less* innocent things, and for a time, I was taken in by them.'

'You mean—?'

I nodded, 'She initiated me, I suppose you could say, into sensations that I had never understood or been introduced to before.'

'I am sure that is the way girls sometimes learn about such matters, always kept so sheltered from the male sex, but you cannot think such things of any consequence to us?'

'Maybe, I do not know. And perhaps if I had left it there, it would have been less important, less harmful, certainly. But I did not. I allowed myself to use this new learning to be encouraged to seduce my betrothed.'

He was somewhat more edgy now. 'And who was he?'

'The heir incumbent to the Viscountcy of Elmbridge, a childhood friend who I did not see as anything other than that, to begin with.'

'So you are telling me you might have been a Viscountess by now, if what, did you cry off?'

'He did.'

His eyes narrowed, concerned at my answer.

I relayed to him all I could of mine and Sheldon's story, how it went, how it ended, how I sought Richards for consolation and revenge. And whilst I knew it was not comfortable hearing for him, I also realised that his attentiveness and reassurance meant that I had done no great harm, yet. Then, when it came to Annalise, I felt the doubt creeping in again and had to will myself on with such difficulty I grew anxious, stuttered over my clumsy words and almost gave up.

'Are you saying you were in love with this woman? This maid?'

'Yes, I am. And I confess that until things changed between *us*, I did not know I no longer was.'

His expression was unreadable, and I might have probed him further before going on if Benedetta had not come into the room then. We both sat up straight and created some distance. I poured a splash of cold coffee from the pot into our cups and tried to look unperturbed. 'Who is it?' I asked. 'Giles?' I mouthed.

She shook her head gravely. She looked almost as white as a sheet. 'I need to speak to you, Signora. It is urgent.'

Marco looked between us both and I shrugged and left the table.

When I had closed the door behind me, I asked, keeping my voice low, 'What is so urgent, Benedetta, and why do you look so mortified.'

'Signora Crivelli is downstairs and refuses to leave unless you speak to her,'

I held a hand to my throat. 'Oh god, she is not.'

'She says she will tell your husband about you, and will not be persuaded to go without you seeing her.'

'Alright, where is she?'

'I left her at the Piano lobby because I didn't want the neighbours to see her.'

I rushed down the stairs at speed. And there she was, already throwing her arms about in frantic gestures as I met her at the foot of the stairs.

'Oh, now you see me! Now you are forced to hear me! You ignore everything! I have patrons hounding me for appointments, Serrano demanding every day—'

'Keep your voice down, for god sake. I live here.'

'You better get yourself to the apartment today or give me Serrano's answer, or I will shout down the house, the street, the Sestiere—'

'Alright! You have made your point. I will come to you later this afternoon. But you must go now, or I shall never come again.'

She pointed a crooked finger at me, 'If you are not there by six, I will return, and this time, there will be no reasoning.'

'I will be there, now go.'

When she left, I sank onto the bottom stairs and sighed into my palms. I had to get out of here, perhaps sooner than I thought.

'Who was that woman?'

I looked up. Marco was standing at the landing and Benedetta was trying to hold him off.

'We better go back up and I will tell you.'

When he turned around to go back up the stairs, Benedetta shook her head furiously. 'No, tell him, no,' she mouthed. I saw her panic-stricken eyes and told him to go on without me, I would meet him up there.

'Benedetta, I have to tell him,' I whispered to her.

'No, no, it will not do.'

'I have no choice. He deserves the truth.'

'He will not want to know *that*. It will ruin it all.'

'That is a chance I have to take. But I will not draw you into it. You shall deny any knowledge, alright? I will protect your name, I promise,' I told her, bracing myself to face him in the drawing room.

He was staring out of the window when I returned to the room, perhaps looking after this unidentified caller. 'Well, who was she?' he asked as I sat down.

It was not the leap I had wanted to make so abruptly, but I saw no point in prolonging it now. 'It was someone I have been working for.'

'Working, here, in Venice?'

I nodded. 'When I first arrived, and to this day, Giles has refused me any money, not a single centesimo.'

'He refuses you money?' he asked, an incredulous frown at his square brow.

'Money, my jewels, pen and paper, as you know, unless he presides over it. I needed money to raise a fare, yet the only thing I had to sell, which he did not take under his close guard, was some dresses that no longer fitted me. I made a trade with the seamstress to sell them for me. In exchange, I would order new ones, and he would settle the account—the only thing he is willing to do, no matter the expense, so long as I don't find independent means to fund my escape from him. I tried to send appeals to my friend and, more lately, my sister, too. But as you know, I have been at a loss for a reply.'

He looked astonished, appalled.

'The dresses raised not a fraction of what I required, and when I ran out of dresses, the only thing I had left to sell was myself.'

He cast me an incredulous look. 'You cannot be serious? Why would you say this? If you do not want to be with me, just tell me. Don't make me sit here and endure all these speeches and contrive things to turn my heart against you.'

'You think I would do this, hurt myself, hurt you, if I was not in earnest.—That it might be easier than facing the longest, most torturous confession I have ever had to make?'

He looked unnerved now, uncertain. Then he crossed the room and grasped me by the arms. 'Then say no more. Say no more, Eleanor. Please, I beg you, say no more. Don't you see? I have already fallen in love with you. I cannot hear another thing. Do you understand me?'

'I'm sorry, I was desperate. I have not done it since we returned,' I said through my tears.

'No, no, shh,' he bid me, and when I would not, he kissed me so I could not speak, and then he took me by the hand and up the stairs to his chamber. 'Lie down with me', he asked.

'I can't, Marco, not until you tell me we will be alright.'

'Do you love me, Eleanor? Tell me the truth?'

I nodded, 'If I didn't, I would not be standing here now in my shame. I would be gone before that woman returns and reveals everything to the whole house.'

'She makes threats to you? Where does she live? I will put a stop to this.'

'No, you cannot. I must deal with this, for I am not going back, I am never going to—'

'Shh, lay down with me. We are going to be alright.'

I collapsed into tears but lay down with him, let him hold me, for I could not keep myself together now. It had all gone so wrong, yet he was still here, but I could not understand why. Why he kissed me and caressed me with his usual tenderness, why he undressed us both and held our bodies in each other's warmth, but when he did no more and tears shined in his eyes, I knew it could not last.

'I would have given you money, every last centesimo, to spare you that. Why didn't you come to me before?' he said eventually.

'I could not ask you for money. We were not even on good terms, and I did not even know I could trust you.'

'Then Dante, you and he have always been fast friends.'

'It is true, but I could not ask him either.'

'You are too proud to ask for money but not too proud to lift your skirt?'

I sat up. 'You think I have any pride at all left when I have to succumb to all your cousin's perversions and demands upon me day in, day out? You think it any worse to be another man's whore when he treats me like one every day, a whore, a broodmare, a child.'

'I don't want to hear what passes between you and him.'

'No, you don't, because it is far worse than what has ever passed between me and any patron. Yes, that is vastly easier. They treat me far better than he ever has!'

He sat up, too, now. 'Stop, Eleanor, I cannot take anymore!'

'And neither could I, and that's why I did the only thing I could other than tying another brick to my leg and putting an end to all of it!' I screamed the words like a madwoman now, sounding so even to myself, and he leapt up and gathered me to him.

'Come, come, do not speak like that; nothing is so bad as that.'

'You only say it because you have never known what it is to be a woman.'

'I say it because it was me that dragged your lifeless body out of the canal! I say it because I think I loved you even then as I blew breath into your mouth and begged you to return to me!'

This brought me to my senses like a sharp slap. 'What? I thought you hated me, disapproved of me.'

'Maybe that would have been better... and alas, it is not true.'

We both collapsed together then back onto the bed, me nursing his sobs, then he nursing mine, and then we slept against the naked comfort of one another, having not moved beyond a kiss, and I knew then that I loved him so painfully I would not recover from losing him.

When we woke, it was on account of Benedetta's hurried shaking of my arm. 'It is four o'clock, Signora. Isabella will soon be home.'

'Four o'clock, oh my, I must go to Signora by six, or she will return. Find my clothes, please, Benedetta.'

'What, where are you going,' Marco said, lifting his sleep-startled face to us.

'I have to go out. If I don't, that woman will come back and reveal all.'

He sat up. 'Then I am going with you.'

'No, Marco, it is better I go alone.'

'You will not face anything alone anymore. Benedetta, leave that, I will dress her. Tell Giacomo to ready the Gondola as quickly as he can.

She went, and he helped me into my stays, tied them, and lifted my dress above me so I could reach into it. 'Marco, I really don't think it's a good idea for you to come.'

'I am not having that woman threaten you and cajole you. I am coming.'

When we got there, I knew I had been right to try to dissuade him. The disgust on his face as we passed beneath the *Ponte delle Tette*, women calling to him from the windows and the streets, making unashamed offers to him as we passed. I saw the cogs of his mind turning, seeing me in the face of all the harlots that accosted him.

'I did not work here,' I told him as the boat drew up. 'I am not a meretrice if that is what you think.'

'What difference does it make?'

'I don't know. Will you wait outside for me, let me handle this?'

'No.'

And so we went into the house together, more offers thrown at him, and he rebuked them with such disgust I felt ashamed of him, of myself.

'Who do you bring to protect you?' Came Signora's chide as we entered the parlour.

'My relative. Now, are you going to give us some privacy to speak, or would you rather an audience?'

She clapped her hands and the girls from the balcony left the room, casting sultry gazes in Marco's direction. Then she pointed to the sofa opposite the one she was sprawled out upon. 'Well, this is unusual. We don't usually have family visits, though if it pleases you. But if you have any ideas, I tell you now there is the bravi at the door listening out.'

'I don't care who is at your door you frightful woman—'

'Marco, please,' I said and turned to Signora, 'I cannot continue with you, Signora. It is impossible. As you see, I am found out already. All that you returning to the house to add to the number who know will achieve is my being taken from Venice by morning.'

She considered me. 'Then why are you here trying to convince me of the fact.'

'Because I do not want that. If my husband finds out, we both lose. I will suffer his wrath, and you will not get another lira from me in any case. You are a businesswoman, Signora Crivelli. Where is the business sense in that?'

'She is not a businesswoman. She is a morally bereft creature who exploits—'

'Marco,' I intercepted again.

'Ah, and yet you do not see me as you see your relative, for I was once as she is, though I admit not of her beauty, and so you see that is why I am reduced to these conditions, because looks do not last and you are forced to find other means. But you see, your relative has the power to change all that and make us both wealthy women. She can earn in but a few years, enough to retire on. She knows that, even if you do not.'

'How much do you want, you offensive termagant?' he demanded.

'Ah, now we are talking sensibly. Well, there is the loss of earnings for the past month, then there is Signor's offer on the table, which alone is worth eleven thousand lire.'

'What?' we said in unison.

'Yes, and that is just my share. He offers you the same per quarter and all other incidentals, if you will only sign, my *Rosa Inglese*.'

He stared at me then, aghast, '*You* are the *Rosa Inglese*?'

'She is.' She smiled at his recognition as if it was some triumph, some great compliment. 'She is on the path to being one of Venice's most sought-after *cortigiana onesta* if she will only see sense in signing to it. Then we might both retire nicely and leave this trade behind if that's what you seek.'

'I told you, I won't do it. All I can give you is everything I have. I have one thousand two hundred lire—'

'You do?' he said, surprised.

Signora Crivelli leant forward in her chair now with a twisted scowl upon her thin lips, 'You insult me with one thousand two hundred lire when I have an offer on the table of eleven thousand?'

'How much do you want?' he asked again, more impatient than before.

'To match my offer, of course, not a centesimo less,' she said haughtily.

'Marco, you need not pay anything. I also have a set of expensive diamonds, and you can take those as well as the one thousand two hundred lire.'

She pulled a face that suggested she was willing to consider this. 'Well, what are they worth?'

'I don't know. I will find out, get them valued.'

She nodded. 'I will come with you. We shall go tomorrow, and if it is worth my while, you will have a deal. Be here in the morning at ten, and do not bring *him* with you.

Marco stood. 'She will not be here in the morning. I will get your money, and you will leave her alone, do you hear me.'

'Or what?' Scrivelli retorted.

Marco's eyes sparked with rage. 'Or I will spend every centesimo I have getting you shut down and put in the gaol house where you belong, and you can enjoy your retirement there, instead.'

She turned back to me now. 'You have until five tomorrow. I don't care if he brings the money or you bring the diamonds. Now get out of my house.'

'Gladly,' he said, snatching my hand and leading me out of the place with such haste that I almost tripped along the flagstones as he waved away women from him. I had never seen him so angry, so unlike himself.

When we got into the boat, I said, 'Marco, you will not give her any money. I will take the diamonds to her. It is the only thing Giles has not locked away. I will tell him I have left them at the Villa and that we will retrieve them when we return to visit Dr Heimlich.'

'If you go near this place again, Eleanor, I will not be able to forgive you. Do you understand? I will deal with her from here.'

'Then will you at least let me give you the diamonds to take to her?'

'I don't want to talk about this anymore. Giacomo, hurry, get us out of here, will you?'

'Alright, I will say no more.'

But it was he who brought it up again when we were halfway back to *Ca' Rosetti*. He had said not a word since we had left the district and only peered thoughtfully into the black water, consumed in his own head. But now, he looked up at me and asked, 'Who is this man that offers eleven thousand lire for you?'

'Why does it matter?'

'I thought you wanted honesty between us. Is that not why you have tormented me with all this talk?'

I sighed. 'It is Serrano.'

His eyes flew wide open, 'Serrano? You have lay with Serrano? My god...'

'I know, it was foolish. I tried to put him off when I recognised him. He gave a false name. I did not know to expect him. And I have not repeated it since, but he will not stop hounding me.'

'Oh, won't he.'

'Marco, you have to stop this. It is not like you!'

'And this is not like you!... Perhaps you are right, we do not know each other well after all.'

'Then perhaps *you* will explain how you know of the *Rosa Inglese*, hmm? No, I didn't think so, because men are happy to use whores whilst looking down on them all the same without any impediment to their character, aren't they?'

'I do not use whores. Not —'

'Until me, you mean? Well, I did not whore myself to you, and you are the only one in Venice who can say that. Not even my husband can pretend I am more to him than a morally acceptable version of the same.'

He looked away. 'I knew because Holland-Bury told me about it, about you—The *Rosa Inglese*. He put a pamphlet on my desk in jest and told me I needed cheering up. If I couldn't have you, I might like to try the latest "trend" upon the market, as he put it. An English substitute for my English tastes.'

'Holland-Bury knows about us?' I could not even begin to approach that matter now.

'No. not about us. No one does, apart from Benedetta. But he knew I was falling in love with you. I could not hide it from him, and he warned me against it.' He let out a sardonic laugh. 'Holland-Bury for once giving me wise counsel—'

'Maybe you should have listened.'

'Maybe I should.'

And then nothing more was said until we got home.

In the morning, he was gone. Benedetta passed a note to me after breakfast and told me he had left early, about six. I tore it open without even dismissing her.

I'm sorry, you were right. I cannot do this. I have left for Milan this morning. I will be gone until you are. Holland-Bury will deal with that woman. I have given him what he needs to undertake the task, so save your money for your journey. He will also see to any other arrangements to assist you out of Venice.

I will never forget you. You have broken my heart.

I fell to my knees and cried unrestrained guttural sobs. Benedetta gathered me up, and Isabella came running into the room. 'What is wrong?' she shrieked at the sight of me.

Benedetta snatched the note from my hands and answered for me. 'She is disappointed, Signora. She thought she had been brought with child, but she was wrong.' She pointed to the bucket of blood-soaked rags.

'Oh, Eleanor, Eleanor, my child, do not despair; it will come. Do not lose faith. Come, come, we shall pray together.'

But I could not pray. I could not do anything but wail as Benedetta forced me up from the floor and put me back to bed.

'Where is Mr Holland-Bury?' I demanded of the attendant when I had searched for him at Marco's office and then everywhere else I could think he might be.

'He has not come in yet, Signora.'

'When do you expect him?'

'Soon, I believe. Would you like me to leave him a message for you?'

'Thank you, no, I will wait.'

It was an anxious wait, but it proved worth the restless pacing and peering out of windows when he finally came up the gallery steps. I saw instantly his eye-rolling disdain at the sight of me when he came through the doors.

I crossed the room to meet him. 'Holland-Bury, I need to speak to you.'

'Not here.' He took me by the arm and directed me into the cloakroom.

'Where is he?' I asked as soon as we were inside it.

'Gone to lick his wounds, nasty ones, it seems.' His glare was accusatory.

'Look, I know he has gone to Milan, he left a note, but where in Milan will he stay?'

'It doesn't matter. He doesn't want to see you, and if you care a fig for him, you will not try to alter that.'

'Holland-Bury, I beg you. I do care for him. I *love* him.'

'Look,' he waved a dismissive hand. 'I am charged with taking care of the gallery and your travel arrangements, not to hear all your sorry declarations. Save them for someone else's ears, for you will find no sympathy here. You have destroyed one of the best men I ever knew.'

I blinked away my tears. 'I didn't mean to. I want to set things right.'

He looked fixedly at me. 'Then get me your passport, and I will send you on your way.'

'Then I will never see him again, I can't—'

'You have done enough harm. Going is the only favour you can do him or yourself, now.'

I had done him harm, though it was unintentional. 'Is he alright?'

'No, of course he is not. Damn, fellow refuses every scrap of interest in him for years, vowing never to love or marry and then, of all the deuced damn choices, falls in love with you! He is devastated. Do you know how many years it took to recover from the loss of his last love?'

I shook my head. 'What happened between them? I mean, I know there was a religious divide, but—'

'She died, though little difference it would have made to their being together.'

'Oh god. I did not know *that*. How?'

He considered me. 'She took her own life.'

'What? I had no idea. Poor Marco. Why did she do it?'

'Because her family forbade their wedding, she was Protestant, and they would not have her marrying into a Catholic family. He converted for her, but still, they would not accept it. They had Marco attacked viciously and warned her if she ever saw him again, they would kill him. She cried off under the threat, but after a time, they secretly planned an elopement. She barely slipped out of the house to meet him when they caught her. She hung herself that night and left a note saying that if she could not be with her love, she had nothing more to live for.'

I was astounded. No wonder the Harpers were so open to having Giles and I—Protestants—amongst them. They had seen the consequences of such divides firsthand.

'So you see, Eleanor, he doesn't need this, another complicated mess of a love interest. It would be bad enough that he could never marry you, just as he could never make her his wife. But what you told him last night destroyed him. He needs time to recover and then, when he does, to find an uncomplicated match, someone he can freely love and who can freely love him back. We both know that can never be you.'

'Alright,' I conceded. 'I see I must leave. I must go first to take care of something, but I will find a way to get my passport and bring it to you as soon as I can.'

His expression softened. 'Then you truly do love him. I am sorry for you both. But it is for the best.'

I nodded. 'Will you tell him that is why I have gone, the only reason I would?'

He patted me lightly on the shoulder. 'I will.'

'I better go. I have matters to attend to.'

'You do not speak of that abbess, do you? I am to go directly and settle that matter this afternoon.'

'I do, but I have these diamonds. I shall have them valued and take them to her. Please do not go. I don't want Marco to suffer any more loss on my account. I will handle her.'

'Well, I am happy to hear it. The damn fool has raised a loan on the gallery to come up with the money she demands. Will you have enough left to travel with, though?'

'Yes. Pay back the loan for him. Promise me you will not go to her and pay it.'

'Well, perhaps it is best to have them valued first. We will see after that if there is a shortfall, and I can pay back the rest if there is.'

'Are you staying to look after the gallery?'

'I was planning to leave Venice next month, but it looks as though I shan't be going anywhere now I have Marco to think of.'

'So you will stay and be there for him?'

He nodded, 'I will. It is about time I did.'

I smiled weakly. 'Holland-Bury, I daresay it makes little difference in the scheme of things now. But I want you to know that I am grateful you didn't tell him about that...that despicable time I accosted you in that alley—'

'And never shall I.'

'Thank you.'

'But tell me one thing…why did you do it? The *Rosa Inglese* hardly needed the custom of a poor fellow like me?'

In the scheme of things, I supposed the shame of this confession made little difference. 'I thought if I could be of use to you, you might have proved willing to share your journey home with me. You will forgive me, but I understand you to have a reputation for being a libertine and thought we could offer each other an exchange. I am ashamed of it. I did not know then how Marco felt about me, or how I felt about him, for that matter. If I had the slightest notion, I would never have even contemplated it, but I desperately wanted to give up the other business. I only did it to raise a fare, and I was merely halfway towards it at the time. I thought for the remainder…'

'I see. Well, you had better go and get those diamonds valued. I will be ready to act when you have your passport.'

I left directly and had Benedetta take me to a jewel procurer in Cannaregio. I watched him inspect them with his looking glass, impatient as he poured over the details. Then he turned to me and said, 'These are not diamonds, they are paste. I will give you nothing for them.'

'You are mistaken, Signor. These are true diamonds, can't you see?'

'They are very good replicas, that I see, but they are paste.'

I took them to three other shops and got the same reply, and even the inns would offer me not above fifteen lira. What was I to do? I could not let Marco pay my debt to Signora, especially now that I knew the pains he had taken to procure the settlement, the time it would take him to pay it back, and his gallery at risk less he should manage it. And nor could I let Signora Crivelli return to Ca' Rosetti screaming down the house with my indiscretions. So I went to her and told her I would sign with Serrano instead, but I wanted to meet him first to discuss the terms. She accepted this, even if boxing my ears with threats and admonishments. She was to set up a meeting directly and send me word of the time.

I had no intention of honouring the commitment to become his mistress in the long term, but I would be gone as soon as my passport was dealt with, and if I could just get him to settle with her and keep her quiet, I could leave without rousing Giles's suspicions or upsetting the family.

A note came the same afternoon: he would see me tonight.

'At last, you have seen reason. This news makes me a very happy man!' said Serrano, gathering my hand and kissing it.

I smiled. 'Well, we have not quite come to terms yet.'

'You want more money?'

'Have a seat, will you, Signor?' I gestured and waited for him to settle into it. 'No, I do not ask for money. You have offered quite enough of that.'

'An apartment of your own?

I shook my head. 'I want two favours of you, Signor.'

'Name them.' He swept an open palm in the air.

'Once you have paid Signora Crivelli her fee, I want you to destroy her. And then, I want you to destroy my husband's trade.'

His expression grew puzzled, as if I was speaking in some unknown language. 'Your husbands trade? But why?'

'Because I hate him, and he has destroyed everything I have ever valued. Now, I shall repay him in kind, that is, if you agree to my offer.'

'Revenge suits you. And you are angry with him, I see that, and as for the old lady, fine, that I have no quarrel with. But it is one thing to bed a man's wife when his back is turned, another to destroy his business. Besides, the contracts are in place between us now. He begins shipping for me as soon as the boat is completed.'

I stood up. 'Very well, Signor, I understand.'

'Where are you going?'

'What sense is there in my remaining if we cannot come to terms.'

He laughed. 'You toy with me.'

My look told him I did not.

'Very well, you shall have what you wish. But you will need to give me time to figure out the best way to deal with the matter. I have valuable tasks he must undertake before I can do as you ask, or the expense to my own interests will be great.'

'How long will it take?'

'I have a clause drawn in to ensure the first run arrives safely before the contract takes enduring effect—an insurance policy of sorts, you might say. I will have to let him set out on the first errand at least before I can intervene.'

'And how long will that take?'

'It is due to leave next week, but it shall not be complete for some months.'

'Is there any chance you can make him go with it?'

'What do you mean, to Brazil?'

'I mean, if I am to be at leisure to tend to you, it would be well for him to be away so I can be at your service, Signor.'

He smiled at this. 'Then, I will see what I can do.'

'Alright,' I outstretched my hand to shake his, '...we have a deal.'

Then he pulled me over to him and into his lap, lifted my skirts and I stayed his hands. 'No, Signor, I am a businesswoman too...once you confirm he shall be gone, you will have what you seek.'

'Come, come, a pledge at least of your earnest. Do you know how I have longed for you?'

'Very well,' I conceded, drawing on the last of my strength to appease him. I took him in hand and let him spend there whilst he nuzzled at my breast, holding back my tears as I forced myself to bring him about.

I tore along the streets of Venice with such rage and disgust as I made my way home.

'Slow down, Signora, I cannot keep up with you,' Benedetta complained as she raced to keep pace with me. For her sake, I slowed a fraction, not knowing how to contain all this rampant fury inside me, not knowing how I would manage the days ahead. I would have to ask Holland-Bury to find me somewhere tomorrow, for I must recover my passport and get out of the place before I proved another love to leave Marco's life by the only exit I could see if I did not get out of here quick.

CHAPTER THIRTY-SEVEN

A Guest.

Eleanor. September 1822.

The following day, once Giles was gone to work, I tried again to pick the lock of his drawer, but to no avail.

'Stop, Signora, Benedetta begged me. 'You know he will hurt you if he discovers what you have done.'

But I paid no mind and bid her to find me some tools to wrench it open with. When she came back half an hour later, it was with Dante.

'Eleanor? What's going on?' he asked me.

'Benedetta, why did you betray me? Dante cannot be involved in this!' I barked.

'Involved in what?' He cast a bewildered glance about the room. 'Eleanor, what are you trying to do? You're not going to ransack his chamber again are you?'

I frowned. 'You know about that?' I said, reflecting on the night I had done just as he said.

'Yes, of course.'

'Who else knows it?'

'Everyone apart from Giles and my papa, I believe.'

I sighed. What did it matter now, anyway. 'No, I am not trying for a repeat, only to open this draw. I have to leave, Dante. My passport and *Carte di Sicurezza* are inside and I must retrieve them.'

'Leave? You mean run away?'

I nodded. 'You know why, Dante, I cannot keep up this charade anymore.'

'I know it is not ideal, but surely you needn't flee? I thought things were better now. You have been so bright and merry I was certain he must be better with you.'

I shook my head. 'Please, Dante, I have no time to explain. I must go, believe me.'

'Where will you go?'

'Home.'

He nodded. 'Alright, I will help you, but let me at least find someone who can do a better job of it before you make a hash of things. Benedetta, go to the locksmith's house in Cannaregio, tell him to come at once and swear him to keep confidence.'

She set off immediately and he held out his hand. I lifted myself from the floor, and he pulled me up and into a hug. 'Eleanor, what is wrong? You are frightening me.'

I clung to him and held him so fast. 'Oh, Dante, so much! So, so much.'

He pulled back to look at me. 'Will you tell me?'

I shook my head. 'I can't. I trust you, I do, but I cannot tell my secrets without revealing the secrets of others.'

'Sounds messy.'

'It is a terrible mess.'

'Where will you go, to your family?'

'It is best I say no more to you, Dante. I don't want to draw you into things you might be questioned about, not because I do not trust you, but because I don't want Giles to hassle you. He knows we are friends; he will suspect I have said something to you, so it is best I say no more.'

He nodded. 'Will you be safe?'

'I will, and perhaps I can write to you someday and confirm it. I will assume a name and send it to the Bottega or something.'

He, too, looked downcast now. 'I will miss you, my friend. You have grown to be quite a little sister to me. Who will I have such mischief with now?'

I smiled, 'I will miss you too, very much.'

'Come here,' he said, hugging me again and pressing a kiss to my forehead. 'You have shed too many tears, enough to fill the canals of Venice, no more. You go and find some happiness, won't you.'

'I will try.'

I sat with him whilst we waited, head against his shoulder, feeling some comfort from being held by someone who could still think kindly of me. Someone who did so by virtue of only friendship, for he was one man who could be relied upon to have no ulterior motive in his kindness to me. I had learned in all my time here, though never declaring or probing further, that he was a lover of his own sex. It was impossible not to know it, however well Marco tried to cover for his slip-ups. I hoped one day he might confess it to me directly so I could comfort him, tell him it made no difference of opinion to me, that I, too, would prove an ally to him. But I supposed now was not the time for it, and when the locksmith arrived and began working on the drawer, I grew entirely distracted, waiting impatiently as he took various tools to the lock until finally, I sighed with relief as the mechanism clicked open and he pulled out the drawer leaving not a mark upon it. 'Thank you!' I said and pulled the drawer from its runner and into my lap.

'By god, what is it, a jewel stash?' Dante said, peering over my shoulder.

'My confiscated ornaments,' I told him as I moved them to the floor. Not paste either, I considered, which was why he had let me keep the stupid diamonds in the first place. I rummaged through the remaining contents and found some papers I thought might be the passports, but on scanning them, I found them to be no more than his correspondence with Dr Heimlich, and as I ruffled through it, I began to despair. 'It's not here,' I told Dante, 'It's not here! Though I saw him put it in here with my own eyes,' I said, tipping the drawer upside down and running my palm in the empty aperture to see if something had fallen out I had not noticed, but there was nothing else.

Dante bent down to pick up the contents and put it back into the drawer, telling the locksmith to lock it back up.

'Is there anywhere else he might have kept it?' Dante asked. 'What about at the shipyard? He has a desk in the office there.'

'He does? Then I must search it. Will you let me in?'

'*I* will get it. You are to stay away from the shipyard or you will alert him. I am always in the office, so it will be nothing for me to look for it when he is out.'

But two days later, after finally having the opportunity to search for it and having been forced to call the locksmith out again to open his drawer, he told me it was not to be found there either. I began to run out of ideas. I had to leave now, I could remain no longer. Serrano had told me by messenger last night that he had failed to get Giles to go away with the ship to Brazil despite all his best efforts. He was set upon some trip, the one I knew to be to Dr Heimlich, and had told Signor that he would not be able to travel so far until he had at least returned from *Villa Rosso*. If that had not been bad enough news, my time was up with the blood-soaked rags now, and my courses should have replaced them, but they had not come at all. I had at first wondered if I could be pregnant. After all, I had not made use of the sponge or alum and mugwort wash, nor even taken my curative tea, with Marco. Nor since. But then I had had none of the symptoms I had suffered before, none of the dreadful sickness and malaise, and so I was sure it was just the distress I remained in as a permanent state of mind now, to blame for it. All the same, I had to be sure.

I had Benedetta seek out an appointment with a doctor in Dorsoduro, the one who had tended Giulia on my request after she had been butchered by the midwife. I had not lain with any but Marco for the entirety of the month. If there was any chance I could be, it could only be his child, and if it was, I would not take measures to interfere with its progression, so I would have to be sure. If I was not pregnant, as I hoped and suspected, then I must make sure Giles or Serrano did not alter that before I could get away from the pair of them. I was running out of techniques to stall them. Use of hand or mouth was already causing Serrano to mistrust me and Giles to get more aggressive. It had seemed not to matter before. I had expected to have the passport by now and be gone. I had no backup plan.

I went back to Holland-Bury that afternoon.

'My passport is nowhere to be found. It is not in the house. It is not at the shipyard,' I told him.

'You have searched the shipyard?'

I nodded, not wanting to put Dante's name in the mention.

'Well then, there is nothing else for it. We shall have to get you another, a forged one if need be. I will need to see what can be done.'

'I cannot wait any longer, Holland-Bury. I have to get out of here, now.'

'Do you want me to find somewhere for you to put up whilst we get it sorted?'

'Yes, as soon as you can.'

'Alright. I will send word to you.'

Then I left, feeling somewhat more relieved as I walked on to the Doctor's house in Dorsoduro. Startled as we passed the hotel Marco had taken me to before, *Locanda San Barnaba*, I noted as I passed it slowly, distracted by the memories contained within its walls. I broke into tears as I wished to go back to that moment and undo it all. No, further still. Back to the day I had ventured to the Ponte delle Tette, so I could decide against it. If I had known back then I could trust him, how he felt about me, it would have all been so very different.

'It will be alright, Signora; do not cry,' Benedetta said, promising to stay with me while the Doctor undertook his examination. But I did not tell her I was not concerned about that, though I kept her close at my side as I lay upon the couch and closed my eyes.

He reached into me, uncomfortable prodding inside, as he pressed my tummy from the outside.

'How long overdue are you?' he asked when he was done.

'A few days, perhaps, why?'

'It is very early to tell. I cannot give you a definitive answer. But the cervix is high and soft, which could indicate you are pregnant.'

'What do you mean *could*? I need to know, Signor.'

'It means, if your courses fail to come within another week, I would be very likely to think you pregnant, though, equally, if your courses return, I would be inclined to think it perhaps the usual presentation of your cervix, for I have never examined you before and do not know what is usual for you.'

'So, I am to be none the wiser than before I came?'

'I can give you the name of a crone who deals *properly* in such matters of unanticipated pregnancy, gentle methods, herbs, if *that* is the urgency? Certainly sooner is better.'

'No,' I said flatly, understanding he thought me considering the methods I had called him out to tend Giulia for.

'Then you may return to me in a fortnight if you do not bleed before. By then, the cervix should have shifted high enough to notice the difference between then and now, and I should be able to give you a firm answer.'

When we got home, I went to Marco's chamber and lay upon the bed, sniffing at the pillow, stroking the sheets he had laid in and weeping so inconsolably I knew not what to do. *I might be carrying your child. How can I visit a herbalist to undo what I don't wish to be undone?*

I stayed on the bed until Benedetta pulled me from it at Dante's return home. I went directly to him. I had already sent a note to Holland-Bury to cancel the lodgings. It was not the time to make such a leap, not yet, not at least until I knew one way or the other. So, I asked Dante if he could help me, to see if he thought Carlotta might take me in on an extended visit to get me out of the clutches of Giles without raising the alarm to him that I was fleeing. I had to think more levelly now, for if he caught me on the run and I was with child, I expected it to go no better than before, and I would lose it. No, this was not the time to raise his temper. I must get through another couple of weeks to know for certain, and then I would know how to proceed. Hopefully, by then, Holland-Bury would have a solution to my lack of passport, and it would all go without incident.

At dinner that night, Dante announced to the table that he had seen his sister earlier and that she seemed a little down in the mouth. Baby Pietro had been teething and restless, and it looked like she could do with a little female company to lift her spirits. Would I consider going to her and staying for a few days to lift her mood?

'I can go to her, Dante. You must not place such burdens upon Eleanor,' Isabella said. 'I will go to her in the morning and stay a few days.'

'Mama, she needs some company of her own age, don't you think?'

'Perhaps, though, I will go anyway.'

I looked at Giles, 'Well, I would be happy to go to her and try to be of comfort if my husband thinks it a good idea.'

All eyes turned on him. 'Well, of course. It will be good for you, too, for you will soon have such matters to contend with yourself, my dear. Indeed, go to Carlotta with Isabella in the morning. I have much to attend to before we set out to *Villa Rosso* next week, so I won't be much about. It is the least you can do, to be sure.'

Isabella looked me over cautiously and said, 'Giles, Eleanor owes us no favour. Are you sure you are up to it, child?'

'I am. In fact, I am inclined to agree with my husband, it will be good for me, too. I know so little about child rearing and I shall have to learn somehow.'

But it was not as easy as I had hoped when I arrived there. Cradling little Pietro and wondering if a version just like he was growing within me. Watching Isabella as she fussed over her little grandson with all the doting admiration that came naturally to her station, knowing that if I was pregnant, this new grandchild would never know the love of its kind and devoted family. Our child would be unknown to them, kept apart by secrecy and shame.

I did my best to hide it, but Carlotta was not so easily fooled by my attempts and was naturally curious about my reasons for seeking such a favour. We were not very well known to each other as it was, though things had always been cordial between us. She and her older sister were the least I had come to know of them all. That she had agreed to the charade in the first place, I knew was solely for the love of her brother and trusting his pleas to be worth the trouble.

'I am sorry to ask this of you,' I told her that evening when we were alone, sewing in the drawing room whilst Isabella settled Pietro to bed. 'It is very good of you to have me, not even knowing why I have asked it... not really knowing me at all.'

She considered me thoughtfully. 'Dante does not often ask for favours and never of this kind. Tell me, is there something between you and my brother?'

'Dante and I?' I asked, surprised but being all too familiar with the frankness of Venetian women than to take it personally. She obviously was unaware of Dante's persuasion, or else I might have laughed it off.

She nodded.

'No, no, nothing of that order. We are dear friends, certainly, but I assure you, no more than that.'

'Well, then, that is a relief. Forgive me, only it is unlike him to beg me to harbour a woman for him. I feared...well, it does not matter. You have given me your answer and I believe you. But pray, why then are you here?'

She was too astute to gull. I would have to offer her something. 'Carlotta, I fear I may be pregnant.'

'You fear it? I thought you wanted to have a family, that it was the answer to the troubles between you and your husband. It is surely a happy possibility?'

I smiled. 'It might well be yet, though I am only a few days late, so I don't want to build my hopes. But I must be cautious, you see—may I have leave to speak intimately with you?'

She nodded.

'You know I lost a child before?'

'My mama did mention it. I am sorry, I cannot imagine the hardship of your suffering.'

'Thank you. But, well, my husband can be quite demanding of my bed and sometimes quite brutal in—'

'I understand, though I am sure you must not permit him to be brutal?'

'He does not ask permission. So, I fear I must protect the possibility of a child until I know better one way or the other. We are to visit the Doctor in Padua next week, and I shall then have an answer. Until then, I must keep him from my bed for fear he will disturb its progression.'

'Of course, you must stay here for as long as you need to. But, Eleanor, surely you must speak to your husband about his manner of—'

'I have tried, believe me. It is my hope that if I get the news I expect to next week, it will be enough for him to see reason and take a cautious approach. I think the doctors' orders shall weigh more with him than my complaints.'

'Of course, well, I will pray that you shall have the news you hope to.'

'Thank you, Carlotta. You are very kind. I truly appreciate you doing this for me. If I might ask, please do not mention this to anyone, not even your mama, for I don't want to cause false hope should I be mistaken.'

'I shall not speak of it to anyone, you may be sure.'

I was relieved but hated deceiving her. It was not a complete lie, but I could not persuade myself it was not a deception. She was his sister, the sister of the man I loved. I could not tell her the entirety of the truth, no matter what the price. If I could not tell him himself, how could I tell her? For I knew that even if I was carrying his child, I would still have to go without mentioning it. It was for that reason I hoped I was wrong and the sole reason I could find, for everything else made me long to hold a piece of him inside me when I was gone from here, to love a part of him forever, even if I must give him up.

But as the days turned in the quiet solitude of Carlotta's house, and I failed to bleed, I began to wonder if it might turn out to be the reality I faced. I looked vigilantly for signs: tenderness at my breasts, the faintest stirring of nausea, a repulsion to coffee, but could detect nothing out of the ordinary and yet I remembered so vividly how I was plagued with these symptoms, how I felt so tired to begin with. Surely it would run this way for me again if it was true? Though I had not known of my pregnancy so early then, perhaps such things were yet to manifest. And so I tortured myself in this debate at length until other matters distracted me.

I had been to the bottega to see if Serrano had left anything for me. Since I had left Signora Crivelli's charge, this was how we communicated now, directly through messengers. I had not been to collect them for two days, and so I expected some implorations for a meeting and meant to put him off too. It was as I had expected, so I sent him a note to say I was indisposed this week and would meet with him when I was in a condition to receive him. One thing I was decided on, was that no other man's seed would taint me now and call into question the potential parentage of a child. Whatever means I could contrive to put them off, I must continue in, and I would be gone soon anyway, and then I would be safe from the risk.

But this proved more complicated than I had expected when Giles came to collect me from Carlotta's later that week to have me attend him at some dinner affair he had been invited to. I was in no fit company to play the prize pig about a table of strangers, yet even that was to be denied me, for I learned in the course of our journey there that it was Serrano's house we had been invited to. An invitation made months ago on the night of Marco's exhibition, yet only now materialised. I knew this was little more than an attempt to draw me out of hiding, and I was furious at him for putting me in such a compromising circumstance.

I stared contemplatively into the water as we journeyed, the lights of the palazzo-lined canal casting amber orbs of colour into the water like golden sunbeams dappling its glassy surface. Then, the boat veered off towards a landing. I stiffened in my seat and wanted to refuse to step onto the jetty as I peered up at the grand Palazzo, brightly lit in the late evening veil of light.

'Run along, my dear. We don't want to be late,' Giles urged me, and I forced myself to follow beside him.

It was a sumptuous palace, grandeur in the décor and furnishings, and it seemed to loom over me and swallow me up whole as we entered the *piano nobile* and were taken into the dining room, equally opulent, hung with dazzling chandeliers and adorned with works of the great artists. A large table set the greater length of the room and every seat taken up on it, bar two.

'Ah, Signor Craythorne, Signora,' Serrano said, rising from his seat, a glint in his eye. 'I thought you were not coming. Sit, sit, we have not started.'

I smiled weakly and wondered how he had contrived to have me sit beside him as he pulled out the chair. Perhaps table etiquette did not apply amongst businessmen, however much they lived as kings here. I sat at the furthest extent of my seat to create some distance between us as he leaned over and made introductions, at first to his wife and then extending to the rest of the table. I could barely look at her as she nodded straight-faced at me. She was younger than I expected her to be, at least twenty years his junior, I suspected. I hoped she was not a loving wife and would instead be grateful for my service to her husband, just as I would be to any who would keep Giles from my bed. And then, as I turned away from her, almost audibly gasping at the recognition of her at the far end of the table, I noticed Tanto and looked instantly into my empty plate before she caught my gaze. It was useless, of course, and when he introduced her and her gentleman companion, I played at my best nonchalance in greeting her as if for the first time, grateful when she afforded me the same courtesy. But I was set asunder by it all. All that remained now was for Marco to appear and my humiliation would be complete.

When the introductions were over and the meal commenced, Serrano commanded my attention, and I had no patience for it. I flashed a glance in Giles's direction and he ignored me, turned back to his neighbour and drank from his glass as he listened to whatever conversation they offered.

'Don't look so put out my little treasure. I had to see you somehow,' Serrano whispered as he passed me the salad platter.

'Not now, Signor, not here,' I said through gritted teeth and filled my plate with leaves.

'But that is half the fun,' he raised an eyebrow and drew a long sip from his glass, and I picked up my fork, trying to find an appetite to keep my mouth full of food and not the words he tried to draw out of me. But when I succeeded in silencing him at last with clipped answers or inaccessibility, I felt his hand in my lap and tried not to leap up in surprise. Instead, I just glared at him, and he smiled widely as he stroked me indecently.

'Sir, please!' I chided from behind the cover of my napkin and felt his hand slip away.

'Later then,' he grinned, and I sat stiffly in my chair and ate all sorts of things I did not recognise, for I could take no wine and oh, how I needed it to come through such a trial as this.

'I like a woman with a healthy appetite, but I hope you have saved a little room for me to fill you,' he whispered to me later as the dessert course was cleared, and I was relieved this drawn-out affair would soon be over with. But when he tapped his glass and stood, announcing there would be dances in the ballroom to follow, I went directly to Giles and begged him that we leave now, for I felt unwell.

'What is wrong with you tonight? I told you this dinner is important, not all his contractors are invited into his home. Now, make an effort. You are embarrassing me,' he said with poorly veiled impatience.

'But, Giles, I do not like it here. Will you at least stay with me?'

'No, I have bridges to build tonight, and so do you. Go and flatter Serrano with a dance, will you? Keep yourself busy.'

And so I danced with him, which, although no joyous affair, at least was public enough that he could not behave indecently towards me. However, when he said he would take me on a tour of the house, I knew instantly what he intended, and I fled to Giles's side to make another petition to leave. When that failed, I begged Giles to dance with me instead, and at least in this I was indulged as he took an opportunity to make a happy show for the company, treating me in the style of the gentleman I knew he was not.

When he led me back, and Serrano sought permission for another dance, which Giles deigned to grant on my behalf, I grew angry. *Fine*, I thought, if you will not protect me, I shall let the Signor have his way! And so I indulged his dances and conversation, laughed at his jokes, and put him off only playfully now.

'You mean to make me jealous with your husband tonight, I think, you little troublemaker.'

'Of course not, Signor. I must keep our cover even if you do not try so very hard to.'

He offered an ambivalent shrug. 'I do not have to. Your husband is putty in my hands, just like all these parasites.' He cast an all-encompassing hand about the room. 'He will say nothing if I steal you from the room this very instant and disappear with you.'

'Then you do not know my husband, Signor, if that is what you believe.'

'Shall we put it to the test?'

I noted the challenge in his eyes. 'No, we shall not.'

'Alright, not yet, perhaps.'

'Not at all. I told you, Signor, I am indisposed, and your wife is in the room. Have a little consideration with how close you stand over me.'

'My wife.' He chuckled. 'My wife pays little notice to such matters. Fear not on that account.'

'I do fear it, Signor. I cannot help it.'

'I do adore your innocence. You are not like the other Courtesans. That is why I had to make you mine.'

I had no innocence left to adore, so whatever it was he saw in me, it could not be that which I had long ago abandoned. 'Well, I do not know what other Courtesans are like, Signor, so I could hardly comment,' I replied, casting a glance in Tanto's direction, remembering the sight of her bouncing in the lap of one of the gentlemen we came home from *La Fenice* with. She had been my greatest example since that night, of how to conduct such business to impressive effect. Whilst Giulia's schooling had proved a practical introduction, Tanto's had been something of a finely tuned masterclass in finesse. Even I had not been able to keep my eyes off her that night, even though I was nervous and embarrassed to fuck my new patron in the same room. In retrospect, I think it was not being so alone with him that helped me accomplish it. Something I struggled with at first in my own apartments, no comforting sight of Giulia or Tanto to reassure me. I turned back to Serrano now.

'You know her?' he was asking, following my gaze.

I shook my head.

'She, too, is in your line, along with the fair-haired lady with Signor Ricci. But they are nonesuch as you, my treasure.'

I smiled and excused myself on account of needing to use the water closet. I had meant it as a ploy to take a break from him; I had not thought him so bold as to follow me into it.

'Signor, get out, what are you doing?' I said as he caught in the door before I could close it.

'I thought you wanted discretion? Now come here. You have tortured me enough tonight,' he snatched me up and pressed kisses to me, and it took everything I could muster to prevent myself from kneeing him in the groin and fleeing from the house. 'Signor, my husband is in the other room. He will notice my absence.'

'And he will say nothing to it when I account for you,' he replied as he clutched at my breasts, and I saw this line was no use, for it seemed to be the very thing that riled him, that grew him stiff in my hand he forced himself into.

'Relieve me, my treasure,' he sighed. 'I can wait no longer. Bring those lips to soothe me and I shall spend quickly and have you back before anyone notices you are even gone.'

I dropped to my knees in defeat and was saved only by a rapping at the door. 'It is Giles,' I whispered, getting back to my feet and tucking my breasts back into my dress.

But it was not, and I listened at the door as he went out, closing it behind him. 'Teresa, my love, can't a man take a pee in peace?' he said, and I knew he spoke to his wife.

'You insult me, Stefano!' came her reprimand. 'It is one thing bringing her to sit at my table, but another to treat our home as a brothel. You ask too much of my tolerance tonight. Now go back to the ballroom before I insist on her leaving!'

I never thought I could be so grateful to meet the displeasure of a patron's wife. I sat upon the floor and began to weep, then I splashed my face with water, patted it dry, checked the state of my dress in the mirror and went back outside before Giles grew suspicious. Though this time, when I returned to the ballroom, Serrano's wife was first to accost me. She paired me to dance with some fellow I did not know, and I accepted it without question, admiring her calmness and grace, wanting so much to tell her I was sorry and knowing I could never insult her pride so.

When the dances finally came to a close, the party still lingered in conversing clusters about the ballroom floor. I could take no more tonight and knew there would be no pulling Giles away from his circle now he had the advantage of Serrano's ear. I stood restlessly by the fire mantle, pretending to listen to the company who were admiring one of the paintings on the wall. I looked up and recognised Marco's painting of the Regatta, the one Serrano had entered the bidding war with Giles over. I felt my heart sink at the sight of it as I remembered him that night in the gallery, exuding such charm and brilliance as he addressed the company and introduced Signora Barozzi to speak. To think that so far back as then, he had felt that way about me and I had not known it. But now, as I played a retrospective review of it all in my head, it seemed so clear. The looks I had taken for disapproval were the expressions of a man contained, forced to replace his true sentiment with a disguise, not so very different as I was doing for the family's sake. Then there were all the other clues: the interruptions, the gestures, the invitations. They were always so formal, or at least so absent any trace of flirtation, that I had not seen them for what they were. His conciliatory attempts to reach me, to help me in the only ways open to him. Even the times he seemed evasive or retreated, I understood now were not to punish or chide me, but to protect us both from what he really wanted to say or do...

Had he been a less honourable man, it might have been more apparent, easier to decipher. But he was the most honourable man I had ever known, so I did not even entertain the notion of interpreting his demeanour in any other way. Oh, how I wished to have understood from the beginning and made better choices—choices that would mean he was still here now.

'I see you done well in the end, my little apprentice. I thought you would.'

I jumped as I instantly recognised the scent of her parfum and felt Tanto's breath at my ear. I turned about to her. 'Tanto.'

'You have come a long way from *La Fenice*, I see. The diamond merchant...impressive catch.'

'Tanto, I am here with my husband tonight, I can't—'

'I know, which is why I have kept my distance, but I didn't want to go without saying hello. Call on me when you will. You remember my apartments, do you not?'

'Yes, I think so.'

'Until then.'

There would be no *then*. I would that there would be now either, I considered, as I watched her slink away.

When we left in the boat, Giles was angry. I had been aware of it all night, though I didn't understand why when I had done all he had asked. When we got into the Gondola to go home, he slapped me around the face as I settled into my seat. 'Don't you ever flirt with the company again!' he growled.

I held my cheek in my palm and looked at him, bewildered. 'I was not flirting, Giles. What do you mean?'

'I saw you playing up to Serrano, whispering with him at the table. When I said you were to be attentive to him, that is not what I meant!'

'I'm sorry. I did only what I thought you wanted me to. I did not want him to think me rude for declining to dance with him or fail to laugh at his dismal jokes, or I thought you would complain about that. It seems I cannot win.'

He sat down in his seat, brooding but placated. 'Just toe the line a little more carefully next time, dear. There is a difference between keeping him amused and giving impressions of flirtation. He is an important associate; I don't want him forming those kinds of impressions I saw in his looks to you.'

'I don't know what you mean, Giles?'

'He has taken a fancy to you, you fool. I knew it from the first, but I do not mind a man to admire what is mine, but I draw the line at any ideas forming beyond it.'

'I shall do only as you instruct me, husband. I did not mean to cause any offence, honestly. You cannot think I welcome the attentions of an old man like he, surely?'

'Of course, I don't, but that is beside the point, you made a spectacle of yourself in the company. Though I hope, my dear, you would not be welcoming any attentions, no matter in which direction they came, irrespective of age or your *preferred* sex.'

I looked away from him now in disgust. 'I welcome no one's, Giles, you know that.'

'Well, I hope you will be welcoming mine when we get home.'

'Home? You are not taking me back to Carlotta's?'

'You can go back in the morning. She will not want you now, it is past midnight!'

My heart sank. I knew the battle I was now to face when we arrived home, and I knew not how to prevent it as I tried my best attempts to appease him with all the tricks I could muster to the exclusion of that *one* act I could not permit. But it was no use. He would not be put off, and when I wriggled from beneath him, barred the way, and conjured up excuses to continue by other means, he grew angry and tried to pin me down. I thought at first he might succeed as he prodded at my thigh so close to success, but I thought of Marco, the child I might be carrying, and I could not let it be called into question for a moment. Sheer good fortune had prevented that calamity in my going away to Villa Rosso, removing all the usual complications I would have faced in such a situation. Had I been in Venice at the time, I would have been forced to consider a whole host of potential fathers, Giles being only one among them. But I had not. I had been only with my sweet, handsome, gentle Marco in all that time. I had bled at the beginning of our trip and never since. By some trick or stroke of fortune, I had evaded Serrano and even Giles since my return, and I was not about to let that alter now, no matter what the price.

'Get off me!' I screamed at him, 'Get off me. I do not want it tonight!'

'Well, I do, and you will do your duty!' he snarled, pinning my thighs down and trying to hold me fast whilst he attempted again. I knew not where the nerve came from, but I drew back my fist and punched him on the cheek as he did, and it shocked him for long enough that I could crawl from beneath him. But as I kicked and clung to the bedpost to get away, he pursued me in a furious rage, grabbing me by the hair and dragging me back to the bed. But I could not allow it. *Not this time.* I knew Mr Harper and Dante at home. If I could make enough noise to wake them, I hoped it would stall his attempt. So when I reached out to the bedstand and grasped the ceramic ornament that always sat upon it, I threw it at the wall, and it crashed as I had willed it, shattering in one hit.

'You stupid bitch, you will wake the house!' he growled, and I managed to crawl to the other side of the bed and get off of it. He chased me, and I fought him now as I had never fought before, punching him, biting him, kicking him as he thrashed me with blow after blow, blood pouring from my face, though I could not tell from where. It was preferable to him having his way, I told myself and carried on fighting, finding things to throw at him whenever they were in reach, turning over the table and my dressing stool to put an obstacle between us. I saw now that he too was bleeding from the corner of his mouth, scratches raised red and angry at his cheek and his throat, the impression of my teeth marking his forearm, and I hoped he might give in now, less one of us ended in killing the other. For I was willing to take that chance tonight. I would not take this anymore. I picked up the fire poker and held it out towards him in warning, steady as a whinstone. 'You dare, you come any closer..' I snapped, and he was unsure. For the first time, I saw him consider not my conviction, but my capable threat. I had never fought back this way before, with such vigour, not since the day the ship departed and he and Digby made a joint effort, and I stood no chance between the pair of them. Even in the early days of our arrival, I did little more than fidget, struggle or run. But we both knew tonight was different. I was willing to lunge, poker in hand.

But I did not need to resort to spearing him with it. Benedetta came running in in her nightcap and shouted out so loud she likely woke the neighbours as well as the rest of the house. It took only moments for Dante and Mr Harper to bundle in after her.

I dropped the poker and tried to cover myself with my torn shift.

'Giles, what is this?' Mr Harper thundered, making out the scene through sleep-glazed eyes. Dante ran over to me and covered me in a blanket. 'What have you done to her, Giles? Look at the state of her!' he howled.

'Me?' he said incredulously. 'You saw her with the poker. I was defending myself from this lunatic!' he lied.

Mr Harper looked between us, unsure of what to believe, for Giles looked every part as ruffled and disarrayed. 'This will not do! You are not a pair of children. Will you brawl so?' Mr Harper fulminated, in a tone that implied though we were precisely that.

'Get your hands off my wife,' he said to Dante as he held me, consoled me.

'Giles?' Mr Harper said, bewildered.

Dante bid me on, 'I am no risk to your wife, you are!' he spat and led me out of the room.

'Giles,' Mr Harper stepped before him. Let him have her wounds looked at. It seems you could benefit from the same and to be set apart for a time. Come on,' said Mr Harper, and I scurried along the hall with Dante.

'Dear god, where are you hurt?' he asked me, sitting me down on the sofa, holding my chin at angles to try to find where I was bleeding from. My nose, my mouth, it seemed.

'I feel nothing. Nothing hurts. Only my head throbs a little.'

'What happened?' he said as he prodded my scalp looking for injuries.

'The same thing that always happens: he takes me against my will. Only this time, I fought him off.

'Why, Eleanor, you married the man. Why fight him now?'

'Because I love someone else! I cannot bear it, Dante. I never want him near me again.'

He paused in his examination. 'Does he know of this other lover?'

I shook my head and it pounded.

'Who is it?'

'I cannot say.'

He pressed a cloth between my hand and my cheek. 'You needn't. It all makes sense to me at last. I wondered why he fled like that—'

I spat a mouthful of blood into the offered basin and wiped my mouth. 'Dante, please, do not ask anymore.'

'He loves you too, doesn't he? I knew it. I saw it with my own eyes but was sure I must be mistaken. Not Marco; he would never...'

'It is a mess, Dante. Which is why I have to go, but I am stuck here without a passport. If I don't get out of here soon, either Giles will kill me, or I will kill him first.'

'That's why you asked me to go to Carlotta. But why are you not there still?'

'He forced me home tonight. He wanted to make use of me and send me back there in the morning once he was satisfied.'

'Beast, he goes to enough whore houses. Why must he be so demanding of you? It is no way to treat your wife!'

'It is no way to treat a woman at all, Dante: wife, whore, it is still an atrocity. But he wants a child, I suppose I am the only one who will do for that task.'

He held me then, and I stained his nightshirt with blood, but he would heed no protest and comforted me despite it, held a compress to my cheek. 'I am taking you back to my sisters. This will not happen again,' he told me.

'But it is so late now.'

'I don't care. You can't remain here.'

CHAPTER THIRTY-EIGHT

Refuge.

Eleanor. September 1822.

My arrival sent the house into the expected disorder, owing not so much to the hour of our arrival as to the state in which I had arrived: my eyes swollen and my body littered with bruises and scrapes.

'Mama mia! Isabella cried, 'Your husband did this to you?' she gasped. 'No, Dante, no, it cannot be.'

'Yes, mama, it is true, though by the look of Giles, she gave as good as she got,' Dante told her.

'Why, why did he do this child?'

'Not now, mama, she is tired and has been through enough. She needs to rest. *I* will explain to you,' he said. 'Just get her up to bed first.'

By morning, the sight of me was doubly horrific, and now I did feel pain. Terrible pain, though from no particular source, just everywhere, I told the doctor when he came. He prodded and palpated at my sore ribs, my abdomen and my scalp with a thoroughness my fragile body was reluctant to permit, but when he pulled the sheets back over me and declared it superficial wounding, I was relieved.

'No, I do not think it serious, but great discomfort is to be expected, especially about the ribs. I can give you something to make you more comfortable for a few days, and I hope to see much improvement by then,' he said as he clipped shut his bag of accoutrements.

'Doctor, is it safe for me to take it if I might be pregnant?' I whispered to him, not knowing who might be lurking outside the door.

'You are pregnant?'

'I don't know, but I suspect it.'

'Would you like me to examine you?'

I nodded and braced myself for this familiar process.

I watched his face, concentrating as he made all the usual preparations. Then I felt his clammy palms pressing, prodding, and then he nodded. 'Yes, it seems you are correct.'

'I am with child?'

'Yes, you are, though very early, I think. Do you still bleed?'

'I have not, for about five weeks now.'

He nodded again. 'That would seem a fair estimation. Then you shall be expectant in, about May.'

The very same I had been due before, I considered. 'Doctor, will the child be alright? It would not have been harmed would it?'

'You took no blows to the region?'

'No.'

'You have checked for bleeding since? Any cramping?'

'There has been nothing I can detect. But I miscarried a child earlier in the year. Will that make the same likely again?'

'What happened? Was there difficulty during the pregnancy beforehand?'

'For the first five months, all was as it should be, I believe, though I was often sick and nauseous, but then I had a nasty fall, and I was not pregnant anymore when I woke up from it.'

He frowned. 'Five months, you say?'

'Yes, I believe that about the time. Why do you say it like that?'

'It is more unusual at that stage, though it happens. You may bleed and it appear to be nothing beyond a heavy bleed before such a term. But, at five months, Signora, the child, would be noticeable, even in miscarrying it. As small as your hand, yes, but identifiable, certainly. You could not just wake and not be pregnant any longer.'

'You mean I would have been aware of passing it?'

'Yes, of course, agonisingly so.'

'But I don't understand. I remember nothing after the fall.'

'Nothing at all?'

'I was still bleeding when I woke. I had been sedated, I believe, for many days. And there were cramps, though only slightly more violent than the monthly type, and I saw nothing of note.'

'Then perhaps you had to have a surgeon remove the dead foetus, or part of it if you had already ruptured?'

'I do not believe so, though a surgeon did attend me. I was on a ship, and he was the only medical man there.'

'Perhaps you were concussed, suffered a spell of amnesia even. I can only surmise. But given your injuries and history, it is wise you take care at this early stage, Signora. I do not know what happened last time, but to take much care and rest now would do you no harm and err on the cautious side.'

'I see.'

'No one knows why some pregnancies succeed and others fail, but what we do know, is the chances are always higher if there is a history of the same. If you were in my charge, not knowing the full history of your former loss, I would have you on bed rest for at least a couple of months whilst it establishes better.'

'So I should not travel?'

'It would be best to avoid it.'

I was both overjoyed and haunted when he left with his assurances that he would not speak of the outcome of *this* examination at all. *It was true.* I was going to have Marco's child. I was going to be a mother after all, yet I now feared for the safety of it. What had really happened on that ship? Could Giles have had the surgeon effect an abortion without my knowing? Had I been so ill because I was no better off than I had witnessed Giulia suffer in the aftermath? Is that why I had been kept sedated? Surely such a frightful disturbance would have woken me? I dreaded to think, yet I could put nothing past him. Was that why he was so determined to see me pregnant? He feared I might no longer be able, so he sought Dr Heimlich to make sure there had been no enduring damage? I had simply presumed it to be the preventative cures that had kept me safe. Before that, I had wondered at Giles's ability. But Heimlich had kept mentioning damage to my cervix; did he know something I did not?

I tried to put it out of my mind as I cradled my stomach in my palm and told it to hold on, that I would do whatever I must to protect it. And then I smiled and cried at the memory of the sensations I had once felt in that space this new child now inhabited. The gentle stirring in my loins that I wished so much to know again. *I must be careful now.* I could no longer travel far, not by ship or carriage. I would not risk disrupting my womb if there was a chance it had been tampered with or weakened without my knowing. I would perhaps have to resort to the convent after all, at least until I knew everything was progressing as it should be.

It was with great difficulty I convinced myself, and Carlotta, to let me out of the house once Isabella had finally gone home to "bring Giles to his senses", she told me, though I implored her not to be harsh. What was the sense in causing the family to be at odds with him now I was to be gone. I wanted no more suffering on my account. I had disrupted the family enough on my arrival. That I would leave things ill between them when they were tied by the bonds of both family and business, I did not want to add to matters. Carlotta assured me that her mother's admonishments would likely consist of her preaching sermons to him about his duties as a husband to take care of me and that I need not be concerned that she would banish him from the house so long as he promised oaths to apologise and to never again repeat his acts.

It might have been amusing to see Giles suffer this kind of correction if it were not so serious a matter. But I put that out of my mind and promised Carlotta that I was only going to the church to pray, and I would be back within the hour, and yes, I would gratefully accept the use of the boat and take Benedetta with me so I might go safely. But the truth was, I was anxious as I pulled my hooded cloak up high over my head. I feared him somewhat differently now I was confirmed to be with child again. But we were not so very far from the gallery here, and I was sure I could go in and out through the back stairs fairly privately.

I went straight up to the office, once Benedetta enquired with the steward if Holland-Bury was in.

I had not expected him to be in company when I arrived and tapped at the door. Less still, did I expect to see Serrano in the seat when he turned about to look at me.

'Ah, the very person!' he said, beckoning me in, and I flushed hot with embarrassment.

'Forgive me, I will come back when you are not busy,' I told Holland-Bury, who looked at me confused before saying, 'What the deuce has happened to you? You look like you've been in the ring with Gentleman Jackson!'

'Not now, Holland-Bury. I will wait in the studio for you,' I whispered, but it was pointless. Serrano was already on his feet, making the very same assessment.

'Eleanor?' he said, daring to pull the hood from about my head, 'What has happened to you? My god, but I only saw you last night.'

'Please, Signor, not here, not now.'

'No need for an introduction then, I see,' Holland-Bury said, wiser than I liked.

'This is who I mean for you to paint for me, Signor,' said Serrano and Holland-Bury's eyes widened.

'Signor, please, where is your discretion?' I scolded him.

'It's alright. This is a man who understands the way of the world. And you would have been so introduced, anyway, for he is an excellent portraitist and will take your portrait for me—though not now, it seems. What has happened to you?'

Holland-Bury shook his head. 'Shall I give you a moment?' A sardonic inflection to his tone.

I said no, and the Signor said yes, and Holland-Bury looked between us, uncertain.

'Alright,' I submitted, '...a few minutes and stay just outside,' I told Holland-Bury.'

'Why, my treasure, do you say such things? You cannot think *I* would harm you. Is that what has happened? Has some ragamuffin done this to you?'

I nodded.

'Who?'

'My husband, Signor. Perhaps now you understand why I could not entertain you last night without risk. I am lucky he did not get to finish the job.'

'Giles is violent with you?'

I nodded. 'Now you see why I asked you to send him away. If he knew the truth about us—'

'He does not though?'

'No, but he suspects your fondness for me, and this was, in part, a result of him thinking I was too much of a flirt with you at your dinner party.'

'I am sorry, treasure. I had no notion things were like that. I will take care of it. I will fulfil my end of the bargain and send him away, no excuses. And I will ruin him, you may be sure. But until I do, I think I must make arrangements for your protection. You cannot stay with him.'

'I am not staying there. I am safe now, with a relative.'

'Alright, you must recover a while and send word to me at the Bottega when you are ready to see me again,' he held his hands up, 'No rush, you take some time to recover. Oh, your beautiful face,' he lamented.

'Thank you, Signor. I will reply when I am able.'

He drew up my hand, kissed it, and excused himself, telling Holland-Bury on his way out to decide upon the terms, and he would be in touch. Then Holland-Bury turned to me, a disbelieving shake of his head. 'I was going to ask what the hell that was all about, but I think I have the measure.—Does Marco know you are his?'

'I am not *his*, Holland-Bury. Why must every man expect a woman to be someone's and never her own self.'

'Alright, calm down. So Giles attacked you then?' he said more sympathetically. I nodded.

'Well, I daresay he was right to object to you being with another man, but it's a damned shabby business to leave you in a state like this. Are you alright?'

'Yes, it is all superficial. And I was not *with* Serrano.'

'Well, I had it very different from him. He tells me he wants me to paint this great beauty he has acquired, an erotic portrait. I hadn't a clue he spoke of you or I would have put him off from the outset.'

'There will be no portrait or further visits to Serrano. I only agreed to it so he would pay Signora Crivelli's settlement and Marco would not fall into debt on my account.'

'But the diamonds?'

'Were paste!'

'Oh, so you mean to take Serrano's money and run?'

'I don't care about Serrano or being his latest *treasure*, alright. I have more serious matters to contend with, which is why I am here.'

'Go on.'

'I need you to help me get into a convent.'

He laughed heartily then. '*Me*, get *you*, into a convent. I'm not sure who will be laughed out of there first.'

'This is not a joke, Holland-Bury. I need protection.'

'You are right, forgive me. But you must see I am hardly the right person to know how to manage that. I haven't stepped foot into a church since Sunday School.'

'It does not matter, they are not to know. Just give them an agreeable story. You are English, as am I. You will assume my husband's role, admitting me there for my melancholy in the hope of my benefitting from a religious course of prayer or somesuch.'

'You cannot be serious?'

'Do I look like I have dragged myself out of my bed when I can barely move without wincing to come and make fun with you, Holland-Bury?'

'No, forgive me. But I don't understand. I should have your passport by Wednesday. You can still make the ship,' he protested.

'I cannot travel now. I am in no fit state.'

'Not now, but in a few days you will be on the mend, surely. I can find somewhere for you to put up until the ship goes if it will keep you out of Giles's way.'

'A few days is not enough. I told you, things have changed.'

'What has changed?'

'I am pregnant, Holland-Bury, and the doctor believes I must take care to rest for a couple of months. I can hardly go rattling about in a carriage or on a ship, or I may endanger the child.'

'Who's is it?' he asked more gravely.

'Does it matter?'

'No, I suppose not.' He sighed, 'Alright, I will go to this convent and see what they say, though how I am to pretend to be a pious sort and convince them you are my wife, I don't know. I am not even Catholic.'

'Nor am I.'

'Is there no one else you can ask?'

'No one else can know.'

'Fine. And let's just say we pull this off, and you have your couple of months' rest, then what? Will you travel then?'

'Yes, of course, I will have to go before it begins to show. You will sign me out in seven weeks' time, say. I will show a marked improvement in spirits by then, and you will declare I am ready to come home. We will ensure it coincides with the ship's departure, and I will leave before anyone suspects my condition.'

'Alright, I will get the passport on Wednesday and hold it here for you until then. It will be blank, so we shall have to fill it out together.'

'Very well, and you will need to ask Dante to lift the floorboards in Marco's attic studio, just beneath the marble as you enter. I have money there for the travel tickets. Once you have the passport, you can get the tickets.'

'So I can repay the loan then, you shan't need anything more?'

'No, you should have paid it back at once.'

'Well, I did not know if a portion would be needed to get you home.'

'No, I have enough money now.' It was true. Serrano's settlement had seen to that.

'Very well, I respect that. I do. It's a shame, Eleanor. In another life, you might have been good together, but not this one. I will send word to you when I know more.'

'Send it to Carlotta's and mark it for Benedetta. I will be staying there in the meantime.'

So, I remained at Carlotta's in the coming days, and when I received a message from Holland-Bury, I packed up my things and prepared to leave for the convent. I had little with me, having spent my time in bed, recovering from my injuries, or so the family thought. They had honoured their promise not to permit Giles to the house until I was recovered, and so I was expecting no visitors when the door knocked and Benedetta said someone was here to see me. I frowned at her, but she said nothing, stepping aside to reveal the answer.

'Marco?' I gushed, bursting into tears, and he rushed over and gathered me up. 'Ouch,' I said, easing him off my bruised ribs.

'Sorry, where are you hurt?' he asked me.

'Where am I not would be the easier question to answer. I thought I would never see you again. I can't believe you are home.'

'I would have come sooner, but I only got Dante's letter last night.'

'Dante? I am sorry, he guessed, I tried to throw him off, but he—'

'It doesn't matter. He is my brother and will say nothing to anyone. He told me what happened at the house. He told me what that bastard did to you, and look at you.'

'I am getting better. There is no real harm done, bruising mostly. The doctor says it looks worse than it is.'

'He shall get more than a bruise,' he said through a stiffened clenched jaw.

'No, Marco, that will not help anyone. He has his share of bruises anyway, from what I am told. It doesn't matter anymore. I am going to the convent, like you said, and I will be safe there. Holland-Bury has arranged everything. I am just packing for it now.'

He raised his eyebrows. 'Holland-Bury arranged it?'

'Yes, I begged him to. There has been trouble with the passport, and I thought it best to wait a while after this, let things settle before I go.'

'Is that still what you want?'

'What? To go to a convent? Of course not, but it will do me good, and I will go home when I am better recovered.'

'I don't mean that. Oh, Eleanor, I don't know how you command yourself to stop loving someone, even when you know you must.'

'Even when you know their shame?'

'Even then.'

I wanted so much to melt at this and betray my feelings for him, but I was trying so very hard to keep to mind what Holland-Bury had told me about his last love and that I could never be the woman he deserved, the woman he could love freely. 'Marco, what I have done is too much to ask for any man's forgiveness. Even I see that.'

'It is not for me to forgive you, Eleanor. You did me no wrong. We were not even lovers then...You did things that you were driven to do to try to escape that brute, even I see that.'

I bit my lip then winced at the pain, 'Marco, don't make this harder than it already is. I cannot give you what you seek. I will never make you happy. I will live forever on the run, forever a married woman and deserter. I am so glad to see you again, truly. So happy to behold the handsome sight of you before I go. I cannot pretend otherwise. But I know this *must* be our goodbye, no matter how our hearts protest it.'

'It does not have to be. Let me be the one to take you away from here. I know it will not be a fairy tale. I know all now, thanks to your honesty. I understand the gift in that, even if it was very hard hearing. But I love you, and I do not care for the cost. I will live out in hiding with you if I must. Just tell me you can forgive me and that you still want me to go with you.'

I covered my mouth with my hand in case it dared betray me. Then, after a lengthy pause where a silent battle commenced within, I said, 'This was never about what either of us wanted, Marco. I will never stop wanting you. But that doesn't mean it is enough. It will never be enough. You deserve more. I have squandered my chance at happiness by giving my hand to Giles, but you are still free to direct your future towards a better path. I will not bring you down with me.'

'Eleanor, love is not something to be commanded by will. You once said it knows no time, and you were right. The timing might be off, but everything else is right when we are together. And that is not beholden to our histories or our circumstances. *Real love*, I think, is made of hardier stuff. You have shown me that. I love you though your past is marked. I love you though you are his wife. I love you for the honesty in which you have confessed things you did not want to speak of—the bearing of your darkness and your light. I don't care how muddled it all is. I want to make something better of it. Will you give me another chance to show you?'

'I cannot. I'm sorry, Marco. I love you, I do. But I will not ruin your life as he has ruined mine. You are free. Stay free, my love.'

'No tears. You have cried enough of those. Just let me love you back, Eleanor. I will always be a prisoner to it, even if you are gone. I know I hurt you by abandoning you and leaving you unprotected for that bastard to brutalise you like this. I should never have gone. I was a coward. Forgive me and I will never leave you unprotected again.'

'I do not want or desire your protection, Marco. I would only ever want to come to you as an equal, and I can never do that as his wife.'

'Come here, let me hold you. I will be careful,' he said, and he leant against the bed and pulled me into the space between his legs, put his arm about me, careful of my ailing ribs. I stepped in close, settling the better side of my face against his shoulder. To feel his warmth again was arresting, and I did not know how I could continue in my attempt to dissuade him when all I wanted was to tell him yes, I forgive you. Yes, let us run off together, for I cannot live without the warmth of your embrace. Let us pretend at being the happy family we have been denied. Let us raise this child just as a husband and wife would. Let's be to our child as your parents have been in raising you: loving, patient, and kind. Let us show them by our example. Oh, how I wanted to make a try of it, but not at such expense to him. Not when there was more he did not know.

'I have missed you. I cannot live without you, you know. I lasted but a week, a very poor show.'

I laughed with him now, though it hurt to rumble my ribs and contort my face into such shapes. 'I missed you too, more than you know.'

And then he kissed me feather light upon the lips, taking care not to hurt me where they swelled at one corner. I knew I should have stopped at that, but if I was to give him up, what harm was there in a last goodbye? So I let him lock the door, watched him remove his boots and then his shirt, and felt myself grow weak at the sight of him. Then he helped me out of my clothes, revealing my bruises and scrapes that made him gasp and his eyes well with tears again.

'He will never hurt you again while I have life in me.'

'Shh, come, lie with me.'

'You are not up to it, I think.'

'Perhaps you are right, but I can hold you, can't I?'

'Yes, let me help you into bed.'

I tried not to wince and complain as I settled awkwardly into it, and when he got in beside me, we struggled for a way to best arrange ourselves so we could manage to merge our bodies as closely together as we could. I ran my fingers through the hair on his chest as he pressed kisses to my forehead and stroked my shoulder.

'Dante said he forced himself upon you and grew violent.'

'He did not succeed. I fought him off.'

'He said that, too.'

'Have you been home yet?'

'No, I came directly. I would have received Dante's letter yesterday, but I moved inns and missed the post. Thankfully, it was conveyed to my new inn last night, and I left immediately.'

'You travelled all night? You must be exhausted.'

'I don't care about that. I am here now with you, that's all that matters. And once I have slept and gathered my thoughts into some better order, I will make arrangements for our leaving.'

'Maybe you should take some time to think about it. Let me go to the convent later as planned. I will spend a couple of months there, and if you still want to go with me after that, I will go anywhere with you.'

'What is the point in that? We know what we want, Eleanor. We have wasted enough time, have we not? I turned my back for a week and look what happened. I will take no more risks. We will leave straight away.'

'I don't want you to make rash decisions. There is so much for you to consider, the gallery for one. I don't think Holland-Bury will remain indefinitely to run it for you, will he?'

'I will sell it if I have to.'

'No, Marco, I will not allow it, not for my sake.'

'For *our* sake. So we might go somewhere and start over anew.'

I felt his hand brush over my tummy and held it there lightly, thinking our child lay beneath these layers of flesh and the warmth of his hand. If he really wanted this and we started over somewhere anew, maybe we *could* be happy. Perhaps I need make no more confessions just now. Maybe our little family could grow into something beautiful, and we might never be discovered. 'Where would we go?'

'That's better.' He kissed me again. 'Where do you want to go?'

'I don't care so long as I am with you, only far away enough that Giles will not discover us, but not so far you are too distant from your family.'

I felt him stiffen. 'If Giles comes anywhere near you again, he will be a dead man, so you will pay no consideration to that.'

I lifted my head to look at him. 'Marco, you must not think of violence. Promise me you will not.'

He looked away. 'How can I promise you that when he does this to you? You cannot expect me just to let this go?'

'Well, I suppose that depends on whether you would rather us go away together or you be locked up for murder?'

'I will not murder him. I will stop some way short of it.'

'Marco, his downfall is to come. Fear not. But it shall not be at the cost of your freedom or conscience. Please, think of your parents, your mama, if you will not heed me.'

He knitted his brow. 'What do you mean, his downfall is to come?'

I faltered, realising my slip-up. He did not know I had signed with Serrano. I promised I would not, and I could not tell him now when he was full of rage, when he was finally back in my arms. 'I just meant that in my jilting him, he shall soon decline and suffer. Let fate take its natural course.'

He lifted my chin to kiss me, then pulled back to smile at me, 'You *are* beautiful and wise, see.'

I felt a shiver of indignity at this deception. After everything we had endured so I could be open with him. And yet, this was not the time for further confession. He was tired, distressed, angry. I needn't add another man to his wanted list, no. It was my hope that one pest would take care of the other, and we might both go off freely. Then I would explain, once we were away from here and all these ghosts. He would not be pleased, to be sure, but he would at least not get himself thrust into gaol for duelling with Giles or Serrano. We might go soon. Perhaps I should give him just another week to think on it and make some plans, and if he was still decided, then I could confess my pregnancy to him and explain why I must not travel very far. Maybe we might settle somewhere in Padua, for now, at least. The journey there was a smooth one along the Brenta, not the rough passage of seas or the rattling about of coach journeying. It seemed a sensible option that should cause no harm to my condition.

So I kissed and caressed him as he fell to sleep, amazed by the sight of him here in my bed. Though I knew I could not leave him here to sleep too long in his sister's house. She was not as constant a companion as Isabella had been with a young child to contend with, but she would look in on me from time to time, and so I had Benedetta keep a lookout. I told her too, to send a message to Holland-Bury and tell him I would not need to go to the convent after all.

CHAPTER THIRTY-NINE

Unbridled Fury.

Marco. September 1822.

'Y ou're back?' Holland-Bury stood, surprised, as Marco came into the office.

'I am. Don't look too pleased to see me. – getting a little too settled as principal, are you?'

'No, not really, my friend. To tell the truth, it's been one headache after another. But tell me, why are you here?'

He sighed and dropped into a seat. 'I had to come home. He attacked her a few days ago.'

'I know. I was supposed to be taking her to a convent today, though she cried off. I hope I am wrong in guessing this is the reason?'

Marco cast him an accusatory glance. 'You knew and you did not tell me?'

'I thought you wanted nothing more to do with her, those were your words—'

He could hardly argue this, they had indeed been his words, even if made in a mist of anger rather than genuine feeling. 'Well, you guess correctly, I cannot do it, let her go. I thought I could, but this last week has proved otherwise.'

Holland-Bury lowered himself back into his own seat now and pinched the bridge of his nose. 'Marco, you have lost your reason, my friend. Even I would not attempt to make something of a wife out of one of my whores.'

'Don't *ever* call her that!' he thundered.

Holland-Bury threw his palms up in submission. 'Forgive me, I should not have. It was disrespectful of me. But Marco, you know I mean only well when I tell you she is no good for you.'

'I know you *mean* well, George, I do, but I am tired of hearing it. You will say not another ill word against her in my presence, whatever your opinion may be. I love her, and that is enough for me. Her past is her past, I accept that.'

Holland-Bury pressed his mouth to his fist before lowering it and peering up at his friend. 'But what if it is not in the past, Marco?'

'It is. She told me everything, George. She did not have to, but she did.'

'Everything? You are quite certain?'

'Listen, you have been a good friend to me this week, and I do not want to come to blows with you; I already have one man to deal with today.'

'Marco—'

'Look, I am tired. I have travelled all night, and I have just seen the woman I love reduced to a wreck of injuries. Please, take nothing personally, George. You know I love you, my friend, but heed my words. Say no more.'

'Alright,' he conceded. 'So what is the plan now?'

'We will set out to Padua next week. I need to find us somewhere to rent that is out of the way, though I have no reason to think he ever goes there. And by the time I have dealt with him later, he will not dare to come after her unless he will have me finish the job.'

'You don't mean to call him out, do you fellow? That's a terrible idea. No, I am not speaking of her now. But on this, I will have my say. What good are you to anyone in irons? Come on, you shall run off with his wife. That must be enough now. S—It is not worth it.'

'I will do enough only to warn him. I am not a fool.—Don't look at me like that.'

'Usually, I would agree with you, and it is I who takes the title, but anyway, what will you do in Padua? Oh no, you don't mean to ask me to stay on even longer?'

'No, George, I do not expect you to give up your life in favour of mine. Though if you would manage just a few weeks longer whilst I get everything settled, I would be much indebted to you.'

'Fine. I wasn't planning on you being back for a little while anyway, so you can count on me until the end of the month.'

'Thank you, George. Now, is there any news on the passport?'

'She couldn't find it. Little difference it would have made anyway. Apparently, travel would only be granted with her husband's permission. I should have a stolen one by Wednesday, if all goes to plan. But I have only asked for one blank, and we will have to fill it out for Padua now, I suppose, so long as there is no difference between the domestic and external format?'

'I do not think so. But perhaps obtain two blanks, just in case.'

'What for? Do you need another?'

'No, I just had mine done for Milan, and it shall last out the year. But just in case we have to move on. I might be willing to box his brains out, but at law, she will still be under his control. If he attempts a cunning approach to recovering her, which is what she suspects, we will have no choice but to flee entirely.'

'Well, let's hope it doesn't come to all that.'

'No. But anyway, get two to be on the safe side.'

'It'll prove double the expense, fellow. I've had a headache getting this far, and it hasn't come cheaply.'

'No matter, settle what you must. But for now, I need the key to the safe. I must look for the deeds.'

His eyes widened. 'The deeds? No, you do not mean to sell the gallery. Tell me you do not.'

'I don't know yet, but I want to get prepared. If Padua works out, I might settle for finding a manager, if not, I must be ready to do what is necessary at the drop of a hat. Anyway, I might need to keep it on a little longer just to settle the loan first. So it won't be so very quick. I shall need to organise another exhibition, see if I can shift a few of those scene paintings. That would sort it out.'

'I paid back the money lender, Marco.—Well, absent the passport cost.'

'What? I told you to settle things with that creature.'

'They are settled.'

'You are certain?'

'I am told so. She was going to sell some diamonds or something, she didn't need the money anyway. Apparently, she has kept a stash under the floorboards in your attic, enough to pay for everything she needs. And so I paid it back and saved you a lot of interest, my friend. The contract is marked as settled; you will find it in the safe.'

'Then I suppose under the circumstances that is one less burden to bind me here. But what do you mean she has money under the floorboards?'

'She said to retrieve it for her boat fares so I could get the tickets on Wednesday when I had the passport in hand. She said to lift the marble, and it was beneath that.'

'She never said.'

Holland-Bury shrugged.

'So when was she to sail for?'

'A couple of months' time. You know she had me in that convent pretending at being a player at the Drury Lane. Dashed hardest thing I've had to manage. I'm telling you, fellow, of all the things I've had to deal with in your absence, that by far was the worst of it.'

Marco let out a laugh. 'I never thought I'd see the day you approached a convent, George, not unless you were on a mission to set up a tryst with a nun or somesuch.'

'I was tempted, my friend, very tempted by the pretty little piece that answered the door. Though when that reverend mother came to speak to me through the hatch, she petrified me, and I swiftly put the notion out of my mind.'

Marco laughed again. 'Oh dear, I needed that laugh, my friend. You shall relay me the full account when I have more time.'

'You are in a rush?'

'I want to go to the shipyard before it gets too late. I don't want to cause a scene in front of my mama. I shall have it out with him there before he returns to the house.'

'Marco, at least sleep on it, my friend. Come back to mine tonight, let your hair down. We will have a few glasses and a game or two. Get your head down. And if you still want to challenge him in the morning, I will go along with you and bear witness to anything that might keep you out of trouble with the law.'

'I will go back to Carlotta's tonight, George, keep an eye on her.'

'She is fine there, and in her state, she is probably better off without you trying to sneak into her bed.'

'Yes, I daresay you are right about that, but I will go and sit up with her at least. Another night, though, before I leave, I promise it. Now, I have to get on my way.'

When he left, Holland-Bury got a clean sheet of paper from the desk and wrote: *Eleanor, have you forgotten what you pledged? If nothing else, at least be honest with him. Don't force me to speak all I know. Go before me.*

The shipyard was busy, horses crowding the wet docks, saws throwing dust into the dry air with impunity. Marco walked towards his father's yard, growing fury in his steps. *Giles is not going to get away with it this time*. He had sat on the sidelines for far too long as it was. Today, he would have his judgement on his treatment of her without censor or invitation.

He dodged his way through moving carts and men lifting logs, tugging at pulleys, and ignored the doffed hats of a few that recognised him from his rare appearances there nowadays. He had not time or patience to be diverted from his cause to stop and entertain pleasantries. He had one mission in mind right now, and *nothing* was going to deter him from it.

When he came to the warehouse bearing the sign *"Rosetti Shipwrights est.1675,"* he readied his words: *Giles, outside, now. It's time you faced a fight with a true match instead of throttling your wife in her bed.*

He suspected he would be in the office where he usually sat pushing paper about, commanding orders at men who undertook all the hard labour that made him riches without breaking a sweat. He headed directly for it, waving a dismissive hand at the men who looked up and greeted him as he walked his way to the small oak staircase that led up to the mezzanine on which the office sat perched on a timber ledge overlooking the warehouse below. He took the steps two at a time and swung the door open wide.

'Marco?' said Dante, looking up from his desk, then standing.

'Where is he?' Marco asked, turning about to see if he had somehow missed him in the warehouse.

'He's not here, brother, you have missed him by an hour or so.'

'Damn it! I should have come directly. Where is he gone? When will he be back?'

'I've no idea. It was an impromptu matter. Serrano demanded a meeting under threat of the contract if he didn't skip to it, so he went.'

He threw his hat down on the desk. 'I will wait,' Marco said, looking over towards his empty chair with contempt.

'Brother, I know what's in your head, believe me. I have wanted to land him a facer ever since. I've only come back into the office now he is out of it. I cannot abide the sight of him. But you know it will expose you both if you dare.'

'I don't care. It is too late for all that, brother; he crossed the line.'

'I know, I do. When I saw her waving that poker at him, I was inclined to snatch it up myself and put an end to it. But think of the family, Marco. Our parents don't deserve to suffer on his account. They will be devastated by all of it. Even you, Marco, they can't find out what has been going on under their noses. Mama will blame herself, and Father will cast you out from under his roof.'

'Look, I know all that. I don't want to cause them distress, which is why I came here and not to the house. Where is Father, by the way? I had hoped he might be out when I got here.'

'Gone down to the woodcutter's office to order some more timbers. Brother, what are you going to do now?'

'I'm going to take her away from all of this. What else can I do? I love her.'

He nodded. 'I know. I can't believe I missed it now I reflect. But you will leave the house in devastation, you realise the cost?'

'What choice do I have, Dante? How else can I protect her?'

'I don't know. But if you can find no other way, Marco, can you not at least do it gently? For their sakes?'

'How?'

'Well, for a start, by not spilling Giles's brains out upon the floor?'

'I don't know how to contain my anger, Dante. It frightens me to be so dispossessed. I think I could kill him. I have watched how she suffered from the day she arrived, and I could do nothing, say nothing...I had no choice then, for she did not invite my intervention and threw me off at every attempt to try, but she has told me the whole now. If you understood the deplorable things he did to force her into marriage, to force her here. I think he has ill-used her many a time, and that is why she ended up so indifferent to such misuse of her virtue.'

Dante stood up and hugged his brother, 'I didn't know he forced her into *everything*. I'm sorry to hear it. I'm sorry to see you like this, Marco. Tell me, brother, what can I do to help? Heaven knows you have always been there to help me when I have needed it. Whatever I can do, I will do it, but will you at least let us think things through more rationally before launching into things we cannot turn back from? There is always more than one way to catch a rabbit. I don't want this to turn any uglier than it already is, and I don't want anything ill to come of you or the people we love. We shall find a way, a better way, between us.'

'Perhaps you are right. Perhaps I must pause to think. I have had no time to think clearly.'

'Stay away from the house a few days more, away from Giles, and if we cannot come up with something better by then, you may still blunder his brains if you wish. But for now, do not turn yourselves over to everyone's knowing; it must be broken gently if it is not to break hearts.'

'Alright, I will stay away and try to gather my thoughts more steadily, but if our paths cross, Dante, I cannot be held to such a pledge.'

'Then get on your way, please, before he comes back. Where will you stay tonight? I will come and see you then. We can talk properly.'

'Carlotta's.'

'No. That is a terrible idea. You know how sharp she is. She will put it all together in a trice if you flaunt it right before her nose.'

'I've already been there. I just want to sit up with her, watch over her.'

'Then let me do it, for god sake. I can call for you in an instant if there is any sign of trouble. Besides, I cannot promise to hold my temper if he dares to venture near her. But I do not think he will. Mother has boxed his ears into contrition, even dragged him to confession, and he says he wants to apologise to her.'

'You believe that?'

'No, but I think he has to play things that way for now. He has been exposed to us all for what he is. He does not have the cover to act from beneath anymore. That has been his greatest weapon, the disguise.'

'She says the same. She does not believe he will come so openly at her now, for he is used to lurking in the shadows when no one is watching. And now all eyes are upon him. Though she thinks she is put at greater risk of having some ruffian snatch her up on his behalf, it would not be the first time.'

'Heavens, you better get her out the way as soon as you can. But perhaps it could be made to look like you had not gone together, a coincidence, however implausible, might soften the blow. But that will only be possible, Marco, if you don't call him out. If he is alerted to what has gone on between you, I think it will only make him more inclined to snatch her away again, for he will understand the threat. Right now, he does not know it. He will think you no different than me in being appalled at his behaviour. Everyone is, don't mark yourself out from the rest of us. Use your cover wisely and keep him in the dark.'

'You always were the calculating one. But I see you are right. If only I can keep some distance, I can wait for the sake of a greater cause, though one day, brother, I shall have my moment.'

'Yes, once all else is taken care of. Now, stay away from Carlotta's. You've been once. It will seem nothing above the ordinary familial courtesy that you should have enquired after her by now, but leave it there. Stay with George for a few nights, or if you can't stomach that, then get a hotel. I will stay at Carlotta's, keeping everyone's eyes cast in the wrong direction.'

CHAPTER FORTY

The Exit Scheme.

Eleanor. September 1822.

'Ah, you got my note then, I see,' Holland-Bury looked up from the painting he was setting into a frame. 'Lucca, you may go. I will call you when it's ready for hanging.'

I waited for the attendant to leave before I crossed the gallery floor. 'I did. I take it Marco has already spoken to you.'

'Yes, and he will not have a word spoken against you. For that reason, I was forced to hold my tongue, but I will not do it anymore, even if he does swing for me over it. You know he went down to the shipyard this morning to settle things with Giles?'

'My god, no, I made him promise. Do you know the way there? I have to stop him.'

'There's no need, he's back now. You've just missed him. Giles was not there, by some stroke of good fortune, and because of that, Marco is not in irons. Will you let him suffer like that for you? You who is shacked up with that old man behind his back, carrying some fellow's child he shall be thrust into keeping.' He shook his head in disgust. 'I thought you loved him?'

'I do. Listen, Holland-Bury, I know why you hate me, and I know why it all looks so terrible from your perspective, I do. But it is not the way you think it is. The child is his. I know this for a fact.'

He let out a snort. 'You cannot possibly know it when you are whoring yourself out all over the place. Why his? Why not your husbands or the diamond traders? Because it suits you to be *his*.'

'No! Because I have only lain with him since I last bled. I own it was by virtue of awaying to the country and being spared the demands of Giles and the patrons, that is true. But it remains the fact. Why do you think I fought my husband off and landed myself in this state? To preserve my knowing for certain that it could not be attributed to anyone else.'

He pinched the bridge of his nose, then looked up. 'So even if it is true that you can rule out Giles, and I do not say it is unlikely since you were abroad for a time, but you cannot deny that I heard with my very own ears what you and Serrano spoke of, and you have seen him since your return.'

'Of course, you did. I wanted you to hear for yourself, for I knew you would never believe me on my word.'

'He said he saw you that night, and you said that was why Giles beat you.'

'He did see me. Giles took me to a dinner party at his house. He thought us flirting, but I was trying to put Serrano off all night, and I succeeded, but Giles saw what he was about, and it riled him.'

'What, so you have an agreement to serve him as his mistress and do not have to lay with him? Is that what you expect me to believe? Because he was full of such descriptions of the 'charms' of his pretty little piece when he begged me to take your portrait, ventured I might do it for the sport, if not the pay.'

'I have submitted to other means to keep him placated, just the once when I could not avoid it when the agreement was made so he would pay off Signora Crivelli. I swear it, ask him yourself if you will, he has lay with me but only once, before Marco and I ever...'

'I don't know what to think.' He let out a protracted sigh. 'I own it is complicated, but don't you see; you have yourself entangled in so many directions now he is forced to untangle things for you. He is talking of selling this place now.—Do you have any notion of how hard he worked to get to this point and bring his dream to life? He's not a rich man like Giles. We artists are not respected or rewarded like men of ordinary trade and commerce. A few of the great names make fortunes, and most of us work tirelessly for survival and an occasional break. He seized that opportunity and didn't squander it like I always do. He invested it carefully, raised loans, and paid them off until he finally got here. And now he will just walk away from it, that's if he doesn't land in gaol first. You will ruin him, Eleanor. I can't let you do that.'

'And that is why I did not tell him any more; he was so angry, so unlike himself, a bloodlust I never thought I'd see on a gentle face like his. But I was frightened that if I confessed to agreeing to the settlement with Serrano, he would go after him, too. I cannot tell him *now*. He is reckless in this head. I must wait until we are away from here so he cannot go and seek out revenge on either of them. I didn't want him to hurry such a decision. I wanted to go into the convent as planned and give him time to consider this properly. But he will not hear it, and now, I see the best thing is for him to be away from Venice as urgently as I.'

'We agree on that at least. Very well, I will hold my tongue for now, for *his* sake. But as soon as you are in Padua, you tell him the whole before he sells the gallery and puts *everything* at stake for you.'

'I assure you, I need no persuasion, I mean to do exactly that. I don't want any more obstacles between us, and I only want him to choose me if he knows all and accepts me on that basis alone—warts and all, as it is said.'

'Then you must not tell him you are pregnant yet. If you really want him to choose you, for you, don't put the matter of a child before it. How will you ever know if he chooses you or his blood if you do?'

He was right in this. He would choose for the sake of the child, and I did not want his choice to be formed on that alone. 'I will withhold it for time enough that he makes his decision as freely as he can, then I will tell him, only, if he chooses me. If he does not, I will go without mentioning a word.'

'Well, let's not jump the gun, but I will let you handle it your way. But think about it, Eleanor, about what he stands to lose.'

'I have thought of little else. I will go now, only I want to say one thing. You are a better friend to him than perhaps even he knows, and though you do not like me, though you surely care little for my thanks, I will thank you anyway, George, for how you have put him ahead of all and tried to protect him, how you have honoured such favours to me in helping me in his absence. I am truly grateful to you, and I hope in time you will see I mean to bring him joy, not trouble.'

I left then, leaving him quite speechless for a change and got Benedetta to find us a boat to make the journey. I supposed Marco already arrived at the hotel, now. He had sent me a note saying he was to stay at the *Locanda San Barnaba* for a few days and he could be reached there. So we headed there by boat and, when we disembarked, walked the streets with Benedetta's navigation, keeping my veil pulled over my head, and staying arm-in-arm with her until we got there.

When I arrived, Giacomo let me in and I found Marco bent over the writing table, a pile of papers before him. 'What are you doing out of your bed?' he said, surprised.

'I could not keep away.'

'You came on foot?' he crossed the room to greet me.

'I could hardly bring your sister's oarsman here, could I? He left me at the church, where she thinks I'm praying. Anyway, I am fine and here with you, where I long to be. Though I think I interrupt you from your matters.'

'I was just writing enquiries to see what I can find for us in Padua. We're too late now to organise anything ahead of us. I daresay we shall have to make do with a hotel for a time, but at least if I get things underway, it needn't be too long. But I can finish up later. For now, I have a more pressing need of your embrace.' He took me by the hand, sat down on the small sofa and patted his lap. I slipped carefully into it, curled up against him as comfortably as I could as he kissed me and stroked my hair, and I listened to his heart beating against my ear. Then I sat up, remembering I had forgotten to give Benedetta the coins I meant to include with my surplus supply of Queens Anne Lace seeds for Giulia. I hardly needed them now, and since I was mindful of the likeliness of Giles going through all my things when I fled, I did not want to leave anything significant about for discovery. So I had sent Benedetta back to the house only yesterday to recover them and destroy all the other incriminating evidence of the solutions and sponges under the excuse of needing more clothes. Today, whilst I stole an hour with Marco, she would take the seeds to Giulia for me since I could no longer be found in that district. Though I had meant to give her some money to take to her too. I had enough of it to spare now, to be sure. And though I had held Signora Crivelli to her part in distributing the ten per cent cut to Giulia whilst I was in her employ, I did not doubt that now I was not, she would feel the absence of those extra coins at a time she needed them most.

'What is it? Are you uncomfortable?' Marco asked.

'No,' I said, 'I need to call Benedetta back. I sent her on an errand but forgot something.'

'Oh, surely I can run it for you later if you give me your instructions.'

'No, you are quite busy enough. Let me see if I can call her back, or perhaps you might send Giacomo to turn her around?'

'I daresay Giacomo is already with her.'

I frowned, 'What do you mean?'

'I mean that we are not the only ones thus engaged.'

'Really, Giacomo and Benedetta are...'

He nodded.

I sat back down. 'She has made no mention.'

'Hardly likely to, is she, and we know all too well why. Such matters must be closely guarded.'

'Then how do you know it?'

'Boys will be boys. Benedetta might have the good sense to cover her tracks, but let's just say that menfolk are not often so discerning.'

'He told you then? How long?'

'He did. He is young, and young men like to boost such things. About a year or more, I suspect.'

'Yes, I suppose they do.'

'I hope you know that I would not—'

'Of course, I know it; you are neither young nor anything like the rest...but—'

'What, say whatever it is that's on your mind?'

'I don't know. I suppose it is quite meaningless talk now, but I know so little of your more personal history.'

'Ah...I see. You've shown me yours and want to know of the indiscretions of my past? I suppose it is only fair. Though I fear I shall disappoint you if you are expecting anything of an epic history. You are the first in a very long time.'

'Your mother told me you were once meant to be married and that it ended tragically. I don't mean to conjure the ghosts of your past in such painful matters,' I said, not wanting him to feel duty-bound to recount the horrific story Isabella had started and Holland-Bury had finished in telling me.

He took a contemplative pause, then said, 'Eliza and I were ill-fated from the start, but we were in love and were willing to climb mountains and do whatever we could to be together. Had I known how it would end, I would have rather we had never met at all. It ended in her suicide, and I have never really forgiven myself for the fact.'

I stroked his cheek. 'It was not your fault, Marco. You cannot account for what someone will do when pressed into such unhappiness and despair. I know that well enough.'

He settled his heavy eyes over the sight of me. 'That was eight years ago, and I meant never to fall in love again after that, and until you came along, it had never been difficult to avoid.'

'Eight years is a long time to be alone.'

'I do not say that I have been entirely alone. There have been other women, but frivolous and fleeting encounters, nothing amounting to—'

'I thought you said you never visited low houses.'

'And I do not, well, not since my Oxford days and even then, but only once.'

'Once?' I frowned, incredulous. 'Why, was it so terrible an experience?'

'It is not appealing to me to accept reluctant kisses from women in desperate circumstances, however well they may play up at disguising them. If I am to lay down with a woman at all, it is because she wants me to and for no other reason.'

I thought of Guistina then and all the talk in class that day. 'And where do you find such women? Forgive me, but if you do not speak of bought women or those with reputations to protect, I wonder—'

'Perchance and rarely, as you say. There was a time when I was much engaged at the shipyard, and there were many more female workers in those days.'

'There are female workers there?'

'Yes, sailmakers, food vendors, the *Calafete* who waterproof the hulls—quite a female workforce back then, though far less in number now.'

'And you would keep company with them?'

'On occasion, if someone took a fancy to me and the feeling was mutual. Then there was a brief and fleeting fling with the Contessa, a widow, I might add.'

'The one who spoke so highly of all your merits at the exhibition? I thought her fond and passionate in her praise, but I own I did not believe at her years—'

'She was perhaps in her forties then, and I assure you her passions lie firmly in the arts themselves. It is long extinguished between us now. But she remains a dear friend. I think you would like her very much. She is an impressive lady, educated to an unusual degree. It was she who gave me the idea to start the ladies' classes.'

'I think you still admire her, perhaps?'

'Yes, greatly, but not in the sense you imply. I was young then. It was before I had ever met Eliza.'

'How did you meet Eliza?'

'I was commissioned by her father to take her portrait, to take all the family's portraits, but she was to have her own to mark her debut, and I suppose she became something of a muse to begin with. And then we grew more intimate, fell in love, and I proposed to her. She accepted, but her family did not. The strength of our feeling had been too ardent to simply give up, as I wish now that we had. So we planned an elopement, which failed and ended in her taking her own life.'

I pressed a kiss to his temple and held it there a moment. 'And that is why you no longer paint in portraiture?'

He nodded. 'I spent years painting her after, as if though she was gone from this world, I could somehow paint her back into life in some other world that existed only within the realms of my mind. It pervaded all my work; even when I took up other commissions, I could not complete them without always digressing into some detail of her, however vague. In the end, as I came more to terms with her loss, it seemed better to move to safer ground. Above the occasional genre scene, I stick to landscapes now, as you know.'

'I am sorry, Marco, that you both suffered so cruelly for wanting nothing more than to love. I find the more I discover about life, the more I realise what a high ransom is asked for something so natural to us as to want to love and be loved in such a world as ours, alas,'

'You are worth the ransom, that I hold to.' He kissed me more indulgently, and I wished we could lie down together now. But a gentle shift in my position was enough to remind me it may be some time before I could manage it. But what was time after this spell of waiting when we had the luxury of forever lying in wait for us?

When we broke from our kiss, I settled back against his chest and asked, 'Had you hoped to begin a family one day, I mean, before things turned out the way they did.'

'I can't say I ever gave it much thought back then. Naturally, in proposing to Eliza, I understood the likely inevitability of such a course, but I was younger then and wanted her for her own sake and saw little beyond that luxury. Though, I have many years since, lamented the loss of that possibility in deciding not to marry.'

'I was told that your mama had made quite the exhaustive effort to try to alter that.'

He laughed. 'Yes, you might say that. I'm sure there was not a suitable woman left in Venice who she had not tried to encourage my interest in at one time. But she has long given up, I believe. Anyway, who are these informants?'

'The ladies at class seem to suspect you in some illicit love affair, and they obviously know you well enough to note the change in you, for they are right, though I had to do my best to dispel the idea.'

He seemed surprised at this. 'They do, and they spoke to you of it?'

'They wanted me to spill the beans on who she is, the irony...'

'Then perhaps it is for the best we are to be gone soon, for they are some of the sharpest-witted women I know, and I daresay it won't take long for them to realise what is between us now if we were to remain.'

'I think Guistina may have an inkling already. Though she did not say so, I felt it in her questions.'

'Ah, well, if she suspects it, it won't be long until she's leading the rest of the class towards the idea.'

'You are well acquainted, I mean—'

'She was one of those matches my mama tried to persuade me towards, but on my part, it was as the others: of no interest to me. She, I know felt somewhat differently and made quite the try. Even after she got married, she made an attempt one day after class.'

'What, to seduce you?'

He nodded, 'About a month or so before you came.—I had only recently branched out into giving ladies classes, though the men's had been running for some years before. I suspected her motives for signing up for it but hoped that since she was wed, she might have given up such notions. I was forced to warn her that if she made another attempt, well, I would not be able to admit her back to the class. Ever since she has been perfectly civilised.'

'You did not welcome her advances, even as a causal interest?'

'No, of course not.'

'But why? She is pretty and accomplished, is she not?'

'Yes, I daresay, but...'

'What?'

'Well, a little more irony, in that I was going to say I have no interest in married women.'

'Well, just this one, I hope. But, before she was married, you could have. I mean, I can't believe you could not find even one amongst the number to suit?'

'I think it was less about them than my own state of mind, and I don't know how you did it, but since you arrived, you have altered that state and rearranged me in ways I did not think possible.'

I reached up to kiss him, but we were interrupted by Benedetta's return, which was perhaps swifter than it might have been, for I supposed Giacomo had likely conveyed her in the gondola. When she poked her head about the door and told me our hour was almost up, I bid her give me five minutes more. 'Argh, I hate being parted from you. I can barely force myself to the door,' I complained once she left.

He sighed and pressed a kiss to my fingertips. 'I know, but it is not long now. And I must get these enquiries out today. If I am swift, hopefully, we'll have a shortlist of viewings to make on our arrival in Padua.'

'Yes, I shall keep my mind fixed directly on that in the meantime, though I will likely return to you tomorrow, if I may?'

'Oh. Now you seek permission,' he teased me and kissed my nose. Dante will sit up with you tonight at Carlotta's. He thinks it will look suspicious if I do, and he is right; my sister is not easily gulled.'

'I know it, but she has already asked if something is between Dante and I, so I don't think he should either.'

'She has?'

'Yes, when he asked her to take me in before, and then he turns up with me in the middle of the night in this state, and now he is to keep bed watch over me? It is not a good idea. She is already full of questions, and it does look very odd.'

'Maybe you are right. It would be better you remain here with me so I can keep you close, but we can find no fitting excuse to account for it.'

'You said yourself, we are to be smart in dealing with this, careful, and I agree. Besides, I am not in any danger at Carlotta's, truly. If I were, he would have made a move by now. He does not want to show his hand to his own family. I told you, his image is important to him, and he takes great pains to show only the side of his face he wants to be seen. He shan't show the ugly one to you, and for now, that will keep me safe. Please, stop worrying. We have much to look forward to and plan. I don't want to waste another breath on him. I see only you and our life together.'

He beamed at me. 'And when we are away from here, so will I. But I cannot rest until I know you removed from his reach. But I better send a message to Dante and call him off if Carlotta's on his tail. You promise me you will stay indoors now? Just until I get things in motion. I will send Giacomo to collect you if you want to come here again, but no wondering about Venice on your own for now.'

'Dante, what are you doing here? You were not supposed to come. Did you not get Marco's message?'

'Charming welcome, that is,' he teased, pressed a kiss to my head and sat down in the bedside chair. 'No, I haven't been home yet. I've only just finished at the yard. I'll be glad when this bloody ship is done with and Giles is out from under my feet. As no doubt will you be.'

'What? He is going away with the ship?'

'What to Brazil? No such luck, but to somewhere else, Antwerp, I think.'

'You know this?'

'There was talk of it. I only caught the gist of his speech to my father, but apparently, Serrano says that if he does not go to Antwerp and deal in his affairs there, he shall withdraw the contract entirely. Got Giles spooked, according to father.'

'I see. Why is he so concerned about this contract, Dante? I mean, I know it is worth money to him, but he has so much already. Why should he care?'

'Anyone would think he was headed for the almshouse the way he punishes the workers to get things installed quicker, but I suppose he has a lot at stake.'

'What precisely?'

'He had to raise a lot of capital to buy a new ship, have us fit it out with all the right artillery, and recruit a load of brutes from the bravi to act as guards, which don't come cheaply.'

This disconcerted me, the hiring of ruffians. It would not be the first time... 'Is all that really necessary?'

'Diamonds are precious cargo. They can't just be loaded onto any old ship. It must be well armed with machines and guards, the risk of pirates must be mitigated against, and smuggling is rife. So he has had to raise several loans to trump the outlay of getting things in a high enough order for Serrano's liking, that much I know. It will all come back to him with dividends once he starts moving them, but Serrano's giving him the runaround, and he has no choice but to pacify him if he can still pull out this late in affairs.'

'Can he?'

He shrugged, 'A mere mortal like me is not privy to such details, but Giles seems to think so, so don't be surprised if he does us all a favour and disappears to wherever Serrano wants to send him.'

This was the news I had hoped for, and though provisional, I knew it would come to pass. Serrano had promised me it, and Giles was vulnerable to his will. I knew not how much he had in his coffers, and granted, much of his wealth would be tied up in property and assets, but the fact he had needed to raise loans meant he stood to lose not only his principal in this venture but interest, too. It might be a far cry from the almshouse, but it was a start. 'Dante, if things were to go badly for him with this contract if he does not satisfy Serrano, how would it affect your family business?'

'It makes little difference to us. Giles pays us to fit and maintain the ships, not to sail them. Our commitment ends there, and he is billed for the work we undertake. So long as he pays us for what we have done, it is no skin off our nose.'

I was relieved to hear this. 'Really? I thought your business somewhat reliant on him?'

'It was to begin with, with the blockades and death of industry here, it is true, we would have gone down too without his patronage, and until he brought you here and showed us what he really is, we in earnest believed him a good fellow, for he is a wise businessman and has been a generous relation, until now. But we are on our feet again and maintain our own small fleet. Anyway, I am sick of talking about business, forgive me, but it has been a very long day, and I came here to find out how you do, not talk about Giles's affairs.'

'Yes, of course, sorry. I am fine, no, better than fine.'

'Now my big brother's back? he said teasingly.

'I am so grateful to you, Dante. I thought I would never see him again.'

'Yeah, like you two love birds can be kept apart. I see what's between you now, though I must have been quite blind for it to have taken me so long.'

'You and me both. You do not disapprove of us, do you, Dante?'

'How can I? I love you both and see you want to be happy, and I want that for you. I just wish you didn't have to run off and leave me behind.'

'I wish that too. I would like us to remain close, though, if we can.'

'Well, that is something.'

'Is there no one special in your life, Dante, that will keep you consoled when we are gone?'

He considered me. 'Not like that, or at least, nothing steady.'

'You know, I always think that if we are fortunate enough to have a chance of happiness, we should make a try for it, even if the odds are not always in our favour.'

'Are we talking about you or me now?' He frowned, and then the door knocked, and I had no time to answer.

'Ah, my big sister and the little scamp,' he said as Carlotta entered the room with baby Pietro resting on one hip. 'Here, let me have him. Come and see your uncle Dante,' he reached out.

'Forgive me for interrupting, but will you help me put him to bed, brother? You always have a trick of amusing him, and he is in a fidgety mood,' Carlotta said, looking between us cautiously.

'Ah, alright,' he said, pulling himself from his chair, crossing the room and pecking me on the head, much to Carlotta's discomfit. Then he swept baby Pietro up in his arms and blew a raspberry on his neck.

We were careful after that not to give Carlotta any other bones to pick, and whilst I was grateful to her for the refuge, it had been a relief to leave when the news was confirmed that Giles had left for Antwerp the very next morning. If there was only one thing I could be glad of in this whole unsavoury bargain with Serrano, it was for this. Not only was Giles out of the way for our departure, but Marco was safe from trying to pursue him, which had quickly become my most present fear on his return, for he did not know Giles as I did. If he had beaten him badly, which I've no doubt he would have given the chance, Giles would not hesitate to set the law on him and press it to take its full effect, family or not. And even if he managed to evade that somehow, Giles would resort to other ways and means—hired brutes, just as he had for his ship. For whilst I was not quite the precious cargo of diamonds to him, I was still *his* wife, and that would be enough if he understood the nature of my relationship with Marco.

So if Serrano's intervention had spared us the risk of discovery, granted us safe passage out of Venice, and spared Marco falling foul of retribution, I could not regret it entirely. And though I would be gone to Padua by the end of the week and never have to entertain his repugnant advances again, I hoped he would still affect Giles's ruin now he had set things in motion. I meant to send him one last message before we set off for Padua to say I had to take a holiday and would return in a month, though, of course, I would not. But it was my hope that if he believed it to be true, Giles might be ruined before he realised I was never coming back. And now I knew the Harpers suffered no business risk from his injury, I rested easier in this hope. What I did not rest so easy on was how I was to approach this matter with Marco when we finally got to Padua.

It was difficult to see how I could put him through anymore after all else. The previous confessions were situated in my past, before we were this to each other, before I knew we were a possibility. Even the dreaded business with Holland-Bury fell into this vault. But it remained precarious that signing with Serrano was very much *after* my knowing, after Marco warned me off and elicited my promises to stay away from Signor Crivelli and her trade. How could I ask him to forgive me for reneging on my promise and so soon? And yet I had to believe that he would, for our happiness was near to complete now Giles was out of the way.

And I felt this instantly as we both returned to *Ca' Rosetti*. No more separation to endure. No more risk of violence or discovery so long as we took care. So we did, for the most part. Marco making busy with covert plans for our departure and covering the gallery, me privately packing up my things with Benedetta when the house was occupied. And when it was not, he would come home at the drop of a hat, take me into his chamber and caress me, make love to me when I grew able, and heal me; I had begun to realise, from so much disappointment. We curled up together afterwards and spoke of the future, our hopes, our dreams and all that we envisioned to be promised to us, and I thought I had found heaven here in Venice when I had first believed it to be the personification of hell. I floated through days and nights, heady with bliss, my heart teeming with gratitude. And I saw it in him, too, the brightness, hope, and easiness, now he had finally stopped brooding, and our plans were coming about. As far as he was concerned, I was *his* wife now, and neither of us needed that to be sworn before a priest, for we had sworn our oaths upon each other's hearts, and all the rest could go to the devil. For no contract on this earth was capable of keeping our love bound, now it was at last on an accelerated path to being set free.

Though we were not quite there yet, and we realised this as we toiled over the decision of what to tell his parents as we all sat up brainstorming, Dante, Marco and I. We were all of one mind in ensuring this might be handled as delicately as possible to protect them from any fallout.

'How about this,' Dante proposed. 'We stick with your idea, Eleanor, you tell them the truth, that you have tired of Giles's mistreatment and mean to run whilst you have the chance, say your goodbyes, etcetera. The timing is ripe, they know now what he is capable of. Then I will say that you cannot set out alone, and I will take you as far as the border, where some relative or acquaintance will come to meet us to take you back home to England.'

'But they will suspect you of no better, Dante, just like Carlotta has,' Marco protested.

'And that is one of the plans' greatest strengths, for they will all be looking in precisely the direction we want them to be—away from yours.'

'I don't want you to suffer such interrogations and accountability, Dante. That is not fair, especially as I will evade my share of the blame,' I said.

'Better that than breaking their hearts, hmm? And anyway, when I return from my escort, they will be relieved that I have not run off with you, Eleanor. They will likely exonerate me at best and, at worst, think I did the only honourable thing I could in seeing you safely out of the way. Either way, it can all be hushed up long before Giles returns from wherever Serrano has sent him.'

I stiffened at this mention and saw it pique Marco's interest.

'Why did he send him to Antwerp anyway?' Marco asked, and I grew nervous at this deviation.

'What does that matter now?' Dante said, and I was relieved. 'He's his little errand boy until he succeeds in the first diamond run, so he can do what he wants. But back to the plan, brother, focus; it's a blessing. It gives us the perfect cover for failing to alert Giles right away. How can you ever get a message to a man whilst he's travelling? By the time he gets the news, it will be weeks past, you will be long gone, and he will likely head straight back to England to look for her since he will be closer to there than here.'

'And you think your parents will not suspect Marco's timely absence?'

'I do, yes, because they always suspect our absences. As much as my mama complains that we shall never wed, I'm not sure she ever really means for us to leave her,' he teased. 'At least she can count on me, eh fellow. There's no risk of that.'

'Dante,' Marco said gently.

'Yes, well, back to the point. I don't think she will suspect your absence for that reason, so long as she has no suspicions about you two already. And if she does, scapegoat here might just deflect them anyway, especially if Carlotta gets her ear. I mean, you only just set off for Milan, what excuse did you give for that vanishing act?'

'I said I had to meet with an art dealer and negotiate on some new paintings for the gallery.'

'Hmm, I was hoping it might be something we could reuse. Perhaps you could have unfinished business with the art dealer? I don't know, think of something. It doesn't matter now. The main thing is the timing. It is all about the timing. I know you two lovebirds are set on drifting off into the sunset on Friday, but I honestly think it a bad idea. You must go first, Marco, on your own and be away before Eleanor even announces her intentions to leave. The first rule of every great criminal: never be found at the crime scene.'

'You'd be dangerous, brother, if you were the villainous type,' Marco jested.

'Well, brother, we all know who got brains and who got the brawn,' he teased before pressing on. 'If you are not even here when all of this unfolds, how can you be suspected of knowing anything? Even if Giles returns here to sniff about when he learns of it? For everyone will say Marco wasn't here and knows nothing.'

'And what about you, Dante? You will be here, and I want you to be above suspicion too, for you do not know him as I do, and he already dislikes our friendship,' I said, thinking this too dangerous.

'Giles is no match for my brother, Eleanor. I know he seems a brute to you because he has a preference for manhandling women, but he is a coward when it comes to meeting a true match,' Marco said, a glint of anger flickering in his gaze.

'I know that, I do. But he will not do his own dirty work, will he? It was not he who snatched me up and stole away with me but a pair of brutes he hired to do it, and even when one of them turned out willing to assist me at the last, he was marched out of the place by pistol point. He might be a coward, but his money makes him a dangerous coward to reckon with. I wish you would heed me, for I have seen so much more than you. Do you think my bruises and scrapes are the worst of it? No, not by a great margin. He is wicked and knows no limits.'

Marco sat up straighter. 'What do you mean, what else has he done?'

'Not now, Marco, just trust me, alright, I know what I speak of.'

'Well, brother,' he turned back to Dante now, 'I shall not have you on the line for this. We will have to go back to the beginning,'

'No, we need not,' I interrupted. 'The plan is almost there. Here is what we shall do. All we have spoken of remains, with the exception that it will not be you who takes me off to the border, Dante, but someone entirely unknown.'

'Well, if they are unknown, how shall we manage it?' he said.

'I will leave a trail of contrived letters between myself and this mysterious helper, plotting my escape and beseeching them to rescue me. I will invent it all, a red herring that can be offered to Giles if he should return with questions. You can tell him that all that remains of a clue is these letters. As for the fellow, we shall take a leaf from Giles's book and hire someone to come to the house and be seen leaving with me. We will have him assume a disguise, so he is at no risk of being traced, either. Then you are here, Dante, Marco is away, and me and the mysterious stranger set out to who knows where, leaving nothing but a trail of cryptic letters in our wake.'

'Not just a pretty face,' Dante winked at me.

'Alright, I think we have our answer,' Marco agreed. 'So I shall pretend to set off for what Milan again, I suppose. Perhaps I'll say a commission arose from my last visit, and I'm to return to undertake it now that the terms have been negotiated. It will give me an excuse to be away at length in its completion. I will leave a few days before, say my goodbyes, Eleanor will compose her missives and then take her chance to go to our parents with her intentions. The fellow will pick her up, we shall have a meeting point where I shall take over and bring you to Padua.'

'Bravo, we did it,' Dante said. 'Of course, there will be much to add to the plans after you bunk, but we've covered the first leg. The rest shall have to wait for another night, for I am quite depleted of brain power.' Dante stood up. 'I love you both. Goodnight,' he said, kissing his hand and waving it at us.

We followed shortly behind and parted on the landing with the same reluctance we did every night, me reaching up on tiptoes to press a goodnight kiss upon his lips, him drawing me in and complaining of me going, me telling him, 'Soon, we shall have every night in each other's arms,' then walking up to my empty floor alone, grateful to have no anxiety of Giles to consider, and sinking into happy dreams of all the tomorrows without him.

Despite contriving a solid scheme, putting everything into place was far from easy under the time constraints of getting everything fired off in synchronicity, and we were both relentless in this final effort and spent little time away from settling one task or another. Marco finding my 'companion', shortlisting houses to let, arranging passports and our carriage to Padua, as well as tying up matters at the gallery in his absence. Me sitting up beneath candle light each night when the house was to bed, composing a series of letters and then Marco helping me with artistic effect and offcuts and examples of his correspondence to postmark them convincingly. So when, on our last night together, before Marco was to 'set off for Milan', he told me he was to go and sink a few glasses with George, I was naturally disappointed. 'Must you go? I shall not see you for another two days, and I am already missing you.'

'I want nothing more than to take you to my bed and hold you close to me for the rest of the day, but I have been putting George off since I returned, and he holds me to the promise. What kind of friend would refuse a fellow a parting drink, especially since he shall be holding the fort, and you shall have your wicked way with me every day after this.'

'Very well, but don't be too long, will you? I want to leave you a parting gift before you go tomorrow.'

'Ah, that was not it?' he teased and gathered me up in his naked arms and kissed the side of my face. 'If I go now, I'll catch him just before the gallery closes. I shall stay with him an hour and rush back to you. You may be sure of it.'

CHAPTER FORTY-ONE

Harlot's Hue.

Marco. September 1822.

'Look, I am going to pay someone to take care of things here for a time, George.

I wanted to give you first refusal, that's all. I thought it might help you out financially, and you know it's likely a temporary position. I shan't keep you here indefinitely.'

Holland-Bury rubbed his chin thoughtfully. 'It's tempting, my friend. I don't say otherwise, and I am grateful for the offer. But you know me, old chap, I was never good at maintaining these punctual affairs, keeping hours and routines; it gets in the way of other pursuits.'

'Which is why I thought it might do you a good turn in keeping you away from expensive vices and actually putting some money in your pocket for a change.'

Holland-Bury smirked. 'I daresay it would, but I remind you I am here on a holiday.'

'I think life's a holiday to you sometimes, George.'

'Not these past weeks, it hasn't been. Look, I need a break—a few days to go on a little bender, restore my spirits, and then I have other work to get on with.'

'You're not still doing those lascivious sketches for those *Holywell Street* presses, are you? George, it is a waste of your talents to sink yourself so. Set your mind to your *real* work and produce another masterpiece, but this time, don't squander the proceeds.'

Holland-Bury tapped the air with a finger. 'I mean to, but for now, it pays well and gives me my free time. Besides, it comes with its own perquisites, and I have a few private commissions queuing anyway.'

Marco rolled his eyes. 'Will you ever change your habits, George?'

'I might,' he shrugged noncommittally. 'You certainly did, and no one could have guessed at that.'

'True. But my habits were not in vice nor draining my chance of a fortune.'

'Look, if you want me to teach your classes or stick my head around the door and keep an eye on the place for you while you're gone, I will, for you. But hire yourself a more reliable fellow for the management, my friend. However much longer I stay in Venice, I mean to make the most of it.'

Then the door tapped, and Giacomo appeared. 'Sorry to disturb you, but someone wants to see Signor Holland-Bury. He won't be put off and means to come up of his own accord if you won't see him.'

Holland-Bury wrinkled his nose. 'Who is this blaggard? We're closing in a minute,' he said, a note of protest in his tone. 'It's not a money lender, is it?'

'No, Signor, it is Signor Serrano.'

Holland-Bury twitched and leapt out of his seat. 'Keep him down there. Tell him I come directly.'

'George, what's he doing here?' Marco said, putting down his glass on the table.

Holland-Bury was already on his feet and heading to the door. 'Ah, just some portrait he tried to persuade me to undertake, but I refused him. I wrote and told the fellow, but he can't take no for an answer. I'll go and tell him in person and give him the message straight.'

Marco frowned, concerned. 'Why would you refuse him? He has paid you well in the past, and for the kind of work you prefer.'

'I told you, I mean to take a break, a holiday, I have enough to contend with—'

'George, what are you not telling me? Why are you in such a fidget?'

'Nothing. Let me go and send him on his way, and I'll be right back in a jiffy.'

'No, send him up here, Giacomo.'

Holland-Bury flushed hot, a nervous tremor in his voice. 'Marco, please, let me handle this.'

'I don't like what I am sensing in you, George. I know you, my friend, and you are hiding something from me.'

'I told you, it is as I said, I refused to be commissioned.'

'But why?—Right, I see I shall have to find it out for myself then,' Marco rose, and Holland-Bury rushed to the door to bar his way.

'Don't, fellow, please, for your own sake, do not.'

But it was too late. Footsteps approached, and Serrano emerged into view.

'Look, I will tell you everything I know if you just let me take this interview privately, Marco, please. I have done all that you have asked of me. Do me this one favour. Say nothing, go outside for some air, and I will explain all once he's gone.'

'Fine, I will wait outside the office, but I shall hear the whole.'

It was too late for any further negotiations, for Serrano levelled with them now, folder clasped beneath his hand. 'Signor Holland-Bury, Signor Harper, it's good to see you! If I might just take a moment of your time,' he said.

'He was just on his way out, Signor,' Holland-Bury as good as shoved Marco out of the way and pressed Signor into the office, 'Come in and sit down, Signor,' he said, slamming the door closed tight behind them and keeping an eye on the glass pane window to see if Marco had gone. He could not see.

'Well, I catch you at last. I know you are a busy man, Signor, but I must insist you reconsider my offer now.'

'Sir,' Holland-Bury let out an exasperated sigh. 'It is as I said before, I cannot. I gave you the names of other artists you can try, but as I told you, I can do no more.'

'You did, and I went, that is why I am here. You won't believe my luck.'

'Oh?'

'Look,' he said, placing the folder he'd been carrying on the table. 'I followed your recommendation to visit that artist, Vitturi, and he showed me his examples. He has a fair hand, but it is nothing to yours.' He leaned forward in his seat. 'But look what I discover in his catalogue. Our very same muse!' He opened the folder to reveal a sight Holland-Bury had not been expecting: Eleanor stood in the nude at a slight angle, turned towards the window as if peering out onto the canal.

He lunged across the breadth of the desk and snapped it shut. 'Not here, fellow, not now. This is a respectable gallery.'

'Alright, alright, keep your head. No one is here, they're shutting the place up.'

'Yes, and I have to get off home, and, well, I see you have no need of my services anyway. You have what you wanted, so now I must get on.' He rose to encourage his leaving.

'But I have not! It is not in the style that does justice. It is but a hint, far too subtle. It is beautiful as is she, and I do not say it is without merit, but I did not buy it for that reason. I bought it so you may begin on the *real* work. She is in no state to sit for it now, but you can work from this and add to it when she is herself again.'

'Sir,' he pushed the folder back across the table as if it posed some threat of bubonic contagion. 'Please, take this away at once. My decision is final.'

Serrano paused, curling his upper lip, then said with a gesturing chop of his hand against the table, making it shake, 'I will pay you thrice what I last offered. You need not take another commission for some time. What do you say? I can do no more.'

Holland-Bury cupped his skull in despair. 'I say no, Sir. Please, you must go now and take this with you.'

'I will go,' he said, rising at last. 'I see you are not in the mood for negotiations. It is the end of the day, and perhaps I have come at a bad time, but I will leave this here for you to...reflect on. You may send it back with your answer when you have had more time to consider it in a better head.' And with that, he pushed it back across the table and turned to leave.

As Serrano came out of the door, Marco burst in after him. 'Who the hell does he speak of, George?'

Holland-Bury snatched the folder up off the desk. 'No one.'

'No one?' Marco repeated, wide-eyed and cynical. 'You turn down good money for "no one." Show me that folder now.'

Holland-Bury clutched it tight behind his back and edged away. 'Marco, you don't want to see it. Please, trust me, fellow. You are making a choice now that you shall regret if you force my hand.'

Marco paced towards him, 'George, by god, I don't want to hurt you, but you will show me that picture, or I will force it from your hands if I have to,' he bellowed.

Then the struggle ensued, and at first, it amounted to a cat-and-mouse dance about the desk, Holland-Bury lunging one way, Marco the other, and then in reverse. Then, once they had repeated this routine several times, Marco shouting to hand it over, Holland-Bury begging him to heed his words, Marco drew back his fist and punched him, knocking the folder from his grasp and getting to it a second before Holland-Bury could. And then, as Holland-Bury pinched his bleeding nose, Marco opened the folder and revealed Eleanor's naked portrait to his sight. He threw it across the room in disgust, shouting 'No!' then he bolted for the door to set after Serrano.

Holland-Bury chased after him, cupping his nose. 'Marco, no, do not! I will tell you everything, just come back. Do not do what you will regret! Giacomo, Giacomo, help me,' he pleaded as he chased Marco down the stairs. 'Hold him back, Giacomo, if you care for your master, hold him back with all your might.'

Looking uncertainly between the two as Marco came bowling towards him, shouting for him to step out of his way, Giacomo outstretched his arms and caught him at the landing. Then Holland-Bury caught up and joined the effort, for one man was not going to be sufficient as Marco thrashed about to free himself with such menace that it took for another two staff and a visitor to the gallery to restrain him, as he called out to Serrano, who was already out the door now. He tried to call him back with a litany of threats and abuses cast into the air, echoing up the dome-covered stairwell. But Serrano did not return, and Marco finally retreated into an involuntary heave of panting breaths as he recovered.

Once he was finally tired out by the force of five men pinning him to the wall, and they were all equally covered in blood that had been left unattended from Holland-Bury's nose, the gallery doors were locked up, and they released him.

He fell to his knees in tears until Holland-Bury persuaded him to return to the office.

'Why didn't you tell me, George? I trusted you...'

'For the same reason, she could not tell you. Look at my face if you want the answer. I'm fortunate you stopped at one hit. I very much doubt the same would be true if you had got your hands on Serrano, would it?'

He puckered. 'She is aware that you know about them?'

'She is. I called her out about it when Serrano approached me. I had given a passing decision in principle that I would undertake the commission to begin with, so I asked about his muse, as I always do. I did not know he spoke of her, but when I did, I refused. I asked her to explain herself.'

'And what did she have to say for herself?'

'I own I took the same stance as you, fellow, and I told her so directly, but I do not think she meant to deceive you. She thought you were not coming back from Milan, and she didn't want you troubling over her debt. She went to have the diamonds valued to pay the abbess off, but they turned out to be worthless replicas. So she signed with him to shut the abbess up and was going to skip Venice, leaving him high and dry. But of course, then we couldn't get her passport, so she was forced to remain and keep him at arms-length, but you see what an eager fellow he is. He doesn't know how to take no for an answer.'

'I shall teach him how.' Marco tensed and slammed a fist onto the table.

Holland-Bury swept a palm through the air. 'And I rest my case.'

Marco refilled both their glasses. 'Alright, go on,' he said, swirling the contents of his glass around.

George took a long sip of his before replying. 'When you returned out of the blue, it changed everything. I told her to be honest, and she said she meant to, but you were in such a high temper with Giles that she thought the timing was ill. If she added to it with her explanation of Serrano, she thought she ran double the risk of seeing you in irons. Which is the only reason I kept my mouth shut, because I could not disagree with her judgement on that.'

He looked up to meet his eyes. 'So, did she agree to sit for the portrait? Did she come with him?'

'No, she knew nothing at all about it. They collided in the office one day, not so untimely as you did just now. It was then she found it out.'

'They were here, together, in this office?'

'Calm down, not like that. It was the day after Giles had ruffed her up. She was in no fit state to...anyway, he caught her here perchance. She'd come to speak of arrangements for the convent, and he was already here, pleading my acceptance. I gave them a few moments to speak, and *only* to speak, whilst she put him off, explained her injuries to him, and so on. There was nothing untoward. She bid me stay outside the door so I could hear it all. She specifically requested it as a condition of speaking privately with him.'

'So you heard it all, what was said?'

He sighed, 'What I told you: He asked what had happened to her. She told him Giles was angered by their flirting at some dinner party he took her to and was partly to blame for his mistreatment of her.'

'What, she was flirting with him and in front of Giles, that's why he beat her?'

'No, well, that's not the way she gave it to me. She said she had been trying to put Serrano off all night, but Giles took offence to how Serrano was looking at her, took it out on her, and not him, I suppose. Look, I don't know, I wasn't there. Anyway, he said he wanted to take her under his protection, and she said no, she was staying with family, but she would hold him to taking some revenge on Giles, and he made earnest promises that he would deal with it or something like that. Then he went and said to send him a message when she was better.'

'She said something similar to me; it makes sense now. She said Giles would fall, but with a conviction, a certainty that made me question it. But she lied when I did. Said she meant he would get his comeuppance in us running off together. But all along, she knew she had placed this in Serrano's hands.'

'I don't know what to say, Marco, I have told you what I know. What will you do?'

He sunk his glass and poured another. 'She has betrayed me, lied to me. I warned her that she was never to step into that bawdy house again or I should never forgive her...' He sighed into his hand. 'But it is my fault. If I had not fled to Milan, it would never have happened. I would have seen to the abbess myself and stopped her from tangling herself up with him. If she is honest with me now and truly has not lain with him, I am inclined to give her one last chance to sever ties with him. But it does not account for why she is posing for these paintings. She never mentioned that in all her confessions.'

Holland-Bury twitched uncomfortably. 'That may be my fault.'

'What?'

'Oh god, I had put it quite out of mind until he brought this in. But here we are. She was looking for a way out of her trade. Or so she told me, well not at the time, but after. At the time, she gave me some fudge about a gambling debt. She wanted to know where she could get work modelling.'

'George, you're mumbling. I don't understand.'

'She wanted work, needed money, and I told her to come to you for a loan, and she wouldn't. I tried to talk her out of the idea of modelling altogether, but when I realised it was an improvement to what she was willing to do for it, I told her where to look and directed her to the academy. She must have followed through on it. I thought the paltry fees had put her off, so I never thought to ask her about it again. I don't know when this portrait was taken, but I know the artist; I can ask him myself, though what little difference it makes, I don't know.'

'When did she ask you this, George?'

'I don't know, ages ago, around the time I blundered and brought the meretrice in to sit for the class. Come to think of it, it was perhaps that which gave her the idea, I don't know.'

'George, that was months ago, and you did not think to tell me?'

'It was before you had declared yourself to each other. It didn't seem important then.'

'You knew how I felt about her even then. You *knew* I would want to know. God, George, perhaps if you had told me she was in difficulty then I could have intervened before it got so bad as all this! She was looking for a way out, an alternative. I could have given her one if I had known so far back as that. Even if it only amounted to paying her fare out of the country, it would have spared her some dignity and all the tangled mess it has become.—Hang on, you knew she was in that line when she asked you about modelling?'

Holland-Bury bit his lip. 'No, not exactly. Oh god, what a mess it all is.'

'How long have you known?'

'Since that day she asked me about the modelling work. After she asked.'

'So months ago then?'

'I'm sorry, fellow, I didn't want to hurt you.'

'Hurt me, why would *you* hurt me?'

'Because she didn't only ask me to help her, she offered me her services in the same breath. That is how I came to know, but not about the rest or the *Rosa Inglese*, none of that.'

He covered his face with his palms, 'Tell me it is not true.'

'I wish I could. But it is the way of it, and I own, I faltered briefly, but look, I refused alright. I swear. I wavered for a moment purely out of surprise, and then I pushed her off of me and left.'

'She threw herself at you?'

'Briefly, not entirely. I kissed her, but only after she offered to go back to my lodgings with me. It was a moment, no more, a lapse.'

'And *you* refused? You expect me to believe that George? I should punch your lights out.'

He held his hands up. 'I did my best by you, my friend, I swear it. You know me, Marco, I am never able to refuse, and I own it was not easy, or even like me, but I did, Marco, for I understood what you felt for her. Ask her yourself if you won't take my word on it. Why do you think I ditched the ladies' class for a time? To avoid a repeat. That was the only reason I let you down, my friend. I took them back up as soon as she cleared off to the country with you…Come on, I cannot bear to see another man cry.' He patted him on the shoulder, and he flinched. 'Look, I wasn't going to tell you at all because I didn't want to see you like this fellow, and I didn't want you to think me meddlesome, but you know now why I was so set against her. Though if it's any consolation, when I asked her why she did it, she said she had only managed half her fare and thought I might share the coach back to England with her. She just wanted to get home and saw another way.'

'Yes, fucking you all the way back to England instead of fucking the whole of Venice in the meantime. You are right: she is nothing but a whore. I am done with it all.'

'Marco, I have never seen you love anyone like this, not even Eliza. Whatever she is, she is more than only that. I have come to the same reasoning lately despite my wanting to get her out of the country and away from you, for I feared it would go badly, as you know I did. Though I own, never so badly as this. But you are to set out to Padua in the morning. All is in place. Go and take some time together to talk all this through and away from Venice and all its demands and distractions. If you suspect her dishonest or cannot forgive her, take her passport and send her back to England and move on.'

'I will send her back to England tomorrow. I have made excuses and forgiven all else, but this? Serrano? You, my own friend, accosted in an alley by her like a meretrice, the very thing she swore herself above. No, I can never trust her after this. I shall go and shed my tears in Padua, away from my family, whilst she is sailing out in an altogether different direction.'

'As you think best, but sleep on it, won't you? You've had half the bottle. Now is not the time for making decisions.'

'Sleep? I think, George, you shall clean up the mess you are in, and we shall go out tonight in your style.'

'Marco, you hate those places, and whilst I'm usually trying to bend your arm, I'm not sure it's the kind of place you want to go to in this head. You'll only be thinking of her anyway.'

'Then stay. I'll go without you if I must.' He sank another glass in one draining gulp.

'Fine, but if you come to regret this, I'll take no blame for it!'

'What difference does one more regret make in the growing list of them I have come to keep account of? But right you are, this one's on me. You are entirely exonerated.'

CHAPTER FORTY-TWO

Christmastide.

Eleanor. December 1822 (3 months later).

'Right ladies, that is time and brings us to our final class of the year. It remains only for me to say it has been a pleasure and to wish you good tidings for the festive season,' said Holland-Bury as we finished packing away our materials. I caught the note of relief in his expression, no doubt glad for a festive reprieve from his gallery duties.

I exchanged the same tidings and farewells with my classmates before setting off into the lobby for Benedetta to cloak me in the many heavy layers that had become necessary at this season.

We had just stepped out of the gallery and were about to get into the boat when Holland-Bury came bounding down the steps behind us and asked, 'Any chance of a quick word before you leave?'

'Yes, one minute, Benedetta,' I said, turning about, wondering in varying degrees of fear and anxiety as to what was owed this unusual request as I stepped aside from the jetty.

'Look, Eleanor,' he said, fixing me with an earnest gaze, a note of apprehension in his tone, 'I thought I had better warn you that Marco will be home for Christmas. He can't ignore his mother's pleas. She hasn't seen him for months, and he has no choice but to ease her suffering.'

'I would not wish it otherwise,' I replied with a light shrug. 'She longs to have sight of him.'

'Well, you know what I mean to ask of you, don't you?'

'Yes,' I sighed, a hint of exasperation. 'To leave him be... etcetera, etcetera.'

'Yes.'

'I shall. Have no fear of that. You think I would take pains over a man who jilted me without even permitting me the chance to explain my side of the story? Even *I* retain a modicum of pride, George. I shall do my utmost to avoid him, as I'm sure he can be relied upon to do the same, and when we are forced into company, I will be civil. Are you happy with that?'

'Thank you. I just needed to give him some assurance, but it seems you are both of the same mind. How are you, anyway?'

'How do you think I am?'

'I didn't mean that, I meant...' he gestured to my tummy.

'Well, you tell me, can you notice anything?'

'Not precisely,' he said, sizing me up with his eyes. 'I suppose you shall pass for filling out a bit, but—'

'Well, thank you very much, George. I know I can always rely on you for tactless honesty.'

'Don't be like that. You look well, very well. It suits you,' he added more sincerely.

I quelled the urge to smirk. 'I'll take that and thank you for asking. Everything seems just as it should be, and I feel so very well indeed I almost do not know myself.'

He smiled. 'That is good to hear. Any news on Giles?'

'Still in Antwerp as far as I know. I do not open his letters, though he sometimes writes to his uncle and I suffer the relay of his words. Serrano means to keep him there indefinitely if he can, but I care not, so long as it is until at least March when the roads are passable again.'

'You will go by road now?'

'Yes, I can afford to now. I have more than enough money. I can even afford a companion to go with me. –isn't that the irony,' I told him, trying to keep the bitter edge out of my tone.

'Well, try to keep Serrano from his sight, won't you? He doesn't need to have that paraded in his view, even if it is all history between you now.'

'I have no intention of doing so. I'm not a fool, George. Discretion is utmost for the sake of the rest of the family if nothing else. The last thing I am likely to do is have him call for me at *Ca' Rosetti* with all the family in residence.'

'I know, but even I have seen you in his box at *La Fenice* from time to time.'

'I am always masked or veiled in public with him.'

'Yes, and to the rest of the world, that may fool them adequately because they know not who you are, but Marco does. He will make the connection. I'm just saying, have a thought for the fact.'

'I will, I shall take care. Serrano is away with his family for the festive period anyway, so presuming he is not to come too much beforehand, I imagine they shall be as passing ships. Now, I must leave you, George. I am on my way to him presently, and he hates it if I'm late.'

Holland-Bury doffed his hat, and I stepped into the gondola. The gondola that was not borrowed or hired but was mine. A gift, along with so many others from the old man I pandered to now. He was certainly an improvement on Giles, and I was left much more at liberty under his charge. Back then, it had been impossible to foresee how it would come to this. The path of the *Cortigiane Oneste*, as Signora Crivelli had always put it. She had been right, though brutal in executing the accomplishment.

I had heard not a peep from her ever since and never asked Serrano what had become of her. There was much I tried not to think of now, including that unhappy night I paced anxiously in my chamber, waiting for Marco to come home from the gallery for our last night together before he left in the undertaking of our plan.

Once I'd grown tired of curtain twitching, I went to bed, expecting him to wake me when he arrived home, but he did not, and when I woke in the morning, Marco was nowhere to be found. His note came via Dante when I went to him in a fit of despair, finding Marco's bed unslept in and fearing he had suffered an accident or some terrible fate befalling him to account for his absence. The result of Dante's search was a downturned face and a sealed scant insult that read:

'You told me you were not a meretrice, and yet you accosted George in the style of one? My own friend? You lied to me. Take your pleasure and go and fuck your old rich merchant and seek your protection there. I am weary of finding excuses for you."

Even Dante had been at odds with me for a time, though we had mended our differences in the days that followed, and even George and I had come to somewhat better terms. I supposed neither of them condoned my actions, but they each knew my earnest love for him and the suffering that followed his departure.—An episode that would have trumped all others that came before it, had I not had the consolation of my pregnancy to keep at the forefront of my mind.—A secret, still, that only Dante, George and Benedetta knew of, but one that was growing harder to conceal every day. Not so very much in my dresses, as George had candidly put it, I had seemed to "fill out", swell, I supposed, back into the busty necklines I had once filled before I came here, a way they never knew to be familiar to me. I had always been gaunt, near skeletal at points, since I had arrived here. But now I recognised my former self in the looking glass, my hair grown back to beneath my shoulders, my cheeks no longer hollowed, my stays no longer hanging loose at my shoulders. I always maintained it was Dr Heimlich's diet and commended it, though I rarely followed it now. Everyone took it as a sign of my return to health in Giles's absence, something no one had taken great pains over.

Serrano had kept his word and detained him in Antwerp ever since, despite his pleas to Serrano to have leave to return in time for Christmas and Carnivale. But they fell on deaf ears, for it was me dictating those replies now, though little that Giles knew it, or that it was all for nothing that he toiled in vain, that his banishment was in my hands and that the contract which kept him hanging on Serrano's every word was already in shreds. For I, too, had kept my end of the bargain, though at first with great reluctance. But Marco's departure eventually left me as indifferent as I had once been before. So I settled for this one inconvenience now. Not for want of money, though it granted it, but for want of seeing my husband as ruined as I had been in his making. It was all I lived for now, at least, until my child was brought safely to my bosom, and then I would have something to live for far beyond all else.

It was the only reason I had not gotten on a stage to Genoa the very day Marco abandoned me. The only thing left that I must remain for. But I was over all that trouble now. The doctors—and I had seen many of the best expertise—were all in unison in their assessment: All was progressing well, and I should be in a fit and safe state to travel now, provided I took care. The farther along I progressed, the risk of losing this child shrunk evermore. Now, I only remained to complete Giles's downfall, which grew ever closer, and once the winter frosts cleared from the city and the roads became less treacherous, I was to depart for home at last, in time to bring my child safely into the world and start anew.

I reminded myself of this as I reflected on the news of Marco's return to *Ca' Rosetti* with the natural trepidation at the thought of seeing him again. I had come through so much. I had grown strong. I had taken command of my life against all the odds stacked against me. A fortnight or so in his presence was nothing to all that. Surely?

But as the excitement grew in the house and it was decorated for the festivities and family began to arrive at *Ca' Rosetti*, I began to question my indifference, reconsidered whether I should revise my answer to Tanto in joining her for the period as she had offered. She had told me it was a lonely time for ladies in our line. Most patrons, being married men were called to family duty, leaving them little company. So she decided to host her own affair and mimic the spirit of family festivity beneath her roof, inviting only her most favoured friends to stay.

I had been surprised to be included in such an invitation, for our acquaintance was still an elementary one. But I had enjoyed having someone I could be myself around. Plain-speaking conversation, no hiding or pretences or feeling like an imposter, as I always did around the art class ladies. With Tanto and her circle, I needn't fear suspicion or judgement at all, for we were in sympathy with each other, and it was that I craved: to feel equal to my company, accepted. Free of the need to lie or make excuses. And amongst them, I did feel equal, and it had helped to resurrect my recently diminished confidence so vastly these past weeks that I felt at greater peace with myself once more. But I feared now that all the pains I had taken to get this far would be jeopardised again in Marco's presence. I must not let that happen...

It had been so long since I had seen him, and I had risen from the ashes of so many disappointments, that I had expected to be able to rely upon some stealthier sense of indifference when I saw his gondola pull into the jetty beside mine.—I had told the family I had hired it with some money sent to me by a friend, for at last I enjoyed correspondence from some quarters and had discovered why I wasn't receiving any replies before. Benedetta had seen Baldassare set aside a letter addressed to me with Giles's mounting pile. It had been a response from my mama asking why I had not replied to her previous letter. Then I knew, all along, he had been keeping them from me. Now, I had all replies addressed to the English consul, bypassing Giles and Baldassare entirely.

I snuffed out my candle to watch him from my window undetected. I was testing the water, I supposed, trying to judge if I had been correct in my assumptions of indifference. The sinking sensation in my stomach unnerved me somewhat, and I could blame it on nothing else, for I had not been sick during this pregnancy, apart from once, when I had eaten a crab without realising I no longer liked them.

So I understood, as I watched him climb out of the gondola in heavy coats and layers that obstructed my gaining a proper view of him, that maybe I was not *entirely* indifferent to him. It perhaps was not helped by the light flutters I had begun to feel in my womb more lately. His child, a constant reminder of both his presence and his absence. However, I had resigned to be happy to nurture a child made in love. For that, I would always be grateful to him. Knowing one day, I could sit down with our son or daughter and tell them that yes, I knew your father well and loved him dearly, even if it could not be…Though now I was to face a more imminent test of my resolution, and though more lately, I felt so very strong, so very settled since I had picked myself up this time, I had never had to put this new conviction to the test.

I listened anxiously to all the excitement rising from below as his family greeted him at the door. I had heard the scrape and clunk of his trunks on the tiles as they were carried to his rooms, but I stayed safely tucked away in mine until dinner was called, and it could no longer be avoided. It was Christmas Eve, and we were to take it early to attend the midnight mass.

'Come, Signora,' Benedetta coaxed me from the dressing table, 'Everyone else is at the table, you keep them waiting.'

'Yes, I am coming directly, but Benedetta, are you certain I am not showing in this dress?' I asked, snatching a final glance in the looking glass at my side profile.

'No, you look bello, now go.'

I took each step with consternation and unnecessary delay. It was difficult to know which disconcerted me the most: the prospect of seeing him again at all or having to endure it under the gaze of such an audience. The whole family had come to stay for the Christmas and Carnavale festivities, including his sisters and their families, an aged aunt and her young godson whom I had never met before today.

'Here she is, said Mr Harper as I looked for my place along the table.

'Buonosera,' I said to all. 'Sorry, I am late.'

'Eleanor, you look beautiful,' said Maria, the eldest of the Harper sisters, 'I have not seen you for so long I hardly recognised you. You are in a great bloom of health,' she said, rising to kiss my cheeks.

I smiled. 'You too look very well, Maria,' I replied, and as I leaned in and glanced across her shoulder, Carlotta looked at me suspiciously, and I pretended not to notice it. She had asked after my pregnancy concerns at intervals since I had left her house all those months ago. I had always told her I had been mistaken, but I knew she had grown less convinced recently.

I headed to my seat without looking in Marco's direction, but then he stood awkwardly as if forced to his feet. 'Eleanor, I hope you are well,' he said, so uneasily I knew I must compensate for his poor effort. 'Marco, you are home', I sang as brightly as I could contrive. I pressed two brief kisses to his cheeks and sat back down. 'I hope your journey was not too treacherous?'

'A little, but I made it in one piece,' he replied, returning to his seat. And I was relieved, for any confusion caused by his clumsy reception had soon been neutralised by mine.

The table broke into conversations all about it in the usual fashion. But I was all asunder inside. The sight of him after so long, the familiar scent of him caught so faintly as our cheeks brushed, it was, for a moment, like he had never gone away. I had to console myself with an inner monologue that pervaded all the conversations I participated in. *No, this does not spell disaster*, I told myself. It is to be expected to be thrown out by a first meeting. It would grow easier now it was done, and most importantly, I had carried it off in adequate style—a narrow rescue, but a rescue all the same.

I repeated these mantras as I sipped on my soup, pretended at my wine glass, wetting little more than my lips by it, and tried to hold the conversations of my neighbours, which I was grateful he was not one of. Though he remained close enough in earshot, so I was careful with my words as I spoke them.

But for all my attempts to avert my eyes from his, to pretend he was not there for the most part—a void in my peripheral vision— there were moments when our eyes caught briefly as I passed along a plate or server at a neighbour's request. We looked away almost instantly each time, yet it would have been better not to see his eyes at all, for they had always had a way of undoing me in their sultry, tawny hues beneath that prominent brow I found so handsome. Yes, he was every bit as handsome as I remembered him, even if less cleanly shaven and his hair a fraction longer than he usually kept it, dark silky tresses hanging level with his square jaw now, not merely at his ear. But even I could not deny this heathen air suited him, made him even more enchanting to my gaze. I forced myself to remember the coldness of his words upon the page that day I realised I would not be going to Padua with him: *"Go fuck your old rich merchant"*, I silently recited, as often as I had to, to moderate the unruly direction of my thoughts.

When I had first received that note, I had gone after Holland-Bury in such a violent fit of fury, thinking he had done it on purpose to set us apart. 'You said you would not tell him!' I screamed, but when he explained all else that had passed that evening, the nude painting I had sat privately for by that academy artist, Serrano's timely arrival and the evidence of the punch he had received from Marco on the nose, I understood he had not been vindictive but pressed into a corner.

'If it's any consolation, when he wrote that note, he had sunk a bottle of brandy and caught not above three hours' sleep. Don't take it harshly; he will regret speaking so as soon as he realises his mistake,' Holland-Bury said when I slammed the note down in front of him.

'What difference does it make? He thinks it, however, he has phrased it,' I replied. And that is what had remained to me ever since: the thoughts, the assumptions that lay behind such ugly words. I held on to them when he caught my eye again and cast my gaze down less patiently to convey my irritation to him. And it seemed to do the trick, for he did not look at me again, or at least I never caught it.

To church, we walked huddled arm in arm, Dante at my left and their aunt's godson, Leandro, to my right, his little mittened hand fidgety as I clutched it. The streets were slippery with frost, but they were walkable with care, and I was mindful to hold tight to him as he tried to wander, attracted to the glistening patches of untrod frost and wanting to skip into them. When Maria came to take over with him, and it was only Dante and I, he turned to me and whispered, 'You're doing well, thank you for your effort.'

'Yes, well, I hardly had a choice with his poor show.'

'I think he is doing not quite so well, Eleanor. Don't be too harsh on him. It has taken everything to get him home, but at least he is here, eh.'

'Yes, you are right. It is worth every trial to see your mother so bright and merry.'

'Well, he always was the favourite, though I never hold it against him, at least not since my tenth birthday.'

I laughed and tapped his hand in reprimand. 'Don't be daft. She has no favourites. She dotes on you just as much, you are the baby, after all.'

'That's what all women say. Is it taught to you in the schoolroom? When you become mothers, you must declare to have no favourites, whether or not you do.'

I laughed out loud quite by accident because his aptitude for accents was always entertaining, and he said this assuming one of an old English stickler, which was very convincing and equally odd, coming from his lips. I could always rely on Dante to cheer me in even the most trying of times, so I kept close to him for the rest of the evening, and it got me through it.

The next day was somewhat trickier, for gifts were exchanged and all the family were at leisure together in the drawing room for most of the day: warming by the fire, playing games of draughts, chess and skittles, exchanging news and memories alike, and I felt like an outsider looking in, however much I was included in it all. It had been made worse by Dante being forced to give me a slightly wider berth today after Carlotta accosted him again with questions over the nature of our acquaintance. 'The good news is,' he said as we pretended over a game of *The New Game of Human Life* in the drawing room, 'that if I am suspected, we are doing a good job of casting eyes away from you and Marco, and the bad news is, I shall have to ease off a fraction since it's a little too close to the truth: right guess, wrong brother,' he teased.

'Yes, you are right. We don't want to raise any such questions more widely. I will be fine, don't worry about me.'

'Well, I should probably spend a little of my time with Marco. I mean, we sat up most of the night, but for appearances, it won't do to seem to be favouring you. It does look suspect if I spend more time at your side when we are under the same roof every day when he has only just returned, and I appear neglectful of him.'

'Of course, I understand perfectly. We must all try to get through this as best we can; that is what matters...how is he, though?'

'I shall tell you precisely as I told him when he asked the same. I shall listen to each of your confidences if you must air them, but I shall keep them in their entirety and will not be pressed in one direction or the other as an intermediary. If you want to know how he is, you shall have to ask him yourself.'

'I suppose it is only fair you are not tugged between us. You said this to him, too?'

'I did, almost word for word.'

'And what did he say?'

'Nice try,' he accused with a teasing finger, 'But you shall have to do much better to catch me off guard.'

'Yes, don't I know it.'

'Look, why don't you just talk to him, ask him how he is? There is no harm in it. You have to keep up appearances somehow because I must confess, it's been a very poor show on both your parts today.'

I sighed. 'I know you are right, but what if he does not want to speak to me and what if I can't speak anything but angry words to him?'

'Well, there is only one way to find out,' he shrugged.

When we finished our game, the second of which I had won in quick succession, he declared he would give us a helping hand, and then he turned about and said, 'I bow out defeated. Perhaps you can better try, brother, come,' he said to Marco, who looked up as startled as I, and came slowly towards us. I could tell instantly from his narrowed gaze in Dante's direction as he grew close, that he did not appreciate it either. But Dante, in his usual breezy attitude, got out of his seat, pressed his brother into it and floated off out of view.

'Do you mind?' Marco asked, settling opposite me now.

'No, not at all,' I said, keeping my gaze levelled at the table. 'Are you any good at *The New Game of Human Life*?'

'Well, I haven't played it since I was eleven, so we shall see.'

'I sense another easy victory,' I said, redistributing the counters. 'Though I suppose it a game of chance, less than skill.'

'I might need a refresher of the rules, I confess,' he said, scanning the fine print in the middle of the board.

'Marco, this is a child's racing game, not Faro,' I reminded him, and we both slipped from our poker-faced rigidity for a moment and a smile crept over our lips.

'Have you been well?' I asked him more seriously once the silence grew too cumbersome.

'I manage,' he said, '...better than before. I would ask you the same, but it seems you have never been better.'

'I also manage, Marco,' I replied, spinning the teetotum.

'Look, since we are forced into conversation and I have wanted so much to say this for the longest time...'

I felt anxious at his words, flashed him a warning glance not to charge ahead so hastily in front of such an audience when we were both still stumbling our way through, but he did not heed me.

'...I have longed to tell you I am sorry for the note I sent you. It was vile and repugnant to me to have spoken so and to you. I have not escaped the shame of the memory for a single minute.'

I busied myself by moving my counter from *the infant* as he spoke, then looked up when I landed on *The Darling*. 'Well, I appreciate the apology. Your move,' I said, gesturing at the teetotum and watching him drop his gaze and pick it up in those strong hands that had once caressed me so tenderly it was painful to remember it. And this is why I did not want to really accept his apology, however earnestly spoken, however rightfully smarting and overdue, for I needed that spark of rage to keep blazing inside me, to stay alight just enough to protect me from any lapse in my defences. For I could not falter again, having been dropped from such a height and survived to tell the tale. But I knew I would have to take care to avoid him if I was not to be so breached, for he was always of an earnest speaking nature, but I was in no head to suffer one of his candid but eloquently set speeches. Too much engagement at that level of intimacy now was only a threat to my sanity, and so I continued in the game, suppressing his attempts to delve beyond the superficial, diverting them at each turn as we played on. And when he landed on the *Good Father*, at precisely the moment I felt the babe stir within me, I thought I might break down entirely and not even make it to the end of this stupid children's board game. And yet was it so very stupid, the way the celestial bodies aligned and chance spun you in and out of its race with the stochasticity of the teetotum. How much really was a case of providence or of skill...

When the game was finally over and he declared the winner, I was only relieved it was done with, and I was at last at liberty to excuse myself and accept gracefully my defeat. I returned to my chamber for the remainder of the afternoon on account that I was tired from our late return home from mass the previous night and needed a nap to refresh me before dinner. But I did not sleep and could not settle to anything, not the book I was reading, not the baby dresses I had secretly begun sewing in undisturbed private moments, not the diary I had filled since the time of his departure, or my outstanding correspondence. I was not to have any respite from the thoughts looping in my head at every turn.

So, in the end, I lay upon the bed staring up into the pelmet and gave in to them. Let myself recall his image to mind, allowed myself to remember what we had once been to each other, and tried very hard to take the view of the bystander looking in, much as I had felt today amongst the family. Not too close, but just close enough not to be absent.

I had used to be so good at that game, my early life had schooled me so perfectly in its art, and I had recovered much of its finesse lately, needing to straddle the divergent paths between my life amongst the Harpers and my secret life with "the rich old merchant" I was fucking. And yet, it was so much harder to contrive for far less yield than it had once so effortlessly provided for. I called upon it now to save me, to get me through this next fortnight until Marco returned to Padua and all could settle back as it was once again.

And then, in the thick of all these thoughts, Dante came into me and I sat up, moved over for him on the bed as we often assumed, backs against the headboard, talking until late.

'So the game went *that* badly then,' he said, patting my knee.

'Why do you say that?'

'God, you are so smooth. I shall have to take care about you,' he teased, tapping a finger to his temple.

'It takes one to know one, I heard it said.'

He grinned. 'Well, it was a simple equation: you up and leaving, added to Marco's sour face, equals a hashed-up attempt to break the ice. I'm sorry. I thought it might help if you both got over the worst of it. It seems I was mistaken, or at least premature.'

'You are not to blame for that, Dante, though as for setting up the scene, I shall not deny I wanted to clump you for it.'

He stuck out his chin to invite it, 'That's fair, I suppose. I deserve it. Go on, take your shot.'

I nudged him with my shoulder, 'I shan't smack you even though you deserve it!'

'Well, you must be contemplative if you give up the opportunity. Is it really so terrible that he is returned?'

'Yes! No. I don't know...but it is hard, harder than I knew it would be.'

'Is there no hope of at least some return to your former friendship, I mean, not all the gooey stuff, but before that?'

'I cannot see how it would be possible after so much.' Then I thought of Sheldon and how we had recovered beyond my expectations. I had even written to him for news of his wedding and received a reply only a few weeks ago. 'I don't know. Maybe it will be possible in time, but I don't think enough has passed yet.'

'Well, it's better than a flat-out, no, I suppose, so I'll take that.'

'Well, so long as you don't take it to him.'

'I told you, I shan't play the pawn between you. But I do hope to encourage you both towards a little greater sense.'

'Ah, now I understand from whence his apology came, from your encouragement.'

'That required no encouragement on my part, and that is the most you shall have from me, so hush those luscious lips with your questions—are you wearing rouge upon them?'

I closed my open mouth then said, 'None of your business.'

'Nice. Subtle but effective.'

'Oh, and what do you suppose I am trying to effect?'

He shrugged. 'I wouldn't dare to suppose, but then I am not the right kind of audience, am I?' he teased, '…though even I can see why a fellow's eyes might just pop out of his head at the sight of you these past couple of days.'

'Oh, can you? Well then, it is a compliment, but do not let your sister catch you admiring my décolletage, or we might be suspected of a very scandalous affair, especially if you are discovered here in my chamber with me.'

'That is a good point.'

We often toyed like this, now there were no secrets between us anymore, not his greatest or my most depraved. It had been the glue that had resealed our fraying friendship in the early days of Marco's departure. It had come out quite by accident at first, but when he realised I was not casting it as an insult but taking the position of an ally, it drew us even closer than before. I understood the loneliness in bearing such secrets as could not be shared with the wider world, nor even your closest kin, and I was happy to play that part in his life now his greatest ally was gone. He missed Marco as much as I did. I knew that. But I hoped I'd proved something of a substitute and support for him in that area of his life, holding his confidences and giving him counsel when he sought it. It was, after all, on my account he must miss him at all. But it had been nice to be able to offer something back in return for all Dante had given to me. He was the dearest thing to me in Venice now and the one I dreaded leaving behind. He promised he would visit me in England, held me to taking him to *The Mermaid* when he did, and insisted he must know his niece or nephew since no one else could. At least, not if his attempts to persuade me to tell Marco about the child continued to fail.

'He has a right to know of his own child, Eleanor. No matter what has passed between you, I know you understand that. I know you are not cruel. I know your heart. Even if you are particularly expert at creating chaos, I know you understand what is right and wrong in the world better than most,' he said in one of his more persuasive speeches.

'Maybe one day, Dante, but the dust must have time to settle before I can think of such things.'

'You know he would be a good father. Do not deny him that because of your differences.'

These words haunted me often because I did know it. It was, in fact, because I knew it, I must ensure that any trace of romantic feeling between us was entirely extinguished before I ever told him. I did not want to complicate things beyond what they already were. If I told him too soon, he would perhaps have a turn of heart directed towards playing that role in the life of our child, and I did not want to tie him down it that way if my heart was still open to him, for then I would forget myself and give in to it, always knowing he was tied to me because of the child. If, however, I waited until we were both fully recovered and strong enough to separate the two, I hoped one day it might be possible to write to him and tell him the truth. Give him the chance to know his child if he so wished. By then, I would hope to be comfortably settled in my own life, so he need feel no obligation to try to protect us. If he saw me well established and his child well provided for, he would not need to feel concerned at his absence. I was to return to England with enough money to establish a modest home now I had been in Signor's service for some months. It would not last forever, and the currency exchange still yielded poorly against British prices, but I would return with enough to start with. But, regardless, one day, I must heed those words and honour his right to know—just not this one.

CHAPTER FORTY-THREE

Frostbite.

Eleanor. January 1823.

'Marco, will you ride with Eleanor? There is not room enough in the boat for us all, and Leandro is set on having his uncle Dante carry him,' said Maria as we queued in the piano lobby, waiting to board with the others. We knew it would take us four Gondolas to convey such a large party to the ballroom at *La Fenice*, where we were headed today for the final festivities before the family returned to their respective homes. But whenever else we had travelled to some Carnevale festival or feast, I had always relied on Dante to pair up with me. And it seemed that was the problem.

Though we had joked about Carlotta's misplaced suspicions, neither of us had seriously considered it a threat of late, with Marco's recent absence and knowing full well how ridiculous a notion it was. But the fact remained that she did not, and it seemed she had not kept her thoughts to herself. For now, her older sister was joining her in her efforts to divide Dante and I whenever possible; interrupting us when we sat together at dinner or in the drawing room, more lately, even following us to our chambers to try to catch us out. Of course, we knew it would result in nothing but disappointment to their investigative efforts, but it had a very unhappy complication: in dividing us, they always contrived to pair Marco and I together to settle the imbalance.

I understood the logic as it must have appeared to them. Marco and I were little disposed to spending above a brief exchange together, and so we were judged safe to be pressed together, whereas Dante and I were always found squirrelled away in some corner of the room, laughing, funning and whispering. We had grown more cautious these past weeks, but it seemed the damage had been done in his sisters' minds, and now they were at the point of shameless intervention.

I settled into the boat opposite Marco with a deep sense of foreboding. Despite our growing more familiar with this routine of being forced into closer proximity lately, we had always been in the direct company of the rest of the party, at the dining table or about the house, not beneath the covered felze of our own gondola with the oarsmen stationed outside our snug compartment.

'You will forgive my sisters, I hope. They are not usually so meddlesome, but I am sure Dante has told you the notions that they have in their heads,' he said once we settled inside.

Snowflakes landed softly on the window pane as we shifted through the frost-sprinkled water and followed the entourage. 'Yes, wrong brother, ironically,' I said, and his eyes flashed at this reference.

'Well, perhaps that is to serve as a blessing, even if poor Dante must suffer their interrogations. I hope you have not been subject to them?'

'Not many, and they have been brief.'

'Well, not much longer, and our party will return to its usual size, and we shall all be spared the inconvenience.'

'That's what this is to you, an inconvenience?' I said, inwardly chastising myself for picking an argument with him on our first plain-speaking opportunity.

'I did not mean that, I meant—'

I glanced away and sighed. 'It's alright. I know what you meant. Forgive me. I am being difficult and I do not mean to be.'

There was an uncomfortable pause before he spoke again, his voice hesitant. 'It is actually a relief to have the opportunity to talk to you in private after so long.'

'Well, we shall have the journey there and back, no doubt. Take your chance now before you are gone again,' I said so clumsily I wished I had not opened my mouth at all. 'Sorry, I am finding this very difficult and making quite a hash of it.'

'It's alright, it is not easy to find the words, is it?'

'I suppose it depends on what we want to say to each other.'

'Well, for my part, I want to say sorry, Eleanor, truly,' he peered at me, his expression contrite. 'Just because things ended badly for us, I had no right to speak to you like that.'

'We all say things in the heat of anger, I know that. But those words have carried with me for so long, I am not sure so belated an apology will erase them from my mind. Forgive me, but it is the truth.'

He bowed his head, a slow, solemn nod. Then he looked up again and said, 'I hope one day they may fade from your mind, and you might remember instead some of the kinder words that passed between us.'

'I hope so, too.'

'You do?' he echoed, brows raised.

'Yes, I don't want to be at odds with you forever, Marco. We are adults and must learn to overcome our differences for the sake of civility.'

'I had hoped for the sake of something more sacred than that.'

I would not meet his eyes and only nodded. 'So, when do you return to Padua?'

'I am not sure. I was supposed to leave last Monday, but I am told the snow is falling too fast in the region, and the roads remain difficult. I would chance the river route if it were not for the fact that it, too, will be frozen over in places.'

'It is a harsh winter here. I own, I had not expected it to be so bad as home, given how hot it is for the rest of the year.'

'Yes, they are not much warmer here, not the winters, only shorter, I find.'

'Well, that I am counting on.'

'Yes, I suppose you mean to resume your travel plans too when it is over.'

'You suppose it, or Dante has told you as much?'

He shrugged. 'Does it matter?'

'Yes, it does to me.'

'Well, in that case, I forced it out of him.'

'Oh? Well, my attempts have been met with stealth,' I said without meaning to, and we looked at each other, half amusement, half awkward.

'So you mean to go before Giles returns? Do you think he will remain away as long as that?'

'I know he shall.'

'I see,' he said stiffly, and I knew he understood the reference. 'Well, I am glad, for your sake, I mean. His absence suits you very well.'

And what of yours? I wanted to say, but I did not. I only smiled and asked, 'How is Padua? I assume you are well settled there now.'

'It is lonely, but it has been necessary. And I have my work to keep me occupied, which at least has been productive. I expect to have the makings of a new exhibition close to completion by the time I return to Venice.'

'And when will that be?'

'I'm not certain yet,' he admitted, his gaze cast to the floor.

But we both knew the answer: whenever I was gone from the place. And so I supposed he deserved a more specific indication of when that might be. 'I hope to go home in March. I am told the Alps too treacherous before, though it is dependent on the timing of spring as to whether it will be the earlier or latter end I make my departure.'

'The latter, I would suspect, in my experience, at least. So you have given up the idea of sailing back and mean to go by road?'

'Yes, I was never fond of sea journeying, as you know, and now I have the means to avoid it, I shall. Of course, there will be the packet at Calais, but at least it is a matter of hours, not weeks, and I am told we might go by steam now and hasten the affair.'

'You have made arrangements then?'

'I have hired the services of a vetturino to take care of those, as well as a guard with a pistol, and a footman. That is as far as I have progressed. I had hoped to convince Benedetta to go with me, but I don't think I have done a very good job of selling England to her. So it seems I must find myself a new maidservant, too. Though how I shall ever find one even half as good as she, I do not know.'

'Well, it's a promising start,' he said, his gaze drifting to the window. 'Venetians are funny like that and have a fancy not to venture too far from home. And I suppose there is always Giacomo to think of.' A shadow crossed his face. 'She likely won't want to leave him behind.'

'Well, I hope I might find one that will not mind venturing.'

'I'm sure it will all work out.'

What, like everything else has for me? 'So, what have you been painting? What will be the theme of this new exhibition? I am sorry I shall miss it.'

'Oh, it's all still very provisional, though it is a mixture of scenes and portraits, so something a little more out of the ordinary for me.'

I was surprised at this. 'Perhaps diversifying is a good thing. Have you brought any of your work with you?'

'No, there seemed little point in lugging so much back for the sake of a fortnight, though I did not expect to have time on my hands waiting for snow storms to clear.'

'I suppose not, but you always have what you need in the attic should you get stuck here in the snow for much longer.—I mean, hopefully not, but just in case.'

'Yes, I must remember to go up there and have a little tidy up. I usually cover everything to spare it from dust and mould at this season, but I overlooked it when I left.'

You overlooked a great deal more than that on leaving. 'It's already done. I mean, I hope I did not take liberties in so doing, but Holland-Bury mentioned it, and so I had Benedetta find me some covers, and I did what I could.'

'Thank you,' he said surprised. 'You have seen much of George then?'

I checked his expression for signs of hostility but only gleaned discomfort. 'No, very little,' I said cautiously, not wanting *that* matter to resurface now. 'I see him only at classes, and I have only lately resumed them, so—'

'I am glad you have not given them up entirely.'

'So am I. I still have a lot of idle time in my day to fill, and it is nice to fill it with something...' I wanted to say: something that reminds me of you, '...something creative.'

'Yes, certainly. I have always found it to prove good medicine.'

I bit my lip. 'You are much missed at the classes, you know, by the other ladies, I mean,' I corrected myself.

He searched my expression before saying, 'Yes, George did mention that. I daresay if I am still stranded by the time classes resume next week, I should show my face. I certainly expect George will be on my case petitioning a longer break from the undertaking.'

'You have not seen him then?'

'Not yet. I came directly to *Ca' Rosetti*, but we write often.'

'Presumably more pleasant exchanges than the one you left for me.' I could not resist it, yet I regretted it instantly, having done so well to temper myself.

He cast his eyes down to his hands which were resting upon his knees, then, after a pause, looked up. 'Eleanor, it was not easy for me to forgive George his part, you know.'

I sighed. 'To be sure, only easier than it was to forgive me mine.'

'Yes, it's true, I don't deny it. To George, vice is a kind of lifeblood, and the female sex is his weakness. The very fact he refused you at all and held fast to his loyalties to me was proof enough of his affection. I only wished he had told me right away, for maybe then,' his voice trailed off momentarily. 'That has been the hardest obstacle to my forgiveness. But I have since realised he was not to know I would break my vow to resist you, so how can I blame him for what I could not then foresee?'

'At least you are honest.'

A flash of irritation crossed his features. 'Unlike you, you mean?'

'I have never been more candid with anyone before, Marco!' I exclaimed, a tremor of injury colouring my tone. 'I meant to tell you all, but you never gave me the chance to explain my side; you just fled...' I swallowed hard, gulping down angry tears that tried to rush forth, determined to maintain my composure. 'And that is what hurts above all else, you didn't even *ask* for my side—'

'Are you saying it's not true?' he demanded, his voice edged with accusation. 'Do you say you did not accost him like a cheap Meretrice, the very thing you claimed not to be? Do you say you honoured your intention not to sign with Serrano? Do you say you are not still fucking him now?'

I dropped my gaze to my lap. 'No. I do not deny any of the charges—'

He pushed his hair from his face and sighed. 'Then what difference would it have made anyway?'

'I don't know. Perhaps it would not have altered anything. I only hoped you might have sought my reasoning, and then you may have better understood.'

'I understand perfectly.'

'Oh, well, enlighten me?'

'No, I shan't be drawn into this.'

'You are already drawn into this! You cannot absent yourself from your own part! You think just because you have leave to run away and hide, you are not part of this? You did not contribute to the creation of this mess? Well, you did, so tell me: what do you understand so well that it was worth abandoning everything we had for?'

'That you are a whore!' he shouted, a temporary lapse in restraint before catching himself and saying more moderately, 'It's who you are now. I cannot change it, and maybe neither could you. But the fact remains, and I cannot live like that, Eleanor. I wanted *all* of you, not to share you.'

'Oh, now that's amusing, you seduce a married woman and expect not to have to share her?'

'No. I never meant to seduce you, I never meant to let my feelings grow for you, I tried to restrain them—'

'And I never *meant* to be reduced to whoring myself out...and yet the fact remains.'

'I am not proud of it, Eleanor.'

'And you think me proud of what I have become?'

He shook his head. 'If your marriage had had a chance, but a glimmer of hope, I would have suffered my feelings in silence for the rest of my days. But it had none, and that knowing weakened my resolve, eroded all I believed would protect me from the risk. And protect you from the risk.'

'I didn't want protection from your love, I wanted protection from your judgement! From the moral double standard you prize so dearly!'

'You think I judge you, but it is not that. I could have forgiven you for what you, in desperate circumstances, believed to be a way out. I could have forgiven you for not coming to ask for help in a house of strangers whom you did not know you could trust to begin with. I could have even forgiven you for seeing an easier way out with George after a time,' he explained, each word heavy with the weight of disappointment. 'But what haunts me in all, is that you did not have to accept Serrano's offer, and yet still you did. Still you go to him now.'

I was stunned for a moment, reading the pain in his eyes. 'I did not want you to suffer for my debt, raising loans on my behalf and risking all you had worked for, for me...'

'And yet for the esteem and value I hold you in, I would have lost any amount, any endeavour, to maintain your dignity and set you free of that path. You are worth more than riches! And yet it seems you cannot see it.' He shook his head slowly in despair. 'I could have recovered the loss of the money. It would have been a willing price to pay instead of having to live with the images in my head of you being so used and degraded.'

I could no longer contain my tears, so I pushed through them: 'I did not think you were coming back. I did not think it mattered. I only signed to settle with Signora Crivelli, and then I planned to leave. I never meant to honour the contract.'

'And now, Eleanor? Now you have your coach and horses booked, why do you still do it?'

I spoke through gritted teeth, 'Because I will not rest until Giles has suffered and lost the way that *I* have suffered and lost. *That* is why I do it now. The *sole* reason I endure it. Because I have withstood worse for far less profit...at least now I might be able to say that it was all worth it.'

His eyes widened with surprise. 'You value revenge over love?'

'No, I value revenge when love is already lost.'

'And you are certain that it is?'

I wiped my face and cast him a questioning gaze. *Could I dare ask?* But before I could reply, Giacomo tapped upon the cover of the Felze.

'I think we arrive,' Marco said, squinting to see out of the window, and we both straightened up to ready ourselves to rejoin the family.

Had that been the extent of our being forced together, I suppose I would have deemed it at least a much-needed opportunity for catharsis and not a complete disaster. But when we arrived at the *Sala Grande*, to the party already in progress, it seemed we were both to be disappointed by any hopes to escape such tensions as we had just endured when the dances were called and we were encouraged to participate in them.

'Oh, I am not minded to dance,' I told Isabella as she ushered me into accepting her husband's offer. Which I had not minded, but had foreseen the danger of agreeing to dance at all ahead of even that. But all were engaged, and it seemed I must not let the family down, and so I gave into encouragement and by the end of the first set, I had danced all the way through with Mr Harper, each of the Harper sister's husbands, a cousin I was introduced to by Carlotta to prevent me accepting Dante's offer, and someone Maria introduced me to in the fastest style I was almost too embarrassed to proceed in it. But like all else, I did.

Marco and Dante had been forced to pair with their sisters and mother for a set, and some other women I did not know. Yet, we were none of us merry for it. Marco and I stumbling over our internal struggles as well as our steps, and Dante being quite aggressively launched in front of anyone's nose his sisters could contrive. I could only be grateful that in all the scheming, Marco had not asked me, and I had been spared that one test of resolve. Or at least it seemed possible we might. But when Dante came to me in the interval and begged me to dance the remaining sets with him before his sisters had him at risk of some poor woman expecting a proposal from him by the end of the night, I gave in and set myself up for the thing I had most tried to avoid.

'You are a very good dancer, Eleanor,' Carlotta accosted us, snatching Dante up as we returned from our set to take a brief sip, '...but it is very selfish of my brother to keep you to himself!' she said pointedly and turned about, 'Marco, you will dance the next with Eleanor, won't you?' she asked. But it was not a question.

'I—' Marco stuttered.

'Of course, you will,' she told him and as good as pushed us both together and steered us to the dance floor. I had always admired the Venetian ladies' fiery spirit, but right now, I wanted to strangle her.

'I'm sorry,' he said as he leaned into a bow. 'They have become quite impossible tonight, they must truly think a real danger exists.'

It did *now*, I thought, as I dipped my curtsey and we stepped into line. *You can do this, Eleanor; it is but a dance* I willed myself.

I did not know the dances so well here. Even where I recognised the music, the sequence of the steps was always somewhat different than I knew them to be at home. Some of the offerings had been merry like country dances, but most had been more sedate or in the style of the German waltz, which still raised hackles in England but seemed to have no such effect here. I supposed it was the Austrian influence, and I did not know what to expect as the orchestra led us in and I readied to follow the example of the other dancers on the floor. Aside from not anticipating the steps, it was the threat of touch I feared the most and hoped to avoid. So far, we had evaded that chiefly, though I had still not entirely recovered from the memory of our cheeks briefly grazing in our welcome at the table on Christmas Eve, or the scent of him I had caught in that stiff exchange. I did not want to be plagued by any other such memories tonight, so I hoped we would not need to grow too close during the course of this set.

It started off so very slowly in a series of bows and curtseys in neat rows, followed by a brief spell of promenade steps that at first allowed me the confidence to think it a more communal dance. Then we progressed as often we might, turning in circles, needing only to press our gloved palms lightly together as we spun towards each other and out to the rest of the audience. There was a charge in even this the first time I felt his glove pressed warm against mine, but it seemed we had unanimously agreed to evade eye contact, and it soon became less startling as we repeated the step.

But then a variation I was not expecting, drew us hands clasped above our heads and the others resting at each other's waists, and I almost pulled back as if from a burning flame. But he recovered our pose, drew me in again, and we were left facing each other, and I soon began to recognise the steps he led me in and realised these were taking us into the Viennese Waltz. *No, of all the dances*, I considered, as we split from the communal pattern and formed into entirely distinct pairs now, hands pressed, waists supported. *Too close.* Then we slowly began to whirl, breaking briefly by reverse turns before the pace picked up, and I did not know what was spinning faster, my body or my mind.

It was easier to start with, to concentrate solely on the steps. The slow waltz was most common at home, and I had not danced the faster waltz often, so as the rhythm accelerated, I tried to remember my footing and how to keep pace, counting in my head as we traversed a corner and overtook another pair of dancers. But once my feet had found the cadence, I had nothing to distract myself with, and I let my eyes find his, which perhaps would not have been so testing had his not been seeking mine at the very same moment.

We stared briefly, then turned in the other direction with the shift of the music and then back again as we faced each other more squarely and caught our gaze yet again, daring to hold it a beat longer this time. But by the time the music reached its crescendo and we grew breathless, spinning and turning so quickly, we seemed to have given up entirely in trying to break our stare, and now it was only the dance that caused it to lapse or break at all. And once we were square again, we found each other effortlessly and grew ever more reluctant to disrupt it for the shifts in the dance, trying to hold on to its intensity as the movement became more and more an irritation, an unwelcome intruder in our smouldering exchange.

Oh, Marco, I cannot take this, I wanted to say. How can you grow more enchanting after all this time away? After so much enmity has come between us. And still, you suspend me in this awestruck condition, and I do not want to fall prey to it now. In fact, I cannot afford to, and I want so much to go now. *Might this be over soon?* And yet my eyes, I knew, betrayed something different, for he too looked mesmerised, and when at last we finally completed the closing steps, he did not release my hand when he was supposed to and I had to pull away to remind him. When we offered our final parting bow and curtsey, we were both altered, and we knew it.

If Carlotta had an ounce of sense, after watching that, she would have put me in the boat with Dante rather than Marco. Though alas, she seemed to either have failed to notice or had misunderstood, for we were pressed to suffer the same fate as the boats were loaded to go home.

But this time, when we settled back into the gondola, it was more difficult to face than before, where I had hoped it would grow easier for our muddling through it on the journey here. But even all that had been undone now, and I did not know how to sit, where to look, what to say as we were faced with the silent proximity of each other after such a charged disruption as we had endured. Our senses still heightened, fragile from their forced awakening, the music still reeling in my head, the heat of our gaze still smouldering in my memory even as my breath fogged before me. For where before I had not known if he sensed it, I believed we were both now fully aware of the danger we were in.

'Are you alright?' he asked me eventually, and I dared to look at him.

'I do not think so,' I confessed, suppressing the urge to weep, my voice cracking over the words.

He offered out a hand and when I took it, he squeezed it gently and did not let it go. I did not want him to, either. 'You are cold; you are shivering,' he said, taking the blanket from behind his seat and pressing it over my lap. 'I don't want to unsettle you, and yet I think we have both been so affected.'

I nodded. 'It isn't your fault. We neither wanted to be forced into such a situation.'

'You didn't?'

'You did?' I frowned, then settled back into the rapture of his contemplative gaze, and this time, there was no music to rely upon, no change of step to disrupt it.

'I confess I am not very fond of dancing, but I could grow to be if that is how it should be done.'

'I thought you a very good dancer, and I am very fond of it in ordinary circumstances, but...'

'Our circumstances are anything but ordinary, I think.'

I dropped my gaze to our hands, which remained still entwined. It seemed surreal to see them so, as if I were looking at a hand that did not belong to me, though it was very much attached to my arm, my senses.

'Do you want me to release you?' he asked, noticing the direction of my stare and drawing my eyes back up to him.

I shook my head. 'I should, but I do not.'

'I should not want to come and sit beside you, but I do,'

I tugged lightly on his hand by way of invitation. He understood it, crossed the space between us, and I shuffled over to make room for him, our hands releasing now through the necessity of movement but finding their way back together as we rearranged ourselves.

'Eleanor, are you alright?'

'Marco, I am frightened.'

'Of me?'

'No, of what you make me feel.'

'I, too, am afraid of the same…but I hope we are not past caring for each other to the extent that we may not learn to be kinder in our dealings?'

'No, I care for you still.'

'Then that is perhaps more than I suspected, though it brings me relief to hear it. I have missed our friendship above all else, and I have wondered since I got here if *that* might still be salvageable—'

'I would like it to be, eventually.'

'Then might we try to return on better terms than we have managed until now? Perhaps without so many prying eyes to satisfy, it might prove easier to try at being more like ourselves.'

I nodded, 'It has been a great deal of pressure to manage under the weight of so much company, and yet now we are without it, I don't quite know what to trust.'

'I know, and it is understandable. I do not attempt to try to seduce you or repeat the errors of our past, so I hope you may take some little comfort in that. But I have watched with great envy as you and Dante grow so fast in your friendship. I long to know if we can grow towards something like it once again.'

'I never want to kiss Dante, nor he I, and I think that makes it all the more conducive to being easy with each other.'

'Yes, there is that,' he laughed a little, '… and maybe we can never enjoy that level of comfort and ease, but I do recall we were once very comfortable together, or at least it seems so, relative to this.'

'Well, it is not difficult to draw the contrast with everything so frigid between us now, and yet…'

'What?'

'It is like the colder things feel between us, the more I long to be held by you and feel the warmth of you, not indecently, I mean, but—' and then he broke free of my grasp, lifted his arm above our heads and gathered me into him.

'Is that better?' he asked.

Do not cry. 'Yes, yes, it is.' And I let myself lean entirely into him, resting my face against the chest I still remembered every bare detail of and heard the thumping heartbeat I had grown to find such comfort in the rhythm of, and at last, it felt like I had finally stepped in from the cold.

CHAPTER FORTY-FOUR

Inquisition.

Marco. January 1823.

M arco felt a tug at his sleeve and turned about as they said their goodnights and departed to their prospective floors. Carlotta was behind him, hissing, pulling strained faces and frowns that seemed to indicate she wanted a word but did not want to have to ask for it in the presence of their parents, who had still not arrived at their chamber along the hall.

He knew, as he conceded and held back in the landing, what this would be about and was reluctant to entertain his sister's complaints any further. But then he *knew* his sister and thought better of it, for Dante's sake.

'Alright, Carlotta. What is it now?' he said with an impatient sigh, keeping his voice low as she began to raise her hands in excited gestures.

'What is it? Are you blind? Did you not see them tonight? And you tell me there is nothing to be concerned with. They cannot be kept apart! He takes no interest in the other women, only her.'

'Carlotta, you know it is often said that we see what we mean to see.'

'Oh, yes, it's all in my mind. Well, tell me then why she is hiding her pregnancy?'

He stepped back, 'What?'

'Oh, you think I am imagining that, too? Well, a woman understands these things, knows the changes in a pregnant body. You have not noticed the swell of her breasts, the glow of her skin, or how fast her hair has grown?'

'An improvement in health is hardly proof of what you claim. She's taking care of herself at last, and it has left its mark upon her after so many months. It was long overdue.'

'Oh, you men know nothing!'

Tilting his head with concern, he lowered his voice and asked, 'Have you spoken to Eleanor about your suspicions?'

'Yes.'

'And what did she say?'

'Well, she denies it, of course. How can she confess when her husband has been away so long that it will raise questions about its fathering? And where will that lead, hmm? To revealing the child is Dante's!'

He laughed now at the irony and wished he could put his sister's mind at ease and explain that Dante was never going to be justly blamed for impregnating anyone. But this was precisely why Dante had never trusted his sisters with his most guarded secret. If this was their response to them thinking him angling at Eleanor, what lengths might they go to to correct his ways if they knew what his private life *really* comprised of?

'How can you find it funny, Marco? Your brother will be disgraced when this gets out and it will, because she can only hide it for so long, and she must have been hiding it for five months at least. Soon, it will be beyond a joke and no one will be laughing if we do not do something about it.'

He counted back in his head. 'Why do you think her five months progressed?'

'Because when Dante brought her to my house with those excuses, just before Giles beat her, I asked her why she had come, and she said she feared she might be pregnant and wanted to keep Giles from her bed, for he was brutal and he might disturb the early pregnancy. She had already lost one child and did not want to increase the risk. So I asked her again some weeks later, and she said she had been mistaken, that her courses had returned and some irregularity must have accounted for it, but I knew she was lying.'

It seemed not quite so funny now. 'And how does that make the child Dante's, even if it's true? She is a married woman, and you said yourself she suspected it whilst Giles was still about?'

'I just know it, Marco, a gut feeling. And I know you have been away and not seen so much, but they are always together, more than before you left. Mama says they sit up together late and pair on every occasion, and you have seen them whispering in corners for the last few weeks. I believe Dante brought her to my house because Giles was onto something between them, and maybe that's the reason he really beat her. And now he is gone, they have been released of the need to take care and have grown reckless in their abandon.'

'Look, I don't know if you are right about Eleanor's condition, but I do know my brother, Carlotta, and it has nothing to do with him, I assure you.'

'Please, Marco, I know you are close, and you will naturally defend him, but will you talk to him? Make him see sense. Please?'

'Fine, I will talk to him, Carlotta, but enough now in hounding him, alright? It will not get you anywhere. Leave the rest to me.'

She nodded, and Marco bid her goodnight and trod the path to his chamber, almost dizzy with astonishment. He held the walls to steady himself as he walked. *Eleanor, pregnant? No*, she would not hide it, not from him, or at least, not from Dante. He changed direction and headed to his brother's room.

'Dante, is she pregnant?'

Dante stiffened as he hung his jacket upon the back of a chair. 'Who are we talking about?' he said, turning around.

'Eleanor, who else?'

'Then, I don't know why you are asking me, for *I* am not *her*.'

'I cannot ask her that. Dante, do you know?'

'I told you, brother, I won't be a pawn.'

'This is serious, god dammit!'

'Not so serious you are not at her chamber demanding answers. Look, I have already had a bad enough night covering for the pair of you and taking the brunt of everyone's suspicions. I'm getting tired of it now. Either talk to her yourself or go back to Padua and stop boxing my ears. I'm going to bed now. I am tired.'

His lack of denial made Marco suspect it must be true, and if it was, there was only one reason his brother was keeping it from him: to prevent hurting him with the truth. Which meant either the child could not be his, or she did not know who had fathered it for the abundance of possibilities to choose from. Giles? Serrano? Some other wretch who spilt his seed for a few sovranos before she parted with the abbess.

Oh god, just when he had begun to think there might be something left to salvage. But if she was carrying someone else's child he would never be able to look at her the same again, maybe not look at her again at all. He should go home tomorrow, come snow or sleet or frozen rivers. He could not suffer any more torment than he had already struggled to come to terms with. It was bad enough she had not given up Serrano or taken the hint that if she would, there remained hope for them, if she still wanted him. He could spell it out no clearer. He would have to wait and see what she favoured the most, what she chose this time: love or revenge. But if this was true, if she was carrying around some other man's issue, there was no point in hoping at all because that was beyond even his capacity for forbearance. How could he bury her past and meet her in the present if she was to carry around a constant reminder of her indiscretions? He had reasoned that there might be a chance of her giving Serrano up after their exchange tonight, but even if she did, would it matter now?

He would have to find a way to ask her, but he knew a direct approach would fail and might even send her running off earlier than she planned to. She was still so hurt and angry, it might take more time and opportunity for her to vent her fury before she was willing to make confessions of that nature, especially when he had lost her faith in the trying.

Her confessions had been important to her; her ability to go through with them had surprised her, and he saw how she struggled in the effort, even if blinded then by his own struggle. He had lost her trust in running off twice now after learning the truth. Why would she give him a third shot at it... and how could he promise not to run again if it was the news he feared it to be? If she was to tell him at all, he would have to build bridges with her and be patient, and he could not do that if he was in Padua. He sighed and sunk onto his bed, still fully clothed.

And what if there was a remote chance, however small, that he might be about to become a father and she set off back to England as she planned to? No, he could not live without knowing. He must stay and find the truth, whatever it was, whatever the outcome.

CHAPTER FORTY-FIVE

Snow Storms Clearing.

Eleanor. January 1823.

T he return of the house to its normal dimensions did, of course, prove the relief we had all been looking to. Though it also provided much more time for us to fill, so many more words for us to find, and whilst we had certainly broken the ice between us now, it remained difficult to move past the surface level of conversation for all our efforts.

It had been better before when Dante was amongst us. But although the Carnavale celebrations had still not entirely ceased in Venice, he too had returned to the shipyard now with his father, which left us either in contrived performance with Isabella, or uncomfortable solitude when she was elsewhere. We no longer even had the disruption of Giles to fear. So these instances became so marked with opportunity that we were often too frightened to remain in each other's company at all and build the bridges we had hoped to that night in the gondola, where we spoke in earnest and held each other in even greater sincerity. But we had not seemed able to return to such a state of intimacy, and I had longed to every moment since. But I seemed always to run contrary to my actual inclination now, as if it could not be trusted.

When he offered me to paint with him, I found an excuse to decline, though I would have done it just to be with him. When he asked me if I would like to play a game of cards at the table, I declined for fear of getting lost in his eyes and forgetting the game entirely. And so I inhabited a world of opposites where I intervened to separate myself constantly from all that I longed for, and in the end, he stopped asking, and I fell dissolute. Which was why, when I readied for my class, and he told me that he would be taking it and that I could travel with him in his boat if I wanted to, I forced my longing and my answer into union.

'Yes, if you do not mind, I would be grateful for your escort,' I told him, and I pleased myself as much as he, I thought, as he smiled at me from time to time and complimented me on my dress and how I was wearing my hair. It felt nice to grow used to seeing him again and feeling his presence about the house, and yet every day, I expected him to announce his return to Padua, so I did my utmost to try not to grow too attached to his presence.

It was still frosty outside, but the worst of the snow had cleared now, and I wondered if there was any further reason to delay his return. At times, I hoped he would just go and get it over with. At others like this, I hoped he might never leave again. And this divergence of mind, hope, and spirit had become a growing burden, as had my realisation that now the family festivities were over, Serrano would have returned from his trip to *Palermo,* and there would likely be a note waiting for me at the Bottega. I would have to go there on my way home, remember not to agree to return in the boat with him, for I did not want to dangle this matter in front of him when I knew now how sensitive he was about Serrano. I would have to take greater care until he left, for even though I always had to exercise care about the family, the secret was no longer so well kept in other circles. I attended him at private parties and dinners, en masque at the theatre, heavily veiled on occasional boat rides to one of his other houses. He had offered to establish me in one of them in Giudecca, an opulent and well-staffed palazzo, but I had declined and opted for our making use of one of his disused casinos in Venice, for I neither wished to leave my surrogate family now Giles was gone, or to be so readily at Serrano's disposal come night or day.

It had made it harder to hide my prolonged absences but also made it easier to keep him at greater arms-length and moderate him somewhat. Though, in general, I need not fear his intimate attentions above two or three times a week, at most, and he, much like Giles had always done, mostly liked to parade me about on his arm like a prize pig. I must be careful now to ensure that *that* scene only played out in the most private circles hereon.

'Marco, you are back at last!' Guistina squealed excitedly as she entered the studio and noticed us talking at my easel. He looked up and smiled, permitted a light grasp of the hands and swift cheek-to-cheek greeting, and said, 'You look well, Guistina. I hope you and the family are enjoying the festivities.'

'We have been, and now I am growing fat with all the dinners and I refuse to continue until lent!'

'You are not growing fat,' he said, and I pretended indifference, but I had always been more on edge around Guistina since finding out their past and felt certain she still would have liked to replace her Cicisbeo with him. She had often been mildly flirtatious in my presence, but it had held no relevance in the beginning. Though she did it with Holland-Bury, too, I reasoned and suspected she was just a flirt and that I was being oversensitive. For though I had no right, I felt jealous that he might be sought in other directions.

Had he already, I wondered now. Had he really been lonely in Padua, or had he found someone to warm the sheets I was meant to be lying beneath? Perhaps some sailmaker woman from the past or even a servant in one of the hotels he had arrived at. I could hardly protest or deign to question the possibility when I was, strictly speaking, doing no better. Though at least in what I was doing there was no feeling or passion involved to pose a risk to my feelings for him, quite the reverse. But if he remained to his habits of not frequenting prostitutes, now his heart was opened, now he knew there was such a thing as love after love, then he might well be at risk of falling for a conquest, even if not intending it.

This troubled me increasingly as I walked to the Bottega to collect my messages after class, for I realised how I suffered from these jealous thoughts, though they were likely entirely unfounded. How then must he have suffered at thinking of all the men who had intimate knowledge of me? I knew that it was not the same, that I took no pleasure in my deeds, that it was a tolerance for suffering repugnance that I had cultivated in my professional endeavours. But I supposed to a man who only fucked for the sake of passion or love, it might be impossible to understand it from any other view. If someone did not appeal to his senses, he could just pass them over for someone who did, or even go without. It was not the same for me. I had endured the advances of the young and old, rich and poor, ugly and handsome alike, never having a say, never being able to pass them over, no matter how much I wanted to. This was an unknown dimension to him, and if he used *his* lens on which to judge *my* acts, he would surely end up tortured by distorted notions of what I felt. Even if he could understand the concept of meaningless sex, even if he did ever pay to sleep with women, he always had a choice in choosing them and would still fail to understand what it was like to have objectionable relations with someone.

Perhaps if he stayed on, I should give up Serrano. If it tortured him so much, however differently I understood the way of things, I would not want to hurt him if he believed it to be of some great consequence. I would like to prove to him otherwise, and yet I was so close to achieving Giles's downfall that I could not lose my grasp; the little bit of power I had mustered to finally give him a dose of his own medicine had been too hard-won to drop it at the last. But did I want to choose revenge over love? Was I making such a choice or only reading between the lines in false hope and fooling myself that he would not set off to Padua any day now? I could not handle such a double blow as his renewed departure and giving up on my revenge on Giles: one of my greatest consolations in Marco's absence. No, I was being hasty and foolhardy in thinking breaking with Serrano now would make any difference at all. I was already tainted in his mind and was not sure anything could restore such damage, for it was already done, and there were things in life that could not be undone, no matter how much wished or willed.

So, I kept that in mind when I broke the seal on Serrano's two messages. The first told me he had arrived back on Saturday and had a surprise for me when I saw him next, and the second asked when that would be.

I sent an immediate return, putting him off until Friday, thinking that Marco, in all likelihood, would be gone by then and I would not be at risk of riling him. Even though he might not see us together with a little extra care, I knew he would suspect it in my absence, for I had noticed how suspiciously he had questioned me about my plans once I declined to go back home with him after class. Where was I off to? he asked. To run some errands, I had told him, but I saw the cogs of suspicion turning in his mind, so I offered some finer detail to put his mind at rest. I have some shopping to do, I explained, which was true because now I was of means again, I could no longer justify walking blindly past beggars in the street as I had been forced to when my circumstances were desperate.

I had money enough now, and though I needed to carefully guard the greater portion for setting up home in England, I could share a little of my better fortune with some of the hungry souls I had grown familiar with here. They, too, had come to know me now and my patterns, and I would often find a young boy called Peppe waiting across the street from the Bottega in expectation of the hot polenta slice I would buy for him at *La Tavola Calda* next door. Then there were the mothers who were constantly toiling in the squares I passed through with scantly fed children hanging off their backs or running about their ankles as they tried to scrub at laundry.

Benedetta and I would fill baskets from the markets and lay them down for them to empty as often as we could. It was a smaller offering than I wished to make, and yet it heartened me to be able to do *something* at last. So I left the bottega and crossed the street to ruffle the hair of the waiting boy as I ordered his hot polenta slice and then headed to the Rialto markets. Once I had refilled my baskets a few more times and deposited them, I headed for my doctor's appointment in Castello, where I received the assurances I hoped to and returned home in more settled spirits.

A letter was waiting for me on my return. It was from the consul, Mr Hoppner, stating that he had received nothing more over the festive period. However, it was likely the season and bad weather causing delays to usual service, and he would be in touch ASAP should anything more be sent for me. I was disappointed. I had received replies from all but Lady W, now. My mother, sisters, Sheldon and Miss Banfield had all written back to me once I had sent them the consular address to go via, but Lady W. remained quiet, and I was at a loss. I feared something ill and decided I may have to resort to prevailing on my mama to enquire after her if I did not get a response soon. I had avoided it so far, not wanting to rock the boat now I knew myself not entirely abandoned by them, but had kept to simple and whitewashed accounts of how things were for me. It seemed pointless to raise their anxieties now that I was to be home in a matter of months. Besides, all the former pleas for help I had once so desperately wanted to send them were no longer necessary, and I was grateful for that now, to have managed to spare them concern. Anything further I wished to explain and elaborate on, I would do it in person on my return; until then, it could keep.

But I had hoped to appraise Lady W. of my plans to return in advance of my journey. Though now, I only wanted news of her health, for whilst I was willing to assume that she had replied to me in all these months, though intercepted by Giles like the others, I was now beginning to grow concerned for her well-being. I *knew* she would not ignore me, so if she did not reply, there must have been a good reason for it.

CHAPTER FORTY-SIX

Fresh Perspective.

Marco. January 1823.

'Dante, I know she is pregnant. Do you know if it is Giles's? Or who the father is?' Marco said when he returned home later that evening.

With a sigh of impatience, Dante fixed his brother's gaze. 'Look, I'm not falling for trickery. I told you we will not discuss this anymore.'

'I am not trying to trick you, brother. I saw her go to Dr Arturo today, so I know Carlotta is right.'

He rolled his eyes. 'Oh, well, that proves it then, for the last time I saw the doctor, he declared the same!' he replied with a sardonic undertone. 'Perhaps she has an ailment or something? Hang on, how did you *see* her going to Dr Arturo's?'

He shifted uncomfortably from foot to foot before admitting, 'I followed her after the class. I know, I am ashamed of it, but I could not help it. I thought she was going to *him*, and I had to be certain.'

'Jesus, Marco, she gets rid of one stalker and now you resume the duty? Why can't you just talk to her openly and ask her all you want to know?'

'I am frightened of the answer, brother. That is why. Even if, by some miracle, she tells me, I fear it will be the news that will break me at the last thread.'

'You think she will not be open with you?'

'Why should she?' he shrugged. 'Look where that has got her so far. I have lost her trust and good faith, Dante, and I am running out of time to win it back. She travels in a couple of months, and I cannot let her go without knowing if there is a reason to ask her to stay.'

'If you still love her, is that not reason enough?'

'Not if she is carrying someone else's child, Dante, I cannot—'

'Well, you will not know if she even carries one at all if you continue to refuse to ask her.'

'I know I frustrate you, brother. I am sorry to bring such burdens to you.'

'Look, you are never a burden to me, Marco, and heaven knows it marks a change from me bringing the same to you. But I am trying my hardest to tread a difficult rope between the confidences and trust of two of my dearest ones and do honour to both your parts. But you are so bloody stubborn the pair of you, I am at a loss to help if you will not help yourselves. If the pair of you spent less time boxing my ears and complaining of the other, maybe you might still have time enough to get the answers you both seek.'

'You are right. I will try harder. We are on reasonable terms but I must try to make a breakthrough with her.'

'Well, I'd give up following her about the streets because I fear that's precisely the kind of breakthrough you might want to avoid.'

'I won't do it again. She did not notice me, and so I have not blundered yet. But if you had seen her, Dante, it warmed my heart as I watched her. She was feeding the poor, and they all seemed to know her. She took time to converse with them and even kicked a ball with some of the children in the square. I find her such a constant contradiction.'

'Aren't we all? Brother, she is a good woman despite all the other stuff. I know her heart, which has perhaps been tainted by wrath and disappointment, but it's like she knows the pain of others, like she can sense its presence. That is how I came to confess to her when Matteo threw me over. She was a pillar to me and my wisest counsel, and I know how rare such generosity of spirit is to find. Don't waste your chance again, Marco; you may not get another.'

It was true. He had always seen through to her heart from the very beginning, even when it was broken and desolate of hope. Maybe it had been this which had prompted his own to begin thawing from its long spell of inertia. He had recognised the pain in her distant gazes, which mirrored his own heartache. Then there was the strength and resilience of character he had watched steadily rise from the wreck of so much adversity and despair, just as he had once had to rise from.

There had been much more than her beauty and clever wit that had reached him. There were depths to her above and beyond the physical he had wanted to travel to. Labyrinths beyond those charming eyes that were always turning in deep thought beyond her gaze. He had wanted to know those thoughts and observations he saw ticking over, and yet so subtly, it was as though they evaded the rest of the company who took her at face value.

It was true; she was always very good at throwing others off the trail of her real thoughts and feelings, often to protect them, he had come to realise. He had come to realise, too, sometimes to protect herself in the only way she could muster. She was doing it still, now, keeping far enough from his reach to protect herself from another disappointment.

He reminded himself that if she was with her child, it was her child, no matter who had fathered it, and it was natural that she would try to protect it. Naturally, she might be reluctant to disclose it to anyone. Maybe that was another reason she had continued with Serrano, to earn what she could whilst she still could, for she had admitted before that she was to return home without the support of her family and would have to find a way to manage on arrival. But with a child in tow, it could not be the one she had since relied on, and now she would have two to support instead of one. He knew her well enough to understand that she would do whatever she must to provide for her child, absent of her husband's support. And however hard it was, it would be preferable to her than accepting Giles's.

Perhaps it was time he tried to understand her predicament with a more objective head. Then, he may have a hope of understanding the logic of her acts rather than just the immorality or betrayal of them. Yes, she had hurt him, but she had not meant to, he was sure. He had been caught in the crossfire of a complicated battle she had been fighting alone. He didn't want her to fight it alone anymore.

CHAPTER FORTY-SEVEN

Re-tuned Melody.

Eleanor. January 1823.

'Ah, there's one for you dear,' Mr Harper said, removing his letters from the salver and passing it on to me.

I put down my coffee cup. 'Thank you,' I smiled, glancing at the hand and recognising it instantly as Giles's. I pushed it to one side, picked up my pastry, and took a bite. This would go with the others I had kept unopened in an ever-growing pile, just so I could leave them behind when I went. So that one day he might find them in my drawer, seals intact, and know that his words were so insignificant to me, and he was so far from my thoughts, that I could not even be bothered to open his missives.

Unfortunately, that did not prevent me from having news of him, however, and I expected at any moment for Mr Harper to declare to have been sent the same and to read it out to the table.

I usually let the words drift over me and suffered them for the sake of offering some small interest and acknowledgement in the company. But this time, Marco was at the table, and I grew more anxious than usual, watching cautiously as his father scanned through some other letters. Then he broke the seal and cleared his throat. 'Ah, word from Giles,' he announced, and Marco looked up from his plate as he began: 'Dear Uncle, please give my best regards to the family. I hope that this finds you all in good health. I am sorry to write to you with such desperate pleas, but the truth is, I am not so well and have suffered some very bad news,' he paused a moment and peered up gravely before reading on, 'I have just had word that the *Maddalena* has gone down off the Puerto Rican coast, complete with its cargo...by god,' he added, I assumed of his own accord, and Isabella held her hand to her throat and gasped. 'Oh no, surely not Edward. Read on,' she ushered with an impatient flapping hand.

'The ship is unrecoverable. The diamonds were sunk by the crew when they realised they were fighting a losing battle. Canons were fired, half the crew were lost in the fight with Confresi pirates, the rest were taken hostage and most likely have been pressed into service, bar the boatswain who escaped at sea, got picked up by a fishing vessel and taken to shore where he raised the alarm. It is a grave disappointment, and I am still finding it hard to take in such news. I need not tell you how much has been lost in this stroke of ill fortune. Had it been any of the other ships in my fleet, the losses might have been slight, but at the very least, this has cost me Serrano's good faith and any future contracts, I fear. For that reason, I ask a favour of you, Uncle, to go to the shipping office and retrieve the insurance deed from the safe and begin drawing on it on my behalf. You will find enclosed a sworn power of attorney for this purpose. I must know what can be recovered and consider any shortfall and how to try to cover it. All of course is made more difficult in my absence, so I must beg leave to return home now and settle things as soon as possible. In the meantime, if you will do whatever you can on my behalf, I would be much indebted...'

I stood up and asked to be excused before fleeing from the room. *Half the crew dead, the others captured?* There was to be no harm to any but he! A contrived contractual dispute, I had been clear about that. No loss of life! *Serrano, what have you done?* I called out to Benedetta to fetch my coat.

'Eleanor?' Marco was behind me on the stairs.

I turned about. 'Marco, I'm sorry, not now.'

Then Dante appeared at the top of them. 'Where are you going?' he asked, and he came bounding down, too.

'I never meant that anyone should be hurt!' I broke into tears and pushed Marco away as he tried to draw in close enough to embrace me. 'I can't,' I held him back. I must go. I will be back when I can,' I said, snatching on my coat, which Benedetta held out to me now she had managed to squeeze past them.

'Please, Eleanor, don't go, not like this,' Marco made a parting plea.

But I was out the door and onto the street without looking back. I ran all the way to *Ca' Serrano*, tears streaming down my face, glacial in the cold wind.

'I am sorry to call here, I said when Serrano's wife came to the door, the Butler unsure of what to do with me, for I was both familiar and forbidden here by the lady of the house. 'Forgive me, but I must see Serrano. I would not have come if it were not urgent. I mean no insult.'

'What has happened?' she asked, unsettled.

I did not know what to say. 'An accident, a ship has been sunk, and I must speak to him, please?'

'He is not here, but you will likely find him on his way back from the *Ducale*. I can tell you no more.'

'Thank you, and please, forgive me.'

I ran back the way we had come, alongside the Grand Canal, telling Benedetta to keep an eye on the water for any sign of his gondola. We were but a few hundred yards down when I caught sight of it, signalled by the bravi guard sat atop. I waved him down, frantic, until he frowned, recognised me, and directed the oarsman to draw towards us.

When it landed, Serrano stood out of it and came towards me on the pavement. Smile wide, arms open. 'Eleanor, what a happy coincidence, I just left your reply at the Bottega, and now it seems I needn't have troubled to, for here you are, as though summoned by my very thoughts of you—'

I backed away from his advances. 'How could you, Stefano? Why did you have to do it so brutally?' I screamed at him, and his bravi guard stood between us before Serrano waved him aside.

'What is this? Why are you so wild with tears? Has something happened?' he attempted to scoop me into his arms and I pushed him away. 'Get away from me, you brute! You are no better than he!' I raged, but then maybe I was no better than either of them anymore, blood on my hands now and how could I wash it away, it could not be undone. I grew hysterical at the realisation, for what did I expect to achieve by coming here? It was already too late. The news must be at least a month old to have even reached us. An image of dead men floating at sea flourished in my mind's eye, and when I began to slap at Serrano's chest to break free of him, the bravi guard swept me up from behind and held me fast about the shoulders and it grew futile to attempt to free myself of him for he was broad and strong, his thick arms the width of my thighs.

Bendetta started up in protests, thrashing her hands about, threatening to call the white coats.

'Gently, Massimo, you know she is precious to me,' Serrano said, palms face down as he pressed them towards the ground, 'Calm down, my treasure, this will do no good. I cannot hear you in such a fitful state.'

'I am not your treasure! You murdering beast! I want nothing to do with you!'

'Murder? What are you talking about, my love? There has been no murder. You are mistaken. Will you get in the gondola and you can talk to me?'

I paused at this news and began to settle. Then, I looked around at the bystanders watching, nodded, and the guard released me. 'Giles said the ship went down.'

Serrano smiled and cast his hands towards the air, 'Well, of course it did, my treasure. That was your surprise, but it is ruined now. I see the news has come before me.'

'Surprise? Do you think I am happy that half the crew are dead, the others captured by pirates? I only wanted *him* harmed, Serrano, no one else! I told you that. How could you? Those men were someone's sons, brothers, fathers—'

'Nobody is dead, innocent one,' he said, and I stared bolt upright.

'Truly?'

'No one is dead. Do you think me a war baron?'

'Truly, they are not?' I asked again, searching his expression for authenticity, and this time, when my tears began to gush with relief, I did not fight him off as he leaned over to comfort me. 'I thought they were all dead because of me.'

'No, no, no, my precious. These things have to look the part if they are to succeed. There were no pirates, only another of my crews commissioned to make it appear so. All the men were released as soon as the ship landed.'

The relief of this was immediate. 'Thank god.'

'You need not worry your pretty little head about such things. I told you I have everything in hand. My word is my bond. Now dry your tears. We should be celebrating, this was *your* surprise, after all.' He pressed a kiss to my head, and I tried for half a smile.

'So what happens now?'

'I claim upon your husband's insurance, and the underwriters shall refuse to settle, for he did not heed my instructions to increase the principal to include the extra artillery I had him add to the ship at the last, or maybe it slipped my mind to tell him that?' he winked, 'So it shall fall void, and then he shall have to find another means to settle with me if he does not want the law at his heels.'

'And will that take long?'

'Most likely, for he shall challenge it, I don't doubt, for it will cost him dear. There was over fifty thousand lire worth of gems in that cargo.'

'And you sunk them?'

He laughed, 'No, no, no. I adore you, my treasure, but I am a businessman. They are on their way to the purchasers presently.'

'And what about the men on board? Will they suffer any loss from this? How will they return home?'

'Seafaring men always understand the risk of going to sea, my love. There is always at stake, much to be lost and gained in such ventures. They will likely enlist on another ship.'

'Signor, that cannot be right. Surely you must do something for them?'

'That is for your husband to deal in.'

'But how can he when he thinks them dead or captive?'

'I daresay a few will find their way home soon enough and fear not; when their bellies grow hungry, they will find their way to his coattails and demand what is rightfully theirs.'

I pondered how to bring him about to the idea. 'But surely, Signor, if they were all to return, wouldn't that be very bad for you too if you are to raise indemnities on cargo that is claimed lost but is not?'

'Always so diligently minded, little one, but you understand not the nature of such matters, such men. Most of the cheap labour your husband procured for the voyage were either smugglers or bravi that had fallen into difficulty with their kinsmen and will not likely want to show their faces here again. The few that were not from such circles may return though, and he will assume those are the ones who have escaped the pirates. Now, enough of this talk, tesoro. We are to celebrate now.'

And so he directed the gondola to turn about, and we headed back down the canal to journey to my casino at the *Ponte del Bareteri*. I braced myself for a long morning, for I had not mentally prepared for this complication. Though having come away with better news than I had expected in ascertaining no blood had been spilt on my account, I could only feel relieved now. So I pulled over my veil, sat back in the gondola with greater ease and encouraged myself into character so I could pretend to be the *precious little treasure* he expected me to perform for him. It was compensatory for the more demanding, dictatorial and *not-so-precious* version he had to deal with in the exchange. I knew he only suffered such alongside the sweetener of my other, more endearing charms. And so when we arrived at the casino and he led me directly to the boudoir, I knew what must be done. And yet, what I did not know was how unbearable it would prove once more as I felt his kisses at my neck, the parting of my thighs.

I had not felt such anxieties since that first odious occasion I returned to him after Marco had fled to Padua. I knew not how to endure the resuming of such duties, still having the taste of Marco's sweet kisses on my lips when I was pressed to uphold my part in the contract. I was pulled into Signor's lap, suspended almost in disbelief that I would have to go through with it all now.

I can't bear it, I cannot do it, I said silently, and I cried as he entered me, keeping my face snug to his shoulder so he could not see my sobs. For I could not perform the usual playacting display of faux exhilaration I usually employed to bring such matters to a speedy close. No, not then and not today. For all I could think of now was Marco and how I wanted not to be this "whore" a moment longer. All I wanted, I realised, was to be worthy of *him*, be *with* him, and yet here I was, Serrano, heaving at my breast as I wiped my cheeks and resigned myself to permit it all to pass. It had not been like this again since that initial day. It had been easy to lie down with him in the interim, disengage my senses and disappear into another realm, another universe, as it all played out in third person. But to suspend one's heart at all was to suspend it in whole, not part, and it was open again now Marco had returned. And that healing wound was ruptured, gaping wide and letting every kind of horror flood my mind so I could not find that bystander who I usually stepped into, for she had fled, and I was here alone to deal in this, to feel it all as he thrust and heaved and spilt into me. And then, when it was over, I threw up into the wash basin, and I knew it was not the child to blame. I was sick at myself, sick at the sight and smell of Serrano as he pressed a kiss to my brow and made his excuses to set off on his way.

I got up from the bed and asked for the sheets to be changed and a bath to be drawn so I could wash the stain of him from my crawling flesh, and as I stood before the looking glass, my naked form before me, I admonished it, disowned it and all the trouble it had ever brought to bear upon me.

Even the sight of my own hands disgusted me as I peered at them through the soap-clouded water, knowing that however many washes I endured, I would always remain unclean. For there was no abluent capable of washing away the sins of the flesh beyond surface level. I may have carried the scent of Orange Flower and Jasmin upon my skin as I rose from the water and stepped into a towel, but the stench of my own conscience was as foul as any gutter or canal in Venice in the peak of a sweltering summers day.

How could I expect him to know how to love me as I was when I could not even bear myself anymore... And then, as I laid out on the clean sheets to cool down from the steaming heat of the water, I felt the shifting inside me, a faint flutter of movement and pressed my palm to my belly and began to cry. *And yet, in all the failures of my flesh, you are the miracle that reminds me of its worth.* My dear child, issue of my love, oh, how you have saved me from utter collapse these past months. How I mean to come through all of this for you, come what may.

I got up from the bed, pulled a shimmy over my head and sat at the writing desk.

"Stefano, I can no longer be at your service. I rescind my part in the bargain. Take back the gifts, and I shall return the money I have left to you."

I wrote, then sealed, and went barefoot down to the hall, placed it on the ornamental table before a vase of calla lilies, turned about and entered the drawing room. I sat at the pianoforte I had been given for my Christmas gift and began to play *con affetto* and lose myself in the endeavour. I used no sheet to guide me but let the music find its way to my fingers of its own accord. It soothed me to hear something so beautiful rising into the room, filling its emptiness with its consonance, to feel it move through me, reminding me that I had the power to create things both good and ill. Walk the path to heaven or hell.

I used to know happiness. Could I find it again? I knew now what must be done. And as I merged deeper into resonance with each revelation, each chord, its medicine carried to that ruptured wound at my heart and I let the pain flow through it and released it in a rush of melodic catharsis. For it was *me* that needed re-tuning now, and I knew that when the music of one's soul had forgotten how to play its clearest brightest notes, it might be reminded by the example of some other kind of magic, how to find its own melody again. And it was time. It was decided. I was ready to choose heaven now and free myself once and for all from the binds of hades I had tangled myself in. I loved Marco above all else and *would* choose love over revenge. Whether Serrano decided to pursue his claim against Giles and complete his ruin once he had read my note of resignation, I doubted, but what I did know was that I no longer cared enough about it. That I was ready to clear anything from our path to happiness and make a final try for Marco. I knew he loved me still. What remained was for me to prove to him I could become worthy of the gift of it. To change my ways entirely from hereon and commit solely to him. Let Giles and Serrano go to the devil without my escort, for I would no longer fester in these low quarters. I wanted to become all that I felt burgeoning within me. A devoted mother and wife to the husband of *my* choosing, and if he would still have me, I would not sway from my course, no matter what. I would do all he needed to show him that before him was no mere whore, but someone who could equally raise their sights in the other direction and be what he deserved. Embody in my deeds all that I felt in my heart. So I let one last crescendo rise and fall before closing the piano lid and rising from it.

When I heard clapping from behind, I gasped, thinking Serrano had returned, perhaps already having found my resignation letter on the hallway table. I turned sharp about in fright, expecting to see him there, but when I saw who stood before me, I could barely believe my eyes.

'Marco?'

CHAPTER FORTY-EIGHT

The Unseen Follower.

Marco. January 1823 (earlier the same day).

'You're not going after her, Marco,' Dante said, creating a barrier between his brother and the door. 'Marco! You know where she is headed,' he warned him.

'Which is why I have to go! He has just had a crew sunk for her, you think she is not in danger in the company of such a man who will stoop so? And in that head she has run off in?'

With a sigh of wavering resolve, he conceded. 'Alright, then I will go with you. But we will tail them and intervene *only* if there is a danger to her. Do you hear me, brother? Only then. This is not an excuse for you to vent your other feelings.'

'Yes, let's go. Giacomo, hurry. I will go on foot. You take the gondola.'

'No,' Dante said, 'You will take the gondola. If she sees *you* following her…' he insisted, leading him over, pressing him into it and fleeing in the direction he had seen her head.

'She will likely be heading for *Ca' Serrano*, Giacomo, tail her at a slight distance for now, but if we lose sight of her, you know where to head,' Marco directed.

'Si, Signor.'

They lost sight of her as she crossed the bridge at *rio di San Lio*, where he knew she would have taken a shortcut through the calle until reaching the *Grand Canal* and crossing at *Rialto*. Usually, they would have overtaken her in the boat and comfortably reached it before she. Giacomo was an excellent oarsman and the canals were fairly quiet, but she was running calamitously along the pavements, and he told Giacomo to speed up.

Though his brother was close behind her, he dreaded losing sight of her. It was all that was keeping him from spinning entirely out of control, focusing his sight upon her hooded figure, a flash of emerald silk weaving through the light traffic. How he wished he could catch the thread of her, turn her back, rescue her from this path of vengeance and the high fee she paid for exacting it. He should have spoken sooner and made his feelings clearer. So many times, he had tried to broach the matter, but her defences were too highly set and barred the way at every turn. Even when he thought there were signs of relent, she would check herself and retreat into stolidity again.

He caught sight of her again when they turned onto the Grand Canal and he exhaled his relief as his eyes kept her in sharp focus. When she approached the gates of *Ca' Serrano*, they regrouped, and Dante, red-cheeked and breathless, climbed into the gondola. As he settled into it, he confirmed he had not been seen and explained the route she had taken through breathy outbursts. Then they both watched on as she knocked, ready to launch in an instant. She was kept at the door, and then Signora Serrano came to it with a frown across her brow.

'Do you think she knows who she is?' Dante asked as they watched the exchange between them, unable to hear it.

Marco's pulse throbbed audible at his throat. 'I don't know, I don't want to think about it. Is she turning her away? Yes, she is walking back. He is either not at home, or his wife has told her so to turn her out. Either way, it is a relief.'

'Yes, hopefully she will have a chance to calm down now before she speaks to him again.—Sorry, I did not mean to—'

'Remind me of the fact? It is nothing I don't already know, but maybe now I might at least have time to get to her first. Set me down up there, Giacomo,' he pointed.

Dante grabbed his arm. 'No. Do you want her to know you have been following her? You are not Giles, Marco, don't be foolish enough to make her question it.'

'Alright, wait until we reach the other side of Rialto.'

'What do you mean to say to her?'

'I mean to ask her to come back with me to Padua right now before the fallout of this disaster comes to bear on her. A whole crew for want of satisfying her need to avenge Giles?'

'It's a damn shady business, to be sure. I can only assume she did not know the toll, for I do not believe for a minute she would have consented to this knowingly. I realise she is incensed with Giles and duly so, but I do not think she would have meant for this.'

'No, and yet this is what happens when you lie with wolves. I am going to get her out of here and see if there is any hope for us once she is away from all these devils.'

Dante patted his shoulder. 'A good decision, brother, however late to the table. Wait, is that? Look, she is waving him down. That's Serrano's gondola coming towards us.'

'Giacomo, steer us back inland,' Marco said.

'Just sit back down, brother. You will be seen. Let's just wait and see what happens. She is safe in the public light of day. We are on the Grand Canal for heaven's sake. It is thick with passers-by. Just sit down.'

Reluctantly, he lowered himself back into his seat but barely, almost squatting at seat level, ready to spring back out as soon as the boat drew close enough to the landing. He struggled to keep sight of her through the passing traffic. Then he saw Serrano get out of the gondola and the guard stepped up to her, and he leapt the yard between the boat and landing, and was almost gone for want of his brother catching him at the last, struggling to the canalside with him on his back.

'Marco, no, it's the bravi. Do you want to end up dead? Giacomo, help me!' he cried out, and Giacomo abandoned his oar and caught Marco by the arm.

'Signor, please come back to the boat. That guard is a beast, it is a death wish,' Giacomo pleaded as they struggled to keep him from fleeing to her.

Marco shoved and struggled against the weight on top of him, roaring, 'Get off me!'

'He's not touching her brother, he has stepped aside. Hold your temper.'

Then Marco lifted his head, refocused on the scene, his eyes wild, his body still trembling with fury, and then he stopped struggling until the sight of her crying and slapping and shoving at Serrano in a fit of hysterics set him determined again. He thrashed beneath their hold. 'Get off me, brother, god damn it, I do not want to hurt you, but you test me now! Giacomo, I warn you! I must go to her!' His chest heaved with exertion and his words strained with desperation as the guard swept her up out of reach and held her fast. But the more violently he tried to free himself from their desperate grasp, the stealthier they held and eventually bundled him back into the gondola, pressing their weight against his back so he could not get up.

'It's alright, Marco. Calm down. He has let her go! She is alright,' Dante told him in gasping breaths. Now, stop fighting us and you will see it for yourself. 'And then he stopped struggling, and as their weight against him eased, he lifted up and saw her get into the boat with them. *No.*

At first, they were only talking, but then he watched her sink against Serrano's chest and thought his heart might erupt from his own. *Eleanor, no. Do not forgive him this, please.*

Then they watched as the gondola turned about to head back the way it had come, with Eleanor still in it. Serrano's arm wrapped around her, pressing kisses to her head.

'Let's go home, brother. There is nothing more to be done here,' Dante said, disappointment in his eyes as he turned away from the sight of her.

'Giacomo, follow them on at a distance,' Marco directed him, 'That's an order!' he spat, still raging.

'Why, Marco?' Dante pleaded. 'You know where she is bound! Why would you do it to yourself?'

Marco's eyes flashed like fire. 'Because I need to see it alright, with my own eyes.'

'She's fine. You saw it for yourself, and Benedetta is with her anyway. What good can come of such needless torture?'

'I must see it! Hold their image in my head, for that will be the only thing I can use to justify all I must let fade to ash now.'

'Brother,' Dante draped a heavy arm over Marco's shoulder. 'I am sorry for it.'

'What choice has she left me?'

'I know...' he shook his head, despairing.

They travelled on, trailing behind Sandolo and fishermen to keep out of sight, but remained close until Serrano's Gondola turned off of the Grand Canal and into narrower waters where they were forced to hold back for lack of traffic. They caught up with them at each turn until, eventually, Giacomo paused and said they had landed at the *Ponte dei Bareteri*. Should he continue?

'Just for long enough to see if they get out. Pause here,' Dante directed him.

Marco had heard not a word, eyes fixed on the sight of the boat as she was handed out of it now, followed by Serrano. Then he stepped beside her, arm at her waist, snaking about it, a kiss upon her ear.

'Marco, it's time we went home,' Dante said gently.

As the boat shifted, he looked up, 'No, I want to see where they go!' he uttered as Giacomo began to row them out of their covert position behind a moored barge a little way from the bridge.

'So this is their little love nest, is it?' he said as he watched the bravi guard lead them to a door further along. They entered it, hand in hand now, Benedetta trailing behind carrying her mistress's discarded hat.

'Whatever goes on beneath that roof, brother, has nothing to do with love,' Dante slapped his back. 'Come on, let's go and take a glass.'

But Marco could not rest at one glass, nor two, as they sat in a coffee house by St. Marks. He uttered assurances to his brother that he was restored now and Dante should not prolong his absence from the shipyard any longer, for their father had enough to contend with today and he would be missed. But he had no intention of leaving and going on to the gallery, as he vowed. Instead, he waited for Dante to exit and summoned the attendant to bring the bottle.

It was Giacomo who pulled him from his seat and rowed him back to *Ca' Rosetti* against his slurry utterings of protest when the bottle was almost empty. Then Marco resigned it was for the best. He would make a start on packing up to leave for Padua, but could not move from his bed where Giacomo had deposited him, head spinning, limbs weak, images of her haunting him in his more vivid moments.

He was not used to drinking in that style of excess as he had often lectured George for. No, a glass or two was usually sufficient for his taste and yet, had it not been for Giacomo's intervention, he would likely have remained there until the place was shut up or he passed out, whichever came first. It took not long to establish the answer, for he was soon out cold, sprawled upon the bed in his clothes and boots.

When he woke and the weight of realisation caught up with him, he got up, steady on his feet at last for his repose and—though not entirely restored—splashed his face with stale water from the jug to startle himself into the present. There was much to do: his trunk to pack and load, an impromptu farewell to make to his mother, and a word with George on his way. But when he went to seek his mother out and learned that Eleanor was still not home, he changed course. He had left her hours ago, so why had she not returned by now? Was it usual for her to spend the breadth of an entire day beneath that roof with him? No, he could not imagine that would carry without at least the suspicion of his mother being raised. *What if things had turned ill after they left? What if something had happened to her?* Could he really depart for Padua without at least knowing she was all right?

He sent for Giacomo.

He stepped out into a menacing rainstorm and pulled his collar up as he made his way beneath the felze. He felt guilty for asking Giacomo to bear its brunt as he navigated them through a mist of vapour, the occasional more furious bursts throwing it down in violent darts pelting the rooftop. When they pulled up to the *Ponte dei Bareteri* where Serrano's boat had been moored, only to find the space empty, he began to panic. She might not even be there still. Had things turned ill again and she got into another fit of hysterics and threatened to expose him for his part in the bad business? What measures would Serrano be willing to take to silence her if she had?

He leapt out and rapped at the door, Giacomo at his side not knowing what to do. Under the direction of his superiors, Giacomo would intervene against his master in service of his best interests, but he was not in the habit of otherwise doing. It had rarely been necessary until of late. Removing him from the coffee house earlier had been difficult enough, but now what? Where was Dante to direct him on the best course as he watched him growing impatient at the lack of answer to the door. But then, the click of a latch was heard, and a manservant opened it just a crack to peer out.

'Yes?' he asked, looking the pair of them over, unable to account for them.

'Is Eleanor still here?'

'No one by that name, Signor. You, I think, are mistaken. This is a *private* house. I cannot help you.' And he pressed the door almost shut before Marco thrust it back open and met the sight of a frowning Benedetta at the foot of the stairs.

'Signor? Giacomo?'

'Benedetta, is she here?'

'Yes, Signor, but you should not be. What is wrong, you look ill?'

'Is she alright?'

'Yes, she is fine, don't you hear her?'

He had not paid mind to the music coming from the house as the door was opened beyond noting that, indeed, persons were inside it. 'Is that her playing?'

'Yes, Signor. You see, there is nothing amiss, all is well. But it won't be if you do not leave before you are seen.'

'Who is in there with her?'

'No one but the servants, honest.'

'Then I beg you let me in, Benedetta.'

'It is not *her* decision,' said the manservant who had opened the door and was looking between them with bewilderment. 'This is my master's house, and he declares no one is admitted.'

Marco gripped him at the collar and Benedetta stepped between them. 'Signor, please, unhand him,' she begged, and he peered at the coward before him trying to wriggle from his grip, his face frozen with horror, and released him.

'Look, I mean to cause no trouble nor to remain here. I just want to see her with my own eyes and ascertain she is alright. I shall go in with or without your leave,' he directed those words at the manservant who stepped back and rubbed his throat. '...but I would prefer to go in peacefully. Will you show me the way, Benedetta?'

She nodded and turned, saying, 'I will tell her you are here.'

He reached for her arm, 'No. Just a glance will be adequate if she does not know I am come.'

'I don't think she heard the door above the music, Signor. She is quite absorbed. I will have to tell her you came, though, just in case the manservant tells his master.'

'Of course, after I have gone.' The last thing they needed now was another messy departure. No, he must avoid that.

But when Benedetta led him to the *piano nobile* and he passed in through the door of a formal parlour and saw her sat, back facing him at the pianoforte, he froze, unable to proceed, unable to turn back. The music altered, reaching his ears differently now, not simply as distant sounds growing more vivid, but with spellbinding intensity and, quite without considering it, he dropped into the sofa he was standing before. He closed his eyes. It was painful to look at her, still in bare dress, layers *he* had removed from her.

'Signor?' Benedetta tapped him lightly and mouthed the word. Marco glanced up, having entirely forgotten she was still there and indicated she leave them, and she eventually withdrew.

CHAPTER FORTY-NINE

Floating.

Eleanor. January 1823.

'Marco, what are you doing here?' I glanced around to make sure no one else had
arrived without my knowledge. 'How did you find me? Who let you in?' I saw
Benedetta hovering outside the open doorway from the corner of my eye and had my
answer. *Oh, why had she led him here, of all places?*

He met my eyes. 'I just had to see for myself,' he said, cheeks tear-stained, or were
they only wet from the rain, I wondered, as I rushed over to him, but he would not
let me touch him, comfort him and shrugged me off.

'How long have you been standing there?'

'Long enough...' He sniffed back tears, 'You play very beautifully, and yet, like
everything else about you, it is but a contradiction.'

'No, Marco, not anymore and never again. If you will have me back, give me one
more chance to show you what can be when I am free of all this, I shall prove to you
otherwise. I own I have lost sight of myself since I came here, but you have found me
now and I mean to show you my better graces. Let me come back with you to Padua
when you go. I am going to break with Signor and I do not care what becomes of Giles.
I want to leave it all behind. I will do whatever it takes to prove myself in earnest and
that I can be so much more than what I have shown you of myself—'

A bitter sneer twisted his features. 'You think I want you now?' he said so coolly I
almost faltered. 'I only came to make sure you were safe, for you have been gone since
morning, and yet I have had to suffer every kind of ill today. It has nearly killed me!'
he thundered.

I reached for his hands. 'Oh, Marco, I am sorry. I did not mean to be away for so
long. Let us leave this house at once and talk elsewhere. Let us go to the Locanda.'

'No.' He pulled them from my grasp and wiped his cheek with his fingertips. 'Since
I am here, though, I would rather like to take the tour.' He cast a glance about the
room. 'I see he has set you up very plush indeed. Come now, won't you show me
about?'

I ignored his sardonic tone and kept my own voice level. 'It is just one of his disused
Casinos; there is really nothing to see.'

He crossed the room. 'You might show me where all the magic happens?'

'There is no magic here but dark arts. Please, let us leave. I beg you,' I said more desperately.

He turned back to look at me. 'Oh, *now* you want to leave? When you have been shut up in here all day in this gilded cage, you proclaim it to be, yet it is clear what you value. So, show me the riches I fade into comparison to and let me at least know my worth. I already have the count at a crew of dead seamen. I see the furnishings are all bright and new here, and *that* is a very nice pianoforte in the latest style.' He ran a finger over the polished wood. 'What of the bedchamber and –'

'Stop!' I cried. 'There are no dead men. It was only theatre to convince Giles. Why do you think I came? Only to ascertain it was not true and no blood was spilt in my name. And it has not been, and I am still smarting from the realisation of how close I came to permitting the possibility. *No more.* I care for none of these things, Marco. I care only for you.' I stayed myself before I came close to adding: and our child.

'Then why have you spent all day here? I am glad the crew have been spared, truly, but if you think no blood has been spilt in your ambitions, then you must not know how *my* heart has bled for all you have forced me to suffer at the sidelines.'

I approached him steadily. 'I'm sorry, Marco—don't turn away from me. Hear me, I beg you,' I grasped his hands and held fast to them until he relented. 'I want to heal every wound I have ever caused you to suffer, soothe every pain, dry every tear, and show you that all the riches or reward in the world could never compensate for the poverty of my heart if I am kept apart from yours a moment longer.'

He snatched away and ran his hands through his hair. 'You have done *too* much.'

'I know.' I fell hysterical now. 'But do not say it is too late, not now.'

'Why, not now? Is there something I do not know? Something you want to tell me?'

I considered this. I did not want to tell a lie, or risk telling him a truth that would force him to accept my petition against his will. I wanted him to choose me freely. I could not bind him into submission by such weighty leverage as his unborn child. I knew him suspicious, Dante had said so and urged me to speak. I had caught his examining glances at my waist, trying to figure it out. I had laced myself tighter since, but now I was in nothing but my shimmy and could only hope the dim evening light was enough to conceal me. I considered him carefully, his eyes full of pleading, but I could not convince myself. So, I chose another line of truth instead. 'I want to tell you that it nearly killed me last time you left, and I cannot do it again, Marco! I have realised since you returned that despite all my trying, I cannot resign myself to a life without you in it. And if I am not mistaken, I think you are of a like mind.' It was not a question, and yet his eyes answered it with a softening of his brow. 'So I am leaving, Signor. I have already written my resignation; you may see it for yourself in the hall.' I pointed, and he glanced in the direction. 'And now I am free, we must both muster the courage to try again, away from Giles, Serrano, Venice. For if we do not, we will never know what has been lost to us... but we will *feel* it, every day and forever. Yes, we both carry the weight of those broken hearts from the ghosts of our pasts, don't we? Is that what you want us to become to each other, ghosts?'

'No.'

'So let us go now and at least *try* to find what is salvageable. If we fail, we shall at least know it was not on account of our own cowardice. But it is my dearest hope and most fervent belief that if we succeed, we will know such great happiness and may at last turn our sights towards a future we had both given up on.'

He sunk onto the piano stool, head in hands, face out of view, but I knew he cried, though he did not want me to see it. And so I sat beside him and stroked the plains of his back until he looked up at me and said, 'Let us go.'

In the Gondola home, I held him close, kissed his rain-damp hair and did my utmost to soothe him, for he was still so forlorn, bent prostate at my lap, and I knew he did not want me to touch him or kiss him in any other kind of manner. Not today, at least. For he was like a child in my arms that needed assuaging, and if he could bear me no closer right now, if all I could do was meet that need, I would do so willingly, gratefully. For this was my doing. My misery had spread like a deathly contagion and this is what I had reduced him to, and it broke my heart to face the consequences thus manifest, for I knew that pain of the heart-induced kind was not inferior to that of its physical counterpart. For when the heart in the chest stopped beating, there was no pain beyond it, *I knew*. I still remembered the stillness as I peered motionless through the canal's murky waters until all faded from me. No, this kind of pain was undoubtedly worse, for it had to be borne, and nursed, and survived through. And *that* was no easy path to tread. But if I had learnt anything from having walked it, it was that if you could bear it and rise from the ashes, even when you thought you could not, there was hope on the other side of it. His love had restored that to me, and now I must restore the same to him. And so I held him close, whispering words of reassurance into his ear, stroking his damp hair and sending prayers of thanks up to the heavens.

When we returned to *Ca' Rosetti*, I had not expected a welcoming party. We walked the stairs as Isabella and Dante rushed out to the landing to meet us. I let go of Marco's arm instantly. Now, was not the time to declare such uncomfortable truths as we would have to face in the morning before we departed the house. He was not fit for such a confrontation or to travel to Padua tonight. I had smelt the liqueur on his breath and felt the listlessness of his movements as I lifted him from my lap and bid him up from the seat. He needed rest and peace tonight, and in the morning, we would discuss things in a better head and decide upon how to handle the explanation of our departure to his parents.

I had hoped that we could sneak back into the house quietly while the family were at the table, that I could settle him to his bed, and that we might be spared an explanation of our coming home together, even if I had yet to find an explanation for my lengthy absence. But as I read the relief and horror on Dante's face at the sight of us and the realisation on Isabella's, I knew we were to be denied that luxury.

'Eleanor, you are home. Marco, what is wrong, my child?' Isabella said, her face grave with concern, Dante at her shoulder. She reached forward to cup Marco's face between her palms to see him better. 'Marco, you are ill, I think? You have been drinking,' she said and then turned to me. 'What has happened?'

'In the morning, mama,' Marco said, '...not now. I am tired.' He gently stepped out of her embrace and proceeded up the stairs.

'Let him be, mama,' Dante said, placing a light hand upon her shoulder, 'Let him sleep it off, eh?'

'But something is wrong. Marco does not drink!'

When all eyes turned back to me, I knew not what to say.

'Eleanor,' she said to me then, a pleading in her eyes, 'Is my son in love with you?'

I nearly fell back on the stair I remained standing on and caught myself on the rail.

'Mama, I already told you, Carlotta is delusional. There is nothing between us,' Dante told her. 'Now, will you let her come up or leave her standing there?'

She stepped aside so I could reach the landing and said, 'I know Carlotta is wrong about you, Dante. I did not mean you.'

My mouth fell open and I realised there would be no waiting until morning, not now.

'Mama?' Dante protested.

And I raised a hand to stay him, 'Isabella, you know your own children, and I cannot speak for him, though I see it would do no good to pretend with you any longer. I do love him.'

She pressed a hand to her throat and Dante closed his eyes and lifted a palm to his forehead.

'I am sorry. It was not intentional, but it is as I said.'

She nodded slowly, stunned by confirmation rather than revelation, I thought.

'Right, I think Eleanor, too, looks tired, mama,' Dante insisted, turning her about.

As she nodded her agreement, I, relieved, walked on and she raised a hand to my forearm as I passed her. 'My husband can know nothing of this,' she said.

I did not know how that would be possible with our leaving in the morning, but I gave a shallow nod and walked on as Dante swept his mother back towards the main level. When I reached the next landing, I paused and headed directly to Marco's chamber.

I found him on the bed, staring into the canopy, coat and boots still on. I pulled his boots off, got him to lift enough for me to undress him, pull the sheets aside, and usher him into them. 'Get some rest, my love. Come to me in the morning. I don't care the hour. We will deal in all then, and as I bent to kiss his forehead, I felt him grasp at my wrist, tugging me gently towards him.

'Don't go,' he said, 'Stay with me.'

'Marco, I cannot, your mama knows—'

'She has understood from the moment I returned. Stay.'

I nodded. I went back to the door to turn the key. Took off my coat, slipped out of my shoes, and blew out the candle, casting all into shadow bar the fire's glow. Then I drew up to the bed, sank beside him, and pulled him into my embrace. I felt the hum of his breath against my collarbone as he curled into me. 'Sleep now, my darling,' I said softly.

And once he slept in my arms, I knew I must get up and go to my own chamber, for Isabella might know now, but I was not to insult her with such liberty-taking. And yet I wanted not to disturb him or leave him at all, and when he shifted in his sleep and lifted his clammy palm from its place at my breast and rested it on my tummy, I felt the little flutters inside me reach up to meet the warmth of his hand and I pressed my own hand over it and smiled. *Baby Harper, meet your father at last.* Then, suspended in the rapture of this beautiful sensation, I, too, grew heady and lost my resolve to go or even undress.

I knew not the hour when I woke with us in the very same position, but when I lifted my head to peer over to the fire it was burned down to a glowing heap of embers, so I assumed it someway after midnight and before the hour of three, though where I could not tell, for its diminished offering of light was not adequate for gleaning the clock face sat upon it. Gently, I lifted Marco's hand from my tummy, carefully rolled his head from my chest and slipped out from beneath his weight. *One more night apart,* I reminded myself as I grew reluctant to go again. *And then we shall know every night in each other's arms and both be healed again.*

I stepped onto the floor as quietly as I could manage, padded lightly over to the fireplace, bent to put another log into the grate and used the poker to work it into the hot ash pile, then encouraged it with a few pumps of the bellows before dusting off my hands, turning about, stepping into the orb of amber light cast upon the rug and searching with my eyes for a sign of where I had left my shoes and coat. When I found them cast into the shadowy half of the room, I crouched to collect them, paused to catch a parting glimpse of him, walked over to the bedside, bent to kiss his forehead, and whispered, 'I love you.'

But as I lifted and turned to go, he reached for me, clasping my hand, and said, 'I love you too,' then he rose, 'Where are you going?'

'To bed, but I will be ba—'

'Don't go,' he pleaded, pulling me close, and I dropped my coat and shoes back onto the carpet, crawled back onto the bed and met the welcome taste of his kiss at my lips, and I returned it, understanding by the manner in which it was delivered, I was no longer restricted to arm's length.

He sat up fully now against the headboard, and though I could barely see his features in the shadowy dimness, I recognised him, knew him restored to himself, felt the heat of his gaze as I freed myself of the bind of my skirts, so I could join him there. And when I reached him again, he kissed me deeper, clutching me to him, and I sighed with such relief to know this pleasure again. How long had I dreamt of this, drawing only from my memory all these months and longing for its re-enactment? 'God, I have missed you,' I breathed into his ear as I felt his kiss upon my throat. And then his hands working the buttons of my dress, lifting my arms as he pulled it from over my head, unlaced my stays as he returned his kisses to my neck causing me to shiver and gasp as I climbed into his lap, palms pressed flat to his chest as I lifted myself enough to help him find me, and when I found the burgeoning tip of him pressed to me, I lowered myself back down again, tentatively, *slowly,* to delight in every sensation of his entry to that place that had longed for only him since the night we floated along the Brenta, thus engaged. We both cried out in pleasure as I landed softly in his lap, a sigh of the pain of longing at last assuaged and pleasure anew replacing it. And when his head fell back against the headboard in a groan too loud to be passable, I hushed him with a kiss and gathered him back into my arms. He pulled the ribbon of my chemise loose to gather the weight of my breasts into his warm, strong hands before breaking our kiss to lift one to his mouth, and now I could not temper my volume either. For I no longer looked for the bystander at my shoulder. I was at last free to dismiss her to the past and *feel everything* with willing abandon. For this moment existed only in the realms of the heavens, and I needn't peer down to my feet to know how far I had risen from its counterpart. I *knew* I was returned. And as we rocked and writhed and clambered to its precipice together in absolute unison, I floated once again. Even when we lay back beneath the sheets, wrapped tight in each other's warmth, I floated still.

Even when we woke again to the shaft of morning light that crept beneath the edge of a broken louvre at the window shutter, I was still adrift as though I had sailed through the hours of sleep in a satiated blink.

I smiled through bleary eyes to meet the sight of him peering down at me, perched on his elbow, stroking the skin at the crevice between my breasts.

'Good morning,' I said, grasping his fingertips and bringing them to my lips.

'It is with the sight of you beside me, to wake to,' he said, bending to replace his fingers. When we broke from the kiss, I said: 'Well, you had better grow used to it, for we shall go to Padua today and know this comfort every morning and every night.'

'Is that truly what you want?'

'It is *all* I want, well, not entirely all,' I confessed, and when he paused and frowned, I brought his hand to my belly and held it there. 'I want to bear the child you have given me, too.'

The shock on his face was a picture to behold, but then it clouded. 'So it is true, you are—?'

I nodded, 'I have been carrying *your* child for the past five months, and I'm not sure how much longer I shall be able to hide that fact, and I look forward to not having to any longer.'

He pulled back the sheets and gazed at the bareness of me, lifting his palm, wonder at the sight before him. 'It *is* true...you *know* it is mine?'

'It is *ours,* and I am entirely certain.'

'But how do you know it?' he asked, a tentative longing in his eyes but a restraint set in his jaw.

'Because you were the *only* one for the entirety of our trip to *Villa Rossa* and all the way until you left for Padua. There was no one in between. Why do you think I would not let Giles near me that night?'

'You knew then?'

'I suspected, but it was too early to be certain, and when the doctor was called to me at Carlotta's, he confirmed my suspicions. I was going to tell you once we reached Padua, but, well, now you know.'

His face lightened and then beamed bright as the morning sun in spring, and we both welled with tears. Eyes heavy, glistening, as he replaced his hand and felt the new dimensions of me, of us.

'I knew you were changed...but I thought you in growing health.'

'It is true. But not only my health is growing...Say hello to baby Harper, who I am told is showing every sign of vitality and is due to arrive in our arms in May.'

He bent to my tummy and pressed a million kisses to it, and I smiled and winced when his lips tickled me into wriggling away from him. Then he lifted up and I felt the shift in his gaze and pulled him above me.

Once the blissful re-enactment of the night before was complete and we spent the remainder of our naked embrace exchanging excited plans to depart, envisioning a future we had neither thought possible, the beckoning reality of the mundane called us to our feet. For before we could leap off into the future of our design, we must face the other tasks that preceded it. The most pressing of which was facing his parents, and though we both dressed with a sense of foreboding at the prospect, we left the room hand in hand, united in whatever may come.

His father and brother were already gone to the shipyard, and we found Isabella in her small garden, making the most of the unusually dry morning and plucking out dead flowers that had gone to seed.

'Mama,' Marco said, and she looked up from the pot she was bent over. She met the sight of our entwined hands with a look of surprise and rushed over to us. 'Release her, Marco! What if the servants see?'

I released my hand from his when I realised he was not going to.

'I don't care who sees mother; I am done caring for such trivialities.'

'Trivial! You think it trivial that you have seduced another man's wife! Your cousin's wife?' She was thrashing her hands about in excited gestures, a realm of the Italian language that still evaded me for the most part. 'Get inside at once,' she directed us, and we went ahead of her as she un-gloved her hands, throwing them down on the ground and marching behind.

I tried to remember Marco's warning as I felt myself distressed at this reception, though she had said nothing to me. 'My mother is all bark and no bite. But be warned, it may be quite a bark until she calms and accepts things, and she will,' he had told me as I grew sick with nerves at having to face such a prospect.

We sat stiffly at the empty breakfast table with the doors and windows shut tight. Benedetta had been ordered to keep all the other servants away from the room.

'Well, what do you have to say for yourselves?' she said, thrusting her palm towards the ceiling.

'Mama, we are not children,' Marco reminded her.

'And yet you act no better?' she replied, quick, clipped.

'Isabella,' I said, my voice cracking over the words, 'I—I am so sorry for any hurt and disappointment this is causing you or your family. I am so very sorry when I have known and loved you as dearly as if you were my own family. You have been nothing but kind and generous to me since I was thrust upon you all, and it breaks my heart to cause you pain, but our intention was never thus. We never meant to fall in love. It was quite by accident, much resisted and yet too powerful to overcome. Loving your son is the only part I am not sorry for; he is everything a man raised in such kindness should be. And I wish I had known him first and things could be done in all the proper ways that would please all concerned. But it is too late for that, and yet not good enough of a reason to give it up.'

'It is the only reason I would ask you to, for I see what is before me, but—'

'No, mama, it is no use. We are decided, and I will not give her up,' Marco told her, firmly but measured.

She looked between us, torn between understanding and bound by duty, it seemed. And I understood such binds so very well I could hardly expect to elicit her agreement or blessing. I meant only to speak earnestly to her heart and seek to preserve the love of mother and son between them. For he and Dante were devoted sons, beloved, and not as I had witnessed family bonds before. Authentic, supportive and beautiful. But this was too much to ask of anyone, and I felt her pain as she confronted not only the scandalous reality of this predicament but all the lost hopes and dreams for Marco's future. The natural urge to one day see him settled in a respectable match, home and family. But I knew, if she could just be patient, in time, all would be delivered in effect, if not in propriety. And she would see her son happy, something I knew mattered to her more than most.

'Your father will disown you, Marco, you know that,' she said.

'I know, and I am sorry, mama, I am. I love my father, despite all our differences—'

'Marco, this is not a quarrel over an army conscription, the shipyard or an art course. This is his nephew's wife!'

'I realise that mama, but what would you have me do? Give up on my chance to love, my happiness, the unborn child I want to know its father?'

She was stunned by this, and so was I, for I had not thought it a good idea to overwhelm her with everything all at once. 'You are going to be a father?' she said, wide-eyed, leaning in as if she had misheard him.

'I am,' he answered, and the pride on his face was impossible to reproach him for as he spoke the words.

She held her hand to her throat. 'I never thought—'

'And nor I, mama.'

'I had given up on it all with you, and we both know your brother shall never...' she said to both our surprise.

'I know it is not the way you would prefer it, mama. It is not as any of us might have preferred the circumstances to run, but I am not giving up my chance at happiness and to be a father, not for anything or anyone. I can only hope that in time, you *and* my father will come to understand.'

'I *do* understand il mio regazzo, I do. But your father...I don't know...'

He reached across the table and rested his hand over his mother's. She peered up at him and asked, 'So what will you do?'

'We shall return to Padua together later, set up a house there and live quietly, in reach of you when you are at the Villa, which I hope will be often.'

She squeezed his hand back. 'And you mean to go today?'

He nodded. 'We must vanish before anything is suspected of Eleanor's condition.'

'A little late for that, Carlotta—'

'I know, Carlotta has already made her suspicions clear, even if she has attributed them in the wrong direction.'

'That at least may be no bad thing,' she shrugged. 'I will be given a break from protecting Dante for a change.'

She definitely knew.

'You don't have to protect us anymore, mama. We are grown men now. You need only think of your own comfort now, and I hope you will take heart in knowing we are happy as we are.'

She nodded. 'I want your happiness, I just hoped it would—'

'Be different, follow the prescribed form?' I interjected, and she nodded. 'I know you and your husband have been very fortunate in your pairing, Isabella, but you know, my life in the prescribed form has run very miserably ever since I met Giles.'

'I know, Eleanor. I see you are unhappy with him, and he does little to help the matter. I realise that not all the strictures of society, or even of the church, are ideal in every circumstance, but we must live amongst it all the same, and my fear is how you both will manage it as outcasts.'

'So long as you do not cast us from your hearts, mama, I think we shall manage well enough,' Marco put in, and she waved him away.

'You know that is not possible, but what about Giles? What am I supposed to tell him?'

'That you know nothing other than that I am in Milan painting a commission, and Eleanor has fled to England.'

I passed her the sealed letter I had prepared for Giles as a decoy.

She searched our faces. 'He does not know anything about this?'

'He suspects nothing, for he knows nothing of me at all, not really,' I answered. 'He has been expecting my flight ever since we arrived, so it will be no surprise to him, I assure you. It is my hope that once he reads this, he too will flee to England in pursuit of me, and so you shall not have to bear his complaint beyond a brief moment, and I am sorry that you do at all.'

'And if he causes any trouble, mama—'

'Marco, hush with such tones of contempt,' she chastised him.

'Forgive me, though I hope you will at least retreat directly to the Villa should he hang about in a miff. And I will come and see you there as you pot your seedlings in the glasshouse for the summer. And by the time they are in bloom, we will have someone else for you to meet then, too.'

She smiled, and then wept, then hugged us both, and warned us to take care before waving us away to get packed.

I had not had a chance to pack a thing yet, and we must be gone before Mr Harper returned this evening. For she knew he would not send us off with any such endorsement and wanted to preserve what she could of her husband and son's relationship and work on him slowly, gradually, once all the dust had settled. Marco reassured me that it was the best way with his papa, to let her soften him by degrees. It was how she had eventually brought him about to Marco's career change, though it was neither quick nor easy.

'I want to see Dante before we go,' I told him as he hugged me from behind and planted kisses over my neck as I tried to pack my clothes into trunks as Benedetta pretended indifference. I was saddened that we could not ask her to go with us just yet, that she would again be forced to break with Giacomo for a time. She had been the dearest of loyal servants and I was sorry to leave her behind, but it was best to raise no more suspicions, and so we must wait until we had news that Giles had been and gone from the place before sending for her. And though we knew not how long that would be, precisely, it seemed that now the frosts had finally cleared, he would likely set out soon, and her delay need not be any worse than the one she had suffered in Marco's recent absence.

'I will send a message to Dante, telling him to meet us at the *Locanda San Barnaba* this evening. We expect not to get very far tonight, anyway. We shall pack up and have our things sent there ahead of us. Take dinner with him in the Trattoria around the corner before we take the boat to the mainland.'

'Yes, yes, that will be nice. Do you think we will get much on our way today?'

He shook his head. 'Not in all this rain the sky threatens, and we shall lose the light early. But I think we can pass the time quite merrily at an inn on the mainland tonight, don't you?'

'Shh!' I whispered, 'Benedetta can hear you.'

'I think the whole inn shall hear you later when I have you to myself,' he teased, sneaking a kiss into the nape of my neck that made me shiver, laugh, and turn about to kiss him.

'Argh,' he groaned. It pains me to leave you for above a moment, but I really must go and see George, get these passports from the safe and find out if he will stay, or at least take interviews for me if he will not.'

'You go now and be back swift and I shall make ready for your return. You will only keep distracting me anyway and I shall get nothing done.'

Besides packing, I had other things to attend to that I did not wish to do in his presence. So I kissed him again and bid him go, and then had Benedetta bring the money and jewels I kept hidden away, the ones from Serrano. I would have them returned to him by the gondolier he hired for me, and once that was conveyed to him with it, I could feel at ease. Though I would only ready it all now. I did not want to alert him before we had crossed out of the city to the mainland. Even if he had returned to the casino and found my letter by now, I expected him to dismiss it lightly, send me some new gift, plead a meeting and try to bring me around again. It had not been the first time I had tried to part with him, and so, until he received the return of his gifts and fees, he would not trouble over it. By then, we would be gone from Venice and he would soon learn of my escape to England.

'Why do you return the money to him, Signora?' Benedetta asked as we counted it out in neat stacks piled on the top of my packed trunk. 'The gifts, I understand. But you earned every centesimo of that,' she said, gesturing at the top of the trunk.

'I want no memory of that man to go forward with me, Benedetta, and I know Marco shan't either, and so it is for the best. I shall keep the thousand lire I earnt before that, though, for I want not to come to Marco empty-handed and leave all the burden upon him. But, I want you to have this,' I said, taking a weighty pile of the coins and putting them into her hand. 'You, too, have earnt every centesimo of that, and it's but a trifle of that which I should like to give to you, but I hope—'

'Signora, I cannot take this. It is too much.'

'Uh ah, you will offend me if you don't. I know not quite what the future holds for us, but I may never be able to be so generous again, so please, while I can, take it and take whichever of my dresses I leave behind.'

Then she let a tear drop and hugged me, 'Thank you, Signora. I am sorry to see you go, but I will hold you to your promise to send for me, and soon, I hope,' she said, pressing a hand to the swell of my tummy.

'Very soon, I promise. I shall be quite lost without you. So take your holidays now and be at ease in the interim, for when you return, you will not be long from having two of us to wait upon.'

She smiled and wiped her eyes.

'And this, I said, taking another pile of the coin, '...will go to Peppe, the boy outside *La Tavola Calda*, for his hot polenta slice each Monday, for he will be waiting. And for the mothers in the square, you know what to do.'

'You can rely on me, Signora.'

'I know I can.'

CHAPTER FIFTY

Crossed Wires.

Marco. January 1823.

'George, you have nothing to be sorry for. I ask you on the off chance and am grateful that you will at least stay to find a replacement. It is more than generous of you after so long. Truly, you have been the best of friends to me these past months, George. I shall not forget it,' Marco told him with a pat on his shoulder.

'And I shall hold you to remembering it,' he avowed.

'Well, it was a long time in the making, fellow, so you might have to remind me once you have settled back into your old habits,' he teased him back. 'It's a shame, George, this new routine suits you well. I have never seen you so bright-eyed since our university days. And look how productive you have been. I had hoped your time at the gallery might have served you, too, in seeing your true capability.'

'And it has, I have seen it, but I don't know if I can remain to the strictures. Besides, I shall be able to afford the time off once I exhibit everything. Are we still on for the spring exhibition? I mean to stay until then and see what can be shifted.'

'Ah, I don't know about my stuff, George. The timing is precarious now, she does not even know she has become my muse. I shall only find out what she makes of the matter when we arrive in Padua tomorrow and she sees the evidence of it all about the place. I will let you know. But, you shall go ahead with yours and the student's work, and I might be able to knock up a couple of more usual scenes before then to add to it, though don't count upon it.'

'No, I daresay you will not be so lonely in Padua with only your paintbrushes for company now. I think I shall be lucky to have a word from you before then, shut up in your little love nest so snuggly. Ah, how the tables have turned. You will still come to it though, won't you fellow?'

'Yes, of course I will, though I shall not be able to stay long. Eleanor will be in her confinement by then and I won't want to be far from her above a day.'

'You, a father, who would have thought it.'

'After Elizabeth, certainly not me. But life is a funny old thing, George. For all our plans, ambitions, and resignations, it has a way of diverting you to unseen tracts. Anyway, I shall have to love you and leave you, my friend. I have already been gone an hour and we have much to do before we set off.' He rose from his seat, shook his friend's hand, patted him on the back, and put his hat on.

'Go well, and if you are not too kept to your bed, drop me a line to let me know you have reached Padua safely.'

'I will. And before you return to England, you shall factor in to stop with us and break your journey.'

'You may count upon it.'

And then he opened the door of his office, taking a final glance as he walked from it, through the studio of vacant easels and down the staircase hung with gilded frames of works he had procured and contributed to and grown blind to in the course of time.

Farewell, my first love, he paused and said to the portrait of Eliza hung above the stairs. *Wish me well. We are both free now.* And he held his hat to his chest for a moment, then continued down the stairs, ready to claim all that was waiting for him. He shook the hands of his attendants and curators on his way out, leapt into his gondola and bid Giacomo make speed for *Ca' Rosetti*.

When he climbed the steps to the *piano nobile*, having noted his father's boat moored at the landing, he braced himself for a difficult parting. He was never usually in before four, and even then, on rare occasion, he considered, a glance at his pocket watch reading the hour as a quarter to three. He would have left the gallery sooner if he'd thought it likely in the least. It was his mama he wanted to protect in all this; he remembered her hard-won struggles to grant him the freedoms he had since enjoyed, but not without toil and toll upon her. For that reason, he must handle this well and stay calm in his dealings with his father now. For he was not going to be swayed or forbidden. He was his own man now, and he had his own woman to think of, and the precious life she carried within.

So when he entered an atmosphere of stiff anxiety, it did not surprise him in the least, not even the sight of Dante widening his eyes at him and shaking his head when he was out of view of the others.

'Mother, father,' he said as he entered the parlour and found them in the anticipated picture of distress.

'Marco,' Isabella looked up instantly at the sight of him with a warning glance, and he saw it was as he feared, though when his papa turned about too and said, 'Son, you are home,' without a note of frustration in his tone, he frowned his confusion. 'Yes father, I came directly from the gallery—'

'You got the news then?'

'News?'

'Marco,' Isabella said, carefully, 'The news that your cousin is returned home and is in a very bad way.'

His mouth fell wide open. 'What?'

His father stood and patted him on the shoulder, 'The doctor says his condition is still capricious, though he has made it this far, so—'

'What has happened?'

'His carriage turned over south of the Alps. God knows he was foolish to attempt them at all in this season, but I suppose all the bad business with the *Maddalena* encouraged him to rush home and make a try for it. He was taken to an inn in Bolzano a week ago, and when he came around, he demanded his valet pack him up in a carriage and convey him back to Venice, broken bones and all sorts, quite against the doctor's orders. His condition weakened as you might expect in such weather, and now he has a dangerous cold on his chest that threatens his recovery.'

'No,' Marco said aloud, and his father put an arm around his shoulders. 'I know, I know, son. It is a dreadful run of luck, and he's not out of danger yet. All we can do now is our best to take care of him. We have sent for the nurse; I think Eleanor is too distraught to manage it.'

'Where is she?' he asked, and his mother's eyes flashed with fear.

Dante stepped into the rescue. 'Come on, brother. I will take you to see them,' he said, guiding him out of the room.

When it was safe to speak, Dante paused and lent in to his ear, speaking at a whisper. 'You cannot breathe a word, Marco; he knows nothing, and now is not the time to flee. He will never forgive you if you go now. I'm sorry for it. She's in an even worse state than you. She's in her chamber, but take care, the servants are next door, keeping vigil over Giles.'

'I should go in there and finish the job and do us all a favour!'

'Marco, I know him a blaggard, but come, he is in a very sorry state and might die.'

'Forgive me, brother, you are right to correct me. I am not myself, but do not forget the state he left her in, will you?'

'You know I don't. Look, you have had the wind knocked out of you. Go and comfort each other, hopefully, that will ease your suffering. I hoped to be toasting the proud father this evening, but—'

'Thank you, I cannot believe—'

'It is but a delay. Hold fast, brother.'

She was slumped on top of the bed when he came in, face red, eyes swollen with tears, Benedetta working fast to set all back into the room from the trunks.

'Marco,' she sprung from the bed and ran into his arms before he could reach her first. He caught her and held her tight against him.

'Are you alright, my love?'

'No, no, I am not. But better now you are here.'

'Have you seen him?'

'Only when he was carried up to the room, I have refused to go into him since. Your family think I am too distressed to see him in such a state, but—'

'I know, it is the same for me. How bad is he?'

'A very sorry state, it is true, and I know that despite all, I should feel some modicum of remorse, compassion, for I am not wicked-hearted, Marco, but—'

'You cannot help hoping that he might clear the path for us all and leave you a widow.'

She nodded. 'I know it ghastly of me, I—'

'No, not after all he has done to you. I feel the same.' He sighed deeply. 'Though I am heavy with disappointment, that one thought gave me hope, yet I also admonish myself for it.'

'Oh, Marco, I thought we might still go today, but your family, for them and only them, I agreed to stay to play my part, but I know not how to anymore...'

'With me at your side,' he told her, kissing her forehead. 'You will lean upon me now. We will have to take care, but every moment we can seek or steal, we shall remind ourselves of all that is still promised to us. We will have to be patient, but as soon as the tide turns, one way or another, I am taking you to Padua, and we will be a family soon. Hold on to that, through all else, as I shall be.'

She peered up with those endearing eyes, and he caught the flicker of hope in them, a glance towards a lifeline, pressed a kiss to her lips, led her to the sofa, and enveloped her in his arms.

CHAPTER FIFTY-ONE

Healing Broth.

Annalise. December 1822.

'Up prisoner,' called matron through the cell hatch, but Annalise could not convey an answer to her, she could not speak at all. She had been in slow decline since Tabby had left eight weeks ago, and the solitary languidness of her days had begun to take their toll. It had been manageable to begin with, whilst she had still had her laundry work to attend, even if a little lonelier when in her cell. But she had been struck by a terrible bout of pleurisy at the turn of November which had rendered her unable to carry out her work at all.

She had not left her bed for the past three weeks. She was fortunate—she had been told by the matron—that her fever had finally broken, for they had feared she might not come through the night. But she had. Though, why, she could not fathom. It seemed to her it would have been kinder to have been swept away with it and be spared the sufferance of another day.

But the physician had given her a Julep and applied leeches to her ribs and the tenderness had begun to subside, her breathing coming easier once more. But swellings about the glands in her neck and an awful sore throat had seemed to replace them over these past few days, and now, when she opened her mouth to speak, no sound beyond a shallow wheeze of air came forth.

'Did you 'ear me, Tullier? You are to be up and ready in ten minutes,' matron repeated.

Annalise wondered what for. All she could do was nod her reply. She had been declared too much weakened by her illness to undertake any work, and it was not Sunday, so she did not expect to be called to hear the chaplain. Nonetheless, she eased herself up, attended the necessaries, and by the time the matron returned to check on her, she was dressed and ready for whatever she was summoned to.

'Right, Tullier,' said the matron, unlocking the cell and pushing a breakfast tray onto her wooden stool. 'You've got a quarter-hour to breakfast, and then I'll be back to collect you for the chaise, so don't dally!'

Annalise nodded, wanting to confirm whether it was as she had feared, that her time was finally up here and she was about to be transported to some godforsaken land. What else would she need a chaise for? But as she opened her mouth to query it, another empty hiss left her lips, and the matron was already gone by the time she had thought to attempt to gesture to her, her inability to speak. She looked down at her tray and after a little contemplation, decided she should probably eat it, for she did not know what might be expected to pass for meals on a prison ship, but highly doubted it would be a better offering than what had been set before her, particularly since she had been put on a fortifying diet for the past three weeks. Instead of the customary bowl of congealed gruel she was used to breakfasting on, she now had a boiled egg, a piece of bread, and an orange to look to, and so she pulled the stool towards her and began on it.

She got halfway through the offering when she abandoned the effort, her throat so sore and swollen it felt unbearable to keep forcing mouthfuls down. What she needed was something warm to drink, to ease her throat, but she had not had a hot drink in all the months of her incarceration, though she was told that at Christmas, that kindly matron often had a pan of mulled wine boiled up, as a one-off treat. And now she would not be about even for that, it seemed.

Where would she be by then? Somewhere on the sea, to be sure. Tabby had once told her of a relative who had been transported to Van Diemans Land, got his ticket of leave after fourteen years, but never returned on account of the sea voyage. It had taken eight months to get there, and the thought of it again was too much to endure by the time he finally earned his freedom. It filled her with no comfort to think of such a journey so terrible, one would rather stay put than be reunited with his loved ones after such a lengthy separation. If that wasn't bad enough to dwell on, she remembered now Mr Langley's words about the need for wives and maids in the colonies. A maid was one thing she could bear, but a wife, no, and to whom? Some former villain or tyrant reigning over them? But what choice did she have in any of it? She must hope her extensive experience in service would deem her more fitting for that role and must try to press in that direction if she was to survive the remainder of her sentence. That, of course, was if she went even so far as to survive the voyage, given how many prisoners were said to die on their way, and her health was hardly at its best of late. With that thought, she forced another suck of the orange flesh down her disobliging throat.

But when matron returned, she threw a parcel upon the bed and asked: 'These yours?'

Annalise opened the paper package to find her own clothes inside them and the two blankets Nancy had given to her in Falmouth, both of which had been confiscated and replaced with plainer, coarser versions on her arrival here. She wanted to ask her what this meant. Surely, she would not be permitted to have them back on the voyage. And then, when she looked up at the matron, her hand was outstretched, clutching an envelope. 'You got your letters aint yer?'

Annalise nodded and took the envelope.

'Well, you can see for yourself then.'

She unfurled the paper and scan read it before retracing the words more carefully, so surreal they seemed to her:

Lady de Whitaker-Hollingford,
Having referred for the opinion of the law officers of the Crown, in the case of Annalise
Tullier, under sentence of imprisonment and transportation, in whose behalf you
interested yourself, I am directed to acquaint you that, in consequence of their report, his
lordship deemed it advisable to recommend the prisoner to his Majesty for a free pardon.
Consequently, the request has been reviewed and the pardon granted by his merciful
Majesty.
Grounds for clemency: that the prisoner is contrite and unlikely to ever re-offend if the
sentence is mitigated.
I am, my Lady, your most obedient humble servant,
G. Lamb.

'Well, aren't you gonna say something?'

Annalise held her hand to her throat. Even if she could have said something, she would not have found the words. *Could it be true?*

'Cat got your tongue? Aye, so it should. Ain't seen many of them in my time. Well, prisoner, let's hope you'll prove worthy of it and we'll not see you back in a six-month.'

Annalise shook her head to indicate that she certainly would not.

'Right, take up your things then. Your patron has hired a chaise to convey you home and it is expected any moment.'

Six days later, she caught her first glimpse of a familiar landscape as she travelled past a signpost for Epsom on the last leg of her journey. It had been hard on her to cope with such a rattling about and so few stops, but she had not wanted to prolong reaching home beyond a moment more than was necessary. She had dreamt of such a moment for ten long months, thinking it would be delayed by another six years and following an eight-month sailing from the ends of the earth. But she had been spared all that, and now could only mean to race home as fast as she could and behold her dearest ones again. And at last, her discomfort and perseverance had paid off, for she was in reach of home, close enough to walk now if she had to, though likely she hadn't the strength, so weary and weak her body had grown these past weeks.

Her newfound freedom had done much to transform her spirits, but the journey had done nothing for her recovery from the illness that still plagued her. The cold December air and chill in the coach and damp sheets at the few inns they had rested in had been wearing her back into a heavy cough, and her voice had failed to return as yet. It had made things difficult until she managed to procure a pencil and paper at their first stop so she could at least communicate her speech in writing when conversing with innkeepers and coachmen. They had all assumed her a mute, and had been accommodating enough, though it had slowed down things she had wanted to hasten, such as procuring her room and enjoying her first night's sleep in a proper bed against a soft feather mattress for the first time in an age. That had been at the first stop in Chard, the only decent inn they had procured on the entire journey. She had taken numerous cups of sweet, warm tea and coffee, washed the grime from her skin in steamy bowls of water poured from the kettle and finally felt clean.

The steam had soothed her congested airways too, and she had spent a time just sitting before the roaring flames of the fire, wrapped in a soft blanket, just inhaling the vapour of the bowl and finding, at last, something capable of soothing her. She slept soundly, too, sinking into the bed and struggling to lift herself out of it in the morning for the luxury of its warmth and comfort. But then she remembered her reclaimed liberty and mustered herself up to meet the coach again and pursue the next round of rattling in the task of reaching home.

And now, here she was, dashing along the Carshalton Road and soon to meet the High Street and all that was familiar to her. Her heart raced with the horse's hoof speed, and she could barely contain herself when she passed the ponds and began to slow. And there it was. *Poppy's Pies*, the sign plate flapping in the wind. A light aglow beyond the windows but the panes too misted with condensation to see in through them. She leapt down from the coach before the groom could get down to open the door for her, forgetting how weak of limb she was and taking his arm to steady herself. It was not physical strength but excitement that propelled her on, and finding the shop shut up, she wrapped on the door.

'We're closed!' Came the reply from beyond it. She could see the shadow of someone behind the counter, and eventually, when she persisted in her knocking, a flood of new light poured onto the shop floor as the jib door was opened up, and someone else came through it and finally unlocked it. It was Poppy.

'By gad! It's you, luv!' she cried, pressing her hand to her chest and bursting into tears.

Annalise smiled and scooped her up into a hug.

'Oh, luv! Thank the dear lord above you are home at last! We weren't expecting you till Thursday, or we'd have been waiting up for you. But bless you, you are here, and that's all that matters! Now come on, let's get in from the cold, she said and dragged her into the fragrant warmth of the shop and locked the door up behind them.

The smell of suet and mulled wine hung in the air, and it made her smile, for she would not be sipping on mulled wine at the Bodmin Gaol now, but here, at home with her friends, in time for Christmas.

'Is it good to be home, luv?' Poppy asked when she turned back to her and then frowned. 'Are you alright, luv? You look ever so pale and you're as quiet as a mouse.'

Annalise nodded and went to reach for her pencil, but then remembered it was of no use to write things out for Poppy. So she tapped at her throat and silently mouthed the words, 'I've lost my voice', three times before she understood her and said, 'Oh! Oh, you poor love. You don't look very well. Let's get you before the fire and I'll send Thomas out for the doctor.'

Annalise mouthed 'no' to this. She didn't want a doctor. She wanted nothing more than her friend's smiles and a warm bed.

She was indulged in this and much more as she was pushed into one of the comfy fireside chairs and a mug of hot broth pressed into her hands. Then, as each member of the household learnt of her arrival, they joined her at the fireside with beaming smiles and kindly words of welcome. Her body was fatigued, her chest congested and lungs heavy, but she was so happy to be in the company of friends, to be sat in her parlour again, she paid no mind to her bodily complaints and settled back in the chair and listened to their talk and progress and news of others not present, with such heartfelt contentment she could not quite believe any of it was real.

In the end, it was Poppy who sent them off to bed and ordered the same for her, saying they had all worn her out and she looked fatigued. She led her upstairs, helped her on with clean night clothes, and tucked her into a bed dressed with fresh linens and warmed with a hot brick.

But by morning, the doctor was called. Poppy complained she looked no better for a night's rest, perhaps worse. She lamented the barking cough that had woken her in the night, sounding frightfully like the croup. Complained she looked like she had wasted away in the light of day: her skin sallow and no meat on her bones. It would not do. The doctor was to come, and that was all there was to it.

'You are emaciated, Miss Tullier. No doubt, the prison diet and conditions have done you much detriment and stripped you of your strength, as is commonly the case in such circumstances. Your lungs are rattling, and your throat is closed in but for the merest pathway. I suspect inflammation of the Larynx, which is why you cannot speak, and pneumonia to the left lung, at least.' Then he turned and said to Poppy, 'I shall bleed her and leach her and leave a recipe for a medicinal gargle and mullion flower ptisan to be taken on the hour. She may also benefit from a poultice about the back of the ribs if her breathing does not improve or the coughing will not cease—liquids only, but plentiful. Warm broths and nourishing soups aplenty, for she is undernourished, and her strength needs building up again. If she has not improved in forty-eight hours, or she deteriorates before such a time, send for me. Otherwise, should she improve, as I expect by then, she shall work herself up gradually to a wholesome diet of fresh nourishing food, and if you can get them from anywhere at this season, a pound of oranges a day will expedite her recovery, to be sure. They might sometimes be found in the markets in London at this time of year when the boats dock in at the Thames from the warmer climes.'

And so Annalise was set up in Poppy's bed with the fire kept burning around the clock, and a single bed from next door was brought into the room for Poppy, and the youngest of the Bartlett children had the Chinese sofa made up for a bed in the interim.

'I shan't 'ave you disturbed in the night for my fidgeting. You're to be kept as comfortable as yer might, and I'll still be close at hand if you should want for something. You need only tap your hand against the bedpost, and I sha' know you call.' Poppy had instructed once the doctor had bled and leeched her and helped Poppy apply a poultice to her back.

And with her lack of speech and listless energy, she could do nothing to protest at all this mollycoddling. So she was forced to accept the many efforts laid on for her in the coming days as the household took turns to sit up with her, bring her warm cups of something or another and hold herbal-scented steam baths below her face. On the third day, Miss Lockheart came and sat with her after teaching her morning class downstairs and brought her some books to keep her amused in those bedridden hours. Anyone would have thought her on her deathbed with all the trouble taken for her comfort and care.

But after a week, she could not deny its efficacy as she felt the congestion dry out, and the swelling at her throat and chest receded into something closer to normal. Her voice had still not returned, but there was a relaxation about her throat now that lent her to believe it would not be long before it would, as the doctor had lately said. She had moved on from the liquid diet to heartier meals and endless oranges, which Poppy had managed to procure through one of the local stage drivers who was in London on his duties at least thrice a week in the course of his routine.—Being a local man and a regular to the pie shop, he was content to procure the oranges in return for the favour of free pies.

However, as the weeks turned and she began to feel more and more like herself again, she believed that it was not the fine nursing care or nourishing diet that had healed her, but the love behind all those efforts that had proved the difference. The comfort of home and the gift of her liberty had instantly transformed her spirits; it only seemed that the body was somewhat slower to return to its former condition. But as the January frosts settled over the village ponds, body and mind were once again in union and great comfort.

To be continued...

Dear Reader,

Thank you for reading my debut series: *Diary of an Obstinate, Headstrong Female.* I hope you enjoyed reading it.

I would be *most obliged* if you would leave me a review.

I am currently working on book 5 in the series and anticipate its completion either, late 2024, or, early 2025.

For further information, please see my website :
https://www.ccburns.co.uk

For the latest updates, follow my Facebook page.

f facebook.com/bluestockingbard

www.ingramcontent.com/pod-product-compliance
Lightning Source LLC
Chambersburg PA
CBHW051940020726
47501CB00001B/205